HER ROYAL HAREM, THE COMPLETE SERIES

CATHERINE BANKS

DEDICATION

Thank you to Avery, my husband and best friend, for his continued support. You're the moon of my life, and I'll always love you.

Thank you to the readers of this series. Your reviews, kind words, and emails to me kept me going during rough times.

Thank you to Michelle F., Jenica S., Ericka S., and Vicki C. You four have helped me immensely with this series, even if you didn't realize it.

As always, thank you to my amazing editor Pauline C. You're the best.

And, last but not least, thank you to my mentor, friend, and all-around amazing person, R.J. You've really helped me this year, and I can't wait to see what 2019 brings for both of us.

ROYALLY ENTANGLED

HER ROYAL HAREM, BOOK ONE

CHAPTER I

I never expected moving into a new apartment would land me in the center of a supernatural harem.

But then, how could I have? I hauled my measly two boxes of possessions up to the second floor, seemingly ordinary apartment. Well-kept. Clean. The manager, Ms. Patty, clearly took pride in her building.

Two thousand dollars a month worth of pride, I reminded myself as I unlocked the door to my new home. It had to be worth it.

When I walked in the door, something felt...wrong. I couldn't pinpoint what, though. Ms. Patty had overseen the furniture delivery the day before, and looking around, I could see everything was placed where I had asked.

Why, then, was unease clenching in my gut? I bit my lip, set my boxes down, locked up behind me, and took a look around the apartment. It didn't seem anyone was here or had messed with anything.

Maybe it was just in my head. After what had happened back in my hometown, it wasn't really any wonder I felt on edge. But as long as Demarcus didn't find out where I was, I should be okay.

I would be okay. Especially, if I kept the necklace my grandmother had given me on. It made me feel safe and always reminded me of my grandmother, who I missed very much.

I wondered what my neighbors would be like. There were nine total apartments, but three of them were vacant currently. When I had asked what the tenants were like, she had just laughed and said, "They're all best friends...for now."

I had no idea what she had meant by that.

Things had been a bit crazy in Jinla with the four main Other clans at war. The mages, dragons, werewolves, and elves had been at war for decades now, but humans like me had no idea why. Jinla was the hub for Others since the four clans had their headquarters based here. Just on my walk from the train station to here, I had seen two elves, a goblin, and two guys I was fairly certain had been werewolves. Grandma thought I would have been afraid of Others, after being attacked by some, but I knew that there were always bad apples in the bunch and I couldn't blame an entire race of Others for one or two bad beings. Plus, I had dated a couple Others and they had been the most loving beings I had ever met.

The four Other clans were ruled with monarchies, unlike the President of our human democracy. A few hundred years ago, we had had a king as well, but now the President worked with the Others' Kings to ensure we kept peace between all races. The Others had huge areas in Jinla for their headquarters, but also a lot of land outside this city. There were entire states owned by one of the Other clans.

After putting my clothes away and popping a frozen pizza in the oven, I turned to my favorite past time, video games. My gaming console was just in sleep mode, so I woke it up and launched my current favorite game, *Ghost 2*. One of my clan members had already created a chat lobby, having been on an hour earlier due to different time zones.

"Yo!" I said in greeting.

"Jo!" several male voices responded.

I didn't have many friends in person, but I had a great group of about ten online friends – my best friends. We talked about everything. Some people didn't understand it, but my virtual friends were the closest people I knew. We had met in person a couple of times, but most of our interactions were through our headsets and in the games.

"Jo, did you see the specs for the new hard raid?" Dragonknight asked. He wasn't really a dragon or a knight, but that was his gamer tag. We created our own gamer tags, or gamer names, when we signed on to the console for the first time. Mine was not creative at all, *Jolie*. Yep, just my first name.

I took my pizza out of the oven and settled onto the couch for the evening.

"Yep, it looks hard, but I'm ready for the challenge," I replied.

Three hours later, I realized that I had in fact, not been ready for the challenge. We said our goodnights and I collapsed onto my bed, waking up with barely enough time to make it to my first day of work without being late.

When I got to work, I rushed into the huge building, and the receptionist pointed at a map off to the right. "Room twenty-one."

There were over ten floors, and I was glad I only had to go to the second floor.

I had landed a writing position with one of the most popular gaming companies. It was a huge honor and a nice pay increase from my last job.

"You must be Jolie," a man in jeans and a *"vampires drool"* t-shirt said.

"I am," I replied and held out my hand.

He shook it and motioned for me to follow him. "Your desk is right over here. Someone will be by in a bit to walk you through the processes we have here."

Once I got started, the work and its processes were simple enough. The day flew by, and after a full day, I clocked out and headed back towards my new place.

On my walk home, I put in my noise cancelling headphones and sent a message to the group chat with the clan. Without telling them any information that could get me in trouble, I hinted at the awesome games I'd gotten a sneak peek of. Just as I hit send, something slammed into my side and carried me across the intersection. I gasped and looked up to find a man carrying me and a bus barreling past where I had just been walking.

He'd saved me from being hit by the bus I had not seen or heard.

How cliché of me to have my nose down and almost get hit by a bus!

He smiled down at me and said something, but I couldn't hear him. I took out my earbuds and asked, "What?"

"I asked if you were okay?" he repeated with a wide smile, setting me on my feet.

He was drop dead gorgeous. Dark brown hair, blue eyes, nice cheekbones and jawline, and muscular, not too buff, but his chest was defined even through his shirt. I mentally checked to make sure there wasn't drool dripping down my chin.

"Yes, thank you."

He set me on my feet and I brushed myself off and smoothed my clothes down.

"I'm glad," he said softly.

"Thank you, again," I said and started to walk away, still in shock.

"Wait," he called and caught up to me.

"Yes?" I asked.

His biceps looked incredible in the shirt he had on. It hugged his shoulders and chest, and was cut in the perfect spot to accent his biceps. Had he lucked out in finding the shirt to fit like that, or did he just make everything he wore look amazing? His dark hair was styled up, his beard and goatee perfectly shaped to his jaw. The clothes he wore were nice, definitely more expensive than the skirt and V-neck t-shirt I currently wore.

"Well, I did save you and I think I deserve a date," he said and stuck his hands in his pockets, thumbs outside of them.

A date? This sexy male wanted to go on a date with me? Hell yes!

"A date, huh? What would this date involve?"

I was glad I came off cool and composed, despite my brain trying really hard to fry itself with the fact I had almost died and this delicious being was talking to me. It had been a few years since I'd had sex, and he was making me think all kinds of dirty things.

"Dinner and dessert."

The way he said dessert made me shiver in delight. I definitely wouldn't mind some dessert that involved him.

"Okay," I agreed, keeping my drool in my mouth.

"Great! This way, milady," he said and bowed.

"May I know the name of my savior?" I asked with a fake accent, staying in line with his "milady" comment.

"Rhys. And you, milady?"

"Jolie."

He stopped and held out his hand.

I looked at it a moment and then asked, "Clan?"

His smile disappeared. "I wouldn't save you just to hurt you."

"It's been a rough few years," I replied stiffly and avoided looking at his eyes. It would take me an hour at least to explain all of the misfortune that I had experienced. And, I really didn't want to go over what had happened last year, the reason my grandmother had given me the necklace.

"Dragon," he whispered.

Thank the Goddess.

I shook his hand and met his eyes. "I'm sorry. I'm not racist. I don't care what you are. It's just—"

He kissed my knuckles and smiled. "I understand."

We resumed walking and I felt his eyes on me as we moved down the sidewalk. Dragons were notoriously observant, so I didn't let it bother me.

"Where would you like to eat?" I asked.

"Me?" he asked, his eyebrows raised. "I don't think a woman has ever asked where I wanted to eat before."

I chuckled. "Well, you saved me, so I owe you dinner."

"What about here?" he asked and indicated the restaurant beside us. It was a nice Italian chain restaurant that served amazing breadsticks. We had one in my hometown.

"Great," I agreed and opened the door for him.

He grinned and walked in.

"Thank you," he said softly to me.

"You're welcome."

The hostess seated us quickly and ordered our food as soon as we sat down. The restaurant was a bit slow, which was good for us.

"So, Jolie. What were you doing when you didn't see the bus racing towards you?" he asked and snapped his breadstick in half before eating it.

Texting my video game clan.

"Texting some friends," I said somewhat truthfully. "I just started a new job today and had promised to message them afterwards."

"Oh, you're new to town?" he asked.

I nodded. "Just moved in last night."

"I wish I had known. I would have taken you on a tour instead of to dinner," he said. His brow furrowed a brief moment and then he smiled. "Maybe I'll stop you from being hit by a car tomorrow and can convince you to go on a second date."

I laughed.

"Let's hope I don't need rescuing again. Once in a lifetime is enough for me."

"You're human, right?" he asked softly and tilted his head. His nostrils flared as he drew in my scent.

"Mostly."

"Mostly?"

"I am, like, a thirty-second Gorgon," I admitted to him. The most famous Gorgon of all, Medusa, was a distant relative of mine. At least, that's what my Grandma had told me. Generally, it wasn't something that I brought up right away, but I wanted to be honest with him right up front. I was hoping it might get me into his bed tonight.

No, stop that, you dirty mind. You are not sleeping with someone you just met.

I'd never had a one-night stand before, not that I was against it, I just hadn't had one before. But, I didn't want to start my life in Jinla with one.

"Interesting," he replied with a smirk.

"What do you do for work?" I asked him, leaning on my elbows on the table to give him a nice view of my cleavage. I didn't flirt often, and I wasn't great at it, but I could get by.

"I'm an architect," he replied.

"That's really interesting," I admitted.

"It can be, yes."

"Do you enjoy it?"

He nodded. "I like creating things."

Our meals came and we ate and chatted. I ordered some wine and before I realized it, I was a bit tipsy. Okay, I was drunk.

"Where to next?" I asked with a warm smile, feeling warm all throughout my body.

"There's a bar right around the corner," he said. "Want to go get some drinks?"

He led the way out of the restaurant and I stumbled when we walked down the sidewalk.

"Easy," he said with a chuckle and put his solid arm around my waist, so his large bicep fit into the curve of my side. I had to resist the urge to explore the muscle with my hands.

"Sorry," I said with a soft laugh. "I guess I had more to drink than I thought."

"Would you prefer to go home?" he asked, stopping and leaning against the side of a building, right next to the alley.

I leaned into him, my breasts pressed against his chest, and whispered, "But I haven't had dessert yet."

His eyes sparked and he leaned down, lightly brushing his lips over mine. "Dessert does sound good right now."

I pulled him down and kissed him deeply, sliding my tongue into his mouth, and wrapped my arms around his neck.

He picked me up and I instinctively wrapped my legs around his waist, our kiss never breaking. He walked down the alley until we were hidden from view, and a distance away from the large trashcan we were using to block us from the sight of passersby. I dropped my legs long enough to let him unzip his pants and put a condom on. He lifted me up again, pushing me against the wall, and slowly entered me, moving my thong to the side to do so. He was big, but not too big. When he was completely buried in me, he moaned and whispered, "You feel amazing."

I moaned and moved my hips with his.

He growled and clamped his mouth over mine, stroking his tongue across mine in sync with the pumping of his hips. My orgasm hit after only a couple of strokes and I squealed into his mouth as we continued to kiss. Stars danced behind my closed eyes as I floated on euphoria that continued as he didn't stop.

I had forgotten how great sex was with dragons. This male was an alpha and the safety and security he made me feel as his arms held me and we became one for a short time, was euphoric in and of itself.

Another wave crashed over me and my fingernails dug into his muscular shoulders.

He nipped my neck gently, my hips bucking against him as he did.

He moved faster and harder, orgasms tearing from me one after the next, but soon he lost his rhythm as he orgasmed.

We broke our kiss, both panting and satisfied.

"Wow," he whispered.

"Mmhm," I replied, euphoria and the alcohol making me beyond happy. This town was starting off wonderful.

We got dressed and I stopped him at the edge of the alley. "Thanks, for tonight."

"Going to pass on drinks?" he asked with a smirk.

"I think dessert satisfied me plenty."

He bowed elegantly and kissed the knuckles on one of my hands. "Then I bid you goodnight, milady." He held out a business card. "And I would love to hear from you again."

I took the card and curtsied. "I shall call upon thee, good sir."

He bent and kissed my cheek. "Seriously, call me. I'd love to take you out again."

"Okay," I said with a nod.

CHAPTER 2

During my morning commute, I hummed along to a song, thinking about my date last night. I would wait at least two days before calling him, if I did at all. He was sexy, but he seemed like he might be super protective, which I didn't particularly like.

That sex had been great, though. Or perhaps that was just because of how drunk I had been and how long it had been since the last time. No, it had been good, and he was damn sexy.

After almost getting hit by a bus, I had done some research and found out there was a great public transit system in town. Now, I was on a bus instead of getting hit by it. The buses were clean and most of the people riding were dressed in business casual clothes. I felt under-dressed in my jeans and t-shirt, but this was my preferred attire and work didn't care what we wore since we didn't have visitors. Plus, as a video game company, we were more about the games and less about impressing suit-wearing corporate types.

My stop was approaching, so I stood up, picking up my backpack from the floor by my feet as I did. The doors opened, and the man next to me snatched my backpack and ran off the bus.

"Hey!" I screamed after him and jumped down and onto the sidewalk

Something blurred as it rushed from behind, whizzing past me, and then knocked the purse snatcher, er, backpack snatcher down. I jogged forward and the blur turned out to be a handsome man with bulging muscles. He turned to look at me, his foot holding the criminal down, and smiled. His eyes were amber, which told me immediately what he was.

Werewolf.

He grabbed the backpack from where the criminal had dropped it and held it out to me. "Here you go," he said with a wide smile.

I took it and smiled. "Thank you, so much."

The werewolf was a few inches over six feet, had a beard and goatee similar to Rhys's, black, slicked back hair, and was obviously of Italian heritage. The leather jacket he had on only added to his masculine appearance, which my inner Jolie was drooling over. This town had a lot of hot guys. I was so glad I had moved here.

Police showed up, but paused when they saw the werewolf with his foot on the guy. "Deryn," they called in greeting. "We've got it from here."

The werewolf raised his foot and stepped back so that he was beside me. "He snatched this woman's bag," he explained. "Lots of witnesses to attest to that."

The police nodded and handcuffed the guy whose eyes were wide as saucers as he stared up at Deryn. Was he scared because he was a werewolf? Or was there another reason? The cops seemed to know him.

"I'm Deryn," he said to me and held out his hand, still smiling wide.

I shook it. "Jolie. Thanks again, Deryn. I don't know what I would have done if he had gotten away with this." I slung my backpack onto my shoulders and pulled my hair out from under the straps. "Do you work near here? I could take you out to lunch as repayment for helping me."

He smirked. "You don't have to repay me for doing what was right. However, I'd love to go out on a date with you."

"I can't go out tonight," I said a bit sadly. I had a raid planned with my clan and I couldn't back out on them. We were determined to beat the hard raid.

"What about making it a lunch date then?" he asked.

I smiled and felt my shoulders rise. "Okay."

He took out a pen, pulled the cap off with his teeth, and held his hand out, palm up. I set my hand in it and he turned it over to write his phone number on my palm. He took the cap out of his mouth and put it back on the pen.

"Text me the time and place and I'll be there," he promised.

I nodded and smiled, glancing down at his number. "Okay."

With a wave, he walked away, head held high, shoulders back, and smiled at everyone he passed by. His butt looked incredible in those jeans and I wasn't the only woman to notice. With one last look, I turned and went to work.

"You're late," Justina said and shook her finger at me. "Lucky for you, everyone is in a meeting, so they won't know." Justina was tall, thin, and gorgeous. She was part Egyptian and part Italian, add in being a dhampir, and she was almost perfect. I had met her when I came to interview over a month ago and we had instantly become friends, texting nonstop since that day.

"Thanks," I said and plopped down into my computer chair. "Some jerk tried to steal my backpack."

"Oh no!" She gasped and rushed to me. "Did he hurt you? Are you alright?" She grabbed my arms, raised them, and spun me around to search for injuries.

I shooed her worries away and sat back down. "A werewolf was on the bus and stopped him for me. So, I wasn't injured at all."

She smirked, a knowing look on her face. "Oh! Was this a sexy werewolf? Not that they make any other kind!"

I chuckled and nodded as I looked down at my hand with his number on it. "Definitely was. He asked me on a lunch date."

"A lunch date! Damn girl, you move fast! Wasn't it just last night that you were with that dragon?"

I blushed and mumbled. "Yeah." Now, I was really regretting telling her about that. I should keep things like that to myself.

"Hey, no judgments here! I try to get two different men each week, though my options are slim lately, but that may be my high standards. Just make sure you give me more juicy details!" She laughed, throwing her head back as she did.

"Where should we go?" I asked Justina. "I don't really know any of the lunch places here."

"Fifth Street Bistro," she said immediately.

I sent a text to the number he had provided, glad that my hands weren't sweaty, since that happened somedays.

Me: This is Jolie from this morning. Thank you again for getting my bag back. How does noon at Fifth Street Bistro sound?

"You need to get pictures of these guys for me," she said. "Work best friends share everything."

I chuckled. "I'll try." I'd love to have pictures saved.

Deryn: Perfect. I'm looking forward to it.

She peered over my shoulder and whistled. "You are so getting laid tonight."

I put my phone away and shook my head. "Stop it."

"I'm jealous," she said and sat down in her chair. "It took me a week to find some good males here."

"I definitely like this town better than my hometown," I said with a smirk and laughed.

The meeting ended and our coworkers came out, chatting and going to their desks, ending our reprieve. Should I feel bad for going on two dates in as many nights? Neither had been premeditated. Neither had been *expected*.

I became engrossed in my work, letting the story take me, and it wasn't until Justina yelled my name that I snapped back into reality.

"What?" I asked, taking my headphones off and looking up at her.

"Lunch!" she yelled at me.

Several people turned to look at us, but I ignored them, leapt to my feet, and grabbed my ID and cash out of my backpack.

"Thank you!" I yelled back and ran out of the office, shocked to find it was five minutes until noon already. On the elevator ride down, I typed in the address and used my maps app to find it. Justina saved me by giving me a location only a block away, so I wouldn't be late.

I walked outside, smoothing my clothes, taking deep breaths to calm down. I had dated werewolves before, and they were great at smelling emotions. I did not want him to think that I was nervous about our date, or flustered. I turned the corner and saw the bistro, it was pretty busy already, and standing outside was Deryn.

I took one last deep breath and walked towards him, confident and relaxed, with a wide smile on.

"Hi," I said to get his attention since he was texting or emailing someone on his phone.

He looked up and smiled. "Hi."

"You wait long?" I asked, despite the fact I was exactly on time.

He shook his head and slipped his phone into his pocket. "Nope. How has work been?"

We got into the long line of patrons, and I turned to face him. "Pretty good, actually. I would have been late for lunch if my friend hadn't shown me the time."

"What do you do?" he asked, tilting his head to the side slightly.

"I'm a video game writer," I answered truthfully.

His eyes widened. "You game?"

I nodded, not surprised that he was shocked by that. A lot of males were shocked to discover that I played video games. They were even more shocked when they found out how much I played. "Yes, I do. Do you?"

"Lots!" he said happily. "What's your favorite type of game?"

"RPGs and FPSs."

"Me too! Have you played *Ghost 2* yet?"

"Only every night since it came out," I said with a chuckle.

"Did you beat the hard raid?"

"Not yet. My clan and I tried last night, but got hung up on the last part."

"That's awesome that you game. I haven't met a girl in real life who games before."

"We're out there, just few and far between."

"That's an understatement," he said and chuckled. "So, what's a gorgeous gamer girl like you doing single?"

He thought I was gorgeous? I knew I was attractive, but I would never have described myself as gorgeous. I had long, dark brown hair that was naturally wavy, high cheekbones, thick lips, and an hourglass figure. Even with how much I played video games, I made sure to work out and eat healthy most of the time, so I was in good shape.

"I just moved here from out of state."

"Really? Maybe I can take you for a tour?" he offered. "Show you the best parts of the city?"

"I would like that," I replied and stepped forward, following the line as it moved.

"What do you think of our city so far?"

"I really like it. I like the diversity here and how everyone gets along." Even though there was a war, it seemed like here, everyone put that to the side. I also liked that there didn't seem to be many vampires here. I was hoping to avoid vampires as much as possible. They were not my favorite race of Others.

"Deryn," a deep voice called.

Deryn turned and scowled at the large male behind him. The male had dark sunglasses on and was a brick wall brought to life.

"What?" Deryn asked, irritated by this male's presence. They obviously knew each other, but that didn't explain why he was upset by him just talking to him.

"You're wanted at headquarters," the male said.

"I'm busy," Deryn snarled. "It can wait."

"It's urgent."

Deryn rubbed his temples. "You guys always say that, and when I get there, nothing important is going on."

"Dan's orders. I'm just the messenger," the male said and shrugged.

Those around us were slowly moving away from Deryn and the newcomer, their eyes wide, and stances stiff. Why were they scared? Was it because Deryn was a werewolf? I couldn't see people in this city being scared of an Other, since there were so many of them here.

"Fine," Deryn said with a sigh. He turned to me and said, "I'm really sorry about this. It's a family matter."

Pack matter, was what he meant.

I smiled. "No problem."

"Dinner, tonight?" he asked. "I'll make it up to you."

"Okay, if it's early." I could go to dinner with him and then get home and raid with my clan afterwards. I would make it work.

He kissed my cheek and inhaled sharply. "I'll send you details later. Thanks for understanding."

He left and people looked at me questioningly. I realized with a sigh, that I hadn't snapped a picture of him for Justina, but it was too late. She would have to wait until later to get a picture. I ordered a quick bite to eat and took it back to work with me.

I ended up staying late at work to help some coworkers with a project, so I didn't even get to go home before my date with Deryn. Justina had been bummed that I hadn't gotten a picture yet, but I promised her that I would try tonight. That had appeased her enough she loaned me a change of clothes for my date. I asked her why she had the clothes in her desk, and she had simply said, "You never know when you'll need them."

I stood outside of the restaurant Deryn had chosen and rubbed my arms against the chill that was starting to set in. A drink sounded really good right now.

"Waiting long?" he asked as he approached.

I smiled and shook my head. "Nope."

He wore a pair of slacks and a button up shirt that accentuated his strong arms incredibly well. Yes, I had a huge thing for biceps. Well, muscles in general.

I wore a nice blue dress, that hugged all the places men appreciated the most. Thank goodness Justina and I were the same size.

"You look amazing," he whispered and leaned forward to inhale my scent next to my chin.

I inhaled his scent back and practically purred. He smelled like pine. "You look great, too."

He quirked his eyebrow. "You've dated a werewolf before?"

I nodded.

"How long ago?" he asked.

"Four years ago," I informed him. Knowing he would want to be sure that he wasn't overstepping another wolf's grounds, I added, "I'm completely unattached."

He smiled wide and pulled open the door for me. "Just what I wanted to hear."

The restaurant was incredible, reminding me of an opera house, with thick, burgundy drapes and low lighting. The host took us to a table that had been marked reserved, and they immediately brought out champagne and two flute glasses.

Deryn raised his glass of champagne. "To new friends."

I smiled and clicked my glass against his. "New friends." I took a long drink and then looked at the menu. It was extravagant and expensive, I wanted to try it all.

"What do you recommend?" I asked and set my menu down.

"The prime rib is amazing," he replied, still looking at his menu.

"I'll have that then," I said with a nod of my head, glad I had a decision made.

He looked up at me and smiled. "I know you'll love it."

"So, what type of work do you do?" I asked him.

"I make a lot of decisions for the family business," he replied. "My dad is the CEO, but he's training me to take over and decided the best way to train me is just to hand me the reins for ninety percent of the operation."

"That sounds like a lot of work," I said sadly. He wasn't that old, but had a lot of responsibility.

He smiled, joy filling him again. "Yeah, but I get a lot of time off to spend with my friends."

"What do you do for fun, besides play games?" I asked.

"My friends and I usually hang out and drink, or play something together. We're all really busy and have high level jobs, so the time we spend together is strictly relaxation time."

That sounded really nice. Sounded like what I needed.

"And why is a sexy, alpha werewolf like you single?" I asked, resting my chin on my linked hands on the table, raised up on my elbows.

"Haven't found the right one," he said with a shrug.

"Well, I'm flattered to be considered," I whispered huskily.

He smiled and mimicked my position. "I'm glad that I found you early on."

"Oh?"

"I know you'll have plenty of suitors knocking down your door once you've been here a while."

"I doubt that, but I'm glad I met you early as well."

He smiled at me, and it warmed me all the way to my toes.

My phone buzzed, and I looked at it.

Dragonknight: We still raiding?

Shit. I had forgotten to message them.

Me: Be on in an hour or two.

Dragonknight: Okay.

"Everything alright?" Deryn asked.

"Forgot to message my clan that I would be late to raid tonight because of our date."

"Do you need to go?" he asked, completely serious.

He would let me leave our date early to go game? This guy was definitely a keeper!

"No, thank you. I let them know I'd be on in a couple of hours."

"I really wouldn't mind," he said. "I know what it's like when you make plans with your clan. Especially, if you and your clan members don't live near each other."

Was he perfect or was I dead? Had that bus actually hit me and everything after was just a dream?

"I appreciate it, immensely, but they understand that I just moved here and I need to meet people in real life."

"My lucky day," Deryn said with a wide smile.

"Your orders?" a waiter asked.

Deryn held open the taxi door, looming over me as I stepped up to him. "I had a great time tonight," he said softly and brushed some hair behind my shoulder.

"Me, too," I said sincerely and stood up on tiptoe to kiss him lightly on the lips. "I'd love to do it again."

He leaned down and kissed me deeply, his tongue sweeping across mine. I leaned into him, as we continued to kiss. He tasted like champagne and strawberries. When we finally separated, I was grinning like a fool.

"Goodnight, Jolie."

"Goodnight, Deryn."

The taxi dropped me off, and I took the stairs up to my apartment, needing some exercise. Deryn was a lot of fun and super sexy. I would definitely be calling him to hang out sometime soon. He was really easy to be around.

Rhys was sexy, but I didn't really know much about him. That was something I could fix by going out with him again, on an actual date. But damn, that sex had been great!

After taking a shower, I sat down to turn my game on, but saw my phone blinking.

Deryn: I enjoyed tonight. Maybe Saturday we could get together to game? I've got a lot of old school games, including some karting games.

I smiled and chewed on my nail as I debated what to say.

Me: I enjoyed tonight as well. That prime rib was amazing. Saturday should work. I'll text you Friday night to confirm?

Deryn: Sounds great. Can't wait to see you again. :)

Me: Same XD

My phone chimed again and I expected it to be him, but it wasn't.

Justina: Did you get a picture?

Me: No. Sorry. Xoxox

Justina: Did you get laid?

Me: No! Geez.

Justina: hahaha lmao

Me: We're hanging out Saturday.

Justina: "hanging out" Nice!

Me: Sigh. I'm not a slut...normally.

Justina: You do you, hun.

Me: Going to bed. Bye.

During lunch, I went to the park and found a quiet place to meditate. All morning I had been warring with myself about whether I should feel bad about dating both Rhys and Deryn, or whether it was fine. I took a deep breath and sat on the grass. Closing my eyes, I tried to make all of the sounds disappear as I relaxed.

Five minutes later, I was groaning and grumbling.

"Meditation works best when you're quiet," a male voice whispered beside me.

My eyes snapped open and I turned to find a male elf sitting right next to me, mimicking my sitting position with his eyes closed. He was handsome, most elves were, and I really wanted to touch the pointed tip on his ear. He was incredibly stocky and looked to be Latino, with warm, bronzed skin.

He opened his eyes and smiled at me, warmth filling his eyes and radiating from him. How could one being be so happy, that it infected another person?

He held out his hand. "I'm Foxfire. Everyone calls me Fox, though."

I shook his hand and smiled back, my shoulder dropped forward, and my breath released in a content sight. "I'm Jolie."

"It's nice to meet you, Jolie. You must be new to town."

"How'd you know?"

"I visit this park often, and this is the first time I've seen you. I would remember if someone as beautiful as you had come through here before."

My smile widened. "Flirt."

He chuckled, stood up, brushed his butt off, and then held his hand out to help me stand. I accepted, letting him pull me into a standing position before I wiped off my butt to get rid of the grass and dirt.

"I'm sorry I interrupted your meditation session," he told me.

I laughed. "It wasn't much of a session, as you could tell."

"Troubles at home?" he asked, the edge of his smile slipped slightly.

I shook my head. "No. Just started a new job here, and I've only been here a few days, so it's been a bit crazy."

He waved toward the park's main path. "Care to go for a walk?"

His eyebrow ticked up a little when he asked, and my heart fluttered.

"I'd love to," I said, hoping I didn't sound as breathless as I felt.

We continued down the path, side by side, the wind whispering through the canopy of trees. There wasn't another soul in sight, and for that, I was glad.

"Do you work, Fox?" I asked, once I'd worked up the nerve. I could flirt with Rhys like a pro, but something about Fox made me feel childish and inexperienced.

He nodded. "I'm on my lunch break right now."

"Me, too."

"Does that mean that I might get a chance to see you again during the week?" he asked.

His eyebrow did that thing again, this time paired with a smirk that made me feel weak in the knees.

"Only if you're very nice," I said, not letting on to my infatuation as I flipped my hair over my shoulder.

"I'm always nice," he replied, and with that, he produced a silver rose out of thin air into his palm. He held it out to me, and I gratefully accepted it.

"Wow," I whispered. "It's beautiful."

"Not nearly as beautiful as you."

So, he was a sweet talker, too! I couldn't contain my smile as I pressed my nose to the flower to smell. It had a muted scent, but it was calming and reassuring, just like his presence.

"Thank you," I said from behind the rose before offering my smile to him directly.

We walked in silence for another five minutes, enjoying the flowers and trees, a small reprieve from the city life that surrounded the park. It smelled clean and fresh here, reminding me of my small hometown and the fields that had surrounded my house.

We didn't get nearly enough time together before he told me he had to get back to work.

He dipped his head forward slightly, then looked up, and asked, "Would you meet me here tomorrow?"

I tucked a strand of hair behind my ear, immediately warm and open to the idea. "I'd like that."

He pulled out a cell phone from his pocket and handed it to me. "If you'll please..."

I entered my phone number and name into his contacts and sent myself a message with his name, so that I wouldn't be surprised if he texted me later.

"All set," I said, handing his phone back with a smile.

He kissed my cheek and waved as he walked away. I twirled the rose as I went back to work and inhaled the slightly sweet smell that it gave off. I might as well have been walking on air as I strode back into the building.

"Who gave you that?" Justina asked.

"None of your business," I whispered, not letting the fact that I had added a third guy already to my phone book bother me. Or the fact that she would definitely have something to say about it.

She rolled her eyes and went back to working.

I sent a message to Rhys, not wanting him to think I had forgotten about him.

Me: Work's been crazy. Dinner on Saturday?

Rhys: I was worried that you had forgotten about me.

Me: No way that I could forget about you.

Rhys: Dinner sounds great. 7?

Me: Okay. You pick the place, and message me the address, and I'll meet you there.

Rhys: Can't wait.

I would spend the day with Deryn, and then go out with Rhys for dinner. I was a single woman and I didn't have any attachments to these men. So, there was no reason that I couldn't date a few of them.

After work, I went out to a nearby bar and sipped on a vodka lemonade while I people watched. It was one of the best ways to figure out what the town was really like, and what went on. There were various races in the bar. Among them were werewolves, elves, dragons, and even some mages. There were way more humans though, our race taking up at least seventy percent of the population of the bar.

"Hello, is this seat taken?" an incredibly deep male voice asked.

I turned and smiled wide. He was hot, incredibly hot. What luck I seemed to be having!

"No, it's not taken."

He sat down and held out his hand. "Hi, I'm Nico."

"Nice to meet you," I said with a smile, but didn't shake his hand, picking my drink up to give me an excuse.

With a flick of his wrist, he produced a playing card. "Would you like to see a trick?"

I turned to face him fully and nodded with a wide smile. "Yes, please."

He snapped his fingers and a red rose appeared, a smile spread, and he set it down on the bar top in front of me. Then, he showed me his hands, front and back. The next instant, he held a full deck of cards and was shuffling them.

I clapped and he chuckled. "I haven't done the trick yet."

"I'm still impressed," I told him.

He showed me the cards, front and back — they looked like normal cards. "Watch closely," he whispered. He shuffled the cards again and then, they changed, the symbols turning blue and purple instead of red and black.

"Wow," I said and clapped again.

He continued shuffling and they returned to black and red. He bowed his head and smiled.

My liquid courage was in full effect at the moment, plus the fact that I'd managed to get dates with some other pretty hot males this week. I hoped three would be enough, but I wouldn't be disappointed if I couldn't add him as the fourth to my phonebook.

"Would you like me to show you a trick?" I asked him.

"You, show me a trick?" he asked.

I nodded. "Yes."

He waved his hand at the bar top. "Please."

I wrote my name and phone number on a napkin, folded it in half, took the glass of water that was next to me, put the folded napkin into it, slid a coaster on top of it, flipped it over so that it was upside down, and then pulled the coaster out. This left my number in the folded napkin inside of the water with no easy way for him to get it.

I stood up and kissed his cheek. "Thanks for the show. Hopefully, I hear from you soon." Quickly, before he could say anything to me, I turned and left.

His laugh was deep, and rumbled all the way across the noisy bar as I left.

I was chuckling to myself as I typed a message into the group chat with my clan, telling them about the joke I had just played on Nico. They all agreed that it was great, and if he figured out a way to get my number, he would definitely call me and I should give him at least one date. I slid my card through the reader to open the apartment building door and replied to another message on my phone, looking down as I walked inside, towards the elevator.

"Jolie!" four male voices called out at the same time.

I jerked my head up and felt a knot form in my throat. Rhys, Deryn, Fox, and Nico stood together in front of the elevator, waiting for the doors to open.

Oh no. They all know each other!

"Wait," Rhys said to the others. "How do you know her?"

"How do you know her?" Fox asked.

"What is happening?" Deryn asked.

I kept my head down and was about to head to the stairs, but the elevator arrived. They walked in first, lining up along the back of the elevator and looked at me expectantly. Rhys held the door open for me. I stepped inside, pushed my floor, and felt as small as a mouse with all of them towering over me. Their stares were heavy, pressing upon me as the elevator moved up.

What was I going to do?

"You live here?" Rhys asked.

I nodded. "Just moved in. Which one of you live here?" I hadn't turned around, worried to see what the expressions on their faces might be.

"All of us," Nico replied with a soft laugh. "We all wondered who the new resident was. I had no idea it would be you."

"So, it seems you've met the four of us already," Deryn said. "Sort of funny, right?"

I spun around, worried they were mad and needing to defend myself.

"I didn't know you guys knew each other. I met you all randomly and..."

"It's okay," Fox said and smiled reassuringly at me.

I wasn't so sure. My floor came up and I rushed out, getting into my apartment and locking my door with a groan. What the hell was I going to do? They all lived here. They all knew each other.

My phone beeped and I wasn't shocked to see it was one of them.

Deryn: We still hanging out tomorrow?

He still wanted to hang out? Had they talked? Maybe he didn't know that I'd slept with Rhys.

Me: Yeah, if you're still up for it.

Deryn: Definitely!

CHAPTER 3

I stood outside of Deryn's apartment and fidgeted with my hair. I had told him I would come over, but now I was nervous. What if they confronted me instead of wanting to hang out?

Taking a breath for courage, I knocked on the door. *Might as well get it over with.*

Deryn opened the door and smiled. "Jolie! Come on in."

"Thanks," I replied with what I hoped was a nice smile.

His apartment was pretty large, at least two bedrooms, and had a huge living room where Fox was sitting, playing a video game.

He turned and smiled at me. "Hey, Jolie."

"Hi, Fox," I said with a little wave, shocked that he was here. Wasn't I supposed to hang out with Deryn?

Fox was playing the newest first-person shooter, a game I had been considering getting, but wasn't certain it was good enough to draw me away from *Ghost 2*.

"How do you like it?" I asked him and leaned on the back of the couch, while I watched him play. Deryn's TV was huge, at least eighty inches. I was totally jealous and possibly drooling a little at how amazing the graphics looked.

Our building had incredibly fast internet speeds as well, so the frames per second were maxed and there was no lag.

"I love it so far. I'm just doing the campaign," he replied, shooting one guy and blowing up another guy with a sticky grenade.

"Haven't given PVP a chance yet?" I asked with a smirk. A lot of the gamers I knew avoided the player versus player aspect of the game for as long as they could, because they became rage monsters. I was also one of the rage monsters when playing PVP, but it took a lot to make me rage.

"He rages worse than anyone else," Deryn told me. "We had to ban him from playing one game because he wouldn't stop breaking controllers."

"I replaced each of the ones I broke," Fox countered.

"Do you guys live together?" I asked curiously.

Deryn shook his head. "No, Fox lives across the hall. He comes over to try the new games that I get, though."

"Sweet," I said and looked at the entertainment center where my eyes widened. "You have every single console," I whispered and headed towards it. It was calling to me. All of the old consoles that I had played with as I grew up, and some I hadn't been able to get.

"Yep," Deryn said with a satisfied smirk. "Even the oddball ones that didn't really have a purpose like the Mini Sub One."

"Do you have games for all of these?" I whispered as I almost began to worship his collection.

"What do you want to play?" he asked with a smirk.

"*Road Bashers 3*?" I asked. It had been a childhood favorite of mine, but it was rare and incredibly expensive now.

"Mind if I stay and play?" Fox asked.

"Not at all," Deryn replied and then looked at me. "Okay with you?"

I smiled and nodded. "It's a party game, after all."

Deryn set up the game and I took a seat on the couch in the middle. Deryn and Fox sat on either side of me and we all grabbed a controller and prepared to play. The music came on, and I immediately got the chills.

"Oh man," I whispered excitedly. "It's been so long since I've played this."

We spent three hours playing *Road Bashers 3*, teasing and messing with each other like the three of us were old friends. They were so easy to be around. It was strange for me to feel so safe and comfortable with them when I barely knew them, but here we were. When we finally decided to turn it off, Fox kissed my cheek and then waved as he left the apartment, yawning.

"That was fun," I told Deryn. I would have kept playing except that I had my date with Rhys and I didn't want to be late for it.

He smiled and nodded. "Yeah, I haven't had that much fun playing a game in a long time."

"I should get home," I whispered and headed towards the door. He trailed behind me, then leaned against the wall next to the door. "I really did have a lot of fun tonight," I told him.

He brushed my hair behind my ear and whispered, "I'm glad." His lips were warm and soft as he slid them across mine. It was a sweet kiss, and yet, it made my hormones rage. "We should play again soon," he whispered.

I nodded and kissed his cheek once before leaving his apartment and running right into Rhys.

"Oh," I gasped.

He smiled. "Hello." He looked up at the apartment number and his smile disappeared as he asked, "Were you on a date with Deryn?"

"I played some games with him and Fox," I explained. "I had planned on going back to my place to finish getting ready." After glancing at my phone and confirming that there was still half an hour before our date, I asked, "Unless you're ready now?"

"Go ahead and freshen up. I need to talk to Deryn really quick," he told me with a smile.

I kissed his cheek and then went to the stairs to walk down to my floor. I threw open the door and almost screamed when Nico was there. I put my hand to my chest and dropped my head. "Mage's Mana!" I exclaimed.

"What?" Nico asked with a chuckle.

"You startled me," I explained and exhaled loudly. "Sorry."

He pushed open the door for me and stepped to the side. "No, my fault." I stepped past him and he whispered, "Your trick was great, but one thing you didn't know..." He snapped his fingers and the napkin I had written my number on appeared in his hand, dry and smudge free. "...I'm a mage."

My eyes widened as I stared at him in disbelief. A mage. Wow. I had no idea.

"Good to know," I whispered and smiled before skipping down the stairs to my floor.

It only took me a couple of minutes to get my hair brushed and touch up my makeup. I did a twirl in front of my floor-length mirror and then went to the living room. As soon as I sat down on the couch, someone knocked on the door.

Rhys smiled at me when I opened it. "You look beautiful."

"Thank you," I replied, stepping into the hall, and turned, closing and locking my door.

He pushed the elevator button and looked at me with a tilted head. "You're an enigma."

"What? How?" I asked.

"You're gorgeous, but single. Normally that's because the girl is crazy. However, you don't seem crazy."

"You've only spent one night with me," I reminded him. "I could quite possibly be hiding my crazy."

He smirked. "That is possible, but you're forgetting that you've also spent time with all of my friends."

My cheeks warmed and he noticed.

"All of them were raving about you," he informed me. "Deryn couldn't stop talking about how much fun he had with you today. This is the first time that I've heard him talk about a girl. It's definitely the first time I've heard him talk about a girl he hasn't slept with."

"How do you know if I've slept with him or not?" I asked defensively.

"We're best friends," he replied. "We tell each other everything."

"So, they know that we..."

"Yes, but not the circumstances or details."

"And what did they have to say when they learned I've dated all of you, but you and I have slept together?" I asked nervously.

"There were a couple high fives, and we all agreed that you're pretty awesome," he said and hit the stop button on the elevator, making it freeze between floors.

I glanced at it nervously and fought the urge to rush forward and hit the button. He walked towards me slowly, stopping a foot or so away from me.

"Why was I the only one you slept with?" he asked.

The others weren't really in situations that allowed for it.

"I just, didn't..." I replied softly.

"But you want to," he stated.

"I'm single," I reminded him. "And I had no idea that any of you knew each other, or that you all lived here. I met four sexy males at different times and they all wanted to spend time with me. I don't think it's wrong that I went out with you all. I don't think it's wrong that I had sex with you. I don't think it would be wrong for me to sleep with one, or all, of the others either. None of us are attached or taken. Am I wrong?"

"No, you are not wrong," he agreed. He reached out slowly and then pulled me forward against him. "I'm not selfish enough or possessive enough to try to make you choose. I wish I was the only one, but you have done nothing wrong and are still doing nothing wrong."

"Glad we agree," I whispered as I swallowed around the lump in my throat and set my hands on his chest, mostly to keep me balanced, but also because I *really* wanted to touch him.

"I am competitive, however," he replied and inhaled. "And you are too good to pass up." His lips were on mine and my hands wound around his neck instantly. He lifted me up and pushed me back against the wall of the elevator. He gripped my butt as he held me, his fingers digging into my skin, but not painfully.

I broke our kiss to kiss his neck and he moaned.

"Not now," he whispered and gently nipped my neck. "Though, the thought of taking you here is very tempting. Tonight, I want to enjoy our date and not lose out on it because dessert was too filling."

I chuckled and nipped his earlobe. "Okay."

He groaned and gripped my butt tighter. "If you do that again, I'll go back on what I just said."

I leaned back and held up my hands in surrender. "Okay."

He kissed me again and then set me down and hit the button on the elevator. "I'm glad that we agree."

"Me, too," I said and exhaled happily. I ran my fingers through my hair and smoothed my clothes down. "I was really worried that you guys would shut me out after you found out what happened."

"No, that's not how we are."

"Good to know."

We stepped outside and were met with several members of the media with cameras on, and bulbs flashing as they took pictures. Rhys put his arm around my shoulders and steered me away from them.

"Rhys, who is this new female? What is she doing in your apartment building? Is she part of your clan?"

"Has the Dragon Clan made a decision about the war?"

"Where was the artifact last seen?"

He didn't respond, and gently propelled me forward until we were away from the building, and across the street.

"My apologies about that. They're vicious at times," Rhys said with a soft sigh.

"Who are you?" I asked softly. "You seem to be someone important, but—"

"No one important," he replied. "They're just trying to get information out of us, but it won't work."

"You guys seem important," I commented as I looked back at the media who were now scowling at us.

He smiled. "Did you just say we are important to you?"

I scoffed, but smiled at him. "I hardly know you." It was strange, though. I did feel close to them. Was I that desperate for affection that I fell for the first guys to give me attention? Was I the crazy stalker chick? Oh no! I didn't want to be the crazy stalker chick.

He waved down a taxi and moved close to me on the back seat. His scent was a mixture of fire and something that I couldn't place, but knew it was a masculine smell. "I'd like to remedy that," he whispered to me.

"Remedy what?" I asked, sidetracked by his delicious scent and body heat.

"Not knowing each other."

"Sounds great to me," I said and looked up into his beautiful eyes. "Are you always warm or do you create extra heat when you want to?"

"I run warmer than a human, but I can create more heat if I want to," he replied.

The taxi pulled over and we climbed out onto the sidewalk. Rhys paid the driver as I stared at the restaurant we were headed into. *Simone's* was not just nice, but swanky. It was a restaurant that people joked only politicians and celebrities went into because no one else could afford it.

"You okay?" Rhys asked and set his hand on my lower back.

"You lied. You are someone important," I said. "Or at least famous."

"Come, our table is waiting," he replied and ushered me forward, completely ignoring what I had said. We stepped inside and the staff immediately led us to our table and brought out champagne.

Rhys smiled at me and said, "Order whatever you'd like."

The restaurant was somehow the perfect temperature. Most of the places I went to were either too hot or too cold, but they seemed to know the exact temperature appropriate. There were far less tables in this restaurant than the ones I frequented, which gave us more privacy to talk.

"Are you part of a mafia?" I asked him.

He smirked. "No."

"An actor?"

"No."

"Model?"

"Not currently, though I did model for a brief time when I was younger for extra money," he admitted.

"A member of the Summit?" I asked since I knew many of the clans had representatives who went to the Summit to meet and discuss issues with the other clans.

"I do not have a seat on the Summit," he replied.

"But you are affiliated with it somehow?"

"Yes."

"You're not a King?"

"No."

I tapped my chin as I tried to think about who he could possibly be that would allow him this much money and the eye of the media.

"Have you decided on what you want to order?" he asked, obviously trying to change the subject.

"I'm debating between the steak that costs twice my monthly income or the chicken pasta that costs more than my rent," I replied with a relaxed and teasing smile.

He smiled back, completely at ease and relaxed as well. "I recommend the steak, medium rare."

I sipped the champagne, and my eyes widened at the delicious taste. "This is wonderful," I told him and took a bigger drink.

The waiter who came over was old, but his skin was unblemished and smooth. He also had sharp pointed teeth that came to his bottom lip. Vampire. "Are you ready to order?" he asked with a slight accent.

"My usual, Vlad," Rhys replied.

"Medium rare steak," I ordered.

"Mashed potatoes?" Vlad asked.

"Please," I replied with a nod.

"Very well," he said and bowed before leaving us to eat the bread I had not even seen him set on the table.

I took a piece and buttered it. "So, what do you do for fun?" I asked Rhys.

"You asked me a ton of questions. I believe, it is my turn."

"Okay," I agreed.

"What do you do for work?"

"I write for a gaming company."

"What do you write?"

"I write the storylines for games. I've got one that I'm working on now, which I think is going to be pretty awesome."

"Really?"

I nodded.

"Do you like it?"

He was so focused on me, it was a bit overpowering, but also exciting. There was the potential for danger with him, but also for him to protect me from danger. The latter was something I desperately needed.

"I love it," I replied with a wide smile. "Not only do I love it, it was a big raise for me to move here and take the job."

"So, that's why you moved to Jinla?"

I nodded.

"What do you do when you aren't working?"

"Usually I play video games."

"Really?" he asked, eyebrows raised.

"Why is that hard to believe?" I asked him a bit defensively.

"I've never met a gorgeous woman who played video games."

"We exist," I assured him, silently pleased he had called me gorgeous.

"Clearly," he replied with a smirk. "What are your favorite types of games?"

"The kind you play," I said and chuckled. "I play a little bit of everything."

"What are you playing currently?"

"*Ghost 2.*"

"Do you play with a clan?"

"Yes," I said, shocked he knew what that was.

"Double standard," he whispered with a smirk.

"What?"

"You were shocked that someone as hot as me would know about clans."

He caught me.

"Possibly," I admitted.

"We have our own clan," he explained. "Deryn will be sad to learn that you already have a clan."

"He knows, actually. I can still play with you guys, but I've been with this clan since the first beta came out. So, I don't have any plans to leave them," I explained.

I chewed on the bread and closed my eyes at the perfect texture and flavor. How did they make bread so perfectly?

"I take it the bread is good?" he asked with a chuckle.

"Amazing," I replied and took another bite.

"What character do you main?" he asked.

"DPS."

"Really?"

I nodded. "And I'm guessing you're a tank?"

He blinked twice and then asked, "How'd you guess that?"

I smirked at him and buttered another piece of bread. "You seem like someone who would prefer a tank."

"Can you guess what Nico is?" he asked softly with a smirk.

"Obviously the DPS," I said with a chuckle. "He would be the one who wants to use magic."

"And what about Deryn?"

"That's a bit harder to guess. He seems like he would be good at all of the classes and would enjoy them all."

"True."

"If you're the tank and Nico is the DPS, then Fox is the healer and Deryn would be your additional DPS," I guessed.

He clapped softly. "Impressive."

"If I were to play with you guys, it would be beneficial if I was an additional DPS player," I replied.

Our food came out and we ate without much discussion. The food was almost worthy of the price tag and deserved to be savored. Once we finished, we didn't linger and left the restaurant, headed back to the apartment building.

"Thank you, for tonight," he told me and kissed my cheek. "I enjoyed learning more about you."

"I enjoyed tonight, too," I replied and smiled happily. I was normally alone or with just one or two friends, but I had promised myself when I came here that I would be more outgoing and make more friends. So far, it was serving me well.

"Next time I get to learn more about you," I said adamantly.

"Deal," he agreed.

We waited for the elevator and I realized how tired I was. I leaned against the wall beside the elevator opening and Rhys played with some of my hair, twisting it around his finger gently and letting it fall away.

The elevator opened and Deryn stepped out. His eyes widened as he took us in. "Were you out together?" he asked.

"Yes, we were on a date," Rhys replied.

"What!" Deryn yelled.

"I told you that I wouldn't let you steal her away from me," Rhys told Deryn. "Besides, all of us are single, so there's nothing wrong with it."

"I didn't say there was anything wrong with it. I just can't believe you took her out so soon," Deryn explained.

"We had already set this date up a few days ago," I whispered, staring intently at the floor.

"Always one step ahead, aren't you?" Deryn grumbled.

"Let's get you to bed," Rhys said to me and ushered me inside of the elevator.

I put my face in my hands and sighed. What was I going to do about these guys? While I said that I didn't see anything wrong with it, part of me did feel bad. I would never forgive myself if I ended up ruining their friendship.

"Jolie," Rhys said loudly.

I jerked my head up and asked, "What?"

"It's your floor," he noted and waved at the open elevator doors.

"Oh, thanks," I said and headed towards the hallway.

He followed me to my door and kissed me goodnight. "Goodnight, my beautiful princess."

"Goodnight, Prince."

His left eye twitched.

Holy monster's teats! No way!

"You're a Prince!" I screamed.

"I...yes."

My hand flew to my mouth as I held in my gasp. A Prince? He was a Prince? What had I fallen into?

"Say something," he begged.

"I'm just in shock," I explained and looked at him again. I really needed to pay attention better to the media. I would have known that as soon as I met him if I had been watching news stories or reading up on the happenings of Jinla.

"Please don't let this change anything," he whispered, his eyes downcast and fists clenched at his sides.

"Why me? You could have any girl that you want. You could have ten or twenty girls if you wanted. I'm no one. I'm nothing special. I'm just a socially anxious gamer."

"You are special. You are kind and beautiful. You are easy to be around. I've never met a human woman – any woman – who was so easy to be around. I'm so relaxed and calm with you. It's nice compared to my normally anxious life."

He was anxious? I supposed he would have a lot of duties as Prince.

"Don't worry," I told him and gripped one of his fists between both of my hands. "Knowing you are a prince doesn't change how I feel about you."

He used my hands to jerk me forward and wrapped his arms around me in a hug. "Jolie," he whispered and sighed loudly.

"Eh?!" Nico yelled.

I jerked away from Rhys and found Nico walking down the hallway towards us.

"Nico," I whispered in shock.

"You told her you're a prince? Why?" he demanded and stood before Rhys with a scowl.

"I didn't tell her that *I* am a prince. She guessed that I am," he explained.

"You still admitted it, though."

"I'm not going to lie to her about it. If she watches the news, she'll find out on her own."

"It's not fair. You've been out twice, while the rest of us..."

"It has nothing to do with fairness," Rhys snapped.

"Guys!" I yelled angrily.

They both turned to look at me with partially opened mouths.

I clenched my fists at my side and through clenched teeth said, "You are not allowed to fight about me."

"What?" Nico asked.

"You are friends. I'm a random chick—"

"You're not a—" Rhys began.

"I am!" I snapped. "I am a random chick and I refuse to become an issue between you friends. If that's going to be the case, I remove myself before there are any further issues."

Without waiting for a reply, I spun around, opened my door, and then slammed it closed behind me.

CHAPTER 4

I had spent my day off of work drinking and playing games in a rage.

"I think you should probably stop for the night," our clan leader said to me after I cursed for a few minutes straight when we lost the match.

I groaned. I couldn't even play video games right. I was ruining everything.

"Fine. See you guys later." I shut down my console and tossed my headset to the other couch. Playing longer would only upset me more, so I knew he was right, but it still made me mad.

The four males had been trying to contact me, but I had ignored them all, not returning any of their texts or calls. I had screwed up by continuing to see them after I found out that they were friends. I wasn't going to do it anymore. I wasn't going to cause issues between friends. I wasn't one of those girls.

I raised my bottle to my lips, but it was empty, not even a spare drop in it. "Dammit!" I growled and stood up. I needed more alcohol. After searching for a few minutes, I finally found my keys and cards, and headed out of the apartment towards the nearest spirits store. I liked the place. The owner was a sweet, old human woman with grey streaks through her hair that reminded me of lightning.

The sidewalk lurched a bit as I walked, seeming to randomly roll beneath my feet and make me unstable.

Or, I could have been drunk. Most likely I was drunk.

On the way to the store, I had to go by the park that I had met Fox in. I looked at it with a mixture of happiness and sadness. They were all so sweet. I had really enjoyed the time I had spent with them and could have seen myself becoming good friends with them

While looking at the park, I saw a huge group gathered, split into four factions, or so it appeared. At the center stood Rhys, Deryn, Fox, and Nico, each standing behind males sitting in chairs. Who brought big wood chairs to the park? What the heck was going on?

"What are they doing?" I asked myself out loud and squatted into the bushes to creep closer. They were still a bit away, but I could hear what they were saying better now. There were so many beings gathered and spread out among the trees. There had to be at least fifty, possibly more since some of them seemed to blur together and then multiply. Who were they all? I had to be extra quiet so that no one spotted me.

"It's been twenty years!" one of the men in the middle yelled. "It's been long enough! You've had long enough to return it to us!"

"What do you expect us to do?" another asked, this one standing near Fox. He had silver eyes and was definitely an elf once I focused hard enough on his features.

"I say we take over. Screw these pathetic humans. Let's kill them until we find our missing-"

"We are not killing the humans," Rhys snapped.

Hearing him defend my kind was a relief, but I did not like where the rest of them were headed with this discussion.

"Why not? They're pathetic! They don't deserve to live beside us," someone else said.

"Kill them!" another said.

My heart hammered against my chest as many began to agree.

One of the older gentlemen, who was seated in a chair at the center, raised his hand, and everyone quieted. "Raise your hand if you agree with killing the humans."

A few started to raise their hands, and I stumbled forward, tripping over the bush I had been hiding behind. Everyone turned, and the four men from my apartment all started to move towards me.

Crap. Thank you, drunken klutziness.

One of the people nearest made a grab for me. I tried to get away from him, but there were others and they were faster, grabbing my arms and stopping me. I squealed in fear and tried to break free, but their grips were too tight.

"Let her go," Rhys ordered them.

One of them released me, but the other two held on.

"Release her," Deryn ordered them with a snarl.

Reluctantly, they released me.

Tears streamed down my face, and I walked up to Rhys who reached me first, having been the closest. I gripped his shirt in my hands and said, "I don't want to die! I'm too young to die."

"Shh," he ordered me. "What are you doing here?"

"I was getting more booze and I saw you guys. Then they started talking about killing us. I don't want to die. I just met you, and I want to get to know you more."

"It's alright," Deryn told me, taking my hand and pulling me away from Rhys. "You're not going to die."

"But, they said—"

"We won't let anything happen to you," Fox said adamantly, smiling warmly at me.

"We aren't going to kill the humans," Nico assured me.

I knew that I should let the conversation drop and be reassured by their proclamations, but I was too drunk and stupid to stop. The words fell out of my mouth before I could stop them.

"I know we're stupid, and I know most of them aren't used to you, but if you give them a chance to learn, I know more will come to love you. Killing the humans won't make them like you. I only met you four, and yet I want to know more about you. If I'm dead, I won't get to learn about you and learn what makes you so amazing. I feel so content when I'm with you guys. It feels right to be with you, even if I can't anymore because you're fighting and I don't want to contribute to that. But, I don't want to be dead."

"Who the hell is she?" one of the men sitting in a chair asked. He had the same eyes as Nico.

"She's our friend," Nico told him.

"Get her out of here," he ordered him.

There was a book open in the middle of their circle showing a necklace with a pendant that looked very familiar. I pulled out of their holds and stumbled over to the book, dropping to my hands and knees to look at it.

"I've seen this," I mumbled and squinted to try to get a better look.

"Don't touch her!" Rhys ordered someone behind me.

"Don't touch the book!" someone ordered me.

I pulled my necklace out from beneath my shirt and tugged the chain over my head before setting it on the book beside the image. I was positive, it was the same necklace.

"Is this what you're looking for?" I asked and looked up at my friends who were standing in a protective circle around me. I hadn't realized how much trouble I was in until I saw that they were all using their powers at that moment to keep others away from me. All of their eyes were glowing and they all held weapons at their sides.

Everyone stopped what they were doing and turned around to face me, and the book.

Deryn dropped to his knees beside me and looked at the book and my necklace. "It's..."

"It is!" Fox exclaimed.

"Where did you get this?" the man with Nico's eyes asked me.

"My Grandma gave it to me. She told me to keep it safe and that it would protect me from vampires." As soon as I said it, I clamped a hand to my mouth.

"Vampires? Is that who hurt you last year?" Rhys asked me.

"Maybe," I mumbled around my hand covered mouth. Maybe I should stop drinking so much alcohol.

Before I could grab the necklace back, the man with Nico's eyes snatched it.

"I need that!" I screamed. "It's the only thing preventing them from finding me!" I crawled towards him, the damp grass soaked into the knees of my jeans. "Please!"

"Jolie," Rhys whispered and placed his hands on my shoulders. "It's okay. You don't need the necklace."

"I do!" I yelled.

"This is a precious artifact to us," Fox whispered, his calming presence helping to push back the hysteria that was trying to build within me. "Please, may we have it back?"

"It's precious to you?" I asked. It was just a necklace. What was so special about it? Aside from it keeping the vampires away from me, Grandma hadn't said that it could do anything else.

"It is very precious to us," Rhys said.

"If it is yours, then I should return it to you," I said firmly. "I'm sorry for being selfish. Please, take your necklace."

A voice began laughing loudly, causing everyone to look around for the source. I already knew. I knew who was coming.

My body shook and my heart beat quickly. My palms began sweating and wrapping them around myself did nothing to help. No. How did he find me so quickly?

Rhys, Deryn, Fox, and Nico stood near me, taking protective

stances. It should have made me happy to know that they were willing to protect me even after what had happened, but it only made me worry about their safety.

"You've revealed yourself, little lamb," Demarcus said as he materialized a few feet away from us. He was tall, thin, and very powerful. His clothing was straight out of the eighteenth century, which he claimed had the best style, and refused to wear anything else.

"Who are you?" Rhys demanded.

"Oh, did you get another protector?" Demarcus asked.

"N-no," I stuttered quickly, getting to my feet.

"Do you remember what happened to the last protector you had? Do you remember how much he screamed? I'll be more than happy to do it again. Come with me now, and tell me how you escaped, and I'll leave these boys alone."

I stepped forward, ahead of the males, and started to walk towards him.

"That's a good girl. Come with me and I'll not hurt anyone," he said with a cocky smirk.

"Jolie!" Deryn called out.

Fox grabbed my arm and stopped me. "No, you can't have her."

"Oh?" Demarcus asked and quirked a brow. "You have a claim to her?"

"She's ours," Rhys growled, his eyes shifted into dragon's eyes and his hands now had thick talons coming out of his fingertips. He came to stand on my right side and I looked at him in shock.

Deryn shifted into warrior form and stood behind me, setting his clawed paws lightly on my shoulders, his claws carefully pulled away from my skin to avoid hurting me. "Leave, or we'll take this as a challenge."

"Everyone," I whispered in shock. Even after causing them problems, they were willing to protect me?

"Do you really want me to kill these boys?" Demarcus asked me, frowning.

I turned to face the males and said, "Please. Please let me go."

"No," all four replied at the same time, not looking at me.

"You are ours," Deryn whispered. "You are our friend. You are important to us. We protect what is important to us."

"If you are hurt—"

"Don't have such little faith in us," Nico said with a smile. "Rhys isn't the only prince."

"What?" I asked, lost.

The four of them smiled at me.

"We're all princes," Fox explained.

"You may be strong, but you aren't strong enough to defeat us alone," Deryn said to Demarcus.

Demarcus smirked and five vampires materialized beside him.

"Clearly, you have a death wish," the male with Nico's eyes said. "Nico, I don't know who she is, but don't disgrace us by losing now that you've made such a claim."

"Just give me the girl," Demarcus snarled. "She's just one, stupid human."

"No, she's not," Rhys growled and leapt forward, attacking Demarcus.

Nico stayed at my elbow, a staff in his hand which had a dark blue jewel on the end of it. I hadn't even seen him grab the staff. Where had it come from?

He set his hand on my shoulder and squeezed lightly. "It'll be okay."

How could it be okay? How could any of this be okay?

"Do you have a cape?" I asked softly, trying to keep my hysteria down as I watched the others fighting.

"Yes," Nico replied and added, "I'll show you it another night."

Demarcus and his vampires were ferocious and everyone moved so fast that I couldn't keep up. Someone was going to get hurt. It was going to be my fault.

"Just give her to me!" Demarcus snarled at Rhys as they fought.

"No!" the four males yelled at him at the same time.

My legs wobbled and I dropped to my knees beside Nico. Something warm and painful at the same time spread from my chest throughout the rest of my body. What was going on? Nico stepped closer to me and began whispering something in what I was pretty certain was Greek. Air shimmered around us and a transparent bubble enveloped us.

"Tell me how you did it!" Demarcus demanded. "How did you escape?"

"It really bothers you that a human girl escaped, doesn't it?" Deryn taunted him, jumping in to back up Rhys. "How could you let such a weak being slip through your fingers?"

"You left the door unlocked," I whispered.

"What?" Demarcus asked. He leapt away from Deryn and Rhys to look at me across the park.

"You left the door unlocked. You and your men thought that leaving me broken and defeated was enough. You thought that I was too broken to have the will to run. You thought that my broken leg would keep me from trying."

Fury began to build in me and I stood up, fists clenched at my sides.

"You underestimated my will to survive. You left to sleep for the day and I walked out of that building and all the way to a hospital. It was your own ego that allowed me to escape!"

Demarcus snarled. "A mistake I won't make twice."

Deryn lunged at him, but Demarcus expected the move and backhanded Deryn, sending him flying into the tree off to his right.

"Deryn!" I screamed, fear clawing its way up my throat. I couldn't lose him. I couldn't lose anyone else to Demarcus.

"Please, stop protecting me," I begged Nico. "Please, let him take me. You hardly know me. I'm not worth all of this."

"We know enough. You're our friend and someone we are all very interested in romantically. We will not let him take you and hurt you. We won't let anyone hurt you."

"You're all fighting each other already. I'm not worth ruining your friendships. I'm not worth getting hurt over. I'm just a stupid, drunk, human girl who doesn't know when to leave well enough alone."

"Ah, you're drunk. That explains a lot," Nico chuckled.

"What's that supposed to mean?" I asked with a glare in his direction. He wasn't phased by the glare, which meant I needed to work on my scary face.

"We can have this conversation another day, when you haven't been drinking. Okay?" Nico promised.

"Stop ignoring me!" Demarcus yelled and lunged towards me. One minute he was there and the next, he disappeared. My eyes widened and a small shriek escaped my lips as he appeared in front of me and tried to reach through the bubble to grab me. I jerked backward, but there turned out to be no need. The bubble exploded outwards in a flash of brilliant sunlight. Demarcus and his vampires screamed once as they disintegrated before my eyes.

Nico picked me up and headed towards the apartment. I gripped the front of his shirt and stared mutely at his neck. What had just happened? It had all been so fast, that I wasn't sure what exactly occurred.

"You're safe," Nico whispered reassuringly. "We killed the vampire who was after you. He'll never hurt you again."

"He's *dead* dead?" I asked and squeaked at the end of my sentence.

"Yes."

"The artifact is returned!" someone shouted behind us. It seemed I wasn't the only one in a bit of a shell-shocked state.

"She saved the humans. She ended the war," someone nearby whispered as we walked through those in attendance.

"You hear that?" Deryn asked, walking on my left side. "You're a hero."

"I didn't do anything," I countered. "You saved me from the vampires."

"You saved us," Fox said adamantly. "Our four factions have been at each other's throats for a long time trying to locate that artifact. You found it and returned it to us."

"We need to ask her some questions," someone said behind us.

"No," Rhys snapped. "She is not well. You may ask her questions a different day. For now, be happy that this human ended the war."

"What's her name?" another person asked.

"Jolie," I replied. "My name is Jolie."

I woke the next morning to a hallway of flowers, mostly roses, but all from different people, if my cursory glance at the cards accompanying them were correct. I stood, transfixed in my doorway as I looked at them.

"You're popular now," Deryn informed me from down the hallway.

I turned to look at him and saw he was not smiling, like he normally did. Instead, he radiated sadness. His eyes could not have drooped more if he was a puppy.

My heart constricted.

"What do you mean?" I asked, my voice barely more than a whisper.

"Most of these are from males wanting to be your suitor," he explained. "You proved that you did not care what race we were, and that you are selfless. Those are important traits in a mate. Plus, you ended the war. You're a hero...heroine."

"I'm not a hero," I whispered. There had to be at least thirty vases here. Hundreds, maybe thousands, of dollars' worth of flowers. "What am I supposed to do with these flowers?"

"Keep them?" Deryn suggested.

"Did any of you send them?" I asked and turned my head away to avoid his eyes.

"No."

"So, if I throw them away, you won't get upset?" I asked and looked back at him.

"On the contrary, I will assist," he replied, his joyful energy returning.

I turned and he smiled warmly at me for just a moment before it wilted again. "You were avoiding us yesterday," he said matter-of-factly.

I nodded.

"Why?"

Rhys stepped into the hallway and stopped when he saw the flowers, Deryn, and me.

"I was avoiding you because I think it's best if I don't associate with you four," I admitted.

"Why?" Rhys demanded. "And you can't lie and try to say it is because we're Others."

"Because you are friends," I answered truthfully.

Fox and Nico walked into the hallway, chatting softly, but froze when they saw the situation.

What were all four of them doing in my hallway? Were they all coming to see me?

"You four are friends, right?" I asked them.

All four nodded.

"I refuse to be the girl who gets between you. I'm not like that. I hate girls like that. I spend ninety percent of my time talking with men. Half of them have stories about a girl that ruined a friendship of theirs. I won't let that happen to you four. You are princes! You have to get along so that your races get along. If I drive a wedge between you—"

"Why do you think that you will cause us to stop being friends?" Fox asked.

I slid down my closed door and wrapped my arms around my bent knees. I was a selfish woman. No matter what they said about the necklace, I was not a heroine or selfless. I was a vile, selfish creature.

"I can't choose," I whispered and placed my forehead against the top of my knees. "I can't choose between you four." I didn't know them that well, but they each offered something different. Rhys was a serious alpha, but had a soft side. Deryn was playful and strong. Fox was sweet and relaxing. Nico was silly and I could tell he was a trickster. I found that in this short time that I had known them, I was already attached to them. Thinking about being separated from them made the center of my chest hurt. Actually, ever since yesterday, my chest had felt strange.

"Does anyone smell that?" Deryn asked, lifting his nose in the air and moving towards me, stepping carefully around the flowers.

"Who said you had to choose?" Fox asked.

"Nico and Deryn both got mad at Rhys and Rhys admitted that he's competitive," I explained.

"We never said you had to choose between us," Rhys pointed out.

"Not yet, but soon you will. I've only been out with you each one or two times. Even if you let me continue to date you, eventually you will make me choose. I don't want to. I want to be friends with all four of you."

"Oh no, she's trying to friend-zone us!" Nico screeched and then gave me a smile. Yep, trickster.

I lowered my knees and picked up the nearest flowerpot. It had petunias in it. The card said it was from Anton and he had given me his phone number. Deryn had been right. These were guys trying to date me. What the heck?

Deryn continued sniffing as he went past me, but stopped and spun towards me. His eyes widened and he jerked the pot from my hand.

"Hey!" I shouted in shock.

He threw the pot out the window at the end of the hallway, shattering the glass.

"What the hell was that about?" I asked him. "Just because you don't like them, doesn't mean—"

A huge explosion rocked the building, making me scream in shock and fall to my side. Deryn picked me up and ran down the hallway.

"Run!" he yelled.

"What's—"

The next explosion made the entire building sway and Deryn

stumbled a step as he raced down the stairway. My arms tightened around his neck and I closed my eyes, praying to whatever god or goddess might be listening to let us survive. I did not want to get crushed by a building.

Cold air hit me and when I opened my eyes, we were across the street from the apartment building.

"Wh-What happened?" I asked and shivered, my heart pounding and my palms damp with sweat, but still unable to release Deryn.

"Bombs," he whispered, his eyes focused on the building and a scowl on his face. "Someone sent you bombs."

"They tried to kill me?" I asked, my throat tightening as soon as I said the words.

"It would seem so," Fox whispered.

I looked around and exhaled in relief to find the four of them with me. "You're all safe," I said, feeling my back relax. Deryn set me on my feet, but kept his arm around my waist, since I didn't think I could stand up on my own at the moment.

"Why?" Fox asked Rhys.

Rhys's eyes had changed to green and gold, like dragon's eyes and he grumbled in a deep and rocky voice, "It seems some aren't happy that she ended the war."

"It will be impossible to find out who sent them," Nico whispered.

"I could have died," I whispered and looked up at Deryn. "Thank you."

He didn't smile at me. He wasn't even looking at me.

"We need to figure out what we're going to do," he said to Rhys.

Rhys nodded. "Yes."

The fire trucks came, and I stepped away from the men to sit on the curb. This was not how I expected today to go at all! I was grateful that they had saved me, but the conversation we had started in the hallway was far from over.

"Do you think my apartment is okay?" I asked them softly.

"The bombs weren't packing much explosive power, but we don't know how many of those flowers had them. We won't know the damage until we go inside," Fox said and knelt beside me. He stroked my hair slowly and it was oddly relaxing.

"I hope my games are okay," I whispered and tried *really* hard not to lean into his hand.

"If they aren't, I'm sure we can find replacements," Deryn assured me. "Your data is all saved under your login, so it won't matter if you have to get a new console."

"Right," I agreed, feeling a little better.

Fox shifted into a red fox and climbed into my lap. My brain was on overload from all of the events, so I didn't even blink at his sudden transformation. Instead, I wrapped my arms around him, moving his head to my shoulder, and buried my face in his fur.

"Cheater," Rhys whispered.

The apartment manager walked over to us and sighed loudly. "Luckily the damage isn't too bad. The door and hallway wall of Jolie's apartment are destroyed, but most of your stuff survived. It wasn't enough to make it through the floor or ceiling of the hallway, so everyone else is good."

"Great," I mumbled into Fox's fur.

"The detectives are there now, trying to figure out who did it," the manager said. "So, you need to stay away from that floor for now."

"We can all go to my apartment for now," Rhys instructed everyone.

The group started to head across, but I couldn't move. Someone had tried to kill me. If Deryn hadn't smelled the explosive and grabbed me, I would be scattered about the hallway. There would be chunks of me with the flowers and dirt. Someone who went so far as to put explosives in flowers didn't strike me as the kind who would give up easily. What would their next attack be? Where would it be? I was in danger, and I was human. I had no way of protecting myself. There was nothing I could do. I was going to die. This was even more frightening than when Demarcus had been after me. At least with him, I knew the danger and what it looked like. This had no face. This had no warning. I was at a complete loss.

Fox leapt out of my arms, and Nico picked me up gently, cradling me against his body. "You are safe. You are alive. We are here for you. No one will harm you while you're with us."

How could he be so certain? They weren't invincible. They could be injured too.

"You'll be killed, too," I whispered.

"Did Demarcus kill us?" he asked.

"No," I admitted reluctantly.

He headed to the apartment building, his head held high as he carried me, the others walked around us in a shield of protection, hiding me from the media as they tried to snap pictures.

"We will not let you die," he told me adamantly.

Something slammed into what appeared to be a translucent shield around the five of us. On closer inspection, I realized that it was a large caliber bullet.

Rhys stepped back, shifted into his dragon form and took to the sky, disappearing into the smoke.

"Rhys!" I screamed.

The three remaining men hurried inside and to an apartment on the first floor that was unlocked. I assumed it belonged to one of them, but didn't ask.

"He'll be fine," Nico assured me.

"Bullets can't penetrate dragon's scales," Deryn said with a small smile.

A dragon's roar shook the building and I clutched Nico tighter. He sat on the couch, keeping me in his lap, and stroked my back.

"Food?" Fox asked me.

My stomach was a knotted mess of anxiety. I shook my head and climbed out of Nico's lap, sitting on a leather recliner that was unclaimed, and curled my legs up beneath me. My heartbeat quickened and I let my body fall sideways, my head resting on the arm of the chair.

"Jolie?" Deryn asked, turning to fully face me from behind the couch.

"Fine," I lied and closed my eyes.

Again. People were being put in harm's way because of me, again. I wasn't special. I wasn't gorgeous. Pretty, yes, but not a ten. Why did people keep getting hurt because of me? Maybe I needed to become a hermit. Could I get internet while being a hermit? I needed internet no matter what. There were too many games I wanted to play that required internet.

The door opened and I flew out of the chair, running to Rhys who had no visible injuries or blood stains anywhere I could see.

"Rhys!" I yelled and threw my arms around him. He hugged me back, pulling me close to his body.

"You find him?" Deryn asked.

"Yes, the police have him now."

"Did you get hurt?" I asked after stepping back from him.

He smiled. "No."

Finally, my heart unclenched and I felt the adrenaline leave me, fatigue setting in heavily. I went back to the chair and lay down again.

Rhys was safe. All four of them were safe. Everything was okay for now.

"What's the plan?" Fox asked. "It's clear that they are after her and aren't going to give up."

"We're going to take shifts," Rhys said. "One of us needs to be with her at all times."

"That's a bad idea," I whispered without opening my eyes.

"Why?" Rhys asked.

"I'm bad luck. Maybe I should leave town for a while. I could take a vacation and wait for things to calm down."

"Or, they could follow you and kill you," Nico said bluntly.

True, but then none of them would be in harm's way.

"I'll watch her tonight," Rhys said. "Nico, you'll have to take her to and from work, since you have a shield. Tomorrow, we'll put the schedule together."

CHAPTER 5

Warm arms encircled me and a warm body pressed against my back. Nature called, or I would have stayed with him. I slid out of bed and stumbled into the bathroom, staring at my worn reflection. The bathroom was immaculate, not a single thing out of place. I opened the top drawer and found spare toothbrushes, the kind that had toothpaste already on them.

"Score."

Quickly, I brushed my teeth, ran my fingers through my hair, and used the bathroom.

When I came back to the room, Rhys still lay on his bed, his shirtless torso on display for my viewing pleasure. And it was *definitely* a pleasure. He had a perfectly shaped chest, one that was all thanks to genetics. His abdominals were so defined, that I could imagine water getting stuck in the grooves.

His room was super tidy as well. He had a few pictures, all of them of the four princes, from toddler age all the way to the present day, during outings and events. I envied their friendship. I envied a friendship that had lasted a lifetime. I had one friend that I'd known since junior high, but we weren't that close anymore.

I crawled back into bed and lay my head on his chest, listening to the beat of his heart, and enjoying his warmth.

He wrapped his arms around me.

"Morning," he murmured.

"I'm sorry I woke you," I whispered and tried to get out of bed.

"Stay," he begged and held me tight.

I stilled and made myself comfortable on his chest again. He was so warm and I felt incredibly safe lying in bed with him. I knew if someone busted into the room, he would protect me, no matter what the danger was.

"Thank you," I whispered. "I should have thanked you all yesterday, but I was a bit shell shocked."

"Are you ready to talk about relationships yet?" he asked, opening one eye to look at me.

"I told you guys, I don't want to come between you all. You've been friends your entire lives. If I did something to ruin that—"

"We all talked last night," he said and opened his other eye.

"Oh?" That was hardly fair. I couldn't argue with them while I was asleep.

"After you fell asleep. We all agreed that we felt a connection with you."

"A connection?"

"It's harder for humans to sense, but we all share a connection with you and with each other."

"Wait, you're bi?"

Not that I cared what they were. It honestly wouldn't change anything.

"No," he chuckled. "The four of us have a warrior's bond. However, with you, we all somehow added you to that bond."

"Warrior—"

He sighed.

"You're not a warrior. You're our—"

"Whore?"

He scowled at me. "Absolutely not. You're like...our queen."

"Queen?" I asked in disbelief.

"Don't give me that scowl," he teased and tapped the tip of my nose with his finger. "Generations ago, the queen would be assigned guards. The guards would develop a warrior's bond between themselves to be able to find each other and communicate easier. The queen and her guards would develop a bond to help her call upon them in times of need and so they could sense her distress."

"I'm not a queen," I pointed out. Not that he didn't already know that.

He ran a hand down his face and sat up. "I'm sorry, I'm not very good at explaining things like this. Nico is better at it. I'll have him explain it to you as you go to work."

"My clothes—"

"I'm going to go with you to your apartment, so you can pack your essentials and clothing."

He stood up and stretched, giving me ample time to admire his muscular back and perfect ass.

"Let me brush my teeth and grab something to eat on the way out the door," he said around a big yawn.

He didn't take as long as I thought he would, but we were still pushing it and I had to rush to pack my things. He had me leave my stuff in his apartment and Nico was there waiting for me when we arrived.

"You're going to be late," he said in a sing-song voice.

"Apparently, dragons aren't morning people," I teased.

"Mornings would be better if they started after noon," Rhys said and yawned. "You got her?"

Nico nodded. "I've got it handled."

Rhys pecked me on the cheek and walked inside, yawning. "I'm going to go back to sleep now," he informed us.

Nico clapped his hands and a bubble appeared around us. A moment later, it disappeared from sight, but I could still sense it because it blocked the wind.

"Ready?" he asked.

I nodded, and we walked out of the apartment building and towards my job, passing by other males and females of various races going to their jobs as well.

"Did you sleep well?" he asked.

"I didn't even feel Rhys move me," I admitted. "I just went to sleep in the chair and woke up in his bed."

My hand flew to my mouth and I wondered if he would be upset that Rhys had slept in the same bed as me.

"Nothing happened, I—"

"Jolie, I know you slept with him already. Plus, this won't work if we all freak out when someone does something with you. We aren't like that. We aren't a bunch of jealous idiots."

"Rhys said you would be better at explaining about the bond," I told him. "He mentioned me being part of your bond, but not the warrior's one. He said something about queens, but it didn't make sense, since I'm just a human."

He nodded. "He always gets frazzled when talking about it. So, he told you about the queen and her guards having a bond, right?"

I nodded. The light changed, so we had to stop at the crosswalk and wait. There were quite a few people walking about and many were looking at Nico. He didn't seem to notice, his hands in his pockets as he leaned against the light pole with relaxed shoulders.

"Normally, there's a big ceremony and they all make the bond as one. We aren't exactly sure how it happened, but you became part of our bond. That's not how it normally works. Normally, our bond is completely separate from the Queen's bond. I did some research on it, but haven't turned up anything yet."

"So, what you're saying is that I'm bound to you guys, but not like a queen would be, more like as another warrior, but still different?"

None of this made any sense to me.

"Sort of," he murmured and chewed on the inside of his cheek.

The light changed and we resumed walking.

"So, is there a way to remove me from the bond?" I asked and looked up at him.

His eyes grew wide and he looked at me. "What? You want to break the bond?"

"Well, if the bond isn't right, shouldn't we get rid of it?"

"It's not as simple as taking off a ring," he explained. "It's painful and it can't be repaired once broken."

"But, if you decided you wanted to bond with me later, couldn't you do it like the Queen's bond? Not that I am saying you should bond with me, since I'm not royalty or anything."

"Theoretically, yes. However, since I've never heard of this type of bond before, I don't want us to break it without knowing the consequences. For all we know, if you break it, you might die."

Nico was very blunt and straight to the point. I liked that about him.

"So, do you guys, feel me?" I asked and tilted my head to the side as I thought about how weird it must be to sense other people when they weren't near you.

"Yes," he nodded. "We can sense where you are and we can sense your mood."

"My mood?"

"Yep. For instance, right now you're anxious and confused. Yesterday, you were having an anxiety attack, but you lied to us about it."

Heat spread across my cheeks. "Oh."

"You don't have to be embarrassed. Anxiety is a common issue, mainly among humans, but Others are known to experience it as well. Next time though, you could just ask one of us to help you.”

“How can you help me with an anxiety attack? They don’t make sense most of the time anyway. Sometimes they just come on out of nowhere, for no reason.”

“Fox is very skilled at helping people with turmoil. That’s why he shifted into his fox form for you when we were outside. He could sense your anxiety spiking and knows that a lot of humans are calmed by furry animals. It did help, until we got into the apartment and Rhys went after the gunman.”

“I wish you guys would see things from my side,” I muttered.

We stopped in front of my office building, and he turned to face me. “So, tell me your side. We don’t know anything about what happened between you and Demarcus, or what he meant about a protector before.”

“I have to go to work,” I said, glad to dodge the topic.

“I’ll be here to pick you up at five. Please, don’t step outside. Just wait for me.”

I nodded.

He opened the door for me, and once I stepped inside, he removed the shield and kissed my cheek. “See you later.”

I smiled and jogged to the elevator to go to work.

“You’ve been holding out on me,” Justina accused with hands on her hips next to her cubicle.

“Uh?” I replied, smartly.

She pointed out the window. “That’s Nico, Prince of the Mages. He walked you to work and kissed you like you were the best of friends. What the fuck? How do you know him? Were you involved in the explosion last night at their apartment building? Are you dating him? Have you slept with him?”

I stood with my mouth open, prepared to answer her, but she didn’t stop the onslaught of questions. So, I closed my mouth and waited for her to stop venting.

She took a breath and looked at me expectantly.

“Oh? Are you done shooting questions at me a mile a minute?” I asked.

“Spill,” she ordered me.

“Yes, I live in the apartment building with them. Yes, I was involved in the explosion. I’m fine though, thanks for your concern.

We are friends. I have not slept with him. We are dating, I think? Maybe?"

Were we? Was what I had with these guys considered dating?

"What happened with the guy you went out to lunch with?"

"We're dating, too. I think?"

This was so confusing. I wished I knew more about the bond we had. How could I have joined their bond?

"You go, girl!" she said and smiled.

After rolling my eyes at her and sitting down, I got lost in my work. At noon, I realized that I hadn't made a lunch and I wasn't supposed to go outside. Justina had brought her lunch, so I didn't want to ask her to go buy me something.

People started whispering loudly and I stood up to see what was going on, to find them all looking outside. I walked to join the crowd and smiled when I saw Deryn shift from wolf to man and head into the building.

"What is he doing here?"

"He's so hot."

"That's the second prince I've seen at this building today."

Justina looked at me with a raised eyebrow.

I smiled and waited until he entered the office, a backpack in hand. He looked over everyone and when he saw me, smiled.

"Hey," he said and maneuvered around the gaping people to me. "Rhys told me he forgot to mention lunch and you were still kind of frazzled. So, I offered to bring you some food." He opened his backpack and pulled out a plastic lunchbox. It had a kid's hero character sticker on it.

"You're the best," I told him and kissed his cheek before grabbing the box from him and heading towards the lunchroom where we could sit at a table and eat.

He followed behind me and asked, "Did you sleep well?"

"Yes. I didn't even wake up when Rhys moved me," I explained. This time not bringing up waking up in his bed and hopefully avoiding that conversation.

"That's good. We were all worried about you," he whispered. He pushed open the door to the lunchroom for me and conversation inside immediately died.

I ignored it and headed to an open table. He sat next to me and turned his chair so he could face me.

"Are you going to eat, too?" I asked.

He shook his head. "I already ate."

The lunch he had brought me consisted of a turkey sandwich, chips, a granola bar, and a fruit snack.

I giggled and took out the sandwich. "You packed me a kid's meal."

He smiled. "I thought you would enjoy it."

While I ate my sandwich, I looked at the others, all staring openly and not caring how rude it was.

"You learn to ignore them," he whispered to me, leaning his elbow on the table and scooting his chair closer to mine.

"Why'd you come in wolf form?" I asked after finishing the food in my mouth.

"You saw?"

I nodded. "I saw you through the window."

He scowled at me. "You shouldn't be standing next to windows. They had a sniper, remember?" he told me harshly.

The sandwich suddenly tasted like sawdust. I hadn't thought about it.

"I'm sorry. I didn't..."

He nodded and brushed my hair behind my ear. "I'm sorry for snapping. I just want to make sure you stay safe," he explained.

"Couldn't they just come into my work?" I asked.

He nodded. "They could."

"What do I do—"

"Fox said that he has a plan for that. He didn't tell us what it was, but he said he would be able to put it into play tomorrow."

"Okay," I whispered and set my sandwich down.

"Hey," he whispered and maneuvered his face in front of mine.

"Yeah?"

"You're beautiful," he said and smiled.

I laughed and shook my head. "You flirt."

His smile widened and he leaned forward to kiss me lightly on the lips. "Truth speaker."

"What's it like to be able to sense me?" I asked softly.

His eyes widened. "They told you?"

I nodded. "It still doesn't make much sense to me," I admitted after a moment of silence.

He ran a hand through his hair and said, "It doesn't make sense to us either. Not that we would have had a problem making you our queen, eventually. It's just...there's usually a process and specific steps needed. None of us know when it happened or who did it. Well, we all did it. It's not something only one of us can do."

"Nico said if we broke it, that I might die," I said with barely any breath.

He turned his chair and draped his arm across my shoulders. "We aren't going to break it, so you don't have to worry."

"But you didn't choose this. You guys didn't choose for me to be added."

"We did, somehow. It's complicated. Like I said, we all did it. Somehow, we all decided to add you. It's just strange that it didn't create the Queen's bond between us and instead added you to our bond, but the bond isn't something that happens against the group's will."

"Will it hurt you if the bond is broken?"

"It hurts whenever a bond is broken."

"Will it kill you?"

He shook his head. "The warrior's bond was created so that if one of us dies, it won't incapacitate the others. It's designed that way so we can protect the queen. We will experience pain at the warrior's loss, but not death."

"So, then shouldn't it be okay to remove me?"

"We don't know. This is uncharted territory. Fox and Nico are in contact with their elders to try to see what they can find out from them and if they know anything. We'll know more soon."

I packed up my lunch and then leaned my head against his shoulder.

"They said you all talked about our relationship," I whispered.

He nodded.

"I'm worried that I'll ruin your friendships."

"You won't," he assured me.

"How can you be so sure?" I asked and tilted my head to look up at him.

He smiled and whispered, "Because the only thing we care about is keeping you near us. We all want you. We all care about you."

"Is that because of the bond?" I asked. Wondering if the bond made them like me more. We did barely know each other, after all.

He nodded. "Partially. We were all interested in you before the bond formed though."

"I can't choose between you four," I whispered. "I'm selfish, I know. I just...can't."

He brushed his lips across my forehead and whispered, "We aren't asking you to choose, Jolie. We are asking you to let us all have you."

I chuckled and shook my head. "That sounds so wrong," I whispered.

"It's not. In the days before humans ruled, the queen didn't have a king or a husband, she had her guards."

"I'm not a queen," I reminded him.

"You can be our queen," he whispered in my ear.

A shiver raced up my spine and it had nothing to do with fear or cold.

CHAPTER 6

"Jolie, are you going to introduce me?" Justina asked with a scowl on her face as she sat in the chair across from us.

"Deryn, this is my friend, Justina. Justina, this is—"

"I know who he is," she said and smiled at him. "He's the famous Prince Deryn of Clan Wolf. One of the first wolves to learn how to talk in warrior form. Beloved of his house. And, one of the most sought-after bachelors in the Others' circle."

He smiled at her. "I like her. She should announce me when we go places."

Justina leaned on her elbows on the table and her eyes flashed red. "Hurt her, and I'll be the first to announce your death."

His eyes flashed gold, but the smile stayed on his lips. "Good to know."

"Justina. Deryn. We are all friends," I growled at them.

"Oh, she's got the growl down," Justina whispered. "Just how much time have you been spending with her."

"Not enough," Deryn countered and then stood up. "I have to go, but remember, stay away from the windows and wait for Nico to come get you."

"Thank you for bringing me lunch," I said and hugged him.

He hugged me back, and then spun and dipped me to kiss me deeply.

People gasped and began talking excitedly.

He helped me stand back up and then bowed to me in a grand

flourish. "Until tonight, my queen." He winked, and then we watched his great derriere leave the room.

I flopped down into the chair and sighed. I was in over my head.

"Why do you have to stay away from windows and wait for the Mage Prince to come?" Justina asked. "What haven't you told me?"

"Well…"

What could I tell her?

"…I ended the war and people weren't happy about that. They tried to kill me twice already."

Her eyes flashed red. "Why am I just now hearing about this?"

For the first time, I found myself afraid of Justina.

"I, um, it just happened last night and—"

"And you have a cell phone capable of texting," she snapped.

"A lot of shit has happened to me, Justina. I'm sorry I didn't text you, but I'm barely keeping it together right now. Please, don't add to it."

Her scowl stayed in place, but she nodded once. "Fine."

"Thank you," I said with a long sigh.

"So, how many Princes are you dating?" she asked with a smirk.

"How much do you know about magic?" I asked her instead of answering. She was a dhampir, after all. She had to know something.

"Quite a bit, actually," she admitted to me. "What's going on?"

"Do you know about the bonds that they develop with Queens and guards?"

Her eyes widened. "Yes."

"Have you ever heard of one developing with the female becoming part of the warriors' bond, instead of developing a separate one?"

"What have you gotten yourself into?" she asked me softly and glanced around at the tables near us. She gripped my arm and pulled me out of the room and down the hall to one of the empty conference rooms. She drew the blinds, locked the door, and turned to face me.

"I met them all individually. I told you about my meetings with a few of them."

"How many are there?" she asked.

"Four."

"All princes?"

I nodded.

She let out a low whistle. "You met the Four Princes of Jinla. The quad of friends that every girl has been dying to break into. You broke into their group in less than a week!"

"I discovered that they all live in my apartment complex with me and they're all friends. They told me that they don't know how it happened, but at some point, they added me to their bond. They said it was not a conscious thing, but it can't be done without all of their consent. So, somehow, I joined their bond. Nico said it is possible I might die if they try to remove me from the bond."

"I've heard of it happening before," she told me softly.

"And?" I asked, my throat dry and the sad look on her face totally not reassuring.

"She removed herself from the bond and died," she whispered sadly.

Great. There went that idea.

"So, they're stuck with me?" I whispered and looked at my pathetic human hands.

"Yes. Though, with your current predicament, it will be a good thing. They will have the uncontrollable desire to protect you."

"How did it happen for the one you know about?"

"They were all protecting the female from something and during the altercation, they expressed their interest in her. The bond formed, but since she was human, it added her to their bond and did not make a Queen's bond. The only perk, is that when she died, they didn't feel it the way they would have if she had been their Queen."

"Do you think it's a defense mechanism to protect them from having a human with a shorter lifespan added? Since our lives are so much shorter?"

She nodded.

"So, does this mean the feelings they feel towards me—"

"The bond deepens the bonds of friendship, but not romantic feelings. Your friendships will grow immensely, but the romance will be something you have to work on with them separate of the bond. One positive of this, it means they won't feel jealousy towards each other when one is with you and not the others."

This was all so insane and out of control. When could this have happened? What could have—

"The park," I whispered in shock.

"What?"

"The night I returned the stolen artifact, an old enemy showed up intent on taking me back with him to torture me. They protected me. They all stood together and told me that I am important to them. They said I was their friend and they would protect me. That must be when the bond developed."

She ran a hand through her hair and thought about it. "It sounds likely that was when it happened," she agreed. "Though, as I'm not one of the participants, I can't be sure."

I pulled out my phone and dialed Nico. He answered before the first ring had even ended.

"What's wrong? You're upset," he said.

Stupid bond.

"I have answers about the bond," I told him.

"You do?" he asked, shocked.

Yes, I was capable of finding things out, too. I imagined sticking my tongue out at him, but he wouldn't see it even if I did.

"Are the others working right now?" I asked.

"No, we're all at Rhys's."

"Can you come get me? I can explain it to everyone."

"What about work?"

"I can't focus on work right now," I admitted.

"I wouldn't be able to focus with four princes waiting for me either," Justina teased.

I glared at her and she laughed.

"I'll be there in a few minutes," he said and hung up.

We went to our desks and I typed a message to my supervisor, letting him know that I wasn't feeling well and would be leaving early. Luckily, I was ahead of my deadlines, so it wasn't a big deal.

"How did you meet them?" Alexandria asked. She was a short, curvy woman with a love for gossip.

"Who?" I asked, feigning ignorance.

"The Princes," she said and rolled her eyes.

"Oh, we live in the same apartment building."

"How—"

She was interrupted by Nico walking inside the room and heading towards me with a determined look on his face.

"I need to go," I told her, grabbed my stuff, and met him halfway.

He hugged me and I relaxed into him, not realizing I was so close to having an emotional breakdown. I was normally really good about keeping my emotions hidden.

The emotions were easier to stuff down, once I touched him, and I smiled at him in appreciation.

"Ready?" he asked.

I nodded and walked beside him out of the building, ignoring the stares of everyone.

"What's wrong?" he asked me. "Aside from what you have to tell us?"

"You guys probably aren't going to be happy about what you hear," I whispered.

"It will all be fine," he assured me.

I wasn't sure.

Once we got into Rhys's apartment, all eyes turned to me. It was too much pressure to have four alpha males staring at me like that. Instead of sitting and letting the pressure build on me, I paced behind the couch and relayed Justina's information to them. When I finished, I continued pacing, waiting for their responses.

"It was likely the night at the park," Rhys confirmed. "We all vowed to protect her."

"Agreed," Nico said.

Tears brimmed in my eyes.

"I'm sorry," I whispered. "If I hadn't gone to the park that night, none of this would have happened. I knew I should have stayed away from you all."

"Fate cannot be stopped," Fox informed me.

"Fate? This isn't fate," I replied with a scoff. "This is my bad luck being pushed on you four. I'm a curse."

Fox stepped in front of me, making me stop walking. "You are not a curse."

"You are jaded by the bond now. You care for me as a friend because of this—"

"We cared about you before the bond was formed," Deryn countered.

"At least you guys won't be in much pain when I die," I said. The only positive thing that came out of all of this.

"You're not going to die," Rhys growled.

"Eventually, I will," I replied. "Way sooner than you all will."

The weight of everything came crashing down on me and I dropped into the leather recliner Rhys had vacated a moment ago. It was still warm from him and I curled up on it.

"Well, at least we know what happened," Nico whispered.

"It doesn't change anything, really," Rhys admitted.

Fox knelt in front of me and smoothed my hair back. "Do you want me to shift?"

I shook my head. While his fox form was comforting, I preferred his human form.

"Can you pet me?" I asked, blushing as I asked for something so ridiculous.

He didn't smirk, laugh, or question me. He just sat on the floor next to the chair I was on, and started petting my hair. "Are you hungry?" he asked softly.

"No," I whispered in response, my eyes closing at not just the soothing touch, but his reassuring presence. How could someone be so calming?

My cell phone rang on the coffee table where I had set it when I came in, but I ignored it. It rang immediately again without the person bothering to try to leave a voicemail.

"Hello?" Rhys answered.

I opened my eyes, shocked he would answer my phone, but also not really caring. I had nothing to hide with them.

"What are you talking about?" he asked. "She's not at work right now. She left early," he said to whoever was on the phone. His eyes widened and he grabbed the remote for his television. "Thanks for calling. We'll let her know you called. No, I promise, she's safe and sound. Bye."

He turned the television to a news station and I stared in disbelief at what was left of the building I should have been working in.

I leapt up and ran towards the door, but Deryn grabbed me and stopped me.

"Justina!" I screamed. "I have to check on—"

"There are no casualties," he said in a loud voice to get my attention.

"They evacuated everyone before it went off," Rhys said and pointed at the screen where the headline said just that.

I slumped into Deryn. "So, everyone's okay?"

They nodded.

My phone rang again, this time it was Justina calling, so I ran and snatched the phone from Rhys.

"Are you okay?" I asked her.

"Yes. Let me talk to Deryn."

"Why?" I asked a bit miffed she wouldn't want to talk to me after almost getting blown up.

"Jolie," she whispered in exasperation.

I grumbled, but gave him the phone.

"Deryn," he answered. He listened a moment and then my phone creaked as his grip tightened. "Got it," he replied and set my phone gently on the table, the screen cracked on one of the corners.

"What?" I asked.

"A package was delivered for Jolie," he told everyone. "Justina knew about the problems and smelled the package because she thought it was odd Jolie would be receiving one after starting so recently. She could smell the bomb thanks to her dhampir abilities and got everyone evacuated. The bomb squad inadvertently set it off after everyone was evacuated."

Another attempt on my life. This time, my entire building had been put at risk. Justina had been at risk. If I had still been there and received that package, I would have been blown to pieces. Why were these people always trying to blow me up?

Fox picked me up and carried me out of Rhys's apartment, despite the guys' protests. He took the elevator to his apartment and once inside, set me on a soft fur rug in front of a fire that had started as soon as we had entered. His apartment had very few decorations and hardly any furniture. I stayed in my fetal position on the rug while he did whatever he was doing in the kitchen.

A few minutes later, he came back and set a cup of hot chocolate on the ground in front of me. Hot chocolate was my favorite.

"Do you have a peppermint stick?" I asked softly, trying so hard to hold it together.

He disappeared and came right back and put a peppermint stick in the cup.

I sat up and sipped it carefully, but it was the perfect temperature. He sat down behind me, his legs on either side of my body, and scooted close enough that I could lean back against him and still drink the cocoa.

"I know this is a lot to deal with," he whispered and pet my hair. "I know there are lots of crazy things going on. This is not how you expected your new life in Jinla to be. I know."

He was right about all of that.

"The bond is something unexpected for all of us."

"Do you hate me for it?" I asked him.

He kissed my temple. "No, Jolie. None of this is your fault. You didn't seduce us and trick us. You didn't do any of this. This, is life. This is fate. You may not believe in fate, but I do. You are meant to be with us. We are meant to be your protectors. I can feel it, deep inside of me, I know this is right."

"My life is a curse," I told him, letting the hand holding the cocoa cup fall to my lap.

"Tell me," he requested.

His phone vibrated in his pocket and he took it out, holding it far enough back that I couldn't see the screen. I didn't care. It was probably just the other guys texting to see what was going on.

"When I was eighteen, I was attacked by a vampire. My boyfriend at the time was a werewolf. He defended me from the vampire. Two years later, a witch and I bumped into each other on the street and she put a hex on me. It put me in a coma for a year until my grandma found someone who could remove it. A year after that, a human went on a shooting spree. He shot me in the leg and I almost bled to death. Last year...last year Demarcus captured me. I had been dating a human at the time. The human tried to protect me, but he couldn't defeat Demarcus and his men. Demarcus tore him to pieces, slowly, and made me watch. I thought I was going to die there. I thought I was done for. Then, I escaped. I moved here, hoping to avoid all of this. I thought it was the town I had lived in. Clearly, I'm just cursed. I'm a curse, Fox. I'll get you all killed if I stay."

"You've had a very unfair life," he whispered.

I nodded.

"Don't you think it's okay to let yourself indulge a little, then?"

"What do you mean?" I asked, tilting my head back to look up at him.

He smiled. "You deserve friends. You deserve happiness. You deserve to be loved."

"Justina could have been killed today. My coworkers could have been killed," I reminded him.

He took my cocoa and set it away from us. "They weren't. Justina is a dhampir. She is very capable of protecting herself. We are capable of protecting ourselves. We are capable of protecting you."

He did something with his phone and pushed it away from us. I watched it slide and he turned me around to face him and brushed my hair behind my ear.

"Do you want to be happy?" he asked.

I nodded.

He brushed his knuckles down my cheek and then leaned forward and kissed me lightly on the lips. Instead of the raging fire I felt with

Rhys and Deryn, I felt a slowly building fire. It was like the fire in the fireplace — small, but warming and relaxing.

I kissed him in return, and he laid me back on the rug, kissing me deeply and slowly, possessing me in a way that I had never experienced before. His movements were slow and deliberate, not rushed and demanding. It was even more of a turn on than the fast and passionate sex I'd experienced before.

He peeled my clothes off slowly and kissed from my toes to my forehead. He settled between my legs and slowly entered me, giving my body time to adjust to his size.

"You're beautiful," he whispered as he began to slide in and out of me. "Your soul is beautiful. Everything about you is vibrant and pure."

How could I be pure if I'd slept with other men before?

"You may not think you're worthy of us or of being our queen," he whispered into my ear, "but you are."

His warm lips covered mine and I lost myself to his gentle and consuming touch.

CHAPTER 7

Fox drew me a bath and while I soaked, the others came into the apartment. I closed my eyes and relaxed, completely at ease. I never knew sex like that existed. I never knew someone could fuck you into calmness.

It was incredible.

"How is she?" Rhys asked.

"Relaxed," Fox replied softly.

"What's happening tomorrow?" Deryn asked.

"Her work won't be open until they can clean up and ensure the building is safe for them to return to," Rhys explained. "Plus, a lot of employees were feeling traumatized over the experience. She's got at least the rest of the week off."

"Fox?" I called, looking for shampoo or soap near the tub.

He walked into the bathroom and knelt next to it. "Yes?"

"I can't find the shampoo or soap," I explained.

He grabbed some bottles in a carrying tray from beneath the sink and set them next to the tub. He started to roll up his sleeves, but I grabbed his hand and shook my head.

"I got it," I whispered.

He nodded and left me alone in the bathroom.

I washed quickly and wrapped the robe he had left me around myself, tying it securely before walking out to join the guys. They were eating pizza and talking quietly. Thankfully, they didn't stop talking when I walked in. That was something I hated.

Deryn held out a plate with two pieces of pizza on it to me and I gratefully accepted it. Everyone sat on the ground, because there weren't any chairs or couches, so I joined them, sitting behind Fox and leaned against the wall. The pizza was warm and delicious, no doubt the best pizza I had ever eaten.

"This pizza is great," I whispered to no one in particular.

"It's from my parents' shop," Deryn explained.

"Your parents own a pizza parlor?" I asked, looking up at him.

"Among other things," he said.

"Well, they're great at making pizza," I praised and took another bite.

"Would you like a drink?" Fox asked me.

I nodded, but my mouth was too full to reply.

He went to the fridge and got out a bottle and brought it to me.

"What's that?" Nico asked.

"It's a cider," Fox replied.

I took a drink of it and moaned. It was a pear cider, pear was my absolute favorite.

All eyes focused on me.

I took another, bigger drink and closed my eyes as the delicious, sweet liquor went down my throat. It was perfect.

"I'll take watch tonight," Deryn said.

"I need to go to speak to my father. I shouldn't be more than an hour or two," Rhys said and stood up.

I drank more of the cider, surprised that I was still so calm and relaxed.

Rhys squatted in front of me and smiled. "You stay with Deryn and do what he says, okay?"

I saluted him. "Yes, sir."

He leaned forward and I met him halfway, kissing him lightly on the lips.

"Stay safe," I whispered to him.

He kissed my forehead and whispered, "Yes, my queen."

Part of me wanted to argue that I wasn't a queen, but I liked hearing them say it. A girl could get used to having sexy men call her their queen.

"Do you want more pizza?" Fox asked.

"No, thank you. I'm full," I replied. A small frown creased my brow. "Did you put a spell on me?"

Fox shook his head and smiled. "No. I promise I wouldn't do something like that."

"Interesting," I whispered.

"Are you ready to go?" Deryn asked me.

"My clothes are at Rhys's," I said and looked down at the robe I was in. Slowly, the euphoria was wearing off, but contentment was its replacement, which I was okay with.

Deryn picked me up and grabbed one of the six-packs of cider out of Fox's fridge. "I'm going to take this for her," he told Fox.

Fox waved as we left his apartment.

"Want to play karting when we get to my apartment?" Deryn asked.

"That sounds fun," I agreed and wrapped my arms around his neck.

"Are you feeling better now?"

I nodded. "Fox is...magical."

He snorted. "I've heard that before."

"Sorry," I mumbled, feeling bad for admitting that I had slept with Fox.

"For what?" he asked and looked down at me as we waited for the elevator.

"I just...don't know what I can and can't talk about with you guys."

"You mean about when you sleep with one of us?" he guessed.

I nodded.

"You don't have to walk on pins and needles with us," he assured me. "Plus, we all knew when we came in that you had slept with him."

"How?"

He cringed. "Uh, we just did."

"Deryn."

"We could smell that you had," he admitted finally.

"Ew," I whispered and scrunched my nose.

He laughed. "Don't worry about it."

"I can walk," I told him. "You don't have to carry me."

The elevator came, and he set me on my feet beside him. "Better?"

Now I felt cold. I wrapped my arms around myself and frowned.

"What's wrong?" he asked.

"Cold," I admitted.

He laughed and picked me up again. "I can remedy that easily."

I wrapped my arms around his neck and nuzzled my cold nose into his neck.

"Cold!" he gasped, but didn't move away.

"Warm," I purred and nuzzled him.

"None of that," he chastised.

"Of what?" I asked, but chuckled and moved my face away from him. "Sorry."

When we got to his apartment, he gave me a pair of his sweats and a shirt to change into. Once changed, I sat next to him on the couch and grabbed a controller.

"Ready to lose?" I asked with a smirk and wiggled the joysticks.

He smirked. "No one beats me at karting."

"Promise not to cry?" I asked.

"Oh! Alright. Let's make a bet. I win and you share my bed tonight. You win and—"

"I win and you give me a massage," I said.

"Deal."

The apartment was warm and I was already feeling drowsy. I had to focus if I was going to win.

The game started and I focused on the track.

"No," I screeched as I started to slide off the edge.

He laughed victoriously and slid around me.

After I was brought back onto course, I raced after him, using every trick and shortcut that I knew.

"Come on. It's like you want me to win," he teased.

Sharing a bed with him wasn't something I was actively trying to avoid, but I was very competitive.

"We've only gone one lap!" I reminded him just as I slid around him and pushed him off the edge.

"No!" he yelled and tapped his foot as he waited for the flying guy to put him back on the track.

We were neck and neck right up to the end and I would have won, but he reached over and grabbed my leg, squeezing and making me squeal and slide off the couch to get away so he couldn't tickle me more. He zoomed by the finish line first and jumped up, pumping his fists in the air.

"Woo! I won!" he yelled victoriously.

"You, cheater!" I shouted and pushed him.

He laughed and laughed and eventually, I started laughing too.

I fell onto the couch and clutched at my sore stomach. "Too much laughing," I gasped.

"No such thing," he said and sat on the ground in front of the couch, leaning his head back so that his head lay on my stomach.

"Deryn, what if—"

"Do you want to go on a date tomorrow?" he asked me.

"Huh?" I asked, shocked by the topic shift and him interrupting me.

"Will you go on a date with me tomorrow?"

"Yes," I agreed immediately. "Are we allowed to leave the apartment, though?"

He smiled. "Don't worry, I'm taking you somewhere very secure."

"Is it a dungeon?" I asked and moved away from him with a fake gasp. "Are you going to put me in a dungeon and give me lotion?"

He laughed and then stalked towards me on all fours. "Dungeons are no fun. They don't give me enough room to chase you."

I had played with werewolves before, so seeing him stalking me was thrilling instead of terrifying. My heart sped as I leapt over the back of the couch to put some space between us.

"Oh no, the big, bad wolf is hunting me. What ever shall I do?" I asked dramatically and continued walking backwards, a shit eating grin on my face.

He got onto his feet and stalked around the couch towards me. "Where will you go, little girl?"

"Well, I'd take you to Grandmother's house, but we both know what happens there," I teased.

He laughed and charged after me.

I squealed and raced around the couch, as fast as I could, and ran into his room. He pounced on me, wrapping his entire body around me as we fell onto the bed, softening the impact, so that it didn't hurt me at all.

He pinned my arms above my head and leaned down to nip the tip of my nose. "Caught you."

"Are you to eat me?" I asked with a fake accent.

He arched an eyebrow. "Very straightforward, aren't we? Most women at least have the decency to wait until I've gotten their clothes off to ask."

My heart quickened and I licked my lips. "I didn't mean like—"

He crushed his mouth to mine and he grabbed both of my wrists in one hand. "Now, you're helpless. What shall I do with you?"

I squirmed, trying to get my wrists free, knowing full well that I had zero chance of doing so.

He wiggled his fingers and said, "I believe you shall be punished for knocking me off the track in that second lap."

"What?" I asked just before he started tickling me.

I laughed and squealed as he tickled me.

"Torturer!" I wiggled and tried to get free.

"Retribution!" he yelled as he continued.

Someone knocked on the door and he stopped tickling me. Rhys walked in and I yelled, "My savior!"

He smirked. "Am I interrupting?"

"He's torturing me!" I yelled and struggled in Deryn's hold.

Deryn kissed my forehead and released me.

"What's up?" he asked Rhys.

"I brought her stuff here," he said and nodded at my bag that was now on the floor.

"Thanks," I replied, but stayed where I was on the bed. Feeling tired. "I think I'll sleep in this," I told them.

"Sleep in whatever you want," Deryn told me.

"Thank you, your majesty," I said and scoffed.

Rhys chuckled. "Deryn, can I talk to you for a minute?"

"No secrets!" I yelled and sat up.

"It's not regarding you," Rhys informed me. He walked over and kissed my cheek. "Go to sleep. Deryn will join you in a few minutes."

"It's still weird that you're okay with that," I whispered, but crawled under the covers.

"You'll get used to it," he assured me before leaving.

"I'll be right back," Deryn said. "Yell if you need something." He kissed me lightly and tickled my sides before running out of the room after Rhys.

I lay on the bed with a smile on my face. The smile slowly disappeared. Four men. I was dating four men who were all friends. They were all bound to me, and I brought nothing to the table, except my body.

What could I do for them? What could I offer them aside from myself? There had to be something or someway for me to prove worthy of them. The more time I spent with each of them individually, the deeper the bonds became, not on a metaphysical level or anything, but in my heart. They were great guys, and it just felt right to be with them. I felt like I was home, despite never having been with them before.

Was this what people meant when they felt like they had a soulmate? Was this feeling of home and rightness the feeling of what soulmates experienced?

Maybe Fox was right. Maybe this was fate. Maybe it was my destiny to be with them.

I scoffed and rolled over. "Right? It's your destiny to be with four men. That's called dreaming," I reminded myself callously.

For now, I would enjoy the ride. Who knew when it would end? If the people trying to kill me had anything to say about it, that ride would end sooner rather than later. It could be tomorrow or the next day and I could be dead.

Or, the men I was slowly falling for could die trying to protect me.

No, I couldn't let that happen. I couldn't let any of them die.

Deryn's date ended up being a trip to visit his pack. I practically bounced in my seat as we drove towards his pack's headquarters.

"You're lively today," he teased me.

"I'm excited to meet your pack," I said honestly. "It's been a long time since I was with a werewolf pack, but when I used to visit, we had all kinds of fun."

"How long were you dating that werewolf?"

"A couple of years, but we lived in a small town and were friends before and after that. His alpha let me go on a hunt with them one time. It was so—"

"They took you on a hunt?" Deryn asked, his eyes going gold.

"Yeah," I whispered, stilling at his seriousness.

"What did you do on the hunt?"

"I rode on my boyfriend's back and watched the rest of the pack take down some deer. Then we went swimming. Why are you acting like they did something terrible?"

"Hunting is a very serious thing for packs. You're not supposed to let outsiders in."

"I wasn't really an outsider though."

"You were lucky to have found such a nice pack," he said after he calmed down.

"Maybe they're just not as uptight as you," I mumbled.

He draped his arm across my shoulders and kissed the side of my head. "My father is the uptight one. He makes sure that we do everything by the book."

"There's a book?" I asked. "Can I read it?"

Deryn chuckled. "There actually is a book, but no, you cannot read it."

"Tease."

We arrived at a huge compound, and the driver opened the door for us. I climbed out and shivered at the weight of hundreds of predators in the same place. My human brain was warning me to run, but I knew better. Werewolves were not killers, not any more than humans were. Truthfully, less than humans were, since they tried so hard to get on the humans' good sides.

We walked into the nearest building and I was shocked to discover it was a gymnasium. There were several people playing basketball and a few people in the stands. Deryn strode to the stands and took a seat, so I followed and sat next to him.

"Do me a favor?" he whispered. "Don't let anyone know we're dating."

"Okay," I agreed immediately.

"Do you want to know why?" he asked.

I shrugged. "If you want me to."

"I haven't told my father about you yet."

"Ah," I said and nodded. "Got it."

The game ended and the players walked to the sidelines to get some water. One of the players looked familiar, but it wasn't until he smiled that I realized who he was.

"Jolie!" he yelled.

I stood up and rushed forward to meet him halfway, throwing my arms around his neck as he picked me up and spun me.

"Martin!" I squealed.

He set me down, but kept his hands on my hips. "Jolie! What are you doing here? You look amazing!"

"I came—"

"She came with me," Deryn said angrily.

I thought Martin would drop his hands, but he just turned and smiled at Deryn.

"Small world, huh? Jolie and I dated in high school. She was my best friend." He turned back to me. "What have you been up to? Why are you out here? You want to see Sharla and the girls?"

"They're here?" I asked and smiled wide. "I haven't seen them in person in a few years."

"They are up at the main house," he said and grabbed a shirt from the bench in front of us. "Sharla will be so excited to see you."

Deryn hadn't moved or said anything since his one declaration. His fists were no longer clenched as he watched Martin.

"Deryn?" I whispered.

He tore his eyes away and looked down at me. "We're going to the main house."

"Great," Martin said with a wide smile.

The house was just one building over and as soon as we walked in, the girls and Sharla saw me.

"Auntie Jolie!" the girls yelled and rushed to me. I dropped to my knees to hug the twin six-year-old girls.

"How are my favorite nieces?" I asked and kissed their heads.

"Great!" they exclaimed in unison.

Sharla stood behind them with a smile, waiting for her turn.

I stood up and she jerked me into a hug.

"Jolie," she whispered. "I got worried when I heard about you ending the war. And your office! Are you safe? You're welcome to come stay with us."

I kissed her cheek. "Thank you, but I'm well protected." I glanced back at Deryn for emphasis.

He was looking at me with his head slightly tilted and a small frown of concentration.

Sharla stepped back and bowed to him. "Prince, my apologies for being rude. I didn't see you enter."

"You are very affectionate to a woman who used to date your mate," Deryn commented.

Sharla smiled warmly at me. "She holds no feelings towards Martin in that way anymore. We had a long talk when we came to Jolie's hometown, and became friends."

"Are you really alright?" Martin asked and set his hand on my cheek. "You look tired and stressed."

"A lot has happened," Deryn said with a bit of a growl in his voice.

The girls darted behind their mother and peeked out at Deryn.

What was with him?

"Can I talk to you, Martin?" Deryn asked with clenched fists.

"Sure." He pecked me on the cheek, smiled at Sharla, and followed Deryn's tense back out of the living room.

The girls pulled me to the couch and climbed into my lap, sharing my lap as well as they could. I ran my fingers through their hair and the fidgety kids stilled and relaxed into me.

"We've missed you," Sharla said. "We got scared when we went back home and you weren't there?"

"I'm sorry. I'll get better about texting you." I promised.

We did video calls once a month, but I never talked about anything serious with them. Most of the calls were the girls telling me things that had happened at school.

Madison shifted into her wolf pup form so I could scratch behind her ears. Tamara did the same, their heads on my thighs.

"What are you guys doing here?" I asked. They lived three states away.

"Martin was offered a job here a week ago. We came to see about finding an apartment near his job."

"So, I'll get to see you more?" I asked with a wide smile and ruffled the girls' fur.

Sharla nodded. "Much more."

I wasn't sure about that. I would visit them, but not often.

Deryn and Martin came back, both scowling.

Sharla stood up, knowing something was wrong since Martin never scowled. He waved at her and she returned to her seat.

"Girls, go to your room," he ordered them.

They whined, licked my cheeks, and obeyed.

Deryn leaned against the entryway, looking at me with that tilted head again.

Martin knelt in front of me, taking my hands in his.

"You should have called me," he chastised.

"You have your family to protect now," I reminded him.

Sharla growled at me. "Jolie. What did we talk about?"

I sighed and turned to face her. "I love you, but I won't put you in danger."

It was Martin's turn to growl at me. "You are so stubborn," he said.

Deryn had taken a step forward when Martin growled.

I took my hands back from Martin and leaned forward to kiss his cheek. "I won't curse you," I whispered to him. I kissed Sharla's cheek and walked to Deryn. "Once things calm down, I'll come visit the girls. Text me your address."

"I'm not just going to—" Martin started and stood up, but Deryn stepped into his path.

I grabbed Deryn's hand and he stepped back.

"He's my friend," I reminded Deryn.

"Why are you treating her like a mate?" Martin asked Deryn, no submission on his face at all despite Deryn outranking him.

"She's under my protection," Deryn said. "She's my friend."

Sharla quirked an eyebrow and looked at me. I found an interesting spot on the ceiling to inspect.

"Then you should understand my protectiveness," Martin said with crossed arms.

Deryn didn't reply. He took me up the stairs, away from the couple. I let him drag me, but pulled my hand free when we got close to an office with its door open and a male voice talking.

Deryn knocked on the door as he walked in. I wasn't certain if I was supposed to follow him, so I waited by the door. A huge man walked over and hugged Deryn with a wide smile.

"My boy!" he bellowed. "How are you?"

"Good, Dad," Deryn replied.

This...mountain, was his dad?

Deryn escaped the hug to grab my hand and pull me into the room to stand before his dad.

"Dad, I'd like you to officially meet Jolie."

As I looked at him, I realized that I had seen him before. He had been one of the four sitting in the park, which must have meant he was one of the Kings and the Alpha.

I dipped my head in submission. "Alpha, it is an honor to meet you."

Suddenly, huge arms wrapped around me and pulled me into a hug against the giant Alpha. He released me, but kept his hand on my shoulders while his smiling eyes met mine.

"You are welcome here anytime. If you ever need anything, just tell me. Oh, and call me Dan."

"Thank you," I whispered and glanced at Deryn who seemed as surprised as me.

"I need to tell you something important," Deryn said quietly. "It's personal."

Dan turned back to me and inhaled loudly.

I rolled my eyes. "I'm not pregnant."

Both Dan and Deryn looked at me with wide eyes.

"I dated Martin and spent a lot of time with that pack," I explained. "Their Alpha always checked if I was pregnant when I came over."

Deryn shut the door and pushed me to a couch I hadn't seen

around his large Dad. I sat and he sat next to me, his body aligned with mine.

Dan sat in a huge leather chair across from us and waited.

"Jolie's become my Queen," Deryn stated. "Well, sort of."

Deryn explained the entire situation, from meeting me until today. I was blushing by the end, unsure how Dan would react to finding this out.

"So, you found your Queen?" he asked with his mouth hidden behind his hands as they linked in front of his face.

Deryn nodded.

"What do you think about all of this?" Dan asked me.

"I'm not sure. It's still sinking in," I admitted.

"Can you feel the bond?"

I shook my head.

"Are you certain these attacks were for her?"

Deryn nodded. "One hundred percent."

"All four princes, huh?" Dan asked and looked at me.

"I didn't know their titles when I met them," I muttered. It wasn't like I'd sought them out on purpose.

He laughed loudly and dropped his hands to his lap. "What do you need from me?" he asked Deryn.

"To keep our connection a secret. We don't want anyone knowing, but I knew I needed to tell you. And, a driver for Jolie."

"A driver?" I asked him.

"Our cars are well enforced with bulletproof windows," Dan explained. "So, they're able to drive you places without you needing the mage."

"Is this all really necessary?" I asked softly.

"Yes," Deryn said immediately.

"I agree to both of your requests," Dan said. "Would you also like a bodyguard? Martin and her seem to know each other and—"

"No," Deryn snapped a bit too quickly.

"I don't have feelings for him," I chastised Deryn.

"I don't like him touching you," Deryn snarled.

Dan tapped Deryn's nose and said, "Enough of that. Unless you take her as a mate, she's allowed to touch others."

"I know that," Deryn grumbled and rubbed his nose even though the tap hadn't been hard enough to hurt him.

"I'll also do some investigating to see if we can find out who is trying to kill her," Dan promised.

"Thank you," I said and looked at Dan. "I'm honored to have your protection."

Dan smiled. "As my son's Queen, you'll have to make appearances here with the pack, once your relationship goes public. You're going to be seeing a lot more of me."

"What does that mean?" I asked.

"Nothing," Deryn said and stood up. "Let's get going. The others are probably getting antsy to confirm I've kept you alive."

"Jolie," Dan called as we stepped into the hallway. I stepped back into his office. "I'd avoid touching other males for a while. He's too stressed out and touching others will only break his control."

"Okay," I agreed.

I jogged down the stairs where Martin was angrily talking to Deryn, who looked just as mad.

"What's up?" I asked.

"Nothing," Deryn replied tersely.

I hugged Sharla and whispered, "Love you."

"I love you, too."

"Stay safe," Martin ordered me and hugged me.

"Love you," I told him instead of responding to his order.

"Love you, too," he whispered.

Deryn was already outside of the house, so I jogged to catch up to him. A car pulled up and he climbed in without saying anything to me. The silent treatment lasted all the way to the apartment building and up the elevator.

We walked into Deryn's apartment to find the other three males playing video games together on his couch.

"How was your trip?" Rhys asked.

"My trip was great, except for the green monster who unexpectedly tagged along," I said with a pointed look at Deryn.

"What?" Fox asked, looking away from his game.

"Deryn got super jealous of my friend hugging me," I explained.

"He wasn't just hugging you. He had his hands on you for longer than is acceptable with a female who isn't his mate."

I rolled my eyes in response. "You're being ridiculous."

"Did you sleep with him?"

"Yes."

The pen in his hand snapped and the ink splattered on his clothes. His eyes didn't just flash yellow – the wolf remained.

"Why didn't you tell me that before?"

"Would it have made you less jealous?"

"No, but I wouldn't have let him touch you at all."

"You can't tell me who I can and can't be friends with. Or, who I can and can't hug. I've known him much longer than I've known any of you. He has saved me multiple times. His daughters are my nieces."

"Okay. Everyone, calm down," Nico said, coming to stand between us.

I pushed past Deryn to the kitchen, grabbed one of the ciders, and chugged it.

"How did it go with your dad?" asked Rhys.

"Great. He loved her, which was expected. He gave her permission to return to the pack whenever she wanted and also gave her a driver and car whenever we need it," Deryn replied as he took his ruined shirt off and tossed it into the trash.

"Wow, that's pretty generous of him," Fox commented.

"I think the fact that she had two wolf pups in her lap and calmed them down better with scratches than he has been able to with intimidation had a big part to play in his decisions. She's unexpectedly great with werewolves," Deryn explained.

I stopped guzzling my cider long enough to ask, "He saw me with the twins?"

Deryn nodded. "He has cameras everywhere."

"Is that why he hugged me when I met him?" I asked sheepishly.

"He hugged her?" Rhys asked and looked at me. "The Alpha hugged you?"

I nodded. "Big bear hug."

"Holy shit, Deryn. Was your dad high?" Fox asked and chuckled.

"I know," Deryn muttered.

"He hugged Deryn when he walked in," I muttered, feeling uncomfortable that they were making such a big deal out of it. He seemed to be pretty affectionate.

"Dan is very affectionate to his pack, but outsiders he is extremely cold to. He still won't give us his full attention and it's been over two decades," Rhys explained.

"Maybe that's because you're all Alphas and threats. I'm just a small human girl," I suggested.

"No, he just likes you," Deryn said. "Dad is never affectionate to outsiders."

"Well, I am pretty special," I mumbled and tossed my now empty cider into the trash and grabbed another. "Can we order pizza?"

"Why don't you wait to drink that until it comes?" Nico suggested.

I glared up at him. "No."

He sighed, but didn't say anything else as I popped the bottle cap off and started drinking it. I sat on Fox's lap and ran my fingers through his hair. It was incredibly thick and, as was usual when it came to Fox, it was calming.

"Want to play a game?" Fox asked me and motioned at the controllers on the table.

I shook my head. "Not right now. Have we heard anything about when my apartment will be ready for me to stay there again?"

"Manager said at least a week," Nico replied.

I let my head drop forward to rest on Fox's shoulder. "Dammit."

"Thought you could get rid of us, didn't you?" he whispered and chuckled.

"No, just not used to not having privacy," I whispered back.

"We can give you privacy," Deryn said. "If you want to be alone, you're welcome to use my spare room."

He was being nice, probably because he realized what a jerk he was earlier.

"Okay," I replied, but didn't move.

Seeing Martin and his family had been a huge surprise and knowing they were nearby made me worry. I didn't want them to get caught up in my problems. I meant it when I told him that I wouldn't come see the girls until after all of this was over.

I finished my second bottle and started to trace Fox's pointed ear, but he grabbed my hand and looked at me with silver eyes.

"That is very sensitive," he whispered to me. His eyes were glued to my mouth and I realized that there was a new part of his body pressing against my lower body.

"Oh," I gasped and jerked my hand away. "Sorry."

He smiled. "You didn't know. It's okay."

"Pizza should be here soon," Deryn called from his bedroom.

Nico was engrossed in the video game he was playing next to us and it appeared Rhys hadn't heard what had happened.

I exhaled in relief, glad they hadn't witnessed my embarrassing action, and climbed off Fox. He kissed my cheek and said, "I'll be back."

I took his vacated spot and let my head fall into my hands.

"Need to vent?" Nico asked me, eyes still glued to the TV as he shot his way through a horde of zombies.

"No," I whispered. "Need to hide."

He chuckled.

"Nico, what do you like? I don't really know much about you."

I felt terrible about it, too. I barely knew them and yet they were already bound to me and protecting me.

"I like video games. I like learning new things and read a lot of books and magazines..."

"He likes science, a lot," Rhys added.

"Really?" I asked, shocked that a mage would like science.

He nodded. "I love science."

"Even though you can use magic?"

"Science explains a lot of things that we don't understand."

"Too bad science can't explain males," I mumbled and walked to get another bottle of cider.

"What about you?" I asked Rhys as I struggled to get the bottle cap off.

He took the bottle and opened it for me before handing it back. "I like video games. I like sports cars, too."

"What do you like to do?" I asked, leaning my hip against the counter while I faced him. He was sitting on a stool and it made us almost the same height.

"You," he said with a wink.

I rolled my eyes and walked back to the couch with him laughing behind me.

"Is Deryn hiding?" I asked Nico softly.

He nodded, but didn't say anything.

The doorbell rang and Rhys went to answer it, opening the door so the pizza guy could deliver the ten boxes they had ordered.

"Did you get pepperoni?" I asked, set my drink on the coffee table, and walked over to the pizza guy and Rhys.

Rhys nodded. "Yes."

"Here's your change," the pizza guy said to him, but his eyes kept darting to me.

Rhys carried the pizzas to the counter and I went to shut the door, but the pizza guy grabbed my arm and jerked me out of the apartment. He slammed the door shut and ran with me down the hallway and down the stairs.

"Let me go!" I screamed at him.

"Shut the fuck up," he ordered me with a growl.

I couldn't believe that the guys hadn't caught up to us. This guy wasn't running *that* fast. Were they not even aware that he had grabbed me?

He threw open the door on the bottom floor and ran right into Rhys. Deryn grabbed me away from the guy while Rhys held him up by his throat with one arm.

Did it make me twisted to be turned on by seeing Rhys strangle someone with one arm? Most likely. Did it stop me? Nope.

"You okay?" Deryn asked me, blocking me with his body from the guy.

I nodded and smoothed down my clothes.

"Who sent you?" Deryn demanded.

The guy was turning purple and opened and closed his mouth with no sound.

"He can't answer when you're strangling him," I reminded Rhys.

Rhys dropped the guy and he crashed to the ground in a heap, gasping in breaths. "I don't know," he said quickly. "I got the job by text and they wired the money."

"What was your job?" Deryn asked.

"Grab the girl and take her outside," he said and started to stand up.

"Nico!" Rhys yelled.

Nico appeared next to us. "You bellowed?"

"Can you create a protective shield around her if you can't see her?" Rhys asked him.

He nodded. "I can create one that will last about five minutes, will that work?"

"Perfect," Rhys said with a smile.

Nico leaned down to kiss me lightly on the lips and when he stepped back, a translucent shield was around me.

"Last kiss in case the shield doesn't hold?" I asked with a smirk despite the fear I felt, knowing that Rhys was going to make me go outside.

Nico scowled at me. "That's rude."

"Alright, pizza boy. Go ahead and grab our girl and head outside."

"What?" he asked and looked between us all.

"Go on," Rhys ordered him. "Go finish your job."

Pizza guy grabbed my arm and pulled me towards the exit, a scowl on his face. I had a feeling that whoever hired him hadn't planned on him living past getting outside, and the guys likely assumed that as well.

"Rhys," Deryn growled as I moved closer to the door.

"She's protected," Nico assured him.

"What if someone grabs her?" Deryn asked.

"Then I'll grab her," Rhys assured him.

"I don't like this," he growled.

I smiled and blew them a kiss. "At least if I die, you won't have to worry about the bond anymore."

"Not funny!" Deryn snapped, but his voice was drowned out by the sound of traffic and people as I stepped outside.

"Now what?" I asked pizza guy who had stopped as soon as we stepped outside.

His phone rang and he answered it. "Yes?"

The person said something and pizza guy nodded along and then started walking in the direction of the park.

"Got it," he said and ended his call. "Looks like you'll be going on a trip," he informed me.

A blue dragon dropped out of the sky and landed in front of me. I screamed and tried to get away, but pizza guy was deceptively strong and held me. The dragon shifted into a female who grabbed me and tossed a sultry smile towards pizza guy.

"Pleasure doing business," she told him. She shifted again and flew up into the sky with me in her claws.

I screamed again, hating heights and being dangled in a dragon's claws was not the way to get over that fear.

A dragon roared below us and I recognized it instantly.

"Rhys!" I yelled.

The dragon carrying me growled and flapped her wings harder. She got up out of the city skyline and a red circle appeared in front of her nose. She blew red mist out of her nostrils and the circle changed into a weird symbol and then we were flying through a portal into a place with lush green grass and mountains.

The portal closed and I stared in disbelief at the land we were in. It reminded me of home, but it couldn't be...

"Why are we here?" I asked loudly, hoping she could hear me.

She didn't respond.

We flew towards the Arle River and I knew without a doubt that we were back in my hometown. Why did shit always happen here?

We flew past the small city where the diner, police station, post office, and city hall sat. We flew over Mr. Archer's fields of corn, past

Ms. Fritz' strawberry patch, and straight to the place of nightmares, my childhood home.

She landed and shifted as she did, ending up carrying me in her arms, which was highly awkward since we were the same height.

"Why the fuck are we here?" I demanded and tried to get out of her arms.

She gripped me tighter and snarled, "Shut up and stay still."

The front door opened and my pulse skyrocketed. A man of average stature with dazzling red eyes and a heart blacker than the midnight sky smiled at me. His jeans were streaked with what was most likely blood, his shirt the same, but his duster was clean. He loved that duster more than anything else in the world.

"Hello, Daughter."

"Why the fuck am I here?" I demanded.

The dragoness set me down and bowed to him. "I've done as you asked."

He tossed a pouch to her and she left as soon as she caught it.

"You're hard to get ahold of," he told me as she walked down the steps of the house towards me. His cowboy hat was pushed up slightly, so he could look at me without tilting his head at all.

"I moved. Everyone knows I moved."

"I don't have your address," he said.

I glared at him. "You have no right to fucking do this."

He turned to mist and closed the distance between us in less than a second. His hand gripped my jaw painfully and he glared into my eyes. "Watch how you talk to me, child."

"Fuck you," I snapped. It wasn't smart to antagonize him. It would be better to bow to him, gravel at his feet. I had done it for twenty-three years. I wouldn't do it any longer. I refused to bow to him.

He backhanded me hard enough to make me fly backwards four feet. I landed on my back and knew the entire right side of my face would be bruised tomorrow. "You disobedient, brat!" he yelled. "You think that just because you're an adult that you can do as you please. That's not how this works!"

Slowly, I pushed myself up to a standing position and wiped the blood from my mouth. He'd held back on that hit, which meant that he needed something from me.

"What do you want?" I asked him quietly.

He smiled. "You're smart, despite being impudent."

I didn't rise to his bait.

"You ended a war that I've been working very hard to keep alive," he told me. "I don't know where you found the artifact, but obviously I need to learn to hide things better."

Him? He was the one who had stolen the artifact?

"Why do you want the war?" I asked.

"The more those four factions fight, the more time I have to raise my army without them coming to look for me."

"Army for what?" What the hell was he scheming now?

"You don't need to worry about that," he assured me. "What you do need to worry about is figuring out how you are going to help me."

"I'm not," I stated bluntly.

His jaw clenched and it took a minute for him to respond. "You're going to use your connections with those four Princes to restart the war."

He'd gone insane. Even more insane than after he was turned into a vampire and gained his powers.

"No," I stated firmly.

He was choking me just like Rhys had done to the pizza guy and I realized that it was definitely not sexy. It hurt. A lot! Especially when you didn't have a chance to prepare for it since the other person moved faster than your eye could track.

"Do not tell me no!" he growled, the human façade he wore breaking as his true self came out. He wasn't human any longer. No, he was a demon in human skin.

"Fuck. You," I gasped out.

He tossed me into the gravel driveway and I screamed in pain as the rocks scraped my arms and hands and a few got stuck into my skin.

"You will do this," he ordered me.

"Or what?" I asked with a gasp. "You'll kill me? Do it. Just fucking put me out of my misery, because I won't betray them."

"Do you need incentive?" he asked with a smirk. "I heard your former werewolf lover moved to Jinla. I could pay his adorable family a visit and—"

"Touch them and I'll kill you," I threatened him.

I knew the blow was coming, but knowing it was coming didn't stop it from hurting. I clutched my side, sure that he'd broken one of my ribs again, and took shallow breaths.

"You are suicidal, aren't you?" he growled.

"I won't do what you want," I whispered. "I won't betray my friends."

"I'll kill them all," he threatened me.

"You can't kill the princes. They're too powerful. Plus, that would put your head right on the chopping block," I reminded him smugly.

He growled and stalked away to pace across the porch.

I took the reprieve to pull out my cell phone and send a message with my location in the group text that Rhys had created.

Dad walked back towards me and I slid the phone back into my pocket while doubled over, so he wouldn't see it before getting up to my knees. He grabbed me by the hair and dragged me into the house. I cried out and tried to grab his arm to take some of the pressure off my hair, but couldn't get a grip. My scalp was on fire and tears filled my eyes.

"Let's see how some time in here treats you," he snarled.

"No! No! No!" I screamed and struggled as hard as I could to get away from him and the closet under the stairs. It was the place of my nightmares. The place he had tortured me and punished me as a child and teenager.

He shoved me in, slammed the door closed and locked it, laughing the entire time.

"Let me out!" I screamed and slammed my body against the door. "Let me out!"

"You can come out when you're ready to do what I ask," he said, his voice fading as he walked away. The front door opened and closed and I knew I was alone.

I curled up into a ball and rocked myself back and forth. The cupboard was small, only big enough for me to be on my knees. It was pitch black.

"You're alive, Jolie. You're alive. He can't hurt you when you're in the closet. They're coming. They'll come for you." I whispered.

It didn't help. No matter what I tried to tell myself, I couldn't stop the panic as it set in. My breathing became rapid and before long, I passed out.

CHAPTER 8

"Let me out!" I screamed for the fiftieth time and kicked the door.

I thought the guys would have been here by now, but I was still locked in the closet. I checked my phone and the group message. My message had gone through, but I hadn't gotten a response and now, I had no service. Figures that the place of my nightmares wouldn't have reception. Even having the phone to brighten up the cupboard so it wasn't pitch black didn't help.

I wasn't a child anymore, but I couldn't convince myself not to be terrified.

I had texted the guys hours ago. Why weren't they here? What were they doing?

The house door opened.

"Fuck you!" I screamed loudly. "I fucking hate you! I hope you die!"

Maybe if I provoked him, he would take me out and hit me or something. At least I would be out of the cupboard.

"That's not very nice to say," Fox whispered from outside the door.

"Fox!" I screamed and then lowered my voice. "Fox, please fucking open the door. Let me out. Let me out!"

"Easy, I'm working on it," he assured me. "Deryn, a little help? There's no key."

The door creaked and then it was gone and light blinded me. Fox sat off to the side and Deryn held the door, which he had ripped out of the stairway.

I scrambled out and ran to hide behind Rhys who was furthest away from the cupboard, next to the door. My body was still trembling and I couldn't get it to stop.

Deryn tossed the door off to the side and they all turned to face me.

"The fuck happened?" Nico asked.

Rhys pulled me in, and I sobbed into his chest. His arms wrapped around me. "What happened?"

"We need to go," I sobbed. "He'll come back."

"Who?" Deryn asked. "Who took you?"

"Boys, this is incredibly rude," Dad chastised them. "When you come to meet the father of the girl you want to date, you shouldn't destroy his property. It makes a very bad first impression."

"Who are you?" Fox demanded.

"Fuck you!" I screamed at him and stepped away from Rhys. "I'm done! Don't ever fucking talk to me again. I'm not yours. I'm not going to do what you want. You can torture me all you want, but I won't help you. I'd rather see you turn to ash."

His smile wilted and he said, "You can leave tonight, but this isn't over."

"I won't help you," I told him. "I'd sooner die."

He moved and I was across the room, pinned to the wall by his arm. The guys moved towards me, but Dad held up his hand to them and they stopped.

"You help me, or I kill them," Dad whispered.

"You can't defeat them all," I gasped.

"No, I can't defeat them all at once, but I can kill them one by one. Which should I start with? The wolf seems mighty fond of you. Perhaps I should start with him? Maybe after I break a few legs, you'll be more obedient."

"Let her go," Rhys ordered Dad.

"Boy, be quiet when family is talking," Dad ordered him.

"Kill me," I ordered him. "Kill me and get it over with."

Dad sighed and shook his head sadly. "I had hoped it would never come to this. Very well, if that's your wish." He drew a blade from his back and I took one last look at the guys and awaited my death.

Death didn't come. The princes attacked as one. Dad cursed, dropped me and disappeared, tucking his tail between his legs as he ran away to stay alive.

I fell to the ground and screamed as my broken rib hit the hardwood floor.

"Jolie!" Fox yelled and rushed to me. He started to move me, but I held up my hand to stop him.

Slowly, I pushed myself up into a sitting position and took several breaths with my eyes closed.

"He won't give up," I whispered with tears in my eyes. "He's going to try to use me. He'll hurt you to force me."

Rhys folded his arms across his chest. Deryn squatted down in front of me, next to Fox. Nico looked around the house.

"That was my dad," I whispered.

All of their eyes widened and Nico focused on me.

"He was turned after I was born," I explained. "He's very powerful."

"We know who he is. We just didn't know you were related," Nico said.

"Why did he kidnap you?" Fox asked.

"He wants the war to resume. He wanted me to use my connections with you to start the war again. He wanted me to betray you. I refused."

"How badly are you injured?" Deryn asked.

"I think at least one of my ribs is broken. It hurts *really* bad to talk or breath. Or move."

"Then shut up," Fox ordered me with a scowl.

The normally happy elf was incredibly angry and it caught me off guard.

"Fox—" I started, but he looked up and glared at me, so I shut my mouth.

"We need to take her to the hospital," Deryn said, despite the fact that all of them already knew that.

"There isn't one for an hour," I said quickly before Fox could tell me to be quiet again.

"I'll heal her," Fox whispered and put his hands on my sides.

"You sure?" Deryn asked, a crease in his brow.

"Just protect me if someone comes," Fox ordered him.

Deryn stood up and spun around so that he was facing away from us, watching for danger.

Fox closed his eyes, inhaled, and his hands started glowing.

"Healing takes a lot of my energy," Fox explained. "I'll be useless in a fight after I'm done, so I don't heal others often."

"You all heal fast anyway," I whispered.

"Shush," he snapped. "No more talking."

I obeyed.

"When I first learned how to heal, I didn't understand the energy it would take. I healed Deryn's broken leg and slept for two days. Deryn thought I'd killed myself by fixing him and freaked out."

"Did not," Deryn mumbled.

"He cried," Rhys said.

"We were four!" Deryn growled.

"My parents spent a lot of time with me to teach me to heal properly. I'm still not anywhere as great as my mother. She can heal a hundred soldiers and just needs an hour nap afterwards. She's amazing."

"And hot," Rhys replied with a smirk.

Nico and Deryn nodded with the same smirk.

"Shut it," Fox growled, but it was obviously a conversation they'd had several times before and he didn't really care.

My breathing became easier and my side stopped hurting completely. I leaned forward and kissed him, just a brush of lips across lips. "Thank you."

"Where else are you hurt?" he asked.

"Everything else is just bruised," I told him and stood up.

"Where?" he asked and saw my cheek.

"Leave it. It's not life threatening," I said and moved away from him.

"Let's go," Rhys said and headed outside.

We stepped outside into an ambush. Fifty vampires stood in a loose semicircle around the porch, their eyes glowing in the moonlight.

"Fuck," I whispered.

"Ready?" Rhys whispered.

"Yes," the three others replied.

Deryn picked me up and tensed, waiting for something.

"Give up and we won't kill you," a tall vampire with shoulder length dark hair said.

Rhys flipped him off, shifted into his huge dragon form, and immediately sent out a wave of fire at the gathered vampires, making them jump back several yards.

Deryn leapt up onto Rhys's back, as did the other two, and Rhys took to the sky. I clutched Deryn tightly and buried my face in his chest as we flew.

What were the odds that I'd be carried by a dragon twice in one day?

"It's okay," Deryn assured me. "Rhys is an excellent flyer."

I didn't respond.

"Why were you so scared when we found you?" Fox asked me. He was lying on his back on the center of Rhys's back, which was just wide enough for it.

"It's stupid and embarrassing," I whispered, "but he tossed me in there for days at a time as a kid with no light or anything. It's terrifying."

"It's not stupid," Nico assured me.

"He's the one who had the artifact," I informed them. "He wants the war because he said that while you are all fighting each other, he can grow an army."

"For what?" Deryn asked.

"I don't know," I admitted. "To take over? He's always been power hungry."

"We need to let the elders know," Nico said and pulled out his phone.

I looked around at the men, sitting or lying on the back of their friend in dragon form, texting and playing games on their phones. I couldn't believe what I was seeing. I burst into laughter and all of them looked at me questioningly, even Rhys's large dragon head turned to look at me.

"What?" Deryn asked.

I waved my arm at all of them. "This scene," I gasped out between laughs.

They looked at each other and slowly smiles took the place of the scowls that had been there.

"Thank you," I whispered and looked at them each in turn. "Thank you for rescuing me, again."

Deryn kissed my cheek. "You don't have to thank us."

"We wish we could have been here sooner," Nico said. "We were attacked as soon as we stepped outside of the apartment building by a group of vampires. That's why we were delayed."

"We came as fast as we could," Deryn assured me.

Rhys snarled.

"Rhys flew as fast as he could," Deryn amended with a smirk.

"So, Lamar was the one who stole the artifact to start the war,"

Fox whispered. "I shouldn't be surprised. I am surprised that he is your father though."

"Only by blood," I grumbled.

"We felt your pain multiple times. What happened?" Nico asked me.

"Well, I talked back and he didn't like that. So, he hit me a few times. Then I told him I wasn't going to help him by betraying you and that really pissed him off. I told him just to kill me, but he decided torture was better and threw me in the closet. He would have left me in there for days before coming to get me to see if I would agree to what he wanted."

"Has he always been like this?" Fox asked softly.

I nodded. "Yes. He started when I was eight...nine? Somewhere around there."

"And you didn't know about the artifact?" Deryn asked me.

I shook my head. "My Grandma gave it to me after I escaped from Demarcus. She just told me it would keep my location a secret from him and keep his group from finding me."

Now I wondered if Grandma had known more than she let on. Maybe she had hoped I would return it to its rightful place.

"Your cheek is going to be really bruised tomorrow," Deryn whispered.

"I know, but at least he held back that hit," I said and sighed. "He may be psychotic, but he won't kill me. I know that much."

Or, at least I hoped that much. He had seemed like he was planning to kill me at the end there.

Rhys landed and we climbed off of him. He switched forms, walked into the apartment building, and hugged me. "I'm sorry we weren't faster."

I scoffed. "I'm just glad you came."

He kissed the top of my head and tears started to fall. Damn him. I had held on during the flight here.

We got into the elevator and the guys crowded around me, placing a hand each on me as I cried. I cried surrounded by four males I was falling for deeper and deeper.

"Who's watching her tonight?" Rhys asked.

"Me," Deryn said.

"I need a shower," I whispered and brushed some gravel off of my arms.

"You have dirt in your hair," Fox pointed out.

I sighed and dropped my head. "Movies are so unrealistic. No one gets rescued looking perfect. They need to show the princesses covered in dirt and grime, not having showered for days."

"You're still beautiful," Fox assured me and kissed my cheek. "Even covered in cobwebs and dirt."

I chuckled and followed Deryn to his apartment, straight for the bathroom. I stood in front of the mirror and looked at myself. My cheek was swollen and I was covered in dirt with leaves and rocks in my hair.

"Gorgeous," I scoffed.

"I think so," Deryn said.

I turned to glare at him in the bathroom doorway. "Sneaking up on people isn't nice."

He smiled. "You just didn't notice me. I've been here for a few minutes." With long strides, he walked across the bathroom and turned the shower on. Steam began to rise and I couldn't wait to get into it.

Without turning around, he took his shirt off and his pants.

"Uh," I said intelligently.

He turned to look at me. "Mind if I join you?"

"No," I replied immediately, waiting expectantly for the last piece of his clothing to be removed.

I was not disappointed when he did.

Blue rupees! He was fucking perfect. How could they all be so perfect? It had to be against the law for them to be perfect and friends and all available for me to touch.

I shed my clothes and got into the shower behind him. The shower was large, big enough that four people could comfortably stand in it and shower together. There were jets in the walls that sprayed your body and a huge sprayer in the ceiling.

I stepped into the water and hissed in pain from the tiny cuts being hit by the water. Deryn turned around and looked me up and down slowly, his mouth curving upwards as he finished.

"See something you like?" I teased and reached for the soap.

He nodded and slid his hands along the tops of my hips. "All of this," he responded and kissed me.

I opened my mouth to him, and he slid his tongue along mine. Damn he tasted good. The kiss deepened and I moved closer to him, squishing his erection between us while I ran my hands along his chest and abs.

"Why were you so jealous of Martin?" I asked him, stepping back and putting shampoo in my hair to distract me for a moment. It didn't take long for the overhead spray to rinse my hair and I cringed when I saw the amount of dirt and debris going down the drain.

"Because, you're my Queen," he replied, putting more shampoo in my hair and massaging it in.

"But you don't get jealous of Rhys or Fox," I reminded him.

"You're their Queen, too."

"So, if another male who isn't part of our fivesome touches me, it's going to make you jealous?" I asked and rinsed my hair.

When I opened my eyes, his face was level with mine. "No one else is allowed to touch you."

"What if I want to be touched?" I asked breathlessly and backed away from him, towards the wall of the shower.

He rested his hands on either side of my head and leaned close to whisper, "Then you tell me." He dropped one hand and slid two fingers inside of me, making me gasp and spread my legs wider for him.

"What if I want—"

I didn't even get to finish the question. He dropped his head and took my nipple into his mouth, twirling his tongue around my nipple and then sucking on it while he continued to finger me.

"Yes," I whispered and let my head fall back.

"What else do you want?" he asked me.

Instead of responding, I dropped to my knees, warm water sliding over my back, and took him into my mouth, surprised at his girth, but luckily able to accommodate it and still take most of him in before drawing back again.

"Fuck," he groaned and watched me.

His dick would feel amazing inside and I couldn't control my selfish desire any longer. I stood up, wrapped my arms around his neck, and climbed on him like a horny monkey, wrapping my legs around his waist.

He adjusted the angle and slid into me, groaning at the same time that I screamed.

"I'm sorry," he whispered as he withdrew.

"For what?" I asked, confused.

"For being a jealous asshole. I'm not usually like that," he replied.

I dropped my hips to pull him back into me. "You can fuck me in apology," I suggested.

He gripped my hips and smiled. "I've never done an apology fuck before."

"We can be each other's first apology fuck," I said with a smile and wiggled my hips.

He groaned and said, "If you keep that up, this will be a short apology."

I chuckled and he gripped my hips tighter before slamming into me.

"Yes!" I screamed.

"You're beautiful," he told me and kissed me deeply.

"Deryn!" I screamed as he pounded into me over and over again, bringing orgasm after orgasm. I had never orgasmed so many times in my life.

He lay me on my back on the floor of the shower, water pelting us from every direction, and flicked his tongue across one nipple while playing with the other at the same time that his hips moved. Everything had become warm and wet, inside and out.

I reached down and rubbed my clit and moaned at the overload of sensations.

"Damn, you're glorious," he growled. Adjusting his position, he gripped my hips and slammed into me harder and faster, bringing another wave of pleasure that had me gripping his shoulders and screaming his name again.

He pulled out of me and orgasmed a moment later.

"Your..."

"Good?"

"Apology is accepted," I replied and closed my eyes, lying on the floor in euphoria.

He chuckled and kissed my cheek as he helped me stand up. We washed each other, taking turns using the bar of soap. When we were done, we dried off and I put on one of his shirts and a pair of underwear.

We sat on the couch and I climbed into his lap, letting him cuddle me while we watched a comedy.

"I'm sorry we let that guy take you," he whispered in my ear. "We hoped we would find out who was behind it all. We didn't think a dragoness would come and steal you away using a portal."

I kissed his cheek and snuggled closer to him. "We found the culprit of this attempt, so it was probably for the best."

"You being injured was not for the best," he growled.

"I'm alive. That's all that matters," I whispered.

"We still don't know everyone who is after you. It obviously wasn't your dad who was trying to kill you. So, we're back to square one."

I hadn't thought about that. He was right.

"Are you hungry?" he asked. "You didn't get to eat any pizza."

"No," I whispered, my thoughts swirling away. "Sleepy."

"We have to go see the elders," Rhys told me.

We were all in Deryn's apartment together, they faced me while I sat on the couch.

Rhys's hands fisted on the back of the leather recliner.

"Okay," I replied, not sure why all four were looking at me so strangely.

"We can't take you," Deryn said, frowning and leaning forward like he was prepared to punch something.

"So, you'll be here alone," Fox explained, putting a calming hand on Deryn's shoulder.

"Oh," I whispered. Being alone wasn't a terrible thing, but having been with them constantly made being alone seem, well, lonely.

"We aren't sure how long we will be. Maybe an hour or two," Rhys said. "We'll try to hurry back."

"I'll be fine," I said, pulling the blanket I had wrapped around me even tighter. "I'll just play some video games."

They all fidgeted. Rhys shuffled from one foot to the other. Deryn stuck his hands in his pockets. Fox chewed on his bottom lip. Nico scuffed the toe of his shoe on the hardwood floor.

"What?" I asked and stood up, letting the blanket fall on the couch.

They glanced at each other and had some type of silent communication go on between them.

They obviously wanted to say something or ask something, but were hesitant to. I stepped forward and hugged Rhys, then went down the line, hugging each of them. They relaxed slightly and they turned to leave.

"Deryn?" I called.

He turned. "Yeah?"

"Can I add my account to your system?"

He smiled and nodded. "Yeah, go ahead."

"Thanks," I replied with a smile for him in return.

"Don't let anyone in," he ordered me.

I locked the door behind them and went to the fridge, grabbed a bottle of cider, and returned to the couch to play some games. It took a bit to get my profile set up on his system, but once I was logged in, a smile plastered itself on my face. I didn't like being away from the guys, but it had been far too long since I'd played games with my clan.

"I've returned!" I said when I joined the party chat.

"Jolie!" four male voices yelled joyously.

"We've missed you," Dragonknight told me.

"Sorry, things got crazy over here. So, are we playing *Ghost 2*, or what?"

"Duh!" Orphan, one of the crazier ones of our clan, said.

"I'm going to be rusty," I said with a sigh. "So, don't expect too much out of me."

"We never do," Turbo said.

Everyone laughed, even me, at his taunt.

The hours past as we played, my mind focused on the game and joking with my online friends. I didn't realize how late it was until Orphan said he was getting off for the night. He was in a different time zone than me, two hours ahead.

"I should get off, too," I said, worried since the guys still weren't back and hadn't text me either.

"Night!" everyone yelled as we backed out of the chat lobby.

They said they would be an hour or two, but it had been four. I didn't want to seem needy, but I was worried about them. Sending a text to the group chat seemed the best option.

Me: You guys okay? You've been gone awhile and I haven't heard from you, so I was worried.

To distract myself, I heated up some of the leftover pizza and scrolled through the movies, trying to find one that would distract me enough not to worry about the guys. Thirty minutes past and I still hadn't received a text or call. Something was wrong. They wouldn't go silent like this and not respond to my messages.

I stood and paced. I didn't know where they had gone. The elders were not people I had been introduced to. Plus, I couldn't go outside on my own. Maybe Martin knew where they were.

Me: Hey, have you seen Deryn tonight?

Martin: No. I thought he was with you.

Me: He went to see the Elders. No idea where that is.

Martin: The Elders have a place in the center of all of the territories. I've never actually been there. Is something wrong? Do you need me to come over?

Me: No. No. I'm fine. Just being a worry wart because I haven't heard from him in a few hours.

Martin: He's really strong, Jolie. I'm sure he's fine.

Me: You're right. Sorry for bothering you.

Martin: If you need me to come over, just tell me.

Me: I'm fine. Thanks. Night.

Martin: Night.

I didn't think Deryn would be okay with coming back to his apartment and finding Martin with me. Hitting play on the movie, I tried to focus on the story and forget about the boys. They were Princes. They were strong and I was just being paranoid.

What would I do if they didn't come back? I hadn't known them long, but they had quickly become part of my life. A big part of my life.

Shouldn't I be able to feel the connection between us? Hadn't they said that it was just harder for humans to use magic, not impossible?

Try as I might, I couldn't feel anything.

I'd fallen asleep at some point, because when they did come back, I was on my side on the couch. I jolted up and jumped over the couch, hugging the first one who came inside, which turned out to be Deryn.

"Hey," he said softly and hugged me back.

I pushed away from him with a fist to his chest, glad that he was back, but also pissed that they hadn't messaged me. Glaring, I asked, "Why didn't you text me?"

"We don't have service there," Rhys said softly, approaching as though to hug me.

I stepped back and said, "Whatever."

They frowned at me. It was frustrating to have four males frown at you at the same time.

I glared at them. Then, turning, I went to the spare room and climbed into the bed. They were safe, which was what I cared about. I wanted to touch them all, but I was letting my anger take over instead.

The four of them stood in the doorway to the room and looked at me.

"We're sorry," Fox apologized. "We would have messaged you or called if we could."

"It's fine. You don't need to apologize," I muttered and pulled the blankets up to cover the bottom of my mouth.

"We do," Nico said adamantly. "If the roles had been reversed, we would have been frantically trying to get ahold of you."

"I'm weak. You guys aren't."

They moved forward, and to my shock, all of them climbed onto the bed so they could all surround me in a square.

"What?"

They didn't talk, just placed their hands on my legs, arms, shoulders, whatever they could reach and closed their eyes. Almost instantly, Nico's breathing evened out as he fell into a deep sleep. Obviously, they weren't going to talk, so I got more comfortable and fell asleep, too.

I sat between Nico's legs on the couch with Rhys and Deryn on either side, and Fox sitting between my legs on the floor in front of the couch. They'd been overly affectionate ever since they returned from the elders three days ago. Every night, they slept in a square of protection around me, making sure to touch me as they slept. No one tried anything sexual, not even more than light kisses were exchanged.

It was frustrating to be celibate again. Okay, I was being childish and selfish since it had only been about a week since I'd slept with one of them, but I was surrounded by gorgeous men and none were trying to fuck me.

The guys laughed at the comedy we were watching, but I wasn't really paying attention. There had been a search for my dad by the four clans, but of course, they hadn't found him. He was exceptional at hiding and disappearing when he needed to.

Nico slid his arms around my waist and squeezed me in a hug. "What's wrong?" he whispered in my ear.

"Nothing," I lied.

"Liar."

He stood up, disturbing the other three, but they didn't complain, just moved out of his way as he carried me to the spare bedroom. He set me on the bed and stood in the doorway, leaning against the doorframe.

"What's up?" he asked, his brow slightly furrowed in worry.

"I don't want to tell you," I muttered in embarrassment and looked down at my hands in my lap.

His hands covered mine and he squeezed them. I looked up into his eyes. He knelt in front of me and smiled. "You don't need to be embarrassed. You can tell me anything."

"You've all been exceptionally affectionate lately," I whispered, staring at his chest. "Which is great. But, none of you have done more than kiss me. What changed? Did I do something?"

His warm hand slid along my cheek, and he rubbed my cheek bone with his thumb. "You've done nothing wrong. We all agreed that we would be okay with all of us sleeping in the bed together and touching you at the same time. However, having other males so close, does make arousal nonexistent for us. That's just not something we are into. We are all wildly attracted to you still."

"I'm being needy and self-conscious," I muttered. "I tried to cure myself of that when I was a teenager. I thought I had, but clearly—"

He kissed me deeply and slid his hands into my hair, gripping the back of my head so that I had nowhere to go except to surrender to him. His tongue slid across mine and I moaned into his mouth, but immediately pulled away, surprised that he let me go.

"The others are right there," I reminded him. "They likely heard that."

Nico flicked his hand towards the door and it shut and locked on its own. He held his fist in front of him and blew into it. A bubble formed out the other end, continuing to grow in size the more he blew on it. The bubble slid along my skin as it engulfed the bed. When it went past my head, I could no longer hear the TV in the living room. Nico stepped into the bubble and pulled his shirt off.

"The others—"

"This bubble keeps the sounds we make from being heard by others. It also keeps the sounds from outside from being heard by us. We can be as loud as we want and they won't hear us," he explained. To prove his point, he yelled loudly and smiled.

No one came running.

The sight of him shirtless was making it harder for me to remember why I was objecting in the first place. Crawling across the bed, he leaned over me, his bare chest right there for me to touch. Without even thinking, my hands went to touch his chest and stomach, stroking the muscles there.

"You're so handsome," I told him and looked up into his eyes.

He smiled and leaned down to kiss me while his hands slid up beneath my shirt and frustratingly stopped at the bottom of my bra. I sat up and ripped my shirt off over my head, then unsnapped my bra. His eyes lowered as the bra slipped off my arms, my nipples already hard from my arousal. He unbuttoned my pants and slid them off with my underwear in one motion. Cool air hit me and I shivered. His pants were still on, which was definitely not what I wanted. Before I could voice my objection, he opened my legs and his tongue swept across my most sensitive parts.

I arched up into him and gasped in pleasure. The amount of sexual frustration and desire I had been feeling made his tongue only necessary for a few swipes before an orgasm ripped through me. His eyebrows rose and he pulled his pants off.

"You should have told us you were so horny," he chastised me.

"Then what, you ro-sham-bo for who gets to fix me?" I asked breathlessly.

His pants gone, he pushed himself into me in one quick movement. The task easy since I was so incredibly wet.

"Yes," he replied. "Or we ask if you have a preference between us."

His mouth closed around one of my nipples just before he slammed into me hard enough for our skin to slap and sting a bit. Too worked up for it to matter, I could only moan my pleasure at the movements. His tongue swirled around one of my nipples while his fingers squeezed and teased my other one. It had been a long time since I'd been so far gone that my orgasms came so quickly. He was gentle with my nipples, but hard with my lower body. He pounded into me so hard that I knew I would be sore tomorrow, but I didn't care. It felt amazing and I was screaming his name and moaning louder than I ever had before.

"I'm really close," he admitted to me. "If you want to switch positions, now is the best time to tell me."

I pushed his chest and he leaned back, letting me get up. He put a condom on and sat back in front of me. Pushing his chest again, he lay on his back and I climbed on top of him, lowering myself until he was fully sheathed inside of me.

He groaned loudly and gripped my hips with his eyes rolled back in his head. I shared the sentiment and took it slow, moving my hips back and forth.

"You are fucking gorgeous," he told me as I rode him.

I smiled at the compliment and rode him harder and faster.

"Goddess, yes!" he moaned.

I screamed as another orgasm tore through me and he groaned.

"You're so wet," he told me. "It's amazing."

With a few more movements, he and I finished at the same time and I lay forward, my head resting on his shoulder with him still inside of me.

"I don't know if I'll be able to tell you when I want one of you," I admitted to him. "I don't want to hurt anyone's feelings or make you guys think that I have a favorite. I don't."

He rubbed my back and said, "We know you don't have a favorite."

"It's still weird," I told him. "Four males all bound to me. I don't even feel the bond."

"How do you feel about us?" he asked, turning his head so he could look at me.

"Way more than I should for only knowing you such a short time," I admitted.

"Come on," he groaned. "Give me more than that."

I cared deeply for them. I was falling in love with all of them. Admitting it out loud wasn't something that I wanted to do, though. I didn't want to admit that I had developed such feelings for them.

His phone rang in his pants and he rolled us over until he could stand up and answer it. "Yeah? Okay. We'll be out in a minute."

"Who was that?" I asked, glad for the distraction from the conversation that we were having.

"Rhys. We're going to go out for dinner and he wanted to also check to make sure that you were okay."

I blushed and whispered, "Doesn't he sense my feelings through the bond?"

Dressing took a bit because my legs were jelly-like. Soreness was already setting in, which did not bode well for tomorrow.

"Yes."

"So, he knows that I was, uh, happy a minute ago."

Nico laughed and kissed my cheek as he put his pants on. "Yes, Jolie. They all know what we did in here, even if they couldn't hear us."

My face was on fire. How could I go outside and face them? This was not something I was going to get used to.

We finished dressing and he pulled me into a hug, resting his head atop mine. "It'll take some getting used to, but eventually, we will all grow accustomed to this and it won't be awkward at all."

Eventually? Even though I knew the bond wasn't something I could break without dying, I hadn't really thought about them being with me for the rest of my life. "You're all stuck with me for the rest of my life?" I asked him softly.

"Not stuck," he said adamantly. "We all chose this."

"Not really," I reminded him. "You all did it, but not really on purpose."

"We all care deeply for you," he whispered. "None of us regrets it."

Not yet, but what would they feel in six months or a year or three from now?

CHAPTER 9

"We're going on an overnight trip," Fox informed me with a wide smile as soon as I answered his knock at Rhys's apartment. He and Deryn came in at the same time, while Nico lounged on the couch. Rhys had taken a call in his bedroom and had yet to return.

"Really? Where?" I asked, excited to get out of the apartment.

"Camping," he said.

"Camping?" I scrunched my forehead.

"What's wrong?" Deryn asked.

"I've never been camping," I admitted. The thought of sleeping under the stars was nice, but being surrounded by bugs was not something I particularly had any interest in. Didn't mean I wouldn't go and enjoy myself, but I was definitely taking bug spray.

"When are we going?" I asked, already making a list of supplies I'd need in my head.

"Today," he said and smiled wide. Fox was perpetually playful, reminding me of a puppy a lot of the time. He was also incredibly smart and quiet most of the time, letting the others make decisions and only voicing his opinion if he really felt strongly about it.

I blinked. Scratch going to the store. "Can you take me to my apartment?" I requested.

"Sure," he agreed. "Rhys! I'm taking her to her apartment!"

"Okay!" Rhys called back from his bedroom. It wouldn't surprise me if he was already packing.

Fox and I took the elevator and walked to my apartment in silence.

His aura and presence were incredibly relaxing and I preferred being alone with him.

"Fox?"

"Hm?" he asked and turned towards me.

"How do you feel about this whole situation? Being bound to me and the others?" Aside from not talking much, he rarely expressed his feelings.

"I would prefer to have you to myself," he admitted with a smirk. "However, I love my brothers, and sharing you with them isn't so bad."

"So, you're fine with sharing me as long as it is with them?" I questioned.

He scowled. "Are you wanting to see other men?"

The absurdity of his question made me burst out laughing. I had to stop walking, resting a hand on the wall as I doubled over in laughter until tears streamed down my face.

"What's funny?" he asked.

"Foxfire, I feel terrible for being shared among the four of you. There is no way in hell I could even begin to consider other men."

He pinned me to the hallway wall and all of my laughter died at the sight of the heat in his eyes. "It makes me very happy to hear you say that," he whispered. His eyes searched mine a moment and then lowered to my lips.

We hadn't kissed in too long, and he seemed to waver on his decision, so I stood up on my tiptoes and kissed him, sweeping my tongue along his lips so he would open them. He pressed me into the wall and returned my kiss, opening his mouth to me and surrounding me in his scent, jasmine and freshly cut grass.

The kiss ended too soon for my liking, but the beautiful smile on his face made it all worth it.

"Come, we need to get you packed quickly so we can be on our way."

The hallway was still burned and there was just a tarp stapled over the hole of my apartment.

"Do you think anyone stole anything?" I asked nervously.

"No, the apartment manager is very good about not letting anyone inside who isn't supposed to be in," he assured me. "If you're worried, you can put whatever you want inside of my apartment. We've been staying in Deryn's apartment most of the time anyway."

"I would appreciate that," I replied and pushed aside the tarp that now made up my door. I longingly gazed at my gaming console, but since Deryn already had one and had agreed to let me put my log in on his, I looked away.

"Would you like me to take your games and console over?" Fox wrapped his arms around my shoulders and whispered in my ear.

I chuckled. "Am I that obvious?"

"No, but it's probably the most expensive thing you have, so it makes sense that you would want it to be safe," he explained, squeezing me once and releasing me before heading toward my games.

He was right, the console and all of the games were the most expensive things that I owned. Was that sad? Should I have other more expensive things? I had never been obsessed with jewelry or makeup. I liked wearing dresses, but hated shopping for them or anything else really. I liked buying presents for people, but hated buying anything for myself.

I was ecstatic that I hadn't had anything against the wall that had been blown up, so I hadn't lost anything in the explosion. Except my privacy.

I headed toward my bedroom and realized that I had nothing on my mental checklist for camping, but the bug spray. "What the hell am I supposed to bring?" I yelled into the other room.

"Clothes!" he yelled back and then laughed.

"Asshole," I muttered. Packing took me a long time, but I figured out to pack jeans, t-shirts, warm pajamas, and underwear.

When I walked out to the living room, I realized that I was alone.

"Fox?" I called.

"Coming!" he called from outside of my apartment. The tarp moved a minute later and he was there.

"What were you doing?"

"I was putting some of your stuff in my apartment," he explained.

I looked around and was shocked to see that all of my valuable items were gone now.

"Wow. Thanks, Fox. I really appreciate you doing that."

He kissed my cheek. "Anything for you, my Queen."

He pulled my bag from me, and pressed a finger to my lips when I went to protest. He hurried back under the tarp before I could say anything. I sighed and followed him to the elevator where I took my bag back. Amused, Fox put up his hands in surrender before we stepped out on the first floor. When we walked into Rhys's apartment, the other three stood in the living room, with a pile of supplies between them.

"Got your stuff?" Deryn asked, looking at my black duffle bag.

"Yep," I said and tossed the bag onto their pile. "I'm sure I'm forgetting something, though."

"Always happens," Nico said with a chuckle. "You get there and realize that you've forgotten something important."

I hadn't noticed until then, but all of them were wearing jeans and t-shirts. Damn they looked amazing. Deryn had the largest biceps, and his shirt accentuated them nicely.

Rhys's chest was the most sculpted, visible through his shirt.

Nico and Fox were sexy, too, and I couldn't stop staring.

"Jolie?" Rhys asked.

"Huh?" I replied, looking up at their faces.

They were all smirking.

Shit.

"Ready to go?" I asked and turned towards the door.

"Our eyes are up here," Deryn whispered as he walked by me.

They all laughed and grabbed the supplies. I walked down in the middle of them, glad to be getting out of the apartment. There was a SUV waiting for us outside the apartment building with Martin leaning against it.

I pushed past the guys and rushed towards him. Martin pushed off the SUV, a wide smile on his face, and pulled me into a tight hug.

"What are you doing here?" I asked from within his hug.

"Deryn called in the request for a driver, and I was the only one available, so Dan asked me to come," he explained.

"Jolie," Deryn growled.

Martin kissed the top of my head and released me to face the four angry males behind me. It seemed that Deryn wasn't the only one who had jealousy issues. Fox's jealous face was the most surprising of all.

"Guys, this is Martin, my best friend. Martin, you know Deryn. This is Rhys, Fox, and Nico," I introduced them.

"Martin, your ex-boyfriend?" Fox asked, taking a step closer to me.

It seemed the best thing to do would be to ignore them. So, I turned around, putting my back to the foursome.

"Do you know where we are going?" I asked Martin.

"Yeah. Deryn sent me the address beforehand. I've actually been there a couple of times. It's a gorgeous place. You'll have a ton of fun," he told me and opened the passenger door of the SUV for me.

Before the guys could object, I climbed inside and buckled my belt. The four jealous males climbed into the back, glaring daggers at Martin who climbed in the driver's seat with a wide smile on his face.

"All set?" he asked them, draping his arm across the back of my seat to turn around and look at them.

"Martin," Deryn growled in warning.

"Great!" Martin said and started the car. "Jo, do you want to pick the music?"

Martin was obviously doing this to rile them up. Why? I wasn't sure, but I was sort of enjoying it. As twisted as that was.

"Thanks," I told him and started shifting through the various stations. "Hey, remember that time that we snuck out of town and went to the country music concert?"

His driving had always been great, so I didn't worry about distracting him. He tugged on my hair and then twirled it around his finger. "Oh, you mean that night that you got so hammered, that I had to pull you off of the stage and you almost puked in my truck?"

"Was that the night that we ended up sleeping in Mr. Archer's corn field?"

He nodded. "We woke up covered in dirt and leaves," he said and laughed. He turned to look at me while we were stopped at a red light. "You still looked beautiful, even covered in dirt." He winked and there were at least two growls behind us. "Oh," Martin whispered and reached into the center console. "The girls sent this for you." He pulled out a bracelet of braided hair.

"What is this?" I asked, confused.

"It's their tail hairs. They took turns plucking hairs from each other's tails and then braided it into a bracelet for you," he explained.

I gingerly took the bracelet and felt tears stinging my eyes. "Oh, wow." It was very soft and was made up of a few different colors.

"They told me to tell you, 'we love you, Auntie Jolie and we hope to see you soon.' They wouldn't stop talking about seeing you for like, a week."

"I wish I could see them more," I mumbled and sniffed against the tears threatening to spill.

"No reason you can't," Martin reminded me. "We're living in the same city now."

"I told you. You know why. And don't for a minute act like a part of you doesn't agree with me."

He sighed and set his hand on my knee. "I'm sorry. I didn't want to start a fight."

"Get your hand off of her," Rhys ordered him with a snarl.

I turned and faced the four, incredibly angry, males. "Hey! You four need to chill out."

"Stop flirting with him," Fox accused.

I rolled my eyes. "I'm not flirting with him. We are talking as friends. He is my friend. He has a mate who he loves and two daughters with said mate. His mate is my other best friend and I love his daughters. I would never come between them, even if there was something between us. But, there isn't! You all are being incredibly jealous, and I don't appreciate it. Not one bit."

Thankfully, the four of them had the decency to look cowed, even though I knew that they likely weren't done being jealous.

Martin had removed his hand, but as he faced forward, watching the road ahead, I saw the smirk on his lips. Did Dan have an ulterior motive in sending Martin to drive us?

"How long will it take to get to our destination?" I asked Martin, turning to face the front.

"About an hour," he answered.

An hour of awkward silence between my males and me. Mine. When did I start thinking of them as mine? They did call me their Queen, and the bond made them my guards.

"Jolie," Fox whispered.

I turned slowly towards him, and found them all staring at me with various expressions, but luckily none looked mad.

"What are you thinking about?" Fox asked.

"Nothing," I mumbled and turned away, looking out the window to my right to avoid all of their gazes.

"She's always been a terrible liar," Martin said to the guys. "She thinks she is good at it, but she's quite terrible."

"We know," Nico replied tersely.

No more words were spoken on the rest of the drive. Our destination turned out to be a gorgeous field of green grass with a few trees and a beautiful lake not far off. Martin helped the guys unload everything and hugged me tightly before leaving.

Standing alone, I looked out over the sea of grass and watched it sway in the breeze.

"We're sorry," Fox whispered behind me.

"It's fine," I whispered back and headed towards the lake.

"Can I walk with you?" Rhys requested.

"Sure," I replied, but still didn't turn to look at him. This land was beautiful, but it reminded me a bit of home.

His fingers laced through mine, and he walked by my side silently. I stopped at the edge of the lake and looked out at the clear water. I could see all the way to the bottom, even far out from the beaches.

"We didn't realize how much it would bother us to see you with another male, since we all share you so easily," he whispered to me.

"I wasn't *with* another male," I reminded him. Seriously, what type of girl did they think I was? Oh, right. A girl that slept with one of them the first night she'd met him and went out with them all in the same week.

"Seeing you touch another male," he amended. "We all laughed at Deryn for his fit of jealousy, but then we all felt it. I understand that you and Martin are simply friends, but it doesn't change how it feels to see a male hugging you."

"So, I can't touch any other males?" I asked.

He sighed. "I would prefer if you didn't, but we of course aren't going to do that. It would help if you would just keep our feelings in mind when you do touch other males. We don't touch other females and wouldn't if you asked us to."

"I'm not going to apologize for hugging Martin," I told him and turned to face him.

He smiled and rested his hand on my cheek. "We don't want you to."

"You keep saying, 'we' instead of 'I'. Why?"

"Because we all agree on these topics. We've all discussed them."

"How could you have discussed this when we were silent in the car?"

"Text message," he replied with a chuckle.

I rolled my eyes, but laughed, too. "I should have known."

He lowered his head towards me, seeking a kiss, but hesitated. "Are you still mad?"

"No," I replied honestly.

"Can I kiss you?"

"You may."

His lips brushed mine and then he kissed me firmly.

"You said you won't touch other females. Does that mean ever?

Like, you four won't sleep with other women the rest of our lives?" I asked him softly.

He nodded. "You're our Queen. You're my Queen. You are the only female for me. If I took another lover, it would divide my attention and you could be hurt or killed due to my distraction. Plus, I care about you and I wouldn't want to hurt you by being with another female."

"What if I said you could?" I asked him. I truly didn't want to know or see them with other lovers, but it just didn't seem fair to them.

"You want me to have another lover?" he asked, his hand still on my cheek.

"No, but you four are sharing one female between you. It's hardly fair."

"As long as you are in my life, and I get moments like this, I will be happy."

His statement made me ridiculously happy and made me feel even more selfish. It should be wrong for me to be so happy that they only wanted me. I was an incredibly selfish creature and I didn't deserve any of them.

"Rhys, can I see your dragon form?" I requested. "I didn't really get a chance to admire your other form the other day since we were running away from vampires."

He kissed the back of my hand and bowed. "As my Queen wishes." His body glowed and then he became a dragon, easily twice the size of an SUV. His scales were red and shimmered in the sunlight with an almost pearlescent quality to them. He had horns on his head and his nostrils were huge. He was magnificent.

I stepped forward and slid my hands along his scales, which were smooth, but very thick. his tail had a few spikes on it, reminding me of a dinosaur I saw in a museum. Did he use it in fighting?

He exhaled and smoke puffed out of his nostrils, drawing my attention. It was definitely warmer up by his head and I waved my hand through the smoke, giggling like an idiot. He lowered his head and I stared into his large dragon's eye, seeing not a dragon, but Rhys.

"You're gorgeous," I admitted to him.

He shifted back and smiled. "I'm glad that you think so. I was worried that you might be scared of me in that form."

"Would you ever hurt me?" I asked him.

He smirked. "Only if you wanted me to."

I laughed and playfully pushed his arm. "Brat."

"Jolie, why did you and Martin break up? You two are very close."

"That's not a story I'd like to relive right now," I whispered and felt my chest tighten as panic started to set in at the onslaught of memories.

"Okay, we don't have to talk about it," he promised and pulled me into a hug. He smelled like he always did and it made me instantly relax.

"Hey, you going to help us set up the tents?" Nico called.

"I guess we should get back to them," Rhys said with a sigh.

"We should," I agreed.

Rhys took my hand, and we walked back to the others to help get camp set up. Once everything was ready, we went to an open area and all of them, except Nico, shifted.

I leaned against Rhys's massive side with Deryn's wolf head on my lap, and Fox lying on my chest with my arms around him. Nico sat next to me, his side touching mine from shoulder to ankle.

"I could get used to this," I whispered as I dozed happily with them.

"We could do this more, but Rhys is a bit too large in his dragon form," Nico replied.

He was right, but I hadn't wanted to say it.

Rhys huffed and smoke rose from his nostrils. I chuckled and patted his scaled side. "It just means we will have to make more trips away from the city, so I can spend time with you in this form."

My butt was starting to hurt, so I set Fox to the side and stood up, stretching my arms up over my head. Deryn stretched and then dropped his front paws down and wagged his tail in an invitation to play.

I reached out and tapped his shoulder before running away. "You're it!" I yelled back to him.

He yipped and charged after me, his long strides ate up the ground between us and he bumped his nose against me.

I turned and ran back after him, but tapped Fox who was just watching us. He squawked in shock and then started chasing after me.

Deryn ran with me, but at the last second, Fox bumped Deryn, making him it. He ran over to Nico and bumped him with his nose and then hightailed it away.

Nico stood up slowly, but then reached back and touched Rhys before running as fast as he could towards us. Rhys growled and charged us, his massive size made each step shake the ground and I stumbled, falling into the grass as he rested his nose against me.

Groaning, I leapt up and raced after Nico, who was the closest to me. He was fast and nimble though, so I couldn't get him, but focusing on him had made Deryn drop his guard and I slapped his shoulder as I ran by, hiding behind Nico.

For at least an hour, I played tag with my guards, only stopping because I was too tired to run more and dropped onto my back, my chest heaving.

"I give!" I told them and raised one arm. "I surrender. I'm too tired to do more."

"Here," Nico said and handed me a bottle of cold water.

Greedily, I gulped it down and exhaled loudly after finishing it. "So, what's for dinner?"

"I guess it is dinner time," Deryn replied after shifting back to his human form. "I'm always hungry, so I wasn't really thinking about it."

"I'll start the fire," Nico said and headed towards the rock circle that we had made for the fire pit.

Rhys shifted back and lay on the ground beside me, his arms behind his head. "That was fun. I can't remember the last time that I played tag."

"Me neither," I admitted and snuggled closer to him, putting my head on one of his arms. "Turtle," I said and pointed up at the sky.

"Turtle?" Fox asked and looked up where I was pointing. "Oh, the cloud shape!" He laid his head on my shins and pointed in the distance. "Monkey."

"That's an octopus," Deryn argued.

"It's clearly a squid," Rhys argued back.

"Rhys, come cook the meat!" Nico called from the campsite.

We all went with him, and I sat on a log that they had carried over, drinking ciders that Fox had brought for me. The four of them went about making dinner, bantering with each other and acting like they would have, if I hadn't been there. It was nice to see them happy and doing something without me being the center of attention. Could it be like this after we defeated my dad and the strangers who were trying to kill me? Could we have a life like this all of the time?

My number one worry was that they would try to make me choose. *I couldn't choose. I loved them all.*

Wait? Love. Had I just admitted to myself that I loved them?

"What is it?" Fox asked, kneeling in front of me. "Why are you scared?"

Stupid bond!

"Nothing," I whispered and knew I was blushing as I looked away from him.

"You can't lie to us," he reminded me. Gently, he picked up my hand and kissed my knuckles. "What is it, Jolie?"

I shook my head and walked away from them, headed towards a set of trees not far away so I could think without them being near me.

Love? Did I truly love them? Wasn't it too early to be in love? The bond had accelerated our feelings, so it was hypothetically possible.

I pictured my life without them and immediately felt fear, anxiety, and a few other things swirl within me that I didn't like. No, I couldn't live without them. Not any of them. There was no possible way to choose between them. And, I didn't want to live without them all either. Thinking about them being hurt sent a pang of pain through my entire body.

Dammit. I was in love with them. All four of them.

"Talk to me," Fox whispered and slid his hands up and down my arms. "What's going on in that head of yours? Your emotions are all over the place."

"I can't live without you," I whispered. "Any of you. You all mean so much to me that thinking of living without you now, hurts."

"We feel the same way about you," he told me. His arms wrapped around me and held me in a warm hug. "You are our world, Jolie. Nothing else matters, but you."

Was he saying what I thought he was? Did they love me, too?

"Dinner is ready!" Rhys called to us. "Get it while it's hot."

Dinner turned out to be hamburgers and hot dogs, which I was perfectly fine with. I made my plate and sat on the log with them all around the fire on other logs.

"What would you be doing right now, if I wasn't in your life?" I asked between bites of my burger and drinks of my third or fourth cider. I had lost count already.

They all tensed and it took a minute for one of them to reply.

"We would be playing games online together, most likely," Fox replied.

"Would you be with females?" I wasn't stupid enough to think they were virgins before me, but thinking about the with another female made my blood boil.

"Perhaps," Rhys agreed.

"Why are you asking this?" Deryn asked, his shoulders tensed.

"It just seems like I have changed your lives too much," I admitted. "Like I've stolen what your life should be like."

"You've invaded our life for sure," Nico agreed. "If we went back in time and could change things, we wouldn't change meeting you or you entering our lives. We are happy with you."

"Our lives were boring before we met you," Fox said.

"You mean it was quiet because you didn't have to keep saving or rescuing a human girl," I said and chuckled. "My life has definitely been noisier since meeting you all."

"What would you be doing right now if you hadn't met us?" Rhys asked.

I shrugged. "Playing games with my clan, most likely. Or trying to find someone to date."

If I hadn't met them, I wouldn't have gotten them tangled in the cursed web of my life.

"You've become entangled in our hearts," Deryn told me. "There is no way for you to leave, no matter how much you might try to hack at the vines entangling you."

I was envisioning myself standing within a heart with vines covering it and wrapped around me.

"You make it sound like it is a prison," I said and smirked. "Being with you guys is anything, but awful."

"We are glad to hear that," Fox said with a smile.

"So, is this what you usually do when camping?" I asked. "You play games, eat some food, and hang out?"

They nodded.

"We also make s'mores," Deryn said and grabbed a bag of marshmallows and sticks.

"I've never had one," I admitted. "I've heard about them, but since I have never been camping before..."

"They're amazing," Fox said and came to sit next to me. "I'll help you make the perfect one."

"There's a way to make them wrong?" How could you make it wrong?

"No, but the marshmallows are best when they're lightly toasted on the outside and melted on the inside. You have to put them in the fire just right."

"You need to light them on fire for a minute to get them crispy," Rhys said and sat on my other side.

"I'm surprised that you use this fire and not your own," I teased.

"He has used his fire when he was craving them and we weren't camping," Deryn told me.

"That was one time and I was hammered," Rhys argued.

"You still did it," Deryn said and pointed at him.

I laughed as the guys made the marshmallows. The first time I tried to roast mine, it melted right off my stick and fell on the ground. They laughed at my pout and told me more stories about times they had gone camping.

S'more in hand, they all watched me with bated breath as I took a bite. The cracker crumbled, but I was able to catch most of the crumbs in my hand as I chewed on the s'more. It was divine!

"It's amazing," I said with a full mouth of s'more.

They all beamed proudly, like they had made it for me personally.

"I know you'd like it," Fox said and ate his in two bites before reaching and grabbing another marshmallow to make a second one.

"What's your favorite color?" Rhys asked me.

"Teal."

"Favorite flower?" Deryn asked.

"Cherry blossoms and hibiscus."

"Favorite holiday?" Fox asked.

"Halloween!"

"Favorite drink?" Nico asked.

"That's hard," I admitted. "I love cocoa, margaritas, and iced tea with a lemon wedge."

"Favorite male?" Rhys asked.

I rolled my eyes. Nice try. "It's so hard to pick," I replied with a groan. "I have so many to choose from."

"So many?" Deryn asked.

"Who is your favorite female?" I asked them.

"You," they said at the same time.

"Do you want to sleep outside or in a tent?" Nico asked me.

"Tent," I replied instantly.

They looked at each other and then back at me.

"What?" I grumbled.

"Why did you say it like that?" Fox asked.

"I don't like bugs," I admitted to them. "I've always been creeped out by bugs."

"Are you scared of certain bugs or animals?" Rhys asked.

"Yes," I mumbled, not wanting to reply.

"And those are?" Deryn prompted.

"Why does it matter?" I asked grumpily. Every girl I knew was scared of bugs.

"If we know what you're afraid of, we can make sure to keep it away from you," Fox explained.

"I'm afraid of losing you four," I mumbled, staring at the last half of my s'more in my hands.

"Why would you lose us?" Rhys asked and squatted down in front of me. He set his hands on top of mine, where I was twisting my s'more around.

"If you wise up and realize I'm not a Queen. Or you try to make me choose. Or you find someone better suited to being a match for a prince. Or if you get hurt, or worse, killed, trying to protect me. Or... damn this alcohol. I wasn't supposed to say any of this out loud."

Quickly, I stood up and stumbled away from the fire and them. Away from the fire and their eyes, I felt cold and rubbed my arms while looking up at the stars overhead. We were such small creatures in the universe. None of us truly mattered in the grand scheme of life.

"You aren't going to lose us," Rhys whispered from behind me.

I turned around and all four of them stood side by side just behind me.

"You can't say that for sure. You don't know what will happen in the future," I argued.

"We know that we all love you," said Fox.

"We all know that you are our Queen," said Deryn.

"We all know that we will do whatever we must to keep you safe," Nico said.

"And we all know that we will do whatever we have to, to keep you in our lives," Rhys said.

"You love me?" I asked softly, feeling like I was flying and falling at the same time.

"We do," Deryn replied and the other three nodded in agreement.

"And you won't make me choose between you?" I asked softly.

"Never," Nico promised.

"I love you, too," I said as I looked at each of them.

They moved forward and surrounded me in a group hug.

"You're stuck with us forever, now," Deryn whispered against my neck.

"Now that you've admitted you love us, we won't let you go," Rhys murmured from my right side.

"Together forever," Fox whispered as he stood in front of me with a wide smile.

I smiled back at him and said, "Sounds like a great plan."

CHAPTER 10

"What do you mean they've summoned me?" I asked Rhys and looked at the other three who were wearing identically blank expressions. They only used blank expressions when they were hiding their true emotions from me.

"The Elders want to meet and talk with you," Fox explained.

"We'll be with you the entire time," Nico assured me.

"Will they hurt me?"

"No," Deryn said adamantly and picked up one of my hands, squeezing it in reassurance. "We won't let them hurt you."

It had been over a week since they had visited the Elders without me. In that time, I'd gotten used to staying in Rhys's apartment, where I was safe and together with all my guys. Even though the room was warm, I felt a chill.

"But, they're the Elders and they can tell you what to do, right? They could order you to kill me?" I'd seen it in a few anime shows and I did not want to end up like those poor women.

"They could order us, but we have free will and none of us would ever harm you," Deryn promised.

"Then you'll get killed for not obeying them," I said and threw my hands up in the air.

Rhys chuckled and took my face in his hands, forcing me to meet his eyes. "They won't do anything like that. They just want to talk to you and meet you. They said they may be able to help you learn to use the bond, which I know is something you want help with."

I looked at them, standing together in front of me. They always dressed like they were going to go out. I had gotten a little dressed up earlier on a whim, even though we hadn't left the apartment since our camping trip. Now, I was glad I had.

"Okay," I agreed. "As long as you'll be by my side the entire time."

They nodded in agreement and I reluctantly followed them out to the car. Martin smiled at me as we approached, but when he saw my face, his smile wilted. "What's going on?" he asked me after getting into the driver's seat.

"She's nervous about going to meet the Elders," Deryn informed him.

"They'll love you. Everyone who meets you loves you. The Alpha can't stop talking about you," Martin said with a smile.

"Will the Kings be there?" I asked and turned to face my Guards.

They all nodded.

"Great. Not only do I have to meet the Elders, but the other fathers too," I grumbled, folded my arms, and slumped in my seat.

"They met you once already, remember?" Fox reminded me.

"Oh yes, when I was hammered and interrupted your meeting," I said, my scowl deepening.

We drove in silence, my mind supplying all kinds of situations which ended with me dead. Martin rested his hand on my knee, where the guys couldn't see it. Even his touch wasn't enough to reassure me.

I envisioned us driving to a dark and gloomy castle, but it was the furthest from the truth. Martin stopped the SUV in front of a gorgeous country estate with perfectly trimmed hedges and a beautiful rose garden.

Martin squeezed my knee for reassurance and I climbed out. No point in delaying the inevitable. My Guards took their places. Rhys in front of me, Deryn on my left, Fox on my right, and Nico behind me. I touched each of their hands briefly and then we walked inside.

Inside, paintings by famous artists lined the walls, each worth hundreds of thousands of dollars.

The guys seemed to know where they were going, making a few turns, going down two flights of stairs, and then stopped before two metal doors. So far, we hadn't seen a single person. Where were they?

"We're with you," Rhys reminded me without turning around.

"We love you," Deryn whispered.

"I love you all, too," I replied, surprised that my voice did not wobble with emotion.

Rhys pushed open the door, and we walked inside. The room was humongous, large enough to hold a concert in, easily. At the moment, there were seven people at the end, all males. I recognized the four Kings from the park, but the other three were definitely no one I had met before. They were old, bent with age, but their eyes held an intelligence and authority that made it clear they were the Elders.

We stopped before them and all bowed. The guys had worked with me on this move a few days ago, for the purpose of meeting the Alphas, but we hadn't gotten a chance to do so before today.

When we straightened, I glanced at the Alphas and Dan winked at me. That helped me loosen a bit and I faced the Elders with no tremors.

The Elders were all different races. The one in the middle had the telltale pointed ears of an elf. The one on the right was the tallest, with a full head of grey hair, and a matching beard. His eyes were golden, a werewolf. The Elder on the left was the shortest, but most muscular, with forearms of a much younger male. He smiled at me and his eyes shifted to a bright green with a slit down the center. A dragon.

"Great Elders," Rhys began, "we present to you our Queen, Jolie." He stepped to the side, taking a place beside Deryn and exposing me to them.

"You are human?" the Elf Elder asked.

"Yes, sir," I replied. "I do have a thirty second Gorgon in me, but no powers or anything."

"Your father is the vampire king, correct?" the Dragon Elder asked. I nodded.

"When was he changed?" The Wolf Elder asked.

"A few months after my birth," I answered and then quickly added, "Sir."

All three Elders smiled and the Wolf Elder said, "We appreciate your respect, but you need only answer, not add 'sir' at the end."

"Yes, sir," I agreed and then cleared my throat. "Okay."

"The Princes indicated that you discovered the Vampire King had stolen the artifact to start the war," Wolf Elder said. "Yet, it came to be in your possession without his knowledge. How?"

"My grandmother gave it to me. I'm..." I paused, unsure how to describe myself. "...I say I'm cursed, but I'm not literally cursed, I don't think. So, unlucky might be better. I've been attacked on multiple occasions by Others. One attack was by vampires who captured me and...hurt me. I escaped and when I told my grandmother what happened, she provided me with the artifact. She said it would keep the vampires from finding me."

"Did it?" Elf Elder asked.

"Yes. The vampires hadn't been able to locate me, until I removed it and relinquished it to the Kings."

"Not without a bit of a fight," the Mage King commented.

"And your Guards protected you and killed the vampires, correct?" Dragon Elder asked, ignoring the comment.

"Correct," I agreed.

"And that is when you believe you created the bond?" Wolf Elder asked and looked at my guards.

"Yes, Elder," Deryn replied.

"Yet, it wasn't a completely conscious decision, correct?" Dragon Elder asked.

"Yes, Elder," Rhys replied.

"Do you feel the bond, Jolie?" Elf Elder asked.

I shook my head. "No. I've tried, but can't sense it."

"Jolie, please come forward," Elf Elder ordered me.

Determined not to upset them, I didn't glance back at my guards. Despite really *really* wanting to. I stepped forward and my guards moved with me.

"Only Jolie," Elf Elder ordered them.

Out of the corner of my eye, I saw Deryn's hand curl into a fist.

They didn't seem like they would appreciate being made to wait, so I walked to them and wondered if I should bow again or drop to one knee.

The three Elders' eyes shifted and began to glow. They covered me in glowing magic of three different colors. Red for the dragon, white for the elf, and green for the wolf. The colors highlighted a rope that went from my chest to the four men behind me. There was no doubt about the bond now.

"We can remove the bond without hurting you," Dragon Elder offered me. "It won't harm your guards either, but you will be removed and unable to develop a bond with any of them in the future, should you desire to, aside from a mate bond."

"I—"

Did I want to remove the bond now?

"Jolie," the four said at the same time.

"You could be free," I whispered to them. "Free to find a Princess worthy of you. Free of my curse."

"You are cursed," Elf Elder agreed and waved at my chest. "A witch's curse."

"We don't want anyone else. We told you this on our trip," Fox reminded me.

"You are more than worthy," Deryn told me. "Right, Father?"

All eyes turned towards Dan who had been scowling. He looked at me and said, "You are worthy."

The other Kings' eyes widened and they turned away from Dan to focus on me. No doubt, trying to understand what he saw in me.

"What's your decision?" Dragon Elder asked.

I chewed on my bottom lip and looked at my four guards. What to do? Free them, or keep them? Was it selfish to keep them?

Definitely.

They had said that they wanted to keep the bond, though. If I freed them from me, they could return to their normal lives. They could be free of the chaos that I brought with me. And I would be miserable. Even though I couldn't feel the bond, just knowing it was there made me happier and safer than I had in years. Plus, I truly loved them. I didn't want to be without them.

"I'll keep my bond," I replied.

All four exhaled and their bodies relaxed, tension leaving them in a rush.

"Would you like us to teach you how to use the bond?" Wolf Elder asked.

"Please," I begged.

Then, I decided to ask for something else, since they were offering to help me.

"Can you remove the curse?"

The three Elders looked at each other, some type of silent communication going on.

"We can," Elf Elder finally said.

"But it will hurt you, a lot," Dragon Elder explained.

"What is the curse?" Dan asked.

"Curse of Antalia," Elf Elder replied.

Dan said something under his breath and looked away. When I looked at the guys, they were all scowling and whispering to each other.

"Breaking that curse will have repercussions," The Dragon King said. "She may not be able to handle them."

Dragon Elder shrugged. "True."

"Don't do it," Rhys ordered me.

"What? Why not?" I demanded, spinning to face him.

"You might die from the backlash. It's not worth it," Deryn explained.

"Listen to them, girl," Dragon King said.

"Let us show you how to use your bond," Wolf Elder said. "Our offer will remain open and you can return, should you want to remove the curse."

"Thank you," I said, feeling irritated to be so close to being able to remove it and yet being told not to.

The Elders took an hour to show me how to find the bond. Finally, I could sense the bond and with it, feel the guys and their presences. Even a slight sense of their feelings.

"The more you practice, the easier it will become and the stronger your sense of them will be," Elf Elder told me.

I bowed. "Thank you."

"What will your father do, now that his secret has been exposed?" Dragon Elder asked me.

"He is power hungry. I have no doubt that he will still grow his army and attack at some point."

"Vampires can't defeat dragons," Dragon King replied confidently.

"He never said his army was vampires," I pointed out.

That had every one of them focused on me again.

"Do you have information you haven't shared with us yet?" Wolf Elder asked.

"This isn't a certainty, I just know how he works. He has worked with other races before. I could see him doing so again. To defeat mages and dragons, he would need more than vampires, and he knows that."

"You five are dismissed," Dragon Elder ordered us. "You may return if you change your mind about the curse, or your bond," he told me.

I bowed and the guys did the same. "Thank you, Great Elders," I said.

Dan grabbed my arm gently before I turned to leave. "Come see me tomorrow," he ordered me.

"As you wish, Alpha," I replied and dipped my head in submission.

He bent close to me and whispered, "Stay close to your Guards. I want you to stay safe."

I nodded once and he released me to return to the guys who immediately herded me out of the building and into the SUV.

Martin drove us out and waited until we were off the grounds to ask, "How'd it go?"

"Good," I replied softly, my brain spinning with everything that had happened. Most of all, Dan's warning words. Did he know something? Or was he just worried?

And I knew I was cursed!

"What's the Curse of Antalia?" I asked out loud, hoping one of them would respond.

Martin looked at me and then had to swerve back into his lane on the road before running into another car.

"How'd you hear about that curse?" he asked, his words tumbling out almost on top of each other.

"It's what I'm cursed with," I said and turned to smirk at him. "I told you I was cursed."

He glanced in the rearview mirror. "Please tell me she heard wrong or is confused."

Deryn shook his head. "The Elders informed us that she has the curse."

"Fuck," Martin replied.

"Anyone going to fill me in?" I asked, but received no response. Pulling out my phone, I searched the internet for the curse and got a ton of results.

Curse of Antalia
Performed by a witch. High level curse.
Curses the victim with a propensity to self-sacrifice, increases likelihood of Others finding them, increases the odds of attacks by Others, decreases moral...

Blah, Blah, Blah. Ah! Here it was.

Removal can be done, but the magical backlash has been known to cause paralysis, coma induction, and even death.

Well, fuck.

My door opened and I jumped, barely holding in a scream. I hadn't noticed the car had stopped.

Rhys unbuckled me and tugged me out of the SUV by my hand.

"Bye," I said to Martin, but he wasn't even looking at me.

We took an awkward elevator ride up to Deryn's, reminding me of the day that I had found out they knew each other and lived with me.

Deryn ordered pizza and they all stood stiffly around the living room. I could barely sense their feelings, but anger and fear prevailed.

"That went better than I thought it would," I said cheerfully with a wide smile.

"You were going to break the bond," Fox whispered. He felt sadness and fear. "Why?"

"I didn't break it," I reminded them.

"It took you quite a while to decide not to," Nico pointed out.

"You're all mad at me," I realized.

"Wouldn't you be?" Deryn snapped.

I shook my head. "No. I would know that you were thinking of me and what would be best for me. That you were trying not to be selfish."

"Selfish?" Rhys asked.

"It's selfish of me to keep the bond. I know that. Especially, now that I know what the curse is."

"You know?" Fox asked. "How?"

I held up my phone. "Internet."

"You were going to break the bond, even though we told you that we love you," Nico argued.

"Yes, I contemplated it."

"Don't you love us?" Fox asked.

"Of course I do!" I yelled. "That's why I was trying to save you. To free you. But, ultimately, I couldn't do it. I couldn't give you up. I can't imagine my life without you in it."

They relaxed, but now I was frustrated, so I stormed off to the spare room, and shut and locked the door. Head in my hands, I sat on the bed.

How could they not understand what I meant? It had nothing to do with my love for them.

"Trouble in paradise?" Burton, my father's right-hand man asked.

I opened my mouth to scream, but he hit me on the back of the head, knocking me out.

CHAPTER 11

"Killing her would weaken them," Burton said angrily.

"We need her as bait and as a bargaining chip. If she is dead, they won't bargain with us," Dad told him.

"They're going to kill you," I mumbled from the chair they had tied me to. At least he had not thrown me in the closet.

"They won't risk your life," Dad replied smugly.

"They're here," Justina said as she entered the room.

"Justina! Help me!" I yelled at her.

"Don't worry, Jolie. You'll be let go once the Princes do as our King asks," she told me with a soft smile.

"Our king? What are you talking about? I don't have a king."

She looked at my dad and then at me. "You may think you don't, but he is our king. It would be smart of you to accept that and join us."

She was working for my father? Why? How? She had never said anything about having a king when we worked together. How had he gotten to her? Dhampirs usually hated vampires.

Dad brushed his hand down her cheek and her eyelids fluttered.

"Oh, fucking gross," I gagged.

"Let's go greet our guests," Dad said with a smile.

Burton untied me from the chair and retied my arms before I could get away. He pulled the ropes extra tight and pushed me forward.

I stumbled, almost falling on my face, but caught myself at the last second and followed Dad and Justina out of the room we had been in, down the hallway, and out onto the porch.

My four guards stood in a line on the front lawn, fists clenched and fury etched into their faces. They saw me and took a step forward, but Burton put a knife to my throat.

"No closer," Burton ordered them.

"Are you hurt?" Rhys asked me.

"No," I replied.

"I wasn't sure you would come," Dad told them, spreading his arms in a welcoming gesture. Then he shook his head and gave them a look of pity. "I'm sure you're likely tired of rescuing Jolie by now."

"What do you want?" Deryn demanded, his eyes boring into Justina who was standing slightly behind Dad, letting him shield her.

"You four are the most powerful, next to your fathers. I need your power," Dad told them. "If you want my daughter back in one piece, you will go to the dedication ceremony tonight and kill the President."

"No!" I yelled. If they did that, their clans would be forced to kill them.

Burton dug the knife into my neck, cutting me enough to make a small line of blood trickle down my neck.

"Quiet," he ordered me.

"We would all be dead before we made it back to get her," Nico told Dad.

"I'm sure you will figure something out. Though, time is running out. You only have two hours before the ceremony starts."

"Are we coming back here afterwards to retrieve her?" Rhys asked.

No! They couldn't seriously be thinking about doing it. It was suicide!

"No, call Jolie's phone after you've done it, and I will give you the location," Dad said, a wide, evil grin on his face.

"How do we know that you won't kill her while we are gone? Or run off?" Deryn asked, baring his teeth.

"You don't, but you can track her with your bond," Dad said with a smirk.

How did he know about that?

"Not if she's dead," Nico pointed out.

"You'll have to take that risk. Or, Burton kills her right now," Dad said.

Burton dug the blade in deeper, making the blood flow faster.

"Fine!" Rhys snarled. "We'll do it. Stop hurting her."

"I knew you boys would see things my way," Dad said smugly. "Off you go."

My four guards turned to face me and as one, they bowed to me, spun around, and left.

I was crying and didn't care if my dad saw or not. Those idiots were marching off to die. They hadn't even taken a moment to debate it or not. They just agreed and left. They were going to lose their statuses and lose their clans, because of me. It was stupid and asinine.

"Let's move," Dad ordered us. "We have a long drive ahead of us."

Burton withdrew his blade from my neck, allowing me to take a deep, stuttering breath. Dad licked his finger and then brushed it along my cut, healing it. If only other pains could be fixed so easily.

The four of us climbed into a truck, and Burton drove towards the city. We parked at an old, abandoned factory, much to my surprise. Dad hated places like this. He avoided them if possible and would rather kill everyone in a hotel to use that as a base of operation. So, why were we here? Was it because it was so unlike him?

Inside the factory was nothing except two couches and a television set.

Burton shoved me down on the couch. "Get comfy. The show will start soon."

They couldn't do it. They had to be smarter than that.

Dad turned on the television and settled on the couch beside me. "Think they'll do it?"

"I hope not," I muttered.

"You better hope they do. For your sake."

"How'd you know about the bond?" I asked him angrily. Only the Alphas and Elders knew.

"I have my ways," he said cryptically.

I rolled my eyes in response and looked at the TV where a crowd was gathering in front of a stage which had a podium on it. There had to be thousands of people there. There really was no hope for them.

Realization hit me...Justina had known about the bond. She'd sold me out!

The President took the stage and started his opening speech.

No sign of the guys. Maybe they were just going to abandon me. That hurt to think about, but it would be better than them dying. I would much rather they left me to my father than to put themselves in such a dangerous situation. I wasn't worth it. I wasn't worth this. The price was too high. I should have let the Elders remove the bond, so that they wouldn't feel compelled to protect me. To ruin everything.

No, it was my dad who was ruining everything. Once again, he was ruining my life.

The crowd began to scream and soon we saw why. The four Princes of Jinla walked down the center of the crowd, bodies glowing with power. Deryn was in warrior form, half wolf and half man. Rhys was also in warrior form, though I'd had no idea dragons could do it as well. Nico had a staff with a glowing crystal on the top in one hand and I realized, he wasn't walking, but floating. Fox had his hair pulled back and in his hands, he carried two swords. They looked scary as shit and hot as hell.

Fuck.

The President held his ground, and stood facing them boldly. His guards had run off. What cowards.

"We're sorry," Rhys said. "We must protect what is ours."

Nico raised his staff, freezing the President in place.

"They're really doing it!" Burton exclaimed in shock, standing up from the couch.

Rhys shifted into his full dragon form and in one swoop, swallowed the President.

"Fuck!" I screamed. How could they do this? What was wrong with them?

"I knew you'd come in handy, eventually," Dad told me, smiling victoriously.

The camera turned off and a screen announcing technical difficulties appeared. Dad turned off the television.

It was over. They were going to be killed. The life I had finally started to love, was just swallowed up with the President. If there was any hope of the guys getting away, I prayed they would survive. Even if I never saw them again, I wanted them to survive.

My phone rang and Dad answered it. "Hello?"

"Let me talk to her," I heard Deryn say.

Dad put the phone to my ear.

"What have you done?" I asked, tears making my throat constrict and making the words difficult to say.

"I love you," he whispered.

Fuck. No!

"This is not goodbye," I growled.

"Is the TV off?" he whispered so softly that I barely heard him.

"Yes."

What did that have to do with anything?

"Good, put your dad on."

"They want to talk to you," I told him.

Dad took the phone back. "Yes, you can come get her." He gave them an address and then hung up, putting the phone back in my jacket pocket.

Burton tied me to one of the beams in the center of the building.

"What are you doing?" I asked him, trying to get free of his hold.

"We can't be here when they show up, or they'll kill us," he explained. He taped C4 above my head on the beam and hit a button, starting a countdown.

"Dad!" I screamed.

"You said she wouldn't be hurt!" Justina reminded him.

"If they get here in time, she won't be hurt. Or, they'll all die together," Dad said and waved as he walked away. "Bye, Jolie."

"Don't do this!" I screamed at him.

There was no way the guys would make it in time. They were probably in a battle right now, trying not to be killed by their fathers. They had done what he had asked and it didn't matter. I was going to die anyways.

Closing my eyes, I reached down the bond to each of them, only able to brush them with my essence, but I knew that they had all felt it. At least I was human, so I wouldn't hurt them like losing a true Queen would when I died.

I let myself sob, a truly ugly cry, since no one would see me. I wailed my despair, knowing they would die for no reason. I was the cause of their deaths.

"I'm sorry," I cried. "I'm so sorry."

No one answered.

I glanced up, checking the timer. One minute and forty seconds. Pulling on my restraints, I tried to break free, but they were too tight and I was too weak.

"Fuck me!" I screamed and closed my eyes.

"Now doesn't seem like the appropriate time for that," Rhys said.

I opened my eyes and gasped. All four were standing in front of me.

"I'm hallucinating, right? You're all most likely dead now. I will be in less than a minute too. This has to be a hallucination. My mind, trying to give me one last goodbye?"

I was rambling, but I couldn't help myself or stop the words from tumbling out.

Nico removed the tape from the C4, took the C4, and ran outside with it. Rhys unbound my hands and the bomb exploded.

"Nico!" I screamed.

"What?" he asked, coming back into the warehouse.

I dropped to my knees on the dirty floor and asked, "Is this real?"

They huddled around me and there was no mistaking their body heat and touch.

"You ate him," I whispered.

They all laughed and Rhys said, "I didn't. We just made it look like I did."

"You didn't kill him?"

"Nope."

I turned to him and punched his arm as hard as I could. "You scared the shit out of me! I thought you were all going to die!"

The tears returned and Rhys pulled me into a tight hug. "We are all alive and well, my Queen."

I kissed him and then hugged and kissed each of the other three as well.

Dan barged into the warehouse with the other three Alphas. We all stood up off the floor and I waited to find out why they were here.

Dan shoved Rhys aside, so he could get to me. Deryn moved forward, but before they could react, he grabbed me in a huge hug. "You're alive," he breathed.

I hugged him back as much as I could with his size, my arms barely making it around him.

"I am," I agreed.

He set me on my feet and set his hand on my cheek. "When they told us what was going on, I feared the worst."

"Thirty seconds later and I wouldn't be here," I admitted to him.

"You can come live with my pack, in my house, if you wish to," he offered.

"What?" Mage King asked.

"She's an outsider," Dragon King reminded him.

"She's human," Elf King added.

"She's my son's Queen, which makes her basically, my daughter-in-law."

"I appreciate the offer," I whispered. "I'm honored to receive such an offer. However, I can't leave my guards."

"Are we sure she isn't a witch?" Dragon King asked.

"It would explain everyone's infatuation with her," Elf King said.

"I'm not a witch," I snapped at them and then remembered who I was talking to. "Sirs."

They all laughed at me.

"Why are you all here?" I asked the Kings.

"The Princes weren't sure who would get here faster, since we didn't know where you were going to be. So, we all came," Dan explained.

I bowed. "Thank you." After standing up straight again, I asked, "Is anyone going to tell me what the fuck went on? I saw you swallow the President, Rhys."

"We called in some favors," Dan said. "You save the city, and country, enough times and they'll do almost anything you ask."

"Everyone, except those watching through their televisions, were warned ahead of time what was going to happen," Fox said.

"You guys shouldn't have done it," I chastised my guards. "You could have died."

"Our lives are yours," Deryn whispered. "Nothing else matters."

"We should go," Dan said. "You sure you won't come live with me?"

"I'm sure."

Dan's phone rang and he answered it quickly. "Yes?"

"We're under attack!" Martin yelled so loudly that even I heard him.

"Martin!" I gasped.

"We're on our way," Dan said immediately and took off.

The other three Kings' phones rang, all with similar news.

"This must have been his plan," I realized. "He got the Kings and Princes away to attack the clans at their bases."

"Let's go!" Rhys growled.

"We can't go to four places at once!" I reminded him. "I'll go with Deryn and you three go with your fathers."

"I don't—" Nico started, but I took his hand.

"Protect your people. Deryn will protect me," I said.

He kissed me deeply and whispered, "Stay safe."

Fox kissed my cheek before darting by with his father.

Rhys's jaw was clenched, as were his fists. "I don't like this."

"I love you," I whispered to him. "And I won't be the reason your people die. They need you, much more than I do right now."

"She's right," Dragon King said. "Obey your Queen, Son."

Rhys pulled me to him and kissed me passionately. "I will come for you," he whispered as he pulled away.

"I can't wait," I replied with a smirk.

He let out a bark of laughter, kissed my forehead, and rushed out.

"Let's go," Deryn said and picked me up in his arms. "Put your face against my chest, so the bugs don't get in your mouth."

I obeyed, having had that exact thing happen once when Martin ran with me. He took off at a sprint and I gripped him tighter. He made a few turns and I realized that we were very close to the werewolf pack.

Deryn flew, making it within a few minutes. Utter chaos greeted us. Werewolves were fighting ogres, trolls, vampires, and goblins.

"You were right about it not being just vampires," Deryn said.

"I wish I wasn't right," I muttered.

"I'm going to take you to the house," Deryn informed me. "Go inside and hide. There is always one person to guard the house, so you should be safe."

I nodded and didn't put up a fight about it. He needed to be able to focus so that he could save his people. He ran me to the door, kissed me deeply, and then shifted and charged at the nearest enemy.

"No!" Madison screamed.

Turning, I caught sight of Madison and Tamara cowering against the side of the building nearest us with an ogre moving towards them.

"Maddy!" I screamed. "Tamara!" Without thinking, I raced towards them. I couldn't defeat an ogre, but I might be able to distract it long enough to get them away from it. I slid around the ogre's side and stood between him and the girls.

"Auntie Jolie!" they shrieked at the same time and clutched at my legs.

The ogre growled at me and then roared in my face.

I couldn't let anything happen to the girls. They were my only nieces.

My stomach and chest were hot, way hotter than usual, but I couldn't focus on that. I had to protect the girls.

The ogre roared at me again, spittle flying from his mouth.

I opened my mouth to roar back, but instead of sound coming out, fire did. The ogre screamed in pain and ran off.

What the fuck?

I had just breathed fire. How? Now wasn't the time to think about that. I needed to get them to safety.

"Come on," I ordered the girls. "We need to get inside the house."

They nodded their understanding and the three of us ran to the house. The door was locked, so I banged twice on it. "It's Jolie and the twins, Madison and Tamara!" I screamed as loud as I could.

The door opened and Sharla screamed as the girls tackled her. She hugged them and they all rubbed their faces on each other. I shut and locked the door and she pulled me down to hug me.

"I couldn't find them," she told me through her tears. "I was going to go out and search for them. Thank you. Thank you."

I kissed her cheek. "No need to thank me."

"Auntie Jolie breathed fire," Madison told her excitedly.

"Shush," I ordered them. "That's not something we need to tell everyone. We need to keep it a secret until I can figure out how the hell it happened and why. Okay? It's very important that we not discuss it."

They mimed locking their lips closed and I smiled at them.

"Who is guarding the house?" I asked Sharla.

"Me," she replied.

"I can't believe he is doing this," I told her sadly.

"Who?"

"My father. It's his army attacking. They're not only attacking the wolves, but the mages, dragons, and elves as well."

She gasped and asked, "Are they going to be okay?"

"I hope so. The Princes and Kings went back to help fight. Deryn is outside fighting right now," I explained.

She gripped my hand, and we cuddled closer together on the floor of the entryway.

Please be okay. Please let my guards be okay.

There had to be a way to defeat my dad. I knew he wouldn't be here, he preferred to send his minions to do his bidding instead of coming himself. That way, if they lost, he was still safe. What was he hoping to gain by this attack? Was he really trying to defeat the four main races with his army? There hadn't seem to be *that* many attackers here. There were a lot, but not so many that I would think the werewolves would be overrun.

Something else was his goal. But, for the life of me, I couldn't figure out what it was.

I sat on the floor, huddled with the girls and Sharla, for what felt like hours. We all jumped when someone knocked on the door.

"It's me, Deryn," he said through it.

Sharla got up and checked through the peephole before opening it and letting Deryn in.

He rushed over to me and picked me up to hug me when he saw me. "You're okay?"

"Yes. You?" I asked as I hugged him back.

"I'm fine."

"The other guards?" I asked nervously.

"No one has been hurt significantly," he told me.

"Who got hurt?" I asked.

"We'll find out when we get home," he said. "Let's head home."

The door opened and Martin came in. His family rushed to him, hugging, kissing, and rubbing their scents on each other.

"Do you need me to drive you?" Martin asked from within the arms of his girls.

Deryn shook his head. "Console your girls. I'll drive us and someone can come pick the car up later."

Deryn led me outside, to a building I hadn't gone into before. Dan was there, talking with a few other people. He turned around when we approached and hugged me. "Did you get hurt?"

I shook my head.

"Good. Take the car over there," he said and indicated a black car. I had zero idea what kind of car it was.

"Send someone to get it later," Deryn told his dad.

Dan nodded and waved to us, resuming his conversation.

There were bodies all over. Thankfully, I didn't see any werewolf bodies among them. Blood and body pieces were everywhere, on the walls, the grass, the concrete, hanging from trees. It was disgusting and terrifying.

The entire drive, I felt like I was going to explode with nerves. Someone had been injured. One of my Guards was injured. Deryn wouldn't tell me who or how bad it was, which was making it even worse. Who was it?

Knowing that they were all alive was a huge relief, but I was still worried about the injury. Others healed so quickly, that injuries were not discussed unless it was serious. Like, an arm being cut off, which they would not be able to grow back.

When Deryn parked, I jumped out of the car and raced to the elevator. It seemed to take twice as long for it to come than it usually did.

I burst into Deryn's apartment and looked over the three inside.

Rhys was the only one with a bandage. I rushed to him and he immediately pulled me into his lap.

"I'm fine," he assured me.

"A shifter with a bandage is not fine," I accused him.

His right arm was bandaged, at least half of it covered.

"It's just a scratch," he said.

"Down to the bone," Nico muttered.

Rhys growled. "Not helping."

I rested my fingertips over the bandage, being sure not to let the pressure hurt him. "You're okay?" I asked softly.

He kissed my cheek and nodded. "I'm okay."

"The battle isn't over," I told them. "This was too easy a win and there weren't that many beings."

"You think this was a test?" Nico asked.

I nodded. I had been thinking about it on the way here.

"Also, I need to tell you something," I mumbled without looking at them.

"What?" Rhys asked and slowly ran the fingers of his good arm up and down my arm.

Getting out of his lap, I stood behind the couch and said, "I, uh, breathed fire."

Silence was not the reaction I had expected.

"Come again?" Rhys asked quietly.

"When we got to the pack, I heard the twins scream. An ogre was attacking them. I couldn't let them get hurt, so I ran over and stood in front of them. The ogre screamed at me and my stomach and chest felt really hot. Then, when I tried to scream back at the ogre, fire came out instead."

"You put yourself in front of an ogre?!" Deryn shouted.

"My nieces were in trouble," I growled at him. "Should I have left them to die?"

"No, you should have yelled for me," he growled back.

"You were fighting already."

"Do you think you can do it again?" Nico asked, stopping our argument.

"I don't know. It wasn't a conscious decision. I wasn't trying to do it. It just...happened," I explained.

Rhys walked to me and said, "Picture a volcano. Then, imagine the fire of the volcano erupting, but out of your mouth."

"You really want me to try?" I asked. "What if I light something on fire?"

"I've got it covered," Nico assured me.

This seemed like a really bad idea.

"Okay," I conceded.

Closing my eyes, I pictured a volcano like Rhys had instructed. I imagined the fire coming from my belly and erupting from my mouth. My stomach grew hot, just like it had earlier, and when I opened my mouth, fire came out.

Nico used a spell to contain the fire, but all of them were staring at me instead of the fire.

"Her eyes," Deryn whispered.

Rushing to the bathroom, I looked in the mirror and the blood drained from my face. I gripped the sink to keep from falling.

Dragon's eyes. I had dragon's eyes.

"I've never heard of something like this," Rhys told everyone.

"We should contact the Elders," Fox said.

"What if it is something bad? They could order her to be contained or they could kill her," Deryn said.

That sounded like a terrible option.

Nico pried my hands open and turned me to face him. "Breathe," he ordered me.

A big breath whooshed out of me and I fell into his arms. What was happening?

Nico held me tightly. "It's going to be okay."

"It's the stupid curse," I whispered and pulled away from him. "You're all in danger by being with me."

"Jolie—"

Someone knocked on the door and everyone went silent. Deryn opened it to reveal the apartment manager.

"There you all are!" she exclaimed. "I've been going to each of your apartments trying to find you. Great news, Jolie. Your apartment is fixed."

"Great," I said with a wide smile, glad that my eyes had apparently returned to normal since she wasn't freaking out. "Thanks for getting it taken care of for me."

She waved and left, but before Deryn shut the door, I walked out of it.

"Where are you going?" Deryn demanded.

"My apartment," I replied without turning back to look at him. I pushed the button for the elevator and waited.

Nico stopped next to me.

"What are you doing?" I asked him.

"Coming with you."

"I don't need a guard in my apartment."

"You were stolen from Deryn's apartment," he reminded me.

"Can't I have some privacy? Some alone time?" I asked angrily. My hands were clenched and felt tingly.

Nico tried to pull me into a hug, but I pushed him back. Or, that had been the plan. Instead, he went flying down the hallway and slammed into Rhys who had just stepped out of Deryn's apartment.

I looked down and gasped at my glowing hands.

"I'm sorry. I didn't—"

Booth stood up and shook their heads.

"What was that?" Rhys asked.

"Mage powers," Nico said. "Somehow, she's using our powers."

The elevator opened and I climbed in, mashing the close button as Nico and Rhys raced towards it.

"Wait!" Rhys yelled.

"Jolie!" Nico called.

Instead of going to my apartment, I went to the ground floor and ran outside. Everything was going to shit. Why was I using their powers? I could have killed Nico.

My phone rang and I was surprised to find Martin calling instead of the guys.

"Hello?"

"Where are you?"

"Why?"

"Because Deryn called me, upset, because you ran off. What's going on?"

He was genuinely worried about me. I couldn't let him come near me.

"I can't involve you."

"Just tell me where you are."

"No. the whole point of me leaving is to stay away from them. You'll just tell them where I am, so they can find me."

"They are freaking out," he said. "Deryn said, 'please' to me. Think about that."

He hung up, which shocked me almost as much as Deryn saying please to Martin.

My stomach was growling and I was a good distance from the apartment building now, so I went into the first restaurant that I saw. It was a chain diner that offered a variety of food. Usually, the food wasn't very good, but most of the people who ate there were either old or drunk.

I was neither of those, but I *was* very hungry and it was really dark now. I hadn't realized how much time had past since we had seen the Elders. It was definitely past dinner time.

There were only a handful of people seated, half teenagers eating fries and drinking soda, and the other half were clearly drunk.

The waitress looked tired, but she still feigned a smile as she took my order and set a cup of hot chocolate in front of me.

It was childish of me to run away. Maybe it was the curse. The website had said the curse increased my self-sacrificial tendencies. If I could just stop worrying and trying to leave them, our relationship would be better off. I needed to text them.

Me: I'm safe.

Nico: We know.

Me: How?

Deryn: Look behind you.

I turned around and the four waved at me from a booth they were sitting at. Instead of getting mad, I laughed. I had forgotten that they could track me. Dad had mentioned that.

Grabbing my cocoa, I walked to their table. Rhys stood up and let me slide in to sit between him and Nico.

"Did you know that dragons love hot chocolate?" Rhys asked me.

"All of them?" I asked, skeptically.

He nodded. "Yep. We have cupboards full of it and every meeting, all of our scariest and most powerful members, drink cocoa while making important decisions."

"Will I get to see your clan or your home?" I asked him.

"Once our relationship is official, then you will."

"Why isn't it official now?" I asked, my eyebrows furrowed. How did you make it official?

"We don't want to put you in anymore danger than we already are. Once we find the people responsible for hunting you, then we will make it official," Rhys explained.

"How did my dad turn Justina?" I asked with a frown and shook my head.

"We were trying to figure that out as well," Fox said, his frown mirrored mine.

"Here's your sandwich," the waitress told me as she set it on the table in front of me. "Your orders will be up soon," she told the guys.

"Thank you," Deryn replied with a charming smile that would make most girls, me included, melt in their shoes.

She left without even caring. She was the first female I had seen who didn't care about them.

Rhys reached for one of my fries, and I smacked his hand.

"Mine," I told him.

I poured ketchup onto my plate and took a bite of my sandwich.

"Feisty," Rhys teased me.

Ignoring them, I ate my food, cleaning my plate completely.

"I didn't know you could eat that much," Fox whispered. "I'm impressed."

The waitress had to make three trips to bring out all of the food the guys had ordered. I sat back and watched them. Four princes, all different races, that got along like brothers. They were all hot, sweet, and incredibly powerful.

"When I saw you on the TV, walking down the crowd, powers on display, do you know what I was thinking?" I asked them.

They paused eating and turned to me.

"What?" Deryn asked.

"You all looked hot as fuck," I replied with a wide smile. "Also, Rhys, I had no idea that dragons had a warrior form."

"You're teasing us at a restaurant," Nico chastised. "Not nice."

"I'm not teasing you," I replied defensively.

"Most dragons aren't powerful enough to have a warrior form," Rhys explained. "It's a unique skill."

The waitress set the bills on the end of the table and before I could grab mine, Rhys did.

"Hey, one is mine," I said and tried to grab it.

He held it up above my head, high enough that even if I jumped, I couldn't reach it. "I'll pay. It's my turn."

"Your turn?" I asked. What was he talking about?

"We rotate who pays for food when we go out," Deryn said and draped an arm across my shoulders.

I snuggled into his side as we walked out of the restaurant. There was no point in arguing with them, they were the most stubborn males I had ever met. We waited for Rhys to pay on the sidewalk with people milling about, going on their ways.

If I was able to use their powers, could I shift into a wolf? Outside the restaurant in the middle of the city was probably not the best place to try.

Rhys came out and we started towards home. We walked by an ice cream shop and I stopped, making Deryn stop walking with me.

"Ice cream?" he asked.

"Please," I requested. I was abnormally hungry, wanting to eat again, even though I had just eaten a full meal.

We crowded into the already busy shop, and I immediately regretted my decision. There was a swarm of teenage girls inside, who all stood up and squealed when they saw the Princes. The girls rushed over, asking to take pictures with them.

One particularly pushy girl, shoved me out of the way so she could take a picture with Deryn. I laughed at her bravado and went to the counter to order my ice cream.

The guy behind the counter was in his mid to late twenties, attractive, and had a ton of tattoos on his forearms. They were gorgeous, well done tattoos and I wanted to ask about them, but didn't.

He smiled at me, putting on the charm. "What would you like?" he asked, and I realized that he was flirting with me.

Hadn't he seen me walk in with the guys?

"What do you recommend?" I asked, returning his smile. Flirting was harmless fun, especially with the guys behind me.

"My place, dinner, and dessert."

Damn he was bold. And his offer reminded me of Rhys when we first met.

"Sorry, I already have plans."

"Well, then I recommend the Sunny Sundae," he said, not fazed by my rejection at all.

"Okay, no nuts," I ordered after looking at the ingredients on the menu. I turned and asked, "You guys want anything?"

They were still surrounded by the girls, but didn't seem bothered. It probably happened a lot.

"Strawberry on a sugar cone," Fox ordered.

"Vanilla sundae," Nico ordered.

"Peanut Butter Rush," Rhys ordered.

"Two scoops of chocolate with caramel sauce," Deryn ordered.

"Got all that?" I asked when I turned back around.

He nodded. "I'll get started."

"Who is she?" one of the girls whispered to her friend while looking at me.

"She is our friend," Deryn informed them.

"Lucky bitch," one of them muttered.

I was.

Bumping into the guys was the greatest set of accidents I had ever experienced. Even with the attempted bombing and sniper, I didn't regret it. They were stuck with me now. The bond was permanent, and I would never try to get rid of it.

A sudden wash of magic swirled in me and as it dissipated, I felt all of the guys and their emotions clearly for the first time.

They all turned to face me, feeling as I touched them through the bond.

"You accepted it," Nico said happily.

"What are they talking about?" one girl asked.

I nodded.

Deryn walked to me and pulled me into a deep kiss.

The girls gasped and began talking in whispers.

"We're supposed to keep this a secret," I reminded him after he released me.

"We still are," he replied.

"Totally unfair," Nico grumbled.

"Rude," Fox said.

We got our ice cream and walked back towards the apartment, eating in a swirl of bliss.

"We were discussing having a schedule," Rhys said between bites of his ice cream.

"A schedule for what?" I asked.

"For us to be with you," he explained. "So that you don't have to have all of us in your apartment at once. We would each take one day during the week and the rest of the week, you could choose who you wanted to protect you."

"A schedule of who will guard me?" I asked, thinking this was a sex schedule. Both of which I was okay with.

"Yes," he replied. "And, so we can get some alone time with you."

"Would I be able to hang out with all of you, even if it was one of your days?"

They nodded.

"Why this decision?" I asked.

"We don't want to suffocate you," Nico said. "This way you have more freedom."

"But, if you go outside of the apartment, you have to take one of us with you," Deryn ordered me.

Shocked wasn't the beginning of my feelings on this development.

"Thank you."

They led me to the park, which was abandoned this late at night, instead of straight to the apartment.

"Why are we here?" I asked.

"Try to shift," Deryn ordered me.

"Oh. Okay."

He took my ice cream cup, which was empty, so I had my hands free.

I had no idea how they shifted, but I closed my eyes and pictured all of the times I had seen a werewolf change. My entire body began to tingle, and then I felt it change.

"Holy shit," Fox whispered.

"Shift into a dragon," Rhys ordered me.

That shift was easier, but becoming a huge dragon was startling and a bit disorienting. I looked down at them, their eyes wide in disbelief.

My scales were a beautiful purple color, a color I had never heard of a dragon having. I shifted back and collapsed on the wet grass, panting.

"This is crazy," Fox whispered. He sat down next to me and said, "Tomorrow, I want you to try some elf stuff. Though, I'm sure you will be able to."

"What should we do?" Nico asked Rhys. "This is a huge discovery. The Elders should be told."

"We could have two go and tell them while the other two stay to guard her," Deryn suggested.

"Will it be safe for the two who go?" I asked.

They looked at each other, and I knew the answer.

"I can take her to my dad's," Deryn offered. "He'll help protect her."

"Are you sure?" Nico asked. "She can shift into a wolf. That's likely to set a few people on edge. It makes her a potential threat."

"We're going to need to start teaching her how to control the powers," Rhys said. "The last thing we need is for her to shift in a restaurant or something."

"Why am I so tired?" I asked.

"You used a lot of magic," Fox explained. "You have to learn to pace yourself and figure out how much you have. We'll have to increase your stamina too."

"Like, by running?"

He nodded.

"I hate running," I groaned.

"Let's get back to the apartment," Rhys said as he looked around. "I don't like being out in the open with her for this long."

Fox helped me stand up and kept his arm around my waist as we headed home. "You're truly an enchanting creature," he whispered into my ear.

I blushed and said, "Thanks."

He kissed one of my flaming cheeks and chuckled.

CHAPTER 12

"We got them to agree to speak to us, with the promise that they would allow us to leave and to return home unscathed," Rhys informed everyone.

"Really?" Nico asked.

Rhys nodded.

"They're not going to kill me, are they?" I asked softly. I was a potential threat to all of them, at least in their eyes. I would never do anything to hurt my guards or their clans, but they didn't know that.

"We won't let them," Fox whispered adamantly.

"When do we go?" Deryn asked.

"Now," Rhys said. "Martin is on his way and should be here shortly to drive us."

"Have you guys finally gotten over your jealousy of Martin?" I asked with a smirk.

"No," they all said at the same time.

"What?" I asked and laughed.

"He has slept with you," Deryn reminded me. "We won't ever not be jealous of someone who slept with you. Especially, not the one who took your virginity."

"Males," I grumbled.

"He's here," Rhys said and headed towards the door.

The schedule had become a great thing for us. I got three days to myself, but usually spent it with all of them, or had one of them come over to have some more alone time. Alone time was a rare commodity for us and it was incredibly necessary to keep everyone sane.

Unknown to them, I kept a record of who came over on my off days, so I could make sure that I wasn't favoring one of them over the others. I didn't have a favorite and I wanted to ensure that they all knew that.

The Elders were alone in the giant room this time, but I was still terrified. The guys stood around me in protective stances before the Elders.

"What have you come to discuss with us?" Wolf Elder asked.

"There's been a recent development in our bond," Rhys started.

"She's using your abilities, right?" Dragon Elder asked.

Our surprised faces made him laugh.

"We know it is possible for humans to do this when they are part of the warrior bond. We did a lot of research into it, after we learned of Jolie joining you four," Dragon Elder explained.

"Uh," Rhys said, stumped since I was certain he had planned out exactly what to say to the Elders.

"Do you have any instructions for us or recommendations?" Nico asked them.

"You need to announce your relationship soon. If someone sees her change, or use the powers, before you announce it, it could be disastrous for you," Elf Elder ordered them.

"We haven't found out who was trying to kill her," Rhys explained.

"It's likely not one person. It's most likely that it is several individuals from all of the clans," Wolf Elder told us. "I would not fret about that specifically and instead just focus on keeping her safe, no matter the circumstances."

"Also, Nico, you should have a talisman made for her, to store some magic power. She is human and her body can't handle using too much magic at once. If she runs out of magic in an emergency, the talisman will provide her an additional source, though it will be tiny," Elf Elder said.

"Thank you," Nico replied. "I will have one created."

"Will the others think I'm a threat?" I asked them. "Will this make them uneasy with me?"

All three nodded.

"However, most will understand that as their Queen, you are not seeking to destroy the Princes' clans, but unite them," Elf Elder said.

"Will you take them as mates?" Dragon Elder asked.

"What do you mean?" I asked him back. Weren't they already my mates? I was sleeping with all of them.

"You are their Queen, yes, but you can also be their mate. You would need to create a mating bond with each of them individually," Dragon Elder explained.

"It comes with risks," Wolf Elder added. "After you create the mate bond, if one of them dies, or if you die, they will feel it ten-fold compared to you being a part of their warrior bond."

"And you have a higher chance of getting pregnant," Elf Elder added. "We aren't sure why, but after a mating bond is created, couples get pregnant much easier, even when using contraceptives."

"Good to know," I whispered.

"Think about it. If you don't take them as mates, they may be required to take a mate by their clans. Princes are often given mates by other clans in a business marriage to unite clans or packs," Wolf Elder told me.

"Wouldn't that distract them from protecting me?" I asked, since they had told me that before.

"Yes, but in this case, the mate wouldn't be as important as you," he said. "And the mate would know that."

That was incredibly crass. I couldn't imagine being someone's mate and knowing that another woman would take priority over me for protection in an emergency.

Deryn told him, "We've already discussed this with our Kings."

They had? Why hadn't they talked to me about it and what their decision is?

"When times are tough, royalty is forced to do many things that they do not like and had not planned to do," Elf Elder said.

"Any other advice?" Fox asked respectfully.

"Learn to control your abilities as fast as you can," Dragon Elder told me. "Once you do, you will be able to protect yourself, until your guards show up, should they not be with you."

I nodded. "I will."

"Ruminate over everything we said. Especially, about announcing it soon," Wolf Elder said.

"Have you made a decision about whether to remove the bond or the curse?" Dragon Elder asked.

"I won't be removing the bond," I said adamantly. "I'm still debating about the curse."

"We are glad to hear about the bond," he said.

"Thank you for your time," Rhys told them.

We bowed and returned home.

"Well, that went much better than expected," Rhys said as he plopped down onto Deryn's couch next to me.

I wanted to ask them about the mate bond, but decided I would do it individually over the next four days, when I was going to see them separately.

"I'm glad they already knew about it," Nico said with a sigh. "My fingers were tingling with magic, worried they might attack us."

"During the days that we are alone with her, we should teach her about each of our powers," Fox suggested.

The other three nodded in agreement.

"Jolie?" Rhys asked. "What are you thinking about?"

"Everything," I muttered.

"It's a lot to take in," he agreed.

"What are we going to do about the announcement?" Deryn asked Rhys. "Should we announce it soon, or hold off?"

"Let's hold off for a bit," he said. "I want to get her powers under control and talk things over with my father before we do the announcement."

"All of the poor maidens are going to be crushed when they hear that you have a Queen," I said with what I hoped looked like a true smile as I tried to lighten the mood and stop focusing on my worries.

"They will be," Nico agreed with a smirk at me.

"My brother can stop being jealous of me once that happens," Fox grumbled. "Once I'm not the top bachelor, he will get more attention from the ladies."

I laughed and they laughed with me. This was better. Laughing and joking was much better than being scared or worried. It was a constant issue with the curse, but it seemed that I might be able to get a handle on it and suppress it a tiny bit.

"Who's hungry?" Deryn asked.

"You're all always hungry," I teased them.

"True," he agreed.

"Let's get Chinese food tonight," I requested. "We always get pizza."

"We haven't had that in a while," Rhys agreed. "Sounds great."

"Let's play something," Deryn said and walked to his video game shelves.

I rushed to stand by him and grabbed the game I had been dying to play. "What about this one?"

"Rumble?" he asked.

"It's four players, so we can take turns with just one person not playing. Plus, it's a lot of fun."

"Oh, I haven't played that in a long time," Fox commented with a wide smile. "I'm totally going to own you all."

"What game?" Rhys asked from the kitchen where he had his head buried in the fridge.

"Rumble," I told him.

He spun around. "Oh, yeah! I'm going to destroy you, Fox."

Fox rolled his eyes. "Bring it on."

After hashing out the order, we all sat on the couch and grabbed a controller. The point of the game was to defeat the other players so that you are the last one standing, by beating each other up. It was a 2D game, but oh so fun.

The game started and everyone immediately went after Fox, since he had claimed that he could beat everyone. He was out of the game quickly, which left three of us. I attacked Rhys, who was defending himself against me when Deryn came up behind him and attacked him.

Suddenly, both turned to me and attacked me, killing me.

"No fair!" I yelled and set my controller down.

They focused on each other again and Deryn ended up winning.

"Take two," Fox said.

Nico took the controller I had set down and joined the game.

"No, you don't!" Fox yelled when they tried to defeat him first again. He jumped over them and defeated Deryn.

"Damn it!"

Fox attacked Rhys, but ended up dying instead.

"No!" Fox yelled.

Nico swooped in at the last moment to defeat Rhys and claim victory. "Yes!" Nico yelled. "Finally!"

"Crap. He finally won for once," Rhys said.

"It won't be the last either," Nico said confidently.

After five more matches, our food came, so we set the controllers down to eat together. We all sat at the dining table, plates and silverware out instead of using the paper plates the store had provided.

"This is nice," I whispered. "I've never had a family meal like this before."

"You've never had a meal at a table with your family?" Deryn asked.

I shook my head.

"What about Thanksgiving?" Nico asked.

I shook my head. "I've always wanted to have a Thanksgiving dinner. Like they have in the movies."

The guys looked at each other and then returned to eating.

"What about Christmas?" Deryn asked.

"My Grandma and I used to trade gifts, but that was it." Though, the idea of buying presents for the guys sounded fun.

"We're going to show you what these celebrations are supposed to be like," Deryn promised me.

"Definitely," Rhys agreed.

Rhys and I stood together in the park, my body coated in sweat from his training, and my clothes stuck to me.

"Done for the day?" Rhys asked.

I nodded. "Please. I am so tired." To accentuate my statement, I dropped to sit on the ground.

There were a few joggers out, but most went by without stopping. That surprised me since Rhys was standing there in a pair of tight sweatpants and a shirt that accentuated his muscular chest. He looked damn good.

He dropped down to sit next to me and kissed my cheek. "You did really well."

"Thanks," I replied and leaned my head on his shoulder.

"What do you want to do next?" he asked.

"Actually, I wanted to talk to you," I admitted.

"Uh oh," he grumbled. "Whenever a woman says they want to talk to you, it's not good."

I rolled my eyes at him and stood up. "Come on, let's go home and shower."

"A shower sounds wonderful," he whispered and slid his arms around my waist. He pulled me back against his front. "You're so beautiful."

"We're in the park, in the middle of the day," I reminded him with a blush.

"Then we best hurry home," he whispered, picked me up, and ran.

I squealed and clutched his neck as we flew down the sidewalk, somehow avoiding all of the people who were walking around. He didn't stop until we were in front of my apartment.

I gasped in a lungful of breath and he set me down to open my door.

"Next time, I would suggest that you don't hold your breath," he chuckled.

"Noted," I whispered.

He shut the door behind us and followed me to the bathroom, but before I could climb into the shower, he grabbed me and pulled me against him again, kissing me passionately. I kissed him back, glad to have some alone time with him where I didn't feel bad about focusing on one of them with the others around.

He slipped my shirt off and moaned when he slipped his hand under my sports bra. He almost tore my pants, ripping them off of me in his haste. I tugged at his shirt and he removed it and his pants.

I stepped back from him, putting a hand on his chest so that he would stay still as I admired him.

"I'm so lucky," I whispered, finally meeting his gaze.

"That's my line," he replied, swooped me up, and dropped me onto the bed, ravaging me and making me scream his name countless times.

"Rhys," I whispered after we were done and cuddling in bed.

"Hm?"

"About the mate thing..." I wasn't really sure how to ask what I wanted to ask.

"The decision is up to you," he whispered and kissed the top of my head. "I would be honored to have you become my mate. Nothing would make me happier."

I jerked my head up and looked at him. "You want me to be your mate?"

He nodded. "Yes."

"What did you talk to your dad about then?"

"The fact that I won't take anyone, but you as my mate. Even if you don't want to become my mate, I won't take one. I won't allow my attention to be divided from you. You are my Queen, my love, and I won't let anything happen to you."

"What do we have to do, to become mates?"

"I mark you with a bite and some magic, and we have glorious sex, and then our bond should snap into place."

"But, when I die, you'll feel it so much more," I reminded him.

"You're not dying."

"I will die before you. I have the lifespan of a human," I said.

"Not once you become my mate," he argued. "You'll have the same lifespan as I do after we are mated."

That definitely changed things. If I could live as long as them, then most of my worry was gone.

"Don't answer today," he said. "Think about it during the week and then decide."

I nodded in agreement and got up to took our shower.

♡

"You've been scowling all day," Nico said and tapped my nose. "What's going on in that head of yours?"

We sat on his bed, having just finished an amazing love making session.

"Do you want me to become your mate?" I asked outright. Nico was so blunt all of the time, I figured it was best to be blunt with him as well.

"Yes," he replied instantly and turned all the way so he was facing me completely. "I would be the happiest mage in the world, if you became my mate."

"What if I became everyone's mate? Would that bother you?" I hadn't asked Rhys about it, but planned to do so soon.

"I don't care if you become mates with the other three as well," he said honestly. "As long as I get moments alone with you, like today, then I'm fine."

"Swear?" I asked, surprised he would be so fine with it.

He nodded. "You are what I want."

"How does one become a mate for a mage?"

"A spell, of course," he replied with a smirk.

"Of course," I giggled. I lost my smile and asked, "Can I have the week to think about it?"

"You can take as much time as you want to decide," he replied and kissed me lightly. "I'll be here."

"You're too good for me," I whispered and kissed him.

"What happened to your mother?" he asked.

"I don't really know," I admitted. "She died when I was a baby, but my family refuses to tell me how she died. Dad had really loved her and her death took a big toll on him. I think that was part of why he became a vampire. I think her death broke the last bit of humanity he had and he truly became evil."

"I wish I could go back in time and save you from your awful childhood," he told me and rested his hand on my cheek.

I smiled and said, "I appreciate the sentiment. However, changing my past, might mean that I wouldn't be where I am today. I wouldn't change anything, as long as it meant I got to be with you."

"Ditto," he replied and kissed me roughly, laying over me and pressing our naked chests together.

"Nico," I whispered.

"Hm?" he asked between kisses on my neck.

"You're squishing me."

He chuckled and leaned up on his arms, taking his weight off me. "Sorry."

"When do I get to officially meet your dad?" I asked him. "I haven't gotten to really meet him or speak to him."

"Whenever you want to," he said. "Though, he's not the warmest guy. You'll like my mom better. She has been asking to meet you."

"Then, why haven't we?"

Was he embarrassed by me? Did he not want to introduce me to them until we had decided about being mates?

"We've been a bit busy," he chuckled. "Plus, I wanted to get your powers under control before we went to meet with them."

"Oh."

I supposed that made sense. It wouldn't look good to meet his parents and turn into a wolf or dragon suddenly.

"Then, we should get back to work on my powers," I suggested and climbed out of bed.

Deryn surprised me by taking me to the pack on his day, straight to the house where Tamara and Madison were waiting to leap on me for hugs.

I hugged the girls and Sharla, but was pulled away by a giant arm, attached to an equally giant Alpha.

He hugged me tightly and said, "I'm happy to see you're safe."

"I am safe," I agreed.

One of the great things about Alphas, was that they could make you feel very safe and loved. Dan was incredibly good at that.

He pushed me back to look at me and asked, "Do you need anything?"

"No, I just came to visit with the pack," I said even though Deryn hadn't told me we were coming here.

"Well, most of the pack are at the sports complex right now. They're finishing up a tournament they had started about a week ago," Dan told us. "Why don't you take her and I'll meet you over there?"

Deryn nodded and opened the front door for me. "Come on, you're going to love it."

The sports complex turned out to be a legit complex with a full-sized baseball diamond, soccer field, and a few other things that I wasn't sure what sport they were used for.

There were several wolves on the field, playing what looked like baseball, but they weren't using bats. They were just using their hands to hit the ball.

To the right of the field, was a set of stands with a ton of spectators.

"Are they all werewolves?" I asked Deryn softly as we approached.

He nodded. "Yes. The pack loves these types of games and come to watch them, even if they live away from here."

That was a lot of predators in one place. Deryn took us to the stands, and we sat next to two identical looking guys with long beards and clothes that reminded me of lumberjacks.

"Stan. Clark. I'd like you to meet Jolie," Deryn introduced us. "Jolie, this is Stan and Clark."

"Hi," I said and waved.

"Hello, Jolie," they greeted me in unison.

"The twins here are two of our top fighters," Deryn told me. "If I'm ever incapacitated, you just run to one of them and they'll keep you safe."

"If you're incapacitated, most of us would most likely be dead," Stan, or was it Clark, joked.

"Good to know," I said and watched the game.

"Is that a human?" someone in the stands asked.

"What's a human doing here?" another asked.

Deryn sat up straight and looked around at all of the stands. Everyone tensed up, people's backs in front of us were barely moving as they breathed.

"Jolie is my friend," Deryn said. "And if anyone has a problem with that—"

"They can take it up with me," Dan finished.

For such a large man, he was sure quiet when he moved. He stood beside me and all eyes fixed on him, even the game on the field had stopped.

"Jolie is an unofficial member of the pack," Dan told them.

"Dad," Deryn said in shock.

Several members gasped and a few started whispering to each other.

"Despite being human, she stood between an ogre and two wolf pups, saving their lives. She has earned her place as an unofficial pack member." He turned to me and smiled. "Hopefully, you'll become an official member soon."

What did that mean?

"Continue the game," Dan ordered them and sat next to me.

"Dan, I..." I didn't know what to say.

He smiled at me and said, "You don't have to say anything, Jolie."

The game didn't last much longer, but it was exciting and fun to watch. Deryn took me back to the apartment and I asked, "What do you have to do to become an official pack member?"

"You would have to mate with someone in the pack," he replied.

"Do you want me to become your mate?"

He laughed. "I thought I had made that clear. I one hundred percent want you to be my mate."

"Even if I'm mates with the other three?"

"Yes."

So far, it seemed that they all wanted me.

"Would we have to wait until after we announced our other bond to become mates?" I asked.

"Either we wait until after, or we mate right before so that we can reveal you as our mate and Queen."

"I'm still not used to that title," I admitted to him.

He chuckled and pulled me to lay on top of him on the couch. "You'll get used to it, eventually."

"If you could have one thing for Christmas, what would you want?" I asked. It was a random thought I had been thinking lately.

"You, with just a red bow on," he said with a smirk.

I laughed and kissed him. "Besides that."

"I don't know. I haven't really thought about it since Christmas is still a few months away," he admitted.

"I'm glad I finally got to go back to work," I told him. The company had found another building to work out of and I had started back yesterday. "I'm going to need to save up money to buy you four presents."

"You don't have to get us anything," he told me. "As long as we have you, we'll be happy."

"I appreciate that," I said.

I had to get them something. I knew they were going to get me something and I didn't want to feel like an ass for not having a present in return. Plus, I loved giving presents to people. I loved seeing their reactions to the presents.

"What do you want?" he asked me.

"You, nude and on my bed," I replied with a smirk.

"You can have that right now," he replied and kissed me fiercely.

Fox was the last one I had to talk to about the mating. Despite him being the sweetest, and quietest, I was most worried about what his answer would be. He had his spurts of seriousness that always threw me off.

We sat in a quiet café, eating breakfast before I had to go to work. He was sipping some tea while watching me eat my omelet.

"You've been wanting to ask me a question for a while," he commented. "Are you going to?"

"How'd you know?" I asked him and set my fork down.

"I just did," he said with a shrug.

We were alone, outside of the café, and there were very few people walking down the sidewalks who might walk by us, so I didn't have to lower my voice.

"Do you want me to become your mate?"

"Duh," he said and rolled his eyes.

"I'm being serious, Fox."

"Me, too," he replied. "I only want you, Jolie. Even if that means sharing you with my best friends, I want you. I want you to be my Queen, my mate, and my best friend."

"What do elves do to become mates?" I asked him.

"I perform a spell that binds us together for eternity," he said nonchalantly.

"Oh, only for eternity?" I asked with a smirk.

He laughed and held one of my hands on top of the table. "One lifetime isn't enough for me to spend with you. I need at least five or more, but would prefer to be with you for eternity."

"You're so good at flirting," I whispered, a blush covering my cheeks and possibly my entire face, and squeezed his hand.

"Just speaking the truth."

"I love you."

He leaned forward and rubbed his nose on mine. "I love you, too."

We didn't generally say it in public, but sometimes I just felt it too much not to say it to them.

"Ready to go to work?" he asked.

"I wish I didn't have to work today," I told him with a pout.

"You could quit and we could go play in the park together," he tempted while waggling his eyebrows.

I laughed and shook my head. "No, you naughty elf. I have to work to get money."

"We have enough money for you," he said.

"No, I have to earn it myself."

"Alright, but let it be known that I offered."

"The offer is appreciated, but I wouldn't feel right not doing something to earn money," I explained.

"Well, I could pay you for—"

I smacked him before he could finish his sentence. "Rude!"

He laughed and pulled me against him, making me tilt my head back to look up at him. "When will you decide about becoming my mate?" he asked me softly. His thumbs were beneath my shirt, rubbing against the skin just above my pants. If I let him continue much longer, I wouldn't make it into work.

"Soon," I promised.

He bent his head and brushed his lips across mine. "I look forward to your reply."

There he was again, serious Foxfire.

"Pick me up after work?" I requested.

"As my Queen orders," he said and bowed to me before walking away.

I watched his lovely backside walk away from me with the stupidest smile on my face.

"Who is that?" someone nearby on the sidewalk asked.

One lucky bitch. That's who I was.

CHAPTER 13

An entire month went by with no attacks or incidents. The guys were just as vigilant as ever in their guarding duties, saying they didn't want to fall into a false sense of security because that was when the enemy would attack.

They were likely right.

"There's a meeting today," Rhys informed me as soon as I opened my door to them. I thought they were just coming over for dinner, but their serious expressions said otherwise.

"Oh? With who?" My heart raced, and my nerves were already on edge.

"Everyone," he replied. "All four clans."

"Why?" I asked. "What's the meeting about?"

"Officially signing a peace treaty," Fox replied.

"You have to sign one? You can't just not be at war with each other anymore?" I asked. It seemed a bit ridiculous to me.

"It's in our rules," Nico explained. "We sign a declaration of war and we have to sign a peace treaty when it's over."

"Okay. So, I need to stay in my apartment until you get back?" I guessed.

"No, we want you to come with us," Rhys explained.

"But, all of your clans will be there. We aren't sharing our relation-ship yet."

"You'll be attending as our friend, and the one who ended the war," Deryn said.

"You're all tense," I noted and it was true. Despite us being at my apartment and them all sitting around, they were rigid and stiff. Worried about something.

"We think someone might try to attack you while you're there," Deryn said.

"You'll be there to protect me, right? So, we shouldn't worry about it. Plus, if they did attack me in front of everyone, it would be a death sentence for them," I replied.

"You want to go?" Nico asked.

"Duh. I keep trying to get you guys to take me around your clans. I want to get to know your worlds better and learn more about you and where you come from."

"One more thing before you completely agree to come," Rhys said.

"It's a formal event. So, you would need to wear a dress," Nico said since Rhys seemed nervous about it.

"I don't have a formal dress," I reminded them. They had all seen my closet and all of the clothes that I owned, which weren't many.

Fox held out a bag that I hadn't seen him holding with a wide smile on his face. "I got you one."

"You bought me a dress?" I asked as I looked inside. The dress was a dark blue, that would go well with my skin color and hair.

"Yes."

"You know how I feel about you buying—"

"You can repay me by letting me remove it later tonight," he said with a wink.

Tilting back my head, I laughed, and shook my head at him. "Incorrigible."

"You love me."

"I do," I agreed. "Fine, give me an hour to get ready."

They nodded and headed towards the door, but Fox ran back and set a box on my coffee table. "Those are your shoes! Love you!"

Before I could say anything, all four of them were gone and I was alone in my apartment.

"Brat!" I called, since I knew he could hear me.

I showered and took the time to curl my hair. Then, I actually did my makeup for once. It took me thirty minutes, but I knew it would be worth it once the guys saw me.

The dress lay on my bed where I had set it after pulling it out of the bag and gasping at its beauty. Fox had exquisite taste and the designer tag on the dress told me just how expensive it really was.

The dress fit me perfectly, hugging my curves and highlighting all of the areas that looked good being round. It was tight enough that I didn't need to wear a bra, and that I had to remove my underwear so there wouldn't be a line in the dress.

Since I never went to things like this, I didn't have jewelry to wear, but I didn't think they would mind.

The shoes fit perfectly as well, which made me wonder if Fox had gone snooping through my clothes and shoes to find sizes, or if he was just great at guessing.

"Jolie!" Rhys called from my living room.

"Coming!" I called back.

I did one more check in the full-length mirror and smiled happily at the woman I saw there. Who would have thought that I would find four perfect males who would fawn over me and meet every wish and desire that I had?

When I stepped out of my room, all four of them froze and stared at me with an intensity that was slightly frightening. Their gazes roamed along my body and four sets of eyes bore into mine. My eyes were doing their own roaming. All four wore black suits with white shirts and I desperately wanted to tear the suits off of them with my teeth.

"So?" I asked, since none of them had said anything.

Rhys was suddenly in front of me. "You would put Aphrodite to shame," he whispered and kissed my cheek.

"You look beautiful," Nico said with a smile.

"I knew that would look amazing on you," Fox said with a wide smile. "It will look better on the floor tonight."

"Alright, stop rubbing it in just because today is your day with her," Deryn growled at him.

I couldn't help laughing at that, but dabbed at my eyes to keep them dry, so my makeup wouldn't get ruined.

"Let's go," Rhys ordered everyone.

Standing in the elevator, all four of them found a place to touch me, their hands rubbing me and driving my hormones insane.

"Unless you want a five-way in the car, you should stop touching me," I threatened them.

Instead, their eyes brightened at the prospect.

"No," I said despite the warmth I felt in my core at the thought. I had meant it to be a threat and a joke.

Their hands moved away and I immediately missed their touches.

Martin whistled from his spot against the SUV when he saw me. He walked to me and bowed. "You've never looked more perfect."

"Hey, no flirting with her," Nico ordered him.

"Not flirting," he replied and kissed my cheek. "She knows what my flirting is like."

I blushed, and Deryn got into the front seat, so that I couldn't sit next to Martin. Martin chuckled and got into the driver's seat. I climbed into the back seat next to Fox. He immediately put his arm around me and began caressing my shoulder with his fingertips.

"You know what her outfit is missing?" Rhys asked.

"What?" I asked him.

He leaned back, draping himself across me and touching my neck. When he sat down, a gorgeous diamond necklace lay around my neck. It was shaped like flowers and vines and had to be worth our apartment building.

"This is too—"

"She needs earrings, too," Nico said and put a pair of diamond earrings in my ears before I could object.

Deryn smirked at me and said, "My gift is on your wrist."

What? I looked down to find a diamond bracelet on my wrist. When the hell had he put that on me?

"I'm worth more than half the city right now," I whispered.

"You're worth more than anything on this world combined," Fox whispered and kissed me.

"We give her presents and he gets the kiss," Nico scoffed.

I leaned forward and kissed him and then Rhys. Deryn was looking at me expectantly, so I blew him a kiss with a wink.

He pretended to catch it and tuck it into his suit pocket.

My smile was instantaneous.

"I love you four," I told them, "more than anything else."

"Alpha said he expects a dance with you tonight," Martin informed me with a glance in the rearview mirror.

"I'll happily dance with Alpha," I replied honestly.

"You have to dance with us, too," Deryn reminded me.

I rolled my eyes. "Oh no, how will I ever cope with having to dance with you four?"

That earned laughs from all of them.

To my surprise, we drove to the estate where the Elders met with us.

"Here?"

"Yes, there's an area behind the house which was designed for events like this. It has enough room for all of our people, as well as a dance floor," Nico explained.

"A bar?" I asked hopefully. I did not doubt for a minute that I would need some alcohol to get my nerves calmed.

"Yes," Rhys said with a smirk.

We climbed out of the SUV and walked together around the side towards the bright lights, music and loud voices. Rounding the corner, I was surprised to see close to a thousand people stretched out over a huge concreted area. White lanterns with a strange blue light lined the area, providing mood lighting. The silvery full moon shined overhead, brightening the area better than anything electric could have.

A DJ was set up off to the side with several people surrounding his table.

As promised, there was also a bar, but not just one - four.

"Booze," I drooled and headed towards one.

Fox stayed by my side and chuckled at me. "Alright, we'll go get you a drink, but once the music starts, you and I are dancing first."

"Very well, Guard," I teased him.

His body tensed and his face dropped all emotion.

"I, uh, I thought I could call you that, since you are...I'm sorry."

He relaxed and whispered, "I've just...you've never called us it before. It was a shock to hear. That's all."

"I won't call you it again," I promised, feeling like an idiot.

He grabbed my hand, stopping me from walking. "No, please. Call me that as much as you want. I loved hearing it."

"Oh," I exhaled. "I thought you were mad at me."

He released my hand and bent close to whisper, "If we were alone, I would show you how much I enjoyed you saying that."

When I glanced down, I could already see what he meant as his erection strained against his pants. My cheeks warmed, and I quickly turned away and hurried towards the bar.

I ordered my drink and then was grabbed around my legs from both sides at once.

"Auntie Jolie!" the twins yelled against my legs.

I dropped down and smiled at the girls. They were wearing matching purple dresses.

"You both look like princesses," I told them and kissed each of their cheeks.

Tamara picked up my wrist, which had their wolf tail hair bracelet on it. "You're wearing our bracelet!"

Both girls smiled wide and I could practically see their tails wagging.

"Yes," I said with a nod. "It is a gift that I will always treasure."

I stood and Sharla whistled. "Martin was right, you look phenomenal tonight."

"You're looking mighty sexy yourself, Sharla." And she was. She had on a tight green off-the-shoulder dress that left little to the imagination.

She hugged me and kissed my cheek.

"Son," the King of the Elves greeted Fox.

Fox bowed. "Father."

"Are you going to formally introduce me?" he asked him while looking at me.

"Jolie, please meet my father, King Katar of the Elves. Father, please meet Jolie," he said.

King Katar picked up my hand and kissed the back of it. "It is a pleasure to formally meet you, Jolie. You are stunning."

I curtsied and bowed my head. "It is an honor to meet you, Your Majesty."

"You should come visit our clan," he offered.

"I would love to," I said and smiled at him.

"We will, soon," Fox agreed.

"You need not wait until her decision has been made," King Katar said. "She may visit as your friend, under my invitation."

Fox's eyes widened, and he nodded.

"Thank you, for the wonderful invitation. I will be sure to take you up on it soon."

He bowed to me and said, "Enjoy your evening."

"Where is she?" I heard Dan ask loudly.

"Father, please calm down. She is here and safe," Deryn grumbled.

I gulped my drink down quickly and pushed through a few people to get to Dan, whose head I could see above everyone else's. "I'm here, King of the Wolves," I called to him.

He spun around and his eyes sparkled with joy. "Jolie," he said and hugged me.

Many people began murmuring at the display of affection between us, and I wondered if it really was so strange for him to act this way to me.

"You and I need to have a serious talk," he told me sternly. "The next time you see an ogre attacking wolf pups, yell for me or the Prince, do you understand?"

I put my hands on my hips and glared at him. "I'll tell you the same thing I told Prince Deryn. I could not leave my nieces in danger."

"You could have been killed," he reminded me.

"But I wasn't," I reminded him.

"You may not be so lucky next time," he argued.

"I appreciate your concern, but I would rather face down an ogre than see him harm a hair on their heads," I said sternly.

"She's mighty brash when speaking to a king," Mage King said as he came up to us.

I curtsied to him and said, "I would not presume to speak to you or any of the others in such a manner. King Daniel and I have a more personal relationship, which allows for the formality."

"Did she really put herself between an ogre and wolves?" he asked Dan.

"She stood between two wolf pups and an ogre and roared back at the ogre," he said proudly.

"And it scared it away?" Mage King asked skeptically.

"No, she was protected by the Prince," Dan lied. "She could have died, had her protection not come fast enough."

"True. Are you known for rushing headlong into danger? Is that why my son is constantly in harm's way?" he asked.

"That's a highly inconsiderate thing to say to the woman who ended our war," Nico told his father angrily.

"He's not wrong," I said and met the eyes of the Mage King. "He is in harm's way a lot because of me. However, it is not because I rush into danger. I try to avoid danger if at all possible. If you think it's wrong for me to protect children, then..." I trailed off and shrugged.

My mouth was getting the better of me. Perhaps spending so much time with the princes and getting desensitized to them wasn't such a good thing.

The Mage King threw back his head and boomed with laughter. He patted Nico on the back and said, "I can see why you like her, son. She reminds me of your mother."

"She does," Nico agreed.

The Mage King held out his hand and I set mine in it, expecting him to shake it, but he pulled it up to kiss my knuckles. "It is an honor to meet you, Jolie. I look forward to you visiting my clan soon."

I bowed my head. "Thank you, for the invitation."

He released me and laughed again as he walked away, shaking his head.

"Well, two more Kings seem to like you," Fox commented from behind me.

"Two?" Nico asked.

"My father seems enamored with her, too," Fox said softly.

"Maybe, I'm just a likeable person," I commented grumpily.

"Jolie," Wolf Elder called.

I spun and immediately dropped into a bow, which was difficult in the dress and the reason I had been curtsying instead.

Fox wrapped an arm around my waist to keep me from falling.

"Sorry," I mumbled and straightened myself and my dress.

"Please, come with me," Wolf Elder requested with a smirk and amusement gleaming in his eyes.

"May I bring Fox?" I asked softly.

He nodded once in agreement and the three of us moved through the crowd with everyone staring at us. Was it the dress? Was it because of Fox or the Elder? Or was it because I was human? There didn't appear to be many humans, but it was hard to tell between shifters and humans when they were not using their powers. Their stares made my heart pound and my palms sweat. They were all judging me, I knew they were.

Rhys winked at me as we walked by and reached through to bond to brush mine. I smiled as we continued on, the nerves leaving me.

My guards were here for me and that was all that mattered. They would protect me. They didn't care what others said about me.

The crowd finally thinned, and I could see the other two Elders waiting at the front. This time, I curtsied instead of bowing and Wolf Elder's lip twitched as he fought a smile.

"Welcome, Jolie," Dragon Elder said in greeting.

"Thank you for inviting me," I said. Despite the guys not saying anything, I was sure they had been the ones to invite me.

The crowd had grown quiet and the music had stopped to allow for the Elders to talk.

"Tonight, we sign the long-awaited Peace Treaty between the Four Clans!" Wolf Elder announced proudly.

Everyone cheered and quieted quickly again to hear more of what they had to say.

"Before we sign the treaty, we have to recognize the one who ended the war," Dragon Elder announced.

"Jolie, please come up here," Elf Elder requested.

Fox squeezed my hand before I walked up to them and curtsied again.

"Jolie, a human with no powers, stumbled into our world and has not hesitated since entering. She returned the stolen artifact, once she learned the item she had been gifted was ours. Then, she protected two wolf pups from an ogre during the day of attacks," Dragon Elder informed everyone.

People murmured behind me in shock to each other.

"We owe you much, but are unable to fully repay our debt," Wolf Elder told me.

"We have been told that you are already accepted by the Wolf Clan," Dragon Elder said.

"She is," Dan replied loudly behind me.

"It has been hundreds of years since a human such as yourself has been born. To repay part of our debt, we offer you this—" Elf Elder paused and a teenage boy ran forward with a black wooden box. Elf Elder took it and held it out to me.

I took it and wondered if I was supposed to open it now, or just thank them for it and open it later.

"Open it," Fox whispered behind me.

The Elders were smirking at me, amusement lighting all of their eyes now.

I opened it and pulled out a necklace with four bright diamonds in a line down the center. They were at least 2 carats each, and glowed with a strange ethereal light.

"It's too much," I whispered and looked up at them with tears in my eyes.

"Each diamond contains power from each of the Kings and the Princes," Dragon Elder explained to me.

Holy shit! They'd just given me an extreme boost of power, should I need it. If I didn't do something, I would start crying and my makeup would be ruined for the rest of the night.

Rhys took the necklace he had purchased for me off and put the new necklace on for me, brushing his hand across my shoulders after he had finished, sending chills down my spine in a delightful shiver.

"From this night forward, you are welcome at any of the four clans and are named Princess of the Four Clans," Wolf Elder announced.

That set everyone off. I thought my legs might give out and was saved by Rhys putting his arm out for me to hold. He took the box from me and held out a beautiful silver crown with branches and cherry blossoms that had pink diamonds in the center of each blossom. Before I could protest, he set it on my head and kissed my cheek.

"Our new Princess!" the Elders announced together.

Rhys turned me around and everyone bowed to me, except the Princes and Kings, who did dip their heads in acknowledgement.

What the fuck had just happened? How? Why? Oh my god.

"Now, to business!" Dragon Elder said.

The Kings went to the Elders and a wooden table was brought out with a large piece of paper, a quill, and inkwell. The Kings each signed the treaty as did the Elders.

Dan held out the quill towards me and motioned at the paper. "We need our savior's signature as well," he told me.

Tonight just kept adding surprises on top of surprises.

I signed my name and everyone cheered.

"Peace has been achieved!" Dan announced and clapped King Katar and the Mage King's shoulders.

Everyone cheered and music was turned on again.

"May I have this dance?" Dan asked.

"I couldn't refuse my Alpha," I said with a wide smile and set my hand in his.

"Even my old man is trying to steal her," Deryn whispered jokingly.

"If I were twenty years younger, it wouldn't be a fight," Dan teased.

My face was certainly the color of a tomato at that comment.

Dan swept me out onto the dance floor and surprised me with an elegant waltz.

"You dance very well," I commented.

"All men should learn to waltz," he said adamantly. "It impresses the ladies." He winked at me and I laughed, then twirled under his raised arm.

"You're hogging her," King Katar teased him and twirled me away from Dan.

Dan bowed to me and walked off into the crowd.

"King Katar," I whispered in shock. "You honor me with a dance."

He smirked as he danced gracefully with me. "You don't have to be so formal with me. I'm not as pretentious as some are. You may call me, Katar."

"Katar, I have to admit, your son is growing mighty jealous of our dance," I whispered to him.

As we spun, he saw Fox waiting on the edge of the crowd, and he chuckled.

"He was never good with sharing his toys," he teased. Then he added, "Except with his best friends. That seems to be the case here, as well."

"Katar, I—"

"Don't get upset," he whispered soothingly. "Our kinds are known to have multiple partners."

"What?"

He nodded and pulled me closer so that he didn't have to talk very loud for me to hear him. "Female offspring are rare and so, there are often multiple men for every woman. We also don't normally mate with humans, but you will be an exception."

"You're okay with me possibly mating with Fox?" I asked in a whisper since people were watching us.

"I want my son to mate with someone he loves, and I believe he loves you," he whispered back.

"I love him," I whispered back and glanced at Fox. "Very much."

"As you should...as their Queen," he replied and kissed me cheek before letting the Mage King take me into a dance.

"We haven't gotten off to the best start," he said with a smile, thankfully dancing with me during a slow song.

"I'm at fault," I whispered sadly. "I don't have the best control on my temper."

"My name is Johann."

"Jolie," I said with a smile.

"You seem to make my son happy," he commented. "I have not seen him smile as much as I have when you are near him. He is focused on his training and his studies again, something he had been neglecting. He is also much more interested in our politics, things I know I can thank you for. You are a good influence on him."

"I can't take credit for all of that," I mumbled.

"Trust me, it is all because of you."

"You were right about me getting him into danger," I said sadly. "Especially with the curse..."

"Will you take him as a mate?" he asked me suddenly.

"I, uh...I haven't decided yet," I admitted.

He nodded. "You should decide soon. Even with this gesture from the Elders, you are still in danger. Being named mate of the four Princes, or even one of them, will greatly increase your safety and make people think twice before hurting you.”

“It is strange to me that you Kings are all okay with your sons mating with a human, especially a human who will be mated to other Princes,” I muttered.

“Polygamy is quite common among Other races. Plus, mages and humans aren’t so different, right?”

“Right,” I agreed.

He kissed the back of my hand and handed me off to the Dragon king. My legs were going to be extremely sore tomorrow, from all of the dancing. I wasn’t going to complain though. How many females got to say that they danced with the four Kings and the four Princes?

“Jolie, you look lovely in that dress,” he told me.

“Thank you, King—”

“Emrys,” he supplied.

“Emrys,” I said, hoping I said it correctly.

He smiled, so I thought I had said it right.

“Emrys, how would you feel if I took your son as my mate?” I asked him.

He laughed. “My son has already told me that he will not mate with anyone else, so I suppose it is truly inevitable.”

“I love him,” I whispered.

He nodded and said, “I know. I can see the love you all share with each other.”

“My turn,” Fox said and held his hand out.

Emrys kissed my hand before setting it in Fox’s. “Visit my clan soon, Jolie. They would love to have you visit.”

“I will,” I promised. Had I hit my head and this was all a strange hallucination during a coma? That had to be the answer. There was no way that all of this was really happening.

“Hello, Princess,” Fox greeted me and guided me through a dance that I didn’t know.

“Hello, handsome,” I replied.

“Did my father behave himself?” he asked.

“Yes, he was very nice.”

“I’m glad. Sometimes he can be a bit...overwhelming,” he whispered. I laughed and before I could reply, Rhys stole me away.

“Rhys,” I gasped.

His lips were turned up into one of the most handsome smiles I had ever seen on him. "You look amazing," he said and pulled me closer against him. With his lips next to my ear, he whispered, "I'm going to have you wear that dress when it's my day, just so I can take it off of you."

Our bodies were pressed completely together, not even air could get between us. Our eyes were locked and I swore there were visible sparks between us. His gaze was so intense, so focused on me, like I was the last person on the planet.

Someone cleared their throat behind us, breaking the spell.

"May I?" an older male asked.

"Certainly, Alfred," Rhys said, kissed my knuckles, and then set my hand in Alfred's.

Alfred and I joined the dance and I smiled as he twirled me expertly, matching and exceeding the younger males dancing skills.

"You're quite the dancer," I complimented him.

"You'll often find that the older males have more experience and can provide more enjoyment," he replied with a wink that made me blush.

Another male cut in.

Then another.

And another.

I danced with a whirlwind of males, rarely getting a dance with any of my guards, though they did occasionally sneak in. The next male I danced with was very stiff and kept avoiding my eyes. He had resisted my attempts at conversation, not that I was a great conversationalist by any means.

Rhys slid his fingers along my side as he danced with another female by me. I turned to look for him and felt a sharp pain in my side. Someone screamed and Rhys's gaze, who I finally found, was wide with fear.

"Rot in hell," the male I had been dancing with snarled in my ear.

My body felt cold and numb and it took a lot of strength to look down. In the center of my stomach was a silver dagger, buried to the hilt. Blood dripped down the dagger, creating a pool on the ground at my feet. I swayed and fell onto my back on the ground. That asshole had stabbed me.

More people were screaming and when I blinked, a dragon appeared over me, roaring. I recognized that roar...Rhys.

He was spewing fire, the heat of it warming me a minute as it built in his dragon belly.

"Shit. Shit. Shit," Fox gasped.

He started to heal me, but Katar pushed him to the side. "Stop. We all know that you won't be useful if you heal someone."

Fox stood up and faced away from me, his body glowing softly.

"You with me still, Princess?" Katar asked.

"Yes," I said and hissed as the movement hurt immensely.

"Okay, stay still and I'll heal you," he explained.

"Help...others," I ordered him.

"You'll die if I don't heal you," he informed me.

Tamara and Madison ran beneath Rhys, sliding to a stop next to me with blood coating their fur. Madison shifted and gasped, "Auntie Jolie!"

"You're related to them?" Katar asked.

"Not by blood," Tamara explained.

"Where are your parents?" Katar asked, his hands glowing as he held them over my stomach.

"We don't know," Madison admitted. "That's why we came to Auntie."

"Stay beneath the dragon," Fox ordered them. "He'll protect you."

"Okay," they agreed simultaneously.

A vampire leapt at Katar, but Fox tackled him before he could touch his father. Four more vampires came and Katar had to stop healing me to draw a sword I hadn't even seen him carrying, and sliced all of their heads off.

Two goblins leapt towards him and Rhys used his tail to smack them away. Once they were gone, he curled his tail around my body, not touching me, but protecting me within his scales.

The female dragon who had stolen me previously, flew into Rhys at an alarming speed, knocking him away from me and into the house fifty yards away.

I tried to watch their fight, but my body wasn't responding to my demands. My chest felt heavy and I struggled to take in deep breaths. Was I dying?

"Jolie!" Fox yelled.

Shit. I didn't want to die. Not yet.

"Jolie!" Deryn yelled.

I stared up at the star-filled night sky and tried to locate Fox's powers within me. If I could heal myself... It seemed impossible, so I went to plan B, use all of their powers. Blinding light from somewhere appeared and I felt like I was weightless. The dagger fell to the ground and I felt my innards and skin healing back together. I took a tentative breath and it didn't hurt any more. *Yes!*

"What the—" someone gasped below me.

I sat up and pressed my hand against my stomach, fully healed. That was going to come in very handy.

Now, I wasn't a liability. I wasn't the damsel in distress that the guards had to protect. I could defend myself. I could heal myself. I was OP as hell!

"Jolie!" Rhys called.

He had shifted back into his man form and ran to me, crushing his mouth to mine.

"Now's not the time for that," I reminded him and pushed him back.

The girls cowered next to my feet in wolf form, staring out at the party, which had been attacked by my father and his army. Thousands of different beings swarmed within the party, attacking the attendees.

Their side was losing, the Kings and Princes were killing things right and left, tearing down their numbers and protecting their people.

King Johann and the mages used fire and sun powers to obliterate the vampires. My father floated above the chaos in a sphere with a woman who was holding her hands out. She must have been a mage.

"We have to defeat him," I whispered.

"You can't use the powers anymore," Rhys ordered me. "Most will just assume the necklace the kings gave you protected you. If you use them more, or individually, you'll be exposed."

"We can't let them kill people," I urged him.

"Stay behind me and we'll help get rid of these scumbags," Rhys agreed.

The girls followed on my heels, watching our backs and walking backwards. Their hackles were raised and they were snarling and showing their teeth, looking like vicious wolves instead of scared children.

As we moved, Rhys attacked the enemy, helping the weaker beings defeat those who were stronger than them.

"You okay?" Deryn called to me while fighting a large ogre. The ogre slammed a huge club into the ground, but Deryn easily avoided it. The club got stuck and Deryn ran up it and sliced the ogre's head off with a sword.

"I'm fine!" I called back to him. "What happened to the guy who stabbed me?" I asked Rhys.

"I killed him," he said with a growl.

"Did you know him?"

He shook his head. "Never seen him before."

"He was a mage," Nico told me as he walked next to me, his staff glowed nonstop as he sent spell after spell into enemies.

"Any idea why?" Rhys asked.

"He was struggling to provide for his wife. We think someone paid him to do it and the money had too much allure."

"How sad," I whispered. He tried to kill me, but desperate people did desperate things when they were at the end of their rope.

"You're too kind," Nico warned me.

"How bad are things?" I asked. They didn't seem so bad from where I could see, plus my dad looked mad, which meant he had to be losing.

"Tomorrow, we need a massive cuddle puddle," Nico whispered to me.

To them, lying around me in a square, with a hand each on me was a cuddle puddle. We only truly cuddled on our individual days.

"Watch out!" I yelled and ducked, pushing the girls' heads down as I did, avoiding the sword swung at us.

Rhys stopped the blade with his arm, dragon scales covering it to protect him. He turned and punched the attacker, a goblin with green mottled skin. The goblin staggered back and clutched his face, which was bleeding heavily.

"Nico, go help," I ordered him.

He bowed his head and whispered, "Queen."

They had been doing that more lately and I wasn't sure that I liked it. I wasn't a Queen. I didn't plan to be one either. Being named a Princess was one thing, but queen? Wait, if my dad was the King of Vampires, then wasn't I technically the Princess of the Vampires? Not being a vampire probably played a role in me not being their princess. Not that I wanted to be part of the vampires.

Something slammed into the shield protecting my dad and then dropped to the ground. I realized it was Deryn. He had jumped at him.

Nico and his father stood side by side, sending spells of various sizes and shapes at the shield, which cracked immediately.

The mage with my dad panicked, released the shield, and tried to run. Nico froze her, while Deryn and Fox attacked Dad with swords.

He had a sword of his own and was very skilled with it, blocking most of their attacks, despite it being two on one.

"You've lost," Katar told him. "Give up now and we'll spare your life."

"No, we won't," Nico growled and leapt into the fray, setting Dad's shirt on fire and attacking his legs.

The three of them fought seamlessly together, never getting in the others way without even talking. A simple look and they'd attack simultaneously, and then separately. It was breathtaking to watch.

Dad had several cuts on his arms and a nasty gash in his side, which he was holding a hand over. Nico knocked him onto his back and Fox ran him through. I turned, too late to avoid seeing it. My father screamed out, the sound dying in a gargle. When I turned back, his body had vanished. He was dead. My father, my torturer, the King of Vampires...gone.

Rhys pulled me into him and gripped my side tightly.

"Why did you kill him?" Katar asked.

"He tortured her," Fox whispered to him. "He tortured her as a child and as a teenager. He tortured her when he stole her from us. I could not let him live."

There were several people laying on the ground, some getting healed and others providing first aid treatment. There were also some who were dead, their bodies stiff and eyes unseeing.

"Girls!" Sharla yelled.

The girls turned and ran to Sharla and Martin who were running in our direction. They had been on the opposite side of the battle from us. I smiled to see the reunited family and felt a deep sadness about my father. He was evil and had never loved me, but he was the only blood family I had left. Mother had died while I was a baby, and my grandmother had died a year ago.

"Let's go home," Deryn whispered. He brushed hair behind my ear and rubbed his thumb down my cheek.

Home. Home was definitely with the four of them.

"Home," I agreed and nodded.

They boxed me in and we took the SUV we had driven to the meeting in, but Deryn drove since we had left Martin to be with his family. I leaned against Fox in the backseat and couldn't believe that we had defeated Dad and his army. His evil influence was gone from the world. Finally.

No one talked as we drove. No one talked as we took the elevator to Fox's apartment. As soon as the door closed, all four crushed me in a group hug. My head was pressed into Fox's chest with Rhys at my back.

"I've never known fear before," Fox whispered. "I thought I did, but seeing that blade in your stomach—" He couldn't finish his sentence and instead buried his nose against my neck.

"We failed you, again," Deryn mumbled into my left shoulder.

"No, you didn't. Who would have thought someone would do something like that with everyone there?" I asked them. "Plus, I wouldn't have let you stop me from dancing with them."

"I didn't even get to dance with you more than once," Nico grumbled.

"Well, maybe we can go to a club one of these nights," I suggested. I hadn't been to a club in a long time.

"Let's change," Rhys suggested and pulled his blood-soaked jacket off.

All of them stepped away from me to remove their jackets and unbutton their cufflinks and their shirts.

Rhys noticed me staring and smirked. "Are we bothering you?"

"Please, don't stop on my account," I teased and leaned against the living room wall to watch. "I'm quite enjoying the show."

"Food, booze, and cuddles in an hour at Deryn's," Fox requested.

Everyone nodded their agreement and then took turns kissing me before leaving.

Fox locked his door and was suddenly in front of me. "I need to know you're alright," he said. "I need to get this dress off of you. The sight of the blood on your stomach is making me uneasy."

I slipped the dress off, shivering as the cold air covered me. He slid his hand along my skin, where there wasn't even a scar from the attack.

"I almost lost control of my powers when I saw him stab you," Fox whispered. "I've never lost control."

"It wasn't a picnic for me either," I chuckled.

"Don't joke about this, please," he requested.

Serious Fox was so unfun, but probably right.

"Sorry," I whispered.

His shirt was still on, so I finished unbuttoning it and took it off, leaning back to admire his body. He unbuckled his belt, unbuttoned his pants, and slid them down slowly, giving me a nice view of his backside as he did so.

His strong arms wrapped around me, trapping me to him. "I love you, Jolie. I love you more than anything. I can't stand seeing you hurt. I can't stand knowing I was right there and you almost died. I was powerless to stop it. I don't like being powerless."

His skin was so soft and his muscles were so hard. It was a contrast that I loved exploring with my hands, and my mouth. I kissed my way around his neck and chest. He grew hard against me instantly and moaned as he took my mouth with his.

"Shower," he growled into my mouth. "I need to get this blood off of you."

"You've got blood in your hair," I pointed out.

We kissed the entire way to the bathroom and didn't stop until we started shampooing our hair. It took a few washes to get the blood off of my stomach, but once I did, Fox relaxed and pushed me gently against the bathroom wall.

"You can't die on me, Jolie. I can't lose you."

"You won't lose me," I whispered. "I'm not going anywhere."

"You deserve so much more than I can give you. You deserve the stars and to rule over it all. Martin may have been your first love, but I, and the other three, will be your final loves. I will never take you for granted. I will never stop loving you. I will continue to fall deeper and deeper in love with you as we grow old together."

"You're the greatest thing to happen in my life," I whispered.

He kissed me ferociously, devouring me in a way that was very unlike Fox. Our sexual encounters were normally slow and calm. That night, it was fast and demanding. He whispered promises to love me forever in my ear as he gave me orgasm after orgasm.

"I'm never giving you up," he told me as he gripped my hips and thrust into me as deep and as hard as he could. "You're mine."

"For eternity," I agreed.

"Say it?" he requested.

"I love you, Foxfire."

His body trembled, his eyes fluttered shut, and he exhaled sharply. "God, that is the most amazing thing to hear."

"Say it," I ordered him, moving my hips to match his movements.

He opened his eyes and stared straight into mine. "I love you, Princess. My Queen. Jolie. I will love you until this universe is destroyed."

"Foxfire!" I screamed as I orgasmed, my muscles tightening around him and making it that much better.

He grunted and buried his face in my hair as he found his release.

CHAPTER 14

No one brought up the battle after they'd all shared their fear with me and promised to keep me safe in the future. No one brought it up, but it was still evident that it was on their minds with the haunted expressions they got time to time as they looked at me. Try as I might, I couldn't help them get over what had happened. How bad would they have been if I had actually died?

"Your dad messaged me again about visiting," I told Rhys while sitting at the table in his apartment.

"I told him that your visit will wait," he replied as he flipped a pancake in the pan. He was naked, except for the apron that he had tied into a cute bow above his butt.

"Why? Why are you keeping me from meeting your clan?" I asked him angrily. "I met Deryn's and Fox's."

"I'm not keeping you—"

"Are you ashamed to be seen with me by your clan members?" I asked, my anger spiraling out of control. Anger had never been a major issue of mine, but suddenly, I felt like tearing someone's arms off.

He spun to me and said, "That is the dumbest question you've ever asked me."

"You're an inconsiderate jerk," I growled at him. "Do you have a female in your clan that you're trying to keep me from meeting? Maybe your most recent relationship? One you haven't gotten over yet?"

He set his spatula down, turned the stove off, and stalked towards me, his eyes shifted to his dragon's eyes and for a brief moment, I worried he might hurt me. I knew he wouldn't, but the fear was there nonetheless. Stupid human instincts.

"There is only you, Jolie. There's been no other girls for me since I saved you that first day. I am not embarrassed by you. I do not have a secret female I'm—"

"Then why can't I meet them!" I shouted, fists clenched at my sides and my entire body tingling with barely contained fury.

"Because we aren't mated!" he yelled back and then straightened and fumbled over his words. "I-I'm just—"

"Why do we have to be mated?" I asked. "What if I chose to never be mated to you? Would you keep me from the clan? Would you break our bond? Stop being my guard?"

The fury I had felt was gone, leaving me weak and tired.

"You'll be safest as my mate," he replied and reached for me.

I stumbled away from him, tripped over the chair behind me, and fell on my butt on the kitchen floor. He tried to help me up, but I smacked his arms away and stood up on my own.

"I've lost my appetite," I whispered. He hadn't said that he would not break our bond or stop being my guard. Would he really do it if I didn't choose to mate with him?

"Jolie," he whispered softly, fists clenched at his sides.

I stopped at the door, clothes in my hand, and asked, "If I don't become your mate, will you break the bond?"

"Are you planning to only mate with one of us? Or only some of us?" he asked instead of answering.

"No, it's all or nothing," I answered truthfully.

"Then no, I won't break the bond."

"But you would if I chose only one or two of you?" I asked, feeling a pain in my chest that I knew was unnecessary. What was going on with my emotions? Why couldn't I get a handle on them?

"I don't know," he admitted. "I don't know if I could be your guard while you were mated to one of the others and not me."

"You're the only one who feels that way," I told him. "The others said they wouldn't ever leave me, no matter what I decided about my mates."

"They'd consider it, too, but wouldn't tell you," he said with certainty.

"Maybe. Or maybe you are finally seeing past the bond and what your true feelings are. Maybe...maybe we aren't meant to be more than friends."

Before he could respond, I ran out of his apartment and up the stairs. I stumbled up the last few steps, but finally made it to my apartment with tears streaming down my face, blinding me.

The door was locked and I hadn't brought my keys with me, so I sat against it, knees pulled to my chest and arms around my legs, and cried.

Why? Why was I so emotionally unstable today? What would I do in Rhys's position? Would I be able to stay if the tables were turned?

Hell, I knew I wouldn't be able to share at all. I wasn't sure how they could all do it as it was.

"Sweetheart," Nico whispered. "What's wrong?"

"Rhys," I sobbed and lifted my head. Nico's eyes were bright with worry, his eyebrows scrunched together. He sat on the floor of the hallway with me, cross-legged.

"What about Rhys?"

"He said—" I didn't want to repeat it. Just remembering the words hurt me again. I threw myself into Nico, who caught me and repositioned me so that I was in his lap sideways, my head on his shoulder and my legs over the side of his.

"It's alright, Jolie. I'm here," he whispered.

"Jolie," Rhys whispered, standing above us. "Let me explain."

"Fuck off, Rhys," Nico threatened him and rocked me in his arms.

"I need to talk to her," Rhys said and moved closer.

"I don't want to talk to you anymore," I sobbed and clutched Nico's shirt.

"Jolie—"

Rhys's body flew down the hallway, slamming into the closed elevator doors. I gasped in shock and looked up at Nico who had his hand outstretched and glowing eyes.

"Don't do this," Rhys begged him and stood up. "Don't start a fight with me over a misunderstanding between her and me."

Deryn walked into the hallway and looked at our tense standoff. "What's going on?"

"Dickbag said something that hurt Jolie," Nico said.

"I'm trying to talk to her so I can explain what I said. It's a misunderstanding," Rhys told Deryn.

"You said you would break the bond," I accused him.

"What!" Deryn screamed at the same time Nico did.

"I said if you only mated with one of us, or not all of us, that I would *consider* breaking the bond."

Deryn punched Rhys in the jaw, knocking him down to one knee. Deryn's body was partially shifted, fur sprouting from his hands and face. I'd seen this happen only twice before, both times when a werewolf was pissed and barely controlling their shift.

"What the fuck, Rhys?" Nico demanded.

"Don't fucking lie!" Rhys yelled at them. "If she only chose me or Fox, would you stay as her guard? Would you stay and watch them together?"

"It would be difficult," Deryn agreed, thankfully fully human again.

"Exactly!" Rhys yelled and rubbed his jaw. "Fuck, that was a hell of a hit."

"What if she chooses to mate with someone else and not any of us?" Nico asked him, fists sparkling with magical energy ready to be used.

"Nico," I whispered. "Nico, don't hurt him." He didn't respond to me. I gripped his shirt and shook him. "Nico!"

"I don't know," Rhys admitted.

Nico was gone. One second he was beneath me, and the next I was sitting in the hallway alone. He slammed into Rhys, his hands released an electrical energy that made Rhys scream out in pain.

"Stop!" I yelled, but they weren't listening.

"I love her!" Rhys yelled at them, panting on the floor while Deryn and Nico glared down at him. "I can't watch her love anyone, but you three!"

"Our bond isn't to be broken! We swore!" Nico shouted at him.

"I know," Rhys whispered.

Nico looked like he was going to hurt Rhys again, so I screamed at them. My scream was loud and high-pitched, higher than I'd ever screamed before. The glass windows shattered, the lightbulbs shattered, and the pictures and vases exploded. The guys dropped to the ground, covering their heads and looked at me with wide eyes.

"Stop fighting!" I ordered them.

"Jolie," Nico whispered.

"Shut up!" I ordered him. "Shut up and listen to me. There will be times that I fight with you individually. It will happen. But, that doesn't mean you fight with each other. You're brothers. You're best friends. I'm sorry. I overreacted. I've been extremely emotional lately. And no, god dammit, I'm not fucking pregnant. I am sorry, Rhys."

Rhys, Nico, and Deryn stood up slowly, keeping their eyes on me.

"I'm sorry, Jolie. I love you," Rhys whispered.

"I know you do," I said and felt the tears as they dripped down my cheeks.

"Can I come hug you?" Rhys asked.

I nodded, since it was impossible to talk at the moment. What the fuck was wrong with me? Why was I overreacting to everything?

Rhys gently slid his arms around my sides and pulled me against his chest. "I'm sorry."

My tears soaked the shirt he had put on and I gripped his back as I cried.

"It's us," Deryn whispered. "She's feeding off our emotions."

"What do you mean?" Nico asked. "None of us are crying."

"Fox is," he replied with a smirk. "He's watching that movie about the dog and fox who became friends. He always cries when he watches that movie."

"Which one of you was mad earlier?" Rhys asked as he rubbed my back and hugged me.

"Me," Deryn answered. "I was trying to do something and it wasn't working like I wanted it to."

"She looked like she was ready to blow the building up," Rhys informed them.

"How can we stop her from getting hyped up on our feelings?" Nico asked.

"I'll ask my Elder," Deryn said. "Wolves have a pack connection, similar to our warrior bond. I'm sure he will have something to suggest."

"I love you. All of you," I whispered into Rhys's shirt, the words getting muffled by it.

"We love you more than anything," Nico whispered.

"Come on, your breakfast is going to be cold," Rhys said and tugged me down the hallway.

Fox popped his head out of his apartment and looked at us with red eyes. "What's going on?"

"No more sad movies!" Nico ordered him.

"What? Why not?"

"Because Jolie can't handle it right now."

"Why are you keeping me from your clan, too?" I asked Nico. "Fox and Deryn are the only ones who have let me go. Rhys said I can't go unless we're mated."

"Ah, that's what started the argument," Deryn guessed.

Rhys nodded.

"I want you to be safe," Rhys reiterated. "After you choose whether to become our mate or not, then I'll take you."

"Why not before?" I asked.

"Because being my mate will ensure that no one tries to challenge you," he explained. "As a mated couple, if one is challenged, it is a challenge for both of them. If you aren't my mate, then anyone can challenge you and I won't be able to help."

"So, if I don't become your mate, then what?" I asked.

"We'll cross that bridge when it comes. First, you have to make a decision. And no, I don't mean right now," he said quickly before I could say anything.

Breakfast was a somber affair, but at least no one was crying or punching each other. I excused myself to sulk in my apartment, curled up on the couch with the blanket wrapped around me.

Too late, I realized that Nico hadn't answered me. These men were slowly driving me insane.

"Jolie," Fox called through the door.

"What?" I replied, my voice muffled by the blanket around my face.

"Can I come in? You're sad and it's hurting me."

Hurting him? Why would my sadness hurt him?

"What do you mean it's hurting you?" I asked and sat up. I still wasn't going to the door to let him in. I needed my privacy.

"We can all feel your pain," he explained. "It's like a sharp stab in the center of our chests."

I had no idea that they felt my pain physically.

"I want to be alone," I told him. "Please. I'll try to stop being sad so it doesn't hurt you."

"Okay," he said with a sigh. "I'm sorry I caused you to be upset earlier."

Fox was always so kind and sweet. Yet, I didn't want to let him in to console me. Why? Sometimes, a girl needs to be alone to thoroughly process her feelings and emotions. And I really needed to process everything.

The guys were all great. They were loving, kind, and protective. They wanted me and me alone.

But, was that really fair? Would it be right of me to stay with them? For me to be with four of them, while they only had one of me?

Knowing that they would feel my death tenfold, did not make me want to agree. No matter what, they would have to deal with my death because they lived longer than I did.

They all wanted to be my mate. I wanted them to be my mates. It should have been a simple answer. Yet, I was hesitant to take that plunge. I felt like I was taking away their futures. I felt like I was ruining their chances of finding mates that would be their equals.

Thinking about giving them up hurt immensely. Picturing my future without them at my side was painful and boring. Even just one of them being gone was inconceivable. I could do it, but I really didn't want to.

Running would do nothing, except put me in danger and cause them to have to rush after me to find me. I wasn't going to do that again. I wouldn't be childish and run away ever again. Though, I wasn't powerless any longer. I could shift into a god damn dragon, after all.

So, that left me with two options. One, break the bond completely. Two, become their mate.

Being their mate sounded like an amazing thing. To know that we were mated, that there would be no others who could break us up or that they, or I, would cheat would provide huge relief to our stressed lives.

The warning the Elders gave us about the chances of pregnancy increasing certainly worried me. I was not ready for children. Not for at least five years. Or more. Definitely more. Truthfully, I never saw myself having children. Would they want children? That was something I would need to ask them. That might be a deal breaker for some of them.

"Jolie," Deryn called through the door.

"I want to be alone," I replied immediately.

"Please," Nico begged.

I opened my door and was shocked to see all four of them standing in my hallway with pained expressions and half of them with clenched fists.

They were wearing tank tops and sweatpants. All four of them. They were different colors and brands, but they still matched.

"Why are you all wearing the same thing?" I asked, completely caught off guard, since they never wore similar things, except when they wore suits.

"We were training," Rhys answered.

"What do you guys want?" I asked softly, resigned to not being alone today like I wanted. They weren't being manipulative or rude on purpose. I knew that. I just wasn't sure why they were being so insistent.

"We want to talk," Nico said.

"What about?"

"Whatever it is that is causing you so much pain and discomfort," Deryn said with a growl and rubbed the center of his chest with his closed fist.

"Is it really hurting you?" I asked in disbelief.

All four nodded.

"Talking isn't going to change my feelings," I muttered. It might make things worse, actually.

"Is it about mating with us?" Rhys asked softly.

I wanted to lie, to keep their feelings from being hurt and keep them from misunderstanding why it was causing me pain. However, lying was out of the question, since they could see right through my lies. So, I nodded.

"What about mating makes you sad?" Fox asked. I expected him to be upset or sad, but he was only curious. Or at least that's how he appeared. They were pretty good at hiding their emotions.

"It's not mating that is making me sad," I explained. "But the options of what to do if we don't mate."

The tension grew, all of them freezing and clenching their fists at their sides.

"What options?" Deryn asked.

A loud groan escaped my lips, and I spun around, stalking back to the couch where I flopped onto my side, blanket still tightly wrapped around me. "I don't want to talk about this," I mumbled around the blanket which I'd pulled up to my nose.

The guys filed in, Fox coming in last and shutting my door for me. Rhys sat on the floor in front of the couch, Deryn sat on the couch beside my head. Nico sat at my feet, picking my legs up and putting them in his lap, so I didn't have to move at all. Fox sat in front of the couch, beside Rhys and turned to look at me.

"I love you four," I told them softly.

"We love you as well," Fox whispered. "Which is why we want to find the source of your sadness and annihilate it."

I chuckled humorlessly. "You can't."

"Why not?" Rhys asked, tilting his head back so that he could look at me upside down.

"This is my decision," I whispered. "I have to come up with the decision on my own. I have to decide what I'm going to do about you four. About the rest of my life, our lives."

"We don't get any say?" Nico asked. He had begun rubbing my feet at some point, I wasn't certain when, but I was thoroughly enjoying his warm hands kneading my feet.

"You all already told me that you want to be my mate," I replied. "I asked you each about it."

"What options?" Deryn asked me for the second time.

I groaned. Werewolves were not known to give up on something once they had the scent. "Mate with you all. Mate with none of you. If I mate with none of you, then I have to decide if I'm going to stay. If I mate with all of you, then I'm taking away your chance at finding a mate of equal standing. A mate worthy of you." Before any of them could say it, I said, "Yes, I'm worthy. Blah. Blah. Blah."

"If you don't mate with us, you might leave?" Fox asked, his brows furrowed and a perfectly executed pout on his face.

"Yes," I replied, not wanting to hide anything.

"You love us. Why leave if you don't mate with us?" Rhys asked.

He was getting mad again, I could see it in his tense shoulders and the way his eyes were glowing.

"Because I can't see you with other mates," I whispered without looking at him. It was incredibly selfish of me.

"Do you just want to be miserable?" Fox asked. Normally that question would be said with sarcasm or anger, but he was genuinely curious.

"No," I grumbled.

"You want to mate with us, but you are considering leaving? Why?" he asked.

"If I don't want children, are you four going to be fine with that?" I asked instead of answering his question.

That got them all to shut up and think a moment.

"I've always wanted children," Deryn said softly. "You really don't want kids?"

"Not any time soon," I explained. "The Elders said that once you mated, pregnancy was almost a guarantee."

"There are preventative measures we can take," Nico said. "There are spells and herbs on top of human contraceptives that we can use to ensure the increased virality is combated. Not every new mated pair gets pregnant. It just increases the chances."

"How am I supposed to have children with all four of you? How will we even know whose it is?" I sat up and let the blanket fall to my lap. "That's so much drama."

"It doesn't matter whose kid it is, we will all care for it and love it because it is your child," Fox replied instantly.

"And we would know whose it is because of the powers it possessed," Nico said.

"I never wanted more than two kids," I said, leaning my head back against the back of the couch. "I'd have to have at least four for you all."

"No one said you had to have their child," Rhys pointed out.

"Why were you so sad earlier?" Fox asked, probing for more information.

"I was thinking about what my life would be like without you four in it."

They didn't seem to know how to respond to that. We sat in silence for at least three minutes before Rhys got up, grabbed four beers and one cider, and brought them back for all of us to share.

"We aren't going to force you to do anything or decide on anything," Rhys told me, his hand resting on mine on top of the couch. "We just want you to know that we love you. We love you more than anything. We would be devastated to lose the bond we share with you, to lose you."

"Can I put off deciding?" I asked quietly. Maybe if I pushed it off a bit, I would have a revelation and know what decision was the right one for me.

"Yes," Fox answered for the four of them. He turned on a movie, one I told him a few days ago that I wanted to watch because it was supposed to be one of the best comedies of the year.

I sat up, put my legs on either side of Rhys, and ran my fingers through his hair. It was thick, but soft and silky.

"Me next!" Fox said and tried to push Rhys away.

Rhys growled at him and held his spot between my legs.

Deryn lay his head on my left leg. I knew exactly what he was doing, but I still obliged. With my left hand, I ran my fingers through his hair, while still running the fingers of my right hand through Rhys's.

Fox grumbled and leaned his head against my knee.

Suddenly, my stomach became queasy. I leapt up and ran to the bathroom, covering my mouth with both hands. For once, I was glad that the toilet seat was up, or I would have thrown up all over the floor.

Someone pulled my hair back, away from my face, and held it while I continued to empty my stomach. When I was finally done, I stood up on shaky legs, stumbled to the sink, and thoroughly brushed my teeth and tongue.

Nico set his hand on my forehead and immediately frowned. "You're burning up."

"Fever," I agreed and wrapped my arms around myself as the chills set in. My body must have known that I was sick and made me wrap up in the blanket ahead of time.

"Let me heal her," Fox said.

"No," I ordered him. "This isn't a wound. It's an illness. I don't want you weakening yourself just because I have a stomach bug."

"There's a bug in your stomach?" Deryn asked with wide eyes.

Four sets of eyes glued themselves to my stomach.

I chuckled and shook my head. "Have you never been around a sick human before?" I asked them.

All four shook their heads.

"I just need a fever reducer, soup, water, and rest," I explained. "It will go away on its own."

"Do you have those things?" Rhys asked.

"No," I realized sadly. What a terrible adult I was. Normally, everyone kept most of those things on hand. I didn't. "I need to go to the store."

I tried to walk out of the bathroom, but a wave of dizziness hit me and I stumbled and fell into Nico who caught me.

"You're not going anywhere," Nico ordered me. He carried me to the couch, wrapped my blanket back around me, and set me in the corner of the couch.

"I need a big bowl or bucket," I ordered him.

He ran to my kitchen and after several moments of banging cupboards and other items, he returned with a big, red, plastic bowl that I usually used for popcorn.

I took it from him and threw up into it.

Fox French braided my hair from my temples to the back of my head, so my hair wouldn't be in my way when I threw up again.

"Nico, you stay with her. We'll go get her what she needs from the store," Rhys said.

Nico nodded in agreement. He took the bowl to the kitchen, cleaned it, and brought it back.

"Do you need a list?" I asked through chattering teeth.

Nico lit a fire in my fireplace with his magic, and held a flame in his hand near me, helping me stop shaking.

"We'll call you when we get there," Rhys said.

Deryn, Rhys, and Fox left, while Nico sat beside me. He held the bowl in his lap, in case I had another bout of nausea.

"Is this something that could be fatal?" he asked with tense shoulders.

"I'm not going to die. It's just the flu," I answered. "Humans get it all the time."

He exhaled and leaned back on the couch. "That's good to know."

"How did Rhys become the leader of your group?" I asked, since I hadn't thought to ask about it before.

"He was always the take charge one of the group. At first, Deryn and he argued about who was the leader in our games and hunts. They butted heads a lot, but Fox was able to act as mediator and calm them down. He has a real gift for calming tense situations and people's emotions. I don't think it was until we were about twelve years old when Deryn finally gave in and acknowledged Rhys as the leader, deferring to him in situations. We still have our say, he isn't the king of our group or anything. He asks for our advice and doesn't order us around in a way that would be rude. He just tells us the plan, and normally it's a really good plan, so we go along with it."

My phone rang, and when I answered, Rhys's face showed up. I had never done a video call with any of them before.

"How are you?" Rhys asked as they walked.

"I'll live," I said and fought back a chuckle at his relief. How had they never been around any sick humans before? I knew they didn't get sick, but it baffled me that none of them had been around a sick human when so many of us inhabited this city.

"We're at the grocery store," Rhys said and turned the phone around so I could see Deryn and Fox, heading into the entrance.

"What are those for?" Fox asked as he faced the shopping carts.

"You'll need one of those," I told them. "It is to put the items you're buying in, so you don't have carry them around in your arms."

Deryn grabbed one and pushed it a bit before a huge smile split his face. "These would make fun sleds."

Before I could stop him, he jumped into the basket of the cart and Fox pushed him quickly through the automatic doors, which thankfully opened in time.

"You've never been to a grocery store?" I asked.

"Princes, remember?" Rhys reminded me. "We had professional chefs living with us as kids. Now, we have our food delivered to us or we go out to eat at restaurants."

Fox pushed Deryn so hard and fast, that he slammed into a bin of oranges, knocking four into the cart with Deryn. Deryn picked them up and began juggling them while Fox continued to push him fast down the produce aisle.

"Do you need anything from here?" Rhys asked.

"No, just—"

"Aren't oranges high in Vitamin C?" Deryn asked, still juggling said oranges.

"Yes," I answered him, knowing where this was going.

"Then we will take these," he said.

Knew it.

Rhys walked to the aisle with medicine and I exhaled in relief. If I could get them in and out, we might survive.

"There's a lot of different medicines and variations," Rhys commented as he picked up a cold medicine and then one for indigestion. "Humans need a lot of medicines."

"Yes, we do. You'll want to get a fever reducer. If they have one for flu symptoms, that will work, too," I said.

"Do you have any of these others?" Rhys asked, pointing the phone at the long aisle of medicines.

"No, but—"

"Get out of the cart," Rhys ordered Deryn.

"Why?" he pouted.

"I need to put the stuff we are buying in it."

"Fine, I'll go get my own," Deryn said, taking the oranges with him.

Rhys looked at Fox. "Catch and put them in the basket. Oh, and hold Jolie."

Fox took the phone and turned it so I could see him. "Hi, Jolie."

"Hi, Fox."

Fox started catching boxes of medicine as Rhys threw them, one after the other. "Hold on, Jolie." He set the phone in the cart as Rhys increased his speed. Fox caught them, then dropped them into the cart. Soon, the phone was covered by medicine boxes.

"How much are you getting?" I asked. It looked like he was buying the entire aisle.

"What?" Fox's voice called and the boxes covering the phone began to move. Soon, Fox's face shown through. "There you are, Jolie. Hiding."

"I'm not there. You know that, right?"

Fox rolled his eyes.

Sitting up was taking a lot of energy, so I lay on my side, my head on Nico's thigh, and propped the phone up on the coffee table in front of me so they could still see my face.

"I got two of everything, just in case," Rhys told me when he got back on the phone.

"I don't need—"

Rhys had started tugging on one of the medicines that were locked up, but it wouldn't budge.

"Sir, you'll have to show me some ID before—" A woman with bright pink hair started trying to explain to him. He ignored her and snapped the lock off to grab the medicine out. She let out an exasperated sigh. "I need to see your identification, please."

"ID?" he asked. "I don't have any ID."

"You don't carry ID?" I asked him. Everyone I knew carried ID.

"No, everyone knows who I am," he said softly.

Did he realize how egotistical that sounded?

"I have an ID," Fox said. "Deryn! I need my ID."

"Why does Deryn have your ID?" I asked. These guys made zero sense sometimes.

"He carries it for me," he said like that should explain everything. He disappeared and then a few minutes later came back with an ID card from junior high.

"This is your junior high school ID," the clerk said, exasperated.

"So?" Fox asked.

"Why do you have a junior high ID?" I asked him with a groan.

"Look at it," he showed it to me. He looked really good. "It's an amazing picture."

The clerk groaned. "Fine, it's got a year on it, so I know you're over the age required. Just take the medicine and go."

"What's on the next aisle?" Fox asked and practically skipped around.

"This is going to take forever," I muttered to Nico and turned my head to look up at him.

He was focused on the phone, watching the aisles and the merchandise. "What is all that stuff?"

"I think we need to take a field trip together to the grocery store, so I can show you guys how us plebeians live," I said with a chuckle and shake of my head. They were basically, reverse sheltered. I was going to have to show them what it was like to be human.

"Okay, this aisle has baby stuff, so I don't think we need—"

I interrupted Rhys and said, "Get the flavored water that has electrolytes in it. That stuff helps with dehydration and will help me feel a lot better, once I can keep things in my stomach. It's also great for preventing and curing hangovers." I had a lot of experience with the latter use of it.

"Why is your face sideways?" Rhys asked.

"She's lying down," Nico informed him. "Focus and get the stuff she needs. Her fever is pretty high."

"Should we grab one of these thermometers?" Fox asked and held up a thermometer.

"Yes," Nico answered before I could.

Shoppers kept stopping to stare and gossip in the background. I couldn't blame them. This was definitely not your everyday occurrence at the grocery store.

"There's a few different flavors of this water," Rhys said.

"Just get two of each," Fox said and started grabbing bottles. "Oh, there's popsicle of this stuff too. I'll grab some."

"You guys are buying way too much stuff," I told them.

"Next aisle!" Fox announced excitedly and rounded the corner to go to the next one.

"Where's Deryn?" I asked, realizing that he hadn't come back after Rhys kicked him out of the cart.

"Here!" he called as he flew by in the basket of a shopping cart, a roll of wrapping paper in his hand as an oar. Rhys turned the phone so I could watch as he slammed into a display of stacked soda cans, that toppled over. Some of the cans busted open and sprayed soda all over the aisle and Deryn.

"Oh my—"

"I'm alright!" Deryn called and leapt up out of the cart with a shit-eating-grin on his face. "That was awesome."

"You're going to have to pay for all of that," Fox told him.

Deryn shrugged. "Okay." He immediately started stacking the cans into the cart he had vacated.

"You guys are insane," I chuckled.

"Okay, we still need soup, right?" Rhys asked.

"Yes, chicken noodle soup please," I requested.

He looked up at the signs and found the soup aisle, which for some reason had a bunch of clothes on one side of the aisle.

"Why are there clothes in the soup aisle?" Rhys asked me.

"Why would you try to get clothes at the soup store?" Nico asked me.

"I don't know," I said.

"Okay, chicken noodle. Chicken noodle. Chicken...ah! Here it is!" Rhys held up a can of soup to the phone so I could see it.

"Yes, that's the right kind."

"How many do you want?" Fox asked.

"Just a few, I—"

"Get ten," Deryn said. "I want to try some."

"Be right back!" I yelled and ran/stumbled to the bathroom to throw up again.

"I need to learn some healing magic," Nico grumbled behind me.

"You don't need to stay with me," I told him. "I really don't want you guys to see me being so gross."

He rubbed my back and kissed the top of my head. "Vomit doesn't gross us out. We've been in quite a few battles and there's a lot of disgusting things that go on there."

"Okay, but I need you to get out of the bathroom," I said urgently, feeling my guts bubbling.

"Okay, I'll go check on the guys and see if there's anything else we need to get," he said and left.

I locked the door and was glad my bathroom was far enough away from the living room that he wouldn't be able to hear the disgusting sounds my rear was making.

After spraying some air freshener and washing my hands, I stumbled weakly back to the living room. Nico wrapped me up in the blanket and helped me lay down on the couch, setting my head on his thigh so he could drag his fingertips along the side of my face. The movements were incredibly calming.

My phone was still showing the store, but it seemed they were finally at the checkout. Rhys set a carton on the belt and it fell over, liquid ice cream spilling out.

"Why is this melted?" Rhys asked angrily.

"Because a stupid dragon who has a high body temperature was holding it," Deryn scoffed. "I'll get a replacement."

"Cleanup at register three!" the clerk called over the speaker. She was in her late fifties at least, and looked beyond bored and annoyed. The guys tried flirting with her, but she just stared at them with indifference as she scanned the items they were purchasing.

"We'll be home soon, baby," Rhys said and smiled at me. "I'm going to hang up now."

"'kay," I whispered my eyes growing heavy.

Nico turned off my phone and resumed stroking my face. "Is this okay?"

"Mmhm," I mumbled.

"How long will you be sick?" Nico asked.

"One to three days."

"Days!"

I nodded.

"We made it back," Rhys said loudly.

"Shush," Nico ordered him.

"I'm awake," I grumbled.

Opening my eyes, I found piles of bags and soda stacked inside my living room. It had to have cost them hundreds of dollars. Maybe even a thousand.

Rhys brought one of the bags to me. It was bulging with different medicines. "I don't know which is the best to use for the current illness you have," he told me.

I dug through the medicines and took out one for flu symptoms. "This one will work great." Before any of them could offer, I opened it, poured the liquid into the small measuring cup, and then quickly swallowed it.

"Do you want us to heat up some soup?" Deryn asked me, placing his hand against my forehead with a scowl.

"No, I can't eat anything yet. My stomach is still too upset."

Fox opened one of the electrolyte waters and set it on the coffee table in front of me. "Here, this way it's available when you're ready for it."

"Thank you. All of you, seriously, thank you."

The last time I had been taken care of like this was when my grandma had been alive. It was nice to have people who loved and cared about me.

"Open up," Nico ordered me, holding the thermometer. I obeyed, opening my mouth and then closed it when it was beneath my tongue. The thermometer dinged and he looked at the temperature it showed. "Hm," he grumbled, pulled out his phone and searched the internet for something. "It's high, but not life threatening."

All of the guys relaxed, breaths whooshing out of them. I had not realized they were holding their breaths.

"Guys, I'm not going to die. It's a common illness. Do an internet search for it. You'll see," I promised them.

"We'll take shifts," Rhys told everyone. "She needs sleep and there are too many of us here. Nico, you want a break or you want first shift?"

"First shift," he said and resumed stroking my face.

"I love you," I whispered to them as I let my eyelids droop.

The three who were leaving pressed light kisses to my forehead as they went. It was sweet and it filled me with warmth and love.

Three days later, I was finally well. The guys still tried to baby me, but I assured them I was healthy again. After a bit more reassuring, they believed me and the next four days were filled with marathon bouts of sex and hours of cuddling. They'd been terrified they were going to lose me and they all needed skin to skin contact with me in their arms to remind them I was safe. In a weird way, they seemed more scared after my flu, than they had after I'd been stabbed.

I wasn't complaining.

CHAPTER 15

"Why haven't you made a decision?" Emrys, King of the Dragons, asked me as we ate lunch at a fancy Italian restaurant a block away from my work. He had invited me suddenly that morning and I hadn't wanted to turn him down.

"Decision about what?" I asked him between bites of my penne Alfredo pasta. It was heavenly, and I wanted to scarf it all down as fast as possible.

"Mating," he replied softly, so those nearby wouldn't hear us.

"I have made a decision, but I haven't told anyone," I admitted to him. I was holding off on telling the guys until it was right. Things just didn't seem right yet.

"Since you haven't told your guards, I'm guessing you won't tell me either," he said with a smirk.

"No, sorry."

"I want you to come visit the dragons," he told me. "I've invited you several times to the den and you have pushed it off time and time again."

"Not because I want to," I told him right away, not caring if I was throwing Rhys under the bus. "Rhys said he doesn't want to take me unless I'm his mate. He said if someone challenges me now, he won't be able to fight with me, but if I'm his mate he will be able to."

He sighed and set his fork down. "He's always been a worrier. I blame his mother. I will have a talk with him. I will ensure that no one can challenge you and you will be safe when you visit. What does it say about us if the wolves can have you over with no problems, but my own son is too afraid of us to have you over?"

"Did I just get him in trouble?" I asked softly and stabbed a piece of pasta.

"No, I figured this was most likely the reason you hadn't visited," Emrys admitted. "Like I said, he's always been a worrier. I will talk to him and then we will have you over. Do you have plans Saturday?"

It was strange to be sitting in a restaurant talking to the King of the Dragons about visiting his clan. My entire life was strange. I had gone from an isolated girl with major daddy issues to the Princess of the Four Clans and Queen of the four Princes. Who knew one necklace would cause so much change?

"Saturday sounds great," I replied with a smile, which Emrys returned immediately.

"Great," he said. He sat still a moment and said, "My son is right, there's something about you, your presence, it's calming. Sitting with you like this makes me feel much more relaxed than I have felt in at least a decade. Are you sure you're human?"

I chuckled and said, "I'm human, but I'm glad I can offer you some relaxation."

I didn't have much to offer, but I could handle offering a calming presence.

"There's my Queen," Rhys said and took a seat next to us after giving me a quick kiss on the cheek.

"I love you," I told him with a smile.

He smiled and said, "I love you, too."

"Dessert!" Fox said as he pulled a chair up to the table. "We need to order dessert."

"Why am I not surprised that you four showed up?" Emrys asked with a smirk.

Deryn grabbed a breadstick and took a big bite before he said, "Because you know that we can't allow our Queen to eat with strange men without interrupting."

"Strange men?" Emrys asked. "Is that how you refer to your uncle?"

"Is he trying to steal our Queen?" Nico asked, sitting between me and Rhys with a chair he stole from a nearby couple's table without even asking them. Their shocked faces were hilarious.

"I believe, that would be between your Queen and I," Emrys teased them with a smirk.

I laughed and enjoyed the banter of the men I loved. This was where I belonged. Wrong or right, this was home. Home is where the heart is, mine just happened to be evenly split amongst the four of them. Something I was perfectly fine with.

"Home," I whispered.

Nico squeezed my hand beneath the table, and the other three winked at me.

Yes, this was home.

ROYALLY
EXPOSED
HER ROYAL HAREM: BOOK TWO
USA TODAY BESTSELLING AUTHOR
CATHERINE BANKS

CHAPTER 1

The four males I inadvertently fell for, were all still asleep when I opened the door to my apartment. We had been up until four o'clock in the morning trying to beat the new raid in *Ghost 2*'s second expansion. My body decided it was ready to get up, and for the first time, the guys didn't wake when I climbed out of the giant bed Deryn had had custom made for us. It was large enough to fit eight people, side by side, which gave us plenty of room since there were only five of us. The mattress was plush and heavenly, as though lying on clouds.

I set the coffee carafe on my kitchen counter and arranged the four boxes of donuts, one dozen in each, lids opened. Before the smells could reach the guys, I grabbed my two favorite donuts, put them on a plate, and took the cup of hot chocolate I had purchased to the couch and set them all on the coffee table.

"Coffee," Deryn grumbled, half asleep, as he stumbled into the living room.

"Good morning," I greeted him and smiled as I enjoyed the view. All of them slept in pajama bottoms and nothing else, their chests and abdomens, rippling with muscle, naked for my viewing pleasure.

He bent down and kissed my cheek as he passed by, mumbling what sounded like good morning.

"You left alone again," Rhys growled at me half-heartedly.

They had been getting better about letting me out on my own now that I could tap into their powers, if needed, and protect myself. However, their protectiveness as my Guards, and lovers, still made it difficult for them to be okay with me going out alone.

"I wanted to surprise you with donuts," I told him and sipped on my hot chocolate.

He kissed my cheek and slid his hand along the back of my neck. "It's a good surprise," he said. Rhys hated mornings more than any of us, but said getting to wake up with me was making him start to like them more. I knew that was a lie, but I enjoyed the flattery.

"Donuts!" Foxfire yelled and raced into the kitchen, grabbing a box, and running over to sit beside me. "Thanks, Jolie," he whispered and kissed my cheek with a wide smile. Fox loved mornings. Well, Fox loved almost everything. He was almost always in a good mood and his attitude was infectious.

"You're welcome," I replied and leaned into his shoulder with mine.

"Did you use a shield?" Nico asked, rubbing his eyes and then stretching to give me a nice view of the muscles over his hips that formed a V and led down to a very fun area.

"No," I admitted.

Four sets of eyes turned to look at me.

"I couldn't figure out how to do it with my hands full," I explained quickly. "But I had scales on the back of my head and over my heart, so if I had been shot at they couldn't have killed me."

It had been months since the last time someone had tried to kill me. You would think stopping a war would endear you to those who had been fighting, but some people had been pretty upset about it. Most of them had been thankful. Hell, they'd made me a princess of the dragons, mages, wolves, and elves and given me a necklace with power stored inside from the kings and princes of each race. I still couldn't believe it.

I touched the necklace and felt the energy thrumming within, a constant reminder of the power I could now use.

"That's good," Deryn praised me. "I wouldn't have thought to use scales on the back of my head."

"That's because you don't have scales," Rhys said with a grumble. "I'm glad you've figured out how to use the scales beneath your hair."

"It wasn't easy," I mumbled. The first few times I had tried to do it, I had covered my entire head with scales and freaked out because I thought I was going to be bald afterward.

"How long can you keep the scales on?" Nico asked around a bite of sugar coated donut.

I waited until I'd finished eating my chocolate bar before answering. "I can hold the scales in a small area, like over my heart, for an hour. If I put it in several small areas, I can hold it for half an hour. I can cover my entire body for fifteen minutes at most."

"The more you use it, the easier it becomes," Rhys said. He gulped down a mug of coffee and added, "It will become second nature and you won't even have to think about it."

That sounded like a great thing to have the ability to do. Instead of focusing and putting scales in the spot you wanted, you could just automatically have it there. I had seen Rhys use scales when fighting hand to hand with Deryn, and Rhys said it just happened automatically for him.

"What are our plans today?" Deryn asked.

"I'm going to the dragons' den today," I told them, waiting for Rhys to blow up...again.

"What?" Rhys asked quietly.

Uh oh. Quiet was bad.

"King Emrys invited me over. He promised me safe passage and that I would be allowed to return whenever I wanted to."

"They aren't faeries," Fox whispered.

"When were you going to tell me?" Rhys asked, his voice a deep rumble from the kitchen where he was standing, his grip on the mug he was holding so tight, that I could see cracks forming already.

"Now," I said with a smile.

"I told you why I didn't want you—"

"I've been ordered to come by my King," I said and stood up, shoving the rest of my donut in my mouth.

"I can talk—"

"If I disobey him now, that's setting a bad precedence with your clan. I can't disobey him. I'm going. So, you need to decide whether you're coming with me, or not."

Without giving him a chance to respond, I hurried to my bedroom to change clothes. Emrys had warned me to wear something comfortable and to bring a jacket. That should have made me nervous, but I knew Rhys would go with me and wouldn't let anything happen to me. They'd told me before that even though their fathers were their Alphas, they could withstand their orders, because they were so high in the hierarchy.

Once I was satisfied with my appearance, I went out to the living room where Rhys sat alone. The others had snuck out without me hearing the front door open or close. Rhys sat on my couch, his arms draped across the back, giving me time to take in his new appearance. He had put on jeans and a t-shirt that said, "Unicorns do exist and they're tasty."

Instead of talking, I walked straight to him and sat in his lap, straddling him with my face level with his. "You're mad at me for leaving this morning," I guessed.

One of his warm arms snaked around my lower back, and pulled me forward so that our chests were touching.

"I don't like waking up to find you aren't in bed with me. I don't like knowing that someone could have hurt you while I was sleeping. I also don't like the way you keep hiding things from me." I opened my mouth to say something, but he squeezed me and then sighed. "However, I know you need to obey my father. I don't think anyone will hurt you while I'm by your side, but I can't help but worry. You're my light, Jolie. I can't lose you."

I kissed him deeply and thoroughly, his erection almost immediate beneath me.

"We don't have time," he growled and nipped his way down my throat.

"He isn't supposed to be here until one o'clock," I told him and ground against him.

"He said he was ten minutes away," he said and nodded at his phone.

"Then we better hurry," I said, wrapped my hands around his neck, ground my hips into his, and licked his neck. Rhys's hot button was licking his neck. One lick and he was ready to go.

Rhys carried me to the bed, stripping his clothes off as he walked. The amount of strength he possessed, to carry me with one arm, while stripping with the other, was a big turn on.

"Later, I'm going to make love to you until your legs quiver so much that they can't hold you up," he murmured in my ear and then thrust into me.

My back arched up and I screamed his name. He stretched and filled me perfectly, his strokes perfectly positioned to hit the spot deep inside of me that built my ecstasy. His strokes built the pressure until I screamed my orgasm and tightened around him with my inner muscles.

He growled and covered my nipple with his mouth, flicking his tongue across it with each pump of his hips.

"Yes!" I gasped and matched his hip movements with my own.

"You're beautiful," he told me as he loomed above me, up on his arms.

"You're perfect," I gasped as another orgasm hit.

"Your ass is perfect," he growled and flipped me over, grabbing my hips and jerking them upright so that the top of my body was down on the bed and my lower body was up on my knees.

He entered me slowly, grunting in pleasure as he did. He reached down to rub my clit with one hand while he gripped my hips with the other. His fingers moved quickly back and forth and it wasn't long before I was gripped by not one, but two orgasms.

"Yes!" Rhys yelled, slamming his hips into mine harder and faster.

His phone rang and he growled, but ignored it, leaning forward to grasp one of my breasts while he finished.

We cleaned up and got dressed, making it down to the car just as the driver was getting out.

"Sorry for making you wait," Rhys apologized, opened the door, and ushered me inside.

"No problem, Prince Rhys," the driver replied stiffly and got back into the driver's seat.

"I should have eaten more than donuts," I grumbled and rubbed my hungry stomach.

"We'll eat when we get there," he promised and slid his hand along my stomach.

"Anything I should be warned about before we do get there?" I asked him. His hand was now rubbing my arm, up and down, slowly. It was relaxing me and turning me on at the same time.

"Stay by my side the entire time," he said. "The females are just as aggressive and possessive as the males, sometimes more so. Don't turn your back on a dragon, it's rude and tells them that you think they're not a threat. Don't ask to ride any of them. Don't approach any of them without them approaching you first."

"Geez," I chuckled. "This is a super serious clan."

He nodded. "We can be."

"Eye contact?" I asked.

"Meet all of their stares. You're a princess, so we want to make sure they don't view you as weak."

"Okay."

The gates to the dragon's den were ridiculously high, stretching up so far that if I were standing in front of them, I would have to lean my head all the way back to see where it stopped. They slid open as we approached and the driver took us down the black asphalt driveway. At first, there was nothing to see. Trees and bushes, but no houses of any kind. A half mile later, we finally approached a mansion with two massive dragon statues on each side of the driveway, one wing of each stretched over to create an archway for us to drive beneath.

"Wow," I whispered as I admired the statues.

"Compliment Dad on those," he told me. "He loves bragging about the statues."

We stopped at the mansion where Emrys stood, waiting for us. I hurried out and walked up to give him a hug. "Sorry we're late."

"Did he have a fit?" he guessed as he hugged me back.

"A bit," I admitted and pulled back as Rhys approached.

"Son," Emrys greeted Rhys.

"Father," Rhys replied.

"You look well," Emrys commented.

"You're not getting out of this with compliments," Rhys told him and folded his arms across his chest. "I'm pissed."

Emrys chuckled. "Of course you are."

"Will we be eating?" Rhys asked him. "We're rather famished."

"I have snacks ready," Emrys said with a nod. "Come on, let's get this tour started." He held out his bent elbow and I slid my arm through his. "Did you know that Rhys used to hate wearing clothes. As a child, his mother and nannies used to chase him around the steps here, trying to get him back into clothes."

"He still hates clothes," I said with a chuckle.

Emrys howled with laughter. "I suppose some things don't change."

"I'm dressed now, aren't I?" Rhys mumbled.

I joined in with Emrys's laughter at that comment, but stopped when I saw the beautiful woman standing just outside the door to the mansion. She had the same dark brown hair as Rhys and the same eye shape. She was tall, willowy, and beautiful. Most of all, she's was intimidating. Something about her screamed at me to run the other way.

Emrys patted my hand, released me, and went to the woman to kiss her cheek. Some of her ferocity diminished at his touch, but not much.

"Jolie, please meet my mate and Rhys's mother, Adelaide. Adelaide please meet Jolie, Queen of Rhys's and Princess of the Four Clans."

That was a lot easier to say than to name each clan. I'd have to remember that.

"So, you're the human who thinks she's good enough for my son?" she asked, a snarl on her lips.

"Mother!" Rhys growled.

"No," I answered immediately. "I don't think I'm good enough. That's one of the reasons that I haven't taken him as a mate."

Her composure broke and she frowned in uncertainty. "What?"

"Jolie," Rhys whispered and moved closer to me.

"I'm human. I'm pretty, yes, but I'm not gorgeous. I have no abilities, aside from the ones I inherited from my guards. I have a decent paying job with some job security, but not enough for retirement. My savings is reasonable and I increase the amount every month, something I plan to continue until I retire. I'll die before Rhys, unless he does something stupid trying to protect me, which I will do everything within my power to prevent. I also have three others who want me to be their mate. I'm not an ideal mate for Rhys. Not by a long shot. However, I love Rhys. I love him more than my own life. I've given him opportunities to leave, to free himself from me, but he loves me, too. I'm not worthy of him or the others. I'm not and I know it, but I can't give them up, because I'm selfish."

Rhys turned me and tilted my chin up, tears in the corners of his eyes. "You are more than worthy of me and are the most selfless person I know."

"She's right," Adelaide said.

"Addie," Emrys chastised.

"Well, she is. It's good that you know this. Know this and understand how lucky you are to have Rhys not only give you attention, but warm your bed," she said and then went inside the mansion.

"Forgive her," Rhys whispered and kissed my cheek. "She's over-protective of me. Always has been."

"That's because you're her favorite," a baritone voice said to my right.

I turned and stared at Rhys's brother. I knew without a doubt that was who he was. They looked similar, but the symmetry of his face was slightly different than Rhys's. He was also taller and larger, something I couldn't believe without seeing for myself. His jeans looked painted on and his tank top was stretched to its limit.

"I didn't know you had siblings," I growled softly at Rhys.

"There are six of us," his brother said with a smile and then bowed. "Greetings, Princess Jolie."

"I'd reciprocate the gesture, but I'm afraid I don't know your name, since someone never said he had siblings," I grumbled. Why had he kept this from me?

"Jolie, meet my younger brother, Andras. Andras, please meet my queen and the Princess of the Four Clans, Jolie," Rhys introduced us.

I held out my hand to shake Andras's, but he pulled me forward with it and hugged me. "Handshakes are for acquaintances. You're family now, Jolie."

Rhys growled low and took a step forward, but Emrys punched his shoulder and reprimanded him. "She's perfectly safe with your siblings."

"He's not worried about me hurting her, Father. He's worried I'll steal her like I did his last girlfriend," Andras said and took a step away from me. "Don't worry, I know better than to try anything with this one. You've made it clear that you love her."

"Oh, your brother stole one of your girlfriends? I should hear this story," I said and smirked at Rhys.

He folded his arms across his chest and glared at me. "My pain brings you joy?"

"Do you wish to have her back?" I asked, smirk still in place.

His arms lowered. "No."

"So, Rhys was sixteen," Andras said, instantly launching into the story, and draped an arm across my shoulders as we walked into the mansion. This mansion was even more luxurious than the Elders'. The chandelier above us looked like it was made with real diamonds and not crystals, but I didn't want to ask for confirmation. The hallways bustled with activity, but everyone stepped aside as we walked, most bowing to us.

Would I ever get used to this?

"Rhys's girlfriend was always into me. I tried to tell him that when he first introduced her as his girlfriend, but he didn't listen. He caught her flirting with me, and me reciprocating, and lost it."

"You mean Rhys got mad at another female for flirting? So, I'm not special?" I teased and gave Rhys a fake pout.

He rolled his eyes in response.

"Ah, but for you, I think he might challenge me. For her, he just told her to have fun and left."

"And what happened to this girl?" I asked Andras, sensing they were not still together.

He shrugged. "Who knows? That was more than a decade ago."

We turned down a hallway and I stopped at the first picture I saw. It was of Rhys and seven others in dragon form posing together.

"That's the entire family," Rhys told me.

"This is your mother," I guessed pointing towards a dragon who looked just as fierce, but less muscular, and had the same piercing gaze.

"Yes. How'd you know?" Andras asked.

"She's a tad less muscular and her eyes are the same," I said.

"Which is Rhys?" Andras asked.

Immediately, I pointed to Rhys. "There."

"That's pretty impressive," Emrys said.

"Why?" I asked. "Rhys has distinct markings on his face. There are two small black spots on the edge of his snout." I reached out and touched the right and left side of Rhys's nose.

"Which is me?" Emrys asked.

I had never seen him in dragon form, but I looked at the picture and pointed at the one on the far left, the opposite side of the family from Adelaide. "Here."

"Holy shit," Andras said. "Which one is me?"

This was harder. I studied Andras' face and then looked back at the picture. I was having trouble between two of them and finally just admitted it to them. "You're either this one or this one," I said and pointed at the two on either side of Rhys. "I think you're the one on the right, but I can't be sure."

"Dad," Rhys whispered.

"I know," Emrys whispered back.

"Why do I get the feeling that most people can't tell dragons apart?" I asked them. "I mean, you're all different colors."

"What?" Rhys asked.

"All of you have slightly different mottling to your colors," I said. "It makes you all different colors despite having the same color scheme."

"That's something only dragons are able to discern," Rhys told me. He looked at his dad and asked, "Do you think it's another ability from being bonded to me?"

Emrys shook his head. "No, I've never heard of anyone outside of a dragon being able to see that much and tell dragons apart without having seen them as a dragon before."

"Well, you keep telling me I'm special," I teased Rhys to try to break some of the tension that had built between us. Just one more thing to mark down as odd about me.

"Come, let's eat," Emrys said and led the way.

"Am I in trouble?" I asked Rhys softly.

He chuckled and linked hands with me. "No, my Queen."

"I feel like you've replaced 'Love' with 'Queen' just because you know it makes me uncomfortable," I mumbled.

"I would never do such a thing, my Queen," he replied and kissed my cheek.

"Liar."

"You're the liar," he shot back in a high-pitched tone.

I rolled my eyes at him. "Real mature."

"I'm rubber and you're glue—" he said and was cut off by Andras's laugh.

"You two are adorable," Andras said.

I looked at the other pictures, all family pictures, and was surprised that there were none of them as children. Did they only leave up the newest pictures? Why not leave up one from each decade?

The dining room we entered was unlike any I had seen before. There was a large table on one side and couches on the other side situated in front of a giant fireplace, the mantle at least six feet tall. The table had silver settings and a full feast.

"Didn't he say he had snacks for us? This is a feast," I whispered as softly as possible to Rhys.

"This is a snack for us," he told me. "You forget how much I eat alone. Now, picture nine of us plus you here. How much food do you think we need for us to have even a snack's worth?"

That did make sense. The Others ate a ton of food, and ever since I started using their powers, I had begun eating a ton as well. Nico said it was necessary to keep the magic reserve in our body. That they required a lot of fuel to keep the storage going. I asked if starvation would cause the reserves to shrink and he nodded.

"Please, sit," Emrys said and pulled out a chair for me next to his at the head of the table. I sat and he pushed me in before taking his place. Rhys sat next to me and Andras sat across from me.

"Food!" Emrys bellowed, the silverware and plates shaking briefly from the rumble that felt like an earthquake and tornado approaching at the same time.

"Coming!" a few different voices yelled. Soon, four males and one female came into the room and took seats at the table. The female was a teenager, or very early adult. One of the males was also a teenager, and the other two ranged between Rhys and the teenagers. They were all wearing sweatpants and tank tops, which made me wonder if they had been training. The female and one of the males looked like Rhys and Andras, but the other two looked much more like their mother.

"Oh, a guest!" the teenage boy said happily. "I didn't know we were having a guest!"

"Quiet," Emrys ordered him.

The boy didn't say anything, but he was still smiling wide and practically bouncing in his chair.

"Swear an oath of silence," Emrys ordered them.

The four newcomers gasped and looked at each other as well as Rhys and Andras.

"Really?" the female teenager asked. She swept her long black, curled hair over her shoulder and studied me. "Is this human pregnant with one of these idiots' kids?"

I laughed hard, getting a disapproving look from Andras. "I like her already," I told Rhys.

He smirked. "I knew you would. You two are similar in several ways."

"Who is she?" one of the middle males asked.

"Obey!" Emrys snapped angrily, his power shooting through the table and making me gasp in pain for a brief moment as it went through me.

"Sorry," Rhys apologized quickly. "I didn't realize he was going to do that or I would have shielded you."

"It's fine," I whispered and rubbed my chest.

"We swear an oath of silence on all things to be said henceforth. Our tongues shall not work to reveal the secrets divulged and our hands will fail should we try to bypass words," all of his siblings said as one.

"I'm sorry, Jolie," Emrys apologized after giving his children one more hard stare. "I forgot that you would be affected by my powers."

"I'm fine," I assured him. "It just stung a bit."

"Father," the female whispered, "we swore."

"Jolie, I'd like you to meet the rest of my children. The impatient female is Rhian. She is the youngest. The fidgeting teenage male is Gavin. He is one year older than Rhian. To Rhian's right is Mawrth and to his right is Brenin. Children, this is Jolie. Jolie is the Princess of the Four Clans and Rhys's Queen."

"Queen!" Rhian gasped. "Why? What? She's *human!*"

"Rhian!" Rhys growled. "Show some decorum. Humans are not less than us."

"When did this happen?" Brenin asked calmly. His eyes were cool and calculating, measuring me in a way that was slightly unnerving. Whatever weaknesses I had, I was certain he could see them all.

"At the meeting when she returned the necklace to us," Rhys answered.

"She's also the other three's queen, isn't she?" Gavin asked, his smile still in place. Was he like Fox and perpetually happy?

"Yes," Emrys replied before Rhys could.

"Are you mates?" Mawrth asked.

"Ew," Rhian whispered.

"No," I answered.

"Not yet," Rhys mumbled under his breath.

"Why is she here?" Mawrth asked.

"I invited her so that she could come see our clan and learn more about us. Also, because I want her to show you something," Emrys told them.

"Dad," Rhys groaned.

"They need to know everything about our clan that they can," Emrys said and I knew that was his way of telling Rhys the discussion was over.

"Let's eat," Emrys said. "Jolie will answer your questions after she eats."

Rhys took my plate and piled it high with food and his siblings watched in silence. As soon as he set my plate down, everyone began scrambling for the food at the same time. Apparently, it was common practice for them to allow guests to get food first. I was perfectly fine with that. The food looked amazing and smelled even better. Roast, mashed potatoes, gravy, rolls, green beans, brussel sprouts, tri-tip, and some kind of fish were all on my plate.

My stomach demanded it be filled with the food, which turned out to taste just as amazing as it smelled. When I scraped the last food off my plate, Rhys took it and added another roll, green beans, and some more potatoes and gravy. He had been doing things like this a lot recently, knowing what I wanted without me saying it. Obviously, it was the bond, but it felt incredibly one sided since I never knew what he wanted unless it was poking me. Heh.

He set the plate down and then chuckled. "I did it again, didn't I?" he asked.

"Yes," I said and patted his hand. "Thank you."

"It's not a conscious decision," he said.

"I know."

I ate my food, enjoying the buttery goodness of the roll slowly.

"She eats a lot for a human," Rhian muttered.

"You'll see why," Emrys told her. "Make sure you drink that glass of water," he told me.

I obeyed, chugging the entire glass before wiping my mouth and smiling at him. "Thank you. That was delicious."

"I'm glad you liked it. Now, let's go outside," he said and stood. Rhys pulled out my chair, but Emrys took my arm before he could.

"Even my own father," Rhys said with a sigh.

Andras laughed and patted him on the back.

We went out a door that I had not seen in the corner of the living room. It led to a rose garden, and just beyond that, a huge fighting arena. A fenced in area large enough for two fully shifted dragons to fight.

"Clear the area!" Emrys ordered everyone.

This time, the order didn't touch me.

"Thanks," I whispered, not sure if it was him or Rhys.

"I can direct it if I think about it," Emrys told me.

"That's handy," I said.

"Especially when you have this many children," he grumbled.

"How do you feel?" Rhys asked me.

"I feel great. Why?"

"He wants you to shift," Rhys said, meaning his father wanted me to shift forms.

"Dragon or wolf?" I asked.

"You can shift forms?" Andras asked.

Emrys's orders had been carried out and only the family and I were at the arena now. "Please, show them," he requested.

Rhys picked me up and jumped over the arena fence in one leap, landing on bent knees on the other side. He set me down and leaned back against the fence.

I walked farther away from him, still not sure of my exact size, and then focused on Rhys through our bond. The bond I had, forked off four different ways, all connected to my heart. I followed the line to Rhys and the magic he carried, which was wild, like Deryn's, but more fierce, and with a lot more fire.

I closed my eyes and let the change come. When I had finished shifting, I opened my eyes and Rhys walked to me. I lowered my head and he set his hand on my snout. "You're gorgeous," he whispered and stroked his hand from my nostril, up over my eye, down my neck, and stopped at my shoulder.

"Holy shit!" Rhian yelled. "She turned into one of us!"

"I've never seen scales that color before," Andras commented. "Can I come in?"

I thought he was asking me, but it was Rhys who nodded. "Yes, you are all welcome to come."

Emrys jumped in first and walked to me, staring into my eyes. "Even her eyes are different. They're very similar to yours though, Rhys."

"How is this possible?" Mawrth asked. "She smells like a human."

"She is a human," Rhys explained. "Since she is human, when we made her our queen, she joined our bond instead of us making a true Queen's bond with her. This allowed her the ability to access our powers."

"Can she fly?" Rhian asked.

"She can, but she isn't fond of it, yet," Rhys said with a smirk.

"Can she breathe fire?" Gavin asked.

I huffed smoke out of my nostrils and Rhys chuckled. "Yes, she can."

"You can shift back," Emrys told me.

I shifted back and then covered my body in scales. "I can also do this, and this." This time, I half shifted, a warrior's shift. I enjoyed Rhys's equally surprised face, a replica of his siblings'.

"I didn't know you could do this," Emrys said and poked at my scales.

"Neither did I," Rhys growled at me.

I let my body revert and exhaled, tired from using so much energy. "It's a lot harder to hold," I told them.

"When did you discover you could do this?" Rhys asked.

"Last night," I admitted. "On accident."

"When the boss killed you the third time we tried to beat the raid, right?" he asked.

I nodded. How had he known that? I mean, I know I had cussed up a storm on the mic.

"I felt your anger and thought I felt you more distinctly in our bond, but wasn't sure," he admitted.

"I can't even do that," Brenin grumbled.

"Can you shift into the wolf warrior form?" Rhian asked.

I nodded. "I can, but I used up a lot of my energy taking the dragon warrior form just now. I need at least five minutes to recover."

"You don't need to shift anymore," Emrys told me.

"So, if one of us takes a human Queen, they'll have our abilities," Brenin said while looking at Emrys.

Emrys nodded. "Yes."

"So, this was to show us, so that we don't make the same mistake as Rhys, right?" Mawrth asked.

"No, this is just to let you know this is possible," Emrys said with a soft sigh. "I swear I raised them to be polite children, Jolie. I blame their mother."

"This was not a mistake," Rhys said.

"Sort of," I whispered under my breath while looking up at the sky.

Rhys growled, but didn't rise to my bait.

"They are very cynical," Emrys said. "It is good to understand the negative in everything, or the possible negatives, so you are prepared for all circumstances. However, they should also understand that some things are shown so they understand what happens, not in a negative way."

"It's okay," I told him and smiled at everyone. "I don't take offense."

"It doesn't excuse them from being rude," Rhys growled at them.

"We're sorry," all of the younger siblings said.

"Come on, let's show her the rest of our den," Andras suggested.

"Why did we have to swear an oath of silence?" Rhian asked.

"Because it is not public knowledge that Rhys and the other three princes have a queen. We are keeping it quiet. We don't want the media finding out," Emrys told them. "So, you are forbidden from telling anyone. As far as anyone knows, she is simply the Princess of the Four Clans. Understood?"

"Yes, Father," all of Rhys's siblings said.

CHAPTER 2

We ended up flying to the next part of the den, which was fun because I got to ride on Rhys's back and look at everything as we flew. The den was huge—hundreds, maybe thousands, of acres in size. They had their own city within the city of Jinla. Amazing.

There was a large building in the very center, which Rhys said was like their city hall where the family heard disputes and prosecuted those accused of crimes. Each clan was allowed their own legal system, but if the crimes were serious enough and happened in the human city they turned the dragon over to the human courts. Rhys said that it had only happened a few times in fifty years.

There were several apartment complexes, housing tracks, and a few other houses far out in the wilderness areas. They raised their own animals for food and grew their own crops, too. That explained the real reason he had never been to a human grocery store before.

I still needed to take them on trips to all of the human places I discovered they had never experienced. It was important for them to understand humans, even if I hadn't met them. Even though they had gone to a grocery store already, I needed to show them the joy of grocery stores with bulk food areas. The second place I wanted to take them was the movie theater, though I hadn't decided between the regular theater and the drive-in theater. I knew that they would get a kick out of both of them. Third was the zoo. We just had to be sure to keep Rhys and Deryn a distance away from the animals so that they didn't frighten them.

We landed in the center of their market area. There were vendors selling produce, meats, seafood, crafts, jewelry, and some cooking various foods and treats.

"You have to try the sweet bread," Gavin said and jogged towards one of the vendors selling pastries.

"It's a whole other world here," I whispered to Rhys.

"Yes. There are many who never go out into Jinla," he whispered back to me.

"So, they never meet anyone outside of dragons?" I asked. That didn't seem like a great way to raise children, never introducing them to the other beings that were out there. Yes, there was evil, but there was also so much to learn from the other races.

"We encourage them to venture beyond our gates, even offer field trips for those schooled here, but there are many who choose to stay here," Emrys told me. "We discuss all the other races and ensure they understand that there are good and evil in all races and no one race is all evil."

"Except vampires," I whispered to myself.

Rhys put his arms around me and hugged me into his chest. "I'm sorry," he whispered.

"Don't be sorry. You saved me from them multiple times," I mumbled into his chest and wiped my tears on his shirt.

"Here," Gavin said, pulling me out of my reverie.

I stepped back from Rhys, reminding myself that we were supposed to be keeping our relationship secret. "What's this?" I asked and accepted the pastry Gavin held out to me.

"Take a bite," Gavin encouraged me.

Rhys nodded that it was safe.

I took a bite and moaned. "This is amazing."

Gavin, Emrys, and Rhys smiled at my reaction.

"I told you," Gavin said with a wide smile and took a huge bite of his.

"I guess I'll need to start ordering these for delivery," Rhys said.

"Lots," I replied and finished eating the one Gavin had given me.

"Oh, let's try the meat stick next!" Gavin said and started to rush off, but looked back at me expectantly.

I squeezed Rhys's forearm, then ran with Gavin to get in line for the next vendor.

"I don't have any cash," I told Gavin.

"Don't worry," he assured me. "I've got money."

It was strange to see Gavin and think that Rhys may have been like him as a teenager. Rhys had been raised in this very area.

"What's your favorite thing to do in the den?" I asked Gavin.

"The festivals," he answered immediately. "They're full of fun and action. You should come to our next one! Our fall festival is in just a few weeks. You would enjoy it, I know you would. If my eldest brother won't bring you, just talk to Dad. I'm sure he'll let you come. I'll show you around if Rhys isn't here," he offered.

"That is a very generous offer," I said with a smile.

"Well, I can tell that my brother cares for you. That must mean you are a special female. He never really showed affection for other females. But, it's like he's drawn to you. Like magnets."

That was partly due to our bond. One of the reasons I considered breaking the bond was to see if they really were in love with me and drawn to me because of me and not the bond.

"I'm pretty drawn to your brother, too," I whispered and glanced at Rhys who was watching me with a smirk on his face while Emrys talked to him.

The line finally moved and we were at the front. Gavin ordered for me and then handed me one of the sticks that had a few different types of meat on it, with some with sauce dribbled on them.

"Go on," he encouraged.

I tried a bite from each of the meats and smiled at him. "These are great!"

His smile widened and his chest puffed out a bit. "I told you."

"Can we go look at the vendors?" I asked. "Christmas is coming up and I think I saw something that would work great for one of my friends."

"Sure," Gavin said and led the way. People moved out of his way without him even saying anything, which made it much easier for me to get through them. Rhys caught up to us and walked behind me.

"What's up?" I asked him, glancing back.

"Nothing. I just wanted to walk with you. If that's alright?"

I reached out and squeezed his hand. "Great." A few females glared at my hand touching Rhys, so I lowered it and faced Gavin again, as he made his way to the first vendor who sold handcrafted items.

"Good afternoon, Princes," the woman behind the table greeted them. She looked to be in her late sixties, but that could mean she was two hundred years old since she was a shifter. "And greetings to their friend."

"Hello, Estella," Rhys said and smiled at her. She picked up a bag that had some tissue paper in it and handed it to Rhys. "Is this my full order?" he asked, peeking into the bag.

She nodded. "Yes. I made sure to follow your guidelines and specifications exactly."

He handed her some money and bowed his head respectfully to her. "Thank you."

"Thank you, for your patronage."

The items she sold were mostly knitted and crocheted beanies and gloves. I eyed one of the knitted scarves, but reminded myself that I was not supposed to be here buying things for me.

"Your items are lovely," I told her with a warm smile.

She smiled in return. "Thank you."

We moved on to the next booth with a younger man selling daggers. I picked up one of the smaller, thinner daggers and admired the design etched into it. "This is gorgeous," I whispered and showed it to Rhys.

"Rhys," the man greeted him.

Rhys nodded at him. "Afternoon, Felix."

"Who have you brought to my booth? You rarely have visitors," Felix said with an arched eyebrow.

"Jolie, this is Felix. Felix, this is Jolie, Princess of the Four Clans."

Felix's eyes widened and he dropped his head in a bow. "Apologies, I didn't know—"

"Please, don't treat me any differently than you do Rhys," I said quickly. "Though, I would like to know how much this dagger is."

"Fifty," Felix said right away.

"What are you going to do with that dagger?" Rhys asked me.

"It's not for me. I was thinking it would make a good present for Fox," I admitted to him.

Rhys smiled. "It would make a good present for him."

"Can you bring me back tomorrow?" I asked Rhys. "I didn't bring cash with me, since I didn't realize I would be shopping."

"You can pay me back when we get home," Rhys offered and handed Felix money. Felix took the dagger from me and wrapped it up, put it into a wooden box, and then put that into a small brown paper bag.

"Thank you. This is just what I was looking for, for him," I told Felix.

He bowed his head. "I'm glad to have been of service."

"I'll just make you a tab and you can pay me back or work it off," Rhys whispered so softly into my ear that I almost didn't hear him.

I gaped at him, shocked that he would flirt with me to that magnitude in the den...in public. "You're shameless."

He winked. "I thought you knew that by now."

"What did you say to make her blush like that?" Gavin asked.

"Nothing," I gasped and hurried to the next vendor.

Rhys picked up a few more orders from vendors we went to, and I found a few more Christmas presents for the other guys. I still had no idea what I was going to get Rhys. Honestly, if I hadn't known that the guys would be happy with whatever I got them, I would have zero idea what to get them. What do you get four rich princes who can purchase whatever they want?

Rhys bought a basket of strawberries and we shared them as we perused more vendors. One jewelry vendor in particular caught my eye and I was mesmerized by the rings she had. Not the rings for women though, but the rings for the men. They were made of a gorgeous, dark metal that shone in the sun.

"Thinking of proposing to someone?" the vendor, a man who looked about thirty, asked me.

"No," I said quickly, not glancing at Rhys. "I just find these incredibly beautiful."

"Thank you," he said. "I make them myself from a type of metal that will never break and so, you can't get them resized ever. You have to make certain that the ring you buy is in the correct size."

"How much are they?" I asked out of sheer curiosity.

"Hello, Paul," Rhys greeted the vendor. "What's she hounding you about over here?"

"Nothing," I replied quickly. "Just telling him how much I admire his work. The jewelry is gorgeous."

Rhys nodded. "He has some of the best jewelry."

"Can you get me something to drink?" I asked Rhys. "I'm really thirsty after all of that food."

He nodded and went towards one of the food vendors who had bottles of water.

"Four hundred per ring," Paul whispered quickly to me. "However, since you're a friend of the Prince's, I will drop the price to three hundred."

"They're gorgeous, but I'm not sure if they're going to work for what I have in mind. Do you have a website or something?" I asked and glanced quickly back to see Rhys heading our way.

"Here's my business card. It has my website, email address, and phone number," Paul said softly. Then, louder, he said, "I hope to see you again soon, miss. Have a wonderful day."

I tucked the card into the bag of my other presents and smiled at him. "Thank you."

Rhys handed me my water and I took a huge drink of it, glad I had asked him to get me some because I truly was thirsty after eating a bunch of sweets and meat.

"I still haven't decided what to get you for Christmas," Rhys told me as we headed toward Emrys, who was waiting on the outskirts of the market area.

"You don't have to get me anything. I've got all I want at home," I said and glanced at him with a smirk.

"I'm going to get you a present. I'm just trying to figure out what is the best gift to give you," he said with a smile and put a hand on my back as he guided me around a small crowd in front of a vendor.

"Something under a hundred dollars," I muttered.

He laughed loudly, his head thrown back, and eyes closed for a moment. "That's hilarious."

I put my hands on my hips and glared at him. "What is so funny?"

"There's no way that you're going to keep us from spending what we want on you. I know the amounts some of the others have spent already, and let's just say that your number is miniscule."

"It's not fair," I whispered. "I don't have a lot of money to spend on you guys."

"We don't need anything."

"Neither do I," I growled and faced him.

"She's talking back to Prince Rhys," someone said in the crowd.

"Does she not know who he is?" another person asked.

"I'm sorry," I whispered to Rhys and walked towards Emrys, feeling like an idiot for forgetting that we were in his clan's home, with tons of people watching our every move. I shouldn't speak to him like I did at home.

Rhys grabbed my arm, spun me around to face him, dipped me to the side, and kissed me deeply. There were gasps, shocked murmurs, and some laughs.

When he pulled back and set me upright, I stared at him in disbelief. "Why did you do that?" I whispered softly.

"I just felt like kissing my girlfriend," he told me and took my hand in his.

Girlfriend? Royalty didn't usually have girlfriends, especially not Other royalty.

"Girlfriend?" someone asked.

Rhys tugged on our joined hands and I stumbled after him, looking at Emrys in shock and worry.

"That's one way to go with things," Emrys whispered and chuckled. "Now, they will just think that you're taking the human route for your relationship, since she's human. And it will allow you to touch her more in public. Pretty smart, kid."

"I have my moments," Rhys replied and stroked his thumb across the back of my hand.

"I don't understand what happened," I whispered. "You guys don't do girlfriends."

"Well, we *do* girlfriends, but not like you're talking about," Rhys teased.

"No, we generally don't, but Rhys has never done things like the majority of us," Andras said. "Normally after we graduate, we don't have girlfriends any longer. Girlfriends are more of a teenage experience for us, since we aren't allowed to have sex until after we graduate. But, since Rhys said you're his girlfriend now, it will spread around the clan and you won't have potential suitors coming after you. Or females, who want Rhys, coming after you for your head."

"I thought we were keeping our relationship secret?" I asked Rhys and glanced at Emrys.

"We were, but I am tired of not being able to touch you. This was an easy way around all of that," Rhys explained and shrugged his shoulders. "Plus, aren't you my girlfriend?"

"I guess," I whispered. "I hadn't really thought about it in those terms."

"Well, now you have," he said with a grin.

"Why didn't you think of it before?" I asked. "It seems like such a simple solution."

"I'm not perfect," he said. "No matter how many times you tell me I am."

"I meant your body was perfect, not you," I teased and spun away from him with Andras and Emrys laughing behind me.

Rhys followed me, his presence causing the hairs on the back of my neck to rise since there was a predator stalking me now.

"Still hungry?" Gavin asked from the line he was standing in.

"What are you getting?" I asked him, ignoring Rhys.

"Sweet bread," he said and licked his lips.

"I want two," I said and held up two fingers.

"I'll pay," Rhys told Gavin. "She'll eat your savings dry."

"Did you just insinuate that I'm fat?" I asked and spun to face him.

He startled me by grabbing me and pulling me against him, his face inches from mine. "You know I didn't, you brat."

"You're in so much trouble when we get home," I whispered to him, trying very hard to swallow my arousal and failing miserably.

He chuckled, the deep sound vibrated through my body and traveled south to cause a warmth I didn't want to experience with his teenage brother right next to us. "You're the one who is in trouble," he told me and nipped the tip of my nose.

"Ouch," I grumbled and rubbed my nose as I pushed away from him. Arousal gone.

"Can I get a dozen breads now and two dozen to go?" Rhys ordered.

"Certainly, Prince Rhys," the baker replied.

"Are you staying for dinner?" Gavin asked.

I looked at Rhys. "I don't know. Are we?"

"No, we have plans tonight," Rhys told Gavin.

"We do?" I asked, not remembering us making plans.

"We're going out with the guys tonight," he informed me. "Didn't Fox tell you?"

He might have told me, but I was most likely a few drinks deep when he did. "I think he told me something around the middle of the raid, but I was drinking by then and..."

"Ah, you were drunk," Rhys chuckled.

"She plays video games?" Gavin asked, his mouth popped open.

"More than I do," Rhys said.

"That's so hot!" Gavin exclaimed.

"Little brother, you need to work on your inappropriate comments," Andras chastised him and gently tapped the back of his head.

"I'm right," Gavin told him. "You know I am. Finding a girl who plays games instead of trying to get you off of them is super rare."

"She's a rarity, alright," Rhys said and winked at me.

"Here you go," the baker said and held out a bag with the two dozen he had ordered to go and a box with the one dozen for now.

I opened the one dozen and took three before handing the box to Gavin. Rhys snagged the rolls from me and I pouted at him. "Hey!"

He held them up over his head, way too high for me to be able to reach. "You have to pay for these," he said and walked back towards his father.

"What price?" I asked and tried to jump up and grab his arm to force it down, but he easily dodged my attempt.

He turned and bent so that his face was level with mine. "One kiss."

"If I must," I said with a dramatic sigh. I pecked him on the cheek and managed to grab one of the rolls from him and run behind Emrys to eat it.

"Cheater," Rhys said, but he was smiling wide and his family was amused as well. Before I could respond, Rhys shoved both of the rolls in his mouth and chewed them up.

"Those were mine!" I gaped at him.

He shrugged. "Maybe next time you'll pay the toll."

"I'm going to come back without you one of these days and buy them. Then you won't be able to stop me," I threatened him.

"I'll keep her company when she comes," Andras said and draped an arm across my shoulders. "She'll be perfectly safe."

Rhys growled and his eyes shifted to his dragon's eyes.

"Rhys," Emrys growled a warning at him.

"And I thought Deryn was bad," I grumbled.

Andras hadn't moved, more accurately, he had frozen at Rhys's growl.

"Sounds like we've got a plan," I said with a wide smile. "I'll come back, Andras will keep me safe, and I'll eat all the sweet bread I can without making myself sick."

Rhys blinked twice and his eyes reverted. "Sorry."

"When do we have to leave today?" I asked Rhys, hoping the subject change would keep him from getting angry about Andras *still* touching me.

Rhys looked at his phone and said, "We should probably head back now."

"Already?" I sighed. I stood up on my tiptoes and kissed Andras's cheek. "Thanks for an entertaining day."

His mouth opened for a moment, but he quickly recovered and smiled. "Come back whenever you want."

I hugged Emrys. "Thanks for forcing his hand, so I could visit. I had a lot of fun learning about your clan today."

"I'd like you to come back and train with us," he told me. "There's a lot of skills we can teach you that Rhys can't show you when the others are around."

That sounded slightly terrifying.

"Okay."

"You're serious?" Rhian asked, appearing out of thin air.

"Rhian, what have we discussed about you questioning me?" Emrys asked her.

"I'm not questioning you, Father. I'm questioning that you're actually going to teach her family secrets. She's not his mate."

"Rhian, come here," Rhys ordered her.

I thought she might argue, but she followed him as they walked away from the crowds to a secluded area that was still within our sight. She had her arms folded across her chest defiantly, but as Rhys spoke to her, she slowly lowered them. He didn't appear to be yelling at her or angry, since his face was relaxed and he kept occasionally smirking. She glanced at me and then looked back at him and nodded once. I thought she would come back, but instead she shifted and flew away.

"What was that about?" Andras asked Rhys.

"Just some brother sister heart to heart," he told us. "You ready to go?" he asked me.

I nodded.

"If he tries to keep you away again, just text me and I'll send a team in to steal you," Emrys called after me.

"Thanks!" I called back and waved to him.

Rhys sighed and handed the boxes of bread to me. "You fit in way too well here."

"You should be happy that your family likes me so much. Well, not your mom." It actually stung quite a bit that she seemed to hate me, even after I had opened up to her.

"She'll learn to love you. She's very protective of me."

He shifted and we flew back to the apartment instead of taking a car from the mansion. I was going to ask him why, but relaxed on his back and watched the city fly by beneath us. Millions of people lived here with different lives and different circumstances. What would the guys be doing if I hadn't moved here?

The wind pressing against me was cold, and I was glad I had worn a jacket, but it wasn't helping my face any. Rhys's body beneath me grew warmer and I lay down on my stomach, pressing my cheek to his warm scales.

"Thank you," I called as loudly as I could. A deep rumble beneath my cheek was his response. He landed on the roof of the apartment building and I slid down his foreleg, landing on my feet with the boxes still safely in my arms.

"That was fun," I told him as I waited for him to shift back. "I think they'd be fun to be around, once they aren't so negative."

"They're always negative," Rhys said and tried to grab the boxes.

I spun away from him with a smirk. "No. You have to pay the fee."

He caught my body with his arms, caging me in against his body. "Okay."

I tilted my head back and he brushed his lips across mine gently.

After releasing me, he took the boxes I offered, opened the door, and started down the stairs to the second floor toward my apartment.

"Jolie," Rhys called.

I stopped in front of the door that opened to my floor. "Huh?"

He set the boxes down and asked, "Did you mean what you said to my mother?"

I nodded.

"Are you still considering breaking the bond?"

His fists were clenched, and he stared into my eyes with a frightening intensity.

I turned and took his hands in both of mine. "I know I'm not worthy of you four. I know this, but I am selfish. I don't want to give you up. The thought occasionally flitters across my mind, but I've decided that I will not break the bond. I love you and hurting you by breaking the bond is not something I want to do. To you or to me."

"How can I show you that you are worthy of us? What do I need to do to prove that to you?" he asked. Gently, he stroked his knuckles down my cheek.

"Self-esteem isn't usually an issue for me," I admitted to him. "I like to think that I am practical about how I look. But, when it comes to being the mate of not just one prince, but four? I'm just a weird human girl who plays games too much. That doesn't sound like someone fit to be your mate."

"What should my mate be like?" he asked.

"Strong. Fierce. Powerful. Someone who will produce heirs for you. I don't know if I want children. And if I do decide to have children, I'm going to have to worry about there being four of you who need heirs."

"Heirs aren't a deal breaker," he told me.

"It's still something to consider. Right now, it might not be a deal breaker, but what about in five years or—"

"I love you. I want you at my side for the rest of my life. I want you as my life partner."

"Well, the rest of my life. You all live much longer than me. That's the other issue. If we become mates, my death is going to be so much more painful and—"

He stepped back from me and sighed. "I really wish you wouldn't talk about your death like that."

"Like what?"

"Like it is a sure thing."

"Everyone dies, Rhys."

"Yes, but you make it sound like you're going to die soon."

"I could. You know what my life has been like. I'm always in danger."

He picked up the boxes and opened the door for me. "You are a handful."

I expected to find at least one of the others in my apartment, but it was empty. "Where is everyone?" I asked Rhys.

He set the boxes on my counter and I quickly stole two more pieces of bread while he dialed one of their numbers. He held the phone up to his ear for a bit and then looked at it strangely before dialing another number. He repeated the process again.

"They're not answering. That's not like them."

"Do you think something's happened?" I asked nervously.

"Yes, but the issue is figuring out what has happened," he whispered and then began furiously typing on his phone. After a minute of silence, he said, "Oh, shit."

"What is it?"

"There's a monster attacking the city. They're out there trying to stop it." He showed me a photo of the three of them standing in front of what looked like a huge ogre with tusks as big as their bodies.

"We need to go help them!" I yelled and moved towards the door.

"You're not doing anything. We can't risk you getting hurt," he told me.

"I'm not staying here. If you try to leave me behind, I will just follow you at a distance."

Our defiant stares met and I could practically see sparks between us.

"Fine, but you have to promise to use your scales and shield. And stay out of the way," he ordered me.

I nodded. "Yes, sir."

He growled, and we hurried back to the roof where he shifted and we flew to the park. Rhys set me down a few blocks away, but still within eyesight of the fight. I stood against a building and set scales over my heart and the back of my head and formed a shield like Nico had taught me.

Deryn was in warrior form and I watched in disbelief as he used his claws to crawl up the back of the giant ogre and began tearing into his back. The ogre bellowed and tried to grab Deryn, but he dodged the ogre's attempted grabs easily.

Nico fired a few different spells at the ogre, making it drop to one knee. Fox used his sword to cut at the ogre, but I could tell that the sword wasn't doing much damage, despite Fox's skill.

Rhys dropped from the sky in his dragon form and wrapped his mouth around the ogre's throat. The ogre yowled and tried to pry Rhys's mouth open, but his sharp teeth dug in. The other three increased their work, taking advantage of Rhys's immobilization of the ogre.

A small child wandered by me, mesmerized by the fight and out into the street. I ran out to the child as her mother screamed and grabbed her. I glanced up and screamed at the hell hound's snout right in front of my face.

What was a hell hound doing here? They were only able to come to this side with a demon's summoning, but I didn't see any demons around.

Deryn slammed into the side of the hell hound and sent it flying into the side of the building where I had been. I wrapped my body protectively around the child and then picked her up.

"Hey, beautiful," Deryn said, then ran to continue fighting the hell hound, which was definitely not down yet.

"Don't get hurt!" I ordered him.

"Yes, my queen!" he called back and punched the hell hound on his nose. The hell hound made a terrible, high-pitched squeal of pain, sounding just like a dog when it's hurt.

The child's mother ran to me and I dropped my shield so she could take her. "Thank you!" she yelled and hugged her child to her. "Thank you, so much."

"Jolie!" Nico screamed at me.

I spun around and had just enough time to put up the shield around the mother, child, and me before the ogre slammed into it with his fists, trying to squash us.

"Fuck you!" I screamed at him.

"Let us out!" the mother screamed.

"I'm protecting you, you moron," I growled at her and backed up slowly, keeping her within my shield as we moved towards the building's entrance. Once there, I dropped my shield so she could carry her child inside to safety.

The ogre grabbed me in his giant hand and screamed in my face.

"Jolie!" Nico yelled.

"I'm fine!" I yelled back and stared into the ogre's eyes. "Put. Me. Down."

The ogre snarled at me and tried to tighten his grip around my body, but I'd changed everything below my neck to scales. He looked confused a moment and then threw me as hard as he could towards the park.

"Rhys! Incoming!" Deryn yelled and ran slightly behind me.

Rhys shifted just in time to catch me and wrapped his body around mine, so that when we landed, I landed on top of him. We slid several feet and then he released me.

"You okay?" I asked him.

"I told you, you should have stayed home."

"That child would have been killed!" I yelled at him.

"Now is not the time!" Nico reminded us, his staff glowing as we faced the ogre, the hell hound who had tried to attack me, and two goblins.

"What the hell is going on?" I demanded.

"A portal was opened to the other realm," Nico said. "I've been trying to close it, but it's taking me a while."

"Can I help?" I asked him.

"Come touch me," he ordered me.

"This is not the time for that," Rhys growled at him.

"Jolie," Nico grunted.

I rushed to his side and placed my hands on his bare forearms. Our connection opened and suddenly, I felt Nico use the connection to take magic from me. I gasped in shock and my grip tightened on his arm.

"Protect them!" Rhys ordered Deryn and Fox.

"You don't have to tell us," Deryn growled and punched the hell hound back.

"Almost there," Nico whispered and I could see it. It was a faint, shimmering oval in the air in front of us. It looked like a tear, but on the other side, I could see fire and several dark bodies moving. How many more would come if we didn't close the portal?

"Nico," I whispered, feeling lightheaded.

"Almost," he grunted.

I would pass out if I let him keep taking my power. I had to do something.

The necklace! I took one hand from Nico's arm and wrapped it around the necklace. Instantly, the power poured through me and into Nico. It felt like lava pouring through my veins, and I would have screamed if I had been able to breathe. His back arched and he gasped, but quickly recovered and used the power to close the portal. Once it was closed, I dropped my hand, breaking contact with Nico, and fell in the grass onto my butt.

"Shit, that hurt," I growled.

"Not out of hot water yet," Rhys growled.

I turned my head and watched Deryn and Rhys pummeling the ogre with their fists, pushing it further and further away from me.

"I got this," Nico said, his eyes glowed with power and his feet floated above the ground. He pointed his staff at the ogre and it disintegrated instantly.

"What the—" Rhys gaped.

"Did he just—" Deryn asked.

"Yeah," Rhys replied.

Fox picked me up and carried me away from the park and towards our building. "Are you okay?" he asked me

"Tired," I whispered and leaned my head against his shoulder. "Siphoning the magic from the necklace to Nico hurt. A lot."

"Are you still in pain?"

"No."

"How was your day at the dragon's den?" he asked.

"No. No. You had a giant ogre attacking you. You tell me what happened first."

"Not much to tell," he admitted. "We were walking home from Deryn's pizza parlor and the ogre and hound started attacking people. We kept them from hurting anyone, but we weren't really making any headway until you and Rhys came."

"His mom doesn't like me," I told Fox softly.

He kissed the top of my head. "She hates everyone, especially if they have contact with her precious baby, Rhys. She's always favored him and in her opinion, everyone is worthless and has no business talking to him."

"Emrys had me show them that I could shift into a dragon and his family thought it was to explain the consequences of the mistake Rhys had made, so that they wouldn't repeat the mistake."

I hadn't realized how much their reactions had hurt my feelings until talking to Fox. He was great at listening and I could really open up to him about anything.

"You're not a mistake," he told me firmly. "I'm sure Rhys already told you that his family is super negative in general."

"Gavin was the only one who liked me."

"I'm sure Andras liked you, too," Fox replied.

I looked up and saw his smirk. "Rhys went all 'Deryn' on him for draping his arm across my shoulders and saying he would protect me if I visited without Rhys."

"'Went all 'Deryn?'" Deryn asked. "Why is my name being used as a verb now?"

"Because you were the first one to get super jealous," I explained.

"I have every reason to get jealous," Rhys said, the rest of them having caught up to us at some point.

"No, you don't."

"If I didn't set the ground rules now, he would be doing everything in his power to steal you from us," Rhys assured me.

"Oh, yes. Because I'm such a prize," I said and rolled my eyes. "You're all so ridiculous."

"He's most likely right," Fox said.

"Hey, you're supposed to be the neutral party here," I grumbled.

"Right. Sorry. So, what else happened?"

"I ate a ton of food. I bought a few presents. And, Rhys announced me as his girlfriend."

Fox stopped walking so abruptly, I almost fell out of his arms, but he held on to me. "You did what?" he asked and spun around to face Rhys who was looking rather sheepish at the moment.

"Well, it just sort of happened. I wasn't planning it or anything," Rhys admitted.

"You announced her as your girlfriend?" Nico asked.

Rhys nodded.

"You asshole," he growled.

"What's wrong?" I asked them.

"We can't all claim you as our girlfriend," Nico informed me. "So, right now the clan, and whoever they tell, thinks you're just his girlfriend."

"Which means, that we aren't supposed to touch you as freely as we usually do," Fox said and set me on my feet with a scowl at Rhys.

"I'm sorry. She was walking with my brothers and I wanted to touch her, but I couldn't and it was driving me insane," Rhys told them.

"How do you think I feel every time she comes to the pack?" Deryn growled at him.

"Guys, this isn't a conversation for outdoors," I whispered, noticing that we were growing an audience.

All four of them resumed walking, storming by me and glaring at each other, even Rhys was glaring. *Oh boy.* I'd definitely stirred the pot on that one. I had no idea they would react that way or that what they said was true. *Whoops.*

CHAPTER 3

"How could you do that?" Deryn growled at Rhys as he paced back and forth in front of my television.

"I apologized and told you that it wasn't on purpose or premeditated." Rhys said again.

"This changes everything!" Nico yelled at him.

"No, it doesn't," he said. "You three can announce her as your girlfriend, too."

"That lie will crumble faster than elf bread," Fox snapped.

"It's not technically a lie," I said, finally joining into the conversation.

"What?" Fox asked.

"You guys are all, technically, my boyfriends. We aren't married. We aren't mated. Yes, we're bound, but aside from that, we are dating. So, really, we are boyfriend and girlfriend." Not that I liked the idea of people hearing that I had four boyfriends. The humans would definitely get the wrong idea.

"If we tell them that, we might as well tell them that you're our queen," Nico argued. "It will spread to the news faster than wildfire."

"He's right," Rhys agreed solemnly.

"And why aren't we telling people that I'm your queen, again?" I asked softly, waiting for one of them to blow up.

None did.

"Because, it could make you an even bigger target. By hurting you, they'll be hurting us, and they will use that to their advantage," Nico explained.

"Won't they do the same with me as Rhys's girlfriend?"

"No, they won't think it will hurt him. Piss him off, sure, but it won't physically or emotionally hurt him for a girlfriend to be killed," Nico said, blunt as ever.

"Glad girlfriends don't count for anything," I muttered and reached for a sweet bread, but Fox smacked my hand.

"We're going out to eat. You'll ruin your appetite," he told me.

"Fine. I'm going to shower," I grumbled and then spun around and said, "and none of you can join me!"

They laughed behind me until I started the water. They were probably still laughing, but the water drowned them out. There was more dirt on me than I realized. I had to wash my hair three times to get it clean. After changing and putting on a bit of makeup, I was finally ready to go and came out to discover all of them gone.

"Hello?" I called. They didn't usually leave me alone without telling me where they were going or where I could find one of them.

I grabbed my ID card and bank card, then peeked my head out into the hallway, but they weren't there either. None of them answered their phones or returned my texts. I sat in my apartment for five minutes, fretting, then finally decided to go search their apartments. We'd recently given each other copies of our apartment keys, so we could get into all of the apartments if there was an emergency. Fox's apartment was empty. So were Nico and Deryn's. I went to the first floor and knocked on Rhys's apartment.

"Hello?" I called.

"Looking for us?" Rhys asked behind me.

I spun around and my jaw dropped open. The four of them wore tailored-to-fit tuxedos. They also all had half face masks on.

"What?"

"You're a bit underdressed," Deryn commented.

"We took care of that though," Rhys assured me. "In my bedroom, you'll find your gown. Hurry, or we'll be late and all the food will be gone."

"Where are we going?" I asked, still drooling over their appearances.

"To a masquerade ball, obviously," Nico chuckled.

"But—"

"No more talking. Go!" Rhys ordered me.

I obeyed, hurrying into the apartment and to Rhys's bedroom where a gorgeous emerald dress hung on the back of the door. It fit perfectly, reminding me of the dress Fox had purchased for me. I slipped on the matching shoes and picked up the mask on his dresser. My mask only covered my eyes, but had gorgeous swirls with diamonds accenting the corners. I tied it on and admired myself in the mirror. I looked amazing. Like a real princess.

I hesitated just a second before walking out of Rhys's apartment and doing a slow twirl for the guys, who all looked appropriately pleased.

"You look perfect," Rhys said and kissed the back of my hand.

"You look like a goddess," Deryn said and bowed to me.

"Come on," Nico urged us. "Our ride is here."

Nico took my hand and placed it on his arm, escorting me outside to a long, black limousine.

"A limo?" I gasped. "I've never ridden in one before."

"Oh?" he asked. "Well, next time I'll have to make sure it's just you and me, so I can show you the real fun to be had inside of a limo."

"If only we didn't have plans tonight," Deryn teased me, "we could show you a good time now."

"Ah, but then the dress would be ruined," Rhys sighed. "So, we must restrain ourselves."

"You guys don't share, remember?" I told them with an eye roll.

"We might if you were the only one being pleasured," Nico whispered into my ear.

I shivered and felt my cheeks warm. *Oh. My. Goddess. Did he? They had!* They never discussed doing sexual things together. I wasn't really into guy on guy action, but the thought of more than one of them touching me at the same time was a *huge* turn on. I clenched my legs together tightly as I sat inside of the limo, trying to keep my hormones at bay. I took a deep breath, and grew serious.

"Should I be prepared for an attack at this dance?" I asked them softly.

Nico patted my arm. "No. This time, you do not need to be worried about anyone attempting to hurt you."

"That's what we said last time," Fox muttered. "Then she got stabbed."

"You'll only be dancing with the four of us," Rhys said. "So, no one will get close enough to hurt you."

I nodded, feeling the tension slip away. Once focused on the task at hand, excitement began building in my stomach.

"I've never been to a masquerade ball!" I told them and tried not to bounce in my seat.

"They're a lot of fun," Deryn assured me. "Lots of eating and then lots of dancing."

"We go to this one every year," Nico said. "It's a fundraiser for one of the orphanages."

"Oh, that's nice," I said, wondering why I didn't know they donated and did events like this.

We arrived at the Galleria, a huge building used for events that cost thousands of dollars to attend. I shuddered, thinking how much money they had paid for all of us to go. Rhys stepped out first, standing on a red carpet with media on each side, cameras flashing as they snapped pictures. Deryn got out next, then Fox, and I realized they were forming the diamond of protection, as I lovingly named it. Their formation shielded me from potential attacks and kept me hidden within their towering heights.

"Ready, beautiful?" Nico asked and kissed my cheek.

"Is my mask on right?" I asked and checked the bow I had tied and the bobby pins I had used to secure it.

"Everything about you is perfect," he whispered. "Now, get out before I tear that dress off of you."

"That's not exactly motivation for me to leave," I muttered, but climbed out with the help of Deryn's hand.

Nico climbed out last, taking the rear position of protection. They didn't always take the same spots in the diamond, except Rhys who always took the front. The other three took different positions depending on the situation.

"Move," Nico whispered.

The guys moved as one, walking down the carpet with a wide smile on each of their faces, turning to the cameras to let them take their pictures. Surrounded by my guards, no one could get a clear picture of me. Someone with wings tried to fly up to get a picture, but Nico discreetly used his powers to knock the person down before they could click their camera.

At the door, a man in a tuxedo and a full-face mask held out his hand. The guys set tickets in his hand, Rhys handing him two tickets, one for me. The man bowed and stepped to the side to let us enter.

The Galleria looked like a ballroom in a movie and intricately decorated for the masquerade ball. Thick, dark drapes hung around the room. A giant chandelier hung over the ballroom. On one side of the room, there was an orchestra playing soft music. The rest of the room was dominated by tables of people snacking on hors d'oeuvres.

We went to one of the empty tables and Rhys pulled out a chair for me. "Queen," he whispered.

"Thank you," I replied, opened my napkin, and put it in my lap.

Rhys sat on my left, Fox on my right, Deryn to Fox's right, and Nico sat across from me, on Rhys's left.

"Did you guys ro-sham-bo for seats?" I asked with a teasing smirk.

"No," Fox answered, avoiding my eyes while picking up his napkin.

"Arm wrestling," Rhys said with a grin.

I looked at Fox next to me. "You beat Deryn?"

Fox scowled at me. "I am an elf."

"I still say he cheated," Deryn grumbled.

"I beat you twice, with both hands," Fox replied with a happy smile.

"Fox, I think you just upped your hot points," I told him.

"My what?" he asked with a tilted head and a frown that made his brows furrow slightly in the middle.

"You know the number given based on how hot you are. Women do it a lot. Sometimes it's like a game and we give points to random guys we see walk by us."

"Women do that, too?" Fox asked with a laugh. "I thought only men did it."

"What's my score?" Rhys asked.

"I can't tell you that," I said and scoffed.

"You're a perfect ten," Fox told me, picked up my hand, and kissed my knuckles.

"Only a ten?" I asked and stuck out my lower lip in a pout.

"Oh, that's a good pout," Nico commented. "Judges?"

"Seven," Deryn said. "I've seen her give much better pouts."

"Eight, but only because she's doing that glistening eye thing even through the mask," Rhys said.

"Ten is the highest you can go," Fox said.

"Women give men bonus points," I informed them. "Tattoos add two points. Well, good tattoos. Sometimes tattoos can be worth negative points, but that's very rare."

"I had no idea that you liked tattoos," Nico said. He had one beautiful tattoo on his chest and one on his shoulder. I constantly ran my fingers over them when he was shirtless, so I was surprised that he hadn't put two and two together.

I nodded.

"What else gives you bonus points?" Deryn asked.

"Accents. Super deep voices. Unique eye colors. Being Alpha, but not overbearing. Basically, an alpha who submits in the bedroom on occasion and isn't one of those super assholes. Doing heroic things, like saving kids or me. Those veins that stick out on your arms when you're muscular. Dimples. Being a kind person in general. Slaying my enemies."

"So, we're like, what? Twenties?" Deryn asked with a smirk. "Since we possess most of those traits?"

"I can't reveal your scores," I told them, "but I can tell you that you all have several bonus points."

"Looks like I need to get a tattoo," Rhys said and winked at me.

"Mm," I purred at him. "Yes, please."

The four guys laughed at me, which I found annoying since I was being serious.

"Every girl is different in how they assign bonus points. For example, tattoos are a plus two, while slaying my enemies is a plus four. Dimples are a plus one. It's all about preference," I explained.

"Good evening, Princes," a tall, stork looking man, said as he stopped between Fox and Nico.

"Evening," they returned the greeting.

"Dinner will be served in just a few minutes. Would you like something to drink?" he asked us.

"Champagne," Rhys ordered, gesturing the number four with his hand. "Bring us a few bottles."

"Of course, sir. Anything else?" he asked.

"Princess?" Rhys asked me.

"I'll have the champagne with you," I replied.

The waiter nodded and disappeared in a hurry.

"Let me fill your water," Fox said, took my glass, and filled it with water from the pitcher on the table.

"Thank you," I replied and sipped from the glass.

"Boys," a distinctly feminine voice crooned. "I was hoping you would be here."

Resisting the urge to spin around and glare at whoever she was, I took another drink from my water glass. I almost spit it out when all four of the guys, *my* guards, rose and walked to her to kiss her on the cheek, just below her mask. They each laid a hand on her arm as they leaned to kiss her cheek, and I felt my anger boiling within me. Who the fuck was she? She had on a bright red dress with lace on the ends of her sleeves and down her cleavage. Her lips were perfectly plump, perfectly shaped, and her lipstick was applied perfectly. I hated her. Okay, that was wrong of me to think, but I was feeling very territorial.

"See you on the dance floor," she told them with a smirk in my direction before she sauntered away.

The guys sat down and I returned to drinking my water, trying to pretend I didn't care to know who she was.

Rhys leaned close to me, his breath tickling my neck. "You realize, that even if you learn to control your expressions, it doesn't matter since we can feel your emotions?"

Shit. I'd forgotten.

"I don't know what you're talking about," I replied in an even tone that impressed me.

"Oh?" he asked and straightened. "Then I guess I won't tell you who she is, if you don't care."

"Not in the slightest."

Of course I cared! Tell me, you bastard!

"Your champagne, sirs and madam," the waiter said as he pushed a cart towards our table. It had four buckets of ice with four champagne bottles inside of them. He opened the first bottle, filled our glasses, and set the four buckets in the center of the table.

"A toast," Fox announced and raised his glass.

We raised our glasses as well.

"To friends, now and forever."

"To the clan!" I said and clinked glasses with Fox and then the others.

"The clan!" the four said and clinked glasses before drinking the champagne.

Nico refilled the glasses and our food came out on real silver platters with silver lids. It was magical, everything I had dreamed princesses did.

A team of servers set a plate down before each of us with the waiter overseeing. Once they were finished, the waiter nodded and they disappeared in the crowd.

"Enjoy," the waiter said and then scurried away after the servers.

"Oh my god," I whispered, wiping the drool from my mouth as I looked over my plate. "This is amazing."

"We thought you would enjoy it," Rhys said and began eating.

Steak cooked to a perfect medium rare, rosemary potatoes, and asparagus with mushrooms sat in perfect proportions on my plate. I had never been one for taking pictures of my food, but at that moment, I wanted to take a picture to document how beautiful the plate was presented. The food tasted even better than it looked. None of us spoke until we were finished ravaging our food like it was the first we'd eaten in days.

"That was phenomenal," I told them and wiped my mouth with my napkin.

"Their chef is world renowned, so I hoped it would be amazing," Fox said.

As if he had been watching us, immediately the waiter brought out dessert, crème brûlée. I had never had it before, but after taking one bite, I vowed to have it again very soon.

"Once you have finished your meals, please make your way to the sides of the room so that we may clear the tables to prepare for the dances," someone announced from behind us.

Fox pulled out my chair and held a hand out to me. I gratefully accepted his hand and assistance standing up. We walked to the side and the guys surrounded me.

People were looking at us and whispering to each other. How could they tell who the guys were with their masks on? I could tell who they were, but I contributed that to being intimately involved with them.

I leaned against the wall with Fox on my left, Nico on my right, and Rhys and Deryn in front of me, but thankfully facing me.

"Who gets the first dance?" Deryn asked.

"We could arm wrestle and find out," Fox taunted him.

"Ro-sham-bo," Rhys said before Deryn could say whatever retort was on the tip of his tongue.

They faced each other, fists held between them.

"Ro-sham-bo," they said in unison, raising and lowering their fists with each word and then on the last one, they made a sign. The signs were either rock, paper, or scissors.

Rhys slapped his flat hand, paper, over Fox's closed fist, rock.

Deryn hit his closed fist, rock, over Nico's two extended fingers, scissors.

Deryn and Rhys turned to each other, closed fists in the center between them.

"Ro. Sham. Bo," they said again, enunciating each word while moving their hands.

They both left their hands in closed fists, rock, so they had to do it again. The same result occurred again. The third time, Deryn switched to an open hand laying parallel to the floor, paper. Rhys hadn't changed, so Deryn won.

"Ha!" Deryn shouted victoriously.

"We all get to dance with her still," Rhys reminded him.

"Yeah, but I get the first dance with her at her first masquerade ball," he reminded them.

"No bragging. That's poor sportsmanship," I chastised him.

"Gentlemen," a deep male voice said in greeting behind Deryn. His voice was one of those that I would have given extra points towards his hot score for.

Deryn stepped to the side, so I could see the newcomer. I knew instantly who he was, Fox's brother. The pointed ears were a big giveaway.

He smiled when he saw me, picked my hand up, and kissed my knuckles. "Princess," he said in greeting.

"Prince Silverowl. It's nice to see you again," I replied.

"You look stunning," he said, eyeing me in silence for several long moments.

So did he.

"What do you want, little bro?" Fox asked through a tight-lipped smile.

"I came hoping to get a dance with the Princess," he said while staring at me.

"Her card is—" Fox began, but I interrupted him.

"I'd love a dance, Silver, but my first must go to Deryn."

"I would never presume to take the first dance," he said with a smirk. "I look forward to seeing you on the dance floor." He bowed and walked away.

"Jolie," Fox grumbled, pouting. "Why did you agree to that?"

"I have to get along with your families. Dancing one dance with your brother is hardly any inconvenience."

"You can't add him to our harem," Fox said adamantly.

I gaped at him. "What? I didn't...harem?"

Our arrangement was a harem, I supposed, but reversed since it was many men with one woman. That did not make me feel any better though. It made me feel like a terrible person.

"I didn't mean it as a bad thing," Fox whispered and pulled me into a hug.

I let him hug me, but his power wasn't working on me for some reason, so I still felt sad.

"None of us are here against our will, right?" Nico asked.

Fox released me so I could turn around to face him. "I'm fine," I lied and waved my hand at him. "Just emotional lately." I really was extra sensitive lately.

The orchestra was set up again and the dance floor was cleared. Right when the music started, a giant hand took mine and spun me out onto the floor.

I gasped in shock and looked up the massive body to the mask. "Dan!" I yelled. "You scared me."

"Hey! I get the first dance!" Deryn growled.

Dan set my hand on his shoulder and held my other hand. "Not tonight, junior!" Dan told him and joined the rest of the dancers seamlessly. After a short while, I finally noticed Dan's eyes studying me intensely. "What's wrong?" he asked as we continued dancing.

"Sorry," I mumbled and shook my head, pushing away all of my negative thoughts. "I've been extra emotional lately. Thank you for dancing with me."

"Have you been practicing shielding yourself from their emotions?" he asked, concern in his eyes and voice.

"Yes. It's not them."

"Well, we all have off days. A lot has happened to you recently. Your life has been drastically changed. It's okay to be overwhelmed, but it is best if you talk to someone about it."

"Yes, sir."

The song ended and he dipped me, making me laugh and smile wide. He was always so happy and playful, just like Deryn.

"Keep my son in line, okay?" he said and kissed the knuckles on my right hand.

"I'll try," I replied.

Deryn took my hand from his father's grip and bowed over it. "May I have this dance, Queen?"

"I'd be honored," I replied.

He pulled me close, his arm wrapped around my waist and kissed me gently, at complete odds with the roughness of his move-ment and the raging desire in his eyes. "I love you, baby," he whispered.

My heart felt so full, it could have exploded. "I love you, too, my wolf."

We waltzed around the room with happy smiles and my worries melted away. The dance ended and Deryn kissed my knuckles before passing me off to Rhys.

"Hello, handsome," I greeted him, standing close to him.

"Evening, gorgeous," he replied, setting one hand on my lower back and taking my other in his free hand.

Our dance was flawless, my eyes never leaving his as we twirled amongst the other dancers. I had no idea how he was able to keep us from bumping into anyone else when his eyes were glued to mine, but it was awesome. I was very glad I'd taken ballroom dancing lessons as a teenager, or this night might have been a disaster.

I saw a flash of red as the woman from earlier spun by us, Deryn her dancing partner. Jealousy surged through me, hot and strong.

"What?" Rhys asked and looked around.

"Nothing," I replied and squashed my feelings.

"May I cut in?" Prince Silverowl asked.

Rhys hesitated a moment, but nodded and let him take me into the next dance.

"I'm surprised you would dance with me when there are so many other females here," I told him.

"My brother is never possessive, but when it comes to you, he's as bad as a werewolf with a bone."

I laughed, picturing Deryn and Fox fighting over a bone. "He's not that bad."

"He's gotten stronger since he met you. He has learned new powers and trains constantly. All so he can protect you," he told me.

The guys trained a lot, but I had no idea he was learning new powers, too.

"You're good for Foxfire. He was beginning to neglect his duties and responsibilities and seemed to be falling into a funk. But, he's much better now. Thank you."

"Uh, you're welcome. Really, I haven't done anything. Fox does far more for me."

The music shifted, signaling the end of the song. "Time's up," he whispered. "See you around."

He disappeared into the crowd and Fox took his place.

"What did he say to you?" Fox asked, entering the dancers' area.

"He said he thinks I'm good for you," I answered honestly.

Fox blinked in stunned silence a moment. "Oh."

"You look great in that tuxedo," I complimented him.

"I look even better out of it," he replied with a cocky smirk and a wink.

I laughed and shook my head at him. "Conceited."

He shrugged. "Honest."

"Well, I happen to like how you look in the tuxedo," I told him.

"Thank you." The music shifted again.

Nico cut in and sighed, "Finally! It's my turn."

I giggled and kissed him. "Hello, Sparkles."

He tensed, hating the pet name I had given him after he had tried to do a new spell and all that happened was some bright sparks coming out of his fingertips.

His hand slid lower, his fingers brushing the top of my butt as we danced. "My fingers are known to make you see sparkles while your head is thrown back and screaming my name."

Heat rushed to my core and I stumbled in my dance with him as my muscles clenched.

"Tease," I growled at him, suddenly out of breath.

"You're so easily worked up tonight," he commented with a frown. "When was the last time one of us pleased you?"

He was always so blunt, never beating around the bush. Sometimes, it still caught me off guard.

"Two days ago," I answered. I had become a bit of a sex addict, wanting it, no *needing* it once a day at the very least. Or, I ended up like this, starved and almost uncontrollable. Despite their assurances that they didn't care if I took one of them away for sex when we were all hanging out, I just couldn't do it. It felt too awkward and wrong to do.

"Come on," he ordered me, dragging me by the hand away from the crowd. The other three pushed off the wall they had been leaning on and followed us.

"Where are we going?" I asked, trying not to trip on the dress with the longer strides I had to use to keep up with him.

"Every male here can smell your arousal now," he explained. "I doubt any of them would try anything, but I'd rather be cautious than continue dancing." We exited the ballroom and entered the foyer. "Plus," he stopped and kissed me fiercely, his arms pulling me against him and his tongue sliding along mine. When he pulled back, we were both breathless. "Plus, we have special plans for you tonight."

"What?" I asked, my brain still stuck on his amazing kiss. He had tasted like champagne.

Our limo pulled up and we all climbed in. Once inside, the four sat together across the limo from me.

"Why are you all over there?" I asked. Normally, we all sat together.

"If we touch you before we get to the apartment, our plan will be ruined," Rhys said.

"I thought you were going to take me in this limo?" I asked, leaning my elbows on my knees and my chin on my hands, giving them a nice view of my cleavage.

All four groaned and averted their gazes.

"Rude!" I gasped at them, sat up, and folded my arms across my chest. "Maybe I'll just ruin your plan and lock myself away to have some alone time."

"No, you won't," Fox said with a smug smile. "You're insanely curious, too curious for your own good. And we won't tell you what it is. So, the only way to find out, is to go along with our plan."

"I don't like when you guys push me away," I mumbled while staring up at the roof of the limo. Self-esteem had always been an issue for me, especially as a preteen. It had gotten better when my boobs finally came in, and even better when Martin and I started dating. But, there was always this little voice, who I lovingly named Bitchtits, who assured me in moments like this, I still wasn't good enough. I blamed Bitchtits for my negative thoughts about other women, too. I tried really hard to be supportive and positive to other women. Women needed to stick together in the gaming community. The industry was heavily dominated by men.

"It'll be worth it," Deryn promised.

My body was wound tight, liquid heat pooled between my legs, and I clamped my knees together.

"Fuck," Rhys growled, his eyes now dragon's eyes. "She smells amazing."

"Her pheromones are exceptionally enticing," Fox agreed and licked his lips, my eyes tracking the movement. He could do some amazing things with that tongue.

All four groaned again and I could see their erections jerk inside their pants.

"Hurry up!" Deryn ordered the driver.

"I'm trying," the driver responded in a growling tone. "I can smell her too, you know?'

"Sorry," I gasped.

"You can't control it," the driver replied, "but maybe think sad thoughts instead?"

CHAPTER 4

Deryn rolled up the window that separated us from the driver.

"Who was that woman?" I asked them, anger and jealousy replacing my horny desire.

"I thought you didn't care," Rhys smirked.

"Rhys," I growled.

"She's the President's daughter," Nico told me.

"How many of you slept with her?" I asked, ignoring the voice telling me I didn't really want to know.

"None of us did more than dance with her tonight," Rhys replied, misinterpreting what I wanted to know.

"I'm not talking about tonight." Though, it was good to hear.

They didn't respond for several heartbeats.

"I did," Rhys admitted.

"I did, too," Nico said.

"Me, too," Deryn said.

Everyone looked at Fox. "Yeah, okay. I did, too. Just once, though."

All four of them. I was a bit surprised, but had expected this.

"I see," I said and nodded. Strangely, I wasn't mad or upset. I was sort of numb.

"You're not mad?" Rhys asked, head tilted to the side and nostrils flaring.

"Or sad?" Fox asked.

"I expected that response," I told them and shrugged.

"Now you're sad...no...irritated," Deryn said.

"How would you have felt if I got up to kiss some guy on the cheek who I'd slept with. Oh, wait, I know since I experienced your reactions to Martin."

"Sorry," they all mumbled, satisfyingly guilty looks on their faces.

The limo stopped and I climbed out before they could get to the door, almost hitting the driver with it as it opened.

Our elevator ride was silent, my hormones squashed. Why was I so moody lately? My period had just ended four days ago, so I wasn't PMSing or pregnant. Was it them? Was I not shielding well enough?

I dropped my shields to allow the guys' feelings to reach me. All of them were worried.

"Why are you all so worried?" I asked in a strangled voice, swallowing thickly.

I put my shields back up and sagged against the elevator wall.

"We are worried about you," Fox said, drawing closer. "Your emotions have been all over the place, my powers aren't working, and you're not talking to us. You've been sad a lot lately."

"I'm not sure what's going on," I admitted.

The elevator opened and we all filed out, going to my apartment. I went to my room, stripping out of the dress, fully aware that I had an audience.

"Peeping Toms," I accused them without turning around. I put the mask on my dresser, smiling at how thoughtful it had been for them to remember that attending a masquerade ball was on my bucket list.

Rhys spun me around, claiming my mouth with his and slide his tongue in. His left hand gripped my butt while his right hand slid into my hair to cradle my head.

"Whoa," I whispered when he pulled back. I thought we would be alone, but the other three were still here.

Rhys threw me onto the bed and took his tie and shirt off. The other three followed suit, removing their ties and shirts and then all four climbed onto the bed.

"Guys, what's going on?" I asked, fire rushing through my veins and pooled in my core.

"We wanted to try sharing," Nico said.

"Sharing?" I asked breathlessly. Four insanely hot men, shirtless, and seated around me was making it hard to breathe or think of anything except touching their bare skin.

Fox pushed me on my back and began kissing me, his tongue slow and precise in its movements, driving me crazy.

Someone removed my thong, the last piece of clothing I had been wearing. All four gasped when my scent hit them, Fox stopped kissing me to look where the others were looking.

"She's so wet already," Deryn said. He bent forward and licked my clit, making me gasp and arch up off the bed.

Rhys latched onto one of my nipples, sucking and nipping. Nico took my other nipple into his mouth, swirling his tongue around my already hard nub.

I screamed out, and Fox took my mouth again, forcing my moans into his mouth.

Deryn sucked and licked me expertly, pushing me closer and closer to the cliff of euphoria.

Having all four of their mouths on me at once was a new experience that I thoroughly enjoyed.

Before I could orgasm, Deryn sat back and wiped his mouth with the back of his hand. "She's really close already."

Fox kissed my neck and bit down just hard enough to make me moan, but not enough to leave a mark.

"Go ahead," Rhys nodded and smirked at the whine I made when his mouth left my body.

Nico sucked harder on the nipple he was playing with and I moaned loudly.

I thought Deryn would finish me, but he removed his pants and thrust into me instead.

"Yes!" I screamed, throwing my head back and my hands grasped Nico and Rhys's thighs.

Rhys, Nico, and Fox removed their pants, too, and I immediately grabbed Rhys and Nico, stroking them in time to Deryn's thrusts. Fox turned my head and I eagerly opened my mouth to accept him.

"Yes," he groaned, arching his back.

I screamed as an orgasm hit, tightening around Deryn, who orgasmed with me.

He pulled out and quickly rubbed my clit, making me orgasm in a few strokes.

Suddenly, all of them were gone, none of them touching me.

"Hey," I started, but realized they were switching positions.

Fox entered me slowly and used a steady rhythm. Deryn cupped my breast and flicked his tongue across it. Rhys stood by my head, and gripped my hair as he pushed into my mouth.

I stroked Nico slowly, wanting to keep him hard, but not finish too early. It wasn't until Fox that I realized they were slipping condoms on right before entering me.

Fox's movements were normally slow, but he gripped my hips and began to slam into me hard enough for our skin to slap loudly. He orgasmed before I did, pulling out to let Rhys take his spot.

I flipped over onto my hands and knees. Nico laid on the bed so I could give him head while Rhys gripped my hips and slid into me until he was fully buried.

Deryn continued pleasuring my breasts and Fox reached under me to rub my clit.

I orgasmed several times before Rhys finished, my legs shaking. Since it was just Nico left, and he was already on his back, I sat down on him. He moaned and his eyes rolled into the back of his head.

"What do you want?" Rhys asked as he kissed my neck.

I rode Nico and said, "Just touch me."

Rhys, Fox, and Deryn moved closer to me, kissing my upper body.

My walls fell and the euphoria and love they felt poured into me. I gasped and gripped Nico's chest to keep from falling forward.

"Yes," Nico moaned. "Now we can fully feel your emotions."

"I love all of you," I whispered, resuming my riding.

"You're our world," Nico told me, adding his own thrusts to meet mine.

"You are the only one that we want," Rhys whispered in my ear, his hot breath making me shiver.

"We will always love you," Fox whispered against my neck.

"We will never leave you," Deryn said.

Nico flipped me on to my back and took control. "Which do you love?" he asked as the pressure grew and grew.

"You all."

"You know the answer we want," he chastised and slammed into me faster and harder. "Who did you love?"

The orgasm was the strongest one I had ever had, shooting fire through my veins. "My princes!" I screamed the answer they wanted to hear and Nico joined with his own orgasm.

Nico fell to my side, panting happily.

"I love my guards," I whispered.

After cleaning up and dressing in pajamas, we cuddled on the couch to watch movies. I was high on euphoria and smiling like a fool.

I never thought they would have sex together with me. I would be lying if I said that it had been anything other than magical.

"Jolie," Fox whispered, drawing my attention to him. He sat on the floor between my legs.

"Yeah?"

"We need to ask you something."

My euphoria vanished as fear took its place. "What?"

Rhys rubbed my arm. "Calm down. It's nothing bad."

"We have an important trip coming up," Fox said. "We'll be gone at least two weeks."

"That's right before Christmas," I whispered sadly. It was supposed to be our first Christmas together.

"We would be back on the twenty-fourth, so we would be home for Christmas," Rhys chimed in.

"Okay, so you want me to stay with the pack?" I guessed. They'd all gone on an overnight trip and the only way they had felt okay leaving me was because I had stayed with the pack and Martin had stuck next to me.

"No, we would like you to go with us," Deryn said.

"I can't leave work for two weeks."

"You're just writing. Can't you telework and send them your updates electronically?" Fox suggested.

I doubted it.

"Please," Nico begged from my right side. "I don't want to be separated from you for two weeks. I might go insane."

I felt the same way.

"I don't know. I'll have to think about it."

"We're going to Mascrol," Fox said with a smirk.

"You're going out of country?" I asked, my palms slick with sweat at the thought of them thousands of miles away, across an ocean from me.

"Easy," Rhys said, pulling me into a hug and rubbing my back. "Calm down."

"You'll be across the ocean from me," I whispered into his chest.

"Come with us," he whispered into my hair. "I can't stand the thought of being so far away from you. Plus, we know you've always wanted to visit Mascrol."

"Please," Deryn begged.

What could I say?

"I'll talk to my boss tomorrow. When would we leave?"

"Sunday the tenth," Fox said with a bright smile.

"It's not a yes yet," I reminded them.

"But it's not a no," he replied and went to the kitchen humming.

Sometimes he was so childlike. It was "serious" Fox that always threw me for a loop.

"Pizza?" Fox asked, phone in his hand.

I yawned and stretched with my arms above my head. "I'm going to call it a night."

Nico followed me to my bedroom and climbed into bed right behind me, wrapping his arms around me to make a safety net of warmth. "I can't stand the thought of being away from you," he whispered and kissed the top of my ear. "It hurts just imagining it."

"Same," I whispered back, stroking one of his forearms where it was wrapped around my chest.

"I'm not trying to convince you," he whispered. "I'm just sharing my feelings with you."

"I appreciate that," I said honestly. "And I know being apart for two weeks, even if you were in the next town over, would still put us all on edge. Or, possibly lose our shit. Not being able to touch any of you for two weeks?" I shuddered.

"Same," he whispered and kissed my head.

"Can I talk to you?" I asked Justin, my boss, popping my head into the doorway of his office. He was in his mid-forties with graying temples and a gnarly scar on his right cheek. Rumor around the office was that he got it in a bar fight when someone suggested that video games were only for children and adults who played were childish.

He looked up and waved me in. "What's up?"

I closed the door and sat in the chair in front of him. His office was covered in video game memorabilia that I drooled over every time I walked by. So many of the items were rare and super valuable.

"I need to talk to you about—"

"Wait, let me guess. You're here to talk to me about the Summit," he said with a smirk. "The two week trip the princes are going on."

"How did you know?" I gaped.

He laughed. "I'm a werewolf."

Then, he did something I had never seen before. He grew wolf ears out of the top of his head, complete with fur. It reminded me of several anime shows I watched and before I could stop myself, I leapt up and touched one of them.

He didn't growl or snap at me, which I took as a good sign. Coming to my senses, I plopped back down into my seat, my cheeks warm. "Sorry."

"You're a princess to our pack. You're allowed to touch us without worrying we will bite you," he said with a smirk. "Though, I doubt Prince Deryn would like seeing you do that."

"Deryn's never done that," I whispered and pointed at his ears.

"I started doing it for conventions. It's easier to let my wolf ears out than to purchase some fake ones," he admitted. "I get a lot of girls wanting to touch my ears and even more when I let my tail out."

I bet he did.

"So, about the Summit?" I said to bring us back on topic.

"You're good to go. Just make sure you email me your work, so I know you're working," he said. "If I declined your request, I know I'd have an angry prince visiting me, and I'd rather avoid that. Plus, you are ahead of schedule on all of your projects and all of your work has been stellar. So, I don't see any harm letting you go."

"Thank you!" I screeched and stood up. "Thank you, so much."

"You're welcome, Princess."

I flinched. "Please, don't call me that here. People will think I'm getting special treatment. I don't want that. I want equal treatment. I want to earn my place in the gaming industry."

"You are," he assured me. "I would have booted you out of here a while ago if your writing wasn't so great."

"Thanks," I said, shocked at the huge compliment. As soon as I left his office, I sent a message in our group chat.

Me: I can go with you.

Deryn: Really?

Rhys: Good.

Nico: Sweet.

Fox: Yes! Woohoo!

Me: Yes, Deryn. My boss okayed it since I'm ahead of schedule on my projects.

Rhys: I'll get the paperwork all in order.

Nico: We should celebrate tonight. Pizza and party games?

Me: Sounds great!

Deryn: You touched another wolf's ears?!!!

Damn, how had he found out so fast? Had Justin really called and let him know? Why?

Me: He grew wolf ears out of the top of his head! Like in that show I've been watching. I just leapt up to touch them without thinking. He's part of the pack, so I'm allowed to touch him. Plus, it wasn't like I touched him inappropriately. It was just an ear.

Deryn: -_-

Me: Jealous monster.

Fox: You're ruining our happy mood! Jolie is coming with us on our trip! We won't have to be separated from her!

Nico: I agree with Fox.

Deryn: We'll talk later.

*Me: *static* what's that? *static* you're breaking up. *static* I think I'm going into a tun—*

Fox: XD

Deryn: >:(

Rhys: lol

Nico: o(^o^)o

Me: BYE! xoxox <3

When I got home, Deryn was waiting for me in the lobby.

"Hey, handsome," I greeted him and kissed his cheek.

"Show me how you touched him," he ordered me and folded his arms across his chest.

"Grow ears," I ordered him back.

Shockingly, he did as I asked and two ears popped out of the top of his head. I reached up and rubbed one of his ears and then stepped back. "That's what I did."

"No wonder he called me," he growled, his eyes now his wolf's eyes.

"What do you mean?"

"That goes into my top three turn on spots," he told me, his body crowding mine as he moved closer. "Touching me like that makes me want to take you right here."

"He hadn't seemed flustered," I told him. "He said he does it at conventions all the time."

"Yeah, and I'm sure he walks around with a hard-on all day."

"I didn't know," I whispered weakly. "I wouldn't have done it if I'd known."

"You grow ears," he ordered me.

Me? I could shift, but I wasn't sure I could just grow ears. "Can we go to my apartment first?" I asked. There wasn't anyone else in the apartment lobby with us, but I still didn't want to do it here.

He nodded, the ears disappearing, and we went to my apartment, which was empty.

We faced each other and I focused on the image of a girl with wolf ears and a wolf tail, but a human body. It wasn't difficult, since I had watched a ton of anime movies with characters like that. My scalp began to tingle and my lower back throbbed.

Suddenly, they just popped out. I screeched since my tail was stuck in my pants and hurriedly pushed them down in the back, to let it out.

Deryn groaned and growled at the same time, something I hadn't ever heard before. "That is so hot."

Hurrying towards the mirror in the bathroom, I looked at myself and had to admit, it was sort of hot.

"Come here, please," he requested.

I walked to him, sashaying my hips so that my tail swung side to side.

His eyes darkened and he got a hungry look, one I recognized all too well. With one hand, he reached up and touched my ear like I had done to him.

Holy fangs! It felt amazing and I moaned out loud, tilting my head so he could rub it more.

"See?" he asked, stepping forward and continuing to rub my ear. "It feels amazing."

"I'm sorry," I moaned. "I didn't know. I won't do it again."

"I know you didn't know. I'm not mad at you. I was at first, but once I realized that you weren't aware, my anger disappeared. However, it is important that you learn about things like this, so you don't repeat your mistakes."

"Deryn," I whispered, "does it feel as amazing when you touch my tail?"

He dropped the hand that had been touching my ear and I whimpered at the loss of his touch. His chuckle quickly followed my sound and then he gently stroked my tail.

A gasp wrenched out of my throat. It caused warmth to flow low in my stomach, a sensation I had not been prepared for. Wow.

"Whoa," he whispered. "I've never done the tail before."

"Too much," I whimpered. "It's so sensitive."

"Did you orgasm?"

I shook my head and swallowed thickly. "Almost," I admitted and reverted back to my human form.

Deryn's phone rang. He ignored it, eyes still darkened.

"You should answer that."

He groaned and put his phone to his ear. "What?" A moment later, he said, "Fine," and hung up. He grabbed my hand and pulled me towards the doorway. I followed, just glad to shake off the sexual tension from a moment ago.

We met the rest of the guys for pizza and games at Deryn's apartment. He released my hand with a smile.

"Jolie!" the three guys yelled when I walked in. Clearly, they had started drinking before we arrived, but I was okay with that. They were all happy drunks.

"Guards!" I yelled back and raised my arms in the air.

Fox popped the top on a bottle of hard cider for me, which I gratefully accepted. They came over and we held our bottles up.

"To a wonderful adventure," I said.

"Adventuring!" Deryn yelled.

"Adventuring!" the five of us yelled at the same time.

Yeah, we were nerds, and we were perfectly okay with admitting that. How I had lucked out to find four hot nerds was beyond me, but I knew better than to look a gift horse in the mouth.

We took a big gulp of our drinks and went to the couch to play games. These games were serious, but we were still having fun. Once we got a few more drinks in us, they would be hilarious and ridiculous to watch. We had recorded ourselves one night and watched, as many of us couldn't keep our kart on the track since we were so drunk. The amount of cussing and swerving karts was one of the most hilarious things I'd ever seen. I had saved that video to my hard drive, ensuring I kept it forever.

The pizza came and we ate while sitting at the table together. It always made me happy to eat at the dining table with them, like we were a family.

"We are a family," Deryn grumbled at me.

I jerked my head up and asked, "What? I didn't say that out loud, did I?"

"I didn't hear anything," Fox scowled.

"Me neither," Nico admitted.

"I heard her," Rhys said.

I have a third nipple, I thought in my head.

Rhys and Deryn rolled their eyes.

"Still nothing," Nico said.

"Me neither," Fox said.

"What the hell?" I growled.

Now I couldn't even have my thoughts to myself?

"It's not like we did it on purpose," Rhys reminded me. "Why did this suddenly start? What changed?"

"I don't know," I whispered and shoved more pizza into my mouth. Sometimes, I was a stress eater. This was one of those times. Who wouldn't be stressed when two of the four men you were dating could suddenly read your mind? Nothing would be secret anymore.

"Got a lot of secrets to hide?" Rhys asked with a smirk.

I glared at him.

"Stay out of my head."

"You're yelling your thoughts at me," he accused.

"We need to talk to the Elders tonight," I said urgently.

"Tomorrow. None of us are in any shape to see the Elders," Rhys countered.

The guys continued eating, drinking, playing, and having a good time, but I just wasn't into it anymore. Slinking off during one of their epic battles, I climbed into Deryn's bed and stared up at the ceiling.

If they all ended up able to hear my thoughts, what was I going to do? Not that I *could* do anything. It would change everything. There would be no freedom. Everything I thought of would be on display for them. I could never surprise them. How were they going to react to hearing my thoughts about the others? Oh, Goddess! I couldn't have sex with the other two now! They would hear everything I was thinking about and, uh, this was so unfair. Just once, it would be nice if just once my fucking curse didn't make things worse.

I jolted up in bed.

"That's it!" I shouted.

"What?" Nico called from the living room.

"Nothing!" I shouted back. Had the two not heard my thoughts? Were they too busy playing or too drunk now?

Rhys likes fingers in his ass. I thought as loud as I could.

No laughter.

No growling.

They couldn't hear me. Perfect. My plan was in place and I just had to keep them from hearing my thoughts until I completed it. Step one, go to sleep now!

♥

"Why is she singing children's songs in her head?" Rhys growled from the back seat of the SUV.

"Stop!" Deryn begged, leaning forward to set a hand on the back of the passenger seat.

In order to keep them from hearing my thoughts, I'd resorted to singing all of the catchy songs that I knew. Children's songs were the best because they were easy to remember and often repetitive with few breaks. Less time for stray thoughts to slip in.

Deryn growled and rubbed his temples. "Martin, please drive faster."

My other two guards sat in silence, barely knowing what was going on.

Martin chuckled from the driver's seat next to me. "You're torturing them for something, aren't you? What did they do?"

"They didn't do anything," I answered and just as a stray thought started to slip in, I started singing my favorite rhyme, over and over. And over.

The SUV stopped and we all leapt out, racing into the Elders' room where they waited for us. I slid to a stop and bowed low, keeping my songs up.

"What's troubling you so much?" Dragon Elder asked.

"Rhys and I can hear her thoughts now," Deryn told him.

"We can't think of any reason why we could suddenly start hearing them, but we can," Rhys agreed.

The Elders looked at me.

"Walls are up. No idea how it's happening," I replied and went back to rhyming.

"What is it you wish to ask us, Jolie?" Elf Elder asked.

Damn. He was so good at reading people!

"Break my curse!" I shouted. "I-I mean, please break my curse, Elders."

"Jolie! No!" Rhys yelled.

"I thought we had discussed this?" Deryn said.

"Please," I begged and dropped to my knees in front of the Elders. "I'm sure that the curse is what did this. I'm sure the curse will continue doing things to ruin my life. No more. I can't have it ruining things anymore. Everything is going so well and I can't risk it. I can't lose anyone else."

Tears streamed down my cheeks, but I didn't move to wipe them.

"Jolie," Deryn whispered in shock.

I could feel the four of them wanting to move closer, but they held their ground out of respect for me and the Elders.

I have to do this. If my curse takes one of you... I couldn't even finish that thought.

"Very well," Wolf Elder agreed. "We will break your curse."

"It is going to hurt and you might very well die, so speak with your guards and then we will take you to the room we use for this sort of event," Dragon Elder told me.

"Thank you," I gasped. Part of me had been sure they weren't going to do it.

The Elders left and I spun around to find a mixture of anger and worry on four gorgeous male faces.

"I love you," I whispered. "I love all of you, individually and together. Thinking of a life where one of you is missing...it's torturous. This curse is always hurting me in the worst way possible. You are what matters most to me now and I know it will target you next. I have to do this."

"What if you die?" Rhys asked, pulling me into his arms and burying his face in my hair above my ear. "What will we do then?"

"You will become kings. You will find mates. You will do what you did before you met me," I whispered and hugged him tightly. "You will do all this knowing that I loved you more than anything and will always be part of you. I'll always be in here," I whispered and touched his chest.

"No!" Deryn yelled. "No!" He flipped a chair over and growled loudly, his body shook and fists clenched.

Without hesitation, I went to him and wrapped my arms around his back. "It's okay, Moon Moon. I love you, too."

"Please, don't. Please reconsider," he begged in a tight voice. "If I lose you, I lose everything."

"You won't lose me," I whispered, trying to put as much assurance into those four words as I could.

I hugged Fox who hadn't said a word and he hugged me back, drawing my scent in deeply before he pushed me to Nico. "I'll see you once your curse is removed," he whispered and turned his back on me.

"Stay strong," Nico ordered me, grabbed my chin, and tilted it up. "You're strong and powerful. You carry a piece of each of us in you. You can survive the curse breaking."

I nodded and kissed his cheek. "Yes, sir."

With one final look at the four men I loved, I went into the room the Elders had gone to.

"It will be okay," Dragon Elder assured me. "We will do everything within our power to keep you safe during this."

Nodding, I went to the bed he was pointing to. Well, not a bed, more of a cot. It was the only thing in the room we were now in. Bare walls, stone floor, and one single cot.

I sat down and they pushed my shoulder, guiding me down onto the cot.

"Close your eyes," Dragon Elder ordered me.

I followed his directions.

"Center yourself."

Done.

"You're going to feel tingles along your stomach and chest. Just stay relaxed. After the tingling ends, you'll feel burning, and immense pain. Stay strong and it will be gone, never to bother you again."

"Okay."

I could do this. I would do this.

The tingling wasn't so bad, and the burning was uncomfortable. The pain wasn't immense...the pain was *excruciating*. I screamed and thrashed on the cot.

The Elders chanted and their powers funneled into me at an alarming rate.

My skin was being peeled off. My muscles ripped apart. My soul torn with claws and knives.

The chanting grew louder, as did my screams.

Nico's words came to me. My soul contained pieces of all of them. I was strong. I had a lot that I wanted to do with my life. I wanted to become an award-winning writer. I wanted to become known in the gaming community. I wanted to claim my mates.

CHAPTER 5

Pain coursed through my body, so I was fairly certain I was still alive.

"When will she wake up?" Fox asked.

"Soon," Dragon Elder answered. "Remember that her experience was painful."

"We know," Rhys grumbled. "We all felt it."

"Not like she did," Dragon Elder said. "You felt one hundredth of the pain she felt."

"You're joking, right? Over exaggerating?" Deryn asked.

"No, we're being honest. She had up solid walls between you all and we added our own as well to protect you," Elf Elder explained.

"I can't imagine dealing with that amount of pain," Fox whispered.

"It must have felt—"

"Like my skin was ripped off, my muscles ripped apart, and my soul shredded," I whispered and opened my eyes.

The four of them sat around my cot, scowls on their faces.

"Who died?" I asked with a small smile.

"You almost did," Dragon Elder told me, coming to stand at the end of the cot so I could see him. "It was very close."

"It worked, right? The curse is gone? I really don't think I could do that again."

He smiled and nodded. "Yes, your curse is gone. We successfully removed it."

"Thank you," I said as tears built and dripped down my cheeks. It was gone. My curse was gone!

"We can't hear your thoughts anymore," Rhys informed me.

"Thank you," I sighed.

I was so glad that I didn't have to deal with trying to hide my thoughts from them.

"Can you sit up?" Fox asked and held out his hand.

I took it and let him pull me up into a sitting position. "I'm so sore," I moaned.

"Can we take her home?" Rhys asked.

Dragon Elder nodded. "Stay safe on your trip," he told me. "Keep your ears open and eyes scanning."

Was he warning me that there was going to be an attack? Was I in danger going with them?

"Thank you. Please, thank the other Elders for me."

He nodded and Rhys picked me up and carried me out to our waiting SUV.

"What happened?" Martin asked. "You've been in there for hours."

"Jolie decided to become suicidal," Deryn growled and climbed into the front seat, slamming the door shut.

"What?" Martin asked.

"I had them remove my curse," I told him with a smile. "It's gone!"

"Your curse is gone?" he asked.

I nodded.

"Why is he upset about that?" Martin asked Rhys.

"Because there was a high likelihood she could have died. They told us that she very nearly died," he explained.

"But she didn't," Martin said.

"Exactly!" I yelled and kissed Martin's cheek as we walked by him. "Glad someone understands."

"Drive," Deryn ordered him, snarling and sitting in his seat with tense shoulders.

There was no point in talking to him in the car, so I would wait until we were home to talk to him privately. He was mad that I had risked myself. I understood that. However, it was my decision and I had done what I thought was right.

"I need to buy luggage," I told Rhys, settling onto the seat beside him.

"Okay, we can go out tomorrow, if you want," he offered.

"Why not tonight?" I asked him.

"Because we need you to be with us tonight," Fox told me. "We need time together without outside distractions."

"Okay."

I could understand their need to reassure themselves that I was okay.

Before we climbed into our cuddle puddle once back at the apartment, I grabbed Deryn and dragged him into the hallway. He was stiff and kept turning away from me and folding his arms across his chest.

"I'm sorry you were worried. I don't like worrying you. But, this was something I had to do for myself," I told him.

"You almost died," he growled.

"But, I didn't."

"I almost lost you," he whispered.

"I'm right here," I whispered back and stepped forward, so that my breasts were pushing against his folded arms.

He dropped his arms and pulled me against his chest and hugged me tightly. "The pain you experienced was too much. Then, we felt you slipping. We felt you dying. I couldn't do anything. There was no enemy for me to kill. There was no way for me to protect you. I was helpless. All I could do was sit there and wonder if the woman I love was going to survive or not."

"It's over. My curse is gone. I'm alive and well. I'm so happy. I never meant to cause you pain or worry. I had to do this. I had to get rid of this curse before it took you from me."

"It almost took you from me, though."

"Deryn, please don't be mad at me any longer. I love you. I love you so much that I would rather put my life on the line, than endanger you," I explained to him.

He picked me up until we were eye level and kissed me lightly before he whispered, "Don't ever do that again. Okay?"

"No problem," I said and smiled. He set me down on my feet, but kept his hands on my arms.

"Please, don't endanger yourself to keep me or the other guys safe. It is our job to protect you. You are my queen. You are the one who matters. Keeping you alive is what is important."

"Do you think the Elder was warning me to expect an attack at the Summit?" I asked. The warning was really bothering me.

"No, I think he was just reminding you not to let your guard down. There are always threats and dangers. If you let your guard down, you will open yourself up to attacks."

"Are we good?" I asked him and looked up into his eyes.

He was frowning still, not a twitch of his lips at all. "Yes. We're good."

"Still love me?"

He rested his hand against my cheek and whispered, "I will *always* love you, Jolie."

"Good," I said with a wide smile and spun around to walk inside.

"Jolie," he said, stopping me.

"Yes?" I asked and looked over my shoulder at him.

"You are my world. I will do whatever I can to keep you safe. Even if you decide we aren't going to be mates, I will still watch over you."

"I will always be grateful to have you in my life. I am beyond grateful to have a place in your heart. I will never take you for granted," I told him. "I love you."

"I love you more than you'll ever know," he said.

He pushed open the door and we joined the others on the couch to cuddle and watch movies.

Tomorrow, I would try to find my final presents for them. I wanted this to be the best Christmas ever. I wanted to ensure that this would be a Christmas no one would ever forget.

I couldn't wait to go to Mascrol. It would be my first long distance travel with the guys. It was going to be the longest I had been on vacation in my entire life. Normally, I only took two or three-day trips. Two weeks was going to be insane. How many pairs of pants would I need to bring? How big of a suitcase was I allowed?

I didn't want to be like some girls, carrying sixteen bags and making others take care of them for her.

"You're chewing on your lip," Rhys whispered. "What are you worrying about?"

"What size bag I'll need and how many pairs of pants I'll have to take for a two-week vacation."

He chuckled softly and patted my knee. "We'll take care of it all tomorrow. Don't worry."

What he didn't tell me, was that I only needed luggage big enough for my bras, underwear, pajamas, and a few pairs of pants. Everything else was being provided for me. Whatever the hell that meant. Part of me suspected I was going to be forced to wear dresses quite often.

"What will I be doing while you're stuck in meetings?" I asked the guys while packing my bag.

The four of them were lying around my room, two on the floor, one on the bed and one across the chest at the end of my bed. The chest was wooden with an ornate symbol, a symbol I had never seen before, and that Rhys, who had given me the chest, said was something I would learn about later. No matter how much I pestered him, he wouldn't tell me what the symbol was, and neither would the others.

The chest had a few weapons, a thick quilt, and a few dragon scales from Rhys inside. Every few weeks, he would add another scale to the chest. He said it was important to him that I keep them in the chest, but didn't explain the significance.

"Martin will be guarding you while we are there," Deryn told me. "He will take you anywhere you want to go within the grounds."

"So, I won't get to go explore?" I asked.

"We'll take you when we can," Deryn promised.

"I'm surprised that you guys are okay with Martin watching me," I teased them.

"We trust you," Fox said.

"We had a long talk with him. So, he understands our expectations," Deryn said with a smile that held no warmth.

"So, you threatened him," I said and shook my head. It wasn't surprising. Alphas in general were protective, but because he was my guard, and I was his queen, it made him even more protective.

"We will come get you every opportunity that we can," Nico assured me. "We would rather to be with you than attend the meetings. They are always boring."

My phone rang and I quickly answered when I saw it was Martin. "Hello, handsome."

"Hello, beautiful," he replied.

Deryn growled softly, able to hear both sides of the conversation.

"Are you here?" I asked in a sultry voice.

"Yes. So, why don't you slip past your four guards and get down here. We can run away together."

"Martin," Deryn growled.

Martin laughed loudly. "He is so easy to rile up when it comes to you. It's almost like he loves you or something."

"I know, it's weird, right?" I said and winked at Deryn. "We'll be down in a few."

"I'll count the seconds until I'm honored with your presence, Princess."

"I'm going to punch him," Deryn said calmly, merely stating a fact.

"Let's go. We've only got a ten-hour train ride to endure," Rhys said, glancing at his watch.

"Ten hours of torturing you four. Yay!" I cheered.

"She's sadistic," Fox sighed while he stood from the bed. "Why must you enjoy torturing us?"

"Stop being so jealous, and I will stop teasing you so much. You four should know that I am not going to leave you for anyone else. My heart belongs equally to you four."

Fox kissed my cheek, his normal, radiant smile back in place. "That was all I wanted to hear."

Rhys grabbed my bag for me and headed out. Fox followed.

I stopped Deryn with a hand on his arm. "Hey."

He turned and smiled at me, a dazzling, happy smile. "Hey."

"Are we good?" Things had been strained between us since I removed my curse. He had been affectionate, but seemed far away whenever he was with me.

He rested his hand on my cheek and nodded, smile still in place. "Yes, baby. I'm sorry if I've been acting weird. I'm just worried about you." He kissed my lips and then linked our fingers.

They were all worried about me, which I didn't understand. The curse was gone, so they shouldn't have been worried any longer.

Nico had held the elevator for us, so we quickly got in.

Martin had the backdoor of the SUV open and helped load the bags before walking to me and bowing. "Princess."

A couple people walking down the sidewalk slowed to look at us.

I smacked his shoulder. "Stop that."

He pulled me into a hug and rubbed his cheek against mine, the stubble on his chin scraping me slightly. "This trip is going to be a ton of fun."

"I hope so," I replied with a tight smile.

Honestly, the Elder's warning still bothered me. Plus, my life had never been quiet or easy.

When we boarded the train, the guys argued over seating arrangements for a minute before resorting to ro-sham-bo.

I took the window seat so I would be able to look at everything as we went.

Nico sat beside me with a victorious smile and draped his arm around my shoulders.

Fox sat in front of me, Rhys next to him, and Deryn and Martin behind us.

"Nico," I whispered.

He leaned close to me. "Yes?"

"How much did you spend on my Christmas present?"

He jolted backward as though I had shocked him. "I'm not telling you that."

I smirked. "You haven't even purchased anything yet, have you? Don't worry. I'm not done shopping either."

"I have your present already," he said. "I'm just not going to tell you how much I spent. That's not something that you share with each other."

"More than one hundred? Two hundred? Three hundred?"

He didn't react to my questions at all.

I tapped Rhys's shoulder. "What about you?"

"Not saying."

"Fox?"

"Nope."

"Deryn?"

"I haven't gotten it yet," he admitted. "But, I am not telling you what I think I am going to spend."

"It's not fair," I grumbled and folded my arms across my chest. "How do I know how much to spend on you, if you won't give me an idea of what you are spending?"

"We wouldn't care if you spent absolutely zero on us. You could put a bow on yourself and lay on the bed, and we would be fine with that present," Nico whispered huskily in my ear.

"Sounds like a great present," Deryn whispered behind us.

I groaned and gave up.

The train whistle blew and it lurched forward. Our journey had officially begun.

Nico pulled me closer to him, pushing the arm of the seat that separated us up and out of the way. I rested my head on his chest, getting comfortable.

We were the only ones in this car of the train, but I felt like someone was watching me.

"What's wrong?" Nico asked. "You tensed up."

"I feel like I'm being watched," I whispered as quietly as possible.

"Do you want to switch seats?"

I shook my head and snuggled closer to him. "No, I'm fine. I know you'll protect me."

He put a shield around us. "Better?"

I nodded, feeling immensely better with the shield around us, and allowed myself to doze on and off.

After two hours of silence, Deryn stood with a groan and paced the aisle.

"Wouldn't you be more comfortable in your other form?" I asked him. I was considering it myself.

"Yes, but it's more boredom than a comfort issue bothering me right now."

"Let's play a game," I suggested.

"What game?" Rhys asked, standing and stretching too.

His shirt rode up, revealing the V of muscles that made women weak in the knees and brought to mind all sorts of fun things.

Martin inhaled deeply and then, sighed happily.

All eyes turned to him and Deryn stood beside him again with tensed legs, ready to jump on him.

I rolled my eyes.

"Don't fret," Martin told Deryn. "I've learned to lock down my hormones when it comes to her. We wouldn't have finished high school if I had let that delicious smell overpower me."

"We almost missed graduation," I reminded him softly.

"We made it, didn't we?" he said and smirked.

"You're really not affected by it?" Rhys asked.

"It's delicious to smell, but a perk to being mated is my mate's scent is super enticing and mutes other females' scents to allow me to resist easier."

"Good to know," Deryn said.

"You're like a teenage boy," Martin accused me. "You saw Rhys's skin and got all worked up."

"First of all, I am glad I'm not a boy because I know I would get boners way too often. Second, it wasn't just skin. It was the V. You know that drives me nuts."

"I really don't enjoy hearing about how much he knows about your turn-ons," Nico grumbled.

"You should be thanking me. A lot of her likes and dislikes are because of me," Martin teased.

"You mean you guys didn't ask him about me or things I like?" I asked, eyebrows raised. If there was a female who could tell me about them, I would have asked. Well, except for the President's daughter. Definitely not her.

"Part of the fun of new relationships is figuring out what the other likes," Fox said.

"Let's play a card game," Nico suggested.

"Only if you swear not to cheat," Fox said immediately.

"I never cheat when we're playing for fun," Nico replied with a devious smirk.

"Aren't most card games only four players?" I asked. I didn't really know much about card games, since I rarely played them.

"We will take turns, like we do with everything else," Deryn offered.

Deep in my heart, I felt a twinge of regret. Before me, they wouldn't have had to take turns. Before I came into their lives, they had four, which was the perfect amount to play almost any game. It was just a good, even amount in general. With me, I brought them to an odd number of five, which wasn't good for anything.

"What's wrong, cupcake?" Martin asked me softly, leaning against the top of my seat.

"It's nothing," I whispered and shook my head.

"Come on, you know you can't lie to me," he chastised.

"I don't want to talk about it," I whispered and glanced at the guys who were discussing which game to play.

"Want to go for a walk to the dining car? We can get some food and bring stuff back for everyone. I'm sure we're all hungry by now," he suggested.

He was trying to get me away from the guys so that I could talk to him. I *really* appreciated that.

"Okay," I agreed, climbing over Nico to get into the aisle, then pushing past Rhys and Fox to the door leading to another car.

"We're going to get some food for everyone," Martin told them.

"Oh, I'll come too and—" Rhys started, but there was a quiet conversation, too quiet for me to hear, and then Martin was pushing me through the door.

Part of me wanted to glance back at them, since it was dead silent now, but I kept my eyes forward and walked with Martin down the aisle of a car filled with passengers. Every single seat was taken and I felt bad we had an entire car to ourselves. The guys probably paid for all of the seats, but I still felt bad for all the people crammed into this one car.

We went into the next car and delicious scents filled the air.

"Food," I whispered and headed forward.

"So, what's going on?" Martin asked. "And don't say, 'nothing' or I'll pinch you until you tell me."

"I was just thinking about how much I've changed things for them. Before, they wouldn't have had to take turns playing games. They didn't have to take turns with a woman. They didn't have to take turns going out on dates. Now, they have to take turns, make schedules, and ro-sham-bo just to determine what fucking seat they're going to sit in."

A woman in a fancy suit, turned and gaped at me for my language. I rolled my eyes at her and focused back on Martin who smiled at me.

"Why the fuck are you smiling when I just poured my deep, inner thoughts out to you?" I growled at him.

"Sometimes you are so dense, cupcake. They love you. They do all of those things because they want to make this work with you. If they didn't want to do it, they wouldn't. They're fucking princes. They don't take orders from anyone, except their king, and sometimes not even them!"

"I should let them go, so they can go pursue other females, but I'm too selfish for that. I can't imagine my life without them. I can't imagine having to see them with another female. It hurts so much, just imagining it. Which then makes me feel worse, since they have to see me with other males."

The woman looked like she was about to faint now.

"If you don't want to hear us, then hurry up and get out of line," I snapped at her.

She gasped and spun around with a harrumph.

"Again, if they wanted to do that, they would. They don't want to pursue other females. And you're not being selfish. You love them."

"What's going to happen at the Summit?" I asked.

"All of the Other races get together and discuss peace agreements, trade requests, and any orders of business the kings might have to bring up. The princes are there to give advice to the kings and assist in making decisions. Really, they just have to listen to all the boring crap and nod once or twice at their fathers. It's *super* boring."

That sounded awful.

"So, you and I are going to be holed up in a room for hours on end, with nothing to do," I said.

"Yeah, too bad we aren't single," he smirked at me. "Then, we could fill the hours with lots of things to do."

"There are children," the woman gasped at us.

"And we didn't say anything bad. Your dirty mind was the one that supplied what you thought we were talking about," Martin pointed out. "We could have been talking about playing two-person video games for all you know."

"Do you think I should take them as my mates?" I asked Martin as quietly as possible. I never knew when someone from the media would be around.

"I can't answer that for you. That is something that you have to figure out for yourself."

"I think I already have," I admitted. "And I need your help."

"My help?" he asked with raised eyebrows. "I can't mate with them for you."

I laughed loudly, throwing my head back at the ridiculousness of his statement. "No, you idiot. I need you to help me get their mating gifts." Like humans gave each other engagement rings, Others gave each other gifts. Normally, it was jewelry, but shifters couldn't wear rings because they would get in the way when they were shifting. I had heard that one shifter lost a finger because she had forgotten to take off a ring before shifting.

"Oh!" he said, drawing out the word. "That, I can help you with."

We grabbed a ton of food and headed back to our car, where the four princes were huddled together, whispering conspiratorially, but stopped when we walked in.

I rolled my eyes. "Oh, I wonder what you were talking about. It couldn't have been me."

"You're always on our minds," Deryn replied smoothly with a sweet smile.

"That was sweet," I told him and kissed his cheek.

"That's not enough food," Rhys grumbled.

"Well, that's all we could get. So, why don't you go get more, if you think we need more," I suggested. "I'm going to sit down, look at the scenery, and eat my blueberry bagel."

"Martin," Deryn called. "Come with me."

Martin set our haul onto a table and went with Deryn and Rhys to get more food.

"You okay?" Fox asked, sitting next to me in the seat. "You felt sad for a bit while you were gone."

"I'm fine," I assured him with a smile. "Just talking with Martin about some stuff."

"Stuff like?" he probed.

"I love you, Fox, but there are some things that I can't talk to you guys about."

"Why not?" he asked with a scowl. "I talk to you about everything. You're one of my best friends. Aren't I one of your best friends?"

"Yes," I replied immediately. "But, I don't feel comfortable talking with one of you about one of the others. You guys are each other's original best friends and I refuse to cause a rift or issues between you. If I have problems with one of you, I am not going to go complain to someone else about it. Remember what happened when Rhys made me sad that one day? He got punched in the face and it wasn't even something that he deserved to get hit over."

"I get your point, but I wish you would talk to me more," he pouted.

"Plus, you guys talk to each other about everything. So, if I told you something about Rhys, you would either tell Rhys or tell one of the others who would then tell Rhys. It would get back to him and then he'd come talk to me about it and want to know why I didn't just talk to him about it in the first place."

"See, you already know that you should be talking to us first anyway. All of us wish you would talk to us about your feelings more. We want to know what is going on in that beautiful head of yours. We want to know when we do something that makes you happy. We want to know when we do something that makes you mad. And we especially want to know when we do something that makes you sad. We hate when you're sad. It creates this pressure in our chests that won't go away. It's incredibly uncomfortable and all we can think about is making you happy again."

I felt bad, but I meant what I had said to him. I wouldn't complain to them about one of the others. It wouldn't be right.

"I'll try to get better about that," I promised.

We ate and played games for a few hours, but I was tired again. I grabbed Deryn away from the game, pulling him to one of the chairs and lay my head on his lap. He pet my hair and hummed a song that I thought sounded familiar, but couldn't place as I fell asleep.

My sleep didn't last long, though. The train slammed to a halt, throwing us forward and onto the floor. Deryn had managed to keep me from hurting myself and helped me get up.

Our food was now all over the floor, chips strewn all over.

"What the hell happened?" I asked.

"Stay here," Rhys ordered Deryn. "Martin and Nico, come with me. Fox, stay with them."

"Stay safe!" I ordered them.

They didn't respond, just walked out of the car to find out what had happened.

A second later, an explosion rocked the train.

Deryn picked me up and curled his body around mine.

"Status?" Deryn asked.

"No answer," Fox growled, putting his phone away.

"Decision?" Deryn asked.

"Out the back," Fox said. "I'll go first."

Deryn nodded and we headed out the back end of the train. Fox took point, throwing open the doors as we went, but as we looked out the rear of the last car, we hadn't found anything except scared people. Fox leapt out of the last car, onto the train tracks, and then leapt up onto the top of the car.

"Oh, fuck," he said, loud enough for the sound to make it down to us.

"Status!" Deryn growled, growing impatient.

"It's a god damn Cthulhu!" Fox yelled. "It's got the first few cars of the train in its tentacles.

"That's not a real creature. It was created by H.P. Lovecraft," I reminded Deryn.

"Well, then how do you explain that?" Fox asked.

Deryn leapt up onto the top of the train car, me still in his arms, and we both stared at the creature attacking the train. It sure as hell looked like Cthulhu.

"Well..." I didn't know how to finish that.

Rhys, Martin, and Nico were battling with the Cthulhu-like creature, trying to save the cars from its tentacles.

"Fox?" Deryn asked.

"I'll go. You stay with her," Fox said. He kissed my cheek and raced across the top of the train cars.

"Do you guys do things like this a lot?" I asked Deryn.

He smirked. "You'd be surprised how often things like this happen to us."

"So, maybe you guys are the problem and not me," I teased.

"Oh, you definitely attract your own danger," he replied. "But, so do we."

Rhys, Martin, Nico, and a few additional Others were fighting the creature, trying to save the people inside of the cars.

"We need to do more training," I whispered. "I could be useful in situations like these."

"Too dangerous. We will never allow you to face something like this," Deryn said, shaking his head.

"I can shift into a god damn dragon," I reminded him angrily.

"We don't care. You're not going to jump into battle. You only need to do things like that to protect yourself. And yes, your nieces or children on occasion," he said.

"Overprotective," I grumbled.

"There's no such thing. We are supposed to keep you safe. Letting you jump into a fight is not a way to keep you safe. Our entire being is set to keep you safe. All we can focus on is keeping you safe. So, no, there is no such thing as us being overprotective. You are the most important thing to us."

"I wasn't looking for a lecture," I grumbled at him.

He smirked and kissed my cheek. "Well, too bad. You got one."

The train shuddered beneath us, the monster pulling on it, forcing Deryn to jump down off of it and onto the train tracks.

"This is not looking good," I commented. So far, my guys seemed to be able to stay out of harm's way, so I wasn't too worried about them. I was worried about all of the people on the train though.

"This is such a pain in the butt," a guy said as he stepped out of the back of the train in front of us. He had long, golden hair, piercing blue eyes, and was carrying a huge sledge hammer.

"Thor? What are you doing here?" Deryn asked.

Thor? Like, God of Thunder?

"Yo, Deryn. I was sleeping on the train when it slammed on its brakes and sent me flying. Now I'm pissed and I'm going to take it out on the squid thing," he explained. His eyes fell on me, in Deryn's arms, and they widened. "Who is this? Did you find a mate?"

"This is the Princess of the Four Clans," Deryn introduced, but his grip on me tightened.

"I'd stay for a longer introduction, but as a resident god, I've got to go handle this," he said, winked at me, leapt up onto the train, and ran down the cars towards the monster.

"Is he really a god?" I asked.

Deryn scoffed. "In his own mind."

Thor leapt from the train, hammer raised, and gave a mighty bellow. The sky filled with clouds and lightning struck his hammer, alighting it and with a swing, the lightning went from his hammer to the monster.

Rhys and everyone else who had been battling it, leapt away just before the lightning struck, saving themselves from electrocution.

"Thor! Warn us first!" Rhys yelled at him.

"I bellowed," Thor countered.

We all watched the monster twitch. After a few twitches, it sank back into the water from where it had come. The cars righted on the tracks and everyone cheered.

"Great, now he's going to be made out a hero again. Let's get back to our car," Deryn grumbled.

"I take it you don't like him very much?" I asked softly.

"He's a good enough guy, just full of himself. Plus, everyone fawns over him like he's something special. I've beaten him before and so has Rhys. He's not perfect, like people think he is."

"Oh, did he steal a girlfriend from you, too?" I teased him, trying to lighten his mood.

He rolled his eyes at me, but then his usual smile returned. "I actually stole one from him a few years ago."

"You're terrible," I said and shook my head. "I had no idea you were a thief."

"I stole your heart, didn't I?" he whispered huskily in my ear.

My hands gripped his shirt tighter and I tensed. "Don't. Tease. Me."

He chuckled and kissed my cheek lightly. "Sorry, baby."

The others came back, Thor with them, chatting and laughing like old friends.

"Thor, this is Jolie. Jolie, this is Thor," Nico introduced.

I stood up out of the seat I had been in beside Deryn and held out my hand. "Nice to meet you."

He took my hand, pulled me forward and hugged me, his nose tickling my neck as he inhaled deeply. "Hello, Jolie."

I heard three growls and two chuckles, one of which was mine. "Hello, Thor." I sniffed his neck and wondered what it was about his scent that smelled so familiar.

"Let her go," Deryn ordered him.

Thor released me with a smirk. "Don't worry, I was only saying hello."

"That's not how you say hello to someone you don't know," Deryn chastised him with a growl.

"It is if you're a werewolf," I said. "Especially a Northern Clan Werewolf."

That got everyone's attention.

"How do you know about that?" Thor asked suspiciously.

"Because that's what I am," Martin said.

Thor spun to face Martin. "I knew you smelled familiar!" He spun back to me. "You aren't a werewolf, though."

"No, but Martin and I dated in high school and I spent a lot of time with the pack," I admitted. I stared at Thor a minute longer before realization struck. I gasped and yelled, "Tim!"

"Tim?" Deryn asked.

Thor flinched. "Oh, wow. It's been years..." He froze, eyes widened, and pulled me forward to inhale the top of my head. He took a few big lungfuls and tilted my chin up with his finger to look into my eyes. "Jo?" he asked softly, recognition finally showing.

I nodded. "Yes, Tim."

"Holy wolf teats!" Martin yelled.

Thor smiled wide, dimples flashing, and he whispered, "Jo," before kissing me deeply.

I tried to push him back, but he was gone the next instant, Deryn having thrown him off of me and against the far wall of our car.

Thor wasn't even fazed. He was still smiling wide and tried to walk back towards me, but Deryn and Rhys blocked his path.

"Jo, how is it possible that you're even more beautiful now?" he asked me.

My cheeks were on fire. It had been a long time since I last saw him. Back then, he was Tim, not Thor, and he wasn't nearly as muscular.

"Don't touch her again," Deryn ordered him.

Martin pulled Thor into a bone crunching hug and Thor returned it. "I didn't even recognize your scent!" Martin exclaimed. "Your appearance and scent are so different!"

"Well, the last time I saw you two was graduation," Thor reminded us.

"You went to school with Jolie?" Rhys asked, for clarification.

Thor nodded. "She was my first love."

"Wasn't that Stacy H?" I asked with a teasing smirk. Stacy was the first girl he kissed and she had been head over heels for him.

"No, it was always you," he said seriously. He turned to Martin. "You let her get away? What the fuck is wrong with you?"

I flinched and Nico and Fox saw it, exchanging a look before turning back to Thor, who was still being blocked by Rhys and Deryn.

"It's a long and unpleasant story," Martin answered without looking at me.

"We've got hours left on this ride," Thor said. He looked at Rhys and Deryn. "How long are you going to keep standing there?"

"As long as we think you might try to kiss her again," Deryn growled.

"Jo," Thor called, "come talk to me."

I squeezed between Rhys and Deryn to hug Thor, ignoring their growls again. "I can't believe it's you."

He chuckled. "I feel the same. They said your name, but I couldn't believe it was you. That you could be *the* Jolie."

We sat at the table and my guards took seats around me.

"You want to tell it?" Martin asked.

I shook my head, dreading this tale already. Thor held out his hand and despite the four males growling behind me, I set my hand in his. Thor could always tell when I was upset. He was very empathic.

"Jolie," Deryn growled softly.

Without looking at him, I reached back and held my other hand out to him. He linked our fingers and quieted.

"Remember how we kept seeing vampires in the area?" Martin asked Thor.

He nodded.

"There was a battle going on between the witches and vampires that we hadn't know about. Jo's dad was King of the Vampires and somehow the witches found out about Jo. We were out in Mrs. Lindstrom's field and they attacked us. It was just the two of us. I killed two of the witches, but another one grabbed Jo before I could stop her. She took Jo to the coven."

Thor's hand tightened around mine, but it was such a small movement, I wasn't certain he had done it consciously.

"Jo, tell your part," Martin said.

Thor turned toward me.

"Um, the witch took me to the coven. They had built a place on the other side of the river and cloaked the building so the wolves hadn't been able to see it. They, uh, they tied me to a post and tried to get information about my dad from me. I didn't know anything, though. They started torturing me to try to get me to break and…"

"We heard her screams," Martin continued for me. "We broke their illusions and I had to barter for her release."

A cost that I had been against and tried to convince him not to agree to.

"What was the cost?" Nico asked.

"That I separate from Jo and we never have a romantic relationship again. If we did, we would both become sterile."

For me, that wouldn't have mattered, but Martin had always wanted children. It was a definite deal breaker for him.

"So, you gave up your relationship to save her?" Deryn asked softly, his anger gone now.

Martin nodded. "But, they had already put a curse on her, two actually, that we hadn't known about."

"What happened?" Thor asked me.

"I was in a coma for a year until Grandma found someone who could break it. Then, just a few days ago, I had the final curse removed."

"And almost died," Deryn growled.

I jerked my hand away from his and stood up with fists clenched. "And I'd do it again," I growled at him. "Don't you get it? These witches put that curse on me when I was eighteen and I just now got it removed. I've been in danger and so has everyone else, because of it."

Deryn reached for me, but Thor pulled me forward so he could hug me. I hadn't even realized that he had stood up.

"What else happened, Jo? Why are you so angry?" he asked as he held me.

Like Fox, he had a soothing presence, and I relaxed into him. "A lot has happened," I whispered. "Some things I don't think I can even tell you about."

"No, she can't," Deryn growled.

"Deryn," Fox whispered, "calm down."

"Stop touching her," Deryn snarled.

"If she wanted me to release her, she'd pull back. You're not her mate. You may be Prince, but you don't get to order me not to hug my friend and packmate."

"She's not pack," Rhys pointed out.

"Semantics. I spent just as much time playing and hunting with her as I did the rest of my pack," Thor said.

He wasn't wrong. I had spent a lot of time with him.

"I'm his queen," I told Thor, looking up into his eyes. "Rhys, Deryn, Foxfire, and Nico are my guards. That's a secret by the way, so please don't tell anyone."

Thor chuckled. "Well, that explains their protectiveness. But, unless you're also sleeping with them, then…"

I glanced down and felt my cheeks heat up.

"Oh," Thor said. "Well, why didn't you say so?"

"Because it doesn't matter," I said and looked up at Thor. "You're my friend and they…" I jerked my thumb at the guys, "…need to get used to seeing me hug my friends, no matter their gender."

"He kissed you," Deryn reminded me.

"Yes, before he knew anything," I countered. "I'm not marked, so he assumed I was unattached."

"I would have kissed you anyway," Thor said with a smirk.

I punched his arm and he released me and sat back down.

"Want to tell me the rest of the story?" he asked.

I did. I started from the end of the witch story and told him about almost everything that had happened to me and ended with coming on the train. I also made sure he knew to keep it secret.

"That's one crazy life," Thor said with a whistle.

"You never told us all of that," Fox whispered.

"Well, now everyone knows," I said and shrugged.

Deryn left, heading into the next train car with Nico following him.

A guy with tousled brown hair stuck his head into the car. "Thor? Alpha wants you."

Thor nodded, hugged me, and headed after him.

I got into my window seat and watched the scenery rolling by. Lush green hills made up the land we were traveling through with no building in sight. It was beautiful and peaceful.

Talking about all of the bad things that had happened to me had reopened emotions I hadn't wanted to revisit, but was now forced to. After what had happened with Martin and the witches, I had distanced myself from people. I didn't want them involved or hurt, so I made myself a hermit. I made friends online in the gaming community and did my best to only let those relationships flourish. But, I had grown tired of being lonely. I needed physical companionship and not just sex, but the hugging and cuddling mainly. Growing up with werewolves had made me affectionate and going so long without touch had been driving me insane. On and off I dated, but I always left when it started to get serious, normally after some awful event reminded me why I was supposed to be away from people. I'd become a recluse up until I got this job in Jinla and had been starving for affection.

Deryn came back and plopped down in the seat next to me.

"I'm sorry," I whispered without looking at him. "I was being selfish again. I hadn't seen him in so long and the urge to touch him and—"

"No, I'm sorry," he interrupted. "You weren't doing anything wrong. And, I need to get over you removing the curse. You are here and fine, so it shouldn't matter."

"Why have you guys been so tense lately?" I asked him softly. "All of you have been worried about me, but I don't know why."

He held out his hand, but instead of taking it, I climbed into his lap and rested my head on his shoulder.

"You've been having nightmares. You cry out and sometimes call our names. You've even cried while dreaming, tears dripping down your cheeks and you'll be whimpering. It's been happening for weeks."

Shit. I hadn't realized they knew about my nightmares.

"Oh."

"What are your nightmares of?" he asked me softly, his voice gentle and his arms a secure band around my hips.

"Death," I replied softly.

"Whose?"

"All four of you."

He tensed beneath me. "What happens?"

"You're protecting me from something and one by one, you all die. I try to stop it, but I can't move. I just have to sit and watch as you're killed."

I was crying, evident by the wet spot on Deryn's shoulder. Deryn turned and licked my cheeks and eye, clearing away the tears.

"They're just dreams, baby. We are all here, safe and sound."

"What if it is a premonition?" I asked.

"We aren't going to die anytime soon," he assured me.

"You don't know that for sure," I argued.

"Do you really think they are premonitions?" he asked.

"No," I admitted, "but it won't stop happening. Almost every night."

"Perhaps it is your own fear getting the better of you," he suggested. "I know my biggest fear right now is losing you. I wouldn't be surprised if I had nightmares about it."

Part of me knew it was because whenever something good happened, something bad usually came next to counter it. I was trying really hard to just enjoy the happiness we had been having, but my subconscious was a jerk.

Now that I was surrounded by love and warmth, I didn't want to go back to being alone. I didn't want to be a hermit again.

"Hey," Deryn whispered and kissed my forehead. "What's going on in that head of yours?"

"Honestly?" I asked.

He nodded.

"After becoming used to being loved and touched again, I don't think I could handle going back to being a recluse. If I lose you, I won't be able to be alone."

"You won't be alone," he promised me. "You aren't going to lose us. I told you, no matter what happens, I will always be here for you."

"Even if I piss you off?" I asked softly.

"Always," he said adamantly, "and forever."

"I already used the lifetimes line," Fox called to him.

"Line?" I asked, feigning hurt. "So, it wasn't true? It was just a line you use on all the girls?"

Fox rolled his eyes at me. "You know it's not."

"Jolie, did you sleep with Thor?" Deryn asked in a whisper.

"No," I answered loudly. "Why would you think that?"

"He said you were his first love," Deryn reminded me.

"I was *his* first love. He wasn't mine. I only slept with Martin from that pack," I explained.

"So, he loved you and you loved Martin?"

I nodded.

"Wait, *that pack*? Were there other werewolves that you slept with from other packs?"

Oops. Spilled the beans. Shit.

"Um," I replied intelligently, totally ready for that question.

"How many other werewolves?" he asked.

"I don't ask you guys about who you slept with before," I countered.

"This is important," he said seriously.

"Why?"

"Because a representative from each of the packs will be at the Summit, so it is better if he is prepared ahead of time with knowing if any of them slept with you," Fox answered for him.

"Doesn't that mean I should let all four of you know if I have slept with others of your race?" I asked.

"Yes," Fox replied immediately.

"Do I have to give you names?"

"Yes," Deryn said.

Fuck.

"Yukio and Zelphar of the elves."

Fox's eyes widened and he blinked in silence.

"Declan and Kylan of the dragons," I said, looking at Rhys.

"Both?" he asked.

"Yes." They were twin brothers who I had dated one after the other.

"Werewolves?" Deryn prompted, growing impatient.

"Tobias, Ezio and..."

What was his name?

"Lorenzo," Martin answered for me.

I gaped at him. "How did you know that?"

"He called me to make sure we were actually over," he explained.

Wow.

"Anyone else fall in love with you? Like Thor?" Deryn asked with a scowl on his face and his body tense beneath me.

"I don't know," I snapped and stood up away from him. "You can't be mad at me about this. You knew I wasn't a virgin before we slept together. Plus, you're not a virgin either."

My anger was building, partly, okay mostly, due to my embarrassment. It wasn't fair for him to get mad at me for things that happened before we got together.

"No one likes hearing the list of prior conquests," Martin offered. "Not even me and we aren't together any longer."

"Or knowing you will see all of them at the Summit," Deryn growled.

"All of them?" I asked, my voice squeaking at the end.

"One big Jolie reunion," Deryn snarled.

I jerked back, feeling worse than if he had physically slapped me.

Tears pricked at my eyes and I whispered, "Excuse me," before running out of the train car.

Rhys I might have expected a comment like that from, but not Deryn.

The train didn't have many places to escape to, but I knew towards the front was a car with glass ceilings and walls, so you could get a full view. I tripped over someone's foot and muttered an apology as I continued on.

Someone grabbed my arm and I turned, ready to attack, when through my teary-eyed sight, I recognized Dan.

"Alpha," I whispered, then sniveled.

"What's wrong?" he asked.

I shook my head. "I don't want to—"

Deryn entered the car, following me, and I pulled against Dan's hold.

"I don't want to talk to him," I begged him. "I just need some time."

He released me and nodded. "Go, I'll keep him."

I went through the next door and just as the door closed, I felt Dan use his power as he said, "Sit!" It was such a strong command that my knees wobbled.

I stumbled forward, right into Thor.

"Jo, what's wrong?" he asked, his eyes scanning my face and then behind me.

"Jus...need space," I said and hurried around him.

He let me go, but was scowling with furrowed brows as he watched me leave.

Finally, I made it to the car and found a seat. Surprisingly, there was no one else in the car. I curled my legs up, hugging my knees as I watched the hills go by.

There was something more going on with Deryn than he was telling me. He had been upset a lot recently. More than he should have been, even with me almost dying and my nightmares.

"The number one thing alphas hate, is not having control," Nico whispered from beside me.

"Nico," I sighed. "I want to be alone."

"No, you don't. Now, listen. Alphas hate not having control. As prince, we have to operate knowing that for now, our fathers have control. And, we know there are some things we don't have control over and never will. Many alphas mate with a submissive because it ensures that we will have control."

"How loving," I scoffed.

"Shush," he ordered me.

"Fine," I mumbled and turned away from him.

"Deryn has always been in control of everything he possibly could be. Then, you fell into our lives."

"Is this the, Jolie fucked everything up, speech?" I asked with a snarl.

"You are incredibly unpredictable, wild, danger prone, and infuriating. You are emotional, independent, and happy to butt heads with anyone, even the kings."

"This is a fantastic pep talk," I grumbled. "Definitely making me feel better."

"On top of all of that, our lives drastically changed. We went from our happy and content foursome to our hectic fivesome."

I stood up and walked away from him. "Then, just fucking let me leave!"

He teleported in front of me and grabbed my shoulders, his eyes fell to the tears on my face and his scowl disappeared.

"Despite all of this, Deryn loves you more than anything else in the world. More than his own pack. Nothing regarding you is controllable. There is always something new for us to learn about you. We all figured we weren't the first Others you had had relationships with, but half of those wolves you slept with hate Deryn. They will use this opportunity to throw it in his face that they had you first. Since you aren't mated and our relationships aren't public knowledge, they can touch you if you allow it. He is once again not in control. You opted to put your life on the line and there was nothing he could do about it. You almost died and all we could do was pace and pray. He is stressed and hasn't been eating well because of it. He also hasn't shifted much lately. It is not an excuse for him saying such a cruel thing to you, but maybe you'll see things from his side if you know all of the facts."

My anger had dissipated, but I was still hurt.

Nico disappeared, leaving me alone with my thoughts.

What he said made sense. I could understand how infuriating someone like me would be to an alpha who liked to be in control of everything. I knew shifters preferred schedules and predictable events because chaos made them a little less in control of their beasts and an out of control werewolf was not something anyone wanted. For someone as powerful as a prince to lose control would be unthinkable. The fact that he hadn't shifted much recently was bothering me the most. I was a shitty girlfriend for not noticing he hadn't been shifting while we were together. He should have been spending at least half of our time together as a wolf.

I marched back to the car where Dan was sitting next to Deryn who was obviously frozen from his father's order.

"Shift," I ordered Deryn.

Dan said," You may go."

Deryn stood up and opened his mouth.

"Shift," I ordered him again before he could speak.

He scowled, but then did as I asked and shifted into his wolf form.

I held open the door for him. "Come on."

Deryn followed me on silent paws to the observation car. I lay on my back in the aisle, looking up at the sky. Deryn sat in front of me, slightly between my legs, head cocked, and looked at me.

I grabbed the fur on either side of his cheeks and gently tugged his head, so he lay down with his head on my chest, muzzle between my breasts. I pet his head with my eyes closed, inhaling his hot wolf breath and letting him breathe my scent in.

"What you said was rude and hurt me a lot," I whispered. He tried to lift his head, but I held him. I didn't continue until he had stilled. "It is not my fault that I didn't meet you until now. Yes, I have had a few sexual partners, but only one I had planned to mate with before you four. The way I see it, you have a few options. You can keep things as they are, withdraw your request to be my mate, but stay my guard, or you can completely cut ties with me. I love you so much, but I don't want to continue causing you misery."

And, I was crying again. Dammit.

His long wolf tongue licked up each cheek, then he shifted, laying atop me, but propped up on one arm so he wasn't squishing me.

"Baby, I'm sorry. I am a jealous asshole. It is not fair of me to take my frustration out on you. You aren't causing me misery."

"You were happy and smiling all the time, wanting to play and be carefree, but now you are mad all the time. That sounds pretty miserable. What's your decision?"

He kissed me deeply, his tongue sliding along mine in a slow caress as he gripped one of my hips, his thumb rubbing over my hip bone.

"I'm not going anywhere. Didn't we just talk about this? You are stuck with me for the rest of your life. I love you and I promise to work on my attitude and worrying. I want you to be safe and that has seemed impossible lately. I will do whatever I need to, to keep you safe, happy, and with me. I'm sorry for what I said. It wasn't fair of me."

"No, it wasn't," I agreed and sniffled.

He kissed each of my eyes, then my cheeks, neck, and my forehead. "I'm sorry." He sat up, pulling me with him, and hugged me tightly. "I'm sorry."

We sat like that for several minutes. As I looked out the windows, I realized the train was heading toward the ocean.

"Does it turn ahead?" I asked, scanning the coast for the direction the train would turn.

"No," Deryn replied, but didn't elaborate.

Before I could ask where it went, I got my answer. We plunged straight into the sea, a shield of magic around us, keeping the water, as well as the creatures, away from the train.

I gasped and clung to him. More people filed into the car, stepping around us carefully as I took it all in, my mouth agape.

"You're beautiful," Deryn whispered. "I'm lucky to have you."

CHAPTER 6

The rest of the train ride was, thankfully, uneventful. We arrived at a land of swaying green grass and a huge castle, the largest I had ever seen.

A bus took us and two dozen other train riders to the castle. I sat between Deryn and Rhys, but kept standing up to lean over the top of the seat in front of me to talk to Dan.

"How old is it?" I asked him.

"One thousand years at least," he answered. "Over five hundred rooms, a huge ballroom, a courtroom, and three pools."

"I'm going to get lost," I whispered and Dan laughed.

Rhys pulled me down in to my seat. "You won't get lost because you will have a guard with you at all times."

"Is there indoor plumbing?" I asked softly.

All of them, including Dan and Thor who sat in front of me, laughed.

"Yes," Rhys promised.

"I'm hungry," I complained.

"There will be a huge feast when we arrive. We actually will only have time to change and then head to the throne room to eat," Dan told us.

"I have to wear a dress, don't I?" I asked with a resigned sigh.

"Yes, but don't worry, the dresses will all be in styles you like," Fox said behind me.

"That's reassuring," I whispered.

"Who is guarding her while you are in meetings?" Thor asked.

"Me," Martin answered. "That's why I'm here."

"If you need me, just howl," Thor told him. "I know she's quite a handful."

"Rude," I growled at him, but couldn't deny he was right.

Deryn squeezed the hand he was holding, having grabbed it at some point, though I wasn't certain when.

"Is there anything I should know before we get there?" I asked Dan.

"Yes," he nodded, "but I don't have the time to teach you everything right now. Just be on your most polite behavior and bow to everyone to be on the safe side."

"Right, being overly respectful is better than being disrespectful, even if I'm ignorant to who is actually important or not," I agreed.

"Right," Dan said.

"My clan kept our relationship a secret, so we are basically at square one. You're just our friend and here at Dan's invitation as Princess of the Four Clans. They will probably want to talk to you or at least say something to you, but I wouldn't worry about it too much," Rhys told me.

"So, no holding hands or anything?" I asked softly, feeling a bit of pressure in the center of my chest knowing I wouldn't be able to be affectionate with them in public.

Deryn squeezed my hand. "No, we won't be able to hold hands once we are there," he whispered.

"We should have had a cuddle puddle on the train before we departed," I mumbled.

"We can do that once we are in the rooms," Nico offered.

"Are we all staying near each other?" I asked, hopefully.

They all nodded.

"We wanted to make sure that you were safe, and that you wouldn't get yourself into trouble," Nico explained.

"I never get myself into trouble," I grumbled. "It finds me."

"One last thing," Dan whispered.

I leaned forward, so I could hear him through the crack in the seats.

"If anyone gives you trouble or threatens you, you tell one of us immediately. There will be a lot of things going on politically, and if they can find a way to use you for their own agendas, they will take it. They will make up a ton of lies about you, if it furthers their cause. So, let us know if anyone says anything that you think is weird or might have been a threat. It most likely will be one."

"Super positive pep talk there, Dad," I teased.

"Dad?" he whispered.

"Oh, uh, I just meant...you know the pep talk...it's like when a dad—"

"I like the sound of that," he said and turned his head to look over the seat at Deryn. "Someday, I would like that to be official."

"Don't look at me," he mumbled. "That's her decision. You know how I feel about it."

"Hm, yes. It's giving me one less chip to bargain with at the table," Dan said. He looked at Rhys. "Did you say the same to your father?"

"What?" Rhys asked, not paying attention to us.

"About not taking a mate for political purposes?" Dan said cryptically, so no one would know that we were actually talking about them not wanting anyone, but me, as a mate.

"Yes," Rhys said with a nod. "Father knows that is my feeling as well. He said that once he saw us together, at the den, that he knew he wouldn't be able to separate us anyway, even if she never takes me for a mate."

"Hm, well, Daughter, I think you and I need to have a talk soon," Dan told me.

"I don't like the sound of that," I grumbled. "Dad-talks never went well for me. They usually ended with me being thrown into a closet."

"Dad won't throw you into a closet," Deryn promised me. "And if he did, I would just rip the door off for you again anyway."

"My hero," I whispered and batted my eyelashes at him dramatically.

"You should call me that more often," he whispered and kissed my cheek.

"And you said *I* have a big ego," Thor scoffed.

"You do. You refer to yourself as a god, Tim," Deryn growled.

"Don't call me that," Thor growled back.

"Boys," Dan chastised them. "No growling at each other. We're on the same side, remember?"

"No, we're not," Thor argued. "We both love her and both want her."

"You can't have her," Rhys growled at him.

"That's her decision," Thor whispered.

"Thor, knock it off," I growled at him. "If you want to spend any time with me, you have to drop the façade of trying to win me."

"I still love you," he whispered.

"As a packmate," I reminded him. "You don't know me anymore. I'm much different than I was at eighteen."

"Packmate?" Dan asked. "You were part of the pack Jolie grew up with?"

Thor nodded. "Yes."

"Did you really let her go on hunts with you?" Dan asked.

Thor nodded. "She would ride on Martin's back, or mine, and we would chase after animals. Normally, if we had her on our back, we would hunt rabbits instead of the deer that the rest of the pack was hunting. Sometimes, we set her down and joined in, but normally we were content to chase rabbits."

"And none of your pack tried to harm her during the hunts?" Dan asked.

Thor shook his head. "Of course not! She's pack."

"But she wasn't marked," Dan pointed out.

"She didn't need to be. We all knew her scent. She played with us and went to school with us. You have to remember that our town had only about six hundred people in the total population. Everyone knew everyone."

"Most of the town was the pack," I explained. "There were very few people living there who weren't pack."

"Your family being one of them," Dan added.

I nodded.

"I'm surprised your dad stayed in that town, with him becoming a vampire and all," he commented.

"Me too," I said honestly. I still wasn't sure why he had stayed when he knew the werewolves would be able to tell he was a vampire. It didn't really make sense, but then again, my dad hadn't made much sense to me, ever.

"Jo, what was the name of that girl that you punched?" Thor asked.

"Jolie punched someone?" Deryn asked, eyes widening.

"Anna Smith. She was talking bad about Others, werewolves especially, and none of them could do anything, but since I was human, like her, I could. So, I walked up to her and punched her right in her raised nose. She cried like a baby."

"Didn't you get in trouble?" Thor asked.

I nodded. "Alpha made me stay away from the pack for a week."

"He made you stay away? Why?" Dan asked.

"Because he knew that I hated being away from them. I grew up like a shifter, craving affection and touch. Being away for a week meant I didn't get any touch, since my mom was dead and my dad was psychotic."

"That's a really harsh punishment," Rhys said with a frown.

"He was trying to teach her not to fight people, like we are always taught," Martin explained. "Plus, I snuck over after a few days to ensure she didn't go crazy."

"That's why you're so affectionate," Dan whispered. "You're basically a werewolf who can't shift."

"I guess so," I whispered.

"Would you have gone crazy?" Rhys asked.

I nodded and looked at Deryn. "I told you that I wouldn't be able to go back to being alone again."

He pulled me into a tight hug and said, "You won't ever be alone, Jolie."

"No, you won't," Thor promised.

The castle was larger than a few college campuses I had been to. Sticking to my spot in the center of my guards, we walked down the hallway to our rooms. My room was in the center of theirs, giving me added protection. In the closet was a month's worth of dresses in various colors and styles. I opted for a silver dress with a snug bodice, but flowing skirt.

Someone knocked on my door.

"Just a minute!" I called as I put on all of the jewelry the guys had given me.

"You look stunning," Deryn said from behind me.

I spun around, my heart pounding in my chest. "Mage's mana! You scared me!"

His smile let me know that he didn't feel bad at all. "Are you ready?"

Now that I wasn't hyperventilating, I looked at him. He had black slacks, a white button up shirt, and black tie and jacket.

"You look hot," I said, stepping forward and resting my hands on his chest.

"Stop looking at me like that or we won't make it to the feast," he whispered and kissed me.

"We could have our own feast here," I tempted.

"You need to eat," Deryn said. "I can hear your stomach growling."

"Sounds like she's thirsty," Fox said with a wink as he, Rhys, and Nico walked in.

"You present me with a gift and then get mad when I want to unwrap it. It's not fair," I fake pouted.

"You can unwrap all four of us later," Nico promised. "First, we need to get some food."

"Wait," I ordered them. "Before we go and I can't touch you all." I grabbed Deryn, since he was closest and pulled him into a deep kiss, and did the same with all of the others.

"Maybe we could be late," Nico rumbled and pulled me back for another kiss.

I pushed him away with a wide smile, glad that I still had that effect on them. "No. No. We need food, remember?" I said to Nico as I walked away.

Rhys opened the door, preventing us from continuing the teasing, and we all filed out. The guys took their positions around me and walked down the hallway confidently, making turns, and arriving without asking for directions.

"How many times have you been here?" I asked.

"Every year since we were five," Fox answered.

"Well, I'm glad you guys know your way around. I'd be completely lost right now other—"

"Jo?" a male voice asked.

I stopped and turned toward the speaker. It was actually two of them, both dragons with identical faces and smiles.

"Declan and Kylan!" I called happily, stepping out of the protection of my guards to hug the twins. "You guys haven't changed at all."

Declan kissed my cheek. "You look gorgeous, like always."

Kylan nodded and kissed my other cheek. "I'm so happy to see you. We were just talking about you the other day."

"Good things, I hope," I said with a smile, squeezing their hands, each holding one of mine.

"Of course," Declan assured me.

"Declan. Kylan. Nice to see you both," Rhys greeted them.

They bowed to Rhys, but hadn't let go of my hand. "Prince," they said in unison.

Kylan turned back to me. "Are you going to the feast? You should sit with us."

"Sorry guys, but I'm sitting with my friends already," I said and indicated my group.

"Well you have to visit with us and catch up," Declan begged.

"I will definitely try," I promised, unsure how Rhys would react to their proposal.

They kissed my cheeks again and headed off.

"You sure you're not a witch?" Nico asked.

"What? Why?"

"They never touch anyone, unless it is to hurt them," Rhys told me.

"What? That's crazy! They're super sweet and really affectionate."

The guys exchanged glances and then we headed back down the hallway. I hated their shared glances, since I couldn't figure out what they were communicating.

The ballroom was ginormous. It reminded me of a warehouse due to its size, but surprisingly, it was warm and inviting. Currently, it was filled with tables and people milling about, talking to each other.

As soon as the guys entered, a group of females rushed over to fawn all over them. More than a few snuck touches in, and some gave brazen offers to visit their rooms later.

"Jolie?" a soft voice asked behind me.

I turned and smiled up at Tobias. "Hey!"

He pulled me forward and rubbed his cheek along mine. "It is you."

He looked and smelled the same. Light stubble on his cheeks, deep brown eyes, and dark brown hair accented his medium-brown skin. Tobias had been the first male I had slept with after Martin. It had taken me a while to take that step and he had been a patient hunter and gentleman the whole time. I had started to fall for him and when I realized that, I had broken it off and left.

"You look great," I offered and kissed his cheek.

"Tonight, I need to talk to you privately," he said urgently.

"About what?" I asked.

"Tobias, good to see you," Deryn greeted him stiffly.

Tobias tensed and bowed slightly. "Prince Deryn."

"Jolie, do you know—" Tobias started, but Deryn draped his arm across my shoulders.

"Jolie and I are friends," Deryn said, his eyes sparking with gold.

Tobias nodded then looked at me. "Promise?"

I nodded. "Promise."

He left and Deryn pulled away from me before he asked, "What did you promise him?"

"To come talk to him tonight," I answered, not wanting to keep anything from him.

"About what?"

"I don't know," I admitted.

Something was up, though. He had seemed nervous, almost scared. Tobias was never scared. And why talk to me? Why not Dan or Deryn?

"Come on, let's go sit down," he said, starting to reach for me, but dropped his hand and instead waved in the direction of the guys. They had escaped the herd of females and now sat at a table with three open seats. Deryn sat beside Rhys, quickly whispering to him, and I sat between the empty chair and Martin.

"You look beautiful," he whispered and rubbed his cheek along mine.

"Thanks," I whispered, rubbing his cheek back for comfort.

Someone slid into the seat next to me and I turned, expecting to find Dan or Thor, but instead found Ezio.

He was one of the most handsome males I had ever seen, even more attractive than my guards. Copper hair, sapphire eyes, and a smile that had me clenching my thighs together to hide my arousal, was coupled with the body of a god.

He waited for me to stop ogling him and leaned his face forward, waiting.

I met him, sliding my cheek along his silky soft skin and practically purred at his cologne-like scent. "Ezio," I whispered.

He pressed our foreheads together and whispered, "Jolie, my love. I've missed you."

Deryn and someone else growled, but neither of us moved.

"I'm sorry," I whispered and pulled back, not clarifying if I was apologizing to my guards or Ezio for prior transgressions. Honestly, it was a bit of both.

Ezio looked at the four scowling faces of the princes. "What's wrong?" he asked them.

Ignoring them, I pushed up Ezio's tuxedo jacket sleeve, so I could see the small scar on his wrist. I flinched at the sight of it, hoping it would have disappeared by now.

Ezio took the hand on his wrist and raised it to kiss my knuckles. "Leave the past in the past, love. I am perfectly fine and healthy."

"A story you didn't share?" Deryn asked me.

"No, I try very hard not to recall that night," I admitted while staring into Ezio's eyes. "The night I almost lost you."

"That's an exaggeration," he said with a smirk.

"Hardly," I countered and looked away from him, the image of the blood-soaked ground coming to my mind.

"Care to share?" Deryn asked.

"No, this is a private event between us," Ezio told him, turning to give him a glare before looking back at me. "Why aren't you mated yet?"

"I'm working on it," I said, trying really hard not to glance at my guards.

"The sooner you have a mate, the sooner you will be safe. My offer is still open."

"Please," I begged him, "let's not open old wounds."

"What do you think happened as soon as I saw you," he whispered into my ear. He kissed my cheek and vacated the chair beside me. I watched him leave, going to a table with Thor, Tobias, Lorenzo, and a few others I did not know.

"What was that about?" Deryn asked.

I looked at him and was shocked to see that he wasn't mad, but curious.

"Nothing," I whispered and clutched at my chest. Ezio had been the best friend I needed after Martin. We would have mated, but I wasn't ready at the time. Plus, he had gotten hurt protecting me and I had left before he was killed.

I tugged on each of our four bonds, reassuring myself with their metaphysical presences since we couldn't touch.

They relaxed a bit and we all turned to watch the kings and Elders walk in. There were a few other older males I did not recognize with them, and all eleven took seats at the long head table.

Dan's eyes roved across the attendees before stopping on me, and a smile replaced his scowl.

The older male in the center stood and the room silenced.

"That's Amos," Deryn whispered. "He's the Leader of the Summit."

"Welcome to the Summit. Thank you, representatives, for attending. This year marks our two thousand five hundredth Summit!" Amos announced.

Everyone clapped.

"We will convene on business for the first three days, then we will hold our tournament. This year, the prize is extremely valuable, one that I know our strongest will be fighting for. However, I won't announce the prize until the first day of the tournament. Now, let the feast begin!"

Servants brought out silver platters of food and set them on the tables, making us wait a beat before they lifted the lid and showed us our meals. Prime rib, cheesy mashed potatoes, broccoli, and pesto pasta.

"It smells amazing," I drooled, and ripped a piece of meat off, tossing it in my mouth. "It tastes amazing."

We didn't talk as we ate, and I surprised the guys by asking for seconds when they ordered theirs. Not only did I order seconds, but I finished them.

Dessert came and I enjoyed my chocolate pudding slowly, letting it melt in my mouth.

"This is the longest she's ever been quiet," Nico said with a playful smile.

I continued my quietness until I finished my dessert. All I wanted was to curl up and take a nap now. However, I didn't get that option since it was now time to dance.

The tables disappeared and before they could discuss who was dancing with me first, Martin pulled me out onto the dance floor.

"When was the last time we danced?" he asked.

"Senior prom," I answered with a smirk as I recalled that night.

His smile slipped and he whispered, "You know that I only agreed to the witches' cost to save you, right? That I loved you—"

I put my finger over his lips. "I know. And I'm happy for you and Sharla. Plus, I love them," I said, knowing he would understand that I meant the princes.

"I can tell," he said, pulling my hand away from his face.

We spun around the dance floor, two friends enjoying each other's company and having a wonderful time.

"My turn," Nico said, grabbed my hand, and spun me away.

"Hello, Sparkles," I said with a wide smile.

He shook his head. "If you weren't so pretty, I might get offended."

"My looks have nothing to do with it."

"Rhys had to leave to cool down," he whispered.

"Why? What happened?" I asked, worried about my dragon.

"He couldn't handle how Ezio and you interacted. Deryn left, too.

The love in his eyes...it is hard to see our most feared and violent fighters fawning over you and professing their love."

"I—"

"You haven't done anything wrong. Though, perhaps next time you should let us know the extent of your previous relationships."

"Jo," Yukio gasped, releasing the hand of the female elf he had been dancing with to grab mine and pull me away from Nico. "Jo, is it really you?"

"Hey, Yukio. It is me," I said and hugged him.

"Who is this human?" the female elf asked, annoyance obvious.

"Princess Jolie of the Four Clans," I said in introduction with a smirk.

"Oh, now you use the title," Nico mumbled behind me.

"Dance with me," Yukio ordered, pulling us into the flow of dancers without waiting for my agreement.

"You look well," he commented.

"As do you."

"Become my mate," he said, making me stumble.

"What? This is the first time that I have seen you in a decade."

"Does it feel like we have been apart that long?"

No.

"I can't. I—"

"You aren't worthy of her," Zelphar hissed, stopping us in the middle of the dance floor.

"Zelphar!" I gasped.

"You think you are worthy of being her mate?" Yukio scoffed.

"Neither of you is taking her as a mate," Ezio growled, abandoning his dancing partner to join the argument.

"Neither are you," Deryn growled. Rhys, Nico, and Fox stood right behind him. When had Deryn and Rhys come back?

They started closing in on each other, fists clenched, tension thick.

"Guys!" I yelled, getting all of their attentions'. "Stop this right now. You know I hate this shit. I'm not a commodity and I make my own decisions."

All looked cowed, thankfully.

"Martin!" I called. "Thor!"

Both appeared next to me.

"Yes, Princess?" Martin asked.

"Thor, keep them from fighting over me."

"As you wish, Princess," he said and bowed to me.

"Martin, take me to my room."

He held out a bent arm and I put my arm through it.

"Good night, gentlemen," I said and marched out of the ballroom with my head held high.

Once we stepped out into the hall I whispered, "I need to get word to Tobias to come to my room to talk to me. He seemed really nervous and like it was important."

"You sure about that?" Martin asked.

"Why wouldn't I be?" I asked.

"He's one of the craziest fighters I know. He's known for his viciousness."

"He won't ever hurt me. Plus, he asked to talk to me and I promised I would talk to him," I explained.

"Fine, I'll have someone find him and send word to come see you. I'm not leaving the room with him there, unless one of the princes comes," he told me with a tone that held no room for bartering.

"Fine."

Once in my room, I changed quickly into comfortable pajamas and put some socks on to keep my feet warm. Martin sent word via a servant and then we waited in the room together.

"You sure caused quite the raucous. I don't think I've ever seen fighting at the feast before."

"I didn't do anything. Those idiots did it by trying to stake a claim to me when they didn't have one," I grumbled.

"We don't have one?" Rhys asked from the doorway.

I sighed loudly. "I wasn't talking about you four and you know it."

They could be so frustrating sometimes. Obviously, they knew I wasn't talking about them. Plus, we had to keep our relationship a secret, or this would have been easily fixed.

"What are you doing?" Deryn asked me, stopping in front of my chair.

"Waiting for Tobias to come. He wanted to talk to me," I explained.

"And you don't know what he wanted to talk to you about?" Deryn asked.

"No. He just made me promise to talk to him tonight."

"You seem worried," Fox commented.

"He was acting scared or nervous. Tobias never acts like that," I explained.

"She's right about that," Deryn agreed.

"How did you tame the twins?" Rhys asked.

"I didn't tame anyone," I snapped.

"You had our most terrifying males ready to fight over you," Fox said.

"That's because they are stupid and as stubborn as you all," I argued.

"I'm going to find Tobias," Martin said, leaving quickly.

"They are all in love with you, still," Deryn said.

"I made it clear when I left them, that it was over."

"What offer was Ezio talking about?" Nico asked.

"That's personal."

"You are supposed to be open and honest with us," Fox reminded me.

"You want to be open and honest? Fine, I want names of every female you have been with, especially if they are here," I ordered them.

That shut them up.

"You've got my list, so give me yours."

"Do you really want that?" Rhys asked.

"Yes, I want to know which of those females you've slept with so when they touch you, I can plan their slow and painful death."

My teeth had changed, my canines lengthening and thickening.

"Easy," Deryn whispered to me.

"You think I am," I snapped, my anger continuing to grow out of control.

"Jolie," Fox whispered, using his power on me.

Why was I so mad? Sure, the situation was irritating, but I was pissed, way beyond what I should have been.

"None of us is mad, right?" Deryn asked the guys, who all just looked surprised. "Didn't think so."

I paced across the room, trying to calm down. Rhys reached out for me, but I jerked away from him. "Don't touch me right now."

Thor knocked and then walked in, his eyes focused on me. "Jo."

"What?" I growled, facing him.

He shifted and rubbed against my legs like a cat.

"No," I snarled, pushing him away.

He tackled me to the ground and licked my face. I growled at first, but as he continued doing it, something in my chest loosened. I relaxed beneath him with a sigh.

He lay down on me, pinning me with his body and huffed loudly.

"Sorry," I whispered.

"What was that?" Deryn asked.

Thor looked up at him and communicated through their pack bond.

I ran my fingers through his fur as he talked, content to relax now.

"How often do you have these anger episodes?" Deryn asked.

"Once a year," I admitted.

"What did you do when you didn't have a werewolf with you?"

"I just need an Alpha of any race, or a werewolf. If I don't, I just let the anger out until I pass out."

"When did this start?" Rhys asked.

"She's always had it," Martin said as he came in. "Those from my pack are more attuned to it because we had to help her often."

"Where's Tobias?" I asked, pushing Thor off of me to sit up.

"He's sick," Martin said with furrowed brows.

"What? He's a werewolf. You don't get sick."

"They quarantined him because of it," Martin said. "I talked to him though and he said he wanted to warn you about the tournament prize."

"What about it?" Rhys asked.

"He got sick, throwing up, before he could tell me and they ordered me to leave."

"What could make a werewolf sick?" I asked aloud.

No one answered, which was answer enough. There wasn't anything that should be able to make a werewolf sick, except a curse of some kind.

And why was he trying to warn me about the tournament prize? I wasn't participating. It didn't matter to me what the winner got.

"Are you guys participating in the tournament?" I asked them.

"Yes."

"It's mandatory."

"We always do."

"Why wouldn't we?"

"What's the prize usually?" I asked. Maybe we could figure out what this year's would be.

"It varies every year," Rhys said. "Last year it was cash. The year before it was a house."

"A house? Someone won a house?" I asked.

"I did," Fox said. "It's here, in the center of downtown. We could visit it, if you want," he suggested.

"You own a house here?"

"We can come back for a vacation sometime," Fox promised.

"So, what could this year's prize be that Tobias would need to warn me about?" I asked them.

"No idea," Deryn said with a shrug.

CHAPTER 7

Martin and I spent the next day playing card games and cuddling together while he was in wolf form. He was really drowsy, abnormally so, and when the guys came back, he rushed off to the bathroom.

"Oh no," I whispered and started to move towards the bathroom, but Fox grabbed me and stopped my progression.

"Get the healers," Fox said.

Someone left, but I didn't see who.

"Let me go," I ordered Fox.

"No, I can't let you get near him and catch what he has," Fox told me, pulling me farther away from the bathroom.

"I was already touching him, all day," I reminded him.

"Hush," he ordered me.

A stranger came in, I assumed the healer, and he took Martin away.

"Is he going to be okay?" I asked, trying to follow them, but not getting anywhere because Fox still held me.

"We'll make sure he has the best healers on him," Fox promised me.

This was not good. I couldn't let anything happen to him. If something happened to him, Sharla and the girls would never forgive me. I would never forgive me.

"What am I going to do now? I don't have a guard," I whispered, leaning back into Fox.

"We'll figure it out," he whispered and kissed my cheek, his power soothing me.

"Fox, come outside," Rhys ordered them. "Jolie, stay inside please."

"No secrets!" I growled.

"We'll be back," Rhys said and shut the door behind him, shutting me inside.

"Rude!" I yelled.

They came back an hour later, but thankfully they brought food with them.

"So?" I asked as I ate.

"Thor is going to guard you," Deryn told me.

"Really? You're going to let Thor guard me?" I asked him with folded arms.

"Yes. We need you protected tomorrow and while we are in the tournament," Rhys said. "Thor is one of the strongest werewolves and one of the few who knows the truth about our relationship, so he won't actually try to mate with you."

"The others wouldn't either," I muttered. "They'd try, but stop when I said no," I told them.

"He'll be here tomorrow morning to guard you," Deryn said. "And we are going to finish as fast as possible so we can get back to you."

At the end of the day, I was beyond bored. Thor had finally agreed to take me out of the room and on a tour of the castle. The castle was simply amazing. There was so much to see.

I waited outside of a bathroom for Thor to come out, when I heard King Johann talking to someone. Slowly, and quietly, I walked around to the entrance of a small courtyard. The courtyard had a single tree in the center with a circular bench around it. Sitting on the bench was King Johann, King of the Mages and Nico's dad.

What shocked me most, was the person he was talking to. Justina. Justina was a dhampir who had been my coworker for a bit before she joined my father and helped him use me to make the guys attack the President. Thankfully, they had overcome it without actually killing the President. Justina hadn't been with my father at the final battle, the one where he was killed. I hadn't really thought much about what had happened to her, but now I was very curious about what she was doing with the Mage King.

"Will you agree to my deal or not?" Justina asked him.

"You aren't giving me much negotiating power," he scoffed.

The stone I was leaning on moved, making my presence known to them both, so I walked in confidently, like I hadn't been snooping.

"What the fuck are you doing here?" I demanded of Justina.

She hissed at me and ran off, leaving me with King Johann.

"You won't tell anyone about this," King Johann told me. "Do you understand? If you tell anyone about this meeting, I will make you regret it."

He was threatening me! Wow. That was not something I expected.

"What were you trying to make a deal with her about?" I asked him. "What could she possibly have for you?"

"That's none of your concern. You would do well to learn to stay out of things that aren't your business and keep your mouth shut. Now, you get out of here before one of your guards comes in," he ordered me.

Asshole. I obeyed, though, knowing I needed to get back to Thor. I stepped out of the courtyard and Deryn and Thor stood there, scowling at me.

"What?" I asked softly, walking by them toward our rooms.

"We heard," Deryn told me. "We heard everything he said."

"If you say anything..." I started, not sure what the Mage King would do. Would he have me killed?

"Don't worry about it," Deryn said and pulled me into his side with an arm around my shoulders. "I'll take care of it."

Thor didn't say anything, just walked on my right side with a scowl on his face. He looked ready to punch someone.

"Why are you mad?" I asked Thor.

"He threatened you," Thor snarled. "That fucking asshole threatened you."

Yeah. He had. I was shocked, too.

Deryn's grip on me tightened and he didn't let up until we were in my room.

"Nico," Deryn growled. "We need to talk. Now."

"I didn't do it," Nico said, but when Thor, Deryn, and I didn't crack a smile, he walked out with Deryn.

"What happened?" Rhys asked.

"If he tries to touch you, I'll fucking kill him. I don't care if he is a king or not," Thor told me. "I'll tear his fucking head off."

"That's enough," I ordered him. "Be quiet."

"What happened?" Rhys asked again, his pupils changing to slits as they changed to his dragon eyes.

"Go talk to Deryn," I told him, feeling tired and unsure of what to think.

What could Justina have that King Johann would want? He said she wasn't giving him much negotiating power, which meant she had the power in the exchange. What? What the hell could she have?

"More shifters are sick," Fox told me. "The healers still don't have any idea what is causing it, but they are keeping everyone comfortable. Tobias and Martin are doing okay. They're still throwing up and sick, but they aren't dying."

"Thanks for updating me," I said and walked into his arms, letting him hold me and try to ease my stress and worry.

"Jolie," Nico whispered from behind me.

I turned around to face him, unsure what he was going to say or how he would react.

"You're my queen, so no matter what he says, or what orders he tries to give me, if they are to harm you, I will not follow them. I will continue to protect you. You are my top priority."

"So, we're okay?" I asked.

He pulled me into a hug and said, "We're great. I love you. I'm sorry my father did something so crass. I can't believe he threatened you. I mean, I believe he threatened you because Deryn witnessed it, and I would have believed it if you had said it. I just don't understand why he did it."

"Me neither," I admitted and tried to burrow into him, getting as close as I could. "Tomorrow is the tournament, right?" I asked. "What happens?"

"We all go to the tournament grounds and they explain the rules, the prize, and what is going to happen in the events. Sometimes we all have to be in there at the same time, so we are going to have you stay with Dan," Nico said. "We know he won't hurt you and he'll protect you from my asshole father if he needs to."

After an extensive cuddling episode, the guys escorted me to the tournament stands. The "stands" turned out to be a coliseum made of stones likely as old as the castle. The coliseum was oval shaped with a set of box seats on one end where the kings and other summit members sat. There was a magic spell in front of their view that magnified the arena, so that even though they were far away, they could see everything clearly.

King Katar of the Elves and King Emrys of the Dragons both

hugged me. King Johann nodded once at me with thinly veiled anger. Shit. I swallowed nervously, but Dan grabbed me in one of his infamous bear hugs and led me to the seat between his and King Emrys's.

"How are you?" Dan asked.

"Worried about Tobias and Martin," I whispered back.

He patted my hand. "The best healers in the world are with them. They'll figure out what is wrong."

The stands were filled with attendees from various races. I scanned the crowd and Gavin waved at me with a wide smile.

"Your family is here?" I asked Emrys, seeing the other siblings and Adelaide.

Andras winked at me and I gave him a small wave.

"Yes, everyone's families are here, but they aren't allowed to sit up here with us," Emrys answered.

"Then why am I here?" I asked.

Amos stood, getting everyone's attention. "Welcome to the Summit Tournament!"

Everyone cheered loudly.

"Today, our strongest and most talented warriors will be put to the test to see who is the best. As I announced at the feast, this year's prize is the best yet!"

The anticipation was palpable, everyone sat on the edge of their seats. Everyone, but my four princes who stood next to the arena with bored expressions on their faces.

Amos motioned at me to come forward. I looked at Dan, but he just shrugged and pushed me to obey. I walked to stand beside Amos, my heart beating faster than a hummingbird's. Why was I up here?

"This year, the winner will obtain the honor of becoming the mate of Jolie, Princess of the Four Clans!" Amos announced.

Now, the princes weren't bored, their expressions ranging from shock to murder.

"Excuse me!" I demanded. "What?"

"Didn't anyone tell you, dear?" he asked. "You're our Princess and unmated, so it is the logical prize. You're a bit old to be unmated still and it's really us doing you a favor."

"I'm not—"

Dan pulled me to my seat and fixed his glare on Amos. "Who made this decision?" he demanded.

"Me," Amos said with a smirk. "Unless you have a reason we shouldn't offer her?"

They knew! That asshole knew I had guards. Somehow, someone had spilled the beans to him.

"The Summit doesn't take kindly to lies and deceit," Amos whispered to me and Dan.

"Fuck y—"

Emrys put a hand over my mouth, stopping me from finishing. "Quiet," he ordered me. "This is a test."

I hated tests. "I didn't agree to this," I whisper-hissed to him.

"As Princess, you don't have a choice. I'm sorry. I didn't think something like this would happen or we wouldn't have named you Princess."

"I know this isn't your fault, King Emrys," I whispered while glaring at Amos.

I looked back down at my guards and they all bowed to me.

"That's them promising to win," Dan whispered to me.

Ezio bowed to me before he hopped into the coliseum's sandy arena.

"Apparently, Ezio, too," Dan mumbled.

Declan and Kylan bowed to me next and I let out a loud groan. "Dammit."

"Why are my dragon twins bowing to you?" King Emrys asked.

"Because they are stubborn assholes," I growled.

Then, to my amazement, Thor bowed to me and leapt in. What was wrong with these males!

"Thor?" Dan asked.

"I'm his one true love, if you ask him," I growled. "He and I never dated or anything, but we grew up together and he always wanted me." I growled again. "Those fucking assholes are going to regret this if they hurt my—"

Emrys & Dan both put hands over my mouth.

"Just be quiet," Dan said with a chuckle

I folded my arms over my chest, pouting and angry at the same time.

"So, Princess, do you have a favorite?" Amos asked.

"No, I don't have *one* favorite," I answered.

I have four.

Fifteen males of various races faced off with each other, but thankfully my four stayed side by side.

"No shifting," Amos ordered them. "No killing. Maiming is fine as long as it is not life threatening. Magic is permitted, but no deadly force. Last five standing will move on to the next round."

What would happen if one of my guys didn't make it?

Dan set his hand on my knee, which had been bouncing quickly. "It'll work out," he said, but I could tell he was worried too.

Ezio faced Deryn, a feral smile on his lips. "You aren't worthy of her."

Deryn smiled, looking completely calm and relaxed. Like he wasn't about to fight for my hand. "She'll be mine," he told Ezio. "She'll be mine and you can take whatever that offer was and shove it."

Oh boy.

"She didn't tell you what it was, did she?" Ezio asked with a smirk. He looked up at me and raised his right hand, now holding a sword. "I'll prove I'm strong enough to be your mate."

"Dumbass," I muttered.

"You and Ezio—" Emrys asked.

"We were together a little over a year," I confirmed. "I broke it off so he wouldn't get hurt again."

"Again?" Dan asked.

"The one scar on his entire body," I whispered, "was gained by protecting me."

"Oh, boy," Dan sighed. "He told me about you. He hasn't stopped loving you."

"I know," I muttered.

An idea popped into my head and before Amos could start the event, I shouted, "I won't have children!"

That got everyone's attention, even my guards.

"What?" Amos demanded.

"I refuse to bear children," I told him.

Two males left the ring, giving up.

"You can't—" Amos sputtered.

"She can," Dan growled.

I had already chosen this course, when I officially decided to take my four as my mates.

"I already have the surgery scheduled to tie my tubes," I told everyone, blushing slightly since I was airing my business with hundreds of strangers.

"Were you going to tell—" Rhys asked.

"Yes," I said before he could finish that sentence with "us."

"When?" Nico asked.

"After I claimed who I was going to mate with."

All four blinked in silence, my declaration sinking in. I had planned to claim them as my mates. I saw the moment they all understood. Their faces grew serious and they all pulled weapons out.

"Let's go!" Rhys growled, swords in his hands. "Start this tournament, now!"

"Begin!" Amos ordered.

Rhys bellowed and in two movements had sliced off an arm from two males I didn't know.

"I've never seen him so aggressive in the tournament," Emrys said. "What did your statement just now mean to them?"

"It's personal," I said softly, blushing.

"You turned them feral," Dan said, eyes fixed on Deryn.

Deryn was fighting against Ezio, their blades making a shower of sparks, arc around them with each hit. Both wore feral snarls as they fought.

Fox had his hands full, fighting Yukio and Zelphar. Both were attacking him in earnest and his eyes glowed as he fought them, not backing down and it looked like he was winning.

Nico was fighting another mage, keeping that mage from attacking my other guards. In seconds, the mage was unconscious and he was moving to his next victim.

The pool went from thirteen down to nine. Thor was unconscious behind Deryn now, though I hadn't seen how it had happened.

Deryn and Ezio were still battling, Rhys was fighting Declan and Kylan. Fox was fighting Yukio, and Nico fought Zelphar.

Dan grabbed my hand, stopping me as I moved forward unknowingly. Declan had cut Rhys's arm and Rhys was now bleeding.

"Emrys," Dan snapped.

Emrys blocked my view, jerking my chin up so I had to meet his eyes. "Calm down!" he ordered me, pouring his power as Alpha into me.

The dragon inside of me had been rushing to the surface and I hadn't known until he said something. I shoved the dragon back down, but it was hard. We wanted to protect Rhys. We wanted to hurt the one who had hurt our guard.

"He's not going to die," Emrys assured me.

"He's bleeding," I growled, my voice much deeper than usual.

"It's fine. I promise that I won't let them hurt Rhys enough to put his life in danger or cause permanent damage. Now, calm down and put her to sleep or everything will be ruined," Emrys whispered in my ear.

He was right. I needed to get a handle on myself. Taking a deep breath of Emrys's scent, I rested my forehead for a brief moment on his chest and let his power help me put the dragon completely to sleep.

"Good," he praised me and we took our seats again. Thankfully, Amos had been too engulfed in the battle to pay attention to me.

Yukio and Zelphar were out, unconscious on the ground, and now Fox was helping Rhys fight the dragon twins.

"Sir," a human male whispered to Amos and handed him an envelope.

Amos took the envelope, reading it quickly so he could look back at the fight. He finished reading it and handed it to Johann. Johann read it and chuckled darkly. "Fitting," he whispered.

"What is it?" Dan demanded.

Johann gave him the letter and as soon as he read it, Dan growled and said, "No. Absolutely not."

"It's her decision," Johann said.

"Oh, this is her decision, but who she mates with isn't?" Emrys snarled after reading the letter.

Clearly, this was about me.

"What is it?" I asked.

"The illness that is affecting the shifters is a poison. There is an antidote, but the price they are asking—" Emrys shook his head. "We can't."

"What is it?" I asked, dreading where this was headed.

"You. We hand you over and they give us the antidote," Johann said.

"There has to be something else that they want," Dan said.

"Seems pretty clear that they only want her," Johann said.

"Why are you being such a dick?" Emrys asked, his eyes glowing.

"Say that again," Johann threatened him, standing up to face him.

"I'll do it," I whispered.

"You fucking heard me," Emrys snarled at Johann.

"I'll do it!" I yelled at them.

"Do what?" Rhys asked from the arena.

Shit, I hadn't realized that I had been *that* loud.

The fighting had stopped, the remaining five males looking up at us.

"The five have made it through!" Amos announced. "Rhys, Deryn, Nico, Foxfire, and Ezio will continue on to the second round."

The ones who had been knocked out were now sitting up, rubbing their heads.

"Thor. Ezio. Declan. Kylan. Yukio and Zelphar," I called down to them.

"Yes, Princess," they called back.

"Restrain the princes," I ordered them.

"What are you doing?" Dan demanded.

The six males followed my orders, grabbing the princes before they knew what was going on.

"What's this?" Deryn demanded.

"I'm saving my best friend," I told them. "I won't let his children grow up without a father."

"Jolie!" Rhys roared.

"Let's go," I told Johann.

Johann nodded and led the way.

"Father!" Nico yelled. "Don't let her do this! Whatever it is, don't let her sacrifice herself! Please!"

Johann paused a moment at the anguish in Nico's voice, but it was just a brief pause before he resumed walking.

Sounds of fighting broke out and I knew my guards were fighting my exes to get free. Johann placed a hand on my shoulder and teleported us out of the coliseum and to the center of the downtown area.

"This way," he told me, walking towards a bakery.

While we walked, I touched each of my guards through our bond and then built solid walls of impenetrable metal, so they wouldn't be able to locate me. They would barely be able to feel me now, which was for the best.

Johann walked into the bakery, straight through the back, and up a set of stairs to a second floor that was empty, save for one person.

"You have the antidote?" Johann asked.

Justina stepped forward and held out a vile of green liquid. "One drop for each victim," she ordered him.

"Thank you," he said and bowed, backing away from me. He paused and asked, "What will you do with her?"

"That's none of your concern," she told him sweetly, twirling my hair around one of her fingers.

He nodded once, bowed to me, and disappeared.

Justina walked around me, looking at my dress and said, "It's a shame that something as beautiful as this will get ruined."

Her hand wrapped around my throat and she threw me up against the wall, choking me. "You. You ruined everything!"

"Boo. Hoo," I gasped out with a snarl.

She chuckled. "I forgot how much I liked you. Well, it sucks for you, because no matter how much I liked you, your father's death has cured me of the weaknesses I had left in me."

Revenge? This was for revenge because of my father's death?

"You're pathetic," I snarled.

She snapped her fingers and chains slid out of the walls, wrapped around my arms and legs, and secured me to the wall. She pulled out a silver knife and sliced it down my arm slowly, making me scream loudly.

"Your physical pain isn't going to cut it," she told me. "No pun intended. I need emotional pain from you. And, I know just the thing."

I watched in disbelief as the bonds between me and my guards became visible. She stroked her finger down Deryn's, making me shiver in revulsion.

"Don't touch that!" I snarled and thrashed against the chains.

"I lost the one male who viewed me as more than a female. The first who viewed me as an equal," she told me with a sigh. "This one, this one views you as his equal. No, as more than his equal. He views you as his queen." She took her silver knife and ran her finger along its hilt. Symbols down the blade began to glow and she used it to slice through Deryn and my bond.

It felt like my heart had been stabbed. I screamed loudly, my body shuddering against the wall as I lost my connection to Deryn.

"No!" I screamed. "Stop!"

She grabbed Nico's bond, squeezing it tightly in her hand. "Now, you will all experience the pain I felt. The loss of the one you love."

The knife sliced through Nico and my bond, and I felt energy leave me, his magic disappearing with the bond.

I tried to shift into a dragon. I still had Rhys, so I just needed to shift.

My scales started to form, but she wasn't cutting my skin. She was somehow cutting through our magical bonds.

"Stop!" I begged. "Please!"

"No!" she screamed at me and cut Rhys's bond, the dragon disappeared from me in an instant, leaving me feeling cold and helpless.

Three of them were gone. Their absence a hole in my chest. An aching and bleeding hole I couldn't repair. Fox was the only one left. I opened our bond and tried my hardest to send him all the love that I felt. I still couldn't use the bond as well as they could, but I could convey feelings, so I sent him as much love and gratitude as I could. I felt his fear. I felt his anger. I felt his love and it was enough. Knowing they loved me was enough.

"Did you know that Foxfire never knelt to anyone, not even his own father, and yet he has knelt for you numerous times, in front of numerous witnesses. He loves you and everyone can see it. Why you? What makes you so special?"

The knife severed our bond and I wailed in sorrow. Fox, my happy and kind Fox, was gone.

They were all gone. All four of my guards were gone. I was alone in my body for the first time in nearly a year. It had been ten months ago that I met them and we developed these bonds.

"Fuck you, you piece of shit," I snarled at her weakly, my body hanging in the chains. "You're just a jealous child who can't handle the fact that the evil asshole who was manipulating her was killed. He never loved you. He was just using you. You were a means to an end. Nothing more."

She wrapped her hand around my throat and squeezed tightly, cutting off my air supply.

Yes. This is what I wanted. Without them, I wasn't powerful. Without them, I couldn't do anything.

"Why give yourself up?" she asked me. "Did you think they would save you?"

"Save. Martin," I gasped out.

"Martin? Martin got affected by the virus? Poor bastard," she said. "Well, at least that antidote will save him. You. You won't be saved."

Now, it didn't matter what happened at the tournament. Now, it didn't matter if I thought I was good enough or not. Now, they would find new mates. They would go back to their normal lives.

"Your torture isn't over yet," she told me with a wicked smile. "No, this is just the beginning." Her hand wrapped around my face and then, I fell into a dark tunnel, spinning and swirling with black mist. There was no down. No up. Nothing, but darkness and cold air.

CHAPTER 8

"How do you feel today?" Justina asked me, her smile happy and warm, like it had been when we'd worked together.

I had no idea how long I'd been here and I didn't really care.

"Were you ever my friend?" I asked. "Or was it all a ruse?"

"Do you care?" she snapped. "You should be more worried about the fact that your wound never stopped bleeding."

That explained my lightheadedness and the weakness throughout my entire body.

"Did you find me because of my father? Or was it just a coincidence?" I really did want to know.

"Coincidence," she said. "How I wish I hadn't gotten to know you, though."

"Just kill me already," I begged her. "You took them away from me. What more can you do?"

"Well, your dad did tell me that torture never worked well on you. So, I suppose I should just put you out of your misery."

Finally. Death was better than this hollow shell I was now. I hadn't realized how much they had filled me until now. How could I live like this?

I couldn't. This emptiness would eat me up.

What must they be going through?

Well, it likely wasn't as bad as I was dealing with, since they still had each other and their warrior's bond.

"I'm going to let you bleed out," she said. "I think it's a fitting death for the person who took a vampire from me." She sliced my other arm open and waved as she left.

"Bitch!" I called after her.

I faded in and out of consciousness, my arms went numb and my body followed that numbness. Soon, I knew I would be dead. Part of me wanted to fight. Part of me wanted to live. But, that part of me was buried beneath the pain and the loss.

There was no one to blame. I had given myself up, knowing full well that I was likely going to die. And, I would do it again. My death for Tobias's and Martin's lives was a small price to pay. They would be furious with me, but I didn't care. They deserved to live. They deserved to continue on in life.

I had never done anything worthwhile. The Others thought I was a hero for bringing them their necklace, but that was purely coincidence. Had I not stumbled into that park, drunk, I would still have that necklace. I wouldn't be here either. I wouldn't have had the four princes bind themselves to me. I wouldn't have seen my ex-boyfriends again. I wouldn't have been the reason that Rhys and the others fought so hard in the tournament.

I was a walking curse. My death would save the princes. My death would save them all.

"Jo!" someone yelled.

It sounded like Martin, but I wasn't sure. My eyes were too heavy. The room stank of my blood and I couldn't move.

"Jo, hang in there," Martin said, his voice far away.

Hang in there? I was hanging in chains and he said, hang in there? I snorted softly at the pun.

The last thing I heard before I died *would* be a pun.

"Stand back," someone ordered Martin.

There was movement all around me and I was pretty sure they had taken me out of the chains, but I was too cold and numb to feel anything for certain.

"Don't die on me," Martin ordered me. "Do you hear me, Jolie? Don't you dare die on me!"

"Too late," I whispered.

"No, it's not," he growled. "You have four princes losing their shit and they need you to come back. I need you. My daughters need you. How are they going to take the news that their favorite aunt died trying to save me?"

"I'm their only aunt," I grunted.

"Stop talking," the other person, male it sounded like, ordered me. I didn't recognize the voice at all, so it must have been a healer.

"I love you," I whispered to Martin.

"No!" he yelled. "Don't give up! Jolie. Please! Don't give up!"

He was safe. That was what mattered. The princes would learn to live without me again. It might take time to adjust, but they would do it.

"She's lost so much blood," the healer told Martin.

"What do you need?" Martin asked.

"We need to find someone who has the same blood type as her," he explained.

"I'm the same," Thor said.

"Thor," I whispered. "Why are you here?"

"Shut up," Martin snarled at me.

"We've been searching the entire city for you," he told me. "Martin found you and we let everyone know. They're on their way."

"Why? Just let me sleep," I requested.

"Hook me up," Thor ordered the healer.

Something stabbed my arm, but I barely felt it.

"Remember when we went skinny dipping in the lake?" Martin asked me. "You were terrified that Mr. Smiton would come out of his house and find us. But, we did it anyway. We were having a great time and then the entire pack showed up to drink from the lake."

I did remember. I was mortified. I had become used to them being naked, but not them seeing *me* naked.

"You were blushing so much, that Alpha was worried you were going to faint," Thor chuckled. "You were redder than a tomato."

"If that water hadn't been so clear, it wouldn't have been an issue," Martin said and laughed.

"Remember when I first met you?" Thor asked me.

Oh, I remembered. He had been terrified of me. It had hurt my feelings and I had stayed away from the pack for an entire week because of it.

"You smelled so good and so weird at the same time."

Oh, gee, thanks.

"I didn't understand what the smell meant until I was older, but it was Martin who convinced me that you were good and to give you another try. I'm glad he did. Every time we were together, it was one of the happiest days of my life. You always made me smile and you made sure that I never felt like a third wheel, even after you and Martin had started dating."

"Remember that time that Delphine stole her clothes from the PE locker?" Thor asked Martin.

"Oh, yeah!" Martin said. "She sent me a text message asking for help and when I came to the door of the locker room, she practically tore my shirt off of me."

"Where is she?" Dan boomed, his feet thundering across the wooden floor.

"She's alive," the healer informed Dan. "Just barely, though."

"What do you need?" Dan asked him.

"We need to take her back to the castle, but I'm afraid moving her will reopen the wounds and—"

"I'll teleport her," Johann said.

Before I could voice my protests, someone picked me up and then set me down on a cold, metal cot.

"I'm sorry," Johann whispered to me. "I'm sorry this happened to you. My son may never forgive me."

I didn't care if his son forgave him or not. He made his bed. He could have teleported me away too, but he hadn't. He had left me because he was still furious that I'd interrupted him and Justina's deal.

"I was trying to work out the deal with her when you interrupted."

"Why didn't you tell them where I was?" I asked, remembering that they had said they were searching the entire city.

"Because I'm an old fool who can't get over his own ego," he whispered.

"Get away from her!" Nico growled, his voice shaking everything around us. I still hadn't opened my eyes and now that I knew he was here, I was glad that they were still closed. I couldn't look at him. I couldn't see him knowing we weren't bound.

"I'm leaving," Johann said.

"Jolie," Nico whispered from nearby. "Jolie, say something."

"Go, away," I begged, my throat constricting as I tried to keep from crying.

"What happened?" he asked. "What cut the bonds?"

"Justina did," I whispered.

"Stop talking," the healer ordered me. "If your presence is going to upset her, then you need to leave."

"Jolie," Nico whispered. "Please, look at me."

"No, it hurts too much," I sobbed.

"What does?"

"The emptiness."

"Leave," the healer ordered him. "You can see her when she's healed."

"No," I told him. "Stop healing me."

"Sorry, that's not something I can do," he whispered. "We need to find another blood donor for you."

"It doesn't matter. Nothing matters," I whispered. "Just let me go."

"No," he said adamantly. "You're in pain, yes, but you aren't going to die. Now, shut up and lie there while I heal you."

I obeyed, mainly because I didn't have the energy to fight. Talking to Nico had reopened the emotional wounds inside of my heart and I couldn't breathe well.

"I'm going to knock you out," the healer said. "It will speed up your healing."

He wasn't asking my permission. He just knocked me out.

When I came back to, my arms were healed and I could not only open my eyes, but sit up. The room was empty and I looked down at my arms, two giant scars ran down the center of my forearms.

That bitch.

"You're awake," the healer said happily.

I nodded.

"Are you up for visitors?" he asked.

"Can I travel yet?" I asked instead of answering.

"Yes," he replied nervously.

"Who do I talk to about traveling back to Jinla?" I asked, wanting to get away from the princes as soon as possible.

"Me," Dan said as he walked in.

I looked away from him. "I want to go home."

"I thought your home was with my son and his friends," he whispered.

I shook my head and tears began to fall. "Not any longer."

"Hope isn't lost," he whispered and pulled me into a hug. "They still love you."

"They're gone," I gasped. "They're gone! My soul, my heart is empty. They're gone and I can't get them back."

It had been what the Elders had told us, that once I removed the warrior's bond, I couldn't get it back.

"The warrior's bond is gone, but you can still become their queen. You can still become their mate," Dan informed me.

"Only the one who wins her hand in the tournament can claim her as their mate," Amos said.

"Leave us," Dan ordered him.

"You don't order me around, King of the Werewolves," Amos reminded him.

"I'm talking with her. This is a private conversation. You can come see her later when I'm done," Dan told him, his body tightening around mine.

"The second round has yet to happen, so you cannot leave for Jinla. You have to wait until your mate is chosen. Once that happens, I will book you on the first train ride out," Amos said to me.

"Fuck you," I grumbled into Dan's chest.

"What?" Amos asked.

I pulled back to face Amos and said, "Fuck. You."

His shock turned into anger and he reached towards me, but Dan stepped between us.

"You will not lay a fucking finger on her. She's my princess. She's my daughter. You will leave now, or I will rip your fucking head off and explain to everyone that you were trying to kill the princess."

Dan was pissed. I felt his body shaking with anger where it still touched me.

"She is not your daughter," Amos spat. "She's hardly even a princess."

"Get out!" Dan bellowed, the room shaking with his voice.

I heard Amos's footsteps retreating and a door close.

"He's right," I whispered.

"Stop. That's enough," Dan ordered me. "You have to come with me to the coliseum. If you don't want to talk to your guar...the princes, then I will keep them away from you for now. They have to finish the tournament, though."

"Why? I'm not their queen any longer. I'm just—"

"Their friend," Dan finished for me. "Their lover. Their love. They will continue to fight for you."

"There are four of them," I reminded him. "They can't all win me."

"Let's go get you a change of clothes," he said, picking me up and carrying me. "And some food, because I'm sure you're hungry."

"I'm not," I whispered. The emptiness in me was so big, that food would just make me sick.

"Let's get you changed. We'll focus on one thing at a time," Dan whispered.

My room was empty of princes when we arrived, thankfully, so I took my time bathing and getting into another one of the dresses that was in the closet. Dan carried me again, this time taking me to the coliseum.

Ezio and Deryn were fighting, while Rhys, Nico, and Fox stood off to the side just watching. The idiots must have decided it was Deryn's job to fight Ezio, since he was a werewolf.

"Jolie," Emrys breathed as Dan set me in the chair between them again. "How are you feeling?"

"Cold," I whispered, pulling my legs up on the chair beneath the long skirt of my dress.

Emrys blew a ring of fire around me and it sat even with my chest, without moving, the flames warmed me.

"Thanks," I whispered, trying to look away from the arena, but unable to do so.

Fox looked up at me and his eyes widened. He took a few steps towards me, as if he would come to the box, but Nico grabbed his arm and stopped him, shaking his head.

They were keeping him away from me. I knew it. I knew they would feel different once the bond was gone.

"The princess is back," someone in the crowd called and that sentence was repeated over and over again by others until the fighting stopped.

"Jo," Ezio called. "Are you alright?"

"I'm alive," I whispered, not sure if he could even hear me, and looked away, glancing down at the flames around me.

"Jolie," Fox called in a rasping voice.

"Finish your fight!" Amos ordered them. "The three of you should be fighting each other while Deryn fights Ezio!"

"I concede," Ezio said, jumping out of the arena. He ran up the stairs until he reached me, kneeling before me. "Jo, say something."

I shook my head, tears welling up. "Please, go."

He rested his hand on my foot a moment, bowed, and left.

"Four left!" Amos announced to the crowd, as though it were exciting.

"We are done," Rhys called up. "We four claim her."

"You can't do that," Amos snapped. "Only one of you will win."

"Shouldn't it be her decision?" Dan asked Amos.

"Nothing has been my decision," I snapped, leaping up and somehow avoiding the circle of flames still around me.

Emrys extinguished them and stood up next to me. "It's alright," he whispered.

"No, it's not!" I turned to Amos and said, "I'm not a god damn pawn for you to use! I'm not someone you can treat like a trophy. I'm a living, breathing, person! I deserve to choose my own mate."

"Then choose," he said and waved at the princes. "Choose one to be your mate."

"No," I growled and looked away from them. "No. I won't choose one."

"Are they not good enough? Do you think you're too good for the princes?" Amos asked.

"Shut up!" Rhys roared at Amos. "Don't you dare talk to her like that!"

"Silence!" Amos ordered him. "At this Summit, I am the head. I am the ruler. I make the decisions."

"Not about my life," I told him. I turned away and walked back towards the castle and my room.

The crowd erupted into shocked chatter and I ignored all of Amos's demands for me to return. I was done. I was done with all of this.

"It's alright, Jo," Martin whispered beside me. "Everything will be alright."

"Please, don't touch me yet," I begged him as he moved closer.

He kept his distance and nodded. "Okay."

"I want to go home," I sobbed. "Now."

"Okay," he agreed. "I'll help you pack."

In my room, he locked the door behind us and started packing my bag. I tried to help, but it was hard to see anything with the tears flowing down my face.

I was pissed at Amos. I was pissed at Johann. I was pissed at Justina. Most of all, I was pissed at myself.

"Jolie," Rhys called through my door. "Please, let us in."

"No," I whispered, packing faster.

"I love you," he yelled. "I don't care who hears it. I don't care who knows. I love you, Jolie. Please, don't shut me out. Don't shut us out!"

"It's over!" I yelled. "The bond is gone! She severed them. She severed them all!"

"Oh, fuck," Martin whispered. "I didn't know. Jolie, I—"

"We love you. We want you to be our mate. We want you to be our queen," Deryn said.

"I'm a fucking curse. I've always been a curse. Justina came here because of my dad being killed. She hurt me because of that. If you'd never gotten involved with me, none of this shit would have happened. Please, just...stay away."

There was silence on the other side of the door, so I assumed they had listened. Finished packing, Martin grabbed our two bags and put his arm around my waist. "Ready?" he asked.

I nodded.

Yes, I was ready to go home. I was ready to go back to Jinla to start over.

Martin opened the door and unsurprisingly, four princes stood in the hallway. Before I could move away, all four dropped to their knees before me.

"Oh, shit," Martin whispered and backed away.

"Stop," I whispered, tears in my ears. "Stand up."

"Jolie Bernardo, will you become our queen?" Rhys asked me. He pulled out a small black box from his pocket and opened it, revealing a diamond ring. It was a human engagement ring.

"I thought I couldn't become your queen," I whispered. "That's why I joined the warrior's bond, because I'm human."

My voice came out steady, which shocked the hell out of me, since I felt like crying and screaming at the same time.

"That only happened because of how we added you. There is a different set of procedures for you to become our queen," Nico said. "And we can do that still."

"You're finally free," I whispered, looking at each of them in turn. "Why bind yourselves to me again?"

"We love you, you idiot," Deryn said with a soft smile, his words soft instead of harsh. "We want to spend the rest of our lives with you."

Could I do this? Could I become their queen? What would it feel like if I was removed from the bond as their queen?

"It would most likely kill you," Nico said.

Apparently, I'd said that last part out loud instead of in my head.

"Do you want to be with us?" Fox asked.

More than anything.

"More than anything," I said, sniffling as tears built in my eyes and my throat grew tight.

"Say what you want," Rhys whispered.

"I want to be your queen and your mate," I whispered back, the tears spilling over. "But, I don't want to hurt you anymore. I don't want to cause you pain. I don't want you to get hurt because of me."

I was trying to leave to avoid this. I was trying to leave so they could move on. They were so stubborn. And, I loved them so much.

"Kitten," Rhys whispered, "that's what it means to be together. We get hurt protecting what and who we love. We were getting injured in the tournament long before we met you. We'll get hurt in the tournament next year and the year after, no matter what the prize is."

"You are the only one we will bow to," Fox said. "You are our equal. You are the most important thing in our lives. More important than each other."

The other three nodded in agreement.

"You're sure?" I asked softly. "You're sure that you want me? This is a lifelong commitment. This is something we can't go back on. If you decide to do this now, you are going to be rescuing me and getting hurt and who knows what else until I die!"

"We're sure," they all said in unison.

"Jo, come on, just give them your answer," Martin groaned.

"What about Amos?" I asked.

"Let me handle Amos," Dan said from behind me, making me jump and spin around.

"For such a large man, you're too damn quiet!" I snapped at him. Then, realized that Emrys and Katar were with him as well. "Oh, hi."

They waved at me and looked at their sons.

"They won't even bow to me," Katar grumbled.

"Jolie," Deryn rumbled.

I turned back to them and said, "I have one condition."

"What condition?" Rhys asked.

"If I become your queen, you have to become my mates," I said. "That way, even if someone breaks one of our bonds, we'll have another one available."

All four surged to their feet and surrounded me with hugs. Their towering figures made for a wall of protection and I felt safe again. Rhys slipped the ring on my finger while hugging me and I sobbed softly.

"It hurt so much," I whispered. "To feel you each taken from me, from my heart. It's so cold. I feel so empty."

"So do we," Fox whispered.

"But you have each other," I reminded them. "I have no one. I'm alone and hollow."

"We're still there, in your heart," Rhys whispered. "But, you don't need to worry. We'll make our vows to you and you'll be bonded with us once again."

"We'll wait on the mating bonds until we get home," Deryn said. "We don't need to rush to make those while we are here.

"Finally!" Dan bellowed and pushed aside Deryn and Rhys to pull me away from them. He looked down at me and said, "Welcome to the pack, Jolie. Welcome to my family."

"Guys," Thor called as he walked towards us with what looked like a newspaper. "This was published today."

Dan took the paper and sighed. "Well, looks like you won't need to make an announcement." He handed me the paper and I read the headline.

Princess of the Four Clans bonded with the Four Princes.

"How did they find out?" Fox asked, taking the paper from me.

"Justina," I whispered. "She probably did it to try to hurt me more. Everyone being told that I was bound to you when she'd just severed those ties *is* pretty fucking painful."

Fox handed the paper to Nico and then pulled me into his arms. "We're here. We'll make our connection again tonight."

"Are you still going back home?" Deryn asked.

For once, he wasn't ordering me around. He was asking what I was going to do. Maybe, our painful experience had done something good.

"I'll stay with you four," I whispered and kissed Fox's neck. "I don't want to be alone right now."

"Good," Deryn said and pulled me away from Fox so that he could hug me. "I don't want to be away from you."

"How do you want to handle this?" Rhys asked.

"We can make an official announcement when we return home that we are her guards and she is our mate," Nico said, hugging me from behind. I turned and wrapped my arms around his neck. "I'm sorry," he whispered to me. "I'm sorry for everything my asshole father did."

"Not your fault," I whispered back, kissing his cheek and inhaling his scent. I wanted to burrow into him so that his scent completely surrounded me.

I pulled away from him and looked at my ring. "So, what's special about this ring?"

All four chuckled.

"Yes, it was expensive," Rhys answered my unspoken question. "It's magically enhanced so that it will expand when you shift forms."

"Will I be able to shift forms as your queen?" I asked, my chest aching as I thought of the dragon being torn away from me.

Warm hands wrapped around mine, stopping me from rubbing my chest. "Yes," Rhys said, taking his turn to hug me. "You'll get your dragon back."

"I was mid-shift and she stole the dragon," I whined. "She took the dragon and all of my heat vanished. I've been so cold since then."

Rhys's body warmed, heat surrounding me. "I'm sorry," he whispered, rubbing my back. "It wasn't a picnic for us either."

"What did it feel like for you?" I asked, my voice muffled as I buried my face in his shirt.

"Like my heart had been ripped into two, and half of it vanished," Rhys said.

"Like the sun was destroyed and our lives were thrown into darkness," Fox said.

"It was as though half of my body was destroyed," Nico said.

"It felt like someone stuck their claws into my chest and shredded me from the inside out," Deryn said.

"They flipped out," Emrys told me. "When the first of them, Deryn, felt your connection snap, he began tearing out of the building, trying to rush to you. But, as each one was cut, they fell from the pain. They were all crawling toward the city on their hands and knees, snarling and cussing. Then they started going berserk."

"It was excruciating," Rhys snarled into my hair.

"Come, let's get into the room so we can talk," Katar ordered us.

Rhys picked me up before I could even take a step and carried me into my room.

"I love you," he whispered softly into my ear. "When our fathers are done, we are cuddling the shit out of you to try to cope with what happened. Okay?"

"Okay," I whispered back. I wrapped my arms around his neck and nuzzled my nose into his neck. "I love you, too."

"So, we came to let you know that Justina escaped," Dan told us.

"Not surprising," I whispered. "She's a crafty bitch."

Rhys sat on the end of the bed with me in his lap, my arms still around his neck.

"How did she sever your bonds?" Katar asked.

"She had a silver knife that she cut them with."

"Did it have any designs on it?" Johann asked.

I hadn't seen him come in and I had no idea when he had shown up.

"It had strange symbols. I didn't recognize them, but I could draw them for you," I offered.

"Please," he requested.

Nico handed me paper and a pen and I turned around in Rhys's lap, using a book as a hard surface to draw on. I tried to draw the knife and the symbols like I remembered, but it wasn't exact.

"I was a bit preoccupied with pain at the time, so these aren't accurate," I mumbled as I drew. After finishing, I handed it to Nico who cussed and held it up for everyone else to see.

"The Blade of Tate," Dan growled. "I had a feeling it was that cursed blade."

"That blade can cut anything," Johann told me. "It can even cut through mating bonds."

"So, what you're saying is that I'm still not safe? That she could cut our new bonds when we make them?" I asked softly, fear sliding up my back and making me shiver.

Rhys wrapped his arms around me and increased his heat once again. "We won't let that happen," he assured me. "We won't let you be taken again. *We* value your life." The last sentence was said with such venom, that it made me flinch, even though I knew he was directing it at Johann.

"What's the plan for tomorrow?" I asked. "Aren't you supposed to finish the Tournament?"

"We will. We will announce that you are their queen, and as such, we aren't going to make you choose a single mate. We will announce that we are leaving you to make your choice for mate at a later date and not force you to make it now," Emrys said.

"Amos—"

"Amos isn't as powerful as he thinks," Johann said. "He's old and has let the power go to his head. It is time we reminded him that he may be there for the reason of keeping us in line, but this is an instance where *he* needs to be put back in line."

"Seems a few of us need that reminder," Nico grunted.

"She needs to eat," Dan told them. "She hasn't eaten since yesterday and she's refusing to."

"I'm not hungry," I whispered and looked at the floor in front of me. Even though they were going to make me their queen, and they were going to become my mates, I was still empty — hollow.

"You have to eat," Rhys growled at my back.

"Martin, can you get some food for her?" Deryn asked him.

"Certainly," Martin said and set my bag on the ground before leaving.

"You were really going to leave us?" Nico asked.

"Yes," I said, not feeling remorseful at all. "I was going to go back to the apartment and try to figure out what I was going to do to with the rest of my life, without you in it."

"You're so damn stubborn," Deryn growled at me.

"Ditto," I replied with a smirk.

Fox sat in front of me, leaning his body against Rhys's legs so that his head could lean into my lap. "We would have followed you," he told me.

I ran my fingers through his hair and said, "I figured you would try, but I was hoping my exes would keep you busy." I froze a moment, my hand buried in his hair and asked, "Did you guys hurt them?"

"Who?" Deryn asked.

"Ezio, Thor, Declan, Kylan—"

"Oh, you mean when you ordered them to hold us so you could run off and sacrifice yourself?" Rhys growled at my back.

"Yeah, then."

"No one was killed or seriously wounded. They got a few heavy hits from us and scratches, but we couldn't punish them when they were following your orders," Fox said.

"Next time you pull something like that, I'm going to tie you up for an entire week," Deryn threatened me.

I winked at him and said, "Promises, promises."

Dan burst into loud laughter and stood up. "I love you, Jolie. You're the only female I've ever seen who keeps my boy on his toes."

I smiled back at him while Deryn scowled at us.

I climbed away from Rhys and Fox to wrap my arms around Deryn's neck and lean into him. "Are you still mad at me?"

"No," he admitted, wrapping his arms around me and burying his head into my neck while my arm covered him. "Having you here, alive, has made my anger vanish."

"Good," I whispered.

"I'd recommend staying in here the rest of the night," Emrys said. "Nico, put up wards."

Nico nodded. "I will as soon as Martin returns with her food."

Emrys nodded and they all left, leaving me and the guys alone in the room. Deryn's mouth crashed into mine, need and worry spurring on his movements. I kissed him back, glad for the physical touch. I tugged at his shirt and he ripped it in half, so we didn't have to break our kiss. My hands splayed across his chest and I moaned at the heat he was giving off.

"No shirts," I gasped, pulling back long enough to order the other princes.

They all removed their shirts and I followed my own order, removing mine as well, but leaving my bra on. Four male chests pressed against me from all sides and I sighed.

"She's so cold," Nico whispered worriedly.

"I told you I was," I reminded them.

"When are we making the bond?" Deryn asked Rhys.

"After she eats," Rhys said. He blew air against my skin and it was so hot that it burned me a moment.

"Ouch!" I gasped and jerked away from him.

"What?" he asked.

"That burned," I told him and turned around.

"Shit, Rhys. You burned her," Deryn said and touched the top of my back.

"I didn't use fire. I just warmed my breath," Rhys told us. He cupped my cheek. "It shouldn't have hurt you at all."

Fox set his hand over the burn and I felt his magic pulse into me, cooling the burn and then giving me relief.

"Thanks, Fox," I whispered and leaned my forehead against Rhys's chest.

"I'm sorry," Rhys said. "I don't know why that burned you."

"She's fully human right now," Nico reminded him. "Without the bond, she's not enhanced by our powers. I think we all got used to her being tougher than a regular human."

"So, we need to be extra careful with her," Deryn said. "Which means, no rough sex."

"Boo!" I yelled, which earned me four rumbling male chests

against my body as they laughed. "Seriously? Where's the fun in that?" I grumbled.

"Uh," Martin said from the doorway.

"We're not naked," I assured him, since he couldn't see me surrounded by the princes.

"You need to eat," Rhys ordered me, stepping away to get the platter of food Martin had brought with him.

Martin handed it over and asked, "Do you need anything else?"

"No, you can go," Rhys said.

"We're good," I assured Martin.

He nodded and left, shutting the door behind him. Nico went to the door, swiped his hand across the doorway, and a silver line stretched from the doorway, all the way around the room, creating the ward.

"Eat," Rhys snarled at me.

"I'm not hungry," I groaned, but sat down at the table where the food sat. Meats, cheeses, fruits, vegetables, and various dips rested on the large platter. None of it looked good.

"Please," Fox begged me, sitting down cross-legged beside me. "We need you to eat and get more strength back or we can't do the binding ceremony."

"Can't we just do it tomorrow?" I asked as I pushed around some of the fruit with my finger.

"You'll be even weaker tomorrow if you don't eat," he reminded me.

"None of this looks good," I complained.

"What do you want?" Nico asked. "I'll go have the chef make whatever you want."

I was being a spoiled brat. Shit.

"No, this is fine," I said with a sigh and chewed on a carrot.

"Seriously, we can go get you something else to eat. The chefs here are top notch and can make you whatever your heart desires," Fox said.

What did I want?

"Nothing sounds good," I admitted after a moment. None of my favorite foods sounded good. Not even dessert sounded good.

"We could get you a protein shake," Deryn offered.

"No," I almost gagged. "There's no way I could drink the entire thing. I'd end up getting sick before I finished it."

"Are you ill?" Fox asked and put his forehead against mine. "No fever."

"My insides are scrambled," I told them. "Did you guys eat?"

They all frowned and looked at each other.

"No, I guess we didn't," Rhys admitted.

"See!" I said victoriously. "It's not just me."

"We need to eat," Deryn said and grabbed a piece of meat. He looked at it and then sighed. "I don't want to eat this. Shit. What's wrong with us?"

"Maybe we need more skin to skin time," I suggested. "Then we can try to eat afterward."

"She might be right," Rhys admitted. "We all lost something and it hasn't really settled into our minds, and souls, that we have it back."

"Can we do the binding now?" I asked. "Without eating?"

"If we use the extra power that's in the necklace," Nico said and pointed at my necklace, the gift I had received from the kings for ending the war.

"Okay, let's do this," Rhys said and held his hand out to me. I took it and let him pull me to my feet.

CHAPTER 9

They said that normally, the queen would take the guards one by one, but since we wanted to conserve magical power and energy, we were going to do it for everyone at once. All four faced me, on one of their knees, and had their heads bowed. I touched each of their heads and then touched the necklace. The necklace glowed, and the magic began to flow into me.

"Will you, Rhys, Nico, Deryn, and Foxfire, become my guards, my protectors, and keep my life safe even if it means giving up your own?" I asked, my voice sounding louder and otherworldly.

"Yes," they replied in unison.

"Will you protect me above everyone else, even above your king, your mate, and your family?"

"Yes."

"Will you promise to love me until our last breaths?" I asked. I had added this part in, going off script.

"Yes," they replied without hesitation.

"I bind you, Rhys, Nico, Deryn, and Foxfire, to me, Jolie, as my guards, as your queen, until our last breaths."

All four looked up at me. "Yes, my queen," they replied.

From my chest, four strands grew, like tentacles, and continued to grow until they connected with each one of the princes. The instant the strands attached to them, energy surged into my body and my back arched as I gasped in pleasure.

Their echoing gasps led me to believe they had felt it as well.

"I am your guard. You are my queen. My sword is yours. My fangs and claws are yours. I will protect you until my final breath," all four said and stood.

"You are my guard. I am your queen," I replied.

The spell ended and the power disappeared, leaving me weak. I dropped to my knees in front of the princes. They reached out their hands and I flopped onto my side on the ground, so they could all touch my body as I tried to catch my breath.

"The necklace will need to be recharged, my queen," Nico whispered.

I nodded in understanding, rolling my head to the side so that I could look at them. "Now, you are all stuck with me."

"Pretty sure it is the other way around, my queen," Nico chuckled and stroked his hand down my cheek.

"I love you four. More than anything," I told them.

Their hands tightened on me. "I love you, too, my queen," they said.

"Is that going to be a common thing now?" I asked.

"Yes, my queen," Deryn said. "It's pretty much programmed into us that we are supposed to refer to you by that title."

"Can't I order you not to call me it?" I asked. If I was their queen, I should be able to order them to stop doing things.

"No, my queen," Rhys said and smirked. "Nice try, though."

"What do I call you?" I asked.

"Guard," Rhys said. "Though, you can still call us prince if you want to."

"So, I can yell, 'Guards, fetch me my crown'?"

Rhys smirked and said, "Yes."

"Really? Do I get a crown?" Not that I wanted one.

"We can get you one, if you want," Deryn offered.

"A really shiny one with lots of diamonds and jewels," Fox agreed.

"Has to be *super* expensive," Rhys added.

"At least half a million dollars," Nico agreed.

"Whoa," I ordered them.

"We definitely need to have it enchanted, which will double its price easily," Rhys said.

"I should really learn how to enchant things," Nico said and rubbed his chin. "I wonder how long it would take me to learn?"

"I'm honestly surprised you don't already know how to do that," I admitted to him.

"I started to learn, but it was boring and I wanted to focus more on combative spells," Nico told me.

"Maybe I should learn how to do it," I said. "It could be a second income for me."

"I really wish you would just let us provide for you," Rhys muttered and folded his arms across his chest. "We make more than enough money individually to provide for you."

"I have to make my own money. I have to contribute in some way. I don't want to freeload off of you guys."

"You could play video games all day," Deryn tempted me.

"That is *really* tempting, but I wouldn't feel right. I would feel like a gold digger or something."

"Remember her face when she figured out you were a prince?" Nico asked Rhys.

Rhys nodded. "I was terrified she was going to freak out and never talk to me again."

"I considered it," I teased him.

"No, you didn't," he said.

"Maybe," I shrugged.

"She was going to faint at first," Rhys told the others. "I thought I was going to have to catch her."

"Whatever," I said and rolled my eyes at him.

They laughed and I sighed happily as I felt their love and happiness through our bonds. *Yes!* Once again, I was full and warm. I finally had them inside of me and filling me up. I didn't believe in fate, but I truly believed they were meant to be part of me. Without them, I had felt too empty.

"Cuddle puddle?" Fox asked.

I nodded. "Yes."

Everyone changed into pajamas and we got into the massive bed, Rhys lying above my head, Nico on my right, Deryn on my left, and Fox at my feet.

Fox hugged my feet to his chest and said, "If you told me that I would be cuddling a female's feet, I would have told you that you were insane. Yet, here I am, cuddling your feet and happier than a wolf with a bone."

"I know what you mean," Rhys agreed.

"If you had told me that I would be in love with four males at once, especially four Other princes, I would have laughed in your face," I told them.

"I still can't believe you turned your ex-boyfriends on us," Deryn grumbled.

"I knew they would do what I asked," I said. "Plus, they're probably the only ones, aside from your father's, who are capable of holding you back for at least a few moments."

"I can't believe Ezio withdrew from the Tournament," Deryn whispered. "He was so set on winning you for a mate and proving himself."

"He could tell that I love you," I said. "He doesn't want to take me as a mate if I won't love him."

"You do care for him, though," Deryn said.

"I'll always care about him, but we aren't meant to be together. I tried to explain that to him when I left, but he was as obstinate as you four are. He was adamant that what happened wasn't that bad and—"

"What did happen?" Deryn asked.

Crap. I'd opened the door for that question.

"We were out on a date," I told them. "He was taking me to dinner at a nice restaurant, but on the way there, an ogre attacked us. He killed the ogre pretty quickly, but it turned out to be a herd of ogres rampaging through the city. When they heard their companion's death yell, they rushed us. Ezio would have been fine, but he was trying to keep me safe. One of the ogres got close to me and he had to try to help, which left him open and the damn ogre drew a dagger and nearly cut his hand off. There was so much blood and his hand was barely hanging on by a thread. Ezio acted like it was a fucking flesh wound and continued fighting, putting his arm into his jacket to keep his hand from completely falling off. I threw up all over and was a mess when he finally defeated them all."

"How many were there?" Rhys asked.

"A dozen at least," I whispered. "I remember counting eleven severed heads as we walked away from the bodies. He had killed a few more without decapitating them though, so I'm not positive how many there were."

"Dan said you got really angry when you saw Rhys hurt in the Tournament," Fox commented.

I nodded. "I was about to shift into a dragon and beat some sense into Ezio. Emrys forced me to calm down, but it wasn't easy."

Rhys slipped his fingers through my hair and said, "I appreciate your concern, but that really was just a flesh wound."

"Maybe you guys just bleed way too much," I commented.

"There was *a lot* of blood at the place Justina tortured you," Nico whispered.

"You went there?" I asked in disbelief. *Why would he go there?*

"Yes," he nodded. "I wanted to see what had almost traumatized Martin.

"What do you mean?"

"He kept saying that he didn't know how you could survive when you had lost so much blood."

"Thor gave me some of his blood," I said. "The healer hooked him up to me somehow, my eyes were closed so I couldn't see, but he let me take some of Thor's blood to keep me from dying."

"I hope we find her soon," Rhys growled. "I'm going to show her the true meaning of torture."

"You say the sweetest things," I whispered with a chuckle and reached up to link our fingers together. "I don't want you guys going anywhere near her."

"Too bad," Rhys growled.

"I order you not to seek her out," I snapped. Something sharp and cold zipped down our bonds and the guys hissed. "Uh, what happened?"

"You gave us a direct order," Rhys said.

"Now, we can't disobey or it will physically hurt us," Nico told me.

"I'm sorry!" I yelled and sat up. "I didn't know. I didn't mean to. I mean, I did, but not like that. Can I take it back? What can I do—"

"It's okay," Fox assured me, grabbing my hand in his. "You meant the order, or it wouldn't have been issued like that. We will abide by your order and not seek her out. However, if we see her, or if someone else finds her, we will still get our revenge."

"Don't forget," Nico said, "she hurt us, too. You weren't the only one affected by her severing the bonds."

"We want our pound of salt, too," Rhys said adamantly.

I collapsed back down on the bed. "Are there any other important things I should know about being your queen now?"

"Even if you order us to, we cannot hurt you," Fox told me.

"Like, even spankings?"

That got all four of them laughing again.

"As long as we aren't actually *hurting* you, we can enjoy whatever rough sexual fun you want. But, if it hurts you, we won't be able to do it," Rhys explained.

"What about choking?" I asked.

Nico let out a bark of laughter and shook his head. "Since when do you want that?"

I shrugged. "I didn't say I did, but I like having options. Choking might be fun every once in a while."

"Oh, boy," Fox exhaled. "I feel like she just became an even bigger handful. How is that even possible?"

"We should all know by now not to underestimate Jolie," Rhys teased.

"Ha. Ha," I muttered.

"Go to sleep, my queen. Tomorrow will be a busy day," Nico said and scooted closer to me, resting his head on my shoulder.

"Can't we just run away?" I whined. "We could elope! You know, run off without telling anyone to become mates! It's super romantic and I'm sure the kings would forgive us."

"No," they all said at the same time.

"So, unromantic," I sighed. "For princes, you aren't very fairytale-like. You're supposed to be super sweet and romantic. You're supposed to sweep me off my feet."

"We do that on a daily basis," Rhys rumbled, his voice heavy with sleep.

I always envied how quickly he fell asleep.

"We can sweep you off your feet tomorrow," Fox said around a yawn.

"Fine," I agreed, feeling my eyes growing heavier as well.

It seemed like seconds had passed by, but when I awoke screaming and crying, the clock showed it had been five hours.

"What?" Deryn asked, growling and throwing his arms around me.

"Sorry," I sobbed and leaned into his touch. "Nightmare."

He pulled my head to his chest and rubbed my back. Nico rubbed my lower back, where Deryn couldn't reach. Fox ran his hand up and down one of my legs and Rhys pet my hair.

"What happened?" Nico asked.

"Memory, not nightmare," I whispered.

"Losing us?" Deryn guessed.

I nodded. All four moved closer to me, projecting their feelings of love down our bond, and soon, my body relaxed and I fell asleep again.

♥

Martin waited in the hallway when we came out and walked next to me to go get breakfast. "How are you feeling?" he asked.

"Pretty well," I admitted and looked at my arms. "I feel stronger today than I did yesterday."

"Good," he said with a sigh. "I was really worried about you."

I hugged him and pecked him on his cheek. "Thank you."

We entered the dining hall to chaos. Hundreds of reporters swarmed around the front half of the dining hall, bombarding Amos with questions so fast, he couldn't even answer them.

"There she is now," Amos declared, a predatory smirk on his face. "You are free to ask her questions."

"Asshole," I muttered.

The princes stepped in front of me, but that didn't deter the media.

"Jolie! Is it true that you bound the four princes to you?"

"Why?"

"What are you after?"

"I'm after some food!" I growled.

"Come," Ezio said behind me. I turned and he linked our fingers together, pulling me away from my guards, and towards a table where my other exes sat.

"Hey," I said and waved at them.

Declan stood to pull my chair out for me and then pushed it in for me as well. He kissed my cheek and returned to his seat. Ezio sat next to me after kissing my other cheek.

"Thank you, for holding the princes back the other day," I said. I opened my napkin and put it on my lap, knowing I was likely to spill on myself since I was wearing a light blue dress that would easily stain.

"Orange juice?" Kylan asked.

"Yes, please," I replied and pushed my glass towards him.

"You are welcome," Ezio said and leaned closer to me. "But, if you ever order us to do something that results in your near death again, I will steal you away and lock you up in a tower where no one will find us."

He wasn't joking. Ezio's eyes were dead serious.

I swallowed and nodded, unsure if my voice would work properly if I tried to use it.

"Yeah," Yukio said, "that was really awful. We felt responsible for your pain."

"Is it true that they're your guards?" Zelphar asked.

I nodded. "Yes, they are."

"I heard your kidnapper cut your bonds, though," Thor whispered.

"She did, but those were ones that added me to their warrior's bond. They accepted me as their queen last night," I explained. It was nice to get to tell people the truth. I really preferred this to keeping secrets.

"Are you going to take them as mates?" Ezio asked, a strange fire in his eyes that I couldn't place. Was it jealousy? Anger?

"I don't know," I lied.

"Liar," he accused.

"I haven't taken them as mates," I said.

"Thor said you were cursed," Ezio commented.

I nodded. "I was."

"So, you weren't wrong when you told me you needed to leave because you were cursed," he said softly.

"I didn't know I had it then. I just assumed I did because of all of the bad shit that kept happening to me," I admitted.

"Still," he whispered, "to know that you actually were cursed back then. I feel like an ass."

"You were a bit of an ass," I teased, "but, you also nearly lost your hand to keep me alive."

"I'd lose my head if I needed to," he told me.

"She's got enough guards," Deryn growled.

"The offer is open still," Ezio said with a smirk and winked at me.

"I am not rising to your bait this time," Deryn said, setting his hands on my shoulders.

Everyone at the table zeroed in on his hands.

"Guys," I growled.

Their eyes moved to my face. "He's one of my guards, remember? He's allowed to touch me. Plus, I'm *not* with any of you any longer. We broke up years ago."

"It still bothers us," Ezio said. "We all love you, haven't stopped loving you, and you've been through a lot. We are all worried about you."

"You don't need to worry about her any longer," Rhys said, coming to stand on my left side. "We'll protect her."

"You'd better," Ezio snarled. "If she gets hurt, or killed, I'm coming after all four of your asses. Princes or not, I don't give a shit. You protect her or I'll kill you myself."

"We'll die before we let her die," Fox promised.

"Good," Ezio said and returned to eating.

I sipped on my orange juice and sighed. Males were so territorial and aggressive.

"What would you like to eat?" Nico asked, squatting down on my right side.

"Waffles, eggs, and bacon!" I ordered, suddenly feeling ravenous.

"Scrambled eggs?" he asked.

I nodded. "Yes, please."

"Anything else?" he asked.

"A kiss?" I whispered.

He smiled and brushed his lips across mine. They barely touched before he was gone, off to order my food.

"What happened with the media?" I asked.

"We gave them what they wanted. We admitted that you are our queen. We told them that we were the ones who asked you, since that is true. We told them that we in no way regret this decision and plan to try to earn your love to become your mates, but that we may not be worthy of being your mates," Rhys said.

"Ain't that the truth," Ezio scoffed.

I smacked his arm. "Hey."

He smiled, but didn't say anything else.

"Is there a shopping area nearby?" I asked Fox, since he had a house in downtown.

"Yes."

"I need to do some shopping."

"For what?" Deryn asked.

"My final Christmas presents. I still have a couple I need to get."

"If you know what they are, you can just tell us and we can have a servant go get them for you," Kylan said.

"I have to get them myself. That's the whole point of Christmas shopping, you buy presents for your loved ones. I only have a couple of things left to get, so it shouldn't take me too long to buy them."

"We can go with you, to provide additional back up, if you want?" Yukio offered.

"That would be most appreciated," Rhys said before I could decline.

"Seriously?" I asked him.

"You have a knack for getting into trouble. Taking you to an area that is open to the public will be a huge safety risk, plus, the media is bound to be there, and fans who will pester us," Nico said.

"Can't you just do your final shopping at the dragon's den? I know you saw a few things you wanted, but didn't buy there," Rhys said.

"No, they didn't have the last few items I need," I admitted.

"Food," Nico said and set a plate of food in front of me.

"Did you cook this?" I asked him.

He nodded.

"You cooked for a female?" Zelphar asked, his jaw hanging slightly open.

"Not just a female," Nico reminded him. "I cooked for my queen."

"Thank you," I said and dug in, moaning as the waffle melted in my mouth. It was super buttery and he had already poured syrup on it. The eggs were also really fluffy and light, just the way I liked them.

"You're the best," I mumbled around the food in my mouth.

"I think so," he said with a proud smirk. Everyone else rolled their eyes.

"Aren't you guys going to eat?" I asked Nico.

"Once you're done eating, we will," he told me.

"Why? Please tell me it's not going to be like this all the time? I don't want to eat while you guys just sit and watch me. That's totally creepy!"

Everyone chuckled.

"No, it won't be a normal occurrence," Fox promised. "For today it is, but we will eat together like we normally do."

"What are we having for Christmas dinner?" I asked.

"Oven roasted goose, mashed potatoes, gravy, brussel sprouts, ham, oven roasted turkey, sweet potatoes, yams, green bean casserole, chocolate mousse pie, and some appetizers," Nico announced.

"Can we come, too?" Kylan asked with a laugh.

I actually liked the sound of that. It made me smile to think of having everyone together to eat and exchange gifts. But, I knew my guards wouldn't appreciate having my ex-boyfriends there. Especially, since we were supposed to mate that week. I knew that males got super possessive the week after they mated. I didn't want them getting into fights and hurting each other. Maybe next year we could, though.

"You guys should all come next year," I said and looked at everyone at the table. "This year is going to be a bit crazy, but next year should be fine."

"We'd be honored to," Ezio said and bowed his head.

"Don't start bowing to me," I whispered and went back to eating my food. "I don't like it."

"Well, you do outrank me now," he reminded me. "You're the princess."

"Still," I whispered.

I finished eating and as one, the guys sitting in chairs stood up and the princes took their vacated seats. My exes took turns kissing my cheeks before dismissing themselves. Servants brought out food for the princes and I took my time to admire them.

They all had dark bags beneath their eyes, something highly unusual in Others. It told me more than they were telling me. They were still feeling the aftereffects of the bonds being removed. Were they also weighed down by our new bond? Did it cause them problems?

"You are scowling awfully hard over there," Deryn commented. "What's wrong, baby?"

"Does the new bond cause additional issues for you? Or added weight?" I asked, since he had opened the door for me to ask.

"No, why?" Fox asked.

"You all have bags beneath your eyes."

"That's because we didn't get enough sleep last night and the day before was very taxing on us," Nico explained. "We'll take a nap today and everything will be back to normal."

"Swear?" I asked.

He nodded. "I swear, my queen."

"You were free of her and then you made her your queen again, why?" Rhian, Rhys's youngest sister, asked.

"Because I love her, baby sister. You are young yet, so you likely won't understand for a few more years at the very least," Rhys replied to her.

"Many years at the very least," Emrys said from behind me.

"*Dad,*" Rhian complained with a whine.

"You guys are needed in the coliseum," Emrys informed us.

"Do I have to go?" I asked with a pout.

Emrys walked around my side, into my range of view, and smiled. "While your pout is adorable, it won't get you out of this."

"Pouting never works on Dad," Rhian told me.

"It works on Rhys just fine," I told her.

"Really?" she asked, her mouth gaping a second. "I could never get it to work on him."

"You've got to look as pathetic as possible. You probably just focused on looking cute, but that won't cut it when it comes to Rhys. You have to look pathetic and vulnerable," I explained.

"Hey!" Rhys yelled. "Don't give her pointers on my weaknesses."

"You've really got to stick the lip out, too," I advised her, completely ignoring Rhys. "As far out as possible and give him the big puppy dog eyes."

"I'll work on it," she assured me and smiled at Rhys. "Love you."

"Love you, too," he muttered and shoveled food into his mouth.

"I'll see you at the coliseum," Emrys told me. "You'll sit in the same spot you have been."

"Okay."

"I've got to keep her away from my family," Fox whispered. "She'll tell them all of my weaknesses and they will exploit them!"

"You could always bribe me," I offered.

"With what?" he asked.

I smirked. "I'm sure you could come up with something."

"Choking?" he asked.

That had everyone laughing and made Deryn choke on the food that had been in his mouth.

"You all seem happy today?" Dan said as he gripped the back of my chair.

"Hello, Father," I said and smiled up at him.

"Daughter," he replied in greeting, a huge smile splitting his face.

"You sure I can't feign sickness to get out of going to the coliseum?" I asked.

"Sorry, not today," he told me, pulling my chair out and helping me to my feet. The boys stood as well, their plates cleaned, and we made our way to the coliseum.

Dan escorted me to our seats, ignoring the looks we received from Amos, who scowled heavily.

"Today is the end of the Tournament," Amos told me.

"Really?" I asked, sarcasm dripping form my tone. I hated that asshole.

"A choice has to be made," he snapped.

"It has been," I snapped back.

The four princes jumped down into the arena to cheers from the stands. They were well-loved by their people, which was something I wanted to learn more about. I knew they were good people, but what had they done to earn their peoples' respect?

"Will you four battle for victory?" Amos asked them.

"No," all four said at the same time.

"We all claim her," Rhys said.

"Let it be known that Jolie Bernardo is Queen of the Four Princes," Foxfire announced loudly.

The crowd was split between cheering and murmuring. I could understand how they felt, even though I knew what they were going to say. Even though I knew we were now connected. It still felt surreal that I was their queen, completely, now. And, soon, I would become their mate.

"Jolie," Dan said to get my attention. "Go down to them."

I walked to the edge of the platform and smiled down at my guards. Wings popped out of Rhys's back and he propelled himself upward, flying straight up in front of me, snatching me into his arms as he went, turned, and floated down to the others.

I stood before them, my heart full with their love, as felt through the bond.

"This concludes the Tournament," Amos snapped, his anger carrying his words sharply across the coliseum.

"Now we can go shopping?" I asked Rhys.

"Yes, now we can go shopping," he agreed.

CHAPTER 10

Yukio, Zelphar, Ezio, Thor, Martin, Declan, and Kylan joined my four guards and me for my shopping trip. Our huge group made quite the scene as we walked around to the different vendors.

The town was old and the buildings were beautiful with ancient styles I knew Rhys enjoyed seeing, with his architect experience. The buildings looked to be made out of a stone, but the stone was in colors I had never seen before. I thought it might be painted, but Rhys confirmed the stone was naturally those colors.

I had had a pre-shopping meeting with my exes, getting them to agree to keep my guards away from me, so I could buy their presents without them seeing the gifts. And, to pay attention to see if they were eyeing any gifts. I was blessed to have these males in my life, continuing to be my friends despite our romantic relationships ending.

"What are you smiling about?" Ezio asked. He wore a pair of sweatpants and a tank top, showing off his muscular arms. I found it a bit hard to keep from staring, but I was trying my hardest!

"Just thinking how lucky I am to have you and the others in my life. A lot of females wouldn't have their ex-boyfriends helping them shop for their current boyfriends," I replied.

"There's always been something about you. Something magnetic," he said. "You make me happy just by being near me. You're easy to be around and my wolf is always calm when I'm with you. Well, except for when I'm having to save you."

"A few shifters have said that to me," I mumbled. Did it mean something? Was there something unique or different about me that called to shifters?

"It's not just shifters," Yukio said from my other side. He held a pendant in his hand that was shaped like the moon and sun together. "You have always made me feel calm and relaxed as well."

"I wonder if it effects humans, too?" Ezio asked Yukio.

"I don't know. I never spent time with her and other humans," Yukio replied.

The jeweler we stood in front of had many beautiful items, but the one thing I needed, I didn't see.

"Excuse me?" I asked the seller.

"Yes, dear?" she asked. She was an older female with gorgeous grey hair that flowed down to her butt.

"Do you have any, um..." I leaned forward so I could whisper without anyone else hearing, "bloodstones?"

"Sorry, no. I would try Klinton. He has a stall about halfway down the alley here, selling potions. He should have some," she said apologetically.

"Thank you, so much!" I said quickly. I didn't want to leave without getting something from here, so I purchased the pendant Yukio had been eyeing, tucking my new purchase into my large backpack I wore.

"I can carry your backpack for you," Ezio offered for the fifth time.

"No, I want to carry it," I said quickly. Plus, one of his presents was inside the bag.

"What did you ask her about?" Yukio asked, coming back to us. He'd gone to talk to Zelphar and Nico when I had started talking to the seller.

"I need a specific item, but it turns out she doesn't have it. She did tell me one of the other vendors here has some. So, on we go!"

Fox caught up to me and asked, "Are you sure you don't want me to give you—"

"Foxfire, I already told you, no." I said with a sigh. "No."

"You've spent quite a lot and I know you don't make *that* much at your job. I just don't want you spending a bunch of money on us because of what you think we are going to spend on you. You don't need to match our prices."

"Go back with Zelphar," I ordered him. "You're going to see me get a gift for you and it will ruin the surprise."

"Yes, my queen," he whispered, bowed, and stopped to let me continue on without him and let Zelphar catch up to him.

"You've always been stubborn about taking money from others," Ezio commented.

"It's not my money. Plus, it doesn't really make it a gift from me if I am using their money to buy it." And, if they didn't like it, I would feel even worse, because then I had wasted their money on something they didn't want. No, I would use my money. Even though it meant dipping into my savings a bit. They were worth it.

I bought a few more items from the vendors, but I was truly looking for Klinton's stand. I finally found it, and ordered Ezio to keep everyone far enough away that they wouldn't be able to hear me and the seller speaking. He stood ten feet away from me, his arms crossed, and refused to let anyone approach.

"How can I help you?" Klinton asked.

"I need bloodstones and I was told you might have some," I informed him.

"I do," he said with a smile. "How many do you need?"

"Five," I said and pulled out my wallet. "How much?"

"Five hundred," he said and bent over as he grabbed something from beneath his stand. "Do you need boxes?"

"Yes, please."

"I charge ten for each box," he explained.

"That's fine."

He set five black boxes on the flat surface of his stall and slid a clear crystal the size of a grain of rice into each one, into a pocket designed to hold them securely. I was so excited to have finally found them, that I was practically dancing in front of his stand.

"I'm so glad I was able to find some," I said and held out my money.

"These are actually the last five that I have, so you definitely came at just the right time."

"Why are they so hard to find?" I asked. Bloodstones were very popular, used by mates of every race.

"This time of year, a lot of new matings happen and so, the demand for the crystals is high. I usually have a large enough supply, but I miscalculated and ran out. Hopefully, I will have another shipment coming soon," he explained.

"That makes sense," I whispered.

"Is there anything else?" he asked.

"Oh, can I have two healing potions?" They were expensive, but they would give you double your stamina for ten minutes.

"Sure. They are one hundred each," he said, grabbed two glass bottles with heart shaped stoppers with pink liquid in them, and added them to my bag.

I gave him the additional money and put the items into my bag. "Thank you, so much."

"Happy Holidays," he said and waved.

"Ezio!" I called. "I'm done!"

Ezio nodded and jogged over to walk beside me. "Find what you need?"

I nodded happily. "I did! I think my shopping is actually complete."

"Jo!" Martin called. "Let's get some food!"

"Food sounds great!" I called back, turning to go back to the others.

"I love seeing you happy and smiling like this," Rhys whispered into my ear.

I squeaked, shocked because I hadn't seen him approach. "You scared me!" I snapped.

He kissed my cheek and said, "Do you think Ezio would let some stranger get this close to you?"

"No," I said and glanced at Ezio who rolled his eyes at me. "Your voice still startled me."

"Well, that squeak was awfully adorable, so I won't apologize for it," Rhys said and wrapped his arms around my waist as he walked behind me. I had no idea how he was able to walk so well with me, considering our height difference, but he didn't even stumble as we went.

"Rhys," Nico called. The rest of our group stood in front of us, blocking my view of whatever had caused them to stop. Rhys kissed my head and then walked through the rest of them.

"What's going on?" I asked Ezio, who had moved closer and stood behind me, so my back was protected. He was tall enough, that he could likely see what was going on.

"Media," he growled. "They're harassing them to get interviews."

"They sure are persistent," I sighed. "And now I'm royally exposed, everyone knows I'm part of the Other royalty now."

Soon, they would know I was even more entangled than before.

Once we announced being mated, I would be hounded just like they were.

"Rhys is handling it," Ezio assured me. "As much as I hate seeing you with someone else, they do love you and are doing everything in their powers to keep you safe."

"Oh, my gosh. Was that a compliment? Did you just give another male a compliment? I didn't even bring my jacket," I said and rubbed at my arms and tilted my head back so I could look up at him.

"What? It's warm," he said with a frown.

"Yeah, but clearly hell has frozen over, so the snow and ice are bound to descend upon us any moment."

"Ha. Ha," he replied, his eyes fixed ahead.

"Why haven't you taken a mate yet?" I asked him. "And don't even try to say it is because of me. Yes, I know you still love me, but that's not the reason. You knew we were over when I left."

"I had some hope that you might come back to me," he whispered. "At first, but you're right. I just couldn't find anyone who could match your perfection."

"Flatterer," I whispered and turned my face down to hide my blush.

"Do you know how hard it is to find someone who doesn't care that you shift into a wolf and that you spend a lot of time playing video games? Girls generally hate playing games and that their guys ignore them to play games."

I hated that. I wished girls would just get online and play the games with their guys. If he spends a lot of time on a game, talk to him about you joining him online. There was always room for a healer on the team.

"Maybe you set your bar too high," I said, but didn't really mean it. Ezio was amazing and any girl would be lucky to have him.

"Thank you," he said and hugged me. "Hearing you say that means a lot to me."

"Say what?" I asked.

"That anyone would be lucky to have me," he chuckled. "You didn't mean to say that out loud, did you?"

"No," I mumbled, but leaned back into his hold. "But, I meant it. Anyone would be lucky to have you as a mate. You're handsome, kind, and a fierce protector. Though, you are a shitty tank."

"Hey! I had just learned to play the game that week. I was a newbie."

"Still are," I teased.

He growled in my ear, but didn't say anything else.

"How long are we going to be stuck here?" I asked with a sigh. "I'm hungry."

"Rhys!" Ezio called. "Wrap it up, yeah?"

Rhys put an arm behind his back to flip Ezio off and I burst out into a fit of laughter. Rhys looked like the prim and proper prince he was, but behind his back he had his middle finger up to Ezio to tell him to shove it. It was hilarious.

"Is that the princess?" someone asked.

"Princess Jolie!" someone else called.

"Crap," I snapped and sat on my butt behind Martin's legs so they couldn't see me.

"You've never been good at hiding," Martin whispered to me. "Somehow you always ended up making noise and would get caught."

"Shut up," I growled. "I'm not ten anymore."

"You sure about that?" he asked and chuckled.

"We have answered your questions," Rhys said. "So, please let us pass and continue on with our day."

Nico took my hand and pulled me up to stand. "I'm going to make you invisible."

"Why?" I asked.

"Because if they see you, they're going to follow us and yell questions at you," he explained. A sphere wrapped around us and I couldn't see him anymore.

"Nico?" I asked.

He grabbed my hand and said, "It's okay. I'm here. We're both invisible to everyone else now. Just follow the others."

"You still there?" Ezio asked. "I can smell you, but I want to make sure that it's not a lingering scent and you've been kidnapped again."

"You're so rude," I grumbled.

"She's here," Nico assured Ezio with a chuckle.

Ezio nodded and followed just behind us, giving us enough space that he wouldn't step on our heels, but also kept the media from following us too closely. Rhys walked into a building that had delicious scents wafting from it.

"Meat," I whispered and followed everyone inside.

Thankfully, there was a huge table available, one that could seat us all. Nico released his spell and pulled out a chair for me, to sit beside him. I sat down and Deryn sat on my other side, leaning over to rub his cheek against mine.

I kissed his cheek and rubbed mine against his. "Hello."

"Hello, beautiful," he whispered. "Did you get all of your presents?"

I nodded and set my backpack on the ground between my legs, under the table. "Yep! Now, I just need to get them all wrapped and ready to give you guys when we get back."

"Where are you living these days?" Yukio asked.

"With us," Fox answered. "She has an apartment in our building."

"You let her sleep in a separate apartment?" Declan asked. "I would have assumed you all kept her in your apartments."

"We usually stay in the same apartment together, but it varies which one we stay in," Rhys told them.

"And, we give her her space when she wants it. As long as she's in the building with us, we're fine," Deryn said.

"Except when she sneaks out to get donuts," Rhys growled.

"They were a gift for you guys, remember?" I said and scowled at them.

"You went out, unprotected, to get them donuts and coffee?" Ezio asked. "I'm not surprised in the least, to be honest. That sounds like something you would do."

"Yes, I would do something nice like that," I said and picked up my menu. The menu was huge and I couldn't even begin to make a decision.

"Deryn," I said to get his attention.

He just nodded and said, "I'll order something for you, baby."

I set my menu down and leaned my head on his shoulder. "You're awesome."

"Don't forget it," he whispered and chuckled. "What do you want to drink?" he asked.

"Strawberry daiquiri, please."

"Okay," he agreed and returned to looking at the menu.

It was weird to think about the fact that I had just been on my first date with Deryn less than a year ago. Things had moved so quickly between us all, but I didn't regret it.

"So, what did you get me?" Fox asked, sitting across the table from me.

"I'm not telling you," I scoffed.

"It was worth a try, right?" he asked and laughed, his infectious smile spreading to my face immediately.

"Jo," Thor called, "did you get the items you were searching for?"

I nodded. "The last vendor had them. So, my shopping is done."

"Great, then after we eat, why don't we go back to the coliseum for some fun?" Ezio asked.

"Sparring?" Deryn asked, obviously intrigued by that prospect.

Ezio nodded. "No weapons or shifting. Just some hand to hand fun."

"Sounds great," Rhys said with a wide smile.

"When do we return home again?" I asked, a bit anxious to get back.

"Next week. We've only been here, what, less than a week?" Rhys said.

Everyone nodded.

"It feels like it's been an eternity," I mumbled.

The waiter brought out bread and took our orders. I ate a piece of the bread, which was unlike anything we had in Jinla, loving the strange, but delicious taste.

"Don't you just love watching her enjoying foods?" Ezio asked everyone.

"She gets such enjoyment out of good tasting food," Deryn agreed.

"Her blissful expression makes you feel happy, even if you weren't the one to make it," Nico said.

Everyone nodded.

I was blushing, bright as a tomato, I was sure. "You guys," I whispered.

"You ever see her eat beef bone broth soup?" Declan asked.

Everyone smiled.

"She sips it with her eyes closed, a small smile on her face, in supreme contentment," Fox said. "It's glorious."

"I like food," I said and shrugged. "I can't help it."

"We enjoy watching you eat," Nico said and patted my leg. "It's one of the few moments where you will drop your guard completely and you're just you."

"I don't wear masks," I argued. "I'm me all the time."

"Most of the time," Deryn corrected me. "There are often times where you put a mask on. Mostly in public places, especially if they are crowded."

"I don't like crowds," I said. "So, what?"

"No one is saying it's a problem, Jo," Martin said. "They're just telling you that in situations you are uncomfortable with, you wear a mask. But, when you're eating yummy food, you are completely defenseless. It's refreshing to see."

Males were so weird.

"Whatever," I mumbled and smiled happily at the waiter as he set my drink down. "Thank you," I said and took a big drink. Strawberries and rum, a wonderful combination.

"Euphoria, that's what that face is," Ezio said. "I don't think I've ever experienced something like that, especially not with something as trivial as food and drink."

"I need to make her open the bond next time she is about to experience something like that," Rhys said. "Then, I'll know what she's feeling and get to experience it myself."

"Wait until you get a mating bond with her," Martin said. "It's ten times better!"

"Are you mating with them?" Ezio asked, a slight frown marking his handsome face.

"No serious talk," I whispered, closed my eyes, and took another drink.

Paradise! Give me non-stop daiquiris, the males in swimsuits, warm sun, and cool water, and I would be set.

"What are you thinking about?" Deryn purred into my ear.

"We should go on a beach vacation this summer," I whispered, feeling my lips tug up in a smirk.

"Oh, are you thinking about me in a banana hammock?" Deryn whispered even quieter.

I burst into laughter, setting down my drink as I bent over and clutched my stomach. "Now I am!" I shouted over my laughter.

"I look good in one," he said and folded his arms across his chest.

"I'm sure you do." I gasped as I tried to calm back down and wiped my teary eyes.

"Your salad," the waiter said, drawing my attention. I was sitting forward, so he couldn't set my salad down.

"Sorry," I said and leaned back. Everyone at the table apparently ordered salad, which I found strange. Most of the time, the shifters didn't eat salads.

"They're part of the meals," Martin said and smiled at me.

"What?" Deryn asked him.

"She was shocked to see shifters eating salads," Martin explained.

"So, I explained that they are part of the meal, which is why we are eating them."

"How'd you know that's what she was thinking?" Deryn asked.

"Was that what you were thinking?" Nico asked me.

"I've known her a long time," Martin reminded them. "She learned about shifters from me and my pack. So, I can read her pretty easily."

"Yes, that was what I was thinking," I told Nico. "I know shifters eat healthy, but normally, they don't eat salads. They'll eat a vegetable with their steak dinner, but not a salad."

"Sometimes we eat salads," Rhys countered.

"Yeah, if they are full of meat or other protein like eggs," I replied.

"She does know an awful lot about shifters," Yukio commented.

"Yes, I do. I grew up with them. I did a lot of research and asked a lot of questions. Even after Martin and I broke up, I still studied as much as I could."

"Why?" Declan asked.

"I wanted to know as much as I could about them. I wanted to make sure that when I interacted with them, I didn't do anything offensive on accident. I wanted to make sure I was as respectful as possible. I really wanted to make sure if I touched a male, in front of his female, I didn't do anything to make her want to rip out my throat," I explained.

"She wouldn't have ripped out your throat," Martin said and rolled his eyes. "It was my fault for letting you come over during the mating week. She apologized to you and you are best friends now, so it's old history."

"She still tried," I reminded him. "And, I wanted to make sure nothing like that happened again. I didn't want it to be my own fault that a shifter lost control."

"That's not just because of Sharla, is it?" Rhys asked.

I blushed and shoveled a huge bite of salad into my mouth, giving him a small shake of my head.

"That's my fault," Ezio said.

"What?" Deryn asked.

"I lost control one night. She blames herself for it. No matter how many times I tell her it was completely my fault, that a shifter should be able to control their beast no matter what, she still won't forgive herself," Ezio explained.

"They were going to kill you," I snapped, slamming my fork down. "You were almost killed by them because of me."

"Whoa," Deryn said and rested his hand around the back of my neck. "Calm down, baby."

"I think we should hear this story," Rhys said softly, then looked at Ezio. "If, you're willing to share it? We can discuss it privately later, if you wish."

Ezio waved his hand. "It's fine. I was young and violent. It is something I've made certain can never happen again."

"Only because I'm not there to provoke you," I muttered, feeling as small as a mouse.

"About a week into our dating, during, um, fun time, she went for my neck," Ezio explained, fumbling over his words as he looked at Rhys and Deryn. "I hadn't had a female do that before. I overreacted, tossing her off of me and immediately shifted. She'd told me she had been with werewolves before, but I didn't realize she wouldn't know that for how early we were in our relationship, she couldn't do something like that. I was out of control, but to make matters worse, someone had called the cops on us because they'd heard her screaming. Pleasure screams are apparently the same to whoever called. So, the cops burst into the room."

"They saw her naked and terrified on the floor and you, in wolf form, on the bed and flipped?" Deryn guessed.

"Bingo," Ezio said. "They moved towards her and that made me more protective. I deemed them a threat and charged to attack them. Several drew their guns immediately."

"So, who died?" Fox asked.

"No one. She leapt between me and the officer I had charged at, and stood, buck-ass naked, arms spread wide, in front of me so the officers who had drawn their guns couldn't shoot me. They were yelling at her to get down and she refused, telling them to get out and taking steps towards them."

"What did you do?" Deryn asked.

"Nothing. I sat there and stared at her in disbelief. I'd hurt her, growled at her, tossed her off the bed, and she'd thrown herself in front of the humans to protect me without a second's hesitation," Ezio said. He looked over at me and smiled. "That was the night I fell in love with her."

I'd been terrified of Ezio in that moment. I had never had a wolf growl at me so viciously before and he was a huge wolf when shifted. But, I couldn't let him get hurt because of a misunderstanding. Those cops would have killed him first and asked questions later. I could see that Ezio had wanted to protect me when the cops moved towards me and I did the only thing I could think of. I stood up to protect him. In his wolf form, he couldn't communicate with them. He had no way of telling them to back off, except to snap his teeth at them. Had I known that putting my mouth over his neck so early in relationship would make him react that way, I would never have done it. I hadn't realized he would think I was being aggressive towards him or trying to hurt him. I was ignorant and there was no reason for it. So, I started researching their behaviors and laws.

"Is that why you only date Alphas?" Zelphar asked. "Because you know we have the highest levels of control?"

Shit.

"Maybe," I mumbled, shoveling more salad into my mouth.

"It's also because she has an Alpha personality," Martin said. "She doesn't see it, but I'm sure you all do."

Everyone nodded.

"What?" I asked.

"You're essentially, a human alpha," Rhys said. "You may let others take charge in certain situations, but you are an alpha, through and through."

I didn't believe that for a moment. I was terrified and indecisive a lot of the time. I had panic and anxiety attacks. I was not alpha material, at all.

"She hasn't realized that eventually, she's going to be Queen of the Four Clans, has she?" Kylan asked softly.

Fucking casuals! He was right! Oh, god. Oh, goddess. No. No. No.

"She's freaking out," Nico whispered.

Queen of the Four Clans. Queen of the Dragons. Queen of the Mages. Queen of the Werewolves. Queen of the Elves. I wasn't any of those things. I was human! I wasn't capable of being queen to one of the clans, let alone all four.

"Baby, come back to us," Deryn whispered from what sounded like far away.

"Someone cradle her in your lap and hold her tightly," Martin snapped.

It sounded like he was underwater. Wasn't he just across the table from me?

Wouldn't it be better if they had queens of their races? The werewolves didn't have a queen, but only because she had died a few years ago. I couldn't hold a candle to someone like Adelaide. She could rule with fangs and claws. I could shift, thanks to being Rhys's queen, but I wasn't vicious. I wasn't a ruler.

Warmth surrounded me. My cold, numb body slowly came back into feeling and heat radiated from my side. What was the warmth coming from?

"It's working," Martin said, still under water.

There wasn't warmth from one spot. No, there was warmth from my side, my cheek, my neck, and my legs. Four places. Four. That was the number of my guards. Four. Four males. Four princes.

"We're here, my queen," Deryn whispered in my ear. "We've got you. You're safe. You're fine. Come back to us."

Back? From where? Where was I? Hadn't we just been at the restaurant? The restaurant. Yes. Then, someone had said something and I spaced out. Right. Attack. This was a panic attack. Okay.

"One. Two. Three. Four. Five. Six. Seven. Eight. Nine. Ten."

"Why is she counting?" someone asked from the same under water place Martin was.

"Shush," Rhys ordered them. His voice sounded closer.

I was alive. I was not hurt. I was not bleeding. I was protected. I was free.

The feeling, sounds, and surroundings came rushing back at once and I buried my face into Deryn's neck, the source of the heat on my side.

"You okay, baby?" Deryn asked.

I nodded. "Sorry."

"Don't apologize. You have no reason to apologize," Fox told me, his hand running up and down my leg.

"Sorry," Kylan said.

"What are your plans for Christmas?" Thor asked Martin loudly, drawing everyone's attention.

"We'll be getting a tree when I get back, it's a family tradition. Then, Sharla will cook a huge meal, which we will eat while the children open their presents," Martin said. "What about you, Thor?"

"I'll be going home this year. I haven't seen my parents in a couple of years," Thor answered. "What about you, Ezio?"

He was changing the topic so we could move on. I loved them, so much.

"Your meals," the waiter said as he, and a few others, brought out trays with plates of food on them.

Deryn set me back in my seat and Rhys and Fox returned to their seats as well.

"Thanks," I whispered.

"Anytime," Nico whispered back and kissed me lightly on the lips.

I didn't even know what Deryn had ordered for me. I was pleasantly surprised to find sushi rolls.

"Sushi!" I exclaimed.

"You weren't paying attention when I ordered?" Deryn asked me with a smile.

I shook my head. "No, but this is wonderful. It's been a long time since I last had sushi."

"Didn't we just have sushi like a week or two ago?" Nico asked.

"Yeah, a long time ago," I said, picked up the chopsticks they had provided, and quickly ate a piece of the first roll. Crab mix, avocado, and cucumber inside. Fresh salmon, avocado smear, masago, two types of sauce, and green onions on the top. It was my favorite type of roll. "So good," I moaned. The other roll had barbecued eel on the top with a dark sauce. I grabbed a piece of it next and popped it into my mouth. "Paradise," I said.

After finishing my sushi rolls, I returned to sipping on my strawberry daiquiri and looking at the males around me. They were all smiling and talking to each other like old friends. Something that, just a few days earlier, had seemed impossible. Now, the strongest of the races were friends instead of rivals. Was this what they meant about me being an alpha? This was definitely what the kings meant when they questioned whether I was a witch.

A smile spread across my mouth as I surveyed my unintentional work. Maybe my life and death situations were meant to provide something good. They provided an opportunity for males who usually fought to get along. To find a common goal.

"Time to spar!" Fox exclaimed.

CHAPTER 11

"Go Rhys! Go Ezio!" I cheered from the stands of the coliseum. The coliseum was completely empty, save for my entourage and myself.

"You can't root for both of them," Fox chastised me.

"Yes, I can."

"Who are you going to fight?" Thor asked Fox.

Fox shrugged. "Whoever wants to challenge me."

"What's your favorite weapon?" Thor asked him.

"Swords, but I do love playing with throwing axes," Fox said.

"Throwing axes sound fun," I said.

"No," Fox said immediately. "You will somehow end up injured if you participate."

"I'm not a klutz," I growled.

Rhys and Ezio were dancing around on the balls of their feet, fists raised in front of their faces. They looked like boxers. They exchanged a few tentative hits from each other and then, they were moving so fast, that I could not track their movements. Their arms moved so fast, that they were just a blur to me.

"Who's winning?" I asked Fox. "I can't see their punches."

"It's pretty evenly matched right now," Fox said. "Rhys may be testing him to see what his style is or trying to find any breaks in his defense."

"Ezio's defense is pretty damn solid," Thor commented.

"Jojo," Declan called in a sing-song voice.

"What's up, Declan?" I asked without turning towards him.

"Nothing, just wanted to come sit by you," he said and plopped down onto the seat next to me. "Who do you think will win?"

"I honestly don't know," I admitted.

"You're supposed to say Rhys," Fox mumbled.

"I would, but you forget that I've seen Ezio in full attack mode. With one hand, he destroyed a dozen ogres. I'm not saying Rhys couldn't do that, too. I just haven't seen him in a fight like that." And hopefully, I never would. I didn't fancy the idea of my guards getting hurt.

"She's so honest," Declan chuckled.

"Who are you going to fight?" I asked Declan. I still couldn't see their movements, but it looked like they were starting to use kicks as well, since their bodies would drop lower sometimes.

"Deryn," Declan said. "I've wanted to spar with him for a long time, but never had an opportunity."

"Me?" Deryn asked. "Really?"

Declan nodded.

"Well, no matter who any of you fight, I know they are going to be good fights. I'm honestly surprised that you've never sparred with each other before," I said.

"They are going to have to call a draw," Fox whispered. "They're just too evenly matched. This could go on for days."

"You think they'll call a draw?" I asked. They were both so damn stubborn, I couldn't imagine them calling a draw.

"Yes. This isn't a typical fight. If this was part of the tournament, neither would back down, fighting until they passed out or were too injured to protect themselves," Deryn answered.

"Declan," I said quickly, spinning to look at him. "I almost forgot!" I reached down into my bag and grabbed one of the packages. "Here," I said with a smile. "Merry Christmas."

"For me?" Declan asked, his eyes wide and mouth slightly parted. "This is a gift for me?"

I nodded.

"Do I open it now? Or wait until Christmas?" he asked.

"It's up to you," I said with a smile and kissed his cheek. "I don't care either way."

"I'm going to wait," he said with a nod of finality. "That way, I will think of you on Christmas and have a piece of you with me."

I had zero idea what to say to that. It warmed me and I found tears in my eyes. "You're so sweet," I finally whispered and hugged him.

"Draw!" Rhys and Ezio called at the same time.

Both were drenched in sweat, breathing heavily, but I didn't see any blood.

"Next," Rhys called and hopped up into the stands.

"Deryn?" Declan asked.

Deryn nodded. "Sure."

Declan set his gift next to me. "I'll get it after my match. I don't want to lose it or have it smooshed if it's in my pocket."

"Okay," I said with a nod. "I'll keep it safe until you return."

Rhys plopped down in front of me and leaned back, so his upper back leaned against my legs. "Hey, beautiful," he said with a wide smile.

"Hello, handsome. Did you have fun?" I asked, giving him a light kiss on his lips, having to lean around him to do so.

"Yes, I did," Rhys answered. "I'm glad we got to do this."

"Me, too," Ezio said from behind me,

I tipped my head back to look at him. "You had fun, too?"

"Yes," he said with a nod. "It has been a long time since I've been matched so well with someone in a fight. I miss matches like this."

"Well, you shouldn't have gotten so strong," I teased.

He chuckled, but didn't say anything.

"Their fight is starting," Rhys said, getting my attention. He sat forward, his arms on his legs as he focused intently on the fighters.

"Who do you think will win?" I asked Fox.

"Deryn," he said immediately.

"I don't know," Rhys said. "Declan is pretty quick."

"Yes, but so is Deryn when he's focused. I think he might let some of his true skill shine," Fox said.

"Deryn is a bit lazy," Rhys chuckled. "Maybe Jolie will finally get to see some of his true skills."

Deryn and Declan faced each other and then bowed. Once they straightened, all humor left their faces as they focused, but I was glad to see that there wasn't any hostility.

Honestly, seeing them getting along so well despite knowing I'd been with the others, made me really happy. They were all incredibly dominant, each definitely alpha material. Maybe that was what I saw in them. Maybe I was drawn to the dominant males because I knew they would be the most able to protect me.

Deryn darted left and I was blown away by how fast he moved. I knew he could move quickly, he was a werewolf after all, but I had never seen him move *that* fast before.

"You weren't joking," I whispered to Rhys and Fox.

"I didn't know he was that fast," Ezio said.

"I'm surprised you didn't want to fight him," I told Ezio.

"I was worried he might hold some animosity towards me. I figured Rhys was the better option. Plus, I always wanted to fight him," Ezio explained.

"Seems that all of you wanted to fight each other," I chuckled.

Deryn was suddenly still and Declan was on his back in the arena.

I stood up, eyes wide and hands clenched, worried that he had hurt Declan.

Declan laughed and leapt to his feet. "Nice job," Declan said and shook hands with Deryn. "I didn't even see that hit coming."

"What happened?" I asked and sat down again. Maybe it wasn't a good idea for me to watch them. My heart was pounding hard.

"Deryn broke his defense and landed a hit right to his jaw," Rhys said. "That was a really nice punch."

"Thank you," Deryn said, sitting next to Fox again. He took his shirt off and wiped the sweat from his forehead. My eyes were glued to him, admiring his exposed muscular body.

"Hey," Fox snapped, putting himself in my line of sight. "Stop drooling."

"I'm allowed to look and admire my guards," I said and folded my arms across my chest.

"Who's next?" Deryn asked.

"Me," Fox said. "Who wants to challenge me?"

"Me," Zelphar said and leapt into the arena.

"Alright." Fox smiled happily as he joined Zelphar in the arena.

"Who will win this one?" Ezio asked, grinning.

"Fox," Deryn and Rhys answered at the same time.

"He's pretty amazing in battle," I whispered, leaning my elbows on my knees and my chin in my hands. I had gotten to watch him battle enemies in the park and at the party when my father and his minions had attacked.

"Oh, so Fox is your favorite?" Ezio asked.

"What?" Deryn asked, turning his eyes toward me.

"She couldn't pick a winner from any of the other fights and didn't praise any of you. Yet, she swoons over Fox," Ezio said.

Fox removed his shirt and looked up at me. "See, plenty of muscles to look at here."

Fox was the most muscular, shorter than the others, but buffer. Somehow though, his bulk didn't hinder his movements and he was very lithe. I supposed, that could be due to his being an elf.

"I'm not going to be able to see anything, am I?" I asked Deryn.

"You mean because they're moving too fast?" he asked me.

I nodded.

"Most likely," Deryn said.

"Shouldn't she be able to tap into your powers to see better?" Ezio asked.

"We've tried it before and it didn't work. You might try now, since you're officially Queen," Rhys suggested.

"Okay." It was worth a shot. I closed my eyes and focused on our bonds, being sure not to touch Fox's, since he would need all of his focus on the fight. I opened my eyes and everything was brighter, clearer, and I could see so many things I had missed before. I could see a single gray hair on Zelphar's head. They started fighting and I was finally able to watch it.

Fox was fast, his fists punching and blocking as Zelphar returned his aggression. There wasn't one on defense while the other was on offense. They were both being offensive and defensive at the same time. The movements were so fast, I supposed that was probably the easiest thing for them. If you were on defense too much, you might get backed into a corner.

"Shit," Ezio whispered. "I've never seen an elf fight before. That's insane."

"Zelphar's holding his own," Rhys commented.

"Not much longer," I whispered. I could see it, the small faltering movements Zelphar made. I was certain Fox saw them as well.

"She's right," Deryn whispered. "Wow."

Zelphar held up his hand and Fox stopped, mid-punch. "I give," Zelphar said. "I can't keep up with your speed."

Fox bowed to him and they headed up to us again. I released the connections, letting my normal eyesight return. Everything seemed so dull and bland now.

"I'm hungry," I announced. "Can we get some food?"

"You're always hungry," Martin chuckled.

"We need to get a bigger refrigerator for all the food she eats now,"

Deryn said and draped his arm around my shoulders. "Maybe a deep freezer."

"As if you four don't eat a ton, too," I said with a roll of my eyes.

"We should get a deep freezer," Rhys agreed. "We could store a ton of frozen meats for cooking meals."

"So you can stop eating so much fast food and takeout?" I guessed. Honestly, it surprised me how much our interactions revolved around food. It seemed strange to humans how much Others ate.

"I love pizza," Deryn complained. "I don't want to eat healthy all the time."

"I never said all the time," Rhys countered. "I'm still going to eat pizza."

"As long as the pizza guy doesn't kidnap me again," I said and laughed at the memory. Now that I was able to laugh at it.

"What?" Ezio asked. "A pizza guy kidnapped you?"

"Yes," I said. "Then a dragoness took me from him and delivered me to my father."

Ezio reached out and took my hand in his. "Did he hurt you again?"

I squeezed his hand and smiled. He remembered! I'd told him about my father when we were dating. "He's dead now. The guys killed him. So, I don't have to worry about him any longer."

No, now I just had to worry about his ex-lover and my ex-friend, Justina. Would she try to come after me again? Would she want to hurt me once she found out that I was their queen once more and their mate? I was betting so. If I was her, I might.

"You're scowling now," Deryn commented.

"Thinking about Justina," I whispered.

"We'll keep you protected," Deryn promised.

"Is it wrong that I feel bad for her? I mean, she tortured me and tried to kill me, but she's trying to deal with her sorrow."

"You're too nice," Ezio chastised me. "She tortured you and severed your connections with the Princes. What if it had been permanent? What if she had severed them and there was no way to get them back?"

He was right...I knew. And, had that been the case, I would still feel numb and hollow, which would probably be driving me insane. Yet, we had been friends. She didn't stop being my friend because she hated me. She stopped because my lovers killed her lover. It was an age-old story that happened again and again.

"We'll kill her if we see her. You know that, right?" Deryn asked.

"I know." I sighed. "I know."

"I have some errands to take care of," Ezio said as he stood.

"Wait!" I ordered him. Reaching deep down into my bag, I grabbed his present and handed it to him. Then, I handed Kylan, Thor, Martin, Yukio, and Zelphar theirs as well.

"You got us all presents?" Yukio asked.

"Yes. I wanted to get you something to thank you."

"Thank us for what?" Ezio asked.

"Being part of my life, protecting me when you had to, loving me, and helping me this week," I said. "You're all part of me, even if we aren't a couple any longer. I still cherish your friendships."

"Friend-zoned!" Thor gasped and clutched at his heart. "No!"

I smacked his arm and he smiled down at me. "Knock it off."

"Thank you," Thor said and kissed my cheek. "I appreciate it. It means a lot to me that you would think of me and buy a gift."

"I'm going to wait to open mine, like Declan," Yukio told me. "Can I call you after I open it, to thank you?"

"Of course, you can," I said and hugged him.

Yukio looked over my head and asked, "Prince?"

"You are all welcome to contact Jolie," Fox said. "Just remember that she's ours and everything will be fine."

"And that we'll kill you if you touch her inappropriately," Rhys said with a bright and warm smile.

The death threat and smile were in such contrast, that I found myself unable to say anything.

"Understood," all of my exes said.

"Hugs," I ordered them.

Each took a turn giving me a hug and Ezio and Declan gave me kisses on the cheek.

"She's like an omega," Deryn said. "She's so calm and happy to see everyone, that we are all relaxed. She's the reason so many dominates were able to get along just now."

"I thought you said I was an alpha?" I asked, feeling confused.

"You're a human alpha, but somehow you've turned yourself into a wolf omega. So much time in the werewolf pack gave you the ability to have the dual personalities," Deryn explained.

I supposed what he said made sense. I still didn't see myself as an alpha personality as a human, but they would be the better judges on that anyway. Maybe I would ask Dan what he thought.

I realized that I hadn't spoken to Nico much that afternoon. I turned and held my arms out to him. He wrapped me up in a warm hug and then slung one arm beneath my knees to pick me up.

"Hello," Nico said with a smile. "What's up?"

"Nothing. Just wanted some Nico time," I explained and leaned my face into his neck. "Mm, you smell good. Like cologne."

"No cologne on," he countered.

"I know. It's just your scent. I love it."

"What did you buy from that mage merchant?" he asked me softly.

"I'm not telling you," I snapped, jerking my head back to look at him.

"If it's something dangerous or something you could—"

"Nico, I'm not stupid. I promise to be careful with my purchases. I'm actually planning on talking with King Katar about it."

"My dad?" Fox asked. "Why?"

"I need help with something magic related," I explained. "And I can't ask you guys. And, I don't really want to use your dad," I whispered to Nico.

"Understandable," he nodded.

"So, I figured King Katar was my next best option. Plus, I haven't really gotten to spend much time with him."

"Why can't you tell us?" Nico asked, frowning.

"Because I can't."

If I told them what I was doing, it would ruin the surprise! The whole point of having my exes with me today was to keep my guards away, so they wouldn't see what I purchased. If I asked for their help in finishing it, they'd know what it was. Why didn't they get that?

"We just don't want you hurt or doing something you could be hurt with. Magic is dangerous," Nico said.

"I'm sure King Katar will keep me safe," I told him and rolled my eyes. "He likes me, remember?"

"Yes, he does," Fox agreed. "He likes your omega, but alpha personality. It intrigues him."

"Oh, so now I'm like a weird science experiment?" My eyes narrowed as I grew defensive.

Did they think of me as some weird human that needed to be observed? Were the kings really nice to me because they liked me being around to see what I might do? I was a bit strange, yeah, I knew that, but I wasn't completely weird.

"That's not what I meant," Fox said. "I meant that it's unique to have a female like you. You're not weird or a freak. You're refreshing. It's nice to have a female who likes the same things that we do. Do you know how hard it is to find a female who plays video games more than we do? Most get upset if we're playing for more than an hour. You'll play even after we go to bed."

"Yes, I'm a video game addict. I know."

"We love it," Nico whispered and kissed my cheek. "It's one of the great things about you."

"We need to play more games," I grumbled. "I haven't played much lately. My clan has started to tease me and is calling me Jolie's ghost. I've been dead to them for months."

"We will," Nico promised.

"This seems pretty easy for something that's so important," I told King Katar. I faced him, sitting at a table in his house, with the bloodstones on the table between us.

"It is easy, but that's because it is something that we wanted to be sure almost anyone could do. Now, take the crystal in your hand, fill it with your energy, and then put a drop of your blood on it. It will soak up the blood and seal it inside," he instructed me.

It was simple and wouldn't take long, but I would have to do the process four times. I didn't like knowing I would have to cut myself four different times.

It was worth it though. I was really looking forward to seeing the guys' reactions when they opened this gift. I knew without a doubt, that it would be the best present I would ever give them.

The bloodstones were small, the size of a grain of rice, and their purpose was to embed them in your skin, to add a piece of your mate to your body, so they would permanently be part of you. Most put the crystal on their wrists, so it was visible, but not in a way that drew your eye. I had seen some people put them on their chests and behind their ears. I wasn't sure where the guys would put theirs, but I was anxious to find out.

The crystal was warm in my hand and it warmed even more as I filled it with my energy. Since I didn't have my own magic, I had to use my energy. Once it was full, I used the needle Katar had given me, and smeared blood onto the crystal. As he had said, the crystal absorbed the blood and turned red. I put the crystal into a small black box, similar to a ring box, but with a groove made specifically for the crystal.

"Doing it one time is no problem," I muttered. "Most are lucky to have just one mate."

Katar chuckled softly. "I think you're pretty lucky."

"I didn't mean it like that." I blushed. I was the luckiest female on the planet. Four hot males, who were princes, and loved me more than anything else. I couldn't ask for more.

"Round two." I sighed, grabbed another crystal, and put it in my hand.

When I was finally done, I let my head fall onto my arms on the table. "Done!" I exclaimed.

Katar patted my arm. "Well done."

"Thanks."

"Are you ready for Christmas now?" he asked as he packed up the things on the table and wiped it down, even though none of my blood had spilled.

"Yes. Now, I just have to wait to give them their gifts," I said. "I need to hide these somewhere so they won't find them. If they see the boxes, they'll know right away what their gifts are."

"Would you like me to put a cloaking spell on them?" Katar asked.

"You can do that?" I asked. "It would stay even after I leave?"

He nodded. "I can make the bag you put them in look like a present box, and you can put it under your tree. Even if they touch it, they won't know the truth. It will last until you take the boxes out of the bag."

"That's amazing!" I exclaimed.

He smiled. "I enjoy talking with you. You let your emotions out, which is refreshing since Others hide their emotions all the time."

"Rhys said I need to learn to use a court face, to hide my emotions when I don't want people to know what I'm thinking or feeling," I said. "But, it's really hard!"

"They're taught how to do it from a very young age," Katar said. "It is not something you will pick up after a month or two. You will have to continue practicing the rest of your life. You are such an emotional creature, that I'm not sure if you will ever be able to do it."

"Thanks for the pep talk," I mumbled.

He laughed and wrapped me up in a hug. "It gets better."

"I hope so. I'm really far behind the curve."

"Let me spell your bag and then I can go fetch Foxfire. I'm sure he's paced a moat around the house by now."

I put all of the boxes into a single black, drawstring bag and handed the bag to Katar. He held it in his flattened palms and whispered some words I didn't understand. Then, the bag disappeared and a beautiful green Christmas box with a red bow appeared in its place.

"So, I just open the drawstring, pull out the boxes, and the illusion will disappear?"

He nodded.

"You're amazing!" I exclaimed again and hugged him.

"Don't start that," Kara said with a sigh. "It will go to his already big head."

Kara was Fox's mother and Katar's Queen and mate. She was tall, slim, and had gorgeous silver hair that flowed tangle free down her back. I envied her hair and her beauty, mostly because she was also super sweet.

"Hello, Kara," I bowed my head in greeting.

She pulled me into a hug and kissed my cheek. "Hello, Daughter."

This was a new thing that I was not used to yet. Deryn, Rhys, and Fox's parents had all begun calling me their daughter. It was a high honor that I didn't feel comfortable having.

"Is Foxfire still pacing?" Katar asked Kara.

She nodded. "He's convinced something is going to go wrong."

"They're so rude," I grumbled.

"They just don't like not being involved," Kara said. "They want to keep you safe, but when you're away from them, holed up with their father, they have no way to help you."

"I'm certain if I screamed, he would come running," I said.

"Try it," Katar said with a smirk.

"Really?" I asked him.

He nodded. "I want to see what his reaction will be. He knows I'm here and that I'm helping you. I wonder how quickly he will run here."

"He's out front, right?" I said.

Kara nodded.

I took a deep breath and then screamed loudly. Fox was there the next instant and had me in his arms before I could even suck in a new breath.

"What is it?" he asked, scanning the room.

"So little trust," Katar said with a sigh. "I'm hurt, Foxfire."

"What?" Fox asked, looking from me to his parents.

"Nothing's wrong," I assured him. "Katar wanted to see how fast you would come here if you heard me scream, even though I'm in his protection."

"It has nothing to do with you, Father," Fox argued.

"Are you ever going to call me, 'Father?'" Katar asked me.

"Sorry," I whispered. "I'm just not used to it yet."

"It's what you call Dan," Kara pointed out.

"I'm used to assembling myself into a werewolf pack. I'm trying," I said. "Maybe it will come easier once Fox and I are mated."

"Did you give her the present?" Kara asked Katar.

He shook his head. "I figured you would want to."

"It's not Christmas yet," I said.

"We're just very excited to give it to you," she said. "I suppose I can wait until Christmas to give it to you. You are coming the morning of Christmas, right?"

"Yes, Mother," Fox said. "We will come here no later than nine o'clock."

"But, we can only stay for a couple hours because we have to go visit the other clans as well," I reminded them.

"Nine to eleven with the elves. Eleven to one with the dragons. One to three with the mages. Three to five with the werewolves. Then, home to do our presents," Fox explained.

"That's a lot of parties and food," Kara said. "Are you going to survive?"

"Hopefully," I laughed. "I'll just make sure to eat small amounts at each place."

"I'll make sure to package you the best foods to take home with you," Kara said.

"Make sure you pack the fudge!" Fox said. "She has to be able to eat your fudge."

"I'll make her her own special batch," Kara promised.

"You're the best," I told her, tapping Fox to put me down so I could hug her.

She hugged me and kissed my cheek as she pulled back. "I'll see you tomorrow."

"Yes," I agreed, hugged Katar, and then picked up the present and smiled at Fox.

"What is that?" he asked.

"A gift," I answered.

"But they said they didn't give it to you yet," he said.

"It's one she cannot open until you guys are opening presents," Katar covered for me. "Don't even think of trying to open it," he threatened Fox.

Fox led me out with our hands linked and kept looking at the present. Was the illusion faulty? Could he see through it?

"What?" I asked.

"I'm just trying to guess what they got you that is that size," he said.

I hid it from his view and said, "No! Don't spoil my surprise! I don't want you to know until I open it."

"Okay. Okay," he said.

Martin waved from the side of the SUV. "All done?"

"Sorry I kept you waiting so long," I apologized.

"No sweat," he said.

"We better hurry home or there won't be any food left," Fox said.

"Aren't they wrapping presents still?" I asked.

"They're done. I made sure they were just now." He held up his phone.

"You can give me some hints about what the guys are getting me," I said with a smile.

He laughed and shook his head. "Nope. You can wait for their surprise, just like you're waiting for my parents'."

"Rude," I grumbled, but wasn't serious. I was glad to wait for their gifts. It was something I was really looking forward to.

"Buckled up?" Martin asked.

"Yes, *Dad*," I said in a childish voice.

"Don't make me turn this car around," he threatened.

"We haven't even left yet. How could you turn it around?" I asked with a laugh.

"He could turn it around literally, so it is facing the other way," Fox said.

"That's just preposterous."

"Sharla said to tell you that when you come to the werewolf den, you better come see us," Martin told me.

"Of course I'm going to come see you! I have to give my nieces their presents. They're going to love them! I'm the best auntie ever!"

"And totally not full of herself," Martin chuckled.

We drove through town, headed towards the apartment building. It was strange, I had been in this town awhile now, but I hadn't really explored it. I'd driven from one place to the next, but never spent time in the places in between. I would have to fix that! The guys and I could start going on walking trips around town to see what stores and restaurants there were.

There I was, focused on food again. It had been increasingly worse since they made me their queen. I was constantly hungry and ate way more than a normal human should.

CHAPTER 12

I awoke to the first Christmas morning with excitement coursing through my veins, but as I woke up, surrounded by four princes, I knew I already had everything that I could ever want. Or need.

"Morning, beautiful," Deryn grumbled in a gravely morning voice.

I rolled over to face him, a smile on my face before I even saw his smile. "Hello, handsome."

He pulled me closer, kissing my forehead gently. "Did you sleep well?"

I nodded.

"Cold," Fox whispered and rolled closer to me. "Why'd you move away?" he asked, pressing his back against mine.

"Where are the blankets?" I asked.

"I threw them off," Rhys said and yawned, stretching his arms and sitting up so that I could see him without moving.

"Hello, Puff," I teased and held out my hand.

He pulled me up with it and gave me a deep, passionate kiss. My body became an inferno and I wrapped my arms around his neck, trying to climb into his lap.

His lips were gone as was his body and I groaned, draping my arm over the edge of the bed where he had abandoned me. "My guard has abandoned me!" I moaned as though terribly upset.

"Either I abandon you, or pee on you," he called from the bathroom.

"We need to get ready," Nico said. "We've only got an hour before our first Christmas."

"Elven Christmas!" I yelled, leapt to my feet, and rushed to take a quick shower. "I can't miss this!"

My shower was shockingly solo, for the first time in months. Taking advantage of the time I had been given, I shaved all my parts, and thoroughly washed and rinsed my hair. After putting my silver and blue dress on, I styled my hair into a braid over my left shoulder and put on some neutral colored eyeshadow and black eyeliner. Satisfied, I walked out of the room to find the guys all sitting on the floor by the tree, staring at the gift I had placed there.

"What, are you *doing*?" I demanded with my hands on my hips.

They leapt away from the tree, guilty expressions on their faces.

"It's only half a day," I growled at them.

"We're sorry," they all said at the same time.

"I can't believe you guys," I grumbled, stomping over to slide my low heels on.

"Everyone ready?" Fox asked.

"Yes."

"Yeah."

"Where's my coffee?"

The last had come from Rhys, no doubt.

"We will pick some up on the way," Fox promised.

"Ready, my queen?" Nico asked.

I looked up from the small handbag I was inspecting and took his offered hand. "Yes, my guard."

We walked out of the apartment building's front doors into a crush of media. They shouted questions, but with so many different voices shouting so many questions, I couldn't understand them. My guards put me in the center of the group and pushed their way through, to the SUV that waited for us. This time, it was a werewolf I did not know driving. Martin must have been home with Sharla and the girls.

I heard rapid gunfire and immediately ducked down and covered myself in dragon scales. The media members screamed and scattered like cockroaches when the light turned on. The guys spun around to face outward, all of them except Rhys, who was looking at his hand, which was coated in red.

"Rhys!" I screamed and spun him towards me, now up on my feet and still covered in scales. The shoulder of his white shirt had a hole through it and a blood stain spread out slowly. "Rhys, talk to me," I whispered.

"My fucking scales didn't automatically cover me," he whispered in disbelief, still staring at his bloody hand. "Ow."

I glanced up, glad to see a shield around us. "Thanks, Nico," I whispered.

"Getting shot hurts," Rhys growled and looked at me. "Seriously, ow."

"You okay?" I asked, opening his shirt buttons so I could move it aside to inspect him.

"Yeah, I'm fine. The bullet went clean through," he said. "It's been awhile since I've had anything pierce my skin."

"My teeth don't count?" I asked with a smirk, trying to get him to snap out of the weird mood that clouded his face.

He chuckled and dropped his hand, the mood gone. "No, those don't count."

"Get in the damn car," Deryn growled at me.

"Nico put up a shield," I said, "and I'm covered in scales."

"Now," Deryn growled louder.

I obeyed, climbing in and tugged on Rhys to come in with me. "Why didn't your scales cover you?" I asked him.

"I'm not sure," he admitted. "I haven't been practicing lately, so maybe I've gotten lazy."

I poked his rock-hard abs and said, "You are getting pudgy."

He laughed, grabbed my hand, and pulled it up to his mouth, kissing my fingertips. "I guess we'll just have to increase our physical activity to combat that."

"Tease," I hissed at him.

Everyone got into the car and we drove away.

"What? No cops?" I asked. "No one is going to go after the shooter?"

"I got him already," Nico said with a smirk. "You okay, Rhys?"

Rhys nodded. "Yeah, but that hurt."

"You're such a baby," I said and rolled my eyes, only teasing him since I was certain it had to have hurt.

"Good thing we're going to the dragon's den today, so you can talk to your dad," Fox said.

"Yeah," Rhys agreed.

"Who was the shooter?" I asked.

"Human," Nico answered as though that explained everything.

"And he's dead?"

"No, he's in police custody," he told me.

"Oh. Okay."

"No, we did not kill someone and just leave their body on the roof of a building," Nico said with an eye roll.

"I don't know!" I snapped. "Every time we've been shot at before, we've just run off."

"No, you've been taken away. One of us has always stayed and taken care of the person or their body," Rhys explained quietly to me.

"Are you still bleeding?" I asked.

"No," he shook his head.

"Good."

"I need coffee," he told the driver. "Please."

"You got it, boss," the driver said, switching lanes as he changed course.

"What is our first meal going to be?" I asked Fox.

"I'm not ruining it. You'll just have to wait to see," he said.

"I'm getting fudge though, right?" I asked.

He laughed. "I'm sure my mother did as she said and made a special batch of fudge just for you."

"She's getting her own fudge?" Deryn asked with an open mouth. "Your mom never gave me my own fudge."

"You aren't her son's future mate," I reminded him.

"Oh, say that again," Fox said, moving his head next to mine. "Say it again, please."

"Future mate," I whispered into his ear.

His body shuddered and he moaned. "Yes."

We went through a drive thru for Rhys's coffee and then continued on our way to visit the elves. My nerves were frayed, not only was I spending my first Christmas with the guys, but with each of their families. It was so much at once. So many new experiences for one day.

Rhys found a spare shirt in the SUV and changed into it, grumbling about guns and scales incoherently. Once he had the shirt on, he linked our fingers together, scooted closer so that our arms were touching, and whispered, "You're going to be fine. One of us will be with you at all times, no matter where we are. If you need to step out and get some air, just tell us."

His words were reassuring and I calmed a bit, not completely, but a bit.

Katar and Kara were waiting on the porch when we arrived. Both had pleasant smiles on, though Kara looked a bit worn.

"She spends all night working on food preparation and then wakes up very early to get the meal ready. She's tired, but she enjoys it. This is her favorite time of year," Fox whispered in my ear.

Our group stepped out of the SUV, Fox in the lead with me right behind him, and the others following lazily behind.

Katar patted his son on the back and pulled me into a hug. "Everything working?"

"I caught them all staring at it this morning," I whispered.

He chuckled. "Fox has always had an insatiable curiosity."

"You're hogging her again," Kara whispered. "Let me get my hug."

"Sorry, dear," Katar said, giving me a wink before letting me go.

Kara instantly pulled me into a hug.

"Can I have my queen back now?" Fox asked, his voice held nothing, but affection for his mother.

"Fine, Son," she said and let me go. "It's time to eat, anyway."

"Food," Rhys grumbled, a growl in his chest.

Everyone turned to face him.

"Rhys?" I asked softly.

"Sorry," he said and wiped a hand down his face. "I'm really hungry."

"We didn't eat breakfast," I explained to Kara.

"Let's get inside and get you some food," she told Rhys, setting her hand on his shoulder and guiding him inside.

"Is he okay?" I asked Fox softly.

He nodded. "We didn't eat yet and he got shot, so his body needs food. He's fine. As soon as he gets food in his belly, he'll be back to his normal self."

Linking our arms, he pulled me inside and then pulled out a chair for me. I sat and my eyes widened in surprised to find my plate already filled with food. Everyone ate in silence, our appetites too ravenous for courtesies. Kara and Katar didn't seem to mind, smiling at each other occasionally as they ate.

"Where is Silverowl?" Nico asked Fox, breaking the silence.

Fox finished chewing the food in his mouth and answered, "He's on an errand. He should be back soon."

"The meal was delicious," Rhys complimented Kara.

"I'm glad you enjoyed it. Do you need any healing?"

I had forgotten that Fox said his mother was the best healer out of them.

"Can you at least give him a check?" I asked before Rhys could decline her offer.

"Jolie," Rhys sighed.

"No back talk," I ordered him.

Kara rested her hand on Rhys's hand and closed her eyes. Light shimmered from her fingers, spreading from Rhys's hand up his arm, and covered his entire body.

Rhys's shoulders lowered, his face relaxed, tension leaving it that I had not even noticed. "Thank you," he whispered.

"Next time, you tell your queen that you are injured," she ordered him, pulling her hand away and the light with her.

"Yes, Kara," he said with a resigned head bow.

"Thank you," I said to her. "Sometimes, they're a bit—"

"Defiant. Stubborn. Headstrong. Bullheaded," Kara supplied.

I laughed while all of the princes scowled at her words.

"Who is ready for dessert?" Kara asked.

"Me!" I said eagerly.

I had not been prepared for the dessert course. Pies, fudge, cookies, and even a cake were laid out on a table in the living room.

"No fudge for you," Fox said, grabbing the piece from my hand before I could pop it into my mouth.

"What?" I gasped.

"You have to wait until we get home and you eat a piece of the fudge she made for you," he explained.

"Fox," I pouted, sticking my lip out and giving him my best puppy dog eyes. "Just one little piece," I begged, ran my hands up his chest, and leaned into him.

His eyes heated and he pressed himself closer to me. His lips brushed against mine as he whispered, "No."

"Gah!" I yelled and smacked Fox on the chest, pushing him away from me.

"Here, baby," Deryn said, holding out a slice of pie with a ton of whipped cream on top.

"At least someone loves me," I said with a glare at Fox before taking the offered pie.

Deryn kissed me softly and gave Fox a cheeky grin.

"Suck-up," Fox growled at him.

I scooped whipped cream off the top of the pie with one finger and licked it off slowly, drawing the attention of four princes.

"Do that again," Fox threatened, "and you won't get *any* fudge."

"Foxfire," Kara growled, "don't you dare use my treats as part of your threats."

"Sorry," he mumbled.

"Busted!" I laughed at him.

Everyone laughed, including Fox.

Andras and Emrys stood at the steps to their house, waiting for us to exit the cars. Rhys tried to hold my hand, but I quickened my step to hug Emrys and kiss his cheek. "Hello, Father."

He kissed my cheek and smiled, warmth filling his eyes. "Daughter, you look well."

Leaning close with my hands on his shoulders to keep my balance, I whispered into his ear, "Take Rhys away and speak to him. Something happened."

His shoulders tensed beneath my hands and he nodded.

I turned to Andras and opened my arms. "Brother."

He snickered. "That is not what I'd like to hear you call me, but I suppose that is the best I will get."

My arms started to drop, disappointment stinging in my chest and my expression tightening.

Andras rushed forward, hugged me tightly, and tucked my face against his chest with a hand on the back of my head. His lips lowered to my ear and he whispered, "I was teasing you. I'm sorry. I didn't mean to upset you. Forgive me? Sister?"

I nodded, but didn't speak, unsure if I could keep my voice even.

He released me to shake hands with Nico and Deryn.

"Jolie?" Fox whispered.

"Where's Rhys?" I asked.

"Emrys took him inside," he said.

I nodded and headed up the steps, only to have my path blocked by an eager teenage boy. His arms wrapped around me and he spun me around, my feet dangling in the air.

"Jolie!" he exclaimed.

"Gavin," I gasped, clutching his arms while smiling.

He set me down, a joyous smile on his face. "I'm so happy you're here! Come on, food's ready."

"Oh, I don't know if I can eat yet," I admitted.

"You will once you smell the meal that has been prepared," he told me, adamantly.

Nico slid his fingers between mine as we walked down the hallway, pulling me to his side as we held hands. "You look beautiful," he whispered.

"Thank you," I replied, glancing at him curiously. While he did give me compliments, he normally reserved them for when we were alone. He also rarely held my hand.

"What?" he asked.

"You're just not usually so affectionate in public," I whispered.

"Does it bother you?" Nico asked.

"No!" I gasped. "Nico, you know it doesn't. I was just wondering what the change in attitude was from, that's all."

"Almost losing you," he whispered a shadow passing over his face. "I thought I had lost you and, in that moment, I saw all of the times that I was rude to you or the times that I wished I had expressed my feelings more clearly to you. I'm not generally an affectionate person. However, when it comes to you, I find myself constantly wanting to hold your hand, hug you, kiss you, at least touch you briefly."

"You're always welcome to touch me," I whispered and squeezed his hand.

He kissed my cheek and whispered, "I will keep that in mind."

The dining room was decorated with garlands, poinsettias, gold leaves, and pine cones. It was rustic and charming at the same time. Rhys's mother looked in my direction and scowled. She said something to the servant she had been talking to and walked toward me. I dropped Nico's hand and took a step away from him, so I wouldn't try to hide behind him, like I desperately wanted to.

"Jolie," she said in greeting.

"Queen Adelaide," I replied and dipped my head. "Thank you for allowing us to come enjoy Christmas with you and your family."

"You are family now," she said and sighed. "Whether I agree or think you worthy or not, my son loves you and I can tell that you love him. I wished he would be with a female dragon, but you are not a bad specimen. I would like to speak to you in private, if you can spare a moment?"

Should I go somewhere alone with her? I wasn't convinced she would not hurt me. She loved Rhys and I was definitely not her choice for him.

"Certainly," I replied and glanced at Nico. "I'm going to speak with the queen for a moment. I'll be right back."

And if I didn't come back, hopefully they would come looking for me.

Nico nodded and whispered to Deryn, who was talking with Rhian. Rhian had a slight blush on her cheeks and a huge smile on her face. The adorable teenager must have a crush on Deryn.

"This way," Queen Adelaide said, spinning and causing her dress to flare around her. She was so graceful and beautiful. I followed close behind her, glancing at the pictures on the walls as we went down a hallway I had never used before and into a study that smelled mostly of Emrys.

She shut the door and spun to face me. "Are you truly going to remove your ability to have children?"

Crap. I had not wanted a discussion like this with her.

"Yes," I answered her.

"Why?"

"There are many reasons," I replied, trying to be vague and hoping she would leave it at that.

"Please, indulge me and let me hear these reasons," she said softly.

She didn't seem mad, but I still wasn't sure if I could trust her.

"I'm going to be mated to four different males. Four different clans. I don't want to have a child with one of them and not the others. What if I only got pregnant with a child from one or two of them? Or, even worse, three of them and the fourth never had one with me. I don't want to have one of them never have a child and see the others with their children. Plus, I don't really want children. I've never viewed myself as a person who would have children. There's so much work and they have to be protected. I can barely protect myself right now."

"And my son is okay with this?" she asked me.

I nodded. "They said that if I wanted to have children, they would all love the children I had, no matter who the father was, but it's just too strange for me to think about. What would the children call them? Uncle? Here, little John, this is Rhys, your uncle and mommy's other mate? It's too weird. I don't want to do that. I would prefer to never have children if that is the only option available to me."

"You're certain that you are going to have this procedure done?"

She didn't seem to be judging me, but she also didn't seem to be upset or angry with me either. Maybe she understood.

"Yes."

She sighed and said, "While I would prefer to have grandchildren from Rhys, I understand your reasoning. If you would like to talk about childbirth ever, I am willing to discuss my experiences with you."

"Thank you," I whispered, shocked by her offer. Maybe she had gotten over her initial reaction of hating me and thinking I was not good enough.

"We should return. I'm certain Rhys will be following your scent trail now to make sure I'm not being rude or cruel to you."

"So, Rhys is your favorite?" I asked with a smirk.

She laughed. "No, he's just the oldest, so I spent a bit more time with him than the others. I had alone time with him, while the others never had that luxury."

We walked down the hallway again and almost immediately ran into Rhys.

"Mother," he said in a worried tone.

"I was perfectly nice to her. Not a scratch on her head."

"She was very nice and just giving me some motherly time. Don't be so mean to your mother," I ordered him and poked him in the ribs.

"Great, now you are teaming up against me?" He groaned.

"There you two are," Emrys called. He walked to his wife and kissed her forehead. "I think we're ready to eat now."

"I am famished," she admitted, leaning into him.

As cold as she had been when I met her, seeing her like this made my heart swell. She truly loved Emrys and I knew that she loved Rhys as well. She wouldn't be concerned with my intentions with him if she did not care about him.

"Are you hungry yet?" Rhys asked me.

"A little," I admitted.

We stepped into the room and the scents of the food surrounded me. A tornado of cooked meats, baked breads, and vegetables swirled around me and made my mouth water. I was definitely hungry again.

Rhys pulled out a chair for me, between Deryn and Nico, and took a seat across from me. I saw Rhian rush to take the seat on Deryn's other side and had to hide my smile behind my glass as I took a drink.

Rhys arched an eyebrow at me, but I just smiled at him and refused to say anything.

As soon as Emrys sat down, everyone began filling their plates with food. I didn't even get a chance to fill mine, Deryn and Nico filled it for me. Fox tossed a bread roll to them to add to my plate and Rhys laughed softly.

"I can make my own plate," I whispered.

"We know, but you like to pile your plate high with potatoes and not enough meat. You need to eat more meat," Deryn told me.

"I eat a lot of meat," I grumbled, but instead of truly arguing with them, because they were likely right, I just dug in. Everything was delicious and I could understand the appeal of having chefs at your house. I wanted a chef at my house to cook for me! If we all moved into a house together, we could pool our money and hire one of the best chefs in the world to cook for us.

I froze, my body completely tense at my last thought. Since when had I begun thinking of their money as mine? Since when did I start thinking about having a house with all of us together? It would make things convenient, but we had never discussed that. Should we? Should we all live together in one house? We could have separate rooms still. Or one huge room that would make it much easier for us to share a bed. We could make the entire room a bed for all of us to share.

"What's wrong?" Nico asked, setting his hand on my knee beneath the table.

I shook my head and shoveled more food into my mouth. I did not want to talk about this right now. I did not want to admit the crazy thoughts going through my head. What would they think about doing something like that? Would they agree? Would they want to find a house for all of us to live in?

I supposed, the thought of being their mate truly hadn't sunk in yet. Yes, the sex part was well understood. Our future though, what were we going to do? Would we find a house to live in together or would we stay in the apartments? Would they want to have one house or would we go to different ones? Would I go certain days to certain houses? Would we have to make a schedule like we had done before?

"Jolie," Deryn said loudly.

I jerked my head to the side to look at him. "What?"

"You cut through your plate," he whispered.

"What?" I looked down and sure enough, I had cut my plate in half. "Oh! I'm so sorry! I didn't mean to. I was just—"

"It's alright," Emrys assured me. "We have more plates."

"What's wrong?" Deryn whispered in my ear.

I shook my head. "Nothing, just got lost in thought."

"Are you sure?" he asked. "We can go outside to talk if you want to."

"No, really. I'm alright. I'm sorry."

Rhys was looking at me with a strange expression. He looked into my eyes and then glanced at his mother and back to me. I shook my head. No, this wasn't because of what his mother and I had discussed.

A servant brought out a new plate and wiped off my place setting, so I wouldn't have any of the pieces of the broken ceramic on the table still. Deryn remade my plate for me and I ate in silence, listening to what everyone else was saying instead of focusing on the thoughts swirling inside of my head.

Everyone finished eating and we continued to another room, this one had a ten foot tall tree decorated with lights, hand crafted decorations, and pine cones. Beneath the tree sat a giant pile of presents. The room had several large couches and we all took seats on it while Emrys stood before the tree.

"Tradition here is to give out presents from youngest to oldest," Emrys informed me.

"Did you bring the presents?" I asked Rhys.

He nodded. "They're under the tree already."

Good. I would have felt awkward opening presents when I hadn't brought any myself for others to open.

"Tonight, however, we are changing it up a bit," Emrys said.

"What?" Rhian grumbled. "Why?"

"Tonight, we want to give Jolie her present first. Then, we will resume our normal course of action," he explained.

"I can wait my turn," I assured him. "It's really okay."

He shook his head, picked up a package wrapped in beautiful teal and magenta and set it on the ground in front of me. "Merry Christmas, Daughter."

Kneeling on the ground, I ripped open the present and opened the box. A gasp escaped my throat before I could stop it. Inside of the box lay a transparent piece of paper with a swirling dragon on it. I knew it wasn't just a drawing though. This was the symbol of their clan, the one that they all had tattooed on them once they could prove that they could shift and were accepted by the clan.

"Is this...are you sure?" I asked, looking up at the King and Queen of Dragons with tears in my eyes.

They both nodded.

"May I?" Rhys asked, holding out his hand.

I nodded, speechless, and handed him the piece of paper. Unlike tattoos done by machines with ink, this was done by magic. Rhys turned me to face him and looked down at my body thoughtfully.

Finally, he turned me and pulled down the right shoulder of my dress, baring my shoulder to him. I kept a tight grip on the front of my dress so that it wouldn't drop lower and cause me to flash his family. Rhys pressed the paper to my shoulder blade and whispered in a language I didn't understand. A brief zip of pain shot through my shoulder and then warmth spread from it until it engulfed my body.

I could feel them. All of them. I could feel all of the dragons in this room and beyond. I was part of their clan.

"Welcome to the Clan of Dragons, Daughter," Emrys said with a wide smile.

Rhys kissed my tattoo and the little bit of pain that had stayed, disappeared.

After fixing my dress, I stood and walked to Emrys, threw my arms around his neck, and hugged him tightly.

He wrapped his arms around me and whispered into my ear, "Even if something happens between you and my son, now you will always be part of my clan. You will always be my daughter. You will never be alone and never be cast aside."

"You're going to make her cry," Adelaide chastised him. She pulled me away from him and kissed my cheek. "Welcome to the clan, Daughter. You are officially our princess and will forever be so, unless you take over ruling and become queen."

That did not sound like something I wanted to do any time soon, but I didn't say that. I just hugged her and said, "Thank you."

"Alright!" Emrys said with a clap of his hands. "Let's open the rest of the presents."

I took my seat on the couch beside Rhys and didn't stop smiling the entire night.

Accepted. They had accepted me.

Everyone loved the gifts I had given them, especially Gavin who swore he would wear the bracelet I'd purchased every day.

We said our farewells and drove on to our next destination. Rhys ran his fingertips over my shoulder, over the tattoo, as we drove while looking out the window.

"Did you talk to your dad about what happened?" I asked, even though I knew they had.

"Yes, he said it is because I've become lazy and just relied on it to happen. I've got to get back to doing things on purpose and not on habit. He's, of course, right."

"Well, I'm glad it's just that," I said with a sigh. I had been worried something might be wrong with Rhys.

He kissed my cheek and whispered, "I'm fine, love. And, even if I were dying, you have my family to support you now."

"What are we, chopped liver?" Fox asked with a scowl.

"Yes, she'll have you as well," Rhys chuckled.

The time with the mages was a somber affair and I wasn't the only one glad to be done when we climbed in the car two hours later.

"Sorry," Nico whispered. "Dad's not been the same since the Summit."

"Because of me?" I asked.

"Because of himself," he snapped. "Because he was so willing to sacrifice you despite knowing how much I love you and how much the others love you. Despite knowing what Dan and Emrys feel for you. He realized what a terrible decision he made and he's not sure how to atone for it."

"Is that why he gave me such a huge present?" I asked, looking at the card in my hand. He had pre-loaded a credit card with one thousand dollars and told me I could use it for whatever I wanted, since he wasn't really sure what I wanted or needed.

Nico nodded.

"Well, you'll have fun with the pack," Deryn assured me. "Dad pulled out all the stops for you."

"You guys really didn't have to go through all of this for me," I whispered, feeling embarrassed.

"Dad heard that you hadn't really enjoyed a true family Christmas and immediately went into action. I could not have stopped him if I had tried," Deryn told me. "Plus, you know how much he loves you."

I did. Dan had been the first to decide I was good for his son and had claimed me for his pack immediately. Though, Emrys had been the first to officially claim me.

We pulled to a stop in front of Dan's house and twin whirlwinds of fur bounded around the truck, barking and yipping for me to get out. I stepped out and they tackled me to the ground, covering my face with puppy kisses.

"Hello, nieces," I said laughing as they continued to greet me.

"Girls," Dan said in a chastising, but kind voice.

They stepped off of me, sat on their rumps, and looked at me with wagging tails. Deryn helped me up and I wiped my face off on the bottom of his shirt.

Dan pulled me into a hug and kissed my cheek. "Daughter, I have been waiting all day for you."

"We told you we would be here at this time," I reminded him.

"I know," he admitted, "but I had hoped you would come sooner."

"Jolie!" Sharla exclaimed, rushed forward, and pulled me out of Dan's arms and into her own.

I hugged her back and kissed her cheek. "Sharla!" I exhaled.

She kissed my cheek and then pulled back to look into my eyes. Her hand whipped out and she twisted my ear harshly, making me cry out in pain. "If you ever sacrifice yourself for me or Martin again, I will skin your hide!"

"Sharla," Deryn growled, stepping forward.

I held out my hand to him and he stopped.

"Sharla," I whispered, seeing the tears in her eyes. "You know that I could not let Martin die. I could not let him die and allow myself to live. I would not be able to look at you or the girls knowing I had let him die. "

"You almost died!" she snapped at me, growling softly, but her grip on my ear released and she buried her head in my neck. "He told me how they found you."

"I'm alive," I whispered and hugged her tightly. "We are all alive and that is what matters."

"Don't you ever do that again," she ordered me, her growl vibrating my entire body.

I stepped back from her and shook my head. "I can't promise you that," I said honestly. "If Martin is in danger and I can prevent his death with my own, I will always place myself in danger."

"You're supposed to let me die for you," Martin said, wrapping his arms around me from behind.

I turned around and hugged him tightly. "There was no way I could let that happen."

"You're so stubborn," he grumbled into my hair.

"That's enough," Dan ordered us. He pulled me away from Martin and put his arm around my shoulders. "Come on, let's go inside and start this party right."

Dan led me inside, but then took me to his office and shut and locked the door.

"Dad?" Deryn called and knocked on the door.

"Give us a minute," he ordered Deryn, the order carrying power enough to make Deryn leave.

"What?" I asked Dan.

"They're right," he told me.

"Who?"

"Sharla and Martin. You cannot sacrifice yourself like that."

"Dan, what would you have done if they said to sacrifice yourself or Deryn dies?" I asked him with hands on my hips.

He growled and turned away.

"Exactly," I said and pointed at him. "I could not let them die. I love them. I had been in relationships with them. I could not let them die. I would do it again. I don't care what pain I endured. As long as they survive, that is all that matters!"

"You matter!" he yelled, the wolf showing in his eyes. He paced back and forth in front of his desk a few times and then turned to face me. "You are not just a human girl. You are the Princess of the Four Clans. You are the Queen of the Four Princes. You are my daughter, though not by blood, but that does not matter to me. You are important to me. You matter to me. Do I want to lose my son? No! But, I don't want to lose you either. I hope I never have to worry about losing either of you. If there is ever a time where you must choose between you and Deryn, I hope that you choose yourself."

"Dan!" I gasped. "He is your son. Your prince—"

"And you mean the world to him. If he loses you, I fear that he will fall into a darkness that I will not be able to pull him out of. When your connection was severed, he collapsed to the ground, like a puppet with their strings cut. He collapsed and cried. My boy never cries. He has never cried in his entire life! Not even as a baby. He would whimper or fuss, but never cry. Your connection was cut and that hard-ass wolf cried and wailed. I feared the worst. I feared you were dead from his reaction. I tried to comfort him, but he was inconsolable. The others were much the same. I have known those four their entire lives, Jolie. I have seen them together and seen them in battles and in times of joy. I have seen them with females, some they thought they might love. I have seen them face down enemies I did not think they could defeat, but they did. I felt my heart breaking for them when your bonds were cut. They thought you were dead. They thought you were gone from them forever. They were desperate, unthinking, and began to rush around to look for you. We had to sedate Deryn. Please, do not tell him I told you. He was shifting uncontrollably. He tried to attack me. He was so beside himself in grief he could not even form sentences."

"Why are you telling me this?" I demanded, tears in my eyes attempting to stream down my cheeks.

"Because, I want you to know how much you mean to them. I need you to know that if you sacrificed yourself to keep them alive, it would eat at them for the rest of their lives. They would never forgive themselves. You are the only thing that matters to them. You are the most important thing to them. I understand the desire to protect them. I'm not saying you should not protect them if you can. Just, please don't sacrifice yourself like that again."

"I will do my best," I replied.

"I almost killed him," he told me, fists clenched.

"Who?" I knew he didn't mean Deryn.

"That stupid fucking Mage King. I wanted to rip his head off and Emrys was right there with me. Had you died, no one could have stopped me. I would have killed him. Nico seemed close to doing it himself. I've never seen him attack his father before, but that night, he sent his father flying into the castle wall and told him if he ever put you in harm's way again, he'd take his place as king."

Holy shit!

"When did this happen?"

"The night you were returned to us," he answered.

The night I came back basically dead. I'd barely survived.

"The princes are powerful beings," he whispered. "More powerful than the kings. They're the most powerful any of us have ever seen and we aren't quite sure how they became so powerful. When someone is that powerful, they usually lose their humanity. But you allow them to keep their humanity. You keep them humble and remind them that there are people to fight for. People who need their help."

I teared up again at his words. I thought I made them weaker, not stronger.

"Promise me, Daughter. Promise me you won't sacrifice yourself like that again," he whispered, setting his hands on my shoulders.

"I promise I will do everything in my power to stay alive," I answered.

He sighed then chuckled. "I suppose that is the best answer I will get from you. Come, let's leave these serious discussions for later."

I nodded and followed him to the living room where we found the twins in wolf form wrestling with Deryn in human form.

"That's something we had never seen before," Dan whispered to me. "He loved children, but he did not engage with the pups often. Now, he plays with all of the pups, letting them jump and climb on him and playing."

Deryn looked up and his wide smile wavered a moment as he took us in. The girls turned to see what he was looking at and rushed towards me. I held out my hand, making them slide to a stop before me. "Shift," I ordered them.

They shifted and stood before me in matching red dresses. "Auntie," they said in unison.

I got down on my knees and hugged them. "Hello, girls."

"We've got to go," Martin told the girls.

"I'll come see you tomorrow," I promised them. "I have awesome presents for you two."

"Yay!" they yelled in unison, hugged me once more, and followed Sharla and Martin out of the house.

"They're very fond of you," Deryn said behind me. "They never want to talk to me about anything other than you."

"They're great girls," I whispered.

"Come!" Dan ordered us. "Time to eat."

"I can't believe how much you've eaten today," Fox said to me.

"I know," I agreed.

"What did the old man want to talk to you about?" Deryn asked, keeping his voice low while Dan talked with Nico.

"It's personal," I whispered and tried to walk away, but he grabbed my arm gently and stopped me. "I'll talk to you later about it," I promised.

"You're upset," he whispered.

I turned to look him straight in the eyes, rested my hands on each side of his face, and whispered, "You are amazing. I love you, Deryn."

He blinked twice and said, "I love you, too, Jolie."

Dan had given me a tattoo as well, making me an official member of the pack. The little wolf was on my left shoulder blade and it was a bit strange being connected to so many people at once, but as we drove back towards our apartment complex, their minds faded a bit into background noise.

Deryn taught me how to block them completely and that was a huge help.

Once home, the guys stood in front of the tree, all looking down at the one present from me.

"Sit," I ordered them.

They obeyed, taking seats on the couch.

I picked up the present, fumbled with the bag, and pulled out the four black boxes.

"Tricky!" Fox exclaimed.

"This was your dad's idea," I chuckled.

"I don't doubt it," he grumbled.

After handing each of them their boxes, I sat on my knees in front of them and smiled. "Open them."

They lifted the lids and all of them stared at it in shock.

Dropping the front half of my body to the ground, I bowed to them. "I'm a lowly human girl. I don't have powers, unless I borrow yours. I don't have much money. I'm not the most beautiful woman in the lands. I don't have much of anything. But, I do have a heart that beats only for you four. I love you four more than anything else in the world. I'm not worthy. I'm far from worthy. I'll never be worthy. However, I can't deny my feelings. I love you four. And, I have one thing to ask. Will you become my mates?"

I had rehearsed the speech for hours, but it still didn't come out quite right. I just hoped they knew what I was trying to say.

"I accept," all four said at the same time.

I looked up and the four of them put the bloodstone beneath their left eye, between the eye and their cheekbones. It melted into their skin until it was part of their body, the crystal showing with a slight glow from the magic and blood within.

Mates. They were my mates. Now and forever.

All four bowed to me and said, "You are my queen and my mate from now until the end of time. None shall separate us. None shall come between us. You are mine and I am yours. My heart, my body, and my soul are yours. I shall touch no other female. I shall love no other female. You are mine and I am yours. Forever. This vow I make you, my mate and my queen."

The magic surged through us all and I cried fat tears of joy, hugging and kissing each of them. We weren't perfect. We weren't going to be safe from danger and problems. But, we had each other and that was all that mattered. And, tomorrow I would have them add their blood to my bloodstone to put under my eye, finishing our bond.

"Forever," I agreed.

ROYALLY
ELECTED
HER ROYAL HAREM, BOOK THREE
USA TODAY BESTSELLING AUTHOR
CATHERINE BANKS

CHAPTER I

"Fly or die!" Emrys roared.

Three of my four guards lay unconscious on the ground, blood pooled beneath them. They were alive, but barely.

Nico panted heavily, cuts all over his body, and his magic fizzling. Soon, he would fall, too.

Emrys and Nico battled the army of vampires and dhampir before us, but there were too many.

"I can't," I cried, my hands shaking and my knees weak. My fear of dying at the hands of the enemy was equal to that of flying in my dragon form.

"If you don't, they'll all die!" Emrys, King of the Dragons, yelled at me. His black hair waved in the wind and specks of blood marred its beauty.

Dozens of dead dhampirs littered the field, and piles of ashes from dead vampires crushed underfoot. Among them were also the bodies of my friends, some dead, and some gravely wounded. On one side of the field Dan, King and Alpha of the Werewolves, battled against six dhampirs while Johann, King of the Mages, battled six more behind him.

Chaos. Death and destruction surrounded me.

"Fly!" Emrys roared. His eyes flashed emerald before he shifted, jumped into the fray, and distracted the enemies to give me a chance to flee.

A dhampir stabbed Nico in the stomach and Nico coughed up blood.

"No!" I screamed, tears streaming down my face.

"Jolie!" Rhys yelled.

I sat upright and blinked the dream away. My cheeks were wet with tears and my hands shook.

Rhys pulled me into a hug and stroked my hair. "I'm here," he whispered. "I'm safe and unhurt."

More arms wrapped around me from behind.

"It was just a dream," Fox whispered and I felt his magic wrap around me, a cocoon of warmth and happiness. It couldn't penetrate the fear and distress I felt.

"I need out," I whispered in a strangled voice.

They immediately released me and slid across the bed to give me space. My feet hit the floor and I wrapped my arms around myself.

Deryn walked into the room in his boxers. He looked amazing, but I wasn't in the mood to admire all the muscles on display. He tried to embrace me, but I dodged his hands and rushed to the bathroom.

I turned the shower on and sat on the floor of the tub, letting the warm water hit me.

For the past two weeks, I'd been having the same dream. Every time I woke up in tears. The guys tried to assure me it was just a dream, just my mind's way of processing all the drama that had unfolded since meeting the Four Princes of Jinla.

I wasn't so sure.

I couldn't fly yet, despite my many lessons with Emrys. Flying scared me. What if I shifted mid-flight? My shifts were unpredictable at times. Plus, the dream just felt too real. I worried it was a premonition.

"Jolie," Nico called.

"No," I replied, knowing he would want to come in.

"You closed our bonds," he said. "Please, release them."

Unconsciously, my mind shut down the bonds between me and my four guards when I experienced extreme emotional situations. They hated when I did it because it reminded them of the time our bonds had been severed by Justina.

I exhaled and released the clamps from each of their bonds. Their worry, pain, and love rushed to me. I gasped and struggled to ground myself for several moments. No matter how many times it happened, I was never prepared for the onslaught of their emotions.

"Thank you," Nico called through the door, then he walked away.

After washing and brushing my teeth, I returned to my room. When I had first moved in, I had a queen-sized bed and a dresser. Now, a custom double king bed took up half of the room and my three-drawer dresser had been replaced by a huge dresser with nine drawers.

Rhys sat alone on my bed, his hair much longer than when I had met him. The side swept bangs reached just below his left eyebrow. He wore a pair of jeans and a black t-shirt that hugged his chest. My eyes caught on the crystal imbedded above his cheek, but I looked at his chest instead.

"Are you going to tell us the full dream yet?" he asked, a scowl pulled his eyebrows together.

I wasn't ready to tell them that the four of them were defeated in the dream. They all assumed something had happened by the way I cried and clung to them the first few times.

Turning, I dug through the dresser for clothes without replying.

He sighed and left the room, a cloud of worry and anger surrounded him and flowed down our bond. He quickly shut down the bond, which made me stumble and slide to my knees on the carpet.

That did hurt!

It took me a moment to compose myself, stand, and find my clothes. Once I finished getting ready, I walked out of my apartment, down the stairs, and out to the waiting black SUV. Overhead, the bright blue sky felt too cheerful for my dark mood.

Deryn and Martin stopped talking when I climbed into the front passenger seat and Deryn looked out his window in the back, giving me the cold shoulder.

I checked our bond and it was open. So, why was he mad?

"Hello, beautiful," Martin said before putting the car in drive.

"Morning," I replied and looked out my own window.

The drive to the pack was tense and silent. I jumped out before Martin put the SUV in park and marched to the house. Deryn didn't follow.

Dan opened the door before I made it to the house. He smiled wide and said, "There's my girl!" He took two steps to close the distance and pulled me into a tight hug.

He made me feel loved and safe, just like an alpha should.

"Hi, Dan," I whispered.

He pushed me out to arm's length and scowled. "What's wrong?" Without waiting for me to answer, he looked behind me. "Where's my son?"

I shrugged. "In the car still, probably."

"Are you two fighting?" he asked.

I sighed. "I don't know. He's giving me the silent treatment and I didn't do anything. Well, that I can think of."

"Did you seal your mating bond yet?" Dan asked softly.

"No," I admitted. "But, we just haven't had time. I've been working a lot and he's been at a lot of meetings with you."

"Have you sealed it with any of them?"

I blushed and looked at my feet. "No."

"Are you having second thoughts?"

"No!" I snapped and looked up to meet his eyes. "Not at all." Not that I could anyway. We were technically mates now, but each clan had different ways of sealing the bond. I hadn't sealed the bond with any of them to fully become their mate.

"Do they know that?" Dan asked, a knowing look in his eyes.

"I, uh...they should," I said and sighed, looking back down. "I guess I haven't really been talking much to them lately."

"Want to talk about it?"

"It's a dream I keep having."

"The same one?"

"Same exact one."

"And they die?"

I met his eyes again. "What?"

He smirked. "He told me you were having a recurring dream and you weren't telling them the full story."

"What if it's a premonition?" I asked and gulped.

"It could be."

I groaned. "Dan, that's *not* reassuring."

He draped his arms around my shoulders and steered me towards the gymnasium. "You need to tell your mates what you see. They need to know so that they can prepare for it. Just in case it is a premonition."

I hated talking about it. My anxiety spiked, and I always cried.

"Fine," I whispered, resigned to do as he said. If it was a premonition, they could prepare better by knowing what happened in the dream.

He pushed open the door, and the sounds of the basketball game inside blasted out to greet us. Many pack members sat in the stands, watching the other pack members playing basketball. Dan led me to the stands, pulling me down to the bench beside him. A few teenagers scooted closer to Dan, talking to him about their schooling.

He was so loved by his pack, it made me smile to see him interacting with the younger werewolves.

Martin and Deryn joined the game and began to play basketball with their pack mates. They moved fast across the court. Human sports didn't entertain me, but when Others played them, it became something else. Something super intense.

"Auntie!" Martin's twin daughters, Tamara & Madison, yelled and rushed up the stands to hug me.

I hugged them back and kissed their heads. "Hello, nieces."

Sharla came and over and sat next to me, picking up Madison to take her spot. "Hey," she said in greeting.

I hugged her with one arm. "Hey."

"When did you get here?" Sharla asked.

"Just a couple of minutes ago," I answered.

A bell sounded, ending the quarter. The guys went to the tables on the sidelines and drank water from the cooler there. Deryn glanced in my direction, then looked away.

I sighed loud and dropped my head.

"What's wrong?" Sharla asked.

"Nothing I want to talk about," I told her and leaned my shoulder against hers.

"I'm here if you want to talk," she whispered.

I nodded, but said nothing. I wouldn't spread my relationship issues around.

"I thought I smelled something delicious," a deep male voice said.

Sharla moved to sit in front of me, pulling the girls down with her, giving the newcomer the place at my side.

I leapt up and threw my arms around Thor, the giant werewolf picked me up as he hugged me. "Thor!" I screeched.

He squeezed me and kissed my cheek. "Jo, I've missed you."

He set me on my feet but kept his hands on my waist. "I've missed you, too," I told him with a wide smile. "What are you doing here?"

"I'm here on a mission for a couple months," Thor explained.

"And I'm just now finding out?" I asked with a frown.

He chuckled and pulled me into another hug. "I just got here, Jo. I hadn't had time to tell you."

"You could have texted me," I reminded him.

"Thor," Deryn called.

Thor turned, draping his arm around my shoulders. "Yeah?"

"Why don't you come play with us?" Deryn asked, his eyes glued to the hand on my shoulder.

"No, thanks," Thor said and sat, pulling me against his side as he did.

Deryn's eyes shifted and his fists clenched.

"So, you gave him a mating crystal, but haven't sealed it yet?" Thor asked in a whisper in my ear. "Why not?"

I blushed and turned away. "None of your business."

"Thor," Deryn growled. "Stop pushing me."

Thor sighed and pulled his arm away. "You're no fun."

I stood, grabbed Thor's hand, and led him down the stands. "Come on, I need to talk to you."

Deryn growled, but didn't follow.

I let the door slam shut behind us, then exhaled and leaned my forehead against Thor's arm. "Damn him," I whispered.

"What's up, Jo? Why is he acting crazy again?" Thor asked.

"I'm not one hundred percent sure, but it's probably a couple things lumped together," I said softly.

"Did you really need to talk to me?" he asked.

I shook my head and started walking towards the back of the pack's territory. "No. I just needed to get out of there. Sorry for dragging you with me."

"Don't apologize. If you need me, I'm here. For *anything*," he said and waggled his eyebrows.

I laughed and punched his arm. "Knock it off."

He laughed and draped his arm around my shoulders again. "So, what's new? What's happened since I last saw you two months ago?"

Two months? Had it really been that long?

"Not much. I've been really busy with work and the guys have been really busy with their clans."

"So, not much alone time?" he asked.

"No," I admitted. "It's partially their fault. Ever since that night, they haven't wanted to be apart for more than a few hours."

"Jo, they lost you. They lost their bond with you, felt it sever. You almost died afterwards and there was nothing they could do about it. It's not something you can just get over."

I knew that.

"It wasn't a picnic for me either," I muttered.

He squeezed my shoulders. "Just give them a break. And mate with them!"

I cringed. "I know."

Thor hugged me and rubbed my back. "It'll be okay, Jo. I'm here, so you can call on me if you need me."

I returned his hug, then pulled back, feeling Deryn's anger. "He's behind me, isn't he?"

Thor smirked. "A hundred yards and closing."

"I'll text you later, okay?" I asked.

He nodded, kissed my cheek, and walked off.

Deryn's anger decreased as he stopped by me. "What did you two talk about?" he asked.

I turned and arched an eyebrow. "Now you're talking to me?"

He stepped forward and rested his head on top of mine, but said nothing.

"If my dreams are premonitions, I don't know what to do. If it comes to pass..." I couldn't finish that sentence.

He slid his hands up my arms and whispered, "Baby, you've had nightmares since we met you. Why are these different?"

"They just feel different. They feel real. They don't feel like normal nightmares."

"When we get home, will you please tell us the full dream?"

I gripped his shirt and pulled myself closer to him. "Yes."

He wrapped me up and held me in silence for several minutes. "I love you, baby. I don't like it when you're upset and hold shit in instead of talking to us."

"Can you please release our bond fully?" I asked softly.

"What?" he asked. I felt it open and sagged into him. "Sorry, I hadn't realized that I had done that."

I nodded and stepped back, rubbing my heart. There was still one bond not open.

"Who else?" Deryn asked and placed his warm hand on my sternum.

"Rhys," I whispered. "He's mad at me."

"Let's head back. It's lunch time," he said, changing the subject rather quickly.

We locked fingers and walked to the house. Being able to touch them in public was nice. It took the edge off the pain when one was closed off to me.

"I'll be right in. Save me a seat," Deryn said, letting go of my hand.

I kissed his cheek and walked inside, shutting the door, but stayed by it to eavesdrop.

"Hey, asshole," Deryn said on the phone to whoever he called. "You're hurting her." There was a pause then he growled, "You closed your bond, idiot."

Rhys released the bond and I felt his worry and apology. I staggered forward and caught myself against the wall while my knees wobbled. His emotions were always so much stronger than the others.

Deryn walked in and rushed to my side. "Jolie?" he asked.

"I'm fine," I whispered. "Rhys opened our bond and it caught me off guard."

He helped me up and wiped a tear away from my cheek with his thumb. "We're all still getting used to the bonds. They aren't the same as our warrior bonds."

"I know," I whispered. "Then we'll be adding our full mating bonds on top of that."

"So, you still plan to mate with us?" he asked.

I reached up and touched the crystal embedded under his eye. "Yes. We've all been busy and haven't had alone time with the right circumstances to seal them."

He nodded. "I know. It's still nice to hear it."

"I'm sorry. I should have made it a priority—"

He silenced me with a kiss and smiled. "It's alright. We know we will be your mates eventually."

I touched the stone again. "Yeah, but people already think—"

"Good," he said adamantly. "Soon we will get yours finished."

"Don't I have to have one for each of you?"

"We don't think so. Nico has been working on getting all our blood and connections into one. He's been having trouble, but we know it's possible."

"I wouldn't mind having four," I said softly.

"Good to know," he replied.

"Lunch!" Dan boomed.

"Food!" Tamara and Madison yelled, raced down the stairs, and past us to the dining room. They didn't live in the house anymore, but they might as well have with how often they were here.

We followed them and took seats at the dining table alongside Dan, Thor, Martin, Sharla, and the girls. Dan chatted with Martin and Sharla while Deryn chatted with Thor. It was a nice home cooked meal and I loved being a part of it.

Looking at the girls, I could imagine Deryn helping his own children cut up their meat or making silly faces at them...like he was doing now. He would make a great father.

But, not with me.

Sorrow filled me, tightening my chest painfully.

"Excuse me," I whispered, set my napkin down, and raced to the bathroom. I gripped the counter and bit my lip to stop the sobs trying to escape.

I deprived them of so much by being their mate. I wasn't worth it. My love wasn't worth it.

Deryn tried to open the door and sighed softly when he found it locked. "Baby, what's wrong?"

I flushed the toilet, opened the bathroom window, and leapt out. Thankfully, I landed in a crouch and the impact only hurt my legs a little.

Thor looked at me from the dining room window, his eyes widened, and he stood up, his mouth opening, likely calling Deryn.

I shifted into my dragon form and jumped up a bit so I was floating above the ground—not really flying, but not touching the ground. I banked left, towards the back half of the forest. I landed in a rolling heap, but somehow avoided injuring my wings. I hated flying as a dragon. It was scary, but I was trying to overcome it with small flights.

Deryn tugged on our bond and I gently placed a shield around it, to prevent him from finding me. I did the same to the others' bonds as well.

What was I going to do? They claimed they didn't care, but part of them did. Part of them wanted heirs.

I didn't want to have four children. Childbirth was painful. Plus, there was always the possibility of having two of Deryn's kids and none of Fox's, or something like that. Nature wasn't fair.

Curling up beneath a massive oak tree, I let out the pain. I sobbed and howled my pain. The pain of knowing I wasn't worthy. The pain of knowing a small piece of them would always resent me. The pain of knowing I cost the men I loved so much.

Nico, Rhys, Fox, and Deryn popped into existence a few feet away from me. All four looked at me while clutching their chests.

"Go," I whispered.

All four dropped to their knees and groaned.

"What's wrong?" Fox asked and started to shuffle towards me.

"How did you find me?"

"We can always locate you now," Nico said.

"I'm not worth this…all this pain," I whispered.

"Stop bottling it up and talk to us, please," Rhys begged.

"Love is stupid!" I snapped. "It makes you do stupid things."

All four cringed.

"You chose me, but why? I don't want kids, but you all do. You all would make great fathers. What if I have two kids from one of you and none for the others? Your lives are run by schedules now. We don't come home and spontaneously jump into bed, not when there's three more of you also being affected by my scent. We haven't had time to even mate, yet all four of you have my crystal.

"Mating may not be the best idea. If my dreams are right, you're all going to die protecting me. You're all going to die because I am a burden. I don't add any substance to your lives. I'm not politically savvy. I'm not magically gifted. I have quirks like being able to tell dragons apart, but nothing useful. I make crap compared to you four. I don't contribute. I'm a hinderance."

"Well, now that you got all of that off your chest, how do you feel?" a squeaky male voice asked.

"Is that—" Rhys began.

"No way," Deryn whispered.

"They're real?" Nico asked.

I turned and looked behind me. A tall red fox with nine tails grinned at me, his tails fanned out behind him proudly.

"A kistune?" I asked and wiped at my face.

He bowed. "I'm Nar, a relative of Foxfire's."

"I didn't summon him," Fox said loudly.

Nar sat in front of me. "He's been complaining about not being able to help you. I thought I could assist."

I almost said thank you out of politeness, but I wasn't thankful. I hadn't wanted to say all of that to them.

"You're trespassing," Deryn told Nar, but he looked more intrigued than mad.

"Technically you brought me here," Nar said. "I've been working on her for a week." Nar looked at me. "You're very strong-willed."

"Thank you?" I wasn't certain if it was a compliment or not.

"Can we have some privacy?" Fox asked Nar.

Nar looked at me and whispered, "Summon me if you're in danger."

"How?" I asked as he started to become see through.

He dropped a piece of paper with a kitsune drawn on it. "Put it on your skin and it'll add a tattoo. Then you'll just need to tap me, uh the tattoo, and I'll help."

He disappeared and I stared at the piece of paper on the ground.

"Jolie," Fox whispered.

I looked up at the four men staring at me. "What?" I whispered.

"We need to talk about this," Rhys said.

"I know," I admitted. I picked up the paper and walked to them.

Nico grabbed my hand, the rest set their hands on him, and Nico teleported us to the apartment. We sat together on the floor of my apartment for a moment, then I moved away from them to the couch before they could grab me to hug me.

They sat on the floor facing me.

"You weren't supposed to hear all of that," I whispered and looked at my hands.

"You should talk to us more," Rhys chastised. "We shouldn't have had to hear that from you because of a Kitsune spell."

"It's not easy for me to tell you that type of stuff. You guys don't talk to me about things like that," I reminded them.

"We talk to each other," Fox said.

"Still not me," I pointed out.

"Stop trying to change the subject," Deryn said.

"Let's start with point one," Fox said, putting up a finger like he was counting. "Love is not stupid."

"We told you that kids aren't important to us," Rhys frowned, his brow drawing together. "You told us you were going to get your tubes tied, and we were fine with that."

"You say that, but if I told you I decided to have kids, you'd be ecstatic," I snapped.

"Yes, of course we would!" Rhys snapped back. "Having a kid with you would be great."

"See!" I yelled and stood up. "You want kids."

Fox stood between me and Rhys and said, "We want kids, but we are fine not having them as well."

"What brought the kids up all of a sudden?" Deryn asked.

"Lunch," I replied and plopped back down on the couch. "Seeing you with the twins tonight."

"We know that sex has been sparse," Nico said. "We're sorry about that. We have told you that you can take one of us away if you want."

"I can't do that." I shook my head and my hands fisted.

"Tell us your dream." Deryn reached out and set a hand on my knee.

I sighed and told them the entire dream. They listened silently through it, then all turned to face each other.

"Dhampirs fighting alongside vampires?" Rhys asked.

"That would be a hell of a fight." Deryn growled and shoved a hand through his black hair.

Fox chewed on a lip and I found myself mesmerized by it. "The dream does sort of sound like a premonition," he said.

"It does," Nico agreed with a sigh. He rubbed his temples and murmured something too low for me to hear.

"I don't want you to die," I whispered.

Rhys pulled me off the couch and into the center of them on the floor. They all hugged me, and I sniffled, trying to hold back the tears.

"We don't care how much or how little money you make," Rhys whispered. "You love your job and that is what matters."

"You do contribute to us. You don't see it, but you have helped shape us into better princes just by being our queen," Fox said.

"Ask our fathers," Deryn muttered. "They'll tell you that we've changed because of you and it's something they appreciate."

"Dan's told me that," I admitted with my words muffled as I pressed my face into Nico's chest.

"If you don't want kids, then we won't have kids," Nico said. "We could always adopt."

"Or, we could get a surrogate," Fox suggested.

"I don't know how I feel about a surrogate," I admitted. If someone was going to carry a child by one of them, while we were together, shouldn't it be me?

"You don't need to feel obligated to have a child with any of us," Deryn said. "We won't ever pressure you."

"If you want to get your tubes tied still, we're fine with that," Rhys told me. "We'll go with you to your appointment if you want us there."

"And, you are worthy of us. We aren't worthy of you. You're way more understanding than any of the other girls we've dated. None of them understood our nuances or our quirks," Deryn told me.

"And there wasn't a single girl who we all liked. One of us would bring a girl to meet the others and some of us wouldn't get along with her. We all love you. We all love spending time with you. You're not a rut in the way. You're another friend added to our group. You're our last puzzle piece," Fox said.

"Why am I so emotional?" I asked angrily.

"Nar," Fox said. "He messed with your emotions to get you to open up to us."

"How long will this last?"

I really hated being emotionally vulnerable like this.

"Until tomorrow or the next day," Fox informed me.

Wonderful.

"Are you second-guessing mating with us?" Rhys asked.

"No," I said immediately. "No. I am not second-guessing mating with you four. I want to mate with you. I'm sorry I didn't make it a priority. I hadn't realized how much time had passed until Thor mentioned it today."

"Thor?" Rhys asked. "You saw Thor today?"

"He's helping my dad with some stuff," Deryn explained.

"How has it been two months?" I asked softly.

"You've been so busy with the new game release that you lost track of the days," Nico said and smiled.

"Wait, that means it's March and we missed Valentine's Day?" I asked.

"We never celebrated it before, and since you didn't bring it up, we thought you didn't either," Rhys admitted.

I was the worst girlfriend ever.

"I'm sorry," I whispered. Turning to my right, I threw my arms around Rhys's neck and kissed his cheek. "I'm so sorry."

"You don't need to apologize," Rhys assured me.

"I do. I've been a terrible queen. I've neglected you four."

"That's enough," Nico whispered and pulled me from Rhys's hold. He tilted my chin up to look at him. "We've all been busy and neglecting each other. Why don't we take Saturday and split the day up, so we can each have some alone time with you?"

"You'll only get a few hours with me like that," I reminded him.

"We will take whatever morsels of time we can get with you," he whispered.

"Especially if it's time alone," Fox said.

"We need to make a schedule again and stick to it," Rhys added.

The other three nodded in agreement.

CHAPTER 2

Rhys pushed open the door to his family's house, and I was pulled away by a rambunctious teenage boy.

"Jolie! Come see," Gavin, Rhys's younger brother, said as he dragged me by the hand down the hallway and into a large living room. The furniture looked centuries old, and the room was filled with older dragons. They all looked up as we came in, but Gavin paid them no mind. He pulled me to a set of double doors on the opposite side which led to a balcony where we could see to the town. "Look!" he ordered me with a wide smile.

Gavin's energy was unrivaled, he made even Fox look slow.

I looked out the direction he pointed and saw the town being decorated.

"Is there a festival coming up?" I asked him, admiring the bright teal designs.

"Yes! It's the Night of the Dragon Festival," he said and bounced beside me. "You're coming right? You'll be here?" he asked and looked over at Rhys who was speaking to Emrys.

"I'm not sure," I admitted. "I didn't know there was a festival."

"Rhys!" Gavin called into the other room. "Can she come to the festival? I can stay with her and—"

"I can chaperone," Andras said, hopping down from the balcony above us to land beside me.

"Andras!" I said and smiled. Andras was Rhys's younger brother by a couple of years.

He kissed my cheek and smiled warmly at me. "We've missed you here, Jolie."

"I was here last week," I reminded him with a chuckle.

"A day is too long to go without seeing your lovely face," he murmured in my ear.

"Andras," Rhys growled across the room. "Stop flirting with my queen."

"Not going to happen," he told Rhys with a wide smile. "She's family now and I like watching you get all worked up."

"What happens at this festival?" I asked Andras and was thankful when Emrys distracted Rhys.

"Vendors, games, fireworks—"

"I'm sold!" I said and smiled at the two younger siblings.

"I should have known you were the cause of all this raucous," Rhys's mother, Adelaide, said as she entered the room. After giving me one hard glare, she turned and smiled warmly at the others in the room. "Welcome," she greeted them.

Andras draped an arm around my shoulders and Gavin linked his hand with mine, protectively. Their reactions were unconscious for them and it made me feel better.

"I'm alright," I whispered to them and they both stepped away from me. At Christmas, she had said she accepted me, but now she was being cold again. Why?

Emrys walked to me and kissed my cheeks. "Hello, Daughter."

"Father," I replied.

"Come. Walk with me," he ordered.

Rhys started to come, but Emrys held up his hand. "Stay with your mother."

Rhys's lip twitched, but he nodded and stayed in the room. Emrys tucked my hand into the crook of his arm and led me away from the house. "Rhys told me about your dreams."

I sighed. "Of course, he did."

"But, he said you flew."

I cringed. "Not really. I floated more than flew."

"And?"

"And I fell, like a chick from a nest. I don't know how I didn't break a wing," I admitted to him.

"Why does flying scare you?"

"It's not flying. It's falling."

He nodded, stopping in front of a piano in the great room where we stood. This one had the same age-old furniture, but looked more lived in and less like a museum. "Then, we need to focus on teaching you to fall properly."

"Come again?" I asked and stopped walking.

"If your fear is falling, then we need to teach you how to prepare for crash landings. We all fall at some point and knowing how to fall is very important."

"Do you think my dreams are premonitions?" I asked.

He shrugged, his eyes darting toward the hallway where the voices suddenly grew louder and laughter flowed down to us. "I'm not a seer. I can't tell you if they are or aren't."

"Should I go see one?"

"I need you to promise me something," he whispered.

"What?" I asked and met his gaze, which seared into mine.

"If I order you to flee, to leave a battle, you must do it. You must promise me that you will flee," he said.

"I can't leave my guards behind." I shook my head, a lump forming in my throat.

"What if leaving will save them?"

"Then I will leave," I agreed.

"Then you need to do as I order. If this battle comes to pass, and I tell you to leave, it is because leaving will help your soon-to-be mates. Understand?"

I nodded. "Yes."

"And, please ignore my mate. She's still getting used to seeing Rhys happy with a woman who isn't her. It's a motherly instinct to hate the woman he loves."

I chuckled and leaned my head against his arm as we walked back. "I'm glad you're so accepting of me."

"I told you. It's some weird magic you have over us. All of the kings discussed it. I think that also bothers Addy. She is pulled to you, but wants to dislike you. It makes it harder on her."

"I can't control it," I grumbled.

"Do you want to come to the festival?" Emrys asked, squeezing my hand that was still on his arm and led me back to the room where the others were and back toward the balcony again.

I nodded.

He smiled. "Good, because I was going to force you anyway."

I laughed, and he left me on the balcony to go talk with the group inside. Gavin had disappeared during the walk, as had Andras. Emrys and one of the older dragons left the room, going somewhere else in the house. Rhys talked with some of the older dragons, his mother at his side, beaming proudly. No one could mistake the pride that shone in her eyes. How could I prove myself to her? Maybe she thought I was playing with Rhys since I hadn't completed our mating bond?

A dragon roared above me. I jerked my gaze up, then quickly leapt to the side to avoid her claws. The female dragon was a light pink color with red tipped claws and spikes. I had never met her before.

She spun towards me and inhaled.

Shit, she was going to try to burn me.

I leapt over the edge of the balcony and shifted into my dragon warrior form, which gave me a scaled body and wings. She growled at me and I roared back at her. My new appearance made her hesitate a moment before she spewed fire at me.

Jumping up as high as I could, I avoided the fire and saw Rhys being held back by his mother and Mawrth.

Why?

I landed on the female dragon's back and flapped my arms and flared my wings to keep my balance. She turned her head and I used my wings to propel me forward and punched her in the eye.

She bellowed in pain and swiped with her front claws blindly.

I landed and immediately jumped up and punched the tip of her snout. Rhys told me it was super sensitive. Judging by her howling, he hadn't been lying.

Shifting into my full dragon form, I bit into the back of her neck, like Emrys had shown me. She stilled and dropped to her stomach, submitting.

I huffed out a breath and looked back at the balcony and the room. Rhys stood just in front of me on the balcony in his warrior's form, his gorgeous wings flared behind him and murder in his eyes.

Mawrth lay unconscious with his arm bent at an awkward angle. Their mother sat beside him, her eyes wide and unfocused.

"Jolie," Rhys said.

I released the other dragon and reverted back to my human form. My body felt heavy from using so much magic. I jumped onto the balcony and Rhys wrapped his arms around me and rested his forehead against mine.

"You did well," he whispered.

"Thanks," I said.

The dragon turned into a beautiful woman in her early thirties with wavy pink hair. She bellowed and reached for me. Before she could touch me, Rhys stepped between us and roared. His roar shook the ground beneath my feet and the glass in the doors and windows rattled. I could sense his challenge, but since he directed it at my attacker, it didn't affect me.

She fell to the ground, whimpering and crying.

Andras slipped an arm beneath my legs and lifted me. "Come, Sister," he whispered.

Rhys knelt before the woman and whatever he said to her, she nodded vigorously in return.

"Where are you taking me?" I asked.

"To get some clothes," he whispered, then chuckled.

I glanced down and gulped. I hadn't realized I was naked. Usually, my powers gave me clothes.

"You're drained, so you couldn't make clothes," he explained.

"Rhys—"

"He's fine."

"He hurt Mawrth," I said, glancing at their brother's body as we walked out of the room. The older dragons wore mixed expressions of shock and fear.

"They waited until Father and I were gone from the room. Had I been there, this wouldn't have happened," Andras said, his grip on me tightening.

"What was this?" I asked.

"A test," he said. "Mother wanted to test you."

"She looked upset," I commented. Shocked and disbelief were the emotions I really associated with her expression.

He nodded. "Rhys yelled at her and shoved her away. And, she didn't know you could shift so well."

"So, she's going to hate me even more?" I guessed, hiding my face from the people we passed in the hallway.

Andras climbed the stairs and stopped in front of Rhys's bedroom. "I don't know what goes on in her mind." He set me down, checked the room, then held the door for me. "I'll wait here," he promised.

I quickly changed into a spare pair of Rhys's exercise clothes that were kept in the drawer. I had to tie the shirt because it was too big and rolled up the sweats, but they would do.

I inhaled Rhys's scent, which somehow still permeated the room despite him not using it. This was where he'd grown up.

His walls were bare and only two figurines sat on his dresser. One was a dragon and fairy playing. The other was a unicorn. Why did he have these? Had someone given them to him?

Rhys roared again and the house shook. I ran out of the room and Andras stayed by my side as we ran back to the room where we had left Rhys.

Emrys stood over Rhys who was slowly getting to his hands and knees. I started to go to him, but Andras stopped me with a hand on my shoulder.

"I will not apologize," Rhys snarled and stood, facing his father with dragon's eyes.

Emrys growled and shifted into warrior form. He punched Rhys hard enough to make him stumble back a step. Rhys straightened and met Emrys's glare again.

"Apologize!" Emrys roared. I cringed back and Andras hugged me, shielding me slightly with his body.

Their mother stood a few feet away from Rhys and Emrys. Her eyes locked with mine and she bellowed, "You!"

She started to move towards me, but Andras stepped in her path. "You've done enough today," Andras growled at her.

She snarled and slapped him. "I am your mother! Your queen!"

I stepped around Andras and stood toe-to-toe with her. "What kind of mother hires someone to attack their son's queen?"

"You're no queen!" she snapped.

"What are you talking about?" Emrys asked me.

"Nothing," she growled and glared at me. "She's delusional."

"When you and Andras left, a female dragon attacked me. She and Mawrth held Rhys back while I protected myself."

"You're a—" she started.

"I saw it," Andras said. "I came in when Rhys knocked out Mawrth. Mother tried to order him to stay. Her order rebounded, and he shoved her to the side to get to his queen."

"She must prove her worth," she said and sneered.

Emrys dropped his hand from Rhys's neck and marched towards us. I had never seen him so mad. It made me nervous and want to hide behind Andras.

He stopped and spun his mate to face him. "She is our princess. She is your son's queen. She is his mate."

She tried to interrupt, but he didn't let her.

"She doesn't have to prove anything to you. I train her. I keep an eye on her. You have no need to do anything. Rhys may be your favorite, but that doesn't give you the right to treat her so poorly."

"She—"

"Has had to deal with enough shit. I understand that you are threatened by her. I understand that you don't like the pull she has on you. She draws us all. Get over it, or you may lose your son. He will not choose you over her," Emrys growled.

"Jolie," Rhys called.

I walked to him and gingerly touched the red welt on his cheek. "Rhys."

He linked our hands and faced his mother who still looked pissed. She hadn't been cowed at all. "She passed your test. Next time, I will kill whoever comes after her."

Her eyes narrowed to slits. "You wouldn't."

"Anyone who wishes harm upon my queen is my enemy. You should remember that, Mother," Rhys growled.

Wings popped up behind him, and he picked me up before taking to the sky.

We flew in tense silence before we landed in front of our apartment building. The media rushed us, clogging the entrance to the building.

"Princess Jolie, what's it like having four princes as mates?"

"Will you be having children soon?"

"Who hurt Prince Rhys? Was it you?"

Rhys growled, and the media members backed off, but didn't stop their barrage of questions.

I walked into the building and took the elevator to my apartment. Rhys locked my door behind us and stomped to the fridge.

Nico and Fox paused their game to look at us.

"What happened?" Fox asked.

"Mother paid Matilda to attack Jolie," Rhys grumbled while looking in the freezer.

Fox rushed to me, lifted my arms and shirt. "Where are you hurt?"

"I'm not," I snapped.

Rhys popped two frozen pizzas in the oven, then leaned back against the kitchen counter to face us. "She easily defeated Matilda."

"What?" Nico and Fox asked in unison.

I rolled my eyes and sat on the couch opposite them. "I've been getting lessons from Emrys, remember?"

"What else happened?" Fox asked Rhys. "You're way too mad for that to be it."

"Mawrth and Mother tried to hold me back, so I couldn't help Jolie," he explained.

"Is Mawrth alive?" Fox asked softly.

"I broke his arm and a few ribs," Rhys said, his eyes shifting for a moment.

Nico ran a hand through his hair. "Your mom is so crazy."

"Who hit you?" Fox asked Rhys.

"Dad. He thought I had disobeyed Mother and shoved her just because I didn't like her saying negative things about Jolie."

"She said bad things?" I asked, not surprised.

"Andras set him straight, thankfully," Rhys said and sighed. "I was too upset to explain it."

"What happened once he got the full story?" Nico asked.

"Emrys yelled at his mate," I answered. "Then Rhys told her he would kill whoever came after me again and they would be his enemy. Add her to my enemy list."

"I had to make sure they understood," Rhys said nonchalantly.

"Can I get a minute alone?" I asked Nico and Fox.

They kissed me on the cheek before leaving the apartment and I locked the door before walking to Rhys. I grabbed his hand and led him to my bedroom, then turned and said, "I know this isn't romantic, but we don't really have time for that."

I pulled his shirt off and slid my hands up his bare chest. Of my four guards, he had the nicest chest.

"You don't have to do this right now," he whispered and rubbed his hands up and down my arms.

"We need to complete our mating bond. We are only partially mated and it's driving you guys crazy," I said. "You are my mate, Rhys. No matter how stubborn and frustrating you can be, I will always love you."

He pressed his forehead to mine and whispered, "I will always love you, too."

I kissed his lips and slid my hands from his chest to the back of his neck, pulling myself closer to him. He broke our kiss, yanked my shirt and pants off, and carried me to the bed. He jerked his sweats off and leaned over me.

"I'm going to mark you," he whispered and kissed my neck,

scraping his teeth gently and making me gasp. "The mark will go around the dragon mark on your shoulder."

He bit my shoulder and magic shocked me through his teeth. I gasped in pain and had to force myself not to pull away. Rhys reached down and rubbed my clit while the magic worked. Distracted, the pain lessened. It had been a week at least since we had sex and I ground against his hand and moaned. He released my shoulder, then kissed me deeply, claiming my mouth with his. He thrust into me and I moaned into his mouth. The connection built as the pressure in my lower body did. He and I orgasmed as the connection snapped into place, making us both cry out.

We collapsed onto the bed together and he pulled me into his arms.

"Finally," he whispered. "You're all mine."

"Well, a quarter yours," I reminded him.

He chuckled. "True."

"Rhys?"

"Hm?" he asked, stroking his fingers up and down my arm.

"Are you really okay with not having kids?" I asked softly.

He rolled onto his side and loomed over me, so he could look into my eyes. "I would love to have a child with you, yes. I would love to see what the two of us created. But, I am also fine not having kids. I understand your worry about not having kids for each of us. Life isn't fair and we would never expect you to carry a child for each of us if you didn't want to. Labor isn't pleasant, and we don't want you to be in pain, even if it would mean bearing children for us. If you bore children for the others, I would love those children like they were my own because they came from you. The choice is completely up to you. I will be fine with whatever decision you make."

I nodded and snuggled into him. "Okay."

CHAPTER 3

Millions of stars shone above me as I slammed to the ground on my back. Air whooshed from my lungs and I gasped for breath.

"Too slow," Tawny taunted me, her golden hair glowed like fire around her. She always looked ethereal, but when we fought, the elf woman looked even more like a goddess.

"Cheater," I panted and groaned as I rolled onto my hands and knees. "You used magic."

"You have magic, too. Use it," she ordered me.

"You okay?" Fox called from the swinging tire he sat on in one of the nearby trees.

"Peachy," I growled and stood. My hair blew forward into my face and I debated cutting it.

"Hold on," Fox ordered me. He leapt off the tire swing and hurried over. With expert and nimble fingers, he braided my hair and used a piece of a plant's vine to secure it. He beamed. "There, now it won't get in your face."

I brushed my lips across his, then faced Tawny again. "Ready."

She snickered and amusement lit her lavender eyes. "No, you're not."

Tapping into my connection with Fox, I channeled his elven powers. The forest came into focus, much sharper than before, and Tawny moved at a slower pace.

I smiled and met her halfway, dodging her punch, and leapt up over her leg sweep.

"Yes!" she shouted and threw a barrage of punches at me. Her smile was radiant and my lips curled to match hers.

She laughed joyously as we fought. Sweat slid down my spine and dampened my hair at the base of my head.

Time disappeared, and I worried I wouldn't be able to keep up, but soon, she raised her hand and stepped back.

"I give," she said. "That was amazing."

I released the powers and fell to my back on the cool grass, staring up at the cloudless night sky. "I'm spent."

Fox lay beside me and unbraided my hair. "That was a huge improvement."

"Finally figured out how to tap into our connection," I admitted.

He nodded. "I felt it."

"I need a shower," I groaned.

"No time," he gasped as he looked at the time on his phone. "Rhys is supposed to be here in two minutes."

Rhys was never late.

"Need an outfit?" Tawny asked.

I nodded. "My body smells, too."

She pulled me up and waved glowing hands at me. The sweat disappeared, my body odor vaporized, and my leggings and tank top were replaced by a flowing elven gown of blue gossamer. The front of the dress was shorter than the back, which gave me freedom of movement and yet still looked gorgeous.

I threw my arms around her and squeezed. "You're amazing!"

"I could have done that," Fox pouted.

Tawny hugged me back, then wiggled her fingers at my face, adding a silver pair of earrings that matched my necklace.

Rhys roared, announcing his approach, and landed thirty yards away in his dragon form, but quickly shifted.

Tawny tensed beside me, her mouth a thin line. "I'll see you next week," she whispered and ran off into the forest.

Her behavior was understandable since she had been attacked by a dragon as a child and still didn't trust them. I wished I could show her their soft side.

Rhys and Fox bumped fists with smiles on their faces. It always warmed my heart to see the friends interact.

Rhys tapped our mating bond to get my attention.

I met his eyes and smiled. Now that we were fully mated, he had calmed down a lot. It was a great relief.

Walking with a bit more sway to my hips than normal, I watched Rhys's eyes shift to his dragon's eyes. I kissed Fox and hugged him. "See you tonight?" I asked.

He nodded. "I'm headed home now."

"Love you," I called as I threw my arms around Rhys's neck.

Rhys picked me up, released wings from his back, and leapt up into the sky. Rhys nuzzled my cheek and said, "I missed you today."

I kissed his cheek and tightened my hold on him. "I missed you, too. Guess what?"

"Chicken butt!" he yelled.

I giggled.

He and Fox had spent a lot of time together lately and it had made Rhys more childlike.

"No," I said. "I was able to use elf powers, and Tawny didn't end up tossing me on my back."

"Nice!" he said.

I looked at the approaching dragon's den, and my heart sank. "Do you think she will ever like me? I thought she had grown to like me, at Christmas, but now we're back to square one." There was no need to specify who I meant.

"Yes," he said. "She just needs a couple months."

I didn't believe him, but I stayed silent.

Andras in dragon form suddenly flew down to us, making me shriek.

"Andras!" I snapped and took a stuttering breath. "You startled me."

"You think I would let some random dragon drop down next to us?" Rhys asked with a half-laugh.

He had let Matilda fight me.

His eyebrows furrowed, and fury zoomed down our connection.

Andras chuckled, a wheezing dragon laugh, then made a purring sound at me.

"Thank you," I said, assuming he was complimenting my dress. "An elf woman made it for me."

"How do you always know what we're saying?" Rhys asked.

I shrugged. "Same way I can tell you apart when only dragons should be able to." I wiggled my fingers at him and in an eerie voice said, "Magic!"

He rolled his eyes, and Andras roared with laughter.

We flew over the house where Emrys stood on the porch. He raised his hand, shifted, and flew after us.

Rhys landed in a grassy area near the town with Emrys and Andras on either side of us. The town was quiet and there were no lights on. What had happened to the decorations? The lanterns? All of the things I had seen just a few nights ago?

After brushing off my dress, I hugged Emrys and then Andras.

"Hello," I said and smiled at them.

"Welcome to the Night of the Dragon Festival!" Emrys announced.

Lights, lanterns, and a huge bonfire roared to life.

I gasped and gawked at the amazing decorations and all of the dragons waiting.

"It's gorgeous!" I yelled.

Gavin ran forward and grabbed my hand, a smile of pure joy on his face. "Come on, Sister!" he shouted.

Rhys nodded once, and I jogged beside Gavin to a vendor selling paper lanterns.

The vendor, a middle-aged man with gray specks in his hair and bright green eyes, bowed to me. "Princess, thank you for coming."

The lanterns ranged from simple floral designs to elegant landscapes painted on them. I took my time admiring them, trying to find one that was just perfect for my first time. The vendor cleared his throat after several moments, making me look up.

He blushed and set a paper lantern on the counter top. It was painted with two dragons flying side by side, soaring through clouds together. They weren't just any dragons, though.

"I hope you don't mind, Princess. I just couldn't get this image out of my mind. It's an image of—"

"Rhys and I flying," I finished for him. A tear slid down my cheek as I stared at the two gorgeous dragons in flight.

Rhys wiped the tear away. "She loves it," he told the vendor. "So much so, that she can't express her gratitude or emotions properly." He handed the vendor some money.

"Can..." I cleared my throat. "Could you paint this again? On a canvas?"

He smiled and nodded, his gray speckled hair bobbing with the movement. "Yes, Your Highness. I'll start on it first thing tomorrow."

I held the lantern up to Rhys. "Isn't it perfect?"

He smiled wide and kissed my cheek. "Yes, you are."

"Are you hungry?" Gavin asked.

I had forgotten he was there. The puppy-like teenager didn't seem to have realized that though. "Yes!" I exclaimed. "Take me to the best vendors!"

Gavin's smile widened, and he took my hand again. More people bowed to me and I looked at Rhys in question as he trailed after us.

"Now that we're fully mated, you are officially part of us," Rhys explained.

I rolled my eyes. "So, the kings naming me princess and me being your queen, didn't count?"

He shrugged. "Guess not."

Gavin and I ate some fried food from one of the vendors on a bench while watching the dragons enjoying the festival. There were hundreds walking around, all smiling, except one woman.

Gavin stood, moving his body slightly in front of mine. "Mom," he said, trying to pull her focus from me.

Her eyes were locked with mine, and I doubted he could do anything to distract her.

I remained seated and nibbled on my food, but tapped Rhys's and my mating bond to draw his attention.

She stopped by Gavin, her eyes still fixed on mine, and said, "You're strange and I don't like that."

"I don't like beating up women who were ordered to attack me because you're too afraid to do it yourself," I said.

Gavin's jaw dropped open and he took a small step away from us.

Her eyes sparkled. "You may dislike me, but at least you finally completed the mating."

I lowered my food. Had that been her goal all along? Had she successfully manipulated me?

I stood. "You had nothing to do with it."

She arched a brow. "Whatever helps you sleep at night, *Daughter*."

I growled and felt my scales begin to cover me.

She leaned forward and said, "He will always bow to me."

My fist connected with her jaw and I gasped, not having planned it, but the crowd's gasp drowned mine out.

She fell to her hands and knees.

"Don't call me, 'Daughter' again until you mean it. And, he bows to no one, but me," I hissed at her.

Mawrth landed beside his mother, and his eyes glowed as he looked at me.

Andras landed next to me and glared at Mawrth. "Don't get involved unless you want me to break your other arm."

Adelaide laughed and stood. "You've got spirit. I'm surprised someone with such a terrible past isn't more broken than you are."

"Love heals a lot of things," I told her.

Rhys and Emrys walked over, but stopped a short distance away.

"Twenty on Jolie," Emrys said with a smirk.

Adelaide looked at her mate in shock. "You think she can beat me?"

Emrys nodded.

She spun to face me. "I challenge you to a Three Bloods Rite!"

I looked at Andras.

"First to draw blood three times from their opponent wins. No maiming or killing allowed."

I handed Andras my food and smiled viciously. "Challenge accepted."

The crowd cheered.

Rhys held our lantern and smiled.

"Why are you happy about this?" I asked angrily.

He walked beside me towards the sand arena. "I have faith you'll win." He leaned closer and whispered, "And I won't bow to anyone, but you."

I smiled and kissed his cheek before turning to Emrys and asking, "Any tips?"

He smirked. "Don't get cut."

I glared at him. "Why do you want us to fight?"

"Because she needs to vent her anger and she hasn't seen your secret weapon."

No. No one except Emrys had seen it.

I glanced at Rhys, then Emrys. "I thought we weren't going to show anyone?"

"You're keeping secrets?" Rhys growled.

I batted my eyelashes. "I leveled up and haven't had a chance to show you my new skill."

"This isn't a game," he growled. "You could have shown me."

"I ordered her not to," Emrys said.

"As my mate, she can tell me anything and ignore your command."

"This was before we fully mated," I explained.

"She drops her left shoulder before using lunging attacks," Andras told me.

I nodded and filed that information away.

Adelaide removed her jacket and stood with her dress tied through her legs and around her waist.

I turned one of my hands into a dragon's talon and used it to cut the back of my dress so it was all one length.

Rhys kissed my cheek then motioned behind him. "Look who just showed up."

Nico, Deryn, and Fox smiled at me from the fence lining the sand arena. I jogged over and kissed each of them. "What are you guys doing here?"

"Rhys invited us," Nico said.

I spun and gaped at him and Emrys. "You planned this?"

Emrys smirked. "No, but we guessed it would happen. There's normally at least a dozen Three Blood Rites at each festival."

"Kick her butt!" Fox cheered.

After another kiss for each of my mates, I went to the center of the ring. Exhaling, I calmed myself like I did before each of my matches with Emrys.

Adelaide snarled at me. "Your pretty dress will look so much better when it's soaking up your blood."

"Talk, talk, talk. Let's go!" I shouted. Opening my connection with all of the guys, I covered myself in scales and roared at her.

She did the same and charged forward.

I dodged her talon hands aimed at my face, dropped down, sliced open her legs with my now werewolf clawed hands, and rolled away.

"First blood!" Gavin announced.

The crowd was split between cheering and booing.

She growled and spun around, dropped her left shoulder, and charged. Andras had warned me, so I easily dodged, but she ducked to avoid my attack. Spinning, she sliced open my shoulder. Cheers and boos sounded.

"Now!" Emrys ordered me.

Creating a magic barrier that she couldn't enter, I closed my eyes and took shallow breaths.

"What is she doing?" someone asked.

"Coward," Adelaide hissed and pounded on my barrier.

Blocking out the sounds, I focused on my change. Dragon's scales because they were the toughest, werewolf teeth and claws because they were the sharpest, elf vision because they saw the best, and mage magic because it was the best for defense and offense. Plus, I harnessed my dragon's size, making myself larger.

The crowd gossiped, and someone screamed when I dropped the barrier and stood to my full height.

"She's huge!" someone screamed.

Adelaide's eyes widened, and she gaped.

"One move and it's over," I said in a frightening voice.

One second, I stood before her, the next, I was across the arena and both of her arms were bleeding.

"I didn't see her move," one of the crowd said.

"What the heck is she?" another asked.

"Holy mother of mana," Nico whispered.

"Did you know she could do that?" Fox yelled at Rhys.

"Jolie is the winner!" Emrys announced and the crowd cheered.

Rhys, Nico, Fox, and Deryn came over to me and then walked around me in a circle.

"She's tapping into all of our powers at once," Nico said, blinking and shaking his head.

"I didn't know that was possible," Deryn whispered, running a hand through his dark hair.

"What do I look like?" I asked, suddenly feeling a little self-conscious.

"Like a goddess," Fox whispered, his eyes wide in appreciation.

Deryn snapped a picture with his phone and smirked.

"Catch me," I gasped, then reverted to my human form and collapsed. My energy was gone, like a candle snuffed out.

Deryn, who stood closest, caught me. "You okay?" he asked, his eyes glowing momentarily in his worry.

I snuggled into him and nodded. "Just takes a lot of energy to do that form."

"Amazing!" Emrys shouted, a huge smile on his face as he walked to me. "That was the best version of that form I've seen yet."

"Maybe their proximity helped," I suggested.

He scratched his chin and nodded slowly. "Possibly."

"Let's find a comfy patch of grass to lie on," Deryn whispered and nuzzled me behind the ear.

"The lanterns," I said and looked at Rhys.

"We still have a bit of time until we launch them," Rhys assured me.

"I'll get some snacks," Fox said and ran off into the crowd with Nico following him a moment later.

Deryn carried me to a small grassy hill, then lay me down beside him, letting me use his bicep as a pillow.

"You were great today," he whispered against my forehead.

"Thanks."

"Do you have plans tomorrow? I thought we could go on a date, just us two," he said.

"I think I'm free. That sounds amazing," I told him, my eyelids drooping lower and lower.

"Rest, my queen. I will guard you," he whispered.

I awoke from my cat nap to the scent of the food Fox and Nico brought over.

"Food," I mumbled sleepily.

"I see she's channeling Rhys in the mornings," Fox teased.

I opened my eyes and sat up, my mates sitting in a circle with me on the grass. "What did I miss?" I asked.

Rhys shrugged. "A few fights, but none involving us."

Fox scooted closer to me and held out a fluffy piece of bread. I broke it apart and ate it slowly. It tasted like buttery clouds.

"How's the crystal coming?" I asked Nico.

He scowled. "It's still not working right."

"Then, maybe I should just get four," I suggested. "I can put two on each side."

"I'm still working on it," Nico said, shaking his head. "Give me a week."

"Okay," I agreed.

Andras sat down in our circle, eating a piece of meat. "How do you feel?" he asked.

"Still tired, but better," I replied.

Gavin landed behind me in dragon form and curled up with his head behind my back. His breath was warm and made me realize how cold I was.

"Gav, can you move your snout closer?" I requested.

He made a purring sound of acknowledgement and did as I asked, then began taking deeper and slower breaths.

I shivered, then his warm breath wrapped around me. "Thank you."

Rhian giggled a few yards away with three male teenage dragons talking to her.

Rhys notice, growled, and stood.

"Leave her alone," I said with a smile. "They're just talking and we can see them from here."

"They—"

"I got it," Andras said and walked to the group with his hands in his pockets and a deep scowl. I had to admit, it was intimidating.

"Overprotective," I grumbled.

"What did you do today?" Deryn asked Nico.

I leaned my side against Deryn and listened to them discuss their day. Fox continued to feed me food and I ate it while being warmed by Gavin's dragon breath.

"Jolie. Where are you?" a male voice asked.

"Who?"

"I'm near. I'll find you soon," he promised.

I jerked awake, heart pounding. Was it a dream? Who was it? The voice did not sound familiar.

Deryn smoothed back my hair, a frown once again in place. "What is it?"

"I think a dream."

"Of?" Fox asked, his serious face on.

"A guy, saying he was near and would find me."

"Threatening?" Nico asked.

"Someone you know?" Rhys asked.

I shook my head. "I didn't recognize the voice and he said it like he was rescuing me."

"And it wasn't one of your exes?" Deryn asked.

I shook my head.

"It's time!" Emrys announced.

"We'll do a sweep," Deryn told Rhys.

Andras had joined us again at some point and stood, too. "I'll go, too."

Deryn nodded and he, Nico, Fox, and Andras went off in different directions.

Gavin growled and flew up into the sky to assist.

"It was probably just a dream," I muttered to Rhys. I hated making them worry over nothing.

He pulled me to a stand, handed me our lantern, and said, "Probably, but your safety is important enough to check it out."

I stayed at his side as we moved through the crowd to where Emrys and Adelaide stood. Adelaide wouldn't look at me.

Wonderful.

Emrys lit his lantern and together, he and Adelaide, released it up into the sky.

Rhys blew out a bit of fire to light ours and smiled. "Ready?"

I took one side gently and nodded. Together, we pushed ours up into the sky and watched hundreds of others join it. Watching the lanterns float together like a swarm of firebugs was just as magical as I thought it would be.

Rhys wrapped his arms around me from behind and rested his chin on my shoulder. "I love you."

"I love you, too. Thank you for sharing this with me."

The group rejoined us a few moments later with nothing to report. We stood, watching the lanterns and enjoying a night of fun together.

"Is it going to hurt?" I asked Nico anxiously.

"Just a little," he said and rested his forehead against mine. "Ready?"

"All my life," I whispered.

My heart stuttered as he smirked at me. He was so handsome, and he was all mine.

Nico placed his hand on my heart and I placed mine on his. Wind stirred around us as he pulled out his magic. Using words I didn't understand, he began the spell. His magic swirled from his hand into my chest, then spread down my arm into his chest. Warmth spilled within me and I could feel his emotions. Love. So much love.

"Yes, I can feel your emotions, too," he whispered and smiled at me.

"It still surprises me how much you love me," I whispered back, a tear sliding down my cheek. "I just hope you feel or understand how much I love you."

Our mating bond felt stronger than our bond as queen and guard. It was intense, more intense than Rhys's mating bond with me.

"Why is our bond so strong?" I asked him.

"It takes it a bit to settle. Don't worry, it won't be this strong forever," he assured me.

"Why is the bloodstone giving you trouble?" I asked. "I know others who have multiple mates and have a single bloodstone."

"I think it has to do with our power levels. I'm able to get two of us, but when I add a third, the bloodstone explodes," he explained.

"Explodes!" I screeched. Now I was really glad we hadn't given it a try the night I had given them theirs.

He sighed. "Yeah. We may need to do two for you."

"I'm fine with that," I assured him.

"Will you put them on the same side?"

"Yes."

He nodded. "Okay. I'll get everyone together to finish the two."

"What if these dreams are premonitions?" I asked. I had had the battle dream and dream of the man talking to me every night since the festival.

"Would you let me take a look?" he asked.

"At what?"

"I can use a spell to see your dreams," he said.

"What are the possible repercussions?" Magic was unpredictable and could hurt more than heal at times.

"It could backlash and hurt me, but you won't be hurt."

I stepped out of his arms. "No."

"Jolie—"

"No," I said, sterner. "I won't let you get hurt."

"It's just a possibility," he said, his brows furrowing.

"Why don't we go visit Fox?" I suggested.

He pulled me back into his arms and said, "I've got a better idea."

I smirked, then squealed as he picked me up and carried me to his room.

"Sex isn't required for a mage's mating, but I haven't had you alone in a while," he said. "I shall take my time ravaging you. Then, I'll fuck you senseless."

"Promises, promises," I taunted with a smirk.

He arched a brow, the bedroom door slammed closed, his front door locked, and a ward surrounded us to keep our sounds in.

"Challenge accepted," he growled.

CHAPTER 4

"Plates!" I yelled, urging my clan members to run to the area in the current map we were playing in *Ghost 2* that looked like it had plates on the wall. This map was a small forest and there were strange dogs prowling around. The tamers protected them and attacked us whenever they could.

"Tamer!" Dragonknight yelled.

"Down," Alex advised, letting us know he had killed the tamer.

"Bones," Turbo said.

We all ran towards the area we had designated with that call sign.

My mates had been summoned to a meeting with the four kings. Something urgent had obviously come up, but their fathers hadn't filled them in. That worried me. I was glad that I had fully mated with all four of my mates now. It settled our group and my mates were happy and content.

"Jo! On your right!" Orphan shouted.

I spun my character and immediately got tossed back by a tamer.

Orphan and Turbo dropped down from a rock that overlooked the spot I was in and pushed the tamer back.

My character stood, no longer dazed. "I'm up," I said.

They killed the tamer and a large chime echoed through the forest.

I groaned and we all said, "Bugs."

Hundreds of knee-high bugs rushed into the forest. Standing back to back, the five of us fired our weapons, lobbed grenades, and used magic to fend off the waves of enemies.

I loved the graphics of the game and reminded myself not to get distracted by the luminescent colored bugs. They looked like a cross between a cockroach and a pug dog, but with a luminescent shell.

We killed the last one and fireworks exploded overhead, announcing our victory.

"Yes!" we yelled. Finally, we had beat that part of the raid, the third of five steps.

My phone rang.

"Be right back," I told the clan and muted my microphone on my headset. "Hello?"

"The kings want to talk to you," Nico said. "Come downstairs and we will pick you up. We're about two minutes away."

"Okay," I agreed, a lump formed in my throat.

"It's nothing bad," he promised.

"Thanks," I replied and hung up. "Guys, I have to go," I said to the clan.

None of them responded to me, still talking to each other.

"Guys!" I said louder.

"Did you see Jo get tossed back?" Dragonknight asked and laughed. The others joined in.

"Yeah, ha ha. Real funny," I said.

No response. I looked at my mic and sighed. I was still muted. I hit the button and said, "I did it again."

"Talked when muted?" Alex guessed.

"Yeah," I admitted.

They all laughed.

"I have to go," I said.

"Bye, Jo!" Dragonknight said.

"Bye," said Alex.

"Later," Turbo said.

"Bye-ee!" yelled Orphan.

I turned off the console, brushed my hair, and checked my armpits for body odor.

Good to go!

Nico leaned against the inside wall of the apartment lobby, messing with something small in his hand.

"What are you playing with?" I asked.

He opened his hand and showed me two bloodstones.

"Are they ready?" I asked.

He nodded and held them out to me. "I just finished adding mine."

I took one and placed it under my eye, just below my cheekbone. It zapped me and then melted into my skin painlessly. I added the second and a surge jolted through our connections, sharpening them.

"Whoa," I whispered.

Nico exhaled. "Well, now we are all official."

"Happy?" I asked.

He smiled and pulled me into a deep kiss before whispering, "Ecstatic."

We walked outside, and the media sent a barrage of questions at us while snapping pictures.

Nico threaded our fingers together and put a barrier around us, silencing the outside noise.

I squeezed his hand in thanks and smiled up at him.

"So, what did you do while we were gone?" he asked.

"Got through the forest part of the raid," I answered.

"Solo?"

I laughed loudly. "No! With my clan."

He smirked. "Fox got through it solo."

I gaped at him. "No way!"

He opened the door of the SUV for me. "I recorded it."

"Hey, gorgeous," Thor greeted me from the driver's seat.

I leaned between the front seats and hugged him. "Hey."

Nico tugged me down beside him with our still joined hands. "When the kings talk to you, I need you to promise to hear them out. Then, think before answering."

"Am I in trouble?" I asked.

He shook his head.

That was a relief.

Thor drove us to an office building in the center of the four territories I had never seen or been to before.

"What's this?" I asked and stayed seated even though Thor already had my door open.

"This is an office we use for meetings in neutral territory," Nico said and climbed out.

Thor looked at me questioningly.

"Something feels off," I whispered. My entire back was tingling.

Nico stood outside my door, next to Thor, and held out his hand. "Come on."

I took his hand, stepped out, and felt a bit better once he put a barrier around the three of us.

The building was ten stories, at least, with lots of windows. It had no distinguishing marks and looked like most of the other buildings down the street we stood on.

Fox waved at me from a window on the third floor, a huge smile on his face. I waved back, then walked inside. The lobby had no attendant, just couches, chairs, and three elevator doors.

Thor pushed the button for the elevators and rocked back and forth on his feet. It was a nervous habit he'd had as a teenager and it made me smile to see him do it still. The elevator opened, and he blocked my view with his body, stepped in, and held the door for Nico and me to enter.

In silence, we stood together in the chrome elevator, watching the arrow move from floor one to floor two to floor three. How old was this elevator not to have digital floor numbers? Was it safe to ride in?

"If we fell three stories in a metal box, would we survive?" I asked Nico.

He chuckled. "This elevator just looks old. It's maintained every month to ensure it's safe. But, yes, I could protect us."

Thor walked out first then nodded for us to follow.

"Why are you acting like this?" Nico asked Thor.

"Jolie said something feels off," Thor frowned, his eyes still shifting down the hall.

Nico looked down at me. "How?"

"My back is tingly, and I feel anxious," I explained.

"We're shielded," he reminded me.

I nodded. "I know."

Thor pulled open a door, and we stepped into an executive board room with the four kings, my other three mates, and Andras.

All eight men stood.

Nico dropped the shield and walked to the side to take a seat next to the other princes.

Dan smiled. "Daughter! So glad you came."

"I had a choice?" I asked and pretended I was headed out.

Thor pulled out the chair that faced the kings and I sat.

"We have a proposition for you," Katar said. "We'd like to offer you a position."

"I have a job," I interrupted.

"Jolie," Nico whispered. "Remember what I asked?"

To hear them out.

"Sorry," I apologized to Katar. "Please, go on."

Emrys took over. "We'd like you to join our council. We haven't had a human on it because most can't, or don't, understand us. You do. You also have some interesting suggestions that we'd like to hear more about."

One of my mates had been talking to them. I looked at them and they all smirked. Maybe all of them had been talking.

"I mentioned your idea about the combined school," Andras said with an excited grin. "I think it's a great idea and wanted to bring it to the council to consider."

"Oh," I said and felt bad for assuming it had been my mates.

"What is your idea for this school?" Emrys asked.

"I think we should open a school, a private school for now, where humans, mages, dragons, elves, and werewolves attend together. They could learn about all of the Others and the Others could learn about the humans and by attending together, they would learn to interact with each other. I was fortunate to have the pack near me and attending school with me. But, here in Jinla, that doesn't happen. Everyone is sectioned off and separated. Since the war is over, I thought it would be a great time to implement it." I looked up at them after saying my piece.

"What ages?" Katar asked, his hand scratching his chin.

"For the trial, I would suggest high school ages because they're easier for you to punish and keep in line. The council would be presented with candidates from each race and they would be vetted before being allowed to go to the school. That way, we wouldn't have someone sneaking in some kid who is actually a plan to make things go wrong. Gavin would be a perfect candidate for attending the school, in my opinion, Emrys," I said.

Emrys nodded. "Gavin would do well at a school like that. It would be good for him to be around other teenagers who aren't dragons. It would give them more of a real-world experience," he agreed.

"There's a lot that would need to be ironed out for this to work," Johann said.

I nodded. "There are a lot of steps to opening an institution like this, but I think it's worth the effort."

"We will begin working on it," Dan said, and the other three kings nodded.

I smiled and felt useful for the first time in a while.

"Back to you joining us," Dan said. "We would pay you and it wouldn't be full time, just once a week for a few hours. Unless, urgent matters come up."

"What would I be required to do?" I asked.

I wasn't against the idea, but I wanted to know what I was getting into.

Johann floated a stack of papers to me while he remained seated. "This is your proposed duty statement. We are willing to make adjustments if you have concerns."

I grabbed the floating papers and reviewed them. It all seemed pretty basic. I would be their fifth member, their tie breaker. I would make decisions and could offer ideas and opinions.

I would be an idiot to refuse.

"What's the pay?" I asked. Knowing them, it would be way too much.

"You'll be compensated at an appropriate rate," Johann said.

"When would I start?" I asked. "If I accept."

"Tonight," Dan said.

"What are the steps?" I asked. A throbbing pain built in my temple and I rubbed at it. What was going on? Where was the pain coming from?

"I, King Daniel of the Werewolves, nominate Jolie Bernardo as human councilor," Dan said loudly.

Magic gathered in the center of the room.

What the heck?

"Votes?" Dan asked.

"Yes," Katar said.

"Yes," Johann said.

"Yes," Emrys said.

"Congratulations, Jolie," Dan boomed.

The magic exploded outwards and punched me in the chest. I gasped and fell backward out of my chair, fighting to breathe.

"Jolie!" several voices yelled.

Everything hurt. I couldn't move.

"What happened? Why did it backfire?" Dan asked.

"That would only happen if—" Johann began, but suddenly everyone was silent and even my mates stopped moving towards me. Everyone stood perfectly still. I blinked at them.

"It would only happen if she weren't human," a deep voice said near me. The owner of the voice bent over me and I stared at a perfect replica of my own eyes. "What's happened to you?" he asked.

"Who are you?" I asked him back from my seated position on the floor.

He pulled me to my feet and I stared at the strange, but beautiful man blocking my mates from me. They were all frozen: the kings, my mates, Andras, and Thor.

"Your memories need restored," the man with my eyes said, drawing my attention back to him. He reached out and tapped behind my ear.

Pain ricocheted in my skull, then the memories came.

Home. Familiar places, people, and things. The memories were in fragments.

There weren't very many of them, since they were only from the time I was born until I was seven years old, but they opened a startling new reality.

My father wasn't the vampire who had raised me. No, he and the old woman had been my foster family. The man standing before me, he was my true father.

"Dad," I gasped.

He smiled and he was even more mesmerizing than I realized originally. "Hello, Jolie. It's time to come home."

Fear struck me at his words. I stepped back from him. "No. You banished me. This is my home."

He looked at my cheek with the bloodstones and then at my chest. "What are these bonds?" He started to reach for them, and I slapped his hand away and stepped back, stumbling over my fallen chair.

"They're my mating bonds!" I snapped. "Don't touch them!" I wouldn't lose the bonds again. Never again.

He looked at the men behind him. "Which of these men think they're worthy of you?"

"Why are you here?" I snapped to get his attention off of them.

The beautiful man, who had come with Dad, held a trident and kept the kings and princes immobilized, but kept casting strange glances at me.

"I made a grave mistake sending you away. It's time for you to return to Atlantis," he said, narrowing his eyes at me.

"Who is this?" Nico asked, barely able to move his lips.

The spell silencing them was wearing off.

"I'm her father," Dad said.

Nico's brows furrowed. "Her dad was a man turned vampire."

"That was her foster family," he explained in a bored tone. "I'm her biological father."

"How did you find me?" I asked.

"I've been tracking you," the beautiful man holding the trident explained. His silver hair was long, reaching down to his waist in a thick braid and his face was angelic. "You heard me talk to you in your dreams, remember? When the magic hit you, we were finally able to pinpoint your location."

"Who are you?" I asked, still confused, despite my memories being back. Memories before you were seven weren't great once you past your twenties.

"Brayden. Your betrothed," he said and smiled. "We were best friends as kids, too. You should remember that now."

"I have mates already," I said sternly.

He shrugged. "What's one more?"

All four of my mates growled, and I agreed with the sentiment.

"I'm sorry, but I don't want any more mates," I told him.

"We're wasting time," Dad said angrily.

"She's ours. You can't take her," Dan growled, his eyes shifted and glowed, but his body was still held immobile and held back his change.

Dad faced him fully. "Jolie isn't human. She's the Princess of the Sirens, and we are separate from you and Jinla."

"Sirens? She's not a siren," Emrys said.

"She's a null," Dad explained. "She can't feed off emotions or sex, but she is alluring. I'm sure you've all felt the pull to her. How she's likeable and her smile warms your heart?"

All eight males' eyes widened.

"Come, or I break your connections and kill them," Dad threatened.

I was fairly certain he wouldn't follow through on the threat, but I didn't want to push him. I didn't want to risk my mates' lives like that. I looked over at them, met eyes with each of them, and remembered the pain when our bonds were severed last time. I couldn't put them through that again. I couldn't go through that again. Looking at my father, I also knew he had the power to do it. His arms crossed over his chest impatiently.

"Can I at least say goodbye?" I asked, my heart tight in my chest.

He sighed. "I'm getting soft in my old age. Fine, but Brayden is keeping them frozen, so they don't try to keep you."

I nodded and walked to Thor who was closest and whispered into his ear, "Keep them safe. Don't let them kill themselves."

"Jo, you don't have to go," he whispered.

"I do," I said and sighed. "Please, Tim. Please, try to keep them safe while I'm gone."

I kissed his cheek and then hurried over to Andras and asked him to do the same. I hugged Nico and kissed his lips. "I'll come back," I promised. "I'll come back as soon as I can."

"He's not lying, then?" he asked.

I shook my head. "The memories are mine. I am a siren, but a null, like he said. They banished me because of it, too embarrassed to keep me in the court."

"Why go now?" he asked.

I smirked. "To keep you safe, idiot."

"I love you, Jolie."

I leaned my forehead against his and whispered, "I love you, too, Nico."

"Please," Deryn whispered. "Please, don't go. Not again. I can't lose you again."

I hugged him tightly and peppered his face with kisses. "I'll come back. I promise. This isn't goodbye. This is just an unexpected vacation."

"I'll find you," he whispered.

I shook my head. "No, even if you tried, you wouldn't be able to find Atlantis. It's too well hidden. Please, just wait for me. I swear on the moon, I will come back to you."

He kissed me deeply and growled softly. "I love you."

"I love you, too." The tears were getting harder to hold back.

Rhys was glaring at Brayden, but dropped his eyes to mine when I stood in front of him. "You sure about this?" he asked.

I nodded. "This isn't a trick. He didn't implant memories. He freed my true memories. I wish I had known. I wish I could have known to warn you."

"How long will you be gone?" he asked.

"I don't know," I admitted. "But, I'll come back as soon as I can. At the very least, I'll send word to you."

I kissed him and rubbed our cheeks together. "Stay safe, Puff. I love you."

"I love you, too, Jolie," he whispered, a single tear sliding down his cheek.

"Don't go," Fox whispered. "Don't go. Don't go. Don't go."

"Foxfire," I whispered and hugged him. "I love you. I love you more than chocolate. I love you more than all the chocolate in the world."

"I'll buy you all the chocolate in the world if you stay," he promised, two tears sliding down his cheeks.

"I love you."

"I love you, too."

I faced the kings and bowed to them, sniffling to hold the tears in. "Please, keep my guards and my mates safe while I'm away."

"Jolie, you don't have to do this," Dan said.

"He's right," Johann said. "You don't have to go."

I stepped back to stand beside my father and wiped at the tears on my face. "I wish things were different. I have to go. I have to obey my king."

"We are your kings. You pledged yourself to us," Emrys reminded me.

"I will return," I told them. "But, please, don't hold your breath."

Dad set his hand on my shoulder and Brayden backed up until he was close enough for Dad to set his other hand on his shoulder. "Thank you for taking care of my daughter in my absence," he said and then the room filled with the men I loved most in the world vanished.

CHAPTER 5

The room Dad teleported us to looked nothing like Atlantis. The curtains were cheap, flimsy material, definitely hotel room quality.

"We're just picking up our things," Brayden said.

All four of my mates were freaking out. Anger, fear, and sadness filtered through the bond in a jumble of emotions. I sent as much love and calmness as I could back to them.

I didn't like this situation either, but Dad was much stronger than they knew. He could turn them all against each other. I wouldn't let that happen.

"What am I expected to do when I return? I don't know anything about sirens or our society," I said, clenching my hands into fists. I wanted to hit something.

"Brayden will be teaching you on our journey," Dad answered and strode to his luggage. "We must take the train and then a boat—"

"And then the Kraken will pick us up," I finished for him. "I remember that much." *Now.*

My entire life had been a lie. Human? I wasn't human at all.

I realized Dad hadn't answered my question. It seemed like they were trying really hard to keep me in the dark.

"Let's go," Dad ordered us.

Obediently, I followed him with Brayden right behind me. At the reception desk, the receptionist bowed and said, "Safe travels, King Dalton."

He nodded once, and we left the hotel. Why hadn't his arrival been headline news?

Outside the hotel, the media rushed us.

"King Dalton! What are your plans in Jinla?" one reporter asked.

"I came to get my daughter. My business with Jinla is now complete," he answered.

"Princess Jolie, what are you doing here?"

"Are you his daughter?"

"Aren't you human?"

"Where are your guards? The Princes?"

"Are you leaving?"

"Princess Jolie?"

"Princess Jolie is unavailable for comment," Brayden said sweetly. A wave of power washed over the media members and immediately, they silenced with huge smiles on their faces.

Sirens were the worst manipulators in the world. They were also excellent liars, one of the many reasons I wasn't looking forward to returning.

"Is there a queen?" I asked Brayden softly.

He shook his head. "You're the only heir."

I hadn't asked about heirs, but that was helpful information to have.

A black SUV pulled up to the curb and before the doors opened, I smelled the passengers.

I ran forward and held my hands up to my dad. "Let me handle this."

His brows furrowed, and he looked around, unsure what I was talking about.

The SUVs driver's side and passenger doors opened, letting Martin and Ezio out.

"Jo," Martin growled and stalked towards me.

Brayden stepped closer, but I pushed him back with a hand to his chest. "Stay out of this," I ordered him.

Ezio and Martin towered over me.

"What is going on?" Martin demanded.

"My memories were sealed," I explained. "I didn't know who I was until he unlocked them just a bit ago."

"Start from the beginning," Martin ordered me.

Ezio stood silently, glaring at Brayden.

"I'm not human. I'm a siren. I'm actually Princess of the Sirens, but I'm a null. Basically, I don't have any siren abilities, so essentially, I'm human. The king, my dad, the guy over there..." I pointed, and

Martin glanced before looking back at me. "...banished me from Atlantis because I was a null. They put me with a human family to be raised. Now he's decided he needs me back."

"You didn't know any of this?" Ezio asked, hard eyes filled with fire stared into mine.

"No, I swear."

His eyes softened a moment, then he returned to glaring at Brayden. I was surprised Brayden hadn't spontaneously combusted into flames from the fire in his glare. I knew Ezio would never harm me and even I moved a step away from him.

"And you're just going? You're leaving your mates behind?" Martin snapped.

"I'm saving them," I growled. "If Dad wants to, he could turn this entire city against each other. I won't be gone forever. I'll be back as soon as I can."

"You won't survive long without your mates. You'll go mad," Martin said. "What's your plan?"

"I have to go to Atlantis, find out what's going on, and then fix it so I can come back home."

"Let me come with you," Ezio whispered, moving so close, our arms touched. "Please, let me come to ensure you're safe."

"Princess Jolie will be perfectly safe," Brayden said and reached towards me.

In less time than it took to blink, both Ezio and Martin had shifted into warrior forms and pushed me behind them. Brayden had his trident out and aimed at Ezio.

"Enough!" I snapped. I shoved Ezio and Martin back and exhaled loudly, trying to release some of the nervousness building. "Please, just trust me. I can't let you get hurt. Please keep the princes safe while I'm gone. And, don't even think about coming after me. You won't be able to find me."

"This is insane," Martin growled and reverted back to his human form.

I hugged him and whispered, "I'll be back. I promise."

Ezio pulled me into a hug. "Please, take me with you."

I shook my head. "They won't let me. The guy with the trident is my personal guard. Plus, I can use my mates' powers still. I'm not defenseless. They have no idea what I can do, so I've got the upper hand."

He inhaled at my neck and I pet his head. "'Come home or I'll boil the sea to find you,'" Ezio said. I looked up and he whispered, "My prince asked me to tell you that."

"Tell him to give me three months," I whispered.

"You have one month, max," Martin whispered. "You go any longer than that away from them and you will all go mad. The last thing we need is those four going mad. It will be worse than when your bonds were cut. Insanity is much harder to cure."

I hugged them each again and returned to my dad who looked irritated.

"Are you done now? Can we go?" Dad asked.

I glared at him. "You're the one who showed up unannounced and is yanking me out of my life. Giving me ten minutes isn't much to ask."

He opened the door of a taxi and waved me in. "After you, Your Highness."

Ignoring his jab, I climbed into the taxi and buckled my belt. Ezio and Martin hadn't gotten into the SUV yet. Martin was on the phone, while Ezio stared at Brayden who also hadn't turned away yet.

"You let anything happen to her and I'll tear your head off," Ezio told him.

"Don't threaten me, dog," Brayden snapped.

"I'm not threatening you. I'm telling you. If you let anything happen to her, I will tear your head off of your body," Ezio said calmly.

"You're in love with her," Brayden realized.

"She's my princess," Ezio growled. "And I will do anything to keep her safe. You should just let me come with you."

Brayden laughed. "Not going to happen."

"Then make sure she stays safe," Ezio said and turned away, showing Brayden his back, and getting into the SUV.

Martin glared at Brayden and got into the driver's seat.

"You've got some interesting friends," Dad commented.

I decided letting him know they were my ex-boyfriends wasn't necessary at the moment, so I said nothing. Brayden finally got his luggage into the trunk and climbed in the front seat.

"What am I expected to do while I'm back?" I asked Dad, since he was stuck in the backseat of the car with me.

"You're expected to be our princess," he said as though that answered anything.

"What does a siren princess do?" I asked.

"Brayden will explain all of that," he grumbled and faced out the window.

I sighed and leaned my head back against the seat. This was ridiculous. If Martin was right, I only had one month to get this figured out. Brayden was my only hope in finding out what was going on.

He had said we were best friends, but I didn't remember anyone named Brayden. There were only a few people I interacted with before they banished me. I needed to get him on my side, but explain there was no way in hell he was going to become my mate.

The taxi dropped us off at the train station and I wasn't surprised to find yet another group waiting for me. I sighed and said, "Two minutes."

"Aren't you popular?" Brayden growled.

"I'm Princess of the Four Clans," I told him. "Yes, I am popular."

"Were," Dad said. "You *were* their princess."

"No, I still am," I told him and climbed out of the car.

The train station was noisy and there were hundreds of people getting on and off trains. Standing to one side were Declan and Kylan, dragon twins I had dated when I was younger.

"What are you two doing here?" I asked as I approached.

"Who do we have to kill?" Declan asked, looking over my head. His icy killer gaze was scaring people and they gave the twins a wide berth.

"You're not killing anyone," I told him and sighed. This was one of the issues of dating such powerful and bloodthirsty beings. "I have to do this. Why do I have to keep repeating myself?"

"You don't have to do this," Declan said.

"We can take you away right now," Kylan said.

"No, you can't. You would shift and then they'd use their powers to make you attack each other or innocent bystanders. Look, while I'm gone you guys need to get together, all four clans, and do research on sirens. And, keep my mates out of trouble. I'm not weak. I'm not human. Plus, they aren't kidnapping me. This is my biological dad and there's something going on that they need me to help them with. I don't know what it is, but I have to see if I can help them."

"How do you know they need your help?" Kylan asked.

"I just do. Please, trust me."

"Princess," Brayden called. "It's time to go."

"That the asshole who thinks you're going to take him as a mate?" Declan growled, smoke seeping out of his nostrils.

Did everyone know what had happened?

"Yes, but I have no intention of taking anymore mates," I said adamantly.

"Make sure he knows that," Kylan said.

"Hugs and then I've got to go," I told them.

"We'll find you if we need to," Declan promised.

After hugging them, I went to Brayden and followed him onto the train. Getting on the train made me remember my last train trip and the Summit.

"Why aren't you part of the Summit?" I asked Dad as I sat beside him in an empty train car.

He didn't respond.

Pulling out my phone, I sent a quick message to the guys. Atlantis likely didn't get cell reception.

Me: I love you. I'll get this handled as fast as I can. I know you're not happy, I'm not either, but I'm doing this to protect Jinla. Sirens are powerful manipulators and Dad is the strongest siren alive. Or, at least he was before I was banished. I'm the only heir and I have a feeling that's part of why they are bringing me back. I'm safe. I'm still connected to you. I can still use your powers. Please, try to relax. I will come back to you.

Immediately, I got responses.

Rhys: I love you.

Deryn: Tell Trident Douchebag I'll cut him to pieces if he touches you.

Fox: I miss you already.

Nico: I love you, my queen.

Deryn: Love you, baby.

I put my phone in my jacket pocket and closed my eyes with a sigh. Couldn't my life be calm for just a few months?

"Here," Brayden said.

I opened my eyes and accepted the worn leather book he held out to me. There was no title or author name.

"It's basic information on sirens," he said.

I opened it and found handwritten pages inside.

"Did you write this?" I asked.

He nodded. "I knew you would need it, when you finally returned."

His cheeks had a slight pink tint to them and his eyes were focused on his hands.

"Thank you," I said and opened it. I thumbed through the pages, reading snippets, and was surprised to find drawings of animals, plants, and maps of Atlantis.

Dad and Brayden talked, but I tuned them out as I read. There was so much information, but none of it answered the big question.

Dad moved to the back of the train car to take a phone call, leaving me and Brayden alone.

Brayden tilted his head as he looked at me. "You really don't remember me, do you?"

"Sorry," I said and shrugged. "Even with my memories back, I don't remember."

"You and I have been betrothed since we were born. I was the only one allowed to play with you."

"I'm sure our betrothal ended when I was banished, so why didn't you find someone else?" I asked.

"Your banishment was a huge shock to me. No one told me until you were already gone. Even now, I don't understand why they did it. Okay, I do, but—"

"You do?" I asked, interrupting him.

He nodded. "Being a null means, other sirens can manipulate you. You wouldn't be a good queen because others could control you."

That did make sense, but it didn't make it hurt any less.

"Part of me always believed you would be back. Or maybe hoped is the better word. So, I never found a mate."

"Well, now you're free to," I told him with a warm smile.

He scowled.

"Brayden, get us something to eat," Dad ordered him, interrupting Brayden before he could say anything in response.

Brayden left, and Dad faced me with an intense expression. "Who are your mates?"

"The Four Princes of Jinla. Rhys of the dragons, Foxfire of the elves, Nico of the mages, and Deryn of the wolves."

"Four?" he asked. He looked at my chest in silence and it made me uncomfortable. "What are the other four bonds?"

How could he see them?

"I'm their queen," I explained.

His eyes widened. "Which came first?"

"What?"

"Which bond was formed first?"

"Well, technically I joined their warrior bond first since I'm hum... wait. I'm not human, though. How come I joined their warrior's bond?"

"You joined their warrior's bond, then they made you their queen, and then you mated?" he asked.

I nodded.

"Do you have issues with the four of them being alphas? With them fighting?"

"No. They're all best friends."

He scowled. "What about interactions with other alphas?"

"Huh?" *What was he asking all these questions for?*

"Have other alphas been affected by you?" he asked in a near shout.

"Well, the kings said I make them feel calm, peaceful. That I'm easy to be around," I admitted, trying not to cringe back from his intense gaze.

I had a feeling I knew where this was going, and I did not like it. Not one bit.

Brayden came back with food and Dad said, "Get mad."

Brayden's brows furrowed, then his eyes blazed and his fists clenched. "Why?" he demanded.

Dad turned to me. "Calm him down."

"Dad, I'm a null. Even if I wasn't, you're too powerful for me to defeat."

He just waited expectantly.

"I don't even know what I am supposed to do," I grumbled. Facing Brayden, I ordered, "Calm down."

He scoffed and rolled his eyes at me.

Now, I was mad.

"Calm down!" I snapped.

Brayden's fists opened, and he staggered a step back.

"Try to manipulate me," Dad said.

No, this couldn't be happening!

"This is probably from my elf mate. He can calm people down," I explained.

"Don't calm me then," Dad said.

"King Dalton," Brayden snapped.

"Oh, right. Sorry," Dad said and snapped his fingers, releasing the anger I hadn't been able to.

Brayden sat down and sighed. "That was interesting."

"Get mad," I ordered Dad. Immediately, I knew it wouldn't work.

"You're not really trying," he growled. "Plus, emotions are easier to manipulate if you channel the emotion from yourself."

I clenched my teeth and said, "Anger!"

Dad's body tensed, and he took a deep breath before saying, "Jolie, you're not a null. You're an empath. You control emotions."

I wasn't a null. I wasn't human. I wasn't anything I thought I had been. Everything was so out of control.

"I don't understand," I whispered. "You banished me because I'm a null. But, now you're saying I'm not a null?"

He sighed. "I was a stupid man and I know there's nothing I could do to make up for what I've done. We tested you extensively and you registered as a null. Perhaps your life experiences unlocked your abilities."

"Well, I've had my fair share of traumatic experiences," I grumbled and folded my arms across my chest.

"Why don't you tell me about your past?" Dad suggested.

We did have a long trip ahead of us. "Fine, but you're getting the abridged version," I mumbled.

An hour later, both Dad and Brayden stared in silence at me, Brayden's mouth agape.

"And that was when you kidnapped me," I said, bringing my story to a close.

"I did not kidnap you," Dad snapped.

"You took me against my will. I didn't want to leave my mates, but I knew you would hurt them to get me to comply. If you aren't kidnapping me, then let me go back to them," I said and met his glare.

"You need to come home," Dad said. "End of discussion."

"Why? You keep skirting the issue. Why are you bringing me home now? You show up out of the blue and take me away. You didn't know I was an empath when you grabbed me. So, why?"

"I don't have to explain myself to you," Dad snarled. "You are my daughter, heir to the siren throne. You need to be in our kingdom, not playing around in Jinla."

"I'm not *playing around*. I have a life there. I have friends. I have a job. I have mates," I snapped back.

"None of that matters. You are princess. You are coming home!" Dad yelled.

"If you would just tell me what it is that's causing you trouble, I could help you come up with a plan before we get back to Atlantis," I said softly, trying to diffuse the tension.

Dad stood and left the train car without another word.

"I'm guessing you aren't going to clue me in either?" I asked Brayden.

Brayden went after Dad.

I sighed and sat down. An empath? I was a fucking empath.

How would the guys take this?

Had I manipulated them? Had that been why they fell so fast for me? Had I manipulated myself? Was that even possible?

I grabbed some of the food and ate in the silence.

Should I call the guys and tell them what I'd found out? How would they react? Would they think I had been lying? Would they treat me differently?

I put my head in my hands and sighed. What was I going to do?

My cell phone rang, and I knew it was the guys before I took it out of my jacket.

Putting on a smile, I answered the video call.

"Hey," I said.

All four came into view, the phone set up in the center of Rhys's kitchen table and the guys lined up in chairs, so I could see them in the phone's field of view.

"What's going on?" Rhys asked, his brows furrowed.

"Um..." I replied and bit my lip.

I needed to tell them.

"I really wish we weren't apart," I whispered and fought against a wave of sadness and loneliness. Tears sprang to my eyes and I blinked them away.

"Jolie," Fox whispered. "Talk to us."

The four of them looked amazing, wearing tank tops and sweatpants. Had they been training? Or working off their frustration from me leaving them?

"My dad just told me I'm not a null," I said, my breathing becoming erratic.

Panic attack. I was having a panic attack. There was no way to stop it, so I just needed to spit out my story.

"I'm not a null. I'm an empath. He thinks I unlocked my powers at some point after one of my traumatic life events. He asked about how our bonds were formed and I think he believes I may have unconsciously manipulated you."

Tears streamed down my face and I forced myself to look at them, so I could see their reactions.

"I didn't mean to manipulate you if I did. I swear. I didn't know about any of this. Even my dad thought I was a null until just a few minutes ago. If I am an empath, I may have manipulated you without realizing it."

"Baby," Deryn whispered.

They didn't look mad. They didn't look upset.

"Baby, you did not manipulate us into loving you. No empath is capable of making someone love them. You may have made us calm down or made us happy, but those just made us fall for you faster," Deryn said.

"You just said I could have made you fall faster," I pointed out, wiping my face with one hand, while the other held the phone.

"You didn't make us fall for you. You just showed us who you are. You showed us how amazing you are," Fox said.

"We aren't in love with you because you used your powers on us," Nico said. "Promise."

"You're sure?" I asked.

All four nodded.

"Have you figured anything else out?" Rhys asked.

I shook my head.

"You have one month," Fox said. "We won't be able to last longer than that."

"I know," I whispered. "Martin told me."

The train door opened.

"I have to go," I whispered.

"Love you," the four of them said.

I stared at my four mates, memorizing the scene to help me get through the next month, and said, "I love you, too."

Before I hung up the phone, I noticed them all glaring at something behind me.

Brayden plopped down beside me and asked, "What did they want so soon?"

"Nothing," I whispered and closed my eyes.

Silence descended, the only sounds coming from the train as it moved along the tracks.

Turning slightly in my seat, I angled myself so Dad and Brayden couldn't see my phone.

Me: Nico, do some research on spells or charms to protect from sirens and empaths.

Nico: Already on it.

Me: Anyway you'd all wait to tell your dads?

Deryn: Too late.
Rhys: Dad said it explains a lot of things.
Me : (
Deryn: <3
Me: Brayden wrote a book with info about sirens. I'm going to try to get some screenshots to you guys.
Rhys: Who's Brayden?
Me: Trident Douche.
Deryn: hehe :)
Rhys: lol
Fox: :O :O :O
Nico: smh
Me: Promise you're going to stay out of trouble?
Rhys: Where's the fun in that?
Deryn: We need distractions right now.
Rhys: You're the one who needs to promise to stay out of trouble.
Me: I never seek out trouble.
Fox: No, but it always finds you.
Me: Why was Ezio in Jinla?
Deryn: He came to talk to my dad about something
Me: What?
*Deryn: *shrugs**

Dad and Brayden moved to a pair of seats in the back of the train car.

Perfect.

I quickly snapped pictures of all the important pages in the book and some less important ones, then sent them through the group chat. I skimmed the book for anything else that seemed important.

Royal Mating

That looked important.

Royals must only mate with royals of other clans. Although it is permitted to have multiple mates, it is strongly encouraged to have a single mate only. Should the heir to the throne wish to have multiple mates, all must pass The Gauntlet. Only those who pass The Gauntlet and prove their worthiness may mate with an heir.*
**The Gauntlet is a four-event tournament usually involving a race, survival challenge, quest, and loyalty test.*

Me: Guys, look...

I sent them a picture of the page and waited for their responses.

Nico: We're already your mates. It doesn't seem logical to put us through this.

Fox: Have they mentioned it?

Deryn: Sounds fun.

Rhys: We should make our own if they don't want us to do it.

Me: SMH. They haven't said anything, but it makes me nervous.

Nico sent me a message directly, instead of through the group chat.

Nico: Send each page of the book in order directly to me. I'll read through it.

Me: We're almost to the ocean. Once there, the Kraken comes, and I won't be able to contact you.

Nico: Do it quickly then. :)

I obeyed, snapping the pictures as fast as I could and sent them to Nico. I got to the last handwritten page and froze with my finger hovering above the picture button on my phone. It was a note from Brayden to me.

Jolie, I don't know if I'll ever see you again, but if I do, please don't deny me. Please take me as your mate. Things aren't as they seem. I'll explain in private if we ever meet. Your father is ill and you're our only hope. ~B

I snapped the pic and sent to Nico with the caption: *WTF?*

Nico: Stay safe, my queen. Keep your eyes and ears open.

Me, to the group: Love you all

What could this mean? Dad ill? What kind of illness? And, how the heck could I do anything for them?

A minute later, Nico messaged me again.

Nico: Kraken? What happens with the Kraken?

CHAPTER 6

The train stopped and after grabbing the bags, we filtered out of the train with the other passengers. There were a lot of vendors along the pathways, something common in port towns. The scent of sea water was incredibly strong and it brought back a surge of memories.

I closed my eyes and let the memories wash over me.

"Almost home," Brayden whispered in my ear.

"Farther than ever from home," I countered and opened my eyes.

He sighed and continued after Dad. I followed close behind, watching the various people walking around. I stopped at a merchant with bread and purchased two rolls.

"Thank you, ma'am," the merchant said.

"Princess, you should have asked me to purchase it for you," Brayden chastised me.

"I'm perfectly capable of purchasing my own items and taking care of myself," I growled at him and ate half of my roll in one bite.

A boat with the siren royal crest sat at the docks, and I headed for it. The boat was small, since all it had to do was carry us past the next island and out to meet the Kraken.

Three men stood at attention when Dad stepped up to the boat and he waved his hand to dismiss them. They returned to their preparations, but froze when they saw me with Brayden. They all bowed to me.

"Back to work," Brayden ordered while glaring at them until they stopped peering at me.

They obeyed, and Brayden helped me get onto the boat. He led me to a bench on the deck and we sat down.

"How did your mates feel knowing you most likely manipulated them?" Brayden asked, his eyes trained in the distance.

"I didn't manipulate them," I spat. "And, they all agreed that even if I had, it wasn't my fault. Especially, since I thought I was human the whole time."

"What was it like?" he asked, his gaze finally meeting mine.

"What?" I asked, furrowing my brow.

"Being human."

My frown deepened. Because of the curse I had before, it seemed as if trouble had followed me at every turn. That had only changed a little since I met my mates. "Terrifying most of the time, since I was in danger so often."

"When we get back, I'll help you get caught up on current affairs," he said.

I glanced at him and found him staring out at the ocean again. Was this his way of telling me he would answer the questions I had from reading the book?

"Let's go," Dad ordered the crew.

Before we were out of range, I sent one last, "I love you," text to the guys, then watched the men scurrying around the boat.

The boat moved away from the dock and out to sea. It had been so long since I last visited this area of the world. I missed the ocean.

Out in the open waters of the ocean, I felt small and insignificant. It was a reminder that more important things lay out in the world. Seagulls called overhead, and they swooped down as I threw pieces of the leftover roll I didn't finish. My father frowned when I giggled.

We passed the island and people on the beaches waved at us, recognizing our seal. It was nice to see the siren's reputation was still good amongst the people.

Five miles away from the island, the boat came to a stop.

Butterflies fluttered in my stomach. I leapt to my feet and raced to the bow, hands gripping the railing as I waited. The water before us churned and then a huge head surfaced, followed by giant tentacles and eyes. I snapped a picture with my phone, then turned it off. Even with my phone off, I still had our bonds, which relaxed me a bit.

The Kraken looked us over, then his eye stopped on me. He shrieked and one of his tentacles shot out and wrapped around me.

Brayden and the other men drew their weapons, but I shouted, "Stop!"

The men stopped as did the Kraken, holding me in front of one of his eyes, dangling above the ocean.

"He's not going to hurt me," I told Brayden.

"Watch," Dad whispered to him.

I turned back to the Kraken and smiled. "Hello, Pookie."

The Kraken screeched again and pulled me to his head. I lay atop his head and pet him, his skin slick and slimy. Most found it repulsive, but it didn't disgust me. The Kraken blew bubbles in the water and closed his eyes in contentment.

"Pookie?" Brayden asked.

"I let her name him," Dad explained. "I did not think about the fact she was a young girl and that would influence her name choice."

"Pookie, are you going to take us to Atlantis?" I asked, despite already knowing the answer.

Pookie screeched and thrashed his tentacles, making the boat rock.

"Easy," I chastised him.

Dad cleared his throat and Pookie quickly wrapped his tentacles around Dad and Brayden, both holding their luggage in one hand.

Pookie piled us atop his head, then bright light surrounded us, and he dove beneath the water. The light around us acted as a shield, providing us air to breathe and kept the water out.

Down we plunged, the sea animals rushing to flee as Pookie descended. I stared up, watching the sunlight fade until all that remained was Pookie's light. Down and down we went, the temperature dropped as we did, and I wrapped my arms around myself a moment before remembering to use my dragon powers to heat my body up.

"Your eyes!" Brayden gasped.

I looked at him and smiled. "My dragon mate's powers. I can do many things a normal siren can't."

"Can you shift?" Dad asked.

I shrugged and looked away from them, watching as a tiny speck of light below us grew brighter and bigger. My ears popped. This trench was the deepest in the world and protected by Pookie.

If the cold, lack of oxygen, and pressure of the depths didn't kill you, Pookie would.

Miles we traveled down until the beacon I had seen came into our line of sight. Pookie swam farther down and then into a huge cave. Lava flowed at the bottom of the cave, hardening when it got to the end of the line. I stopped using my dragon powers since it was warm enough now. Not far from here was a giant volcano and this was one of a couple offshoots for the excess lava that kept it from erupting.

A light ahead snagged my attention away from the lava. A hole in the cave had a silver glow surrounding it. It was the portal to Atlantis.

Pookie stopped and the light moved off his head and to the cave floor. I waved to Pookie, then stepped through the portal between Dad and Brayden.

Atlantis had been a bustling city with vibrant colors of plants, grasses, and animals. I had spent hours each day collecting flowers in every hue of the rainbow.

The Atlantis before me now was not what I remembered. It was like they had thrown a monochrome blanket over everything. No flowers grew. The grass was gone and only dirt remained. A few animals skittered about, but at least three-fourths less than my last visit.

I covered my mouth to hold back my gasp, and Brayden looked at me with knowing eyes. Was this what he meant? It did look sick.

Two guards in royal uniforms, deep blue with silver swirls on the shoulder to signify rank, stepped forward and bowed.

"Welcome back, Your Majesty," the guard on the left said. He had three swirls, indicating his rank as Captain of the guards.

"Thank you, Captain. Any news to report?" Dad asked and headed down the dirt path towards our castle. Even the castle looked sickly.

The Captain glanced at me, then stood and followed just behind Dad. "None, Your Majesty."

"Exactly what I wanted to hear," Dad replied.

The second guard fell into step behind Brayden. He looked familiar, but I couldn't pull the memory out and it was too rude to just stare at him. I was certain I knew him, though. Why wasn't the memory there? Dad had given me my memories back.

We stepped into the castle and I had to stop, more memories flooded my mind so quickly, that I couldn't see the present.

Within the memories, I saw times where I played with a young version of Brayden, as well as the guard beside me, Sam.

"Princess?" Sam asked.

"Jolie," Brayden whispered and set his hand on my forearm.

The memories faded, and I gasped for air. Had I been holding my breath?

"I'm okay," I whispered. "Memories overwhelmed me a moment."

Sam's eyes flashed with anger as he looked at Brayden's hand on me, then he turned away to hide it.

"Let's get you to your room," Brayden said and removed his hand.

Dad and the Captain had disappeared into the castle, likely going to Dad's chambers.

Trailing my fingertips along the walls, I took in my home. It was so much more depressing than it had been.

"What happened?" I asked softly.

"Let's get you to your room first," Brayden said.

I turned to Sam. "Sam, where are all the sirens?"

Both he and Brayden tensed, and Brayden spun around to face us. "How do you know his name?"

"He was in the palace a lot and we talked while waiting for our dads to finish meetings," I said.

It wasn't a lie, we had done that, but we had also spent much more time together aside from that. I felt like Brayden couldn't know that for some reason, though. He had said he was the only child *allowed* to play with me.

Brayden stared at Sam, but Sam just stared back with a bored expression. Brayden resumed walking.

"The others don't visit the royal grounds much anymore," Sam said now that Brayden had turned away.

"The merchants don't come?" I asked in disbelief.

Sam shook his head.

"Where are they?" I asked.

"Shelnam," Sam answered.

Shelnam was the town where all their houses were. It made sense to stay there if they didn't want to be in such a drab area. I was going to need to make a trip out there soon, to talk to the people.

Brayden stopped in front of my door. "Your quarters, just as you left them."

He was right, they looked just like they had before I'd been banished. Rainbow colored walls, unicorn bedspread, pink furniture, and stuffed animals everywhere.

"You're dismissed," Brayden told Sam.

Sam looked at me and I nodded once. "You can guard my door," I told him. Sam bowed, then took up a position on the wall opposite my door.

Brayden shut the door, and I made a privacy shield that would keep our conversation private. Brayden's eyes widened at the emergence of the silvery bubble.

"No one will be able to hear us now," I advised him. "Spill, all of it."

He sighed and leaned against the closed door. "Your father is ill. He's been battling it since you left and we think your presence might help cure him."

"Ill how?"

"Dementia," he said.

I plopped on my butt onto the bed and gaped at him. Normally, dementia was a human-only issue, but if it affected an Other, things could get very bad. A siren being affected by it was terrifying. He could use his powers on people without understanding what he was doing. Someone with low level powers wasn't an issue, but my father could put the world under a spell without realizing what he was doing.

"How bad is it?" I asked.

He ran a hand through his hair and sighed. "I've been able to keep him from doing anything too serious, but there have been a few close calls. It's getting progressively worse each week for the past two months. If we can't stop it, the Elders are considering taking extreme measures."

They would have to kill him. Nothing else would work.

"What can I do?"

"Spend time with him, just be happy and by his side. You're our last hope."

"Does he know all of this?"

Brayden nodded. "Yes. He's the one who suggested that bringing you home might help."

Something about that statement didn't ring true.

Maybe Dad wanted to spend his final days with me as his only family left alive. Or, maybe Brayden was lying.

"Why is everything so ugly and cold? Why don't the people come here anymore?"

Even if he had a few episodes, it didn't explain all of this.

"A month after you left, the dementia hit hard. He demanded to know where you were and killed a guard who said you were gone.

During a lucid moment, he ordered all the colors destroyed and forbid the merchants from coming on the royal grounds."

"Why?"

"They reminded him of you."

"If you had just told me this, I would have come."

"But you would have brought your mates."

"So?"

"We're trying to keep King Dalton as calm as possible. Having strangers might set him off."

"You're hiding something," I said, realizing it just before I said it.

"I understand that you don't want any other mates, but I think it would be best if we let your father continue under the assumption we are courting."

"I'm not taking any more mates," I said adamantly. I didn't care how sick my father was, I wouldn't take on another mate.

"You and I both understand that, but let's keep it between us."

Part of what he said made sense, but I got the feeling he still held information back from me. I couldn't pinpoint what it was about him, but I didn't trust him.

"Why didn't you come get me sooner?" I asked. "If this started right after I left, you could have gotten me back right away. It's been over twenty fucking years."

"We hoped with time, it would improve. We were wrong, but he had some periods of lucidity that gave us hope. Plus, we couldn't find you. It wasn't until the newspaper with your picture announcing your bonding that we located you as living in Jinla."

"Dad didn't know about my bonds when you got to me," I pointed out.

"He just forgot," he said, truthfully.

"How long are they giving him before they make their decision to kill him?"

"Two weeks," he replied softly.

"Weeks! That's not enough time for me to do anything."

"It's all we have."

I pulled my knees up to my chest and hugged them. Two weeks to try to cure my father's dementia. A father I hadn't seen in over twenty years. I popped our shield and sighed.

"I need someone to teach me how to use my powers. Find someone, today," I ordered him.

He scowled, but bowed and left the room. I waited three minutes past the time he had left before opening my door and peeking outside.

Sam stood on the opposite wall still. His lips turned up in a smirk for just a moment before he turned serious again.

"Get in here," I whispered and held the door open.

He walked in, scowling. "How can I—"

I threw my arms around his shoulders and hugged him. He was a lot bigger than he had been at nine, but he still had the same mischievous gleam in his eyes.

He hugged me back and the tension melted from him. "Jo," he whispered.

I held my finger up, locked the door, then put a privacy shield around us.

"What the fuck is going on, Sam? Give it to me straight."

"You're in trouble, Jo. We're all in trouble," he said.

I could hear the dramatic music in my head and shook it to rid myself of the ridiculousness.

"Spill," I ordered him. "No one can hear us now."

He leaned against my bright pink dresser with his hip and said, "I need to ask something first."

"Fine," I sighed.

"Are you going to mate with Brayden?"

"No, but that stays between us for now. He said we should let Dad keep thinking we are courting."

Sam scoffed and rolled his eyes. "I bet he did."

"Sam," I growled.

He tensed. "Your eyes changed color."

I rubbed my face and sat down on the rainbow rug beneath my feet. Sam did the same. "I have four mates. One wolf, one dragon, one mage, and one elf. I have access to their powers. When I'm mad, my eyes shift sometimes."

"Alphas?" he asked.

"Yes."

He nodded. "You wouldn't be able to settle for less."

"What?"

"You're an alpha amongst the sirens. So, you would need alphas as mates, too."

"I answered your question," I reminded him.

"I don't have any proof for what I'm about to say, but I know it's true. Brayden has some type of magic, not siren based. Mage most likely. He is using powers to control King Dalton. He wants to take over Atlantis and he wants you as his mate."

"Why do you think he is controlling Dad?"

"The night before you were banished, King Dalton told the guards to prepare Brayden's things to be removed from the castle. I don't know where he was going to send him, since both of his parents had died the year before and Brayden was only ten at that time. Brayden had a long discussion with King Dalton in the king's chambers, just the two of them. Hours later, King Dalton came out and said to move Brayden to a room closer to him and you were banished the next morning. Brayden hasn't left his side since. King Dalton has lucid moments and I've been privy to them a few times. It's like he comes out of a spell. It's not like dementia."

"Why haven't you told anyone?" I demanded.

"With no proof, I would only endanger my position and then I wouldn't be able to keep an eye on the king."

"Do you know what he has planned?"

If we knew his plan, we could find a way to counter it.

"No. I think he plans to use your father to try to force your hand at mating. He seemed to be planning to have the king killed. I was able to convince the Elders to search for you, finally."

"It was your idea?"

He nodded. "I hoped you might break the spell."

"Why do you think Brayden is after me if you're the reason I'm here?"

"Because once he found out, he made arrangements for The Gauntlet to be prepared for him to participate."

"When?"

"I don't know."

"I won't take him as a mate. What can I do? Can I go to the Elders?"

"Siren law is clear, to be the Princess's mate, they must pass The Gauntlet."

"My mates are in Jinla," I said, my heart beginning to pound. What could I do?

"If they don't pass—"

"Take me to the Elders. I'll see if I can talk sense into them. I understand the law, but I'm clearly an exception since I was banished."

"I didn't think you'd recognize me," Sam admitted, changing the subject.

I smiled. "How could I not recognize my best friend?" My smile faded, and I said, "Brayden told me he was the only one allowed to play with me and that we were best friends."

Sam's expression grew fierce. "Glad your memories came back"

"That's why I believe you," I whispered. "I didn't get all my memories back from Dad and Brayden was lying to me. The rest of my memories came back when I stepped into the castle with you."

His eyebrows furrowed. "This is not good. No. He's more powerful than I thought if he could make King Dalton do that."

I agreed. "Sam, I need to get a message to my mates."

CHAPTER 7

"The Gauntlet will go forward as planned," one of the three Elders said.

Brayden stood on my right. He'd seen me heading out of the castle with Sam and had followed us. Now, I saw a smirk on one corner of his mouth.

"Elders, I already have mates. They won the Summit Tournament for my hand—"

"Then they should have no problem winning another," another Elder said.

My hands clenched into fists at my side. "I was banished. I should be free from these—"

"You are the Princess of the Sirens. And, you are not above the law."

"At least wait until I'm able to get them here so they can participate," I begged.

"You have two weeks until the Gauntlet," the last Elder said.

"Sirs, you're going to allow four alphas to come to Atlantis when the king is in such low health?" Brayden asked, taking a step forward.

"My father will be fine. My mates will cause no trouble," I promised.

"Tamed them?" Brayden asked and smiled.

"They aren't the ones who need tamed," I muttered and turned away, remembering I wasn't supposed to alienate Brayden. I turned back with a smile and said, "Please, Brayden. Help me out? That's what best friends do, right?"

His eyes sparkled and he smiled.

Hook. Line. Sinker.

"Okay," he agreed. "As a favor to my best friend."

I smiled wide, radiating happiness. I watched in disbelief as it spread throughout the room until everyone was smiling.

Whoops.

"I'll get a message to your mates," Brayden said with a warm smile that I would have believed was genuine, had I not smelled his lie. He had no idea I could smell lies.

I smiled back and said, "Thank you." Before I could lose my composure, I turned, and Sam fell into step beside me as we walked back towards my room.

"Jolie," Brayden called.

I stopped and turned to him, my smile back in place. "Yes?"

"Will you join me for dinner tonight?" he asked.

"I planned to eat with Dad," I said honestly.

"Ah, well another night then," he said.

I nodded. "For sure."

His smile warmed at that and he turned away.

"I want to see Dad," I told Sam.

"He's in his chambers," Sam said and pushed open the door to the castle.

I put the privacy shield around us as we walked down the hallway. "He isn't going to send word to my mates. I really need you to do it. Can you? Can you get word to them without Brayden finding out? I don't want you to risk yourself."

He smiled and said, "I haven't survived here the past twenty-three years without you just by my good looks."

I laughed and shook my head. "You haven't changed one bit."

He flexed one of his arms. "I've gotten more muscular. "

"I meant your ego," I scoffed.

"Is there anything you'd like me to add to my letter?" he asked.

"Tell them not to hurt the Kraken and to prepare for fun after all."

"They'll know what that means?" he asked.

I nodded. "They will."

We stopped at Dad's door, and I dropped the shield. "I'll leave you to your time with your father," Sam said and walked back down the hallway.

I knocked on the door, Dad said, "Enter."

I opened the door and peeked my head inside. Dad sat at his desk, looking at some papers there.

"Hey," I said cheerfully and smiled. I locked the door behind me, slid my foot along the doorway to seal it with a ward, then walked to the chair in front of his desk and sat.

He looked up and smiled. "Jolie, I'm happy to see you."

"I thought we could eat dinner together," I explained.

He stood, his posture suddenly rigid. "I don't have time." His hands moved along the top of his desk while he kept his eyes locked with mine.

What was he doing?

His fingers found paper and pen and he wrote something with his eyes still fixed on me. I peeked over and it took all my control not to gasp.

Kill him.

Stepping around the desk, I grabbed the paper as I stood before him, hiding it in my hand. I hugged him and said, "I understand." I spun, the crumpled paper in my hand, and marched out of his chambers.

I would kill Brayden, but first, I needed to learn how to control my powers. The Captain, whose name I still hadn't gotten, approached. His stride was confident and proud as he moved down the hallways of the castle. I didn't remember him from my childhood, which bothered me. Was he a plant by Brayden?

He bowed to me. "Princess Jolie. Can I help you?"

"What's your name?" I asked.

"Stevens."

"Captain Stevens, I'd like to go to Shelnam. Can you arrange transportation?"

His brows furrowed. "Brayden didn't mention you going to Shelnam. Perhaps I should contact him and—"

"Is Brayden Prince of the Sirens?"

"No."

"Am I not Princess?"

"You are."

"Then why do we need to involve Brayden at all?"

"He is your guard and—"

I stepped closer to him and said, "My guards are ten times the Other Brayden is. You've sworn to serve the royal family, have you not, Captain Stevens?"

He swallowed and nodded.

"Then, I suggest you remember who is *actually* part of the royal family."

I spun and marched out of the castle. Captain Stevens followed me, but I had no interest in waiting for someone to get me a horse. I focused and opened my bond with Rhys a bit more. Wings popped from my back, both tipped with a claw.

Captain Stevens gasped and stumbled a step back.

I turned and smiled at him, knowing my eyes were now slitted dragon's eyes. "I'll return shortly."

Crouching first, I leapt up into the air and used my wings to propel me higher. My fear over falling was gone. I couldn't explain, but with all of my memories back, I felt more like myself and the fear was no longer there. I turned towards Shelnam and flapped my wings. Flying was definitely faster. It took me one-fourth the time riding would have.

As I flew into Shelnam, I was excited to see color again. Beautiful flowers bloomed along all of the windowsills of every building. The fields beyond were lush and green, like I remembered, and dozens of small creatures in every shade of the rainbow ran about.

The merchants and citizens froze when they saw me. I minimized my link with Rhys and let my wings disappear.

An old woman, bent with age, hobbled towards me with a cane in one hand. "Princess?" she asked.

I nodded.

The town erupted in cheers and my name being yelled. Children ran up to me, wide smiles on their faces.

"Who is in charge currently?" I asked.

"I am," a tall man with cerulean eyes, tattoos covering his arms, and shaggy brown hair said as he approached. He had a warm smile and I recognized him immediately.

"Colton!" I yelled and rushed to him.

He opened his arms and embraced me. "Jo," he whispered. "You're all grown up."

I tilted my head back to look up at him, well over a head taller than me, possibly taller than Rhys. "So did you."

He touched the bloodstones below my eye. "Mated?"

I nodded and stepped back from him, so I didn't have to tilt my head so much. "I need to talk to you."

All happiness fizzled out of him and he said, "Yes, we have much to discuss."

"First, I need food," I advised him.

He smirked and gestured at a building to the left. It had a simple sign which had a drawing of a bowl with steam on it. Mr. Bloomswort and his wife had owned it when I was last here.

Colton pushed open the door and I walked in, inhaling the familiar aromas of spices and seafood. It was empty, which was good because I needed to talk to Colton privately.

Mr. Bloomswort hobbled from the back, a bit grayer than I remembered, but not much different. His eyes widened and he bowed. "Princess."

I hurried to him and hugged him. "No bowing, sir."

He patted my cheek fondly. "It's good to see you."

"She's come for food," Colton told him.

"Coming right up! Take a seat," Mr. Bloomswort said and went back to the kitchen.

The tavern looked exactly the same, even the same tables.

"You look good, Jo," Colton commented.

I looked up and smiled. "Thanks. So do you."

"What are you doing back? I thought you were banished?"

"It's sort of complicated," I said and sighed. "And I'm not sure which story to believe."

"He's very powerful," Colton said.

"Who?"

He smirked. "Your betrothed."

I pretended to gag, and Colton roared with laughter.

"Shit is so complicated," I told him.

"I can imagine. I've been trying to keep the citizens out of it all, which basically equated to us not leaving this town."

"Thank you, for keeping them safe," I whispered.

"Jo, he's not just a siren. He uses magic unlike any I've seen before," Colton whispered.

I nodded. "He's controlling my dad."

Colton sighed and ran a hand through his already disheveled hair. "Shit. I thought he was, but hoped it really was dementia."

Mr. Bloomswort brought out an appetizer of oysters, then went back to the kitchen.

I ate one, as did Colton.

"What are you going to do?" Colton asked.

"Wait for the cavalry to arrive," I mumbled.

"Cavalry?"

"They're making my mates participate in the Gauntlet."

"But, you became mates while banished. They shouldn't have to participate."

"I know!" I said and groaned. "I think he's got the Elders under his control, too. Or at least, mostly."

"So, your mates are coming here?" Colton asked.

I nodded.

"And you think they can defeat him?"

I sighed and ate another oyster. "Yes, but I'd like to be the one to do it. If I could be sure I could defeat him alone, I would do it before they arrived. However, I know better and will wait for them to back me up."

"Will they be able to pass the Gauntlet?"

I laughed. "They'll pass easily. They'll probably play around to have more fun during it."

"What can I do?" Colton asked. "You didn't come here to see me."

"No, but it was a nice surprise to find you here," I said and smiled at him. "I need a teacher."

"A teacher? In what? You're a null."

I smirked. "Nope, I'm an empath."

His jaw dropped. "Oh, fuck."

"What?" I asked, my brows furrowing.

"Do you know anything about empaths?"

"Only what Trident Douche told me," I said, using Deryn's nickname for Brayden.

Colton laughed, then said, "Wait here. I'll get someone who can teach you."

I nodded and watched him leave. Nico would have yelled at me for being so trusting of Colton. I couldn't explain it, but I just *knew* he was on my side. Maybe it was an empath ability.

"Here you go," Mr. Bloomswort said and set a platter of fish tacos on the table. "Want some water?"

I nodded. "Yes, please."

I ate all of the tacos and drained my water before Colton returned. He came in, then held the door for the woman he had brought with him. The woman was so tall, she had to duck to step through the doorway. I'd forgotten that most sirens were tall. Somehow, I'd gotten the short stick.

Though she always had been a tall kid, she was no longer lanky, but curvy and gorgeous now. She had dark eyes, dark hair, and a rack that made me feel inferior for a moment.

"Jojo!" she said, smiling.

"Leona," I said and stood.

She hugged me, and I hugged her back.

"You two hungry?" Mr. Bloomswort asked.

"Yes, sir!" Leona boomed, released me, and sat at my table.

"I thought you were getting me a teacher?" I asked Colton.

Leona frowned, then stuck her lip out in a pout. "I'm not good enough for you?"

"You?" I asked. "You're an empath?"

All three sirens in the room shushed me.

"That's not publicly known," Leona explained.

Well, this trip just kept throwing surprise after surprise at me.

Leona eyed me. "I'm pretty shocked you're an empath, too. I never even got a hint of it from you when we were kids."

"Probably because you spent most of the time trying to catch the boys," I teased.

"While Colton was trying to look up skirts at all the girls' underwear," she accused.

"I'd ask about your underwear, but I see the bloodstones," he said and sighed dramatically.

"I'd have to be wearing some to comment," I said and winked.

He groaned and clutched at his chest, flailing backwards dramatically. He sat back up and asked, "Would you be interested in a third mate, possibly?"

I smirked. "I have four already."

Leona and Colton blinked in shocked silence.

"You think they can pass the Gauntlet?" Mr. Bloomswort asked as he set fried fish nuggets and calamari on the table.

I nodded. "They enjoy challenges."

"Explains why they ended up with you then," Colton teased me.

I threw a piece of calamari at him, which he caught and ate with a smile on his face.

"You see Sam?" Leona asked.

I nodded. "He's off on an errand for me."

"So, what do you know about empaths?" Leona asked while eating fish nuggets.

I set the book Brayden had given me on the table and opened it to the page on empaths. "This is all I know."

Leona and Colton inspected the book and Colton asked, "Who wrote this?"

"Trident Douche."

Leona looked at me with a quirked brow, then burst into laughter. "Brayden!" she gasped and pounded the table with her fist as she continued laughing.

Colton shook his head as he read it. "He doesn't know about empaths. The other info is right, for the most part, but not the stuff about empaths."

Leona pulled a pen from her pants pocket and scribbled out some information Brayden had written, then wrote a full page of notes. I tried to read it, but she tore a blank page from the back of the book and continued writing information down.

"Wouldn't it be easier just to give me a book that is already written?" I asked.

"They don't exist. All empath books were burned decades before we were born. It is now past down from empath to empath verbally," Leona explained.

"Why?"

"So outsiders won't find out what we can really do. If they found out, they would capture us and make us work for them," Leona said.

"Why are you writing it down for me, then?" I asked.

She smiled. "You're my princess. Who better to break tradition for?"

"Will you also teach me?"

She nodded, writing furiously. "Trident Douche is likely on his way here. I'm giving you what I can, so you can read and prepare for our training session tomorrow."

"Where am I supposed to meet you?" I asked.

"My house," Colton said. "Same place I grew up in, you remember?"

I nodded.

"Tomorrow, after breakfast," Leona said. "Read this all tonight and prepare mentally. Okay?"

"Okay," I agreed and felt my nerves building again. I really wished the guys were here.

Leona closed the book with the new pages inside and gave it back to me. I tucked it into my jacket, glad for its small size.

Not even a minute later, Brayden walked in. He glared at Leona and Colton's backs before walking to me with a smile. "Jolie, you should have let me know you wanted to visit. I was worried something had happened when I couldn't find you. And Captain Stevens was shouting nonsense about you having wings."

I pulled my wings out behind me, fanning them as far open as they would go. "It wasn't nonsense."

All present stared at my dragon wings with wide eyes.

"Plus, I wanted to visit with some of the townspeople I knew from when I lived here. Despite you being my best friend..."

Colton and Leona's eyes hardened, and their jaws clenched.

"...I did have a few others I played with. Leona and Colton were two of them."

Brayden scowled at the backs of the two sirens, who hadn't bothered to acknowledge him.

"I didn't know you played with the commoners," Brayden said.

"There's a lot you don't know about me," I said with a pleasant smile. "It has been over twenty years since we last saw each other."

"True," he said and smiled warmly, "which is all the more reason for us to get to know each other again."

Colton tensed, and I kicked his shin under the table while never breaking eye contact with Brayden. "Yes, we should. Let's meet for breakfast tomorrow," I suggested.

His smug smile was aimed at Leona and Colton who couldn't see it. "Sounds great."

I batted my eyelashes. "Could you pay for my food? I don't have any currency."

Brayden looked at the plates. "You ate all of that?"

"I burn a lot of energy with my double connection to the four alphas," I said, stood, and patted my flat stomach. "I should lay off, so I don't get fat."

"You look perfect," Brayden said with a leering smile.

I never wanted to gag so much just from a look before. I held my smile in place while Colton and Leona avoided eye contact.

Brayden put the money down, golden coins with a clam stamped on them, then pulled open the door for me.

I hugged my two friends, tucked my wings in to get out the door, then winked at Brayden. "Race you home." Immediately, I flew up into the sky and raced to the castle. I found a maid and asked her to fill my tub with warm water, so I could take a bath. Then, I locked my door and secured it with a ward, just to be sure. Safe, I slid into the warm water and began reading Leona's notes.

CHAPTER 8

I survived breakfast with Brayden, managing not to throw up despite his lewd glances and comments, then hurried back to my room. I needed to get to Shelnam without Brayden finding out.

How?

Pacing back and forth, I tried to think of a plan. I could turn into a wolf, but there weren't wolves in Atlantis, so I'd get a lot of attention. Same problem with a dragon and even a fox. And, I hadn't tried turning into a fox yet anyway.

Nico hadn't taught me an invisibility spell, so that wasn't a possibility either.

I didn't know the staff or whose side they were on, so trying to use them wasn't a great option. I wished Sam was back.

I tapped my bonds with each of my mates and they tapped them back. At least they were okay, for now. While I felt mostly certain they could pass the Gauntlet, I was a little worried. I knew Brayden would participate and he'd cheat however he could.

I should just kill him before the Gauntlet even started. To do that, I needed to get to Leona for my lessons.

Screw it, I'd fly there again and if Brayden tried to stop me, I would kill him. This was my home, my kingdom, and I wouldn't let him back me into a corner.

I put the book in a bag and marched determinedly out of the castle. A few guards looked at me, but none tried to stop me. I flew as fast as I could and landed on the far side of town to avoid as many townspeople as I could. I knocked twice on Colton's door, then pushed it open.

Colton and Leona sat at the dining table with papers scattered across its top.

The house hadn't changed, except all of the pictures save for one were gone. He still had the same dull brown couch, the same seashell chandelier, and the same picture of four dirty, smiling kids, hanging on the ice box. I put up a ward, then walked past Leona and Colton to the ice box. Sam, me, Leona, and Colton stood together, all covered in mud, and smiling like idiots.

"You remember that day?" Colton asked.

I nodded. "It was my last day here." Not that we had known that at the time.

"We'd played for hours in that muddy creek," Leona said and chuckled.

Something small and shiny in the background caught my eye. I squinted and leaned closer, then used Fox's power to enhance my eyesight.

There, in the background of our picture stood Brayden, glaring at us with shining eyes.

"Oh, shit," I whispered. I pulled the picture down and set it on the table, atop some of their papers. "Look."

"What?" Leona asked.

"We see it every day," Colton said.

I pointed at Brayden. "Brayden with glowing eyes."

They leaned forward and then Colton grabbed a magnifying glass and they both cussed.

"Do you think he is the reason I was banished? Sam thought so, but could it be because of him?" I asked softly.

"If so, why let you come back now?" Leona asked.

Suddenly, it clicked. "Because he can't claim the throne unless we're mates," I whispered. "He's going to go after my mates. I know he is."

I started to head for the door, but Leona stopped me. "We need to train first. You're a loose cannon right now."

"He's going to kill them!" I shouted.

"You said they're strong, right?" Colton asked.

I clenched my jaw, but replied, "Yes."

"Just give me a couple of days. Colton and I will come with you afterwards to help," Leona promised.

I checked the bonds, and everything felt fine. "Okay," I agreed.

"You read my notes?" Leona asked.

"Yes." I didn't understand all of it, but I'd read it all.

"So, we can sense emotions, including sensing when someone is using a false emotion to hide their true emotions. We can also manipulate other beings emotions."

"Just like sirens," I commented.

"Yes, sirens can manipulate emotions, but they can't sense emotions. Empaths can, depending on their power level, manipulate more beings than sirens at a time. One more thing we can do that sirens can't? Manipulate our own emotions to empower ourselves."

"Really? That would have been nice to know all these years," I said.

"Your ultimate power though, is addiction," Colton said

"What?" I asked.

"People crave happiness. Generally, empaths are happy people and people want to be around us. They will crave happiness like a drug because being happy releases chemicals in your brain that drugs do and, they end up craving you," Leona said.

"How do I prevent someone from being addicted?" I asked.

"You have to lock down your powers. It sucks, but it's the only way. Luckily, it's not hard to lock them down," Leona explained.

"Okay, none of this sounds terrifying, though. Colton made it seem like I was going to self-destruct."

Leona smirked. "Because I haven't told you our ultimate weapon. Mind manipulation."

"Like sirens?"

She smiled wide. "Better. We can make people see whatever we want them to."

"Hallucinations?"

She nodded. "And I think you're powerful enough to pull it off on a mass scale."

My eyes widened. "So, I could make a group of people think they're seeing one thing, while another is happening?"

Leona and Colton nodded.

"Blue rupees," I whispered.

"What does that mean?" Colton asked.

I gaped at him a moment, then remembered they didn't have internet or electronics. They all made a trip to the mainland at least once in their lives, but they couldn't use any of that stuff here. "Oh, guys. I forgot how sheltered you are here!"

"We're not sheltered," Colton scoffed.

"You're missing out on hundreds of video games! We've got to figure out how to get internet down here," I said, considering how we could possibly accomplish it.

"I think we have more pressing matters to attend to right now," Leona said.

I sighed and rubbed my face with both hands. "You're right. Teach me everything."

We made it four hours with no distractions, then my stomach wouldn't shut up. After a quick meal at Mr. Bloomswort's tavern, we returned to do more training.

My training consisted of me trying and failing to manipulate Colton's emotions. I did figure out how to shut down my powers, which was a huge relief to everyone. Five more hours of training left me mentally and physically exhausted. I kept nodding off and Leona decided to stop the lessons for the day.

"I haven't learned anything," I argued, trying to sit up with arms made of lead.

Colton pushed me down on the couch and shook his head. "You're done for the day. Go to sleep. We'll stay here and make sure Trident Douche doesn't show up."

Leona draped a blanket over me, then she and Colton returned to the kitchen table to go over the papers they'd been looking at when I arrived. I hadn't even thought to ask about them.

♥

"Baby, open your eyes," Rhys whispered.

"Rhys?" I asked and opened my eyes. I stood in a dark room with no furniture and no windows. There was no light source, yet I could see. Rhys, Deryn, Fox, and Nico sat in front of me.

"What's going on?" Nico asked. "You used a lot of power today."

"Training with my new powers," I explained. "Wait, where are we?"

"You pulled us into a dream world with you," Nico explained.

"Yes!" I yelled. "Finally, I did something with my empath powers."

"My queen, focus. What's going on?" Fox asked.

Uh oh, serious Fox was here.

"Trident Douche isn't just a siren. He has other abilities. He is controlling my dad. Possibly others, too. I think, I don't have proof, but I think he's the reason I got banished."

Since this was my dreamscape, I pulled up the picture and made it poster sized for the guys to easily see it. It appeared in my hands and I held it out to them.

"That's me, Colton, Sam, and Leona," I explained. "That angry boy in the back is Trident Douche. This was the day before I was banished. I think he started controlling my dad then."

"He's packing some serious power then," Nico said.

"If he banished me, but now brought me back, it must be because he can't get the throne without becoming my mate."

All four growled.

"I think he plans to kill you," I said and swallowed. "Sam is on his way to get you. They're going to make you participate in the Gauntlet."

"Challenge accepted!" Deryn yelled and the other three smiled.

"Focus!" I snapped. "He won't want you to make it. I don't know what kind of powers he has. I'd tell you to stay away and let me kill him, but—"

"You know we won't listen," Rhys said.

"That, and I would prefer to have you as backup," I replied.

"Are you safe?" Fox asked.

"I think so," I said.

"Can we trust Sam?" Deryn asked.

I nodded. "When you get to the Kraken, call him 'Pookie' and open the bonds with me. He should sense it and let you down with Sam by your side."

"Pookie?" Nico asked with an arched eyebrow.

"I was five!" I snapped.

"You named him?" Fox asked.

I nodded.

Rhys walked to me and rested his hand on my cheek. I leaned into it. "Baby, please stay safe until we get there."

"I'll try my best," I promised. "I need you here in two weeks, no later."

They nodded in understanding, then took turns kissing me. I didn't want to end the dream, but felt it crumbling around the edges.

"I love you," I whispered.

They bowed. "Love you, too," they said in unison.

Leona, Colton, and I sat in Mr. Bloomswort's tavern, eating and chatting, when Brayden and Captain Stevens burst in with a few guards behind them.

"Arrest them," Brayden ordered the guards.

I stepped into their path. "On what charges?"

"Kidnapping the princess," Brayden said.

I folded my arms across my chest. "No one kidnapped me."

Captain Stevens tried to move around me, but I stepped into his path again. "I order you to leave this establishment at once!" I shouted.

The guards, Brayden, and Captain Stevens spun and walked out.

"Whoops," I whispered to Leona and Colton.

We walked out and Brayden glared at us. "Where did you learn to do that?"

"I've always been able to," I lied.

He snarled. "Arrest them, now."

I had had enough of his shit. I shifted into my wolf warrior form and growled loudly. "Take one more step and I'll kill all of you!"

Everyone froze and gaped at me. Merchants, townspeople, guards, even my friends stared.

"I am Princess Jolie of the Sirens, and I am heir to the throne! Guards, arrest Brayden and take him to the dungeons."

They turned, but Brayden dodged them, then ran to me. I tried to slice him with my claws, but the bastard was nimble and he avoided them.

"No!" Leona yelled.

Brayden touched my head and he filled it with his power. Nothing existed, but Brayden.

He was a god, no *the* god! I should bow to him and...

Four golden lights pierced the haze in my head.

"No!" I screamed and clutched at my head.

"You're mine," Brayden whispered, a cool hand touching my forehead.

"Jo!" Colton yelled, but his yell was cut off by the sound of flesh hitting flesh and his breath whooshed from his lungs.

"Stand," Brayden ordered me.

I obeyed. The little fucker thought he had complete control over me. He was wrong.

I met his eyes, then slammed my knee into his balls as hard as I could. He gasped and clutched himself. I punched him in the face with dragon scale covered hands.

He stumbled and fell onto his butt, his eyes wide with fear.

I shifted into my dragon form and roared. Arching my neck, I inhaled to shoot fire and destroy Brayden.

Cold water splashed against my face, making me gasp and open my eyes.

Brayden stood before me, a smug smile on his face. We weren't in the town anymore. Stone floors, iron shackles on my wrist and ankles, and pitiful moaning all pointed to me being in the dungeon.

"How?" I asked weakly. My arms and legs were chained to the wall, preventing me from choking his stupid neck.

"I took control of Leona. I always thought she was an empath, but couldn't be sure until you helped me confirm it today," Brayden said.

"I'm going to kill you. I don't know what you are, but I'm going to rip your head from your body and burn you until you're nothing more than ash!" I screamed.

He chuckled. "You've always been a spitfire. Sadly, you can't fight me this time."

He set his hands on my face, from temple to jaw on each side, and began to shove his power into my head again.

I screamed and thrashed, but I couldn't stop him. He was right, I was too weak to fight him. I slammed my bonds closed, just in case he could get to the guys through them.

"I'm sorry," Leona whispered somewhere nearby. "I'm so sorry, Jojo."

I fed Brayden another strawberry, then ate one myself. We sat in the royal gardens, now just dirt with a pond of silver fish.

Something wasn't right. I couldn't fully understand what it was, but I just knew something wasn't right.

Brayden said we were betrothed and destined to be mates, to rule Atlantis together. Yet, I had two bloodstones beneath my eye. One only got bloodstones when they were mated. So, that had to mean I had mates. But, I didn't remember having mates. I couldn't feel them. I couldn't sense anything. If I had mates, where were they? Why was I with Brayden if I had other mates? And, shouldn't they be participating in the Gauntlet?

So, why did I have bloodstones if I didn't have mates?

"You keep getting sidetracked and spacing off," Brayden whispered, rubbing a fingertip down my cheek. "What are you thinking about?"

"It's so quiet here," I said to change topics. "I miss the festivals."

"You want a festival?" he asked.

I shrugged. "It's been so long since I've been to one. I remember how fun they were as a kid. Isn't there a holiday coming up? A festival soon that we could participate in?"

"No, but we could hold a festival once the Gauntlet is over," he suggested.

"If you win," I said. "I don't think you'll want to have a festival if you don't win."

He didn't seem to hear me.

"What do you want to do today?" I asked him.

"I have to go to the arena today," he said and stroked a finger down my arm.

"Can I come?" I asked and scooted closer to him. "I don't want to be away from you."

He smiled and cupped my cheek. "Kiss me and you can."

I blushed and turned away. "You know the law. You can't be my mate until you win the Gauntlet."

His smile disappeared, but it quickly returned. "You're right."

"So, can I go?" I asked and leaned my head on his shoulder.

"Not today, love. Why don't you find the seamstress to have her make a dress for the day of the Gauntlet?" he suggested and stood.

I pouted and stood too. "Okay."

He pulled me into a hug and kissed the top of my head. "Don't worry, I won't be gone long."

After walking me back to my room, he left to go on his errand. I flagged down a maid and asked her to fetch the seamstress.

The seamstress arrived shortly thereafter. "How can I assist you, Princess Jolie?" She was an old woman with leathered skin and shoulder length grey hair.

"I need a dress for the Gauntlet," I explained. "It needs to be beautiful, but also something I can maneuver in."

"Maneuver, Princess?" she asked.

"Loose around my legs and a high slit on at least one side," I explained.

"Color preference?"

"Dark blue," I said, knowing it was a color that men said I looked good in. A memory tugged at the edge of my mind, but I couldn't access it.

She nodded and pulled out a measuring tape, immediately getting to work. Once she was done with my measurements, she left to start making my dress.

Four simultaneous taps at my mental wall made me gasp in shock.

"Princess Jolie?" a young guard called through the door. "You're needed outside," he said, his voice shaking with nervousness.

A roar shook the castle and I hurried out to the guard. "What is it?" I asked him.

"Hurry," was all he said before turning and sprinting down the hallway.

I followed, running alongside him out of the side door to the courtyard. Four males stood side by side, facing Brayden with murder in their eyes.

"Where is she?" the werewolf in warrior form asked.

"She is not—" Brayden began, but I hurried to his side.

"What's the meaning of this?" I asked angrily.

"Jolie." All four males breathed a sigh of relief.

"You need to go back inside," Brayden told me. "It's not safe for you here."

I looked at him and scoffed. "I am Princess here, not you." Facing the four newcomers who were scowling again, I asked, "What do you want?"

"Jolie, what's wrong with you? It's us," the short, muscular elf said.

A guard stepped out from behind them and said, "These are the guests who will be participating in the Gauntlet."

I looked more closely at the men. They were all very handsome. And, they were all definitely alphas. They would make for decent mates, if they passed the Gauntlet.

I nodded. "Your rooms are prepared and waiting for you. If you'll follow me, I'll—"

"What did you do!" the dragon yelled at Brayden.

Brayden smiled smugly. "Jolie, come here," he ordered me.

I scowled, but walked to his side. I did not like to be ordered around and he knew that. He draped an arm around my shoulders and the four males growled. "Brayden, I—" I started, but he interrupted me.

"Jolie is my betrothed," Brayden informed them.

"Only if you pass the Gauntlet," I reminded him. "Not that I doubt you."

"Baby," the wolf whispered. "You're stronger than him."

"Come," I ordered the visitors. "Let's get you to your rooms."

Without waiting for anymore disruptions, I headed into the castle. The four followed me silently. Inside the hallway, guards watched us. I hadn't seen so many guards in the castle before, which meant Brayden had called them in. We walked to the visitor rooms, and I pushed open one of the doors and walked inside. All four entered without waiting for my invitation, the last one, the elf, closed the door.

I spun around and threw my arms around the nearest one. The five of us were connected, which made me believe they were the mates my bloodstones were connected to.

"I'm sorry," I whispered into his ear, feeling like an idiot for just throwing my arms around him, but it was my body's desire to touch them.

"You don't recognize us," he realized and hugged me tightly. It was the wolf.

"I do and I don't. I am pretty certain that you are my mates and we're connected, but I can't remember your names or anything about you. I suspected Brayden was lying to me, but I don't remember anything other than living here and him being betrothed to me since we were born."

"You locked down our bonds, so he couldn't get to us," the mage said.

"What?" I asked. "I don't know what you're talking about."

"This is incredibly powerful magic," the mage whispered.

"How do we break it?" the dragon asked.

"You could try kissing me," I suggested and smirked up at the wolf holding me.

He didn't hesitate. He pressed his lips to mine and with a hand on my upper back and one on my lower back, pulled me against him as tightly as he could.

When we separated, I smirked and said, "Well, it didn't work, but at least it was enjoyable."

"Baby," he whispered and touched my lower lip with his thumb. "We told you to stay safe."

"I'm alive," I said. "I'm still here...somewhere. I hope."

"I can break it," the mage said. "But, he'll know immediately that it's broken."

I stepped back and shook my head. "Not yet. I need you to win the Gauntlet first."

"So, you and he didn't..." the elf asked and trailed off.

I shook my head. "He may control me to a certain extent, but I am still me. I know I'm not his. I know I have mates." I tapped the bloodstones under my eye. "I know I belong to others. Plus, it is against the law to have sexual relations before they win the Gauntlet."

"At least there's that," the elf sighed.

"It's hard to explain. It's like he took segments of my memory and locked them up, so I can't access them. I get feelings, like about you four, but I don't know your names or what happened to me."

"Where's your friend? The one teaching you about being an empath?" the mage asked.

"Who?"

He scowled.

"You were with two friends," the dragon told me. "People you knew from your childhood."

My brows furrowed, and I tried to get the memory to surface, but it wouldn't. My head began to throb, and I clutched at it.

"That's enough," the mage said and pulled me against his chest with a hand to the back of my head. "Don't try to think any harder or you'll hurt yourself."

"I'm sorry," I whispered and felt tears stinging my eyes. "I wish I could break this now, but I need to be sure I can get rid of him when I do. He needs to pay for what he's done. Even if I can't remember exactly what he has done right now."

"We know what he's done," the wolf said with a snarl. "We'll make sure he pays."

I believed him. Looking at the four males before me, I believed they could win the Gauntlet and defeat Brayden.

Someone knocked on the door and the guys quickly moved so that I was hidden behind them.

"Enter," the dragon called.

"Is she—"

The door was shut and they moved aside so I could see a guard.

"He's a guard—" I started, but he rushed forward and hugged me.

"Jo," he whispered. "Jo, you're alive."

"Sort of," I mumbled as I inhaled his familiar scent. Who was he?

"She doesn't know who you are," the dragon told him.

The man released me and jerked backward. "No. He got you?"

"Brayden? Yeah."

He snarled and ran a hand through his hair. "Dammit. I knew I shouldn't have left you alone. What about Colton or Leona? I couldn't find them and—"

My head felt like it had cracked as images of the two sirens he was talking about slipped through the barrier Brayden had put up. I yelped and fell, but four pairs of arms caught me at the same time, cradling me between them all.

"Dungeons," I gasped out. "They're both in the dungeons."

"You cracked the spell a bit," the mage told him. "Crap."

"I have to go," I gasped and pushed away, tears in my eyes again.

"We'll win the Gauntlet," the elf promised me. "We'll free you from his spell."

I nodded and dashed outside, running down the hall and into Brayden. I cried and hugged him. "There you are! I was so scared! I thought you were gone."

"Why would I be gone?" he asked, petting my hair.

"I heard a guard say you were gone. I must have misheard him," I lied and looked up at him, batting his eyelashes. "Are you done at the arena? Can we have dinner together?"

He smiled wide and ran the back of his hand down my cheek. "I'm done with work. Let's go get some dinner."

I nodded and let him escort me, arm in arm, to the dining hall.

CHAPTER 9

Brayden kept close to me, meeting me for every meal and insisting that I accompany him to the meetings he held with the Elders. I knew he was keeping me from seeing the four males, my mates, but I did not call him on it. The Gauntlet wasn't too far away, and I couldn't risk Brayden finding out that his magic wasn't working one hundred percent on me.

Dad stayed holed up in his chambers, refusing to see me. I tried not to let it bother me, but I was getting really worried about him. Why wouldn't he want to see me? I was his daughter, his heir. He went so far as to order me to stay out of the wing of the castle his chambers were in.

I suspected Brayden had a hand in Dad's actions, but I did not have any proof.

Brayden and I walked in the garden and I saw the four males on the far side, their bodies glistening in the sun with sweat from working out. I was sad that I hadn't been able to see them practicing, but knew I couldn't voice that opinion.

They headed in our direction, putting shirts on, which made me want to pout even more. Brayden draped his arm over my shoulders and pulled me against his side. If I acted different, he would know I wasn't completely under his control, so I played along, sidling up closer and smiled up at him.

"How can I help you gentlemen?" Brayden asked them.

All four were glaring at him. The wolf's eyes were glued to his arm around me.

"We were hoping to talk to the princess," the dragon said.

"Me?" I asked. "What about?"

"We wanted to talk to you in private," the dragon said.

"She will not be left alone with four outsiders," Brayden said. "You could kill her."

"We won't kill her, and you know that," the mage said with a scowl.

"I'm her guard, so if you want to talk to her, you have to talk to her with me present," Brayden told them with a smug smirk.

"What if I met with them in my office?" I asked Brayden. "You could stand guard outside my door to ensure they didn't try anything."

"No," Brayden said and glared down at me. "I will not allow you to be with them, alone."

I returned his glare and said, "You know I don't like being ordered around."

His gaze softened, he smiled, and put a hand on my cheek. "Sorry, sweetheart. I just want to make sure you are safe. If you were injured, or killed, I would be devastated."

"I don't think they have any ill will towards me," I said and looked at the males once before looking back at Brayden. "It's a normal protocol for the heir to meet with royals of other areas. They're princes, right? I should have met with them individually when they arrived."

"No," Brayden said again.

I pushed away from him and put my hands on my hips. "You can't change protocol."

"You can't put yourself in danger. We are so close to the Gauntlet and to our mating," Brayden whispered.

"They are also participating for my hand," I reminded him. "It's better for us if we show them proper courtesies."

"Come," Brayden said and grabbed my hand.

The four males moved a step forward, their eyes glowing.

Brayden's trident appeared in his hand and he aimed it at them.

I stepped between them and raised my hands. "Whoa. Stop. No fighting."

"We apologize," the elf said, and the four males backed up two steps, though their eyes didn't stop glowing.

Brayden's trident disappeared, and he put his hand on the small of my back and pushed me away from them. "Have a good night, gentlemen."

He hurried me along, and I barely had a chance to turn and look back at them. They looked furious and sad at the same time. My heart ached seeing them like that, knowing that I was the cause of it.

"You should be more respectful of the visiting royals," I told Brayden. "There was nothing wrong with them asking for a meeting with me."

"You are still too naïve," Brayden snapped. "Those males are dangerous. They are powerful and together, they might be able to overpower you."

"I'm not defenseless," I reminded him.

He smirked. "I know."

We walked into the castle and towards my room.

I paused in front of my door and turned to face him with a serious scowl. "The next time you order me around in front of other royals, I will have to punish you. You are not prince. You do not have power over me."

He opened his mouth to protest, but I held my hand up.

"I don't care that you're my guard. No one tells my dad what to do and you won't tell me what to do either. Are we clear? If you can't follow those simple rules, I will find a new guard."

Brayden's eyes hardened, and my head began to throb. "No. That won't do at all. I can't have you being so strong willed against me."

The pain intensified, and I dropped to my knees. "What are you doing?" I gasped.

He set his fingers on my temples and I began to black out. "Making you a bit more compliant. We've still got a week left until the Gauntlet and I don't want those assholes ruining my plans. I've worked too hard for too long to have them waltz in here and ruin it all."

The pain became so unbearable that I fainted.

"Princess Jolie," the dragon prince said and bowed to me as I walked by him.

"Good afternoon, Prince," I replied in greeting and dipped my head.

"Can I help you?" Brayden asked him.

The dragon smiled. "No, I was just out for a walk around your castle and wanted to say hello to the gorgeous princess as we passed each other."

I blushed. He thought I was gorgeous?

"You've said your greeting, now excuse us. We have things to do," Brayden said.

I glanced at the dragon prince as we walked away, and he winked at me. Before Brayden noticed, I turned back around. We continued down the hallway towards the dining hall.

Brayden pushed open the doors but froze when we found the mage prince and the werewolf prince sitting at one of the tables. They stood when we entered and bowed to me.

"You aren't supposed to bow to others of similar stature," I chastised them.

"We will always bow to you," the wolf said and smiled sweetly.

"What? Why?" I asked, unsure what he meant by that.

The mage pulled out a chair and smiled warmly. "Would you like to eat with us?"

I moved a step forward, but Brayden put his arm out. "No," he answered.

"Brayden, what's wrong?" I asked, looking at the two princes and then at him. He acted like they were a danger, but they didn't seem like they might be aggressive towards me.

"I don't trust them," he told me.

"We won't hurt her," the wolf said with a smile that wasn't exactly reassuring.

"It's just a meal," the mage said and tilted his head as he looked at Brayden. "Surely you can't think us sharing a meal with the princess is a problem? We weren't suggesting you leave. We understand, as her guard, that you would be standing at her back the entire time."

"Why don't you have guards?" I asked.

"We have no use for guards," the wolf said. "They would just slow us down."

"Please," the mage said. "Join us for a meal."

"It's only proper courtesy," I whispered to Brayden. "Please stop making a scene."

He was silent a moment and then he relented and pulled a chair out for me, one several away from the princes. I sat and smiled happily.

The mage took his seat beside the wolf and they smiled at me.

"So, Princess, what do you do for fun here?" the wolf asked.

"I like to go for walks and read," I answered.

"You don't play games?" the mage asked.

My head throbbed a moment, but it quickly passed.

Weird.

"No," Brayden said. "We don't."

"Sounds pretty boring," the wolf commented.

"Books are rarely boring," I told him.

"Do you have a library?" the mage asked.

I nodded and smiled wide. "Yes! It's quite large."

He smiled back. "I'd love to see it. Perhaps after we eat, you could show me?"

"I would love—"

"Your meal, Princess," Brayden said, interrupting me.

A servant set plates in front of me and the two princes, then set two more in front of the two empty chairs across from me.

The dragon and elf princes walked in and took the empty seats, smiling at me.

"Hello, Princes," I said in greeting to them.

"Hello, Princess," the elf said. "You look lovely, as always."

Heat spread along my cheeks. "Thank you."

"Eat," Brayden said. "I have errands to attend to."

"You could just go on your errands while I eat," I said and put my napkin on my lap.

"We'd be happy to keep the princess company," the wolf said with a wink at me.

Be still my heart! I might melt into a puddle of goo in my chair if the four sexy males didn't stop flirting with me.

"Out of the question," Brayden said.

"Why not ask one of the other guards to guard me while you go on your errands?" I asked him.

"No. That's final," Brayden snapped.

I frowned at him. "Okay. You don't have to snap at me."

"Such rudeness aimed at your princess is uncalled for," the elf said and tsked his tongue. "I can't remember the last time I heard of a guard acting like that with a royal."

"We've known each other since we were born and he's my betrothed," I said. "Sometimes he forgets the boundaries guards are supposed to follow."

Brayden said nothing, but I knew he was probably mad.

"I'll eat fast," I said and glanced at him with a smile. "Then we can go on your errands."

"Thank you," he said and relaxed slightly.

The princes didn't seem to like my response.

We ate and they kept casting weird glances at me. What were they thinking? What was going on with them?

"Thank you for joining me for a meal," I said as I finished and stood.

The four stood and bowed to me.

Why were they bowing? They shouldn't have been bowing to me.

"I hope you have an enjoyable night," the elf said.

"You as well," I said and smiled at him. He smiled and it lit up his entire face.

Damn, they were so handsome.

"Come," Brayden said and nudged me forward.

I obeyed, heading out of the dining hall despite the strange desire to stay and not only talk to the four princes, but touch them. I hadn't even kissed Brayden, so why was I having these strange desires with these males I barely knew?

"You shouldn't trust others so easily," Brayden chastised me.

"I wasn't trusting them, really. It is proper for me to meet with them. I'm not sure why you trust them so little. They don't seem like they hold any aggression towards me. If anyone, it seems like they hate you."

He scowled. "I don't care what they think about me."

"You've been acting strange lately," I whispered. "What's wrong? Are you worried that you won't win the Gauntlet? Or are you worried that you might have to share me with another male?"

He stopped and turned to look at me. "What do you mean share you?"

"Well, it is written in the laws that the winners of the Gauntlet get to claim my hand. Winners, as in plural. So, if you and one or two of the others win, then I would be mated to all of you," I explained.

"Where did you read that?" he asked, his brows furrowing and fists clenching at his side.

Why was he mad? That was the way our laws were written hundreds of years ago.

"It is written that way in the laws," I said. "The original laws from our inception here in Atlantis."

"We'll see about that," he snapped and resumed walking.

"You can't change the laws," I said and hurried to catch up to him.

He stopped again and faced me. "Do you want one of those other males as your mate?"

"I didn't say that," I said and hoped I wasn't blushing again.

"We have been betrothed since birth. Why would you want to change that now?" he asked, sounding hurt.

"I don't want to change it, but the laws are the laws and we must follow them."

"Sometimes laws are meant to be changed. Sometimes laws become outdated and need a refresher," he countered.

"You don't just go change the laws when they don't suit you," I said with a scoff. "Besides, they may all fail in the very first round for all we know. Stop worrying so much about the laws. You should be focusing on training and ensuring you're prepared for the Gauntlet."

"Don't worry about me," he said and smiled. "I've been preparing for this day my entire life. I will win the Gauntlet and I will make you my mate."

For the first time, I didn't like the idea of being his mate. There was something dark and sinister lurking beneath his cool exterior. What would happen if he lost?

His gaze softened and he hugged me. "I'm sorry. I am very stressed out about the Gauntlet and I don't like having outsiders in Atlantis. It sets me on edge."

"They've done nothing that might be portrayed as indecent, hostile, or marked them as suspicious," I said. "Why are you acting so hostile towards them?"

"You don't see it," he said. "They're up to something. They are plotting something."

His eyes were glowing with anger and I was fairly certain that he was the one plotting something. What? I had no idea, and that frightened me.

As the sun set, I had Brayden take me to my chambers, feigning tiredness.

At my door, he hesitated, his brows pinched in worry. "Are you sure you don't want me to get a healer?" he asked.

I patted his cheek and smiled. "I'm sure it's just the nerves from the upcoming events. I am going to lie down and read a book until I fall asleep."

"Do you want me to stay with you?" he asked.

Tamping down the spike of fear, I smiled wider. "Always trying to break the rules, naughty boy. No, I'm sure you have things to take care of. Just post a soldier outside my door if it will help ease your worry. I won't leave my chambers."

He nodded and brushed his thumb over my cheek before barking orders at nearby guards and leaving.

I released a breath in relief and quickly locked my door behind me. It wouldn't do to have Brayden or the guards barge in. Especially, since I wouldn't be in my room.

Tapping on the walls lightly, it took me a couple minutes to locate the switch. The wall opened, and I stepped through, standing in a narrow passageway that wove all around the castle. Only Dad and I knew about these secret passages, this secret was only for the royal family. Dad said it was a safety precaution in case even the guards turned against the royal family. I was immensely grateful for it now.

I shut the opening to my room and followed the path, which was just wide enough for me to walk. I bet the elf prince's shoulders would get stuck if he tried to walk here.

There was something about those princes, something that drew me to them. I needed to talk to them, to find out what it was.

I paused at the piece of the wall that would open to the elf prince's room. He seemed the kindest of them all. I just hoped I wasn't wrong about them. I hoped I wasn't walking in to a death trap.

I strained to listen, to see if he was in his room.

"I'm telling you," the elf said, "I can feel her. She's close."

"He's right," the mage prince said. "But, I can't just teleport to her. She's probably with Trident Douche."

Trident Douche? It only took moments to realize they meant Brayden.

A giggle escaped before I slapped my hand over my mouth.

"What was that? That sounded like Jolie," the dragon said.

I pushed the lever and the wall split open. I smiled at the four princes who stood in varying stances.

The dragon prince moved towards me, but I backed up, my eyes widening. He froze.

"Wait," I pleaded. "I just wanted to talk."

The elf peered behind me. "Where's your guard?"

I shrugged. "He thinks I'm sleeping."

The mage waved me in. "Come in and I'll put a spell up so no one can hear us."

I nodded and stepped into the room, activating the switch so the door closed over the passageway. Inhaling, I drew in their four distinct scents and shuddered. They smelled familiar and good...no, great.

"Jolie," the wolf prince whispered and lifted his hand towards me, like he was going to touch my face, but then lowered it with a pained expression.

His pain was palpable. I wanted to touch him, to ease his pain, but I couldn't.

"First name basis?" I asked with a cheeky smirk. "I didn't realize we were so close already."

"Fuck, she's even worse than when we arrived," the dragon said, and his hands curled into fists at his sides.

"Jolie," the elf said softly. I turned to face him. "Do you remember us?" he asked.

I scowled. "You're the Four Princes of Jinla. Here to participate in the Gauntlet for a chance to become my mate."

"We are already your mates," the wolf said.

I rolled my eyes. "I think I'd remember having mates."

Especially ones as hot as you.

"Why can't we just kill him now?" the dragon asked, his eyes glowing angrily.

I took a step back, my mouth opening in surprise. "Kill? Who are you planning to kill?"

He held his hands up in surrender. "No one. I'm sorry. I'm just upset because you don't remember us."

"You really think we are already mates?" I asked and all four nodded. "If that's true, why don't I remember you or have a bond?"

"Your guard isn't what he seems," the wolf growled. "He's manipulating your memories."

I shook my head and backed up another step. "No, Brayden would never do something like that to me. He's my best friend."

Their jaws tensed and they all averted their eyes from mine.

"Prove to me what you're saying is true," I ordered them.

"We—" the mage began.

"Prove it or I will have you sent away and you'll lose your chance to participate in the Gauntlet," I threatened them.

The mage walked up to me and turned me so I faced the mirror on the wall. He pointed at my cheek. "If you're not mated, why do you have bloodstones?"

"There's nothing there," I told him. "You don't have bloodstones either."

His hands sparkled a moment, then it disappeared so quickly I thought I had imagined it.

"Nico, how is that possible?" the wolf asked. "How can he make her sight different?"

"I don't know," Nico growled and stomped away from me.

The elf touched my cheek, his fingertips warm. "You have two bloodstones right here," he said. He took my hand and pressed my fingertips to the same spot. For the briefest of moments, I felt the hard edges of the bloodstones, but then it was gone.

I shook my head. "I'm sorry. I—"

The elf hugged me and stroked my hair. "Don't worry. We will figure out a plan."

I melted against him, his body warm and his embrace...loving.

Another body wrapped around me from behind and without looking, I knew it was the wolf.

Every instinct told me to stay, but my brain forced me to jump away from them.

"No," I whispered, my body shaking with need to touch them. "I don't know you. You can't hold me or touch me in such a manner."

"Does it feel like you don't know us?" the dragon asked. He reached out slowly, giving me time to pull away, but I stayed still. He set his hand against my cheek and I leaned into it. "We are all connected," he whispered, then bent and brushed a feather light kiss across my lips.

Desire speared through me. My hands wrapped around the base of his neck and pulled him closer. He wrapped his arms around me and kissed me again, this time hard and fierce, his tongue sweeping across mine.

He tasted like...home.

I jerked away and held a hand out, warding him off. "No! No. We aren't supposed to do anything like that until you win the Gauntlet." Backing up, I hit the lever and the wall opened.

"Don't go," the wolf begged, his eyes pleading and filled with sorrow.

"I'm sorry," I gasped, hot tears splashing down my cheeks. I stepped back into the passageway and hit the button, closing the wall before they could get to me. I ran, my hand over my mouth to hold in the sobs. Once back in my room, with the wall closed tight, I collapsed on my bed and cried.

Kissing the dragon had felt right, familiar. It didn't feel like it was my first kiss, but my hundredth with him.

Were they right? Were they my mates? Or was this some type of ploy to trick me into trusting them?

They hadn't seemed to be acting. Their reactions had been too real, too pained to be faked.

If that was true, what did that mean? Was someone else manipulating me?

They said it was Brayden, but I refused to believe that.

I shook my head back and forth hard.

No, it couldn't be Brayden. He would never do something like that to me.

Would he?

He had been acting strange and had been so adamant about me not spending time with the four princes. Was he trying to keep us apart so I wouldn't discover that I was connected to them?

After changing into pajamas, I lay beneath my covers and touched my lips. The kiss had definitely been enjoyable.

Brayden stopped by later that night, but I ignored his knocking. The door unlocked, and I tensed. Since when did he have a key to my room?

He bent over me and kissed my cheek. "Sleep well, Jolie. Soon, we will be mates. And, those princes will be gone for good."

Gone?

Brayden pulled my blanket up higher and I snuggled down into them, keeping my eyes closed, feigning sleep. He stayed a bit longer, before he finally left. He was going to hurt them. I had to stop him.

At lunch, the princes joined Brayden and I again. They didn't act any different than they had been, thankfully, so Brayden was still left in the dark.

"Any plans today?" I asked Brayden as I ate a piece of fruit.

"I have some business with the Elders to attend to," he said.

"Would it be alright if I stayed behind?" I asked. "It's *so* boring."

He eyed the princes, but they were all very interested in their food at the moment.

"Very well. You may stay, but I need you to stay in your room with guards outside your doors and you not to let anyone inside. Understood?" Brayden said.

"Awfully pushy for a guard to his princess," one of them muttered, but I couldn't tell which one.

"I understand and agree," I said to Brayden, acting like I hadn't heard the prince. "Thank you. I want to finish that book I started yesterday."

"Are you finished eating?" he asked.

I nodded.

"I will escort you to your room then," he said and held out his hand.

I let him help me stand out of my chair, then slid my arm through his with a smile I hoped was warm. "Always the gentleman," I said and tugged him towards the door. "Let's go, so you can get to your meeting. I know you'll be there for hours, since any meeting with the Elders takes at least three."

Brayden sighed. "I fear this one might take four or five."

"Anything I should know?" I asked him, stepping out of the room and into the hallway without looking back at the princes, despite the burning urge to do so.

"No, it's nothing important. They just like to discuss things for hours at a time, no matter how trivial," Brayden said.

Brayden stationed two guards outside my room and waited until I closed and locked my door before leaving.

I waited five more minutes before slipping out of my room and into the secret passageway. My nerves were fried by the time I reached the elf prince's room, my hands shaking slightly.

"Rhys, calm down," the elf said. "It's hard for all of us to see her touch him."

"It's all an act," the wolf said. "Didn't you see her flinch when touching him?"

"It was super subtle, but she did," the mage said.

I knocked twice on the wall, then activated the switch and smiled at them. The dragon was looking out the patio doors and the other three sat around a table in the center of the room. Things were thrown around, like someone had a tantrum.

"Hi," I said nervously.

"We weren't sure you'd show," the mage said.

After closing the secret door, I faced them and said, "I don't believe you yet, about us being mates, but you're in danger. I don't know what he is planning, but Brayden intends to hurt or kill you."

The elf pulled out a chair at the table and waved me forward. I sat, and he kissed my cheek before taking his own seat.

"We know," the dragon said, still looking out the doors. "We are prepared for his attack."

"I want to stop him, but I don't know how. He keeps hiding me away from the others and won't even let me talk to the Elders without him. There's no reason for that, except if he is hiding things from me."

"We appreciate you wanting to help, but we want you to just stay safe," the elf said. "We wouldn't have let you come here like this, except it's taking a toll on us not to have physical contact with you."

Their eyes were bloodshot, which was abnormal for Others.

I stood, walked to the elf, and slowly set my hand on his cheek.

His eyelids fluttered closed and he exhaled a shaky breath. I reached over with my other hand to touch the mage's neck, since he was the next closest.

He set his hand atop mine and sighed with a smile on his face, then closed his eyes.

"Come on," I coaxed the wolf and dragon who were staring at me. "I only have two hands, but you can come touch me. In appropriate places."

They didn't hesitate, both walking to me and putting a hand on each of my arms.

Joy and love surrounded my heart and I felt our connection.

"We really are mates," I whispered in shock. How were the bonds blocked? Why would Brayden do that? Why would he make me forget my mates?

"Yes, my love. We are," the wolf whispered in my ear.

I leaned back against the wolf and dragon and let their love surround and fill me. We had to stop Brayden. No matter what.

"You should return to your room," the dragon whispered against my hair.

"Five more minutes," I whispered back.

The elf pressed his hand over mine on his cheek and with all four touching my skin, I felt happy and content for the first time in weeks.

What was I going to do?

"I don't want you to leave," the mage whispered, "but we can't risk him finding out you know. The last two times you broke part of his spell, he made it worse, to the point that you didn't even know us."

"What?" I asked in disbelief.

"It's too much to explain right now," the mage said. "Just, trust us. We're working on a plan and we know that he is likely to attack us or send people after us. We aren't weak and we work together, so none of us will be caught unaware or alone." He stood from his chair and the others retreated a step back, so only the mage was touching me or in my line of sight. "Please, Jolie, stay safe. We can protect you, but not while you're with him, away from us. Would you consider letting me stay in your room with you?"

"He'll see you when he comes in the morning," I said, swallowing roughly.

"I can use an invisibility spell," the mage explained.

I shook my head and chewed on my lip. "I didn't want to tell you, but...he has a key to my room. I don't know when he had one made or how he got it, but last night when I didn't answer him because I was pretending to sleep, he unlocked my door and came in."

All of them tensed. I felt the tension in the room like a blanket pulled over my head.

"Did he touch you?" the dragon asked quietly.

I didn't like the way he spoke. I didn't like this quiet side of him. "No. He kissed my forehead, but he didn't touch me inappropriately."

"If he tries, or if you feel that you're in danger with him, scream, and I'll come," the mage said.

"We'll all come with him," the wolf promised. "If you're in trouble, the four of us will come protect you."

"I wish the Gauntlet was here already, so we could just get this shit over with," I grumbled and leaned my forehead against the mage's chest.

He slid his fingers into my hair and gripped the back of my head. "Me, too, love. Me, too."

The other three joined us again, all touching me where they could, and we stood like that for another couple of minutes.

"I need to get back," I whispered.

"Do you want me to teleport you back?" the mage asked.

"Okay," I agreed.

"Wait," the wolf said. He leaned forward and kissed me lightly on the lips. "Goodnight, Jolie."

"Night," I whispered.

The elf and dragon gave me kisses as well, all of them feather light and sweet. It drove me crazy.

The mage linked our fingers together and then teleported us into my room. I tensed, waiting for Brayden to jump out and catch us, but he didn't. Everything was quiet.

"Thank you," I whispered to the mage. "Thank you for caring for me."

He kissed me and leaned his forehead against mine, our noses barely touching and whispered, "I love you, more than anything else in the world. I lost you once and I won't lose you again. Stay safe, my queen." He kissed me again, then disappeared.

What did he mean that he had lost me once?

I ate dinner alone, mulling over everything, then sat in silence in my room until I was exhausted and ready to sleep.

I went to bed and my dreams were filled with the princes, my mates, and when I woke, I knew they were not dreams, but memories.

CHAPTER 10

"Welcome!" the announcer yelled. "This is the first Gauntlet in over thirty years!"

The crowd cheered, and I shifted nervously on my throne. Dad sat beside me on his throne, a huge smile on his face.

The arena was located on the outskirts of Atlantis and rose more than two hundred feet high on the outside. The inner walls were over eighty feet high. It was oval shaped, with a raised platform on the southern side. Dad and my thrones sat on the raised platform, giving us the ability to see the entire arena easily. Plus, it separated us from the citizens.

The attendee seats were filled, which wasn't surprising since not much happened in Atlantis. This was the most interesting thing to happen in decades.

The four outsiders stood in the center of the arena, side by side, with Brayden a bit away from them. Brayden had his trident in one hand, the base resting on the sandy arena floor.

"Who do you think will win?" Dad asked.

"The four newcomers," I answered honestly.

Dad looked over at me. "Them? You don't think Brayden will win?"

"I hope not," I whispered.

Dad's eyes widened, but I put my finger to my lips and shook my head. This was not the place to discuss this.

"The first event is a race," the announcer said. "The race will begin here, go to the fountain in Shelnam, and then return to the stadium."

The announcer showed the participants and attendees a bird's eye view of the path.

The mage raised his hand and asked, "Is magic permitted?"

"I'm getting there," the announcer grumbled. "The rules for the race are as follows: no killing and no involving anyone not part of the race."

The mage smiled and cracked his knuckles.

My other three mates stretched and jogged in place to warm up. Brayden's trident shrank down to pen size and he put it in his pocket.

Well, now we knew where he kept it. I never knew it shrank like that.

"Get ready," the announcer called.

The wolf shifted into his warrior form and stood ready at the line. The dragon let wings out of his back and stood between the wolf and mage. The elf's body glowed when he took his place.

Brayden's eyes widened as he looked at them, and I saw worry for the first time. He hadn't been able to compare himself to anyone aside from other Atlantis inhabitants. He had no idea what these four princes were capable of.

"On your marks!"

They all stood at attention, except the mage who was examining his fingernails.

"Get set!"

Their bodies tensed. The entire arena was silent as the audience sat in rapt attention.

"Go!"

A horn blew and all took off without the mage. He looked up at me, winked, then snapped his fingers. One moment he was in the arena, the next he was at the fountain in Shelnam, then with one more snap, he stood back in the arena, just a step before the finish line.

Teleportation!

I tore my eyes away from him to find Brayden just making it to Shelnam, a rather impressive time by Atlantis comparisons. The others, however, were already running back into the arena. He was no match for them in speed, it seemed. The four friends crossed the finish line side by side, so that they were all first place and Brayden came in last. Brayden panted and scowled at the four smiling princes.

"The four princes win with a tie," the announcer said, disbelief coloring his tone.

I restrained from cheering, despite the urge to do so.

"Next is a battle," the announcer said, coming back to his usual character. "Weapons and magic are permitted. No killing. If you kill your opponent, you're disqualified. Winner will be by knockout, yield, or incapacitation. I have the right to stop the battle if I think the person is incapable of protecting themselves."

Brayden pulled out his trident and the crowd cheered. The elf and wolf drew swords from seemingly thin air, while the dragon shifted into warrior form, and the mage made a staff appear from the center of one palm.

"Ready?" the announcer asked.

The five males raised their arms in acknowledgement.

"Begin!"

Brayden raised his trident and pointed it at the four standing across from him. They didn't move. He smiled victoriously and walked towards them with his trident still raised.

"It appears Brayden has frozen them!" the announcer yelled as the crowd cheered loudly.

Brayden moved closer and still the four didn't move.

"No," I whispered. This couldn't be it. They couldn't lose so easily!

The mage tilted his head to look at me and he smiled.

Brayden moved to stab the mage, who was still looking at me, but his trident hit an invisible wall.

The mage turned to face Brayden and said, "You caught me off guard with that once. I'm not stupid enough to fall for it again."

The wolf and dragon raced forward together, attacking Brayden simultaneously. They moved around each other with no sounds and yet never bumped into each other. They ducked when one swung, or jumped when needed, with no verbal communication. Had they known each other a long time and just knew how the other fought? Or did they have some type of mental communication?

Brayden tried to freeze them with his trident's power, but the mage was protecting them. He fought back, but he couldn't defeat two of them. His eyes flicked to me and suddenly my legs were moving, carrying me away from the throne I had been sitting on. I walked to the edge of the raised platform, over two hundred feet above the arena floor.

The elf looked up and his eyes widened when he saw me. "Rhys, switch!" he yelled.

The dragon, Rhys, spun and raced back, while the elf ran by him to attack Brayden.

I stepped forward and fell.

People screamed.

I screamed.

Rhys leapt into the sky with newly sprouted wings and caught me. "I got you, baby."

I clutched him and gasped for air. "He...he tried to kill me!"

"He knew we'd be distracted and want to protect you," Rhys said and set me back before my throne. "He just didn't know it wouldn't help him."

I sat down and Dad reached over to squeeze my arm.

Rhys bowed to me and flew back down to the fight, his entire body rigid with anger. He landed behind Brayden and shifted into a huge dragon. He roared, and fire spewed from his mouth, covering the entire arena, including his friends.

People screamed again.

Had he killed the other three? Had he murdered his friends just to kill Brayden?

The fire disappeared, and my three mates stood, unscathed, bathed in a silver light. The mage must have protected them.

Brayden lay on the ground, water surrounding him in a protective spell all sirens knew. The left side of his face was burnt as were his clothes.

Rhys reverted back to his human form and said, "Next time you try to hurt my mate, I'll swallow you whole."

The water evaporated in a wisp and Brayden moaned.

The announcer raced down to Brayden and checked his vitals. "He's alive, but unable to continue. He loses and the Four Princes of Jinla win."

Some in the crowd cheered, but most stared in disbelief.

"Your Highness," Sam said and knelt before me.

"Did you do as I asked?"

He nodded. "Yes, Your Highness."

Aside from memories of my mates, I had a few memories of my childhood return last night as well. Among them were my best friends: Sam, Leona, and Colton.

"Announcer!" I called.

He looked up at me, stepping to the side as healers came out to tend to Brayden.

"The quest is ready," I informed him.

His eyes widened, and he looked at Brayden's unconscious form. "But he—"

"He is unfit to continue," I said. "Or do you think I should lower myself to accept subpar mates?"

He stuttered and sputtered a moment before composing himself. "Very well, let's move to the third event, the quest."

"Quest?" Rhys asked.

I walked to the edge of the platform and addressed everyone. "Something precious to me has been hidden in Atlantis. You have twelve hours to find and bring this precious thing to me."

"Do we get any clues?" the mage asked.

"It's from my childhood here in Atlantis. And, it's something I would die for." I said, praying it was enough of a clue for them to figure it out.

"Wait!" Brayden snarled, limping towards the center of the arena. "I'm participating, too."

"Very well," I agreed without hesitation. "Your time begins now."

Brayden hobbled back out.

Rhys took to the sky in his dragon form. The elf ran from the arena. The mage teleported out, but I had no idea where he went to. The wolf looked up at me for a long moment, then a huge smile split his face and he turned into a wolf before running out of the arena.

"Shall we get some food while we wait?" Dad asked.

"I can't leave the arena," I reminded him.

"Sam, have another guard fetch us food," Dad said.

Sam nodded and went to the nearest guard to order him to do so.

Pillows were brought out and I gratefully accepted two, putting them on my throne and sighing at the relief on my butt. "Much better."

Dad chuckled. "We should put some padding on these thrones."

"It would make them much more comfortable."

"I'll have someone work on that after the Gauntlet," Dad promised.

"Sounds great," I said. I didn't want to point out that I wouldn't be here long. Once we defeated Brayden, I was out of here. I had no desire to rule Atlantis.

"Here you go, Your Majesty," one guard said as he and three other guards set up a buffet of food on a table before us.

I filled up my plate and ate it quickly, filling my plate up for a second and then third time before I was full.

"Quite the appetite," Sam commented.

"Shut up," I ordered him and growled.

"Do you think any of them will be able to figure the quest out?" Dad asked.

"I hope so," I muttered. "If anyone can do it, I think the Princes of Jinla can."

"You have high hopes for those four," Dad commented.

"Yes, I do," I agreed.

"Brayden isn't a bad person," Dad said. "He's strong and he is a siren."

"He's not just a siren. I don't know what else he is, but he's something else, too," I whispered.

"Why do you think that?" Dad asked. "You haven't even been home for a month and you think you know him better than I do after over twenty years?"

"Yes," I said bluntly.

"The princess may be on to something," Sam whispered at my side.

Dad glanced at him, then focused back on me. "He is your betrothed," he reminded me.

"I was banished, so he should have stopped being my betrothed," I said. "Honestly, has my banishment even ended? Is the Gauntlet necessary since I'm still banished?"

Dad frowned as he thought about it. "I guess that's true. I never un-banished you."

"Don't!" I hissed. "If I stay banished, it might come in handy soon."

"How could being banished be handy?" Sam asked.

"You never know," I whispered.

I chewed on a bread roll as we continued to wait and I thought about the four males who had come. They were obviously friends and they worked flawlessly together. How did I fit into the equation? Did I fit flawlessly as well? What if my memory never came back? What if Brayden found a way to permanently break me?

They were my mates, that was obvious by the two bloodstones beneath my eye that carried blood from two of them in each one. It was interesting that they did two in one instead of four in one or just four individual stones. Perhaps I hadn't wanted to have four stones.

"Would you like some dessert?" Sam asked me.

I nodded emphatically. "Yes, please."

He nodded at the guard who had brought us back the food and the guard hurried off. It was nice having guards to do things for me. But, I would prefer not to have guards and to be free. Would I still be free if the princes were my mates? Would we have guards or servants? Where did we live? I had no idea where or what was going on when it came to them.

"With four mates, that greatly increases my chances of becoming a grandfather," Dad said. "It's hard for siren females to conceive, so four mates would definitely increase those odds."

"Could you not talk about my sex life?" I growled.

"Children are important. We need to continue the royal line," Dad said.

"Well, then why didn't you just remarry?" I asked.

"There is no one who can compare to your mother," he whispered, and a wistful expression crossed his face. "She was perfect."

"She was," Sam agreed.

"I wish I could remember her," I whispered. I wished I could remember a lot of things.

"She loved you," Dad whispered. "More than anything else in the world. She would be proud to see you as you are. You're a lot like her. So proud and beautiful. She never backed down when she truly believed in something."

"Definitely sounds like our Jolie," Rhys said.

Sam, Dad, and I jumped at the sudden appearance of Rhys, the mage, the wolf, and the elf.

"What are you doing here?" I asked. "You haven't completed the quest yet, have you?"

Leona and Colton stepped from behind them and I flew into their arms. "You're okay!"

They hugged me back tightly.

"You're not," Leona whispered. "And it's all my fault."

"It's not your fault," I assured her.

"We need to defeat him. Now," Colton said.

"Dad, they won. They found what I'd hidden. You need to announce them as the winners," I said urgently.

Dad nodded, stood, and opened his mouth, but no sound came out.

"Not. So. Fast," Brayden hissed. He held a dagger to the back of my father and glared at us.

"You've lost," I told him. "You lost the Gauntlet and you've lost Atlantis. Just give up."

"No!" he snapped. "This is my kingdom and I will not let these scumbags ruin it for me!"

Sam moved back behind the thrones, his position hidden from Brayden.

"This is not your kingdom! Atlantis will never bow to you," I growled.

"You aren't even princess," Brayden said with a sneer. "You're still banished."

"Even if you win today, then what? You think I'm going to sit demurely by your side while you rule?"

"No, I'll kill you as soon as we're wed," he said.

My four mates growled and took a step closer, but Brayden stuck the knife against my father's back, making my dad hiss in pain as it pierced the skin.

"Not a step closer," he ordered them.

"You're pathetic," I growled. "You can't even fight me yourself. You have to resort to using a hostage. How do you think you can rule Atlantis when a poor, defenseless girl like me frightens you?"

"You don't frighten me," he said and scoffed. I could smell the lie instantly.

"Fight me, then," I challenged him. "You win, and you get Atlantis. I win, and you die," I said.

He thought about it. "Your mates aren't allowed to interfere."

I rolled my eyes. "Obviously. I challenged you to a duel, not to fight all of us."

"Deal," he said and lowered the knife.

The idiot had no idea what he'd done. Rushing forward, I grabbed him by the front of his shirt and tossed him sideways, away from my father. The elf was nearest him and he attempted to stab him, but Brayden rolled out of the way.

The men began attacking him, four of them against just Brayden. Brayden did something to me that made me cry out in pain and clutch my head. Brayden's power cracked into the wall I had built around my bonds and surged down Rhys's bond.

"No!" I screamed.

Rhys froze, his eyes rolling up into his head a moment, then he began to attack the wolf.

"Nico!" the wolf yelled as he protected himself against Rhys.

The mage, Nico, cursed and ran to me. "It's now or never, love."

I tried to say something, but Brayden sent more power into my head and tried to get to Nico's bond.

Nico whispered a spell quickly beneath his breath and slowly, painfully, began to push Brayden out of my head.

"Just a bit more," he whispered as I screamed.

Slowly, the pain eased and when it did, I was alone in my head again. But, the memories were still locked away.

"You kill me and she'll never get her memory back!" Brayden hissed. He lay on the ground with the wolf holding him while the elf held a sword to his throat.

"I can't remember," I whispered and looked up at Nico. "I don't remember still."

"Unlock her memories now!" the mage bellowed, his body glowing as he struggled to control his fury. Sparks fizzled at his fingertips.

I giggled and they all looked at me. "Sparkles," I said and looked right at Nico. "You're Sparkles."

"Yes," he whispered and turned to me. "Do you remember?"

"She won't. I've locked them down too tightly," Brayden said smugly. "I reinforced them after Sam put a crack in it."

"We should just kill him," the wolf snarled.

"If you do, I'll never get my memories back," I said softly. I would never know what happened to me. Or who I was.

"We can make new memories," the elf said. "I would rather have you, without your memories, than risk him hurting you more."

"I don't even know your names," I said with tears in my eyes, momentarily blinding me. I hurriedly wiped them away.

"Nico," the wolf said, "I have an idea."

Rhys took the wolf's spot, holding Brayden down, so the wolf could walk to us. He whispered in Nico's ear, then looked at me with a smile.

Nico thought about it for several tense and silent moments, then nodded. "It might work." He stood before me and I shrank back at his intense stare. His gaze softened and he brushed my hair away from my face. "This might hurt, but I'll try to minimize that as much as possible."

The wolf stood beside Nico and me, a warm smile on his face. "Just try to relax, okay?"

I nodded. These males were not likely to try to hurt me. At least, not on purpose. They were my mates, whether I remembered fully or not.

Nico placed his fingers against my temples and closed his eyes. "Okay," he said.

The wolf set his fingers atop Nico's and took a steadying breath before closing his eyes.

I followed suit, closed my eyes, and waited.

I saw myself standing on a bus, looking at a strange electronic device. I had always wanted to ride on a bus. The bus stopped, and as I reached for my bag, a male snatched it and ran off the bus. I heard myself yell, but then I saw the bag snatcher on the ground, under a foot.

"This was the day I met you," the wolf's voice whispered in my head.

An arm appeared, holding my bag out to me, as I walked to him. I looked happy, but there were heavy bags beneath my eyes and my body seemed frail.

I was seeing the wolf's memories!

The image changed to me sitting across from the wolf at a restaurant. The dress I had on was pretty and I chatted with him about something…a game of some sort.

More memories played, some were very intimate, and I felt my face flush since Nico was likely seeing them as well. Deryn. The wolf's name was Deryn.

"Sam, swap with Fox," Deryn ordered him.

The memories stopped, but Nico kept his fingers on my temples.

"You okay?" he asked.

I nodded.

"Any new memories?" he asked.

"No," I replied softly. "But, I think it's helping."

The elf walked over. He was the shortest of the four, but extremely muscular. He was also the happiest of the bunch, radiating joy, even now.

"Ready, cupcake?" he asked.

"Yes."

He set his fingers on top of Nico's and we all closed our eyes.

The first memory was me, sitting in a park with crossed legs and closed eyes, grumbling to myself. It looked like I was trying to meditate. The elf sat beside me and we talked, then walked around the park together. Another memory showed me sitting on a sidewalk, looking scared and sad. The elf's body shrank down and he crawled into my lap. Another memory, me standing while Fox, that was his name, and the other three bowed to me. Four princes bowing to me.

The shell around my memories cracked more.

"No!" Brayden yelled.

"Rhys," Fox said. "Your turn."

Rhys took his place and funneled memories of fun, pleasure, and fighting. He was always fighting for me. Even with the bond closed, I could tell he loved me. It was evident in how he always kept an eye on me wherever we were and in how he would caress me while I slept.

They all loved me.

Rhys stepped back and wiped away a tear that had fallen from my eyes. "Did I hurt you?" he asked.

"You love me, so much," I whispered.

He smiled. "We do."

The shell cracked a little more, allowing a few memories to slip out. The memories weren't nice ones, but painful experiences of mine. A woman severing my bonds with the princes was the first, and the second was of me trapped in a cupboard of some sort.

I whimpered, and Nico began to funnel his memories to me.

"Yes, there are lots of painful memories."

He showed me a memory of me being stabbed at a party.

"But, there are also happy ones."

This memory was of a holiday event, all of us together and laughing, while eating desserts.

The shell broke apart and my memories rushed forward. Nico broke contact with me and gasped in pain as he fell to his knees.

New hands touched my head and slowed the memories, letting them funnel through at a pace that was not as painful. When the last memory was set in place, I opened my eyes to find Leona holding me.

"Leona," I whispered, my voice hoarse as though I'd been yelling.

"I owed you," she said softly.

"Did-did you see them?"

She nodded. "I'm so sorry that you endured so much."

"You've ruined everything!" Brayden screamed.

Everyone froze. Nico was weak from helping me and couldn't counter him.

Brayden shoved Sam and Fox away and stood. "This isn't over," Brayden snarled at me.

Leona's hands dropped, and I was able to move. I faced Brayden and sang the lullaby my grandmother had taught me. At the time, I thought it was just a lullaby, but now I knew. It was a type of siren's call, but one for empaths to use against sirens. It enraptured them.

Brayden jerked back, his eyes wide. I continued to sing, power pouring from me in waves. His legs trembled and he screamed. He stabbed his trident in its small, pen-sized form into his leg, breaking my hold and fled.

I collapsed to the stone floor of the platform and smiled. He may have escaped, but I was back to my old self.

CHAPTER 11

Brayden had escaped Atlantis, but that was no longer important.

Dad stood before me, scowling as he looked at me and my four mates. "You are princess here," he said.

"Technically, I'm still banished. Plus, I have my hands full back in Jinla," I said.

"I don't think she could survive a month without her video games," Nico whispered.

The other three chuckled in agreement.

I would have argued, but he was right.

"You can make someone else your heir," I said.

"Any suggestions?" he asked me and sat on his throne.

"Sam," I said without hesitation. "He is one hundred percent loyal to the royal family. And, he's a decent fighter."

Dad tapped the arm of his throne, a solid gold and jewel covered monstrosity, as he thought about it. "Very well."

"I'd like to leave tomorrow morning," I told him.

He sighed and his eyes dropped to the floor at my feet. "Okay."

"If it's alright with you, I'd like to come visit from time to time. I know I'm banished, but—"

"Your banishment is lifted. You may visit as often as you'd like. And, you will always be Princess of the Sirens," Dad said and smiled wide, wrinkles forming at the corners of his eyes.

I bowed. "Thank you."

He looked at my mates. "She's all I have left. She's a handful and she's bound to get you into a lot of trouble."

"Rude," I muttered.

"Please, do all you can to keep her safe," Dad said.

"She's not just our mate, but our queen as well," Deryn told him. "We will do everything we can to keep her safe."

Dad nodded, pleased. "Since you are leaving tomorrow, we must have a feast tonight."

He always loved feasts, having them as often as he could when I was a child, so this was no surprise.

"Sam!" Dad yelled.

Sam entered the throne room, having been standing just outside the doors. "Yes, Your Majesty?"

"Tell everyone we are having a feast tonight! Tell the chef to get to work, immediately."

"You're leaving tomorrow?" Sam guessed.

I nodded. "I need to return home."

He scowled and said no more, turning and marching out to follow Dad's orders.

"Go and rest," Dad said. "I'll have Sam collect you when it's time for the feast."

We all bowed to him then walked to my chambers. My body and mind were still reeling from everything that had happened. Plus, I'd used my powers and that had significantly drained me.

We lay on my bed, my head on Rhys's stomach as he slept perpendicular to me. Fox and Deryn slept parallel to me, spooning their bodies to mine, while Nico lay at my feet, hugging them like a teddy bear against his chest.

"Thank you," I whispered to them. "Your memories were just what I needed."

"You need to rest," Fox whispered and stroked my hair.

"You four have no idea how much your love means to me. I don't think I can ever express how much I love you. I owe you so much. You've done so much for me in such a short amount of time."

"And we'll keep doing them, for the rest of our lives," Deryn whispered, his voice groggy with sleep.

"Sleep, my queen. We have plenty of time for everything else. But, you need to recharge," Rhys ordered me, his chest rumbling beneath my head.

♥

The feast and dance afterwards had been a ton of fun. We invited the entire Atlantis population to the royal courtyard and Dad reinstated the merchants' rights to sell once more. It brought some color back, but there was still a lot of work to be done. We ate, drank, and danced, celebrating my mates, the defeat of Brayden, and the new heir.

Leona pulled me aside, near the end of the feast, and held out a leather journal. "You should take this."

At first, I thought it was the journal Brayden had given me, but this one was larger, a true journal size.

"What is it?" I asked as I accepted it.

"Everything we know about empaths. I wrote it all down for you," she said with a smile.

I hugged her. "Thank you, Leona."

"Anything for you, Jojo."

"I'm going to miss you," I whispered into her chest.

"What about me?" Colton asked.

I turned and hugged him. "You, too."

"Am I just odd man out? Or are you mad since I'm heir now?" Sam asked.

I giggled and hugged him, then stepped back to look at the three of them. "Thank you, for everything. I couldn't have wished for better friends."

I bowed to them and several people nearby gasped.

"We don't bow to each other," Sam said, parroting something I had said to them as a child.

I stood and held out my hand, palm down and horizontal. "Friends forever."

They placed their hands in a stack atop mine and said in unison, "Friends forever."

We converged for a group hug and I had to wipe my eyes when I stepped back. "Keep each other safe. That's an order from your princess."

They smiled and nodded.

I clutched the journal to my chest and sniffled. "If I stay longer, I'm going to cry."

"Come, my queen," Fox said and slid an arm around my waist. "You need to pack or we won't leave on time tomorrow."

"Until we meet again," Colton said.

My three childhood best friends bowed and left.

"We'll come visit," Fox promised.

I sniffled again and wiped at my eyes. "I know."

Rhys, Nico, and Deryn sat on the floor in my room, talking quietly when we entered.

I sat beside Deryn and leaned my head against his shoulder. "What's up?" I asked.

"We were discussing how your title affects things," Deryn explained.

"Does it?" I asked.

"Yes," Nico said and nodded. "For one, you can't be the human council member."

"Right, since I'm not human."

"You could be the siren council member, but you would need your dad's approval for that," Nico continued.

"I can ask before we leave," I said. I set the journal Leona had written for me in the center of our circle. "Here is everything known about empaths and some general siren knowledge as well."

Nico opened it and began reading. He paused and looked at me over the top of the journal. "This says you have difficulty getting pregnant."

I nodded. "We are almost infertile. One in three sirens are actually infertile."

He went back to reading.

"I need to pack," I said and stood. A suitcase had been brought to the room for me. I packed the dresses the seamstress had made. They were too beautiful to leave behind. I also packed my copy of the picture Colton kept on his fridge, plus a few trinkets from my childhood.

I put the packed suitcase by the door, then sat in Rhys's lap, leaning my head against his chest.

"Dan destroyed the office," Rhys whispered.

"What? When?"

"When your dad and Trident Douche left with you. He roared and threw a chair through one of the building's windows. Then he broke the table and threw a couple more chairs before Deryn got him to stop."

"You're telling me that Deryn was calmer than Dan?"

Rhys nodded.

"He blamed himself for you being taken," Deryn said. "I haven't seen him lose it like that in a long time."

"My dad and Rhys's dad weren't much better," Fox said. "They were glowing and shifting. I don't think I've ever seen my dad so angry."

"I'd be pretty angry, too, if some random guy teleported into what should have been a safe place and interrupted my meeting," I said.

"By contrast, we were pretty calm," Nico said, eyes still glued to the book.

Wow. I knew they were fond of me, but I couldn't believe the kings would be so upset over losing me.

"They were probably mad that Trident Douche had been able to freeze them," I said.

Rhys shook his head. "It was you. They love you like their own daughter."

Three alphas roaring with rage and throwing tantrums when their son's mate was taken. It was a sight I would love to have seen. It was also hard to believe.

"I can show you the video when we get home," Deryn said. "I can see that you still don't believe us fully."

"Would you, if the tables were turned?" I asked.

"I suppose not," he agreed.

"I don't think you're lying," I added. "It's just hard to believe it was because of me."

"You can make people hallucinate," Nico whispered, eyebrows nearly touching his hairline.

"Supposedly, but I wasn't able to do it when training with Leona."

But Leona had been able to do it to me when Brayden took us to the dungeon.

"Scary," Fox whispered. I looked at him and he smiled. "Not you. The power."

"It is my power, it is part of me," I said, stood, and walked to the vanity. Nothing about me had changed physically, but I felt different.

"We'll have to see if we can find an empath to train you," Rhys said.

"There aren't many of us," I explained. "Leona, old lady Anthea, and I are the only ones, as far as I know."

"Maybe we need to offer Leona a job?" Nico asked and looked up at me.

I looked at him in the mirror's reflection. "You're scared of me," I realized, whispering the words because they were painful to say.

"You're powerful, even more so with our powers also at your

disposal," he said carefully. "You need training, so you don't accidentally do something."

He hadn't denied being scared of me. Wonderful.

Nico set the book down and came to stand behind me. He met my eyes in the mirror. "I'm not scared of you. I'm scared of uncertainty, and your new powers make you an uncertainty. You could enthrall Jinla without meaning to. You could project your nightmares and make us think they are really happening. I'm most worried about you doing something you'll regret and end up wallowing about it. You are a wonderful person and I want to keep you happy and safe as long as I can. I know you would never forgive yourself if you hurt Gavin or one of the others. I'm going to go find Leona."

"She's probably at her or Colton's house in Shelnam," I said.

Nico hugged me from behind and kissed the top of my head. "Okay."

It was hard saying goodbye to my friends and Dad. Nico created a protective shield and we stepped through the portal. Nico's shield kept us from drowning as we entered the undersea cave.

"Pookie!" I yelled, then whistled.

"A Kraken pet," Deryn chuckled. "You should add that to one of your game's storylines."

"That's a good idea," I said seriously, a story already forming in my head.

Pookie swam to us and shrieked in joy when he saw me. He quickly used his magic to surround us and brought us to rest on his head.

I patted him and murmured praises as he swam out of the cave and up the trench. Instead of waiting for our boat, I had Pookie take us all the way to the shore. People screamed and fled the beach. Many took pictures and I couldn't wait for the headline tomorrow in the newspaper.

Pookie used a tentacle to lift me off his head and bring me to his eye level.

"Thank you. You're the best Kraken ever," I said.

Pookie made a cooing noise and set me down on the beach next to my mates, who had leapt off Pookie when he stopped. I waved and

Pookie waved a tentacle back before diving into the waters and disappearing.

"Ready?" Fox asked.

"Wait for it," I said, a smirk on my lips as I stared out to sea.

"For what?" Rhys asked, squinting as he looked out.

Pookie shot up and out of the water, his entire body in the air for a moment before he fell back down.

"Goodbye," I whispered and laughed, surprised the Kraken remembered me teaching him to do that.

"Your Highnesses," someone panted behind us.

We turned and looked at the wolf before us, panting hard.

"What is it?" Deryn asked.

"The alpha has lost it. He's destroying your house," the male panted.

Rhys shifted, and we climbed onto his back. As fast as possible, we flew to the pack.

The house was completely destroyed when we arrived and Dan, in warrior form, stood in the rubble howling.

I leapt from Rhys, letting dragon wings form to slow my descent and landed in front of Dan. He looked at me and cocked his head, pausing his howling.

"Dan, what's going on?" I asked.

Martin, Sharla, and the twins stood off to the side, safe, but upset.

Dan growled and walked up to me. "You can't be her. She's gone."

"I'm back," I assured him. "Smell me."

He did and his eyes widened.

"Jolie?" he asked. "I heard you were dead."

"From who?" Deryn asked as he came to my side.

Dan pulled Deryn into a bone-crunching hug and shifted back to human form. "Son, you're alive!"

Deryn hugged his dad back. "Dad, what's going on?"

"We received word that you'd been killed in Atlantis. Your bonds are gone," Dan explained. He opened his mouth, then closed it. "No, they're back now."

"Search the compound!" I screamed. "He's here!"

Someone laughed off in the distance. Rhys roared and took off after him, but Brayden had a few tricks up his sleeve. With a burst of light, he disappeared.

Dan pulled me into a hug, inhaling my scent deeply. "I'm sorry, Jolie."

"Why are you apologizing?" I asked, hugging him back.

"We let you get kidnapped. We've become lazy and overconfident."

I patted him. "You have no reason to apologize. They surprised us all. Besides, I needed to go home."

He pushed me back. "So, it's true? You're a siren?"

I nodded. "An empath, actually."

"So, you're Princess Jolie of the Sirens and Four Clans of Jinla?"

"Apparently," I said and sighed. "My life is always so complicated."

Thor and Ezio ran from the gathered pack's mob and hugged me between them. They rubbed their faces against mine silently.

Deryn growled and they both released me.

"Sorry," Thor said and canted his head to the side in submission.

"Jolie, you're okay," Ezio said and hugged me again.

"I am," I assured him.

He released me and looked at Deryn. "No disrespect."

Deryn sighed and rubbed his hand down his face. "She's your alpha female. I get it."

Dan looked at the rubble at his feet. "Guess we're getting a new house." He looked over, meeting my eyes. "I thought I had lost you and Deryn. I thought you were dead."

I thought he had used Leona to make me hallucinate, but this made it apparent that Brayden had the powers of hallucination as well, too.

"He's a manipulator," I said. "He makes you do and believe whatever he wants."

Dan asked, "And what about you?"

"Me?"

"You're a manipulator, too, right?"

I supposed I was.

"I guess, technically. But, I haven't been able to."

Dan shifted again. "Get off my land."

"What?" I asked, staring in disbelief as Ezio and Thor shifted and growled at me, too.

Tears slid down my cheeks.

"You're no longer welcome here," Dan said, snarling.

No. This wasn't real. Dan wouldn't do this.

I had to be hallucinating.

Closing my eyes, I focused on the magic within me. There,

Brayden still had a piece of magic inside my head. He'd camouflaged it well, but now I had it. I squashed it like a bug and opened my eyes.

Dan cradled me in his arms, worry lines marring his forehead.

"Hello, Alpha," I whispered.

He rested his forehead against mine. "Daughter, why are you crying?"

I told him, and he wiped my tears away.

"You are pack. Forever," he whispered.

Dan held me for several more minutes, even growling at Deryn when he tried to get close. Everyone left us alone and for the first time, I felt what a father's love should be. My true father loved me and I couldn't blame him for banishing me, since that had been Brayden's doing. Yet, I still hadn't felt true, fatherly love until Dan.

"Where?" Emrys roared.

Dan leaned back and scowled at Emrys who shoved wolves who were too slow to move out of his way. Dan stood, releasing me, and took a step back.

Emrys's eyes were dragon's eyes and smoke billowed out of his nostrils. He growled and Dan backed up more, his hands raised.

"What's going on?" I asked softly, not looking away from Emrys as he approached.

"Same as me," Dan whispered. "His alpha protective urge is in full swing. Someone must have reported your return and he rushed here. Normally, this would be an act of war, but I know what he's going through."

"What is that? What are you going through?" I asked.

"We thought we had lost our daughter. Thought we would never see her again, thanks to our failure to protect her. Her return is something we have to see. We have to smell and touch you to ensure that you are real. We have to know we didn't completely fail and that you are truly here. Truly safe."

"Shouldn't you be happy instead of angry about my return?" I asked. Emrys was almost to me now, his eyes glued to mine.

Dan chuckled. "The fury is for those keeping us from you or trying to take you away."

Emrys stopped before me and reached out a trembling hand. I stepped forward and wrapped my arms around him, my head against his chest.

He inhaled my hair at the top of my head and a single sob broke free before he wrapped me up in his arms and held me silently.

I let him hold me as I had with Dan, letting him absorb my presence.

"Daughter," he whispered. "Are you hurt?"

"I'm fine, Father," I replied and smiled up at him. "I told you I would come back."

He set his hand on my cheek and tears glistened in his eyes. "I thought I'd lost you. I've never lost a child and I thought you would be my first. Those two siren males surprised me and I realized, for all my lectures to you about remaining aware, I was not."

"Dad says he's sorry by the way. He was under mind control, but he still feels bad about breaching your territory," I whispered.

Emrys smiled. "You are back and safe. All else is irrelevant." He looked over my head and scowled. "Dan, what happened to your house?"

"Jolie!" Katar yelled.

"Oh, sure, everyone just breach my territory. No problem," Dan said, throwing his arms up in a gesture of frustration, but he smiled at the same time.

"You know why," Emrys said. "Would you have stayed away if she were at my place?"

Dan waved his hand dismissively.

Katar reached for me, still with Emrys's arm around me and Emrys growled.

Katar growled back and began to glow.

"Whoa!" I yelled. "Emrys!"

Emrys stopped snarling and shook his head. "Sorry." He released me and went to stand beside Dan.

"Jolie," Katar whispered.

I turned and bowed. "Your Majesty."

He went to grab me for a hug, but Kara, Katar's mate and Fox's mother, snatched me first, embracing me tightly.

"Jolie," she cried, tears streaming down her face. "You're really back."

Katar growled, and Kara flinched, releasing me quickly so Katar could hug me. "I didn't realize he was so far gone," she whispered.

"I didn't know elves had the same problem," Emrys said.

Kara nodded. "It's very rare, that's why I didn't think about him having it."

Katar held me, then pushed me out to arm's length. "If you ever sacrifice yourself for me, Emrys, or Dan again, I'll lock you in my cells for a month!"

I smiled and said, "I missed you, too, Katar."

The rage left him and his shoulders slumped. "Father," he whispered and hugged me again. "You can call me father."

"Do I get to hug her now?" Kara asked with her hands on her hips and one eyebrow arched.

Katar released me to allow his mate to hug me. Kara smacked the back of my head.

"Ouch!" I yelled.

"Stop trying to be the martyr! I'll follow through on Katar's threat. I won't hesitate to lock you up," she said.

"They'll do it," Fox called.

I turned, realizing my mates had stayed back throughout the entire ordeal. They stood beside Martin and his family, watching us while leaning against the wall of the building they stood before.

"Dan, what did you do to your house?" Kara asked.

Dan rubbed the back of his neck sheepishly. "Uh—"

"He decided it needed more bedrooms," I said. "Since I'll be trying to provide an heir or two."

"What?" all four of my mates asked, pushing off the wall and moving towards me.

"I'm not exactly the same person as I was when I left," I explained. "Getting my memories back and truly unlocking my powers has changed me." I looked at the alphas and smiled. "I've decided that I want a little Jolie running around. To see my child spoiled by not just one grandfather, but all of you makes it even more appealing."

"You mean it?" Deryn asked, his eyes alight.

"I can't promise to give you each an heir. I can't even promise to have one, since sirens have low fertility, but I know you will all love my child, no matter who the father is."

Deryn picked me up and crushed his mouth to mine. He set me down and the other three hugged me.

Kara hugged me and whispered, "I may be able to help increase your fertility."

"Okay, but not until we deal with Justina." *And Brayden.* The last thing I needed was to put a child in danger. Plus, there was still the worry of my dhampir war dreams.

"We can wait as long as you want," Fox said.

"She is back, the rumors were true," Johann said, appearing next to Nico.

"Yes, she is," Nico said, since everyone else was too busy glaring at Johann to respond.

"How strong are your empath abilities?" Johann asked.

"I'm powerful, but I don't have the ability to use many of my powers yet," I admitted.

"Would it be better to detain her?" he asked.

"Try it," Dan growled, his eyes turning amber.

Johann raised his hands. "I'm just asking a question."

"She's able to contain her powers," Nico told him.

"We have a teacher coming in a few days," Rhys added.

Johann nodded. "Smart. It's not a good idea to allow an untrained siren to run around."

"Afraid I might ensnare you? Make you like me?" I asked with a scowl.

He smiled, and I was shocked at the difference a smile could make. He looked...fatherly instead of scary.

"I already like you, which I'm sure you know."

I did.

"Your powers were at work from the time you met Rhys," he whispered to me.

"How do you know?" I asked.

He teleported to stand beside me and whispered into my ear, "Because I loathe sirens, yet I can't find any other emotion for you besides admiration. You wanted nothing more than to be loved and here you stand, four princes as your mates and their alphas loving you as if you were their daughter. This isn't a fairy tale and yet you seem to be headed to your happy ever after."

Johann disappeared, leaving me staring at my feet.

He wasn't wrong.

"What did he say?" Nico asked.

"I need a minute," I whispered and backed away from them.

"Jolie," Emrys called my name like you would a child about to do something bad.

"I just need some time. Some space," I said. "I won't leave the wolf lands. Just...give me some space." I let out wings and flew towards the forest, shutting down my bonds with my mates as I searched for a place to think alone. A few miles into the forest, I came to a small waterfall. It had a large boulder at its base, which served as a perfect place to sit. I sat atop it and closed my eyes.

Johann wasn't wrong. This was too good to be true. Yes, bad things had happened, but overall my life was great. Were my powers at work, unbeknownst to me? Was I slowly brainwashing them? Was there a way to reverse it?

"Hello, child," a woman's voice said.

I opened my eyes and my mouth dropped open. A woman floated beside the rock I sat upon, her body see through.

Johann's comment about this not being a fairy tale popped into my head. "Are you my fairy godmother?"

She laughed and said, "I'm your mother, dear."

My mother?

"Siren mother?" I asked.

She scowled. "What other kind is there?"

"Long story, never mind. What are you doing here? Aren't you dead?"

"I bartered with the Goddess to be able to come to you when you most needed me. So, tell me what troubles the Princess of the Sirens?"

"Where do I start?" I sighed.

"What is upsetting you right now?" she asked, sitting down on the rock beside me. I was surprised she didn't pass through it.

"I have four mates and their families love me. Well, most of them. One of them suggested that it might be because my siren abilities were active even without me knowing. That I used my powers to make them fall in love with me."

"We are generally more appealing to others. People do have a tendency to fall for us faster, but it's not a power we control. Sirens are alluring. That's just how we are. We can't stop it."

"What if I did use my powers without knowing?"

"Does it matter now?" she asked. "If they're already your mates, then they must truly love you. Our abilities don't make someone fall in love with us permanently. We would have to keep using our powers constantly or keep them in a trance to do that. You may have unconsciously put out vibes, but you didn't make them fall in love with you."

"How do you know?"

"Because I had the same issues," she said.

"What about making them addicted to you?" I asked. "I was told we could make them crave being around us so much that they become addicted."

She nodded and said, "It can happen. We radiate joy and people crave that, especially in a world full of darkness. However, it is difficult to make people addicted. I doubt you made anyone an addict because that power is the hardest to learn."

"Mom, I'm afraid. I'm afraid Johann is right, and my powers created this world for me."

Her arm wrapped around me and it felt very real. "I promise that you did not make them fall in love with you. I promise that you are a good person. I can see your soul and it radiates with a goodness necessary for an empath. Keep your heart open and do what you think is right. Your mates love you so much that they interrupted our reunion."

"What?" I asked and looked behind us.

"Who is that?" Fox asked, his voice awed and his eyes wide.

"This is my mother," I whispered and stood.

She stood with me and curtsied. "Hello, Sons. Thank you for keeping her safe. I know you'll continue to do so in the future."

"How are you here?" Nico asked.

"Bartered with the Goddess," she replied. She glided around my mates, looking into each of their eyes and each one, she gave a nod of approval to. "These four will do. I can assure you that their love is true and you didn't bespell them into loving you. Do you have a teacher? He will have to be sure to teach you how to and how not to tamper with their clans' bonds. It is possible for you to tap into them and cause all to become enraged or calm, depending on your desire."

"Leona is coming to teach me," I said, filing away that terrifying possibility for later.

She smiled. "Little Leona. When she was born the entire Kingdom cried, because she *made* us cry. She is one of the strongest empaths I've ever met."

"I'll let her know you approve," I said.

She turned and looked at Nico. "Johann hates sirens. He will never accept us. So, keep an eye on him when Jolie is around. He may like her right now, but his hatred is deep for sirens."

"What happened to make him hate us?" I asked.

She smirked. "He doesn't enjoy losing fights, especially against a young girl who wields no weapons. He doesn't like when people are more powerful than him."

"You fought him?" Fox asked, eyes wide.

"At a Summit Tournament," she replied with a nod.

"Wait, the sirens used to attend?" Rhys asked.

She scowled. "What do you mean *used to*? We've been attending since the Summit was founded."

"They haven't been part of the Summit since we've been attending," Rhys said.

She spun and faced me with a fiery glare. "You tell your father to begin attending again or I will find a way to haunt him."

"I will," I promised, thinking that Brayden must have stopped the sirens from attending the Summit, too.

She mumbled under her breath while looking skyward.

"Mother," I whispered.

Her eyes dropped to mine and she smiled. "There is so much light in you, Jolie. But, there is also darkness. Do not let the darkness take over. If that happens, you may not come back. You have abilities beyond mine. You could destroy the world."

"No pressure," I whispered, my face feeling flushed.

"Boys, you can prevent this by acts of love or even friendship. Keep her happy and safe. If she slips, call her back with your light. Remind her of your love and the things she cherishes. Understand?"

All four princes nodded.

She made a strange sign with her hand and a box popped into existence before her. She held it out to me and said, "This is Selene. She was my familiar. Put her on your forearm and call upon her when you need aid. She's snarky, but powerful."

Inside the box lay a piece of paper, like the one Nar, the kitsune, had given me, but this had a drawing of a unicorn.

"A unicorn? Are you telling me that this is a real, live unicorn?" I asked, mouth agape.

She smiled and nodded. "She's the last of her kind, as far as I know. They're very powerful. I know she'll be an asset to you."

"Thank you," I said and closed the box's lid.

"You and your mates need to talk," she said. "I love you, Jolie. I wish I had gotten to see you grow up, but I am proud of the woman you are." She kissed me on the cheek, then disappeared.

CHAPTER 12

We didn't talk, instead we opted to go home and nap.

Strangely, the four of them opted for their own apartments, leaving me alone in mine. I could tell they weren't mad at me, so I didn't complain nor question them. Sometimes we all needed a little alone time to rejuvenate ourselves, and I totally understood that.

After napping, I popped in an old survival game I hadn't played in years. It was a relatively simple game. The goal was to survive as many days as possible. You had to gather supplies, hunt for food, and defend yourself against monsters on occasion. I had a small base where I had two machines set up that, when I was near them, allowed me to create special gear. I also had a permanent fire pit that I just had to add wood to because you had to keep a fire going at night or the monsters would get you. It didn't require a ton of focus, but it still brought a smile to my face.

Deryn walked in a couple hours later and sat behind me, putting his legs outside of mine and letting me rest my back against his chest.

"I haven't seen this game in a long time," Deryn commented and kissed the side of my head. "I used to love this game."

"I love it because it's fun, but relaxing," I said as I picked flowers in the game.

He rubbed my arms gently as I played, and we stayed like that for a half an hour. Then, I turned on a stand-up comedy show I had been wanting to watch. Deryn lay on his side and I lay down in front of him on the couch, scooting back against him so he could wrap his arms around me and cuddle me. It was the first time I'd been able to relax and laugh with just one of them in a while.

"This is nice," Deryn whispered.

I nodded in agreement. It really was.

"Dad really loves you," he whispered. "He was so scared when he thought he'd lost you. He was in so much pain."

"Scared?"

He nodded. "Since your pack bond was locked by Trident Douche, you couldn't feel it. He was so scared. You've become a part of his life, one he looks forward to. The thought that you would no longer be in his life was what really scared him."

Being part of their lives was great and knowing Dan truly cared for me made it even better.

I ordered ten pizzas, then sent a message to the group chat to let the others know.

Deryn continued to cuddle with me until the others came, then he went to my kitchen and grabbed beers for his friends and a cider for me.

Fox sat at my feet and rubbed them while watching the movie I had put on. It was the newest super hero action movie, one we had planned to go see in the theaters, but never got a chance to.

Deryn lifted me so he could sit at my head and let me rest it on his thigh. Rhys and Nico sat on the couch between Fox and Deryn, my body draped across them.

I bolted upright and looked at the couch. "When did you get this?"

It wasn't my couch. My couch had only fit three people at a time. This one had enough room that I could sit between Rhys and Nico without being squished. It was the longest couch I had ever seen.

"Oh, right!" Deryn said and smiled. "I forgot with everything going on, to tell you. This was made by Ezio. He gave it to us as a mating present."

Ezio had started to dabble with furniture making towards the end of our relationship. I'd never seen a finished piece though. It was made from a single log that he'd added cushions to and applied a lacquer to the log that made it shine and prevented us from getting splinters. It shocked me that he had gone out of his way to make something like this for us. It wasn't that long ago that he had disliked Deryn.

"What did my dad say to you?" Nico asked, scowling.

"He's convinced I've been using my powers since I met you. It's the only explanation for my happily-ever-after and him liking me," I said.

"What changed your mind about kids?" Deryn asked.

"When I was young and still living at the palace in Atlantis, I would help out with the babies. I loved taking care of them and wanted lots of kids. When my memories were gone, my life after that was filled with danger and despair. I didn't want to bring a child into that. I don't want to bring a child into that. I want to see you playing with your children and see our kids with their grandparents. Your clans have been at war, but now we are at peace and I know they would cherish them and spoil them, even if they aren't their biological grandchildren. I hope I'm able to have children and I hope I can have one for each of you, but first, we need to find and kill Justina and Brayden."

"We will," Rhys promised.

The doorbell rang and Fox answered it, getting our pizzas from the delivery man, and set them on the coffee table. We all eagerly dug in and watched the movie. I sat between Nico and Rhys on our giant couch and relaxed. There were lots of things I could worry about, but now wasn't the time to worry about them. Now was the time to enjoy our peace, no matter how temporary it might be. If this adventure had done anything, it had made me realize that I needed to cherish the time I had with my mates. Our lives were chaotic at best and I never knew when me or my mates might get separated.

The four sites on the screen looked very similar, but their location was the most important factor. Two of them were close to the dragon's den, too close.

"Not those two," I said and pointed out the ones I was discussing.

Dan nodded and made a note on his paper.

The four alphas had made me part of their council, as the siren representative, and today was my first meeting. True to their word, they'd been working on my academy suggestion. One of these sites would be the school's location and once I chose, the big planning would begin.

I stared at the map with the two remaining sites' locations marked. One was in the center of the city near the park I had returned their necklace at. The other was in a warehouse district.

"This one. It's near food, a park, and has more transportation options," I said and pointed at the one by the park.

They nodded in agreement and Dan made more notes.

"We obtained some copies of rules and regulations handbooks from several schools. I'd recommend highlighting rules you want added to your school's handbook and writing new ones as well. Once you have these prepared, we will all review and make our own suggestions," Johann said.

He handed me ten booklets, and I set them on the growing stack of documents I had to take home.

Rhys opened a new presentation and put it on the large screen in front of us. "Here are a few options for the architecture," he said. "I can modify them if you need something changed."

He scrolled through a few.

"Stop!" I yelled as he moved to the fifth slide. "This one," I whispered. The drawing called to me and it took me a minute to realize why. "You incorporated something from each of the four clans in this one. It's perfect."

He pulled out the paper copy and handed it to Dan who looked at it closely, before giving it to the other alphas.

"Vote?" Dan asked after they'd all looked at it.

"Approved," the other three alphas said.

"Rhys, you are cleared to begin in depth work on this one," Dan said.

"Understood," Rhys replied and took the paper back.

"Any other business?" Dan asked.

No one spoke up.

"Today's meeting is adjourned," Dan said and stood up with a groan and stretched.

The other alphas stood as well and packed up their papers. I looked at my stack and sighed. So much work.

"Ready, Princess?" Rhys asked and added my documents to his stack.

I nodded and waved to the alphas. "See you later."

They waved back, and Rhys and I headed out of the office and down to the SUV where Thor waited for us. He hugged me and bumped his fist with Rhys's before climbing into the driver's seat.

"How was your first meeting?" Thor asked.

"I've got homework," I muttered, but honestly didn't feel bad. I was excited to get this school started and for the kids to learn about each other and actually be ready to go out into the world and interact with any race.

"What's on the agenda for the rest of the night?" Rhys asked.

"I have to work on my story proposal," I said.

"For your game proposal?" Rhys asked.

I nodded. It was the first time that I had come up with my own story idea and planned to pitch it to the company. To say I was nervous was a gross understatement.

"Aren't you going to the tournament tonight?" Thor asked.

"What tournament?" I asked back.

Please don't let it be more fighting. I had had enough with fighting tournaments. Not that I doubted my mates, but I just wasn't ready for more trouble.

"The huge video game tournament," he said, looking at me in the rearview mirror.

"FighterCon? FighterCon is tonight?" I screamed and pulled out my phone. How could I have forgotten about the biggest video game tournament in the country?

I checked the clan group chat and almost squealed out loud. Three of them were on planes right now, headed to Jinla.

"They're coming!" I screamed.

"Who?" Rhys asked.

"Dragon, Orphan, and Turbo! They're on their way now," I explained.

"Wait, your video game clan members are going to be here in person?" Rhys asked.

"I told you guys about this months ago," I reminded him.

"I'd forgotten with everything that happened," he whispered and gazed out the window.

I sent a text to the clan chat: *Can't wait to see you!*

Thor dropped us off and promised to come pick us up at five to take us to the convention center.

I tapped my foot anxiously as the elevator went up to my floor and Rhys chuckled.

"What?" I asked him.

"You're like a kid waiting to get candy."

"It's been years since I last saw them!" I explained. "And, I haven't been able to play online as much either. So, I'm super excited."

"I can't wait to meet them," Rhys said and smiled. He set down the stack of documents he had been carrying on the floor of the elevator.

"What?" I asked. I hadn't planned on introducing my clan to my mates. Not that I cared or didn't want them to meet. It just wasn't part of the plan.

He arched a brow. "Planning to ditch us for your friends?"

I rolled my eyes at him. "No, I just hadn't thought about it. Last FighterCon we met at, I had been single and my life wasn't always in danger. So, I didn't think about you guys coming this time."

"We're going," he said and folded his arms across his chest.

I got distracted by his biceps a moment, then met his eyes. "Okay. I wasn't trying to ditch you. I really just didn't think about it."

"You don't think about us?" Fox asked behind me and clutched his heart.

I rolled my eyes at him and walked out of the elevator. "You guys are ridiculous sometimes."

Fox pecked me on the cheek and smiled. "You love us."

I smiled. I did love them.

"What's got her all frazzled?" Fox asked, following beside Rhys as we walked to my apartment.

"She's got a big convention tonight and her clan members are coming. She wasn't planning on introducing us," Rhys said.

"That's not what I said!" I snapped.

Rhys smirked, and I realized that he was messing with me. I gave him my best glare and reached for my door handle, but it was suddenly not there. I fell sideways into Deryn who just laughed.

"It's nice to see you, too," he said and hugged me.

I stood on tiptoe and kissed his cheek. "Hello, Moon Moon."

"That's a big stack of crap," Deryn commented as Rhys walked in.

"Showering!" I yelled to them and ran to the bathroom. I could hear them talking and laughing and smiled as I turned the shower on.

"Mind if I join you?" Nico asked.

I screamed and spun around with scales covering my body.

He laughed so hard that he doubled over and clutched at his stomach.

I punched his shoulder as hard as I could with my dragon scale covered hand. "You jerk!"

He rubbed his shoulder, but didn't look remorseful at all. "You should be able to sense me teleporting near you with our bond. I shouldn't be able to startle you like that."

"I still can't quite figure out how to use the bonds," I admitted and looked down at my feet.

"It's okay. It takes some getting used to. I can help you. First, let's get in the shower so we aren't late," Nico said.

I nodded and stripped quickly before climbing into the shower. He climbed in behind me and wrapped his arms around me, pressing his body against mine as we stood under the warm water.

"I missed you today," he whispered in my ear.

"I missed you, too," I said and rubbed one of his forearms that was latched around me, just below my breasts.

"What are your plans tomorrow?" he asked.

"Hanging out with the clan for a bit, most likely," I said.

"Well, how about I take you out for a dinner date? Just you and me."

I turned around and wrapped my arms around his shoulders, linking my fingers behind his head. "That sounds wonderful. Where are we going to go?"

"Wherever you want," he said and kissed the tip of my nose.

While I thought about what I wanted, he tilted my head back to get my hair in the water and rubbed it a bit so it got completely wet, then he added shampoo and lathered me up.

"I'll let you know tomorrow," I said. "I can't think about tomorrow's food yet."

He rinsed my hair out and then washed his hair while I soaped up my body. "How was the meeting?" he asked.

"Good. I'm really excited about this school. I think it's going to be really good for the kids," I said, then playfully pushed him with my hip out of the water so I could rinse.

"It's a great idea. I can't wait to see how it goes," he said.

"Nico, is there something bothering you?" I asked him.

He scowled a moment, then sighed. "Yeah. I had an argument with my dad."

"About me," I guessed.

He nodded. "He really hates sirens."

"Well, I can't change what I was born as. It's not like I chose to be a siren or an empath," I grumbled.

"I know. He's just an ass," he said. He pushed me back against the wall of the shower, putting a hand on either side of my head. "And I don't care what he says. You're fucking perfect."

"I'm far from perfect, but I appreciate the compliment," I said and kissed him on the lips softly.

"I wish I could show you how I see you," he whispered and kissed my neck. "You're perfect for me, Jolie."

Him and three other guys.

"And it makes sense that you would be perfect for the others as well," he said, as though he heard my thought. "We all like pretty much the same things, so us all liking you isn't much of a stretch."

"Does it make it less romantic for me to say that you're all perfect for me?" I asked and bit my lower lip.

He focused on it and groaned. "Stop teasing me, you butt. We have to get out and we don't have time for fun."

"Sorry," I said and chuckled. "I wasn't doing it to tease you."

"And no, it doesn't make it less romantic," he replied and shut off the water.

"Hurry up!" Deryn called through the door. "Your pizza is getting cold."

After drying off, I walked out of the bathroom, naked, since I hadn't brought a change of clothes with me.

All eyes turned to me and I stared in shock at a male I didn't know standing in the living room. His eyes were not on mine, focused a bit lower.

Nico set his hand on me and teleported us to my bedroom.

"Who is that?" I asked and knew I was blushing.

"He is a friend of Rhys's from the architectural company he works for," Nico said. "He's a huge gamer, too, so he is going to go with us."

"Well, he definitely got an eyeful," I grumbled and dug through my drawers for some clean underwear.

"Sorry, I didn't know he was here or I would have teleported us to the room from the bathroom," Nico said.

I waved my hand dismissively. "It's fine. He's not the first person to see me naked on accident."

"I don't want to know," Nico said and sighed.

I laughed and got my underwear, pants, and bra on, then stared into my closet. I had more than a dozen geeky shirts and I couldn't decide which one I wanted to wear tonight.

"Tough decision?" Nico asked.

I looked at him over my shoulder. He was dressed now, probably teleporting to his apartment to grab clothes and then back again while I stared at my closet. "Yes, it is."

"Can I pick for you?" he asked.

"Sure," I said and stepped back.

He smiled and looked at each of my shirts, then shuffled through them again one more time before making his selection. It was a shirt that said, "Not all maidens need saving."

"Not sure this applies to me," I grumbled. "I seem to always need saving."

"You didn't need saving when you fought against Rhys's mom," he reminded me.

"I needed saving from Trident Douche," I snarled and tugged the shirt on over my head.

He rested his hand against my cheek and whispered, "It hurt so much when we realized that you didn't know who we were. I wanted to slaughter everyone in Atlantis, I was so mad."

Nico wasn't prone to bouts of rage, so his statement surprised me.

"I'm glad you didn't," I said and set my hand atop his on my cheek.

He kissed me and then rubbed our noses side to side. "Me, too."

Rhys walked in and said, "Sorry about that. I should have warned you he was coming over."

"It's fine," I assured him and went to my dresser to grab my hair brush.

Fox walked in and grabbed the brush from me. "Let me."

I sat and let him brush my hair. Rhys and Nico went out to the living room, leaving me alone with Fox.

"How was your day?" I asked him.

He brushed out my hair slowly, being sure to get all of the tangles. "It was fine. I made some new charms and Mom is going to sell them."

"Nice," I said softly, my body completely relaxing with Fox being with me and brushing and stroking my hair like he was.

"Is there anything we should know about your clan members?" he asked and set the brush down. His fingers wove into my hair and he began to braid it.

"Not really. They're homebodies like me, but they are good people."

"Races?" he asked.

"Oh, uh..." I thought about it and said, "Human. They're all human." I hadn't really thought about them all being human until now.

"Are you going to tell them that you aren't human?" he asked, releasing my hair now that it was braided.

"I don't know," I admitted. "I mean, if they ask I won't lie, but I don't want to just bust out with, 'hey, guess what? I'm not human.' It would be a bit weird."

He shrugged. "I don't know your friends, so I can't say for sure. Just know that we don't care."

I stood and kissed him. "I know, Kit." I had started calling him Kit, since he turned into a fox and was childlike most of the time.

"Ready?" he asked.

I nodded, and we walked out to the living room. I snatched a slice of pizza from the almost empty box and ate it quickly. "Sorry about earlier," I told the guy. I still didn't know his name.

He stood, and I almost took an involuntary step back. He was tall, like super tall.

He held out his hand and smiled. "It's okay. I'm sorry I startled you. I'm Austin. I work with Rhys."

I shook his hand and grimaced immediately. Vampire. He was a vampire.

He dropped my hand and stepped back quickly.

"What was that?" Rhys asked, concerned.

"She's been a vampire's donor," Austin said. "Other vampires can read it from touching her."

"I wasn't a donor," I growled.

He dipped his head in a sign of apology.

"Is he talking about that vampire we killed in the park?" Fox asked.

"No, this one is still alive," Austin said.

Damn him. He just didn't know when to shut up.

"Jolie," Deryn growled.

"I've got to keep some secrets, so you'll still think I'm interesting," I said with a wide smile, trying to play it off.

Nico sighed and looked up at the ceiling. "There is always something new to learn about you."

"I'm mysterious like that," I said and wiggled my fingers at him.

"Do we need to kill this vampire?" Deryn asked.

"I don't think so," I said.

"It's not a claiming mark," Austin said. "It's just something vampires can sense when they touch her. It's like a mark, but it's nothing serious."

"I think we should kill him," Rhys said and Deryn nodded.

"Not tonight," I said and grabbed another slice of pizza. "I've got games to play and friends to see."

"We've got a bit of time, so don't choke that down so fast. You have time to actually chew it," Deryn said.

I didn't respond to him, but did slow down.

Everyone took seats around the room and I pulled out my phone, checking my messages.

Dragon: I have arrived!

Turbo: me too

Orphan: Psh. I've been here. You're all late.

Me: I'll be there around 5:20. I'm bringing some people with me.

Turbo: You have friends?

Orphan: Aw, I thought we were your only friends.

Dragon: More souls for me to consume in battle!

Me: You all better be on your best behavior.

All three sent back, "LOL."

This night could turn out to be very interesting.

I scrolled through the news sites, seeing what the headlines were and stopped at a picture of us riding Pookie. "Hey, look." I showed everyone the picture.

"Is that a Kraken?" Austin asked.

"His name is Pookie. And yes."

His eyes widened, and he gaped at me. "You're the siren princess everyone is talking about! Holy shit! I didn't realize she was the one you guys are mated to."

"Wasn't that headline news when my dad picked me up?" I asked.

Nico nodded. "Front page of every paper. Jolie, savior of the four clans is also Princess of the Sirens."

It was possible my clan already knew I wasn't human then. I scrolled through some more, then stopped at an article about Nico with a picture of him and a beautiful woman. The headline was asking whether he was cheating on me or not.

"Did you see this?" I asked Nico and showed him my phone.

He snatched it out of my hand and sighed. "Seriously? They seriously put an article in here about this?"

"We need to talk?" I asked him with an arched eyebrow.

He looked at me and gave me his famous stare. "Really?"

I smiled and took my phone back. "Just checking."

"You know we'd kick his ass," Fox said.

"Actually, I don't. Guys are always looking out for each other. You might cover for him," I countered. I knew Nico hadn't done anything. I trusted him, but I could also sense his feelings through our bonds, so I knew how he felt. If he had been cheating on me, I would have felt his sexual arousal and release through the bond.

Nico shook his head and smiled. "I am so glad you're not a normal girl."

"I should be offended by that statement, but I'll take it as a compliment," I told him and winked.

Austin laughed and said, "I can see why you like her, Rhys."

"Are you going to play any of the games?" Fox asked me.

I nodded. "There are two that we always play. I suck at them, but I do better than most of the scrubs who show up. And a third game that I play every single tournament I can."

"You may have your hands full this time," Rhys said. "Austin is a pretty good gamer."

I looked at him and said, "We'll see. I'm always up for a new battle."

He smiled. "Challenge accepted."

They chatted a bit more and then it was finally time to go. We piled into the SUV with Austin up front beside Thor. Thor looked back at me, and I smiled. Yeah, I knew he was a vampire. I was good.

"Ready?" Thor asked.

I nodded. "Let's go!"

The guys chatted amongst themselves while I stared out the window. Having four mates wasn't normally an issue, but I was worried that being royalty was going to cause problems tonight. If it had just been me, I could have disguised myself so I wouldn't be noticed, but there was no disguising them. They were easy to spot because they stood out no matter where they were. Who knew having hot mates would cause trouble?

"We are going to go in through the back, so we can avoid the media hounds," Thor advised us.

"Sweet," I said, despite knowing that the people inside would be a problem as well.

"You're worried about something," Nico whispered in my ear.

"Just worried we're going to cause trouble because we're royalty," I said. "Normally I walk around and only those who know me from being part of the gaming community talk to me. Now, people are likely to stop us because of being royals. I just don't know if I can handle it."

Being in big crowds wasn't my favorite, but when it was a large group of people who loved the same thing as me, in this case video games, it was easier. Now, I didn't know what would happen. I had no idea what to expect.

CHAPTER 13

We made it all of ten feet before my mates were recognized. There weren't usually many women at FighterCon, but there were still more than a hundred. And as we entered the main room, a dozen women rushed towards us.

"That's my cue to leave," I said and slipped away, weaving my way through the crowd until I made it to the sign-up sheets.

"Hello," the volunteer at the table said with a friendly smile. She was young, eighteen years old at the most, but exuded power. She was a mage, but I'd never met someone who leaked magic power like her.

"Hi, I'd like to sign up for some of the tournaments," I told her.

She held out a pen and waved at the six clipboards with papers on them before her. "All sign-ups are still open. Just put your gamertag and your cell number, in case we need to contact you."

"Thanks," I replied and took the pen, filling out the sign-ups I chose. After finishing, I gave her back the pen and looked at the main stage where many others were gathering, but no battles had started yet.

She looked at my name on the sign-up sheet nearest her and her eyes widened. "You?" she whispered. She put her fingers in her mouth and whistled loudly.

The announcer, who had been midsentence, stopped and turned to look at her. His eyes locked with mine and he smiled wide.

Uh oh. Whenever Nathan, the announcer, got that look, there was going to be a huge ordeal. Having his gaze on me made me very nervous.

"The Princess of Fighters is here!" Nathan told the crowd.

I hated that nickname. He'd coined it when I won the first year.

"Our StreetBrawler champion, two years running, has just arrived. Come on up here, Jo!"

The crowd cheered, and I groaned. He'd done this last year, too. Damn him.

After climbing the stairs, I walked to the center of the stage where Nathan stood. I waved to the crowd with a smile, ignoring the jeers since most were friendly goads.

"We were worried you weren't going to make it, Jo," Nathan said.

"Why is that?" I asked.

"We weren't sure if a Princess would be allowed to come," he explained.

"Gaming is my first love," I replied and smiled wide. "Plus, my mates are with me."

"Think you can retain your title of Champion?" he asked.

"I'm ready to find out," I answered, and the crowd cheered. Looking out at the audience, I saw my clan members standing together in the front. I jumped down off the stage and hugged the three of them.

"What took you so long?" Orphan teased. He smiled down at me with dark brown eyes that twinkled with mischief. He was always full of mischief and puns. His puns were epic.

"And what's with the huge entourage?" Dragon asked.

"Being a princess causes a lot of problems when I go out in public," I said with a shrug.

"Can't you sing them away or something?" Turbo asked. He was the shortest of the group, though taller than me. He had brown hair that was so dark, it looked black. He also had the longest and thickest eyelashes I'd ever seen on a man. I was jealous of them, personally.

"You guys know about me being a siren?" I asked.

The trio nodded.

"Everyone knows," Dragon said. "It was on every news outlet."

"Well, I don't have true siren abilities, so I couldn't sing them away," I said with a laugh.

"Jo!" Orphan yelled and pulled me into his chest.

I looked back over my shoulder. Rhys knelt with his knee in a guy's back on the ground behind me.

"Hey, babe," Rhys said to me.

"What..."

"That guy was about to hit you," Orphan explained and released me.

Rhys smiled at Orphan. "Thanks for moving her."

Orphan smirked. "I can't lose my teammate right before a match."

I punched his arm and he laughed.

Rhys let the guy up and I asked, "Fern, are you ever going to get over this grudge?"

Fern was a little older than me and had been Champion the year before I won. Now, he hated me. He wasn't truly dangerous. Just a bit of a drunken idiot.

"I hate you," he growled.

Rhys growled and Fern flinched away. "You try to hurt my mate again and I'll do more than knock you down. Got it?"

Fern nodded and pushed off into the crowd.

"He's one of your mates?" Turbo asked.

I nodded. "Guys, this is Rhys. Rhys, this is Orphan, Turbo, and Dragon."

He shook their hands, but looked at Dragon the longest, for the second time that day having to look up at someone, since Dragon was seven feet tall. "What are you, a third dragon?" Rhys asked.

"Quarter," Dragon answered. "No shifting, sadly."

"You would have made one hell of a dragon," Rhys said with a wide smile.

"Psh, I am an awesome dragon."

Dragonknight was part dragon? I'd never known that. I thought he was human the whole time.

"There you are," Fox said, squeezing between two guys to get to me. "Look, I got you a gift." He held out a keychain that had my favorite female fighter from the game *Underlook*. She had a mechanical rabbit she used to stomp on people and also had a shield to protect teammates.

I took it and squealed. "Thank you!" I kissed Fox and put the keychain in my pocket.

"Mate two?" Turbo asked.

I nodded and introduced them.

We watched the matches, chatting about them, and I felt like myself. Finally.

Nico slid up behind me and wrapped his arms around my waist. I leaned back against him as I watched Dragon fighting Deryn on *Street*

Brawler. Deryn was a decent player, but there was no way he could beat Dragon.

"You look happy," Nico whispered in my ear. "It's a good look on you."

I linked my fingers with his where they lay on my stomach and said, "I am happy."

Deryn lost, but he didn't get mad like usual. He actually laughed and shook hands with Dragon. He jogged over and kissed my cheek before heading off towards one of the other gaming areas.

"Jo versus Austin!" Nathan announced.

I patted Nico's hands, and he released me. I jogged up the steps and held my hand out to Austin, ready this time since I knew what he was.

He shook my hand and said, "I've been looking forward to this."

"Hopefully I won't disappoint you," I said, took the chair on the right, picked up the controller, and chose my character.

Nathan was providing commentary, but I tuned him out. The only thing that mattered was the game. Focused on the screen, I debated my first move. I had no idea what Austin's play style was like. But, I decided to start off aggressive, since that wasn't how I usually played. If he knew about me or had seen me play before, he would expect me to block and wait for him to attack.

The match started, and I sent a flaming ball across the screen. He had started to rush me and hadn't prepared for my attack, so it hit his character.

The crowd erupted.

Pushing forward, we exchanged blows, but I was able to block or parry most of his. He jumped up and I smiled. Noob. Hitting the buttons in the correct order, I activated my characters super. My character jumped up, hitting his in the jaw, then delivered seven more punches midair before throwing him across the screen. His character hit the ground and died.

I didn't avert my eyes from the screen as I waited for the second round to start. This time, I waited for him to make the first move. He surprised me by dashing across the screen and grabbing me, then tossing me backwards. As soon as I landed, I leapt up and sent a fire ball at him. He parried it and stood, waiting. Challenging me.

Fireball. Parry. Fireball. Parry. Super fireball. I smiled smugly, but that disappeared as he parried all four hits of the super fireball.

Son of a bitch!

He was good and before I knew it, he defeated me.

Shit.

Tied one to one, this next match would decide the winner.

Our fight was intense and I was losing. I had one ace up my sleeve and it was time to use it. He activated his super and I parried every hit, then activated my super. He lost to a crowd screaming in disbelief. He set his controller down and exhaled loudly while running his hand through his hair.

I turned and held out my hand. "Good game."

He shook my hand and smiled. "Thanks. You, too."

The next contestants climbed onto the stage, so I hopped down.

Deryn and Fox high-fived me.

"You almost lost," Dragon said. "You need to play more."

"You're rusty as fuck," Turbo said and laughed.

"I won," I said and shrugged.

"That was a nice move," Orphan said.

I smiled and turned to watch the next contestants.

After a few uneventful bouts, Nathan announced the next match and I knew I was doomed.

"Dragon versus Jo!"

"Well, I'm dead," I whispered to Nico.

He kissed my cheek and said, "Just go have fun. Who cares if you win or not?"

He was right. I just needed to have fun. I climbed up the steps and sat in the chair.

Dragon sat down and said, "You better try your hardest."

I rolled my eyes. "Duh."

We looked at our screens and waited for the match to start. He was an aggressive fighter usually, but I just wanted to have fun. So, I ran at him and did a spinning kick. He blocked it and punched me with a hard uppercut that took half my health.

I danced backwards and hit the crouch and then stand buttons multiple times to taunt him.

He let out a booming laugh, then dashed across the screen and hit me with an eighteen-hit combo that ended round one.

He charged me at the beginning of round two and I did everything I could to block or parry his hits. I was successful for a bit, but tried to punch him and he caught me, throwing me back into the corner and began juggling my body with kicks.

"Dammit! Stop juggling me!" I yelled with a wide smile.

He stopped, then squatted and punched me once in the shin, killing me.

"Dragon wins!" Nathan yelled.

We shook hands and climbed off the stage, laughing.

"I'm going to go play *Dank Souls*," Orphan said.

"I'm up soon for *Soulsbourne*," Dragon said and headed in that direction.

"Are you playing in the *Dank Souls* tournament?" Nico asked.

I shook my head. "No. I was going to do the *Soulsbourne*, but I'm super rusty." Even if I would never admit it to Turbo.

"Let's check out the vendors," Deryn suggested. He took my hand and pushed his way through. I followed behind him until we cleared the crowd.

We walked side by side down the vendor stalls, pausing to look at various items. We were halfway down the second aisle when I stopped and turned around. "You're taking turns, aren't you?"

"What?" Deryn asked, setting down the *Dank Souls* figurine he had been looking at.

"You guys are taking turns being with me tonight," I said.

He nodded. "Yeah."

"Why?"

"We all talked and agreed that we don't get enough alone time with you. So, we decided to take turns. Doesn't matter if it's five minutes or a full day, we just want to prioritize one-on-one time with you."

"Because I want that?" I asked.

"No," he said and pulled me into his arms. "Because *we do*." He kissed me, then smiled. "You always look so beautiful when you're happy."

Pushing away from him, I continued down the aisles with his hand in mine. He stopped me to look at something and I leaned into his side. Ever since we'd mated, Deryn had calmed down and reverted back to the happy and playful guy I'd met. I was so happy to have him back.

"Moon Moon," I said to get his attention.

He looked at me with a smirk. "Yes?"

"Do we have an anniversary date?"

He frowned and thought about it a moment. "I suppose the day you asked us to be your mates would count."

"Would you prefer to have separate anniversary dates? To use the dates that I mated with you instead?"

"I don't know," he said and shrugged. "I hadn't really thought about it."

"Well, just think about it," I said. Turning, I spotted a figurine I'd been searching for for years. I rushed over and picked it up. "Yes!"

The seller was helping someone else, so I waited patiently for my turn. Deryn wandered over and looked at the figurine. "Isn't that the one you've been looking for?"

I nodded.

"How can I help you?" the seller, a middle-aged man with grey hair and a grey beard asked.

"I'd like to buy this," I said and held out the figurine towards him.

"Three hundred dollars," he said.

"Three hundred? It sold for sixty," I growled.

"Yeah, originally it sold for that, but now it's a collector's item and hard to find," he said. "Three hundred is my price."

Dammit. I didn't want to spend that much, but I really wanted the figurine.

"We'll take it," Deryn said and held out his credit card.

"Deryn," I grumbled.

The seller boxed it up and handed it to Deryn. "Thank you for your business. Have a great day."

"Why did you do that?" I asked him.

"You wanted it. You've been looking for this thing for months. It's a gift, so accept it gratefully."

"Thank you," I said and hugged him. "Thank you."

He smiled and kissed me. "Anything for you, baby."

"Hey," Rhys said, meeting us at the end of the vendors.

"Hello," I replied. "What have you been up to?"

"I watched a few battles and played some of the demos set up," he said.

"I'm going to go find Fox," Deryn said and took my figurine with him.

Rhys held out his hand. I threaded my fingers with his and we headed back to the *Street Brawler* tournament. Normally I had issues getting through the crowds, but Rhys easily made his way, pulling me after him. We got a spot at the front and Rhys pulled me around to stand in front of him. He draped his arms over my shoulders and rested his chin atop my head. Relaxed and at peace.

Having them like this was great. Having my mates calm and happy made me happy.

I just hoped it would last.

"It's the final round!" Nathan announced. "Dragon versus Octane!"

Octane? He had dropped off the gaming world a few years ago. He was great, though a little intense.

The battle was relentless and long. They almost went to time, both of the first two rounds. They each won one round, so this one would decide the winner.

Dragon looked calm as ever, but so did Octane.

Turbo and Orphan found us in the crowd and came to stand by me.

"This is a great match so far," Turbo said.

I nodded.

The third round started and neither player moved. There was a tense silence for thirty seconds, and then Dragon moved. They battled magnificently, hitting, blocking, parrying, and yet they remained even on health. They continued battling, then Octane activated his super. The crowd filled with loud yells of, "Oh!".

But, the super missed somehow.

Dragon activated his super and that was it. He won the match.

The crowd went wild and I joined them, screaming and clapping.

Dragon got his trophy and check from Nathan, then yelled, "I am victorious!"

We chuckled, then I hugged him when he made it down to us. "That was awesome!" I told him.

"Luck," Orphan said. "How did his super miss?"

Dragon shrugged. "Scrub mistake? Whatever, I won."

"Let's celebrate!" Orphan said. "There's got to be a bar nearby."

"There's one just across the block," Rhys said.

"To the bar!" Dragon shouted.

We began walking toward the exit and Rhys whistled loudly. Nico teleported to me, making Turbo jump back in surprise. Deryn jogged over with Fox at his side, their hands full of new bags.

"What did you buy?" I asked curiously.

"No peeking!" Fox said and hid the bags behind his back.

Following Dragon and Rhys, we walked into the bar Rhys had mentioned, but Dragon, Orphan, Turbo, and I stopped immediately.

The bar was closer to an opera house than a bar. There were hardly any people inside and the ones who were there were obviously much older than us.

"Let's go somewhere else," I suggested.

"What's wrong with this place?" Rhys asked.

"I didn't bring my top hat and monocle with me," Turbo said and my clan laughed.

"There's a great dive bar two blocks away," I told everyone. "Let's head there."

"A dive bar? You *want* to go to a dive bar?" Fox asked, scowling.

"I'd rather not pay fifteen for a beer," Orphan said with a scoff.

"Come on," I prompted them and went back outside.

They followed, but Rhys, Fox, and Nico were scowling and talking amongst themselves too quietly for me to hear several feet back from us. Through the bond, I sensed that they were confused, but nothing else.

The dive bar had loud music and several people outside were smoking.

We showed the bouncer our IDs, except for the princes who just walked by him like he didn't exist. He didn't stop them.

Once inside, we went to the bar to get our drinks.

"Turbo paid two years ago and last year was Orphan," I said. "So, looks like it's my turn."

The bartender was a beautiful woman with flowing hair. She ignored us to look at the princes. "What can I get you, Your Highnesses?"

Deryn stepped up behind me and put his hands on my shoulders. "What do you want, love?"

Her eyes widened as she looked at me then him but didn't say anything.

"Four beers for us, then whatever you guys want," I said, feeling annoyed.

"There's a bench table outside big enough for all of us," Turbo said. "I'll go snag it."

"I'll come with you," I said and followed him out to the back patio. There were about ten people in the back, but most were sitting at the small tables with groups of two to four.

We sat at the table and Turbo turned to me. "You sure you're happy with those guys?" he asked.

"Yeah, why?"

"You just don't seem like you have much in common."

"We do. They play games just not as much as us."

"You mated with filthy casuals?" he asked in mock horror.

I laughed and nodded. "Yeah."

"They seem to legit care about you."

"Yeah? You can tell after four hours?" I teased.

He nodded. "They spent the whole night making sure you were happy. They stayed with you, but not to try to keep guys away, just because they like you."

"You can tell all that?"

He smirked. "I'm pretty perceptive, even if I tend to run headlong into battles."

Nico teleported behind me and Turbo cursed. "Could you stop that? You're going to give me a heart attack."

Nico smirked. "Sorry." He set down a mug of beer for me and one for Turbo.

The others joined us with their own beers. I raised mine and the others followed. "Congrats, Dragon!"

"Congrats!" everyone said.

We drank and talked for hours. It was well past midnight when we decided to leave. I hugged my clan and said goodbye as they climbed into a taxi.

My mates stood several feet away, leaning against the bar's wall, just watching me.

"What?" I asked and stumbled towards them, giggling. I was both drunk and exhausted.

"You're different with them," Rhys said.

"What? How?" I didn't try to act different.

"You didn't stop smiling the entire time we were here. Even when you were complaining about a game, you didn't stop smiling," Deryn said.

"We never talk about anything serious. Our entire relationship is based on having fun. We use each other to escape from reality most of the time," I explained.

They hadn't moved from their spots against the wall of the building. So, I walked to them, standing just in front of the quad. "Let's go home. I'm tired and I drank more than I should have."

"Okay," Fox said and picked me up. "Let's go home."

CHAPTER 14

"Jolie, put the knife down," Fox whispered with his hands held out placatingly.

Knife? When had I picked up a knife? We'd walked home from the bar and...that was the last thing I remembered, coming home from the bar.

"Something's wrong," Deryn whispered.

"I can see that," Fox snapped.

"Jolie," Rhys said.

I turned and faced him, adjusting my grip on the kitchen knife.

"Put it down," he ordered me, using his alpha voice.

"That shit doesn't work on me!" I snapped.

"Time to sleep," Nico whispered behind me.

I spun, but he put his hand over my mouth and covered my face with the cloth he held. I had no choice but to inhale, and the chloroform did its job and knocked me unconscious.

Brayden had been right, they were trying to control me.

The effects didn't last long, but it was long enough for them to tie me up and transport me to the wolf den. They had put me in a containment cage meant to hold loup wolves, wolves who had lost their humanity and were crazed and attacked anything and everything.

"Let me go!" I screamed and struggled against my restraints.

Nico, Fox, Rhys, Deryn, and Dan stood outside the cage, all scowling.

"Mind control," Dan said. "Which means that asshole is nearby."

"Not necessarily," Rhys whispered. "She told me he was able to communicate telepathically with her. He could be doing this from far away."

"How do we stop it?" Fox asked.

I turned my skin into scales and snapped the ropes holding my arms. "Let me out!" I screamed and breathed fire.

Nico put up a barrier around the cage, keeping the fire safely away from them.

Those jerks were going to pay for imprisoning me!

"I am Princess Jolie of the Sirens!" I yelled at them. "Release me or you will be declaring war!"

"How long until Leona gets here?" Deryn asked.

"Tomorrow was what she said," Fox answered.

The bars of the cage were made with extremely strong metal. How could I escape? How could I get out of here?

"When did this start?" Dan asked, moving closer to the cage.

I shifted into a wolf and snapped my teeth at him.

He scowled and his eyes shone gold. "Sit," he ordered me.

My body trembled, but I held my head up higher and growled. No. I would not obey him.

"I'm not shielding her," Deryn said.

"It started when we got back from the bar," Fox answered Dan. "She was drunk and happy one moment, then grabbed a knife and tried to stab me."

I shifted back to my normal form. "You won't be able to keep me here forever," I threatened. "I'll escape sooner or later."

Dan arched an eyebrow. "How do you think you'll escape?"

"He's coming for me," I said and smiled. "And he'll kill you for imprisoning me."

"Let him come," Rhys said and growled, his eyes turning into dragon's eyes.

Shifting my hand into a wolf paw with claws extended, I reached through the bars and tried to grab Rhys, but he was just out of my reach. I screamed and swiped my clawed hands at him.

They always stayed just out of my reach.

The five males left the room, and I was alone. I screamed angrily and thrashed against the cage. I sat and began blowing fire on the ceiling of the cage. All metal melted if heated to a high enough temperature.

Covering myself in dragon's scales, I jumped up out of the hole in the cage. Then, I leapt straight up through the house, through three floors until I made it out into the open air.

"Jolie!" Dan yelled from inside the house.

I was finally out of Nico's range, so I teleported to the park and immediately shifted into my combined form. The princes would come and when they did, I would destroy them.

As expected, the four males found me quickly. They stood in a line before me, scowling.

"Just let me go," I said angrily.

"Go where?" Rhys asked.

"Home," I said.

"Your home is with us," Fox said softly. "We are your mates."

"You tricked me," I snapped. "All of this is a lie."

"I'm going to tear his head off," Deryn snarled.

"Why do you think that?" Nico asked me.

"Brayden freed me from your spell," I explained. "He showed me what you've been doing to me."

"He's the one manipulating you," Fox said calmly. "You can feel us through our bonds. You can sense our feelings. We love you."

"I don't feel anything now, thanks to Brayden," I snarled. "You can't toy with me anymore."

"Yep, I'm going to kill him," Deryn muttered.

"You have our bloodstones," Fox whispered. "You can't fuse them unless it's voluntary. We did not force you."

I reached up with clawed fingers. "I'll remove them."

Nico held out his hand and metal cables wrapped around my arms, pinning them so I couldn't reach my face. When had he learned to do that?

I screamed in pain and Deryn punched Nico's shoulder.

"Ow," Nico said.

"You're hurting her," Deryn growled at him.

"Would you rather she clawed the bloodstones out of her face?" Nico asked.

Deryn growled in response.

"I didn't think so," Nico grumbled and rubbed the spot Deryn had punched.

I shifted into a dragon, my scales protected my bones as I did, and the metal cables fell away. I roared and spit flames at them.

Rhys shifted and roared back, making me cower and take a step back. He was the most dominant male I had ever met. He grabbed the back of my neck with his teeth and bit down, hard enough to hurt, but not hard enough to draw blood.

I was supposed to submit. Part of me wanted to submit. But, Brayden had shown me how manipulative they had been. I couldn't stay here. I had to leave.

Dropping down slowly, he believed I was submitting, but as I neared the ground, I leapt up and clawed his eye nearest me.

He roared in pain and stumbled back two steps.

I shifted into my combined form as the other three approached and fought them in earnest. None of them had drawn weapons, but Deryn and Rhys took warrior forms to better protect themselves.

Nico used a spell to freeze me, but I teleported across the park and out of his range.

"Who taught her to teleport?" Nico snarled.

I couldn't just run. No. I had to defeat them. I had to rid the world of their manipulation so no other girls fell for their ploys.

In my combined form, I charged Deryn, cutting his shoulder and kicked Rhys in the chest when he tried to grab me.

If Brayden hadn't blocked their bonds, I would feel their pain. I was glad he had thought to block them.

Where was Brayden? He had said he would come for me.

Fox tried to use plant vines to tie me up, but I burned them before they could touch me, then used my powers to tie his legs with vines. He cursed angrily and tore at them.

Rhys tackled me from the side and pinned my hands above my head while he sat on me. "Stop trying to hurt us."

"You must die!" I screamed.

"He's controlling you!" Rhys yelled. "Don't you see that? He is controlling your mind and you are letting him."

Drawing in a big breath, I exhaled fire, but Rhys just laughed.

"Your fire doesn't hurt me, Sunshine."

I shifted into my warrior wolf form and rolled us over, so I was atop him now.

Deryn wrapped his arm around my throat and squeezed, cutting off my air. "Don't fight me. Just go to sleep. Please."

I clawed deep gouges into his arms, digging in until I scraped bone.

He growled, but held on, his arm tightening even more.

I collapsed in his arms and held my breath.

"Fuck!" he yelled and pushed me onto my back on the ground.

"Deryn!" Nico snapped.

"She's not dead," Deryn said. "I didn't kill her."

My eyes snapped open and I exhaled fire. He jumped back, yelling in pain. Fox ran to him, using his healing magic to treat the burns.

I stood and faced Nico. His anger was palpable.

"I'm done. You're not yourself," he said. His body began to glow, and I knew I was in trouble.

I opened my mouth and began to sing. All four screamed and clutched their heads. Brayden had taught me a song to hurt whoever heard it. It hurt anyone who wasn't a siren.

The four males clutched their heads as I sang, and blood began to drip from their noses.

Nico lifted his hand and a clear ball formed around me, cutting off all sound. My singing didn't penetrate the ball.

Fuck!

I pounded my fists against the ball, but nothing happened. They were talking and wiping their faces off while staring at me.

My breathing became erratic as I felt the ball closing around me, taking away the air I needed to breathe. I pounded on the ball and screamed, my breaths quickening along with my heartbeat. Fear consumed me, and I tried to shift into a dragon, but the ball was too small. My body reverted, and I screamed. I fell to the ground, gasping for breath.

The ball disappeared, and I gulped in fresh air. That had been too close. I needed to take him out first.

While digging my fingers in the grass, I silently aimed a tree root behind Nico. He squatted down in front of me and I raised my hand. The tree root shot up out of the ground and pierced Nico through his back and out of his chest.

He gasped, and his eyes widened in disbelief as he looked at the root.

"Nico!" Deryn and Rhys yelled.

I turned and ran, headed out of the park, but a force field cut me off, sealing the park off from the rest of the city. Glancing back, I saw Nico with one hand raised, a determined look in his eyes. His other hand pressed around the root and the blood stain spreading outwards from the injury.

I raised my hand, preparing to jerk the root out, but Fox punched me in the side, making me gasp and drop my hand. I hadn't even seen him.

He pointed his sword at me and snarled. "Stop! Jolie, just fucking stop!"

"Not until you're dead," I whispered.

I tried to teleport but couldn't. I walked slowly up to Fox who watched me, but stood still. I snatched his second sword from his hip and pointed it at him.

Tears slid down his cheeks and he whispered, "Please don't do this."

I screamed and swiped at him with the sword.

He easily deflected it. "He's manipulating you, but you're still in there. I know you are. Fight him, Jolie! Fight him!"

I screamed again and attacked, our swords clanging together as he blocked my strikes.

Dammit, they were too strong!

Deryn approached, a sword in his hand. "Baby, you're stronger than him. You can break his hold on you."

I attacked him and yelled, "I only need to break your hold!"

Rhys stood with Nico, his arm around him to keep him standing.

I raised my hand, but Deryn's sword grazed my arm, making me jerk back.

"I am your queen!" I yelled. "Obey me!"

"You can't order us around when you've closed our bonds," Fox said behind me.

I spun and tried to cut him, but he deflected my blade easily.

Out of the corner of my eye, I saw someone new approaching. No, not some one, but multiple people. It was the kings.

"Leave!" Deryn ordered them. "She's not herself."

"That's why we are here," Katar said.

I brought my sword down, aiming for Deryn's shoulder since he was distracted.

Dan caught the blade with his bare hand, blood dripping to the ground as it cut into his palm. "No," he said and pushed me back. "I won't let you hurt them."

"One is about dead," I said. "I'll finish them off, too."

Johann looked over at Nico and his eyes darkened. "Enough playing around." He whispered something and a red circle with magic runes appeared below me. Chains slid up out of the circle and wrapped around my legs and arms.

I tried to pull free, but electricity traveled from the chains into me. I screamed and fell to my knees, my vision swimming.

"Stop it!" Deryn yelled.

"Stop hurting her!" Fox snapped.

"This is the only thing her kind understands," Johann growled.

"And all you understand is defeat at the hands of women," I snarled and began singing, my voice directed at him.

He screamed and clutched at his head, which made the circle and chains disappear.

I shifted into my combined warrior form, well aware that my strength and energy were quickly running out.

Dan and Emrys shifted into their warrior forms and attacked. I kept singing, my voice and powers aimed at Johann, so he couldn't use his magic on me. Fighting the two kings was difficult, but Dan was trying his hardest not to hurt me.

Johann collapsed, so I stopped singing.

"How can you let them do this to me?" I asked. "How can you stand by and let them control me?"

"Brayden is controlling you," Leona said.

I spun around and stared at her in disbelief. "What are you doing here?"

"I came to train you," she said. "If you broke Brayden's hold, you would remember."

She's a traitor. She is trying to steal the throne.

I snarled. "You're after the throne, aren't you?"

She rolled her eyes. "You and I both know that I would suck as a ruler. Come on, Jojo. Fight him!"

Jojo? She called me that when were kids.

She wants to keep you chained to the princes.

"I won't be their pawn!" I screamed at her. "I thought we were friends! Why are you helping them?"

Johann tried to put me in a shield, but I held out my hand and made the vine in Nico's chest move, which caused him to scream in pain.

Johann dropped his hands and glared at me. "I should just kill you," he snarled.

"Try it," Nico panted. "I'll destroy you."

Even while I was killing him, he was protecting me from his father?

It's a ploy.

Leona stopped before me and smiled. "Hello, Jojo."

"You're a traitor!" I snapped.

"You're stronger than this," she whispered. "Let me help."

"Help me by killing them," I said.

She began to sing, and pain engulfed my body. I opened my mouth and sang louder than her.

"Barrier!" Dan yelled.

Johann put a barrier around me and Leona, our songs now contained to only hurt each other.

Louder and louder I sang, but Leona was more experienced and with just a different pitch, she broke my concentration and pain engulfed me like being thrown into lava.

I screamed and clutched my head. The princes yelled and tried to come to me, but the kings held them back.

Leona continued to sing, walking closer and closer to me. My legs gave out and I fell to my hands and knees, still screaming.

How could a melody that sounded so sweet cause so much pain?

Kill her!

Brayden. That was his voice. Why wasn't he helping me? Where was he?

"He isn't here," Leona whispered. "He is using a connection he made with you to control you. You can break it and free yourself."

"He's trying to free me from them," I sobbed.

Leona set her hand on my head and whispered, "If that were true, why isn't he here?"

There was logic to her words.

"Let me help you," Leona whispered.

I looked up into my friend's eyes and asked, "Who can I believe?"

She smiled and asked, "Have I ever let you down?"

No. No, she hadn't.

She bent down and whispered in my ear, "Fuck you, Douchebag. She's not yours and never will be. Run and hide, because once we find you, you won't survive."

Kill her!

No. I wouldn't kill Leona.

Leona began singing again, her words sliding into my skull and slithering around my brain. It should have felt wrong, but it felt nice. Her powers wrapped around a piece of something in my mind and her voice rose. The louder she sang, the tighter it wrapped, until it snapped the foreign piece and my mind became its own once again.

Free. I was finally free of Brayden.

I lay on the grass, letting my brain re-acclimate to what was real, what was truth. Brayden had used his powers on me from far away. He had been able to convince me that my mates were manipulating me and needed to die. I had hurt them. I had almost killed one of my mates!

"Nico!" I screamed, jumped up, and ran towards him.

Johann stepped between us and snarled, "I'm going to kill you."

Nico lifted his hand and used his magic to knock his dad out of my way. "Try it and I'll kill you," Nico threatened Johann.

I didn't deserve to be defended by him. I rushed to his side, tears streaming down my face, and reached out to touch his cheeks. "I'm so sorry. I'm so so sorry, Nico. I almost killed you. I was going to kill you. Please tell me you're okay. Please don't die on me."

"He's going to be fine," Katar said and knelt behind Nico. "Kara is on her way and she's going to fix him up."

I turned to Deryn and cringed at his clawed-up arm. "I'm so sorry. I know saying it doesn't help or change anything, but I really am sorry. I can't believe I did all this. I can't believe I hurt you so badly."

Deryn pulled me into his chest with one arm around me and whispered, "You gave us a really big scare. I wasn't sure if we would be able to stop you."

"I'm sorry," I whispered into his chest and sobbed.

"We know," Rhys whispered behind me. "We can feel you again with our bonds."

"How was he able to tamper with our bonds?" I asked, not moving from Deryn's hold.

"He didn't touch the bonds, just blocked them," Johann said with a deep frown.

"Are you okay?" I asked Rhys.

He nodded.

"Fox?"

He nodded, too.

"Are you okay?" Leona asked me.

I stepped out of Deryn's embrace to hug Leona. "Thank you. You saved me."

"You saved us all," Nico wheezed.

"Stop talking," I ordered him. His mouth snapped shut and my hands flew to my face. "I'm sorry! I didn't mean to order you. You can talk, just please don't. I don't want you hurting any more than you already are."

"Calm down," Nico whispered and smirked at me. "I'm not dead."

"Jojo, are you okay?" Leona asked again.

I nodded. "I'm fine. You destroyed whatever that was in my head. Now, I'm free of Brayden."

"I really am going to kill him," Deryn said.

"Get in line," Nico grunted.

"Will he be able to do this again?" Dan asked.

I turned and fresh tears appeared in my eyes. I dropped to my knees and bowed to them. "Please forgive me."

"Stop it," Dan ordered me. "You didn't do anything wrong. You were being controlled by that jerk." Dan pulled me up and hugged me.

"You really did save us," Rhys said to Leona. "Thank you."

"You've definitely improved in your fighting," Emrys said and patted my back. "I'm very impressed."

I chuckled and wiped at my tear stained face. "Thanks."

"Okay, who am I healing?" Kara asked as she walked into the park.

"Nico first," Johann said.

Kara patted my cheek as she walked by and knelt in front of Nico. "Did you piss off an elf?" she asked him with a smirk.

"No, just my mate," Nico said and chuckled, then started coughing and wheezing.

"Let's get you patched up," Kara said.

"Will you be able to heal him fully?" I asked her.

She smiled. "Do not worry, Daughter, he will be fully healed and just in need of rest."

"How do we prevent this from happening again?" Johann asked Leona.

"I'm going to teach her how to protect herself," Leona answered.

"Can you teach us how to protect ourselves?" Dan asked. "I don't want that asshole messing with us either."

Leona nodded. "Yes."

"When did you learn those songs?" I asked softly.

"A few years ago. I'll teach you some," Leona promised.

"I don't think her learning new songs is a good idea," Johann grumbled.

"It's better for her to learn all of our songs and abilities," Leona argued.

"I disagree," Johann argued back.

"Good thing you don't get a say," Rhys growled.

"We should all have a say. A siren, especially an empath, is danger-ous. Look at what she did today, even untrained. Think about what she will be able to do once she is trained!" Johann yelled.

"Dad, shut the fuck up!" Nico snapped. "It's better if she is trained. Just like it's better for a mage to be trained."

"If you weren't injured, I'd kick your ass," Johann said with a scowl.

"Try me," Nico threatened. "I've been wanting to kick your ass for months."

"Boys," Kara chastised. "I'm not going to heal you just so you can fight each other."

"Your son has had a very bad day," Katar reminded Johann. "Today is not the best day to test his patience."

Johann glared at me once more, then teleported away.

"How did you know to come here?" I asked Dan.

"We felt our sons freaking out and rushed to them, assuming something was happening to you," Emrys said.

"There, all healed," Kara said and stood.

Nico stood up and I took a tentative step towards him. He pulled me into a tight hug and rubbed my back. "I'm fine, Jolie."

I clutched his shirt and sniffled. "I'm sorry."

"Stop," he ordered me.

I obeyed, leaning into him and letting him hold me.

"So, where am I staying? Not that this park isn't beautiful, but I'd prefer to have a house to sleep in," Leona said.

"Let's go get some food," Deryn suggested.

"Come to our house and I'll cook you some food. And, I'll whip up a special potion for Nico," Kara offered.

"Sounds great," I agreed.

Nico offered to teleport us, but Kara refused, stating he needed to rest. So, we waited for drivers to pick us up and take us.

"How did you find us?" I asked Leona.

"You started singing before a barrier was put up. So, I went in the direction the song had come from. It led me here," she explained.

"If we'd known you were coming today, we would have had someone meet you at the station," Deryn said.

Leona shrugged her shoulders. "I like exploring places and don't get enough exercise normally."

"Where is Leona staying?" I asked Nico, whose arms I hadn't left.

"I would offer for you to stay with me in my apartment, but I don't have a spare room."

"She is going to stay in Deryn's spare room," Nico explained.

"Speaking of houses," Dan said. "Are you going to stay in those apartments now that you're mated? Or are you going to buy a single house?"

I had been wondering that as well, but kept forgetting to bring it up.

"What do you want to do?" Nico asked me, peering at me sideways.

"It would be nice to have a single house for all of us to be in together," I said. "But, with individual rooms still."

"Where would we buy or build it?" Deryn asked.

"I don't know," I admitted.

"We could buy some land in a neutral area," Fox suggested.

"What about a beach home?" I asked. "I know the sirens own some land not too far from Jinla along the beach."

"We could have several homes," Fox said. "I have one home and—"

"Where would our main home be?" Rhys asked, interrupting Fox.

"Actually," Dan said, getting our attention. "I already bought you guys some property."

"What?" we all asked at the same time.

He rubbed the back of his neck with an awkward smile. "I was going to give it to you as an anniversary present. It's right outside Jinla, in neutral territory."

"How much land?" Deryn asked.

"Fifty acres," Dan answered.

"Fifty!" I gasped. "Why so much?"

"Well, if you do have kids, they're going to need room to run around and play," Dan said.

"And it gives us lots of space to build a karting track!" Deryn yelled.

"Real life karting?" I gasped. "Sign me up!"

"I'll pull up some maps and pictures while we are eating," Dan said with a happy smile.

I hugged him and kissed his cheek. "You're the best father-in-law ever."

"I heard that!" Katar and Emrys yelled.

I chuckled and the guys laughed, too.

"What would you like to eat?" Kara asked.

"Fudge!" I yelled.

Everyone laughed.

"You can't eat fudge for a meal," Fox scolded me.

"Why not?" I pouted.

"How about I make a surprise meal?" Kara offered.

"That would be best," Rhys said.

Our drivers arrived and we all traveled to the elf's territory where Kara cooked a huge banquet. Everyone ate and laughed and spent time together.

We had to find our enemies soon and kill them. But, at least we had each other. Leona fit in perfectly and it was like she had always been part of our group. She teased the guys more than I did, and it was nice to have another girl around.

Life was hard, but with friends at my side, I knew I could get through any situation.

EPILOGUE

Nico and I stepped into Deryn's apartment to find Leona and Deryn locked in an intense karting battle. I'd introduced Leona to video games and she had become as obsessed as me.

Nico wrapped his arms around me from behind, pulling me back against him. I listened to his steady heartbeat and it relaxed me.

After I'd almost killed him, I had spent a few days attached to his hip. Thankfully, the others hadn't been bothered by it, understanding my need to be with him. I still apologized when I thought about it, but he always reassured me he didn't blame me. I had been under mind control after all.

The game ended with Deryn winning by throwing a shell at Leona right at the finish line. Deryn cheered.

Leona groaned. "I'll get you one day," she promised.

"Time to go," I said, drawing their attention to me.

Leona jogged to me and pulled me from Nico's grip to hug me. "Hey."

I hugged her back and smiled. "Hey."

She punched Nico's shoulder as she walked by him, and out the door. The guys had been a little worried about another girl living with us, but like me, Leona had grown up surrounded by males and quickly became just another "guy" in the group.

Plus, she was one of my best friends and respected that they were my mates. They would never stray from me, and she would never try to make them. Besides, they weren't the one she had her eye on.

Once outside the building, we all smiled at Thor who waited by the SUV for us. Instead of returning to his previous job, he'd opted to stay as our driver and bodyguard. Martin had accepted a less dangerous job within the pack, at my urging. Thor said he stayed because he wanted to ensure I was as protected as possible, since both Brayden and Justina were on the loose.

"Hey, Thor," Leona said in a husky tone, her chest puffed up a bit more than normal and her shirt dipped down, exposing more of her cleavage than it already had been.

His eyes dipped for a brief moment, then he met her gaze. "Hello, Leona."

"Just ask her out already," Nico whispered as we climbed into the SUV.

Thor growled softly, but made no comment.

We were finally going to see our new house. Rhys and the others had explored the land Dan had purchased for us, and picked out the place our house would be built. Then, Rhys had forbidden us from returning. He drew up the designs and plans for the house and wanted to surprise us all once it was done being built.

"What if it's just a big penis?" Leona asked me.

I snorted. "Maybe if Deryn had drawn it."

Deryn pouted. "Rude."

"Where's Foxfire?" Thor asked.

"He's meeting us there. He had something to take care of with the elves," I answered.

Deryn and Nico sat on either side of me, each of their legs touching mine. Deryn draped his arm behind me. "Are you nervous?" he asked.

I shook my head. "No, I'm excited. I hate moving but moving into our forever home is worth it. Plus, it will be nice to be in our own house, away from the media."

"Oh, shit! Speaking of media," Thor said. He blindly grabbed for a remote in the center console, then hit a couple buttons. A TV screen flipped down from the roof of the SUV. The screen turned on, showing Dad and Sam standing before a podium with a dozen or so microphones strapped to it, and cameras flashing from the room before them.

"Greetings, I am King Dalton of the Sirens. I come before you today with several declarations. First, yes, it is true that Jolie, Princess of the Four Clans of Jinla, is my daughter and Princess of the Sirens. She has given up her title as heir due to her already heavy responsibilities with the other four clans. She has a set of wonderful mates, and I am very proud of the woman she has become and the things she has, and will, accomplish." He set his hand on Sam's shoulder and smiled. "Sam is our new heir. He is devoted to the Sirens and is one of Jolie's most trusted friends."

The media began yammering, but Dad held up his hand and they quieted.

"Sam and I will be rejoining the Summit next year and apologize for our inactivity the past two decades. We will no longer turn a blind eye to the darkness that is spreading. It is time for all races to work together and bring peace and prosperity to all corners of the world."

"King Dalton," a reporter called out. "Is Jolie still banished from Atlantis and no longer princess?"

Dad smiled, his eyes full of love and joy. "My daughter is no longer banished. She and her mates are welcome to visit us at any time. And, she is, and always will be, our princess."

"He's going to make me cry," I sniffled.

Deryn squeezed my shoulders and Nico patted my leg.

"Why was she banished? Did she break your laws?" another reporter asked.

"Sometimes, we do things as parents, thinking it will be for the best of our kids. Then, we realize we were wrong and must ask for forgiveness. My daughter has forgiven me, and I will do all I can to ensure all sirens are protected and given the best opportunity to excel in the future."

"That's all the time we have," Sam said, stepping forward. "Thank you."

Thor hit the button and the TV flipped back up. I leaned my head back, looking at the roof of the SUV. It was insane to think about how different my life had been a year ago. So much had happened. So much had changed.

We turned down a road that had recently been paved, but were stopped by Rhys standing in the center of the road.

We climbed out, and he took my hand in his. "Are you ready, my love?" he asked, then kissed my cheek.

I nodded, then we all continued down the road on foot. Foxfire jumped out of the tree line next to us in his fox form. He shifted into his human form, kissed my cheek, and fell into step beside me.

Leona and Thor walked behind us, their arms so close that they no doubt brushed occasionally.

The trees opened and I gaped at the monstrosity before us.

It had four floors, what looked like a helipad on the top, but was most likely a place for dragons to land and take off, two massive wood and iron doors, and over forty windows just on the front. It had wood and rock on the outside, making it look like a cottage. A *giant* cottage.

"It's so big and beautiful," I said, my free hand going to my chest.

"I've heard that a time or two," Rhys said with a smirk.

I smacked his arm, then looked up at him. "It really is magnificent. I love it."

He kissed me and said, "I'm glad you like it. Come on, check out the interior."

"I like it, too," Fox said.

Rhys chuckled. "What about you two?" he asked Deryn and Nico.

"We're reserving our judgment until we see what it's got inside," Deryn replied and Nico nodded in agreement.

The inside was made to look like a cottage as well, with thick, dark wood beams along the ceilings. The first floor had a huge living room, a game room with enough TVs for six people to have their own consoles, and an area with a huge TV for group games, a room with a pool table and foosball table was beside that room, and then a theater with reclining leather seats and projector. There were also a few guest bedrooms.

The second floor had all guest bedrooms. The third floor held rooms for each of us, including Leona and two extras, and a room on one side of the house made to fit a bed all five of us could sleep in comfortably or even just relax in. The bathroom was enormous, more of a public bath than a bathroom.

"What's on the fourth floor?" I asked while still admiring the bath. He'd even had a spa built in.

Rhys led me upstairs, pushed open a set of double doors, and I gaped.

A huge ballroom took up the entire fourth floor.

"Why not have this on the first floor?" Leona asked. "People are going to walk through your personal areas to get here."

He shook his head and pointed at the other end of the room where another set of double doors stood. "That is an elevator from the rear of the house. People will come down a different road than you used, which will deposit them to that elevator."

"You thought of everything," I whispered and pulled him down with a hand on the back of his head to kiss him.

"You forgot the one thing I requested," Nico objected.

Rhys pulled away from me and smiled at his friend. "That area is underground. I figured that it was safer to have it there."

"What?" I asked.

"Nico's lab," Rhys replied.

Nico took off in search of his new playground.

"I'm going to check out my room," Leona said. "Thor, can you come help me rearrange some of my furniture?"

"Sure," he said.

I gave her a knowing smile and she winked at me before trotting off with Thor on her heels.

"Mira," Rhys said loudly.

"Yes, Prince?" a disembodied voice replied.

"Ballroom music, please," he requested.

"Acknowledged," the voice said.

Music began playing, and Rhys swept me into a dance around the room.

"You made it a smart house?" I asked.

He nodded, continuing to lead me in a dance I remembered learning from my father as a young girl. Having my memories back was great, because I remembered all of my ballroom lessons.

"She's programmed to do lots of things. Try it out," he offered.

"Mira?" I called.

"Yes, Princess?" she replied.

"Play my favorite song," I ordered, a smirk on my face, thinking I had thought of something he wouldn't have programmed into her.

"Acknowledged," she replied.

My favorite song began playing.

I halted our dance and blinked back tears.

Rhys caressed my cheek and whispered, "Welcome home, Sunshine."

ROYALLY ENRAGED
HER ROYAL HAREM: BOOK FOUR
USA TODAY BESTSELLING AUTHOR
CATHERINE BANKS

CHAPTER 1

JOLIE

"Stop trying so hard and just do it," Leona said with a shake of her head. "It's like fighting. You don't focus on what move to make next, you just block the kick and punch the guy in his stomach."

"Yeah, once I know how to do it," I argued, but focused and tried again.

Fox sat on a patch of grass in front of our house, growing pieces of vines and braiding them in a long rope. I attempted to change his attitude, to make him angry, but he just kept smiling and braiding.

I sank to my knees on the grass with a sigh. "I'm pooped. I can't do anymore."

Leona patted my shoulder and sat beside me. "Your stamina is improving at least."

"My stamina of not being able to do anything? Wonderful." I hung my head.

"Lunch!" Rhys called from inside the house.

Fox turned and smiled at me. "Done for today?"

I nodded.

He picked me up under the armpits until I was standing, and then kissed me. "Good, because I have something fun planned for us."

"Okay." I returned his smile despite still feeling a bit defeated. We hadn't seen any trace of Justina or Brayden, aka Triton Douche, in four months, and while I was glad to have time free of danger, it worried me. I was certain they were planning something and I wanted to get stronger, so I could be an asset in their defeat.

"Make sure you eat protein," Leona ordered me as she followed us into the house. "And a bit of sugar."

"Yes, ma'am," I said and saluted her.

"I'm going out," she said and headed for the garage behind the house. "I'll be back tonight."

"Oh, are you on your way to visit a werewolf with a special hammer?" I teased.

She smiled, undaunted by my teasing. "You know it! I'm still trying to convince him to use that hammer on me."

Fox burst into laughter.

"Have fun!" I called to her as we walked inside.

"What's so funny?" Deryn asked Fox.

He shook his head. "I am not repeating that."

"What's for lunch?" I asked, kissing Deryn on the cheek before following him down the hallway.

"Not sure. Nico made it," he said with a shrug.

"Nico cooked?" Fox's eyes widened and then he ran down the hallway, disappearing from our view.

Nico was a great cook, so I totally understood Fox's desire to get there and start eating.

Deryn linked our hands and squeezed. "You okay?"

I looked up into his handsome face. His dark eyes were focused, the corners pinched in concern.

"I'm fine. Just tired from using so much magic. Also, frustrated because I still didn't accomplish anything," I said and frowned.

He squeezed my hand again. "You're improving. Leona told me you are."

"Not fast enough," I whispered.

We made it to the dining room, and found Rhys, Fox, and Nico sitting at the table. The table had several main dishes and side dishes.

"What's this?" I asked. "What's the occasion?"

Nico stood with a wide smile, his eyes sparkling with warmth. "No occasion. I just felt like cooking you a delicious meal."

I walked to him and gave him a deep kiss. "It looks and smells delicious."

He pulled out a chair for me and pushed it in when I sat.

We chatted about random things while I stuffed my face. Once finished, I relaxed back in my seat with a satisfied sigh. I gazed at Nico "That was amazing."

"I'm glad you enjoyed it." He kissed my cheek and began cleaning up.

"Let me clean," I said and tried to push him out of the way.

He smirked. "How about we clean together?"

I nodded and took my place at the dishwasher. He scrubbed, I put the dishes in, and when they were done, we would both put them away. It was a system we'd worked out recently.

"Come on," Fox said. "It's time for our date."

"Date?" I asked.

He nodded. "Remember? I said I had something fun planned for us."

"Right!" I agreed, smiling wide. I kissed Nico and then followed Fox out of the house. "Where are we going?" I asked.

"It's a surprise," he said. "You'll see when we get there."

We went into the garage, a huge building with room for eight vehicles. Currently, there were four, one for each of my mates. I had asked about getting my own car several times, but they preferred that I rode with one of them. Plus, Thor often drove us around anyway.

Fox's car was a sleek, silver sports car. I had no idea what the make or model was, just that it was pretty and *super* expensive.

He opened the door for me, and I climbed in.

"Ready?" he asked as he started the vehicle.

I nodded and buckled up.

Our fun date ended up being a trip to a karting place. The guys were planning on building one at our house, but kept arguing over details, so it wasn't finished yet.

Fox paid for us, completely ignoring the looks the women at the counter were giving him. I brushed my thumb over the mating crystal beneath his eye, and he kissed my palm. "I love you," he whispered with a wide smile.

My heartbeat became erratic and I returned his smile. "I love you, too, Foxfire. So much."

His smile turned cocky. "I know."

I laughed and smacked his chest lightly. "Butt."

"I do have a nice one," he said and glanced over his shoulder. "Though, I notice you looking at Deryn's more."

I rolled my eyes. "Yes, you have a great ass. And, I do look at yours a lot. I just do it when you aren't looking." I winked. "I can't let your ego get too big."

We walked to the track, and I realized that no one else was there. The entire place was empty.

"Did you buy out the entire track?" I asked him. Not that it would surprise me. My mates were stupidly rich.

He nodded. "Yep."

Not a single ounce of remorse. That was my Fox.

He helped me put on a helmet, and then we climbed into a couple karts.

A teenage-looking male walked towards me and said, "Head over to the start line. There will be a horn signaling you to start. You get ten laps. I'll wave a flag for the final lap and then the finish flag. Got it?"

I nodded and saluted him. "Yes, sir."

He rolled his eyes and stepped back so I could go.

There was just a gas and brake pedal, plus the steering wheel of course. I could drive a manual transmission, but I was glad that the kart was so simple. I lined up in the middle of the starting line and Fox pulled up on my left.

"I'm going to destroy you," he said with a wide smile.

I opened my mouth to reply, but Deryn replied before I could. "Not a chance! This time, you'll eat my dust!"

I turned and stared in shock at my other three mates, all in karts lined up beside me.

"You guys!" I yelled.

They chuckled.

"I wanted to surprise you," Fox said. "I originally planned for it to be just you and me, but it's just so much more fun when it's all of us."

"Tonight, you and I can have some alone time, since you sacrificed our date," I told him.

"Now, I'm jealous," Rhys said.

He wasn't. My mates were never jealous of each other. Something that my brain had a hard time understanding. Just the thought of them with another woman made me see red.

"Easy," Fox said and reached over to rest his hand on my forearm.

I exhaled and shook my head. "Sorry."

"We're yours," he whispered. "You don't have to worry about that."

I smiled at him. He always seemed to know what I was thinking. "I know. Sometimes just imagining it is enough to make me mad."

"Well, stop imagining it," he said and laughed.

I kissed the back of his hand and then put the visor on my helmet down. "Prepare to lose!" I threatened all of my mates. I turned to Nico. "No magic."

He pouted. "I wasn't planning to, but fine. I'll play fair."

"Only if he is winning." Rhys chuckled, and Nico flipped him off.

"Ready?" the bored teenager asked while chewing on some gum.

"Ready!" we all yelled.

I gripped my steering wheel, a huge smile splitting my face.

The horn sounded, and I slammed my foot down on the gas. The kart was much faster than I thought, and I squealed in delight as it shot forward. I bumped into Deryn, shooting him a wide smile as I continued on. The first turn came up, and I didn't slow down. I waited until I was right at the turn to slam on my brakes and jerk the steering wheel to the side, making the kart drift around the corner.

"What!" Fox demanded as they chased after me.

I laughed loudly, but it was cut off as Rhys caught up to me. I swerved in front of him, preventing him from passing me.

"Hey!" he yelled.

"Cheater!" Deryn yelled.

"It's called winning!" I yelled back.

"We've been played!" Nico yelled. "She's raced here before!"

"No one asked!" I reminded them, drifting around the next turn.

I had come here twice before I moved to Jinla. I'd been trying to figure out where to live and what apartments to apply for at the time.

Deryn and Fox were on either side of me as I drifted, and I couldn't help the joyous laugh that escaped my lips.

"It's on!" Fox yelled.

"Already thought it was," I teased, letting my words float over my shoulder as I took the hairpin turns before us.

Nico shot past me, and I gasped. "Cheater!"

He winked as he held the steering wheel in one hand, flexing his free arm's bicep. "Nope. Just pure skill, baby."

"Isn't that my line?" Rhys asked, slamming into Nico's side and making both of their bodies shudder from the impact.

I heard the teenager who worked there sigh, but didn't look for him. I knew we weren't supposed to hit each other, but I also knew if we broke the karts, we would pay for replacements.

I charged after Nico and Rhys with Fox and Deryn on either side of me.

The teenager waved the final lap flag, and I was too busy laughing at my mates' shenanigans to care that I came in last. I clutched at my stomach as I continued to laugh.

"Again!" Fox yelled as I pulled past the finish line.

"This time I won't go easy on you," I teased, driving my kart back to the starting line.

He said something in another language and we all lined our cars up. Nico winked at me and I saw his fingertips glow slightly. What was he up to?

The horn sounded and we all took off. All of us except Fox, who was stuck at the starting line.

"Nico!" Fox yelled.

Nico laughed, and I high-fived him as I drove beside him.

Fox's kart was finally freed from Nico's magic and he raced after us.

Each race had different results, but each was just as fun as the last. After the tenth race, I parked the kart to get some water and take a break. The guys continued racing, and I took a seat on the viewing deck to watch them.

"They're so gorgeous," one of the girls said. She had long blonde hair that brushed her hips and startling blue eyes.

"I bet they're amazing in bed," the other girl with tanned skin and brunette hair said.

The girls looked to be in their early twenties, but I wasn't sure. They were both beautiful, but neither had a bloodstone. They caught me looking and just stared back.

"They are amazing in bed," I said. "Mind blowing."

Their mouths dropped open.

"You're their mate?" the blonde asked.

I nodded.

"Wait! You're the Siren Princess!" the brunette shouted.

I nodded again.

They took seats at my table.

"What's it like?" the brunette asked, her eyes wide and cheeks slightly reddened.

"What?" I asked.

"Being with four males?" she clarified.

"At times, frustrating. Think about your relationships and how you have to take into consideration their feelings and wants. Now, multiply that by four," I said.

The brunette cringed.

"But, I love them and they love me. They're a lot of fun, as you can see," I motioned at them laughing and racing each other still. "They're the most caring males I've ever met and do all they can for their people."

"Can you make people fall in love with you?" the blonde asked. "Is that how you snagged them?"

Anger boiled within me, but I quickly shoved it down and shook my head. "No, we can't make people fall in love with us. If that were true, I would have had a mate long before I met these four."

"And that would have been a pity," Nico said from the chair he now sat in beside me.

The girls yelped and jerked back in shock at his sudden appearance.

"What's up?" I asked, turning to face him with a smile.

He kissed my cheek and then trailed a finger down my jawline. "Just wanted to touch you."

That was something we'd both been doing a lot lately. I smiled and kissed his lips lightly before looking at the other three, still engaged in an intense race. "Thanks, for coming."

He stood and kissed my forehead. "Anything for you, my flower."

He disappeared and was in his kart in the next instant.

"Whoa," the brunette whispered.

"You get used to the teleporting," I said with a smirk.

"No, you weren't kidding about them loving you. He really does love you," she said, her eyes slightly unfocused.

"What are you?" I asked.

She blushed. "Human, but I can see auras. When he was with you, his aura was pink, full of love. I rarely see that, even with couples who have been together for decades."

"Survive a few life and death situations together, and your bond runs pretty deep," I told her. My smile didn't waver despite the bit of pain that flared in my center. So many painful memories. Especially, the one of me trying to kill Nico.

All four karts slowed and I shoved the memories away, letting the joy fill me again. "Want to hear some stories no one else has?" I asked the girls.

The karts resumed their intense speed.

I told the girls a few funny stories, ones I knew the guys wouldn't care about being shared, and then walked down to the track. All four were removing their helmets and putting them away.

"Dinner?" I asked them.

"Dad invited us over," Deryn said.

I smiled. "Great! I haven't seen Dan this week."

"I know. He keeps reminding me," Deryn muttered. "'It's been four days since I saw her. It's been five days, Deryn. Deryn, where's my daughter,'" Deryn said, mimicking his father.

My mates' parents loved me, all except Nico's father, Johann, anyway. It had taken quite awhile for Rhys's mother, Adelaide, to accept me, but I had finally gained her approval.

"I know you've been wanting to see the twins, too," Rhys said.

Rhys was talking about my ex-boyfriend Martin's twin daughters. I was their unbiological aunt, and I tried to see them at least once a month. But, the last two times I had visited the werewolf den, they hadn't been there.

"Are they there?" I asked.

Deryn nodded. "Yep, Dad confirmed that they are there tonight."

My smile widened. "Great! Let's go."

I climbed into Fox's car and let him drive me, since it had been his idea for us to go on the date. He held my hand as we drove, and I relaxed in the passenger seat. Fox was a great driver, calm and attentive.

He parked at the werewolf den, and we waited for the rest of the guys to arrive before we headed to the house. Dan opened the door and pulled me into a giant hug.

"Hello, Father," I whispered against his incredibly wide chest.

"Daughter, you've been gone too long. You need to visit me more often," he chastised.

"I'm sorry. I've just been busy with my lessons," I explained.

"I told him," Leona said from inside the house. I couldn't see her because Dan's massive body was filling the entire doorframe.

"How did I know you would be here? You heard free food and couldn't stop yourself, could you?" I teased her.

"You never look a gift horse in the mouth," she reminded me.

Dan stepped aside and let me enter the house.

When I'd been at Atlantis, Dan had been tricked into thinking that I had died. In his grief, he had destroyed his house. Now, he had a brand new house, one that had rooms for me and my mates to stay in, as well as two additional rooms for our potential future children. He'd also built a much larger dining room, a play room for children, and two living rooms.

"Your new bed was delivered," Dan informed me.

"Really?" I asked and started to head up the stairs.

"Auntie Jolie!" twin girls yelled as they raced out of the children's room near the stairway. Their noses were still in the air, tracking my scent. They rushed over and slammed their little bodies into me.

Martin and Sharla walked out of the room and both hurried over to hug me.

Sharla pinched my arm. "You've been gone too long!" she chastised me, giving me her mom voice.

"I just talked to you two days ago," I reminded her.

"But I haven't seen you in over two weeks!" she said and pouted. "I missed your face."

"She does have a beautiful face," Martin said. Martin was Sharla's mate and my ex-boyfriend.

Sharla growled and pulled me into her arms. "No, I won't share her. You had her for years before I did," she said.

I chuckled and patted her back. "We need a girls' night."

"I don't know if I like the idea of you two going out together," Deryn said, eyeing Sharla.

"I'd be there to keep an eye on them," Leona said, draping an arm around both of us.

"That makes me even more nervous," Deryn said.

"Girls' night!" I shouted.

"Tonight?" Sharla asked, smile wide and eyes gleaming.

"Yes!" Leona and I agreed.

"Oh, boy," Dan said softly.

"You need a guard," Martin said.

"We can take Thor," Leona said and smirked.

"Not a chance!" I yelled at her.

"Who are we going to take then?" Sharla asked. "I'm not taking Martin. Leona can't take Thor. You can't take any of the princes."

"How about me?" Ezio asked, walking in from the dining room. His copper hair glowed and his sapphire eyes focused on me.

"Ezio!" I breathed. Even mated to four gorgeous and powerful males, Ezio still affected me.

He hugged me and slid his cheek along mine. "Hello, Jolie."

"Why didn't you tell me you were in town?" I asked, inhaling his scent that reminded me of cologne.

"Sorry," he apologized and kissed my cheek.

"Great!" Dan said. "That settles that. Ezio will go out with the girls to protect them. Everyone's happy."

"I don't know about everyone," Deryn muttered.

I turned and arched a brow at him.

He smiled and pulled me away from Ezio to kiss me and nuzzle my neck. "I can't help being jealous."

"Moon Moon. I'm yours. We're mated," I reminded him.

"Yeah, but look at him," he whispered. "He looks like a god."

I burst into laughter and only stopped when Deryn nipped my neck.

"I'm sorry," I said, trying to contain my laughter. "But, you know I'm not one to be unfaithful."

"I know," he whispered, his hand snaking around my lower back to pull me closer to him. "I'm trying to work on my jealousy."

"As long as you're working on it, that's all I ask for."

"Come, let's eat," Dan said. He clapped a hand on his son's shoulder. "I need to speak to you after we eat."

Deryn nodded. "Okay."

We made our way into the dining room and took our seats. Dan and Deryn sat at the heads of the table. I sat to Deryn's right and Nico sat on my right. The table was set with a bunch of food and pitchers of tea and lemonade.

I reached for the lemonade, but Nico beat me to it, filling my glass for me.

"Thanks," I said and kissed his cheek.

Everyone filled their plates and ate, chatting about random topics. I listened and relaxed. This was what I had always wanted my life to be like. Surrounded by those I loved, enjoying life, and just being happy.

Nico set his hand on my thigh and rubbed his thumb across it slowly and gently.

I leaned my head against his shoulder for a moment while chewing. Our connection was so much stronger now. Apparently, trying to kill him had helped us. Who knew?

There was an explosion outside the house, so close that the dishes rattled on the table. Nico and Deryn wrapped their bodies around mine, protecting me in case anything came near us. The next second, all of the males, except Fox and Martin, were gone. Martin and Sharla each held one of their daughters and Fox was behind me.

"What is it?" I asked, trying to look outside.

"Shelter," Martin growled and spun around.

Sharla followed him, and Fox nudged me after the family.

I didn't want to go hide in the shelter. I wanted to find out what was going on.

"Once you're inside, I'll find out what's going on and—"

"All clear," Ezio said as he entered the house, saving me from going into the shelter. "Jolie, you should come outside."

I hurried out and came to a stop by Rhys. He linked our hands together, squeezing mine for reassurance.

"They caught me away from home," Johann gasped.

He had blood coating his shirt and dribbling from his chin.

"Mom?" Nico asked.

"She's at home. She is safe."

"Why come here?" Dan asked.

"I teleported to Nico," Johann explained.

"Katar is on his way," Rhys said.

Johann groaned, his eyes squeezing shut as he tensed from pain. "It's too late."

I dropped to my knees beside him. "Stop talking," I ordered him. I set my hands on his chest and opened my bond with Fox to begin healing him. His internal injuries were much worse than any of us knew. That's why he was giving up. He was bleeding internally and had several broken ribs and a pierced lung.

Johann set his hand on top of mine. "Take care of him. He's going to need all the help he can get to be king," he whispered.

"No," I rasped, tears welling in my eyes.

Fox knelt and ran his hand along Johann's chest and stomach. "He has extensive internal injuries," Fox told Nico.

"Dad," Nico whispered and knelt by him. "Who was it?"

"Dhampirs," Johann said. He looked at me. "Your dreams might be premonitions after all."

Shit. That was not what I wanted to hear. In my nightmares, my mates died.

Nico's body was beginning to glow. His fury and grief were beginning to consume him.

"Take care of each other," Johann whispered to Nico and gripped his hand. "Don't make the same mistakes I did."

"Dad," Nico whispered.

Johann took a big breath, held out a ring to Nico and then all of his remaining magic siphoned into it. Johann's body fell limp to the ground just as Katar came up.

Katar dropped next to Johann and set his hands on Johann's chest. "Dammit! No!"

Kara hugged Nico and whispered something in his ear, but Nico didn't seem to hear.

"I need to check on my people," he said as he slipped on his father's ring.

"Do you want me to—"

He disappeared before I could even finish my question, but luckily Fox had set his hand on Nico's shoulder and went with him, so at least he wasn't alone.

Rhys pulled me to my feet and hugged me. Johann hadn't liked me much, but he was my father-in-law and he had been a good king. Plus, I could feel Nico's grief through our bond and it hurt me.

"Where are the dhampirs?" I asked Rhys, trying not to cry.

"Dead. He said he managed to kill them and then teleported here," Rhys whispered.

Dan knelt beside Katar, tears in his eyes as he stared at his dead friend.

CHAPTER 2
JOLIE

Rhys took me inside and gave me a warm mug of tea. I sipped on it silently, staring at the floor.

Johann was dead. Dhampirs had killed him. I couldn't let my mates die, too.

"He just needs some time," Rhys said. "Fox will help him deal with his initial grief."

Shouldn't I have felt worse about Johann's death? He was my father-in-law. But, he had said so many things to me.

"He's closed our bond," I whispered and rubbed at my chest.

Rhys nodded and rubbed my back. "He's doing it so you don't endure his grief."

"I should be helping him," I said.

"You will. For now, he needs to deal with it with his family and Fox. Your time to help him will come. You should still go out tonight," Rhys said.

"Really? You think I should still go out?" I asked.

He nodded. "Yes."

"Come on. Now's the perfect time to go out for a drink," Leona said with a wide smile.

"There's nothing for you to do right now," Rhys said. "I think it would be best if you went out with your friends."

"Are you sure?" I asked. It felt wrong to go out after such a tragedy.

Rhys nodded. "I'm sure."

"Okay," I agreed with a sigh.

"Ezio!" Sharla called.

"Yes?" he asked, walking down the stairs.

"You ready to take us out?" she asked him.

He looked at me a moment and then said, "Yeah."

"Keep a close eye on them," Rhys ordered Ezio.

Ezio glared at him, but said nothing.

I set my tea down and kissed Rhys. "Love you."

He rested his hand on my cheek and smiled. "I love you, too."

Ezio drove us to Leona's favorite bar. It was a decent sized place with a dance area and served drinks with plenty of alcohol for the cost. It also usually had patrons around our age and good music. She had forced my mates and I to go several times since she'd arrived in Jinla.

Leona sauntered up to the bar, smiling at Rowdy, the owner and bartender.

"Hello, gorgeous," Rowdy greeted her. He looked at me and Sharla. "You brought more beautiful women for me to meet?"

I rolled my eyes. With Leona around, men forgot about any other women with her. I had met Rowdy multiple times, but he only remembered Leona.

"They heard you had the best drinks in town, and we desperately needed a girls' night," Leona told him.

He picked up a silver shaker and flipped it around a few times before catching it. "What are you girls having?"

"Three of your special drinks," Leona said.

"I'm going to find a dark corner to stand guard in," Ezio said, his breath stirring my hair.

"Okay," I said. "Sorry you were relegated to babysitting us."

He smirked and kissed my cheek. "I'll babysit you anytime you want."

I laughed and joined Sharla and Leona on barstools at the bar.

"You good?" Leona asked.

I nodded. "Ezio's making himself scarce so we can enjoy our night."

Sharla smirked. "He's still got a thing for you."

"He also knows he can't have me and he respects me enough not to really try anything," I said. And, it was true. He may flirt on occasion, but he wouldn't actually try anything. One, he knew I would turn him down. Two, he didn't really want to deal with fighting my four mates.

"Could you stop hogging all the hot guys?" Leona asked me with fake irritation, her brows furrowed. "Do you know how hard it is to find a single guy who isn't in love with you?"

Sharla tossed back her head and laughed.

"Stop looking at werewolves and you'll find some," I teased.

"I saw clips from the Summit. You've got all the hottest guys in love with you," Leona said. "If I didn't know your siren abilities were locked back then, I'd assume you lured them somehow."

I rolled my eyes at her. "You know that's not what happened."

"I know. You're just too damn likable!" she said and sighed. "You were as a kid, too. I wanted to hate you, but you were just too nice and too much fun."

I smiled triumphantly. "Say it."

"I love you," she said. Then grumbled, "Jerk."

Sharla and I laughed loudly, but were cut off when a guy draped his arms around Sharla and my shoulders.

"What can I buy you beautiful ladies?" he asked.

"Some space?" Sharla asked and pushed his arm off her shoulder.

"Oh, don't be like that," he said and moved closer to me.

"We'll pass, thanks," I said and smiled sweetly. "We're on a no-guy type of night."

"Just your luck, I'm a yes-guy type," he smirked, thinking he was clever.

"The ladies have been nice and now I'll be rude. Move the fuck on," Ezio growled.

I turned, finally able to catch a glimpse of the guy now that his arm was gone. He was cute, middle-aged, and not cowed by Ezio at all.

"I thought this was a no-guy night?" he asked me.

"He's the muscle," I said. "He doesn't count."

"Plus, she's already tasted that several times," Leona whispered around her drink.

I glared at her.

Rowdy slid my drink to me. "Here you go."

"Thanks!" I said and took a big gulp. It was fruity, sweet, and amazing.

"Leave the girls alone," Ezio said. "Now."

"Whatever. These old hoes aren't that pretty anyway," the man grumbled.

Before I could stop him, Ezio punched the guy. The guy fell to the ground, unconscious.

Leona cheered and Sharla clapped.

"Ezio," I whispered, my mouth agape. He very rarely lost control.

He looked at me and his cheeks reddened slightly. "What?"

I shook my head, mouth still open, but didn't respond.

"I don't care if you're mine or not. I'm not letting some asshat disrespect you. Your mates wouldn't let him, and I'm their stand in."

"I bet he'd stand in for other things while your mates are gone," Sharla whispered in my ear.

"Shut up," I growled at her. I looked at Leona. "You're a bad influence on her. I shouldn't let you two hang out anymore."

Leona pouted, and Sharla cackled loudly.

"I'll be back," Ezio said as he carried the unconscious guy away from us.

"Another drink," I ordered Rowdy. He looked at my full glass, and then his eyes widened when I downed it in two gulps.

We waited until Ezio was back inside and at his post, leaning against the far wall, before we made our way to the dance floor. Sharla, Leona, and I danced along to the music, the alcohol flowing heavily within our systems now.

A guy tried to dance with Sharla, but Leona and I maneuvered between him and her, dancing right up against her. He took the hint and left.

"You're the princess!" a male voice gasped to my right.

I turned and eyed the guy who didn't look old enough to be in the bar, especially with such wide doe eyes.

"Yeah?" I said, unsure why it mattered.

He bowed his head slightly. "I'm Steven, a friend of Mawrth's. I'm a dragon," he said.

Mawrth and I weren't exactly on good terms, so I narrowed my eyes. "Nice to meet you," I said.

"Um, is Prince Rhys here? I actually need to talk to him about something," he looked around, searching for him.

"No, he's not here right now. Do you want to tell me, so I can tell him? Or you can give me a number, and I'll have him contact you." His hands were shaking slightly, which made me nervous.

I looked at Ezio and once our eyes met, he headed my way, moving through people easily.

"Um, I'd like to tell him. It's sort of urgent and dangerous," he said.

"Dangerous for who?" I asked, my body tensing. I could fight if I needed to, but I didn't want any bystanders getting mixed up in it. Or Leona and Sharla.

"Everything okay?" Ezio asked, stopping by me.

Steven's mouth dropped open. "You're Ezio!" he said, his eyes sparkling.

Looked like Ezio had a fan.

"Yeah. Who are you?" Ezio asked.

"He said he has a message for Rhys and it's urgent and dangerous," I told Ezio.

Ezio's body tensed just as mine had. "Why don't we talk about this outside?" Ezio suggested.

"Okay," Steven said. He gave me a smile and then walked ahead of Ezio out of the bar.

"That was weird," Leona whispered behind me, her mouth right by my ear.

I spun around, ready to punch her before I caught myself and tried to calm my now racing heart. "Dammit! Don't do that."

She smirked and then it slipped away. "What could he want?"

"It was a weird interaction," Sharla said, standing beside Leona. "He seemed to idolize you and Ezio."

"I'm sorry. My business always ruins our fun," I grumbled.

Sharla patted my shoulder. "Let's get another—"

Sharla's words were cut off as a huge explosion went off outside of the bar, breaking the glass windows and shaking the ground.

"Ezio!" I screamed, racing around the panicked bar patrons, most having ducked down and covered their heads. I didn't bother waiting to see if Sharla and Leona would follow. They could protect themselves. My only concern was Ezio.

I jumped through the broken front window and searched the street for him. There was a smoking hole in the center of the street, I guessed that was where the bomb had detonated.

"Ezio!" I screamed, my ears still ringing from the blast.

Wind from above pushed down at me. I jerked my gaze up and glared at the dragon hovering there. It had to be Steven, since they'd just stepped outside together. In his paw, I saw Ezio's unconscious body.

I roared and shifted into my dragon form, leaping up into the air before I'd fully shifted. Teeth bared, I flew at the dragon, ready to tear him to pieces and get Ezio back.

He backed up, eyes wide with panic, and then shifted back to human form and dropped to the ground, holding Ezio in his arms.

I landed, but stayed in my dragon form, snarling and growling at him.

He set Ezio on the ground. "I grabbed him and tried to get clear of the bomb, but he got hit by some debris," he told me. He took several steps away and raised his hands, palms out.

I shifted back to human form and knelt by Ezio. "Ezio," I said, trying to keep myself calm. "I need you to wake up. Someone could hurt me." I wasn't actually worried about myself, but hoped it might incentivize him to wake up.

He had several cuts that were already healing, but nothing that should have knocked him unconscious. I lifted his head gingerly, feeling around it for a lump or blood, but found none.

"He'll wake up in a few minutes," a deep voice said.

I spun around, crouched over Ezio's body and snarled, my teeth lengthening and thickening into wolf fangs.

He looked like a cross between Nico and Brayden. In his hand he held a metal staff with a silver glowing orb on the end of it. Mage.

I tugged on my bond with Nico, but he'd shut it down so tightly that I wasn't sure if he could feel it. I tugged on my other three bonds, hoping they would all come.

"Who are you and what the fuck do you want?" I snarled.

He smirked. "You don't know who I am? Why, is Daddy dearest keeping secrets?"

"I don't know you or your dad," I said. "Why did you hurt Ezio? What do you want?"

"Sweet, sweet, Jolie," he said, beginning a slow walk around me. "You're so naïve. My brothers and father must really be keeping a lid on my existence. It's sad really because if you'd been prepared, you could have prevented this."

He lunged for me, and I covered my body in scales and grew wolf claws. Nico popped into existence at my side and put a shield up, which his weird doppleganger leapt away from before touching.

Nico held his staff and glared at the guy. "Are you hurt, love?"

"No, but he knocked Ezio out somehow. There was an explosion and Ezio won't wake up," I said.

"He'll be fine," Nico assured me, still not taking his eyes off of the attacker.

"Brother!" the guy said and smiled wide. "I thought provoking your mate might force you to make an appearance."

Brother? He really was related to Nico.

Nico held his glare a moment longer and then turned to face me. His eyes were red, from crying no doubt, and glimmered with fury. "Can you teleport to the den?" he asked me.

I set my hand on his cheek and said, "I'm not leaving you."

He smiled and turned his head to kiss my palm. "I wasn't suggesting you leave me. I just need to know."

I nodded. "Yes."

"Where are the girls?" he asked.

"Inside the bar," I answered, keeping a wary eye on Nico's brother who stood with his arms folded, tapping his foot, and glaring at us.

"Sharla! Leona!" Nico yelled. "Here, please."

Both ran from the bar to dash inside Nico's shield. Sharla knelt at Ezio's side and inspected him.

"You have to talk to me eventually," Nico's brother said. "I won't stop until you do."

"Don't test me, Klaus. Have you spoken to your brother?" Nico asked, his lip twitching as he held in a snarl.

"Brayden?" Klaus asked.

Nico nodded.

I turned and stared at Nico in shock. Brayden was his brother? He hadn't told me that! Why was he keeping secrets? What the hell!

"No. Why? What did he do this time?" Klaus asked.

"He's on my kill list," Nico told him. "He tried to steal my mate and forced her to forget me."

Klaus's eyes widened. "He was the one trying to steal the siren throne?"

Nico nodded.

Klaus looked at me. "You're the siren princess?"

I nodded.

He sighed and said, "I'm sorry. I wasn't going to hurt her. I didn't realize it was you that was involved. Had I known, I wouldn't have frightened your mate."

"What do you want?" I asked him.

Klaus ignored me, focused on Nico. "I need to talk to you, Nico. There are things happening and—"

Nico cut him off. "I don't have time for this. Dad's dead. I've got shit to do."

"What?" Klaus asked, his face void of emotion and his tone neutral.

"Dhampirs killed him," Nico said and cleared his throat as emotions built in him.

"When?" Klaus asked.

"Today," I answered and slipped my hand in Nico's.

"I'll find you again later," Klaus said. He looked at me and then met Nico's glare. "Keep her close."

He disappeared the next instant.

"Teleport us to the den," Nico ordered me.

"Wait!" Steven yelled. "I need to speak to the prince!"

Nico dropped the shield and staggered forward a bit. I stood before him, letting him lean on me in a way that appeared he was simply cuddling me and kept him from looking weak.

"Come with us," I told Steven. "If you try anything, I'll kill you."

His eyes widened and he nodded before jogging over to us.

"Everyone put a hand on each other. Steven, pick up Ezio," I said.

Everyone obeyed and I teleported us to the den, just outside of Dan's house. Dan threw open the door and growled, eyes fixed on Ezio.

"Easy," I ordered Dan. "Let us explain everything."

"You're bleeding," Dan growled.

I was?

"It's a superficial wound," Nico said. "It should stop bleeding in a moment."

"Why are you so weak?" I asked him softly.

"Used a lot of power too quickly just before you summoned me," he explained.

"Where are the rest of the guys?" I asked.

"Helping my people prepare for my father's funeral," Nico said.

"Dan, can you take Nico to our room?" I asked.

Nico started to object, but Dan put his arm around Nico's waist and pulled Nico's arm around his shoulders. "Don't argue with your mate. She's got that crazed look in her eye," Dan whispered.

Thor stepped out of the house, glaring at Steven.

"Thor, can you take Ezio inside?" I asked.

I tugged on Rhys's bond and he tugged back.

Thor took Ezio and frowned. "What happened?"

"Mage," I said. "Nico said he's fine and will wake up soon."

Thor nodded and left.

"Rhys is on his way," I told Steven. "You can wait in the dining room until he arrives."

Steven nodded and followed me inside.

Martin stood from the couch and hugged Sharla.

After getting Steven to the dining room, I returned to Martin and Sharla. "I'm sorry," I whispered and looked at my feet. "I didn't mean to put your mate in danger."

"It wasn't your fault," Sharla said.

"Just being around me is dangerous," I said.

Martin pulled me into a hug. "It's alright."

"We're good?" I asked as I rubbed my face on his shirt.

He rubbed the center of my back and nodded against my hair. "Yeah."

"What's going on?" Rhys asked as he entered the house.

I pulled away from Martin and rubbed a hand down my face. I was so tired. I hadn't realized it until now. "A friend of Mawrth's said he has to tell you something and it's dangerous," I explained. "He's in the dining room."

"What happened?" Rhys asked, his voice a deep growl as he touched the side of my head.

"Talk to him first. Then, I'll tell you," I said. I rubbed a hand down my face again.

"Go to our room," Rhys whispered and kissed my cheek. "I'll be up as soon as I'm done with him."

I nodded and then scowled as I looked around the room. "Where's Leona?"

"She snuck off with Thor somewhere," Sharla said and smiled. "I doubt you'll see her the rest of the night."

I laughed and shook my head as I made my way up to the second floor and then to the room we used while staying at the werewolf den. Nico lay on the bed, still clothed, but asleep.

As quietly as possible, I climbed into bed with him. He stirred slightly, slid an arm beneath my pillow, and then spooned himself around me. Within a minute, I was fast asleep.

CHAPTER 3

JOLIE

Johann's funeral was short and emotional. Mages burned the bodies of their dead, so my four mates and I stood and waited until his body was gone. Nico stayed longer to take care of some stuff, but sent us away.

Back at the house, Deryn turned on a movie, and pulled me down onto his lap. He nuzzled my neck and asked, "What's going on in that beautiful head of yours?"

"Nico never told me he has brothers," I whispered. "He never told me Brayden is his brother."

Deryn's head snapped up. "Trident Douche?"

I nodded.

"He didn't tell us that. Are you sure he's—"

"He confirmed it when talking to his *other* brother," I said. I took a deep breath and whispered, "It made me realize that there is a lot I still don't know about you guys. I'm a shit mate."

His arms tightened around me. "No, you're not. We're just very secretive. It comes from years of training by our parents. We don't mean to keep secrets or things from you."

I paused the movie since we weren't watching it anyway and straddled him so I could fully face him. "Tell me something about you that I don't know," I requested.

He thought about it and asked, "Have I ever told you about my mom?"

"No," I said, focusing intently on him. I had wanted to ask about her before, but was worried it was a heartbreaking story and didn't want to upset him or Dan.

"Mom was full of fire. She was always working on something and was adamant that things got done, if she believed in them. Dad and Mom became mates when they were sixteen. Her parents were pissed, but Mom put her foot down and told them two more years didn't matter. She loved Dad and that's what was important. When Dad became alpha, they praised their match, which irked my mother so much.

"One day there was an attack on the den. Vampires. Mom didn't want to let everyone else fight while she just sat back and worried. You remind me of her a lot, actually. Anyway, she went out of the house to help fight and protect the weaker wolves in the pack. The vampires ganged up on her, and before Dad or I could get to her, they killed her. Dad went crazy, murdering everything he saw. I was lucky enough to get the wolves away, so there were no casualties on our side. Dad mourned her for months, probably longer than that to be honest, but that's what I saw."

"How old were you when she died?" I asked softly, linking our hands.

"Eighteen," he said. "Dad keeps a smile on his face, and I know the pain isn't as bad for him now, but to this day, I hear him talking to her."

I couldn't imagine losing a mate after so long. The pain I felt when our bonds were severed was torture enough, but for them to actually die...

"Dad loves you, Jolie. You're the daughter he never had. You saw it the day we came back from Atlantis. He keeps pushing me in training and is pushing the rest of the pack as well, preparing for war. He told me that if someone steals you again, he's going to be ready to 'knock their fucking doors down and take you back.'"

Tears burned in my eyes, threatening to fall, but I blinked them back. Dan was amazing, and I needed to do something for him. To show how much I appreciated him.

Deryn pulled me forward, hugged me tightly, and rested his forehead on my shoulder. "That's why I hate that you put yourself in danger so much. I can't lose you, too. I can't watch you die, while I'm unable to help you. But, you keep getting hurt. You keep rushing into things. I love you, Jolie. I love you more than anything else in the world."

I snuggled closer to him and whispered, "I love you, too, Moon Moon."

He chuckled and kissed the side of my neck. "Are you hungry?"

"Just a bit more cuddling?" I requested.

He fell to his side, pulling me with him, and we quickly tangled our legs together. I let him wrap the top half of my body up in his arms. We lay like that for who knows how long, only separating when Nico cleared his throat.

"I, uh, sorry, but can I borrow her?" Nico asked, rubbing the back of his neck.

I stood, and Deryn smiled.

"You know you don't have to ask," Deryn said.

Nico nodded, linked our hands and teleported us to his bedroom.

"What's up?" I asked him. "How are you holding up?"

He ran a hand through his disheveled hair, and I noticed the bags beneath his eyes. "There's so much to deal with during this transition period," he said. "It's just...a lot."

"What do you need from me?" I asked, stepping closer to him. "How can I help?"

He smiled down at me and pressed his forehead to mine. "Honestly, I just wanted to lie with you a bit."

I tugged his hand and climbed onto the bed. He took his shoes off and climbed on after me. I waited until he laid down on his back before snuggling up against his side and resting my head on his chest.

"I love you, Nico."

He wrapped one arm around my side and squeezed. "I love you, too."

"Do you want me to play with your hair until you fall asleep?" I asked, already reaching up.

He snuggled closer to me with a happy smile and nodded.

I ran my fingers through his hair, my fingertips feeling along his scalp as I did. It wasn't long before he was asleep and softly snoring. I tried to climb out of the bed, but his hand snatched out and grabbed my wrist. "Please...don't leave," he whispered, his eyes fluttering open.

I hurriedly climbed back onto the bed and snuggled into him. "Okay," I said. "I'll stay with you as long as you want me to."

"Forever," he whispered. "Forever sounds good."

"Forever and ever," I whispered back.

"I'm what?" I screeched, staring at Nico in disbelief. We'd woken up the next morning and the bags beneath his eyes were thankfully gone now.

"You're Queen of the Mages," Nico said again. "Since I'm King now and you're my mate..."

"Oh," I breathed.

He chuckled and said, "It's not the end of the world. There really isn't that much that you need to do."

"I just..." I didn't finish the sentence. I was going to say I hadn't planned for this to happen so soon, but Nico hadn't planned for this either. His father being murdered is what caused it.

He wrapped his arms around me and said, "I know. It's going to be okay. We'll get through this together, right?"

I nodded, turned, and smiled at him. "Right. What do you need me to do?" I asked.

"Tomorrow, I need you to come with me to speak with the elders of the mages and start learning about my race," he said. "There's a lot that you don't know, and I want you to be prepared."

"Nico, why didn't you tell me that you had siblings? Or that Brayden was your brother?" I asked him, stepping out of his hold.

He sighed and rubbed the back of his neck. "I didn't know until we were restoring your memories. I felt his magic and the bond we shared then. He's my half-brother and Dad never told me about him. I confronted Dad when we returned, and he confirmed that I have not one or two, but six half-siblings."

Six? Wolfsbane! That was a lot of unknown siblings.

"And why didn't he tell you before?" I asked.

"Because he'd left on not-so-good terms with the women and had only stuck with me and my mother. So, most of the women hate me and my mother," he explained.

"You don't think one of them could be responsible—"

"It's a possibility," he said with a nod. "Especially if Brayden hooked up with Justina. She is a dhampir, after all."

If they'd joined forces, it could be a very, very bad thing for us.

"Hey, stop fretting about the future. We're going to just focus on today and what needs to get accomplished now. Right?" he said.

I nodded and stepped into his arms. "You are lucky you're pretty," I mumbled into his chest.

He laughed, a true laugh, and I felt my heart soar. It was the first time I'd heard that type of laugh in a week at least.

"He is rather pretty," Deryn teased from the doorway.

"What's up?" Nico asked him, turning away from me.

"Just came to get you for food," Deryn said.

I finished getting ready and then followed them to the dining room where a huge feast was ready.

Leona sat with Thor beside her, their heads close together, and adorable smirks on their faces. They were an adorable couple. Now that they were officially dating, Thor had been at our house almost every night.

"What's the plan for today?" I asked as I sat.

"I'm hiding at the house today," Nico said, sitting on my right. "I need some decompression time."

"Actually, I was hoping you would come with me today," Thor said as he faced me.

"Me?" I asked, looking at Leona who was piling her plate with food.

"I'm going to visit my pack with Martin. We thought you might want to go with us," Thor said.

"Your pack!" I screeched, excitement coursing through me. "I haven't seen them in years!"

"I'm coming, if you go," Deryn said.

"She's not in any danger with my pack," Thor said and I could tell he was holding back an eye roll.

"I didn't suggest she would be. I just want to meet your alpha and talk to some of the wolves there," Deryn explained.

"Trying to find out if I'm hiding secrets?" I asked.

He kissed my cheek and took the seat on my left. "No, gorgeous. I just want to find out more about the pack and your involvement."

Thor and I exchanged a look that let me know I wasn't the only one not buying it. Whatever his reason, I had nothing to hide.

"I'm sure Alpha would love to meet you. He'd always said he'd love to meet whoever could handle me as a mate," I said.

Thor chuckled and began filling his plate.

"When are you going?" Deryn asked.

"In about three hours," Thor answered. "Martin is finishing up some work and then he'll swing by to pick us up."

"Sounds great!" I said.

After eating, I went to Fox's room and lay with him on the floor. He gently stroked his fingertips up and down my arm, his eyes focused on the ceiling above us, and his thoughts somewhere unknown.

"What's up?" I asked him. "You're rarely quiet and so serious."

"Just thinking about your dreams," he whispered.

I rolled onto my side and rested my head on his chest, wrapping my arms around his torso. "I won't let it come true," I whispered.

He kissed the top of my head and whispered, "As long as you are safe, that's all that matters."

"No. I don't...can't live without you. I need you all," I said, tightening my grip.

"We're working on making ourselves stronger. You should summon your new friends soon. So you can work out whatever deals you may need before a time of crisis," Fox said.

He was referring to the two magical tattoos now on my forearms. One was of a fox, a kitsune to be exact, named Nar. The second was of a unicorn and had been given to me by my mother.

"I'll do that this weekend," I promised.

"I love you, Jolie. I love you more than I thought was possible to love someone. Nico's father dying reminded us that we aren't invincible. And, that we must be as strong as possible to keep you safe. We've almost lost you a couple of times, and I won't let it happen again. When I see Justina, I'm going to tear out her heart and shove it down her throat."

Fox's eyes were bright with power and his body was tight, coiled for a fight. I had never heard him say such threatening things before. I was shocked and sadly, smug that it was because of me.

"When you didn't remember us at Atlantis, I was furious. It hurt so much to have you look at us like strangers again, to not see the love you usually show when you look at us. Plus, you had shut down our bonds so tightly I couldn't feel you. It was terrible."

I squeezed him. "I'm sorry. I know I've caused you a lot of trouble since we met."

He chuckled. "That's an understatement. But, the thing is, I wouldn't trade a moment of it. Having you in my life is worth any amount of trouble you might bring."

"You're so sweet," I whispered, leaned up, and kissed him.

"How long until you have to go?" he asked and kissed me again, his hand roaming up my side.

"We have at least an hour," I said in a breathy voice, my lower body already warming in anticipation.

He sighed. "Only an hour? I shall have to make it a worthy hour then."

He flipped us over and with me pinned beneath him, he kissed me deeply, pressing his lower body into mine and making me all too aware how happy he was to be there. When we had mated, it had been incredibly passionate and when the bond snapped into place, it was bordering on overwhelming. Ever since the mating, sex between us had been incredible. Not to say that it was in anyway unenjoyable before, but Fox was usually more sensual than sexual overall. Lately our love making had been so intensely passionate, my mind refused to process that this was the same man. Fox undressed me slowly, sensually, but with a feverish need edging into each of his motions. He kissed along each piece of skin as he exposed it, licking and teasing my naked body as he stripped me down. As he came to my pert nipple, he flicked his tongue over it teasingly then took it into his mouth and sucked hard on the sensitive peak. I moaned and arched up into his skilled touch.

"Are you too worked up for this much foreplay?" He asked as he slid two fingers deep inside of me, his eyes widening when he felt how very wet I already was.

"Yes," I whispered, arching as his fingers began to slide out of me.

"Damn, baby, you are supposed to tell us when you are this wet and ready."

He stood in one smooth motion, making me reach for him and start to beg him to come back to the bed. I lost all my words as his shirt fell to the floor and his upper body was revealed. As his hands went to the top button of his pants I slid my fingers down my body and began touching myself while he undressed. His eyes tracked my movements and I watched his body spasm against his still closed zipper. I continued to work that oh so sensitive nub while his pants fell to the floor next to his shirt. He was suddenly on top of me, kissing down my throat and collarbone.

I kept working that sweet spot at the top of my center even as he slid his erection within me. He filled me and stretched me and made my body spasm around him with that initial thrust. One thrust, two, three, and he found a rhythm. We both moaned at the same time. I could feel the orgasm building both from where my fingers still teased my body and the deep strokes of Fox as he pushed in and out of me.

"Damn, Jolie! You haven't been this wet in a long time." He began to thrust into me harder and faster and the orgasm broke over me in a wave of dizzying heat and release. And still he pushed into me. As the orgasm subsided I tapped him on the shoulder with a devious smile. He pulled out slowly and rolled to his back beside me, still rock hard and waiting for his own release.

I rolled to my knees and kissed him deeply, then straddled his hips and lowered myself over him, blissfully enjoying each inch as his body was sheathed inside mine. I began to rotate my hips in a slow rise and fall. It only took him a bare minute to catch the rhythm of my hips and match it with his own slow and even strokes. I knew he was close and so was I but I wanted to make the moment last, as we only had an hour to enjoy one another's company. I leaned back until he almost slipped out of me, then rode forward across his body and rocked my hips back and forth over his shaft while I kissed him deeply.

"Now. Please, Fox. Now. I'm so close."

"Me too, Jolie."

I felt his hips arc into me as I rode his body down and suddenly we were both crashing over that glimmering edge. I fell forward into his arms and we both lay there, panting as we tried to catch our breath and find feeling in our limbs again. It may have been a short hour but we were both sated.

CHAPTER 4
JOLIE

I sat in the front passenger seat while Martin drove. Deryn and Thor sat in the back seats, talking quietly, too quietly for me to hear.

"Are you excited?" Martin asked.

I nodded, thinking about Abraham, the alpha. "I haven't seen Abraham since I moved out of my dad's, er, step-dad's house."

"He's always asking about you."

"He was such a great alpha," I said. "I am lucky to have been part of your pack."

"You like him better than my dad?" Deryn asked.

I spun and stared at him. "What? I didn't say that."

"You talk about him in an almost reverent tone," he said.

"He was my first alpha and he treated me like one of them," I said. "He made me feel wanted when I was unwanted at home."

"You didn't answer my question," Deryn pointed out.

"I don't like one more than the other. I like them differently," I said.

"How?" Deryn asked.

"Abraham was like my cool uncle. Dan is like the father I always wanted," I said. "Not sure if that makes sense."

Deryn nodded and relaxed back in his seat. "Yeah, it makes sense."

I was glad, because I didn't really want to discuss it anymore. It wasn't fair to ask who I liked more. That was like asking a parent who their favorite child was. Or asking the child who their favorite parent was. Or asking who my favorite mate was.

We entered the pack's compound and people rushed out of their houses to come see us. There were many I had never seen before, but so many I knew were still there.

I climbed out of the SUV and was immediately inundated with hugs and cheek kisses. I was in the middle of a group of girls I'd known in high school when Abraham stopped before me.

I turned to face him fully and smiled up at him. "Alpha," I whispered and bowed my head respectfully.

He tilted my face up and tapped the bloodstones. "Mated?"

"She is," Deryn said.

All eyes turned to him. Deryn stood a bit away from us, his posture relaxed, but his eyes hard as he focused on Abraham.

Abraham turned to face him and asked, "You're one of her mates?"

Deryn nodded. "I am."

"I suppose he might be alpha enough for you," Abraham said. "Though, I always rooted for Ezio."

Deryn's lip twitched as he held back a snarl.

"Alpha," I said in a reprimanding tone.

Abraham turned and embraced me. "I've missed you, child."

I hugged him back and rubbed my face on his shirt, a habit I still couldn't break. "I missed you, too."

He pushed me back and turned to face Deryn. "You came to speak with me?"

Deryn nodded. "Privately, please."

"This way," Abraham said and waved Deryn towards his house. Deryn turned towards me and opened his mouth, but Abraham cut him off. "She's safer here than with any other pack. This is *her* pack."

Deryn scowled. "She's not—"

"She's ours," Molly, a shorter female werewolf with a shaved head said and wrapped her arm around my waist. "None here would harm her."

"Come on, let's go hunt!" Linus called and several shouted in approval.

"No," Deryn growled. His growl and word were laced with command and it caused everyone to still. "I won't allow her to hunt with you."

I scowled. "Deryn, I hunted with them for years."

"You know we wouldn't let anything happen to her," Thor said and walked to stand behind me with Martin on his right.

"I can't risk it. Jolie, please stay within the compound," Deryn ordered. He turned and walked into the house without another word.

"What the hell was that about?" I asked Thor, looking up at him.

He was scowling and looking at the house Deryn had gone in to. "I don't know."

"Well, if we can't hunt, let's play!" Linus said, not missing a beat.

I walked to Linus, hugged him, and then slapped his arm and yelled, "you're it!" as I ran away.

The pack scattered, some turning into wolves while most stayed human. The pack ran about the compound, swerving around buildings and dodging the person who was *it*. With over fifty people, the game became a squealing and laughter-filled event. Not once did someone get mad or growl about being tagged. That was one of the biggest reasons I loved this pack. Everyone got along. Abraham created a sense of belonging, and we all genuinely enjoyed being around each other. Sure, there were bumps in the road or drama, but they were rare occurrences.

I ducked out of Linus's reach as he tried to tag me, laughing as he chased me around a building. I ran into Deryn, and Linus ran into me.

Linus staggered back, his head bowed. "Sorry." I could smell the fear wafting around him.

I grabbed Linus and tugged him around Deryn. "Hurry!" I yelled.

Linus ran after me and Deryn stared at me with a scowl.

"Deryn's it!" I yelled, finally releasing Linus's hand now that he was away from Deryn and the scent of his fear was gone.

Deryn exhaled, letting his head drop forward a moment, and then he raised it with a full smile in place and raced after me.

I screamed and dodged around Linus and then Thor who was closest.

Deryn tagged Thor. "Thor's it!" he yelled.

Thor chuckled and ran after one of the other pack members who was closest. He chased after a toddler, but then swerved around the toddler to tag an adult. We liked the kids to be involved, but tried not to make them the targets so they could just enjoy the chase.

Deryn slid his hands around my waist and pulled me back roughly against the front of his body, stopping me from running. "You look so beautiful right now," he whispered. "Seeing you with your face lit up with a smile and enjoying yourself with wolves is a definite turn on."

I pushed away from him and kissed his cheek. "You can be turned on later. I can't lose!"

Martin raced towards me, and I ran away from him. A big grey wolf stepped out in front of me, and I tripped over him, landing on my butt next to him.

He growled a moment and then nuzzled my cheek.

"Sorry," I whispered and rubbed at my sore butt as I stood.

The wolf shifted, and I immediately threw my arms around the old man. He'd become fully grey while I was away, but there was no doubt that it was Peter, the second-in-command of the pack.

"Peter!" I squealed as I hugged him.

He hugged me back and chuckled. "Hello, troublesome human."

"I'm not human," I said when we separated.

He winked. "You'll always be the troublesome human girl I chased out of my gardens."

Deryn had stopped, standing several feet away from us.

"Peter, meet one of my mates, Deryn. Deryn, this is the second of the pack, Peter."

Deryn stepped forward and shook hands with Peter. "Nice to meet you."

Peter bowed his head. "Nice to meet you, too. I hope Jolie's not too much trouble for you."

"She's definitely a handful," Deryn said with a smirk, and draped his arm around my shoulders.

"That she is," Peter agreed and chuckled at my frown.

"So, you came to learn a bit more about Jolie's past with us?" Peter asked.

Deryn nodded. "Yes."

"She's quite a girl," Peter said, making me blush. "Take care of her, understand? I don't want to hear anymore sad news related to her."

Peter pinched the tip of my nose, smiled, and then shifted back into wolf form and trotted away.

"They really love you here," Deryn said.

"Are you surprised?" I asked, looking up at him.

He smirked. "No, but it is shocking to see a werewolf pack so readily accept a non-werewolf into it."

"It surprised me when I was younger, too," I admitted. I pulled Deryn to a nearby porch and sat on it with my legs dangling over the edge. "The first time Martin brought me to meet everyone, I was terrified. I thought they were going to eat me. I mean, I knew many of them from school, but I didn't know what they would be like here. As soon as Martin introduced me to Abraham, he pulled me into a hug, kissed the top of my head, and told me I was always welcome to come.

I cried a bit, but honestly, they saved me. I was so broken from the vampire father who raised me and abused me, I'm not sure what type of person I would have turned out to be if Abraham hadn't brought me into the pack."

"He told me a bit about how you were in the beginning," Deryn said. "I'm sorry you had to endure so much as a child."

I kicked my legs back and forth and smiled. "It's okay. It made me who I am and whatever the path, it led me to you."

He bent and kissed me. "I love you, Jolie."

"I love you, too. But, I don't understand why you wouldn't let me go hunt," I said.

He sighed. "I didn't want you to go off somewhere and possibly get into danger while I was talking with Abraham."

"Thor and Martin would protect me," I reminded him.

"Yes, but it's not their job," he said.

"As my friends, it is," I countered.

"I'm sorry. I wasn't trying to be a rude jerk earlier."

"Can we go hunt now?" I asked. "Since you outrank them all, you should be fine hunting with them, right?"

He nodded. "Yes."

"Hunt!" I yelled and jumped down from the porch.

Several people yelled and others howled, and within a minute, most of the pack was waiting before me.

"Hunt!" I yelled again.

Deryn shifted, and I climbed onto his back. "Martin, lead the way!" I said.

Martin, and the rest who weren't already in wolf form, shifted and then Martin howled. Everyone, including Deryn, howled in response and the hairs on my arms stood up. Martin ran towards the trees and Deryn followed. Thor ran on our right, and I smiled over at him. He let his tongue loll out the side of his mouth as he ran, and yipped happily.

Into the trees we ran, and I hunkered down on Deryn's back, gripping his furred neck and holding on with my legs. He ran in the center of the pack, letting others take charge of the hunt.

There was some yipping, and then I saw the herd of deer ahead. Deryn slowed a bit more, letting more of the pack race past him to take the deer down. The first deer was taken down, and Deryn slowed to a stop.

I patted his shoulder and then lay on him fully and sighed. "Wolf fur is so soft and warm," I purred.

He lay down, carefully, so I didn't fall off his back, and huffed softly.

"Thank you, for coming hunting with us," I whispered.

Cinnamon, a brown colored wolf, trotted towards us with blood on her muzzle. She yipped at me and dropped the front half of her body down and wagged her tail. I darted off of Deryn and tackled her. She rolled with me and nipped at my hands and arms, but never hard enough to draw blood. We stopped rolling and squared off, me standing and her in a playful bow.

Deryn growled softly.

"She's not going to hurt me," I told her. "Cinnamon and I have known each other since junior high. Right, Cinn?"

Cinnamon yipped and stood on her back legs, letting her front paws rest on my shoulders as she licked my face.

"I missed you, too," I whispered and hugged her.

Deryn shifted into his human form. "This isn't normal," Deryn said softly. "I've never seen a wolf pack act like this."

"Just because it's not normal for you, doesn't mean it's not—"

"I don't mean just my pack. I've visited dozens of packs and spent weeks with them. I've seen them interact with humans who had married into the pack. None of them accepted the human like they accept you. This pack treats you like a pup. No, not a pup... I don't know! They treat you unlike anything I've seen!" Deryn yelled.

Cinnamon dropped down to all four feet and faced him. She tilted her head and yipped at him.

"She's not pack, though," Deryn said. "I appreciate the sentiment, but she's not in your pack by marking or connected through a mate."

Cinnamon yipped again.

Deryn's brows furrowed. "She...what?"

"I had a temporary mark," I answered, guessing what they were talking about. "Abraham marked me when I started coming around and then removed it when I turned eighteen."

"Why?"

"To protect me, I think, but it didn't help since my dad was a vampire," I explained.

Deryn's brows were so deeply furrowed, I worried he would have permanent lines. "He marked you, but then removed it? You were part of this pack, but then left it. Now, you're part of my pack."

"Permanently," I said with a wide smile.

He looked up and the frown disappeared, replaced by a wide smile. "Yes."

I ruffled Cinnamon's ears. "They were my family. Still are."

"A werewolf pack that took in a human. Just...because?" he whispered and shook his head. "Who treated her like a wolf, despite her being nothing of the sort."

"She's always been special," Martin said, standing behind me in his human form. He ruffled my hair and smiled down at me.

"Dinner!" Abraham yelled.

"We just ate," Martin chuckled.

"I didn't," I said. "And, I'm starving."

Deryn shifted, and I leapt onto his back again. He ran back to the house and then shifted into human form before linking our fingers and walking into the house.

Dinner was full of laughter and stories from my first encounters. Deryn listened, but he didn't smile much. He didn't look mad, but like he was thinking really hard.

The trip home was quiet, and we stopped at the den to visit Dan. Deryn and Dan went to Dan's office and left me downstairs.

"What's wrong?" Sharla asked, bumping her shoulder against mine.

We both sat on the floor with one twin in each of our laps. Madison was in my lap, curled up in wolf form while I stroked my fingers through her fur.

"Deryn's been acting really weird today. He can't understand why Thor and Martin's pack treats me like they do. I just don't get why it bothers him so much," I admitted.

Sharla shrugged. "When you're used to something being done a certain way, having it done any other way is strange and you won't understand it."

"Yeah, but I just don't get it in this case. So what if they treated me like pack? So what if they still treat me like pack even though I'm in Deryn's now? What does it matter?" I asked.

"Maybe he'll explain it later, once he figures out how to properly explain himself," she suggested.

I hoped so.

"Have you talked to Ezio, since that night?" Sharla asked.

I sighed and shook my head. "No."

"Why not?" she asked.

"It's not on purpose. I just haven't had the time," I explained. "I've been so worried about Nico."

"How is he doing?" she asked.

"Better. He's stressed with all his new duties and the transition," I said. "But, he seems to be doing better now."

"Jolie?" Ezio asked, peeking his head into the living room. He smiled and then saw the pup in my lap, so he squatted down to hug me. "How're you?"

"Good," I said. "How are you? I'm sorry I didn't call you."

He kissed my cheek, then sat back, crossing his legs. "You're busy. I know how it is. Plus, I was fine the next day. The spell was just some type of sleeping spell."

"I can't believe all that happened," I mumbled.

"You're always full of trouble," he teased me. His smile faded a bit, and he leaned forward to smell me. "Where have you been? You smell like a bunch of strange wolves."

"I went and saw my old pack," I explained.

"Martin's pack," Sharla clarified.

"Oh," Ezio said. "How was that?"

"Fun," I said, then glanced at the stairs that led to Dan's office.

"Deryn with Dan?" Ezio asked.

I nodded.

"Talking about you?" he guessed.

I shrugged. "I'm guessing so. Deryn was talking to the pack a lot and then went straight to Dan when we got here."

"Well, I wouldn't worry about it," Ezio said. "I'm sure it's nothing."

I leaned back against the couch and closed my eyes. "I'm so tired," I whispered.

"Just close your eyes and rest," Sharla said. "Ezio and I will stay here and make sure you're safe."

"I can't move anyway," I whispered. "I've got a sleeping pup in my lap. It's against the rules to move now."

Sharla chuckled. "Right you are."

Strong arms picked me up against a comforting body. "Warm," I whispered.

"I'm sorry I left you for so long," Deryn whispered.

"'s okay."

"Did you have fun today?" he asked.

"Mmhm," I mumbled, eyes still closed.

"What was Ezio doing?" he asked.

"Huh?"

"He was lying on the floor in wolf form near you," he explained.

"Protecting me," I said.

"Protecting you...inside the house?" he asked. I didn't need to see him to know he was smirking and trying not to laugh.

"I'm danger prone," I mumbled, burying my face against his chest.

"You are," he agreed.

He set me down on a big warm bed and I snuggled down into the blankets. He spooned his body around mine and kissed my head. "I love you."

"Love you, too."

"Promise?" he whispered.

I chuckled and snuggled closer to him. "Promise."

CHAPTER 5
JOLIE

I woke to lips kissing their way from my shoulder, to my thigh, and then was pushed onto my back and my clothes removed.

"Morning," I whispered with a chuckle as I opened my eyes, looking down my body to see Deryn sitting with his face above my stomach.

"Morning, beautiful," he whispered. He lowered his head and kissed the bottom of my stomach and then traveled lower.

I gasped as he licked me and within minutes was moaning his name.

He slid inside of me, and I growled with pleasure.

"You're the most beautiful woman in the world," he whispered. "You're a queen, *my* queen, and I need to make sure you know that."

He pumped his hips, and I arched up to meet him.

"There are lots of people in the house," I reminded him.

He leaned down and whispered, "Then you better be quiet." He kissed me deeply and thrust into me fast and hard.

I bit into his shoulder to hold in my scream as I orgasmed.

"Oh, baby, you're so wet."

"I've been wanting you for a few days," I admitted as I panted with his thrusts.

"You know you just have to ask," he said.

I pushed his chest, and he lay on his back, so I could take control. I sat down slowly and he groaned. "You know how I feel about asking when you're all with me," I said, raising myself up and down slowly, enjoying the feel of him filling me.

He gripped my hips and met my movements with his own. "We need to teach you to communicate telepathically, so you can just ask one of us specifically."

"But, the others would know when we left the room together," I said, throwing my head back as I orgasmed. I tightened around him and couldn't move as much.

"So?" he asked. "It's not like they don't know we have sex?"

"It's different," I growled.

He spun me around, pushing the top half of my body down onto the bed and raising my lower half up until I was on my knees. He slid his hand along my butt, slipping his hand around my hip bone, gripped it, and then thrust into me.

I bit the sheets and screamed into them as he pounded me from behind.

"You're so sexy. You have the most perfect ass I've ever seen," he growled.

He made me orgasm three more times, and then slammed into me one more time, finishing with a loud groan.

We lay in each other's arms for a bit and then took a shower. Dan hugged me when we entered the dining room.

"Morning, Father," I said as I stepped out of his embrace.

"Morning, Daughter," he said with a wide smile. "Hope you're hungry, because I had a feast put together."

I looked at the empty table and he laughed.

"Not in here, girl. The dining hall," he said and pushed me out of the room. I walked outside, and he led me to one of the many buildings that made up the den. This one was used when they wanted the entire pack to gather together. Dan held open the door for me, and I stepped inside to find all of my exes, my mates, and the other kings. There were a few other people I didn't know as well from each of the four clans, but I was surprised to find them all here.

"What is this?" I asked Dan.

"Business meeting," he said with a smirk.

"This is a trap," I said and folded my arms across my chest. "What do you want?"

"Sit and eat," Dan said, turning away from me to head to the front table where the other kings were.

"Deryn," I growled.

He chuckled. "Well, I was hoping our morning fun might put you in a better and more receptive mood," he said.

"So, you only slept with me to butter me up?" I asked, putting a hand to my heart. I was totally faking it. I knew Deryn and I knew that wasn't why, but it was fun to occasionally mess with my guys.

He pulled me into his arms, dipped me, and kissed me senseless. "You know exactly why I slept with you."

"Because I'm pretty?" I asked.

He chuckled and stood straight, bringing me with him. "Yes."

Nico teleported to me and kissed my cheek. "Hello, gorgeous."

"Hi, Sparkles," I said and kissed his cheek back.

"Ready for fun?" he asked.

"I'm deducting five points from all of you for this deceit," I said.

"Five points?" Nico asked. "That many?"

"Fine, I'll make it ten points," I said and walked by him.

"What are the points for?" Thor asked.

"It's their experience points. They were all really close to leveling up, but now they've lost some points," I said. It was really just a silly thing we said and didn't mean anything.

"Don't I get points for this morning?" Deryn asked.

"No," I said as I took my seat beside Rhys. "You ruined it."

Rhys chuckled and kissed the top of my head. "I warned you guys she wouldn't be receptive if you surprised her with a meeting like this."

"What is this about?" I asked him. "You could be my favorite."

"You don't have a favorite," Deryn scoffed.

"I could," I mumbled and pouted. They all knew I wasn't being serious, though. I could never be so petty.

"Let's eat!" Dan said.

Several wolves from the pack wheeled out carts with trays of food. My mouth watered, and I picked my fork up expectantly. As was usual now, my mates piled food onto my plate and then made their own. I ate most of what they had given me, then leaned back in my chair with a satisfied sigh.

"Most of you know why I've summoned you," Dan said.

I turned and glared at him, but he just smiled at me.

His smile disappeared and he said, "Our spies have obtained information about our enemies."

That didn't narrow it down. I had quite a few enemies now.

"A large contingent of dhampirs have been spotted in a remote area about twenty miles outside of Jinla. They've been seen transporting large crates of weapons and there've been rumors that some local people have been kidnapped by them as well," Dan said.

"Why haven't we destroyed them yet?" Ezio asked.

"Because we don't want to kill the soldier ants until they take us to their hive," Nico said.

That did make sense.

"So, how do we find the hive?" I asked.

"We put a tracking beacon on one of them," Dan said.

I laughed. The sound boomed out of me and grew louder, and I laughed until my stomach hurt.

"What?" Rhys asked.

"We have all this magic and power and you used a piece of technology to track them?" I gasped for breath. "They most likely scan for magic, but I doubt they'd think to scan for pieces of technology."

I could picture Brayden's furious face when he learned how they were tracked.

Speaking of Trident Douche...

"Have there been any sightings of Trident Douche or Bitchface?" I asked.

There were a few growls around me.

"Not yet," Katar said. "We're searching for them, but have no leads so far."

They were likely hiding, like the rats they were.

"So, why was this meeting orchestrated? Why did you have to trick me into coming?" I asked.

"We have a plan," Dan said. "And—"

"I'm not going to like it," I finished for him. I sighed. "Hit me with it."

"The only way to draw them out is with bait. They won't come out for anything other than their objective," Dan said.

"Me?" I guessed.

"Not you specifically. Your heart," Katar explained.

I glanced at my mates, and then narrowed my eyes at the kings. "No."

"It will work," Dan said.

"You can't guarantee their safety," I growled and stood. "And, that bitch could sever the ties again!"

"We won't let that happen," Deryn assured me.

I spun to face him. "You don't know that! You can't guarantee that! She has that fucking knife and she will cut our ties. Don't you remember how painful it was? Don't you remember how it felt to lose…" I couldn't even finish my sentence. My chest tightened and pain coursed through me. Not true pain, but the memory of the pain. A memory that I could not get rid of.

All four of my mates moved towards me, but I created a shield around myself, keeping them at bay.

"When did she learn that?" Fox asked.

"I will not risk you four. I will not risk any of you. I will not have our bonds severed."

"We're mates. She can't break our bond as mates," Deryn said.

"You were the one who was so adamant about me not removing the curse because of the risk it held. You were the one who held a grudge afterwards," I reminded him, my voice rising and my anger with it. I felt my body heating up and smoke curled from my mouth. "Why are you so quick to risk yourself now? Have you forgotten what it was like?"

"No," Deryn ground out between clenched teeth. "I remember."

"Perhaps you don't remember well enough," I said. My body was glowing as my power rose to the surface. "If you want to risk yourselves, I will have no part in it. I will have no part in this."

"Jolie," Dan said. "Calm down. We aren't—"

"Pain and loss can be forgotten. I understand that. I understand that it dims with time. I knew things were too good to be true. I knew Johann was always partially right."

"Jolie," Nico warned. "Stop."

They didn't remember what it felt like. They didn't remember the horrible gaping hole that had formed with their bonds gone.

"When you've come to your senses, I'll return," I told them.

With a whispered goodbye, I teleported myself away from my mates. I teleported to the other side of the world. And, once I landed, I closed down our bonds as tightly as I could. It hurt so much that I curled into a ball on the ground. I cried and ugly sobbed as I clutched at my chest. I would not lose them. Not again. Not ever again.

CHAPTER 6

NICO

Jolie had been gone for three days, and we still couldn't locate her. The pain was excruciating and nothing except her being back by my side would fix it.

We had fucked up before, but never this badly. I knew she wouldn't like the idea, but had no idea how upset she would be. I'd tried to explain it to the others, but they were adamant that the plan would work.

Yes, it would work, but Jolie was also right to worry about our bonds. Having our bonds severed had been one of the most painful things I had ever felt, and I couldn't even begin to imagine how it had felt to her, to have four of them cut.

I'd tried every spell I could think of, but still had no luck in finding her.

"This is stupid!" Fox yelled, clutching at his chest.

"We have no one to blame, but ourselves," I whispered.

"She's overreacting," Deryn growled, his fists clenched at his sides as he paced the living room of our house.

"Is she?" I asked, looking at my three brothers. Though we had no blood relation, they were my brothers through and through.

"What?" Rhys asked, turning away from staring out the window. He'd been staring out the window most of the time, like he thought if he just stared, he would see her coming back.

"She had four bonds cut. Four. Imagine our pain four times over. Then, we bombard her with a meeting like that, to tell her we are going to risk ourselves to draw out the people who have caused her the most pain in the past two years. I think she's reacting pretty appropriately for who she is. I'm more surprised that she didn't destroy anything." The amount of power she had been building, had it been released, would have had catastrophic repercussions.

"She's made her point," Deryn growled. "Why hasn't she come back yet?"

"Are you still planning to use yourself as bait?" I asked Deryn, already knowing the answer. Neither he or Rhys responded. "Then, she hasn't made her point."

"This is—" Rhys began, but I cut him off.

"She doesn't know how else to explain or show us the pain she endured. She is doing what she thinks is the best way to bring us to our senses. What if she volunteered to be used as bait? How would you feel?"

Rhys, Deryn, and Fox all growled.

"Exactly," I whispered, my hand balling into a fist at the thought of her being used as bait.

"Doesn't this mean that she's experiencing this pain four times over as well?" Fox asked, rubbing his chest with the heel of his palm.

I nodded. It was something that worried me the most. She was likely in so much pain, that she might not be able to protect herself.

Rhys's phone rang and he answered it with a grumble. His entire body went rigid and then he turned on the television in the room to the news station.

"Reports are flooding in of people in Rulan experiencing pain so intense, that they are curled into balls all over, clutching at their chests. Doctors have confirmed that the cause is magical, but have no idea where the source is," the reporter said. They panned to a video showing people lying in the streets of several cities, crying and clutching their chests.

"Fuck," Fox said, turning to me.

I nodded. "She's there."

"Authorities are trying to pinpoint the location of the spell's origin, but have so far been unable to do so," the reporter continued.

"Do you have a spell to shield us from that while we fly closer?" Rhys asked me.

"Yeah," I said breathlessly. She had no idea she was causing others to feel her pain. She would be devastated to learn about it. We had to get to her before someone died.

We all headed to the roof, and Rhys shifted into his dragon form.

I'd wanted to give her more time, but we had to get to her and stop this. We couldn't let people suffer just because we were being stubborn assholes.

CHAPTER 7

JOLIE

I felt them drawing near, but didn't stop them or try to conceal myself. I wasn't certain how they had found me, but I wasn't worried about that.

The pain was so intense, I couldn't move. I had wanted to return yesterday, but hadn't been able to do anything other than sob on the floor. No tears came anymore, my body was dehydrated and my stomach was completely empty.

Deryn tore the door off its hinges and tossed it out into the hallway. He stood there, his eyes blazing, and looked around the room until he found me. Once his eyes landed on me, the fury was gone, replaced by pain and sadness.

Nico rushed in, pushing Deryn aside and dropped to his knees beside me. "Release the bonds," he ordered me.

I opened my mouth, but all that came out was a wail of pain.

"Dammit," Rhys growled.

Nico grabbed me, but as soon as our bodies came into contact, the pain spread to him, and he fell to the floor beside me, his mouth open in a silent scream.

Fox, Rhys, and Deryn dropped to their knees, clutching at their chests.

Fox had tears streaming down his cheeks and he shuffled on his hands and knees closer to me. "Jolie, release the bonds. Do it. Now. You're hurting others. You're projecting your pain and the others in this city are hurting just like you are."

Fuck.

I was so close to blacking out as it was. I didn't have much time left. How had my power spread? How had others been brought into this?

I took a deep breath, and with a mighty heave, released the bonds. Their energy rushed into me and I fainted.

♥

"Jolie," Nico whispered, his lips pressed lightly to my ear. "Wake up. Please, love. Please wake up. I can't lose you. I can't lose anyone else."

Hot drops splashed the side of my face. Nico...was crying?

My entire body hurt. Everything felt heavy and strange.

Just opening my eyelids took a huge amount of effort.

Nico's tear-filled eyes met mine and he smiled. "Hello, beautiful."

I'd fucked up. I was only supposed to leave them for a day, make them relive the pain that they'd felt when we had lost our bonds. Or, at least as close to that pain as I could.

"Drink this," Fox ordered me, holding a cup of liquid up to my lips.

Nico helped me sit up, and I drank the strange green juice. It burned as it went down, but once in my stomach, I felt it healing me.

I had no strength to hold myself up, but Nico held me effortlessly.

Nico stroked my hair while Fox stroked his thumb across the hand he held.

My throat wouldn't work yet. I closed my eyes and relaxed at their touches.

"She's awake," Nico said.

"Has she said anything?" Rhys asked.

He sounded like he was across the room. Was he mad at me? Was he avoiding me? I couldn't feel them in the bond, despite it being open.

"No. She's still healing," Fox answered.

"We need to go," Deryn said, his footsteps coming closer.

Nico lifted me in his arms, and I leaned my head on his chest.

"Roof?" Fox asked.

"Yes," Deryn said.

Nico walked to the door, pausing by Deryn as he reached out.

I flinched as his hot hand touched my skin. He jerked his hand back and scowled. "She's so cold."

"Who's there?" a deep voice shouted from somewhere downstairs.

"Go," Rhys said.

All four headed up the stairs and to the roof. Rhys shifted and the three climbed on to his back. Nico set me on Rhys's back, looping an arm around my waist and pulling me back against his chest.

The potion Fox had given me was working, but I didn't have the strength yet to hold onto Rhys. Deryn sat in front of me and I reached up a trembling hand, brushing my fingertips on the edge of the back of his shirt, since that was all I could reach.

He turned and his brow furrowed. He scooted back, closer to me, and said something to Nico, but I couldn't hear. It was only a moment later that my eyes rolled up into the back of my head.

I woke still in Nico's arms. He was walking, but the only sound I heard was my blood rushing through my body.

He set me down on something soft it felt like a bed and started to move away, but I grabbed his arm, holding him as tightly as I could.

He slid down next to me, wrapping his arms around me.

Warmth from my other side began to fill me. Fox was healing me.

I opened my eyes and met his tear-filled ones.

Slowly, I opened my mouth and said, "How..."

"Shush," Deryn ordered me. "Don't talk yet."

"Sorry," I whispered, tears welling again and spilling over and down my cheeks.

Nico shushed me and kissed my forehead. "Don't apologize," he whispered. "We're the ones who are sorry. We're jerks and we are sorry."

"I'm sorry," Deryn whispered his lips next to my ear and his cheek against mine. "I'm sorry."

Maybe it hadn't been for nothing? Maybe, they understood what I'd been trying to say.

"I'm an ass and I'm so sorry. I always screw shit up with you," Deryn whispered. "I shouldn't have tricked you like that. I shouldn't have agreed to that plan. I knew you wouldn't like it, and yet I went along with it anyway. I'm not fit to be your mate."

I grabbed his arm, squeezing as hard as I could. He rubbed his face against mine and I felt the dampness from his cheek.

"Someday, I'll learn to actually look at things from your point of view. I'll try to get better. I'll try to think things through before acting. I can't lose you. And, I know you can't lose us either. We won't be using ourselves as bait. Okay? We promise," Deryn whispered, sniffling.

Nico moved away from me, his body replaced by a warmer one as Rhys lay beside me. He slid his hand along my cheek and rubbed his thumb over my cheekbone. "We're sorry, baby. We're so sorry."

"I shouldn't have run off," I managed to say, new tears streaming down my face. "I'm sorry," I sobbed.

When would I learn to stop acting without thinking? When would I learn to stop being so damn childish?

"Shush," Rhys ordered me. "Just lay and heal."

"Did you eat at all?" Deryn asked.

"No," I whispered, sniffling. "No food or drink."

Just pain. Lots and lots of pain.

"Drink this," Deryn ordered me.

I opened my eyes and let Rhys sit me up before drinking from the offered cup.

This cup held a potion that helped restore magic reserves and healed the body faster than others. It also tasted like shit.

I swallowed it, and then coughed a few moments.

Rhys kissed my temple as he held me up. "I'm sorry."

"I'm sorry," Deryn said.

"I'm sorry, too," Fox said.

"Me, too," Nico said.

"We won't use ourselves as bait," Fox said.

"Promise?" I asked as I looked at each of them.

They all nodded.

"We promise," they all said.

"I'm sorry," I said and started crying again, wrapping my arms around Rhys's neck, and then hugged Deryn. Fox leaned forward across my body to hug me and let Nico do the same.

"No more talking," Deryn said.

Rhys lay me back down and then spooned his body around mine. "Sleep, Jolie."

Deryn spooned his body on my other side and before I could ask where Nico and Fox were going, Nico used a spell to put me to sleep.

When I woke, I sat on the edge of the bed, staring down at my hands.

"What's up?" Deryn asked groggily, wiping at his eyes as he sat up beside me.

"I'm sorry," I whispered.

He pulled me onto his lap and wrapped me up in his arms. "We all get a little carried away from time to time."

"I can't lose you," I whispered, tears streaming down my face.

His hold tightened, and he kissed the top of my head. "You won't."

Rhys sat up, his eyes still closed as he pulled me from Deryn's lap, and into his. Deryn held one of my hands, and I took several deep breaths to relax.

"We need to find them, but there has to be another way," I said.

"We'll think of something," Rhys replied in his grumbling sleepy voice, eyes still closed. He was so not a morning person.

"They'll slip up eventually," Deryn said. "The bad guys always do."

"What day is it? Don't you guys have work?" I asked, trying to look around Rhys for the clock on the bedside table.

"It's Saturday," Deryn answered.

"Shoot, I have to go to see the elves today," I said, jumping from Rhys's lap. My legs wobbled a moment, but they held me up. After a quick shower, I felt back to my old self.

Fox was the only one left in the room when I finished changing. I'd been instructed to dress fancy, so I put on a red backless dress I had recently purchased. It was a little snug in the stomach, but not uncomfortably.

"What's up, buttercup?" I asked with a smile.

He held out his hand, a scowl on his face.

Serious Fox was never a good sign.

I went to him, set my hand in his, and let him pull me down to sit in his lap.

He nuzzled me behind my ear and whispered, "Promise me something?"

"Hm?" I asked, my pulse hammering at his deep and quiet tone.

"If you want to leave, if you want some space, at least take me with you. Let me be nearby so if something happens, I can get to you. You could have died. I don't know what I would do if you died. Probably destroy something."

The thought of Fox destroying something was almost funny. Yes, he was strong and powerful, but he was so often relaxed and non-aggressive, it was easy to forget.

"I'm sorry," I whispered, nuzzling his neck and placing a gentle kiss on it.

"Don't apologize. Just, promise me?"

"I promise," I whispered, wrapping my arms around his neck and squeezing.

"You're my world, Jolie. We screwed up. We did forget how painful it had been. We did forget what it was like to lose you. I don't want to condone your tactic, but it worked. We all remembered what it was like, how awful it was. I don't want to be separated from you again. Never again."

Hearing him admit that what I had done had worked made the guilt lessen. Not that I liked hurting them, but I was glad that what I had done had succeeded.

"Never again," I agreed, squeezing him.

He stood, supporting my weight with one arm beneath my butt, while I kept my arms around his neck. "Now that we got that serious business out of the way, let's go have fun!"

"What are we doing today?" I asked.

"Elven fun!" he said.

I looked up at him, and he just smiled brightly, radiating happiness and warmth.

"Whatever you want to do," I said, resting my head on his chest as he carried me.

"Whatever I want, huh? Well, in that case we aren't leaving the house for a week," he said in a rumbling whisper in my ear.

"Naughty elf," I quipped.

He chuckled. "Dad will kill me if I don't bring you home. Mother has been demanding to see you, too. She's got something up her sleeve and I'm not sure what it is. It's worrisome."

"Your parents love me," I reminded him. "I'm sure it is fine."

"I think they like you better than me," he said with a pout.

I bit the sensuous lip he had stuck out, and he growled, his hold tightening.

"Tease," he grumbled when I released his lip.

"Not a tease a promise for later," I replied.

"We don't have to stay long, right? We could pop in, give greetings, then come back home, right?" he said.

"You can wait," I said, jumping from his arms as we got to the garage.

"I *can*, but that doesn't mean I want to," he replied, unlocking his car.

I climbed in and buckled up. They'd only recently stopped using drivers for everything. Dan had argued with Deryn for hours about us needing to use a driver, but we'd won out in the end. We still used drivers for some things, but for the most part the guys drove now.

"When did you learn to teleport?" Fox asked as he started the car.

I shrugged. "A while ago."

"And why didn't you tell us?"

"Because I figured it might come in handy at some point," I replied. And, I had been right.

"What else do you know how to do?" he asked, backing out of the garage.

"Well, I did learn this new thing with my tongue, and—"

He groaned and then laughed. "You're such a brat."

"You love me," I said with a wide smile.

He shifted into first and headed away from the house. "That I do, my love. That I do."

"So, what does elven fun consist of?" I asked.

"A party," he said.

"For?"

"Uh, for a special event," he said, skirting around a proper answer.

"Fox," I said in a growl.

"Dad's birthday," he said.

"What! I don't have a gift for him. We have to stop somewhere first and—"

Fox shook his head, stopping me. "We have a gift. I got one that is from both of us."

"What is it?" I asked.

"Well, I can't tell you yet. We have to talk to my mom first," he said, his brows furrowing and his grip tightening on the steering wheel.

Was that fear?

"What is it, Fox? Why are you scared?"

"It's probably nothing. I'm just being paranoid," he said.

"Fox," I moaned and leaned against the door. "You're doing that thing again."

"I know!" he said and sighed. "Look, I can't say anything until we see Mom. Okay? The others will be there, too."

"The others?" I asked.

"You know, your other mates," he teased. "Or am I just so handsome that you forgot about them?"

I chuckled and leaned over to kiss his cheek. "You are very handsome."

"Deryn still has the best butt, though. That irritates me," he grumbled.

I burst into a fit of laughter. I couldn't help myself. I laughed so hard that I clutched at my hurting stomach.

"Laugh it up," he grumbled.

"Kit, you have an amazing ass, too. I don't understand these complexes you boys have. You're all fucking gorgeous and could get any girl you wanted."

"There's only one girl I want," he said. "And she keeps staring at Deryn's ass as he walks by."

I bit my lip to keep from laughing again. "I look at yours when you walk by, too."

"Not the same," he grumbled.

"You also lose all self-control when Rhys has his shirt off."

Well, in my defense, Rhys had a perfect chest.

"Are you feeling self-conscious?" I asked, leaning over to rest my head on his shoulder.

"What about me is better than them?" he asked.

"Well..." I blushed and turned away from him.

"Well?" he asked.

"You are the biggest," I said.

His eyebrows rose and then he laughed. "I am."

"You already knew that," I said.

He shrugged. "It happens. When you know guys for your entire life, at some point you see their junk."

"So, there you go," I said.

"So, I just need to walk around airing my junk out to get you to look at me?" he asked.

I burst into another fit of laughter. "Please, don't," I begged.

He smirked. "Oh, alright. I'll keep it contained until it's needed."

"You're the sexiest elf I know," I told him. "If that counts for anything."

He smiled, a purely dazzling, happy smile. "That does. Thanks."

"You're welcome."

CHAPTER 8

RHYS

"Still having issues?" Dad asked as he entered.

I lay on my back in the gym, sweat dripping from my body, and my breathing coming in great, heaving pants.

"Yes," I admitted with a groan.

He sat down beside me, staring at the wall of the gym, but really just looking off into space while he thought.

I waited patiently, knowing he was thinking and needed a moment to get his thoughts in order.

"Have you told Jolie?" he asked, glancing down at me.

I winced. "No. I was going to the other day, but then the shit hit the fan and—"

"Did you apologize to her?" he asked.

I sat up and glared at him. "You were in on the plan, too," I reminded him.

"I was against it, but willing to do what the majority voted," he said. "I told you Jolie wouldn't go for it."

I sighed and rubbed a hand down my face. "I don't think I've screwed up so badly before," I told him. "She was right. We had forgotten how painful it was."

"I hadn't," he said. "You were utterly destroyed when your bond was cut. I should have recorded it so you could rewatch the absolute terror and pain on your face when it happened."

"I'll tell her soon," I promised, wanting to change the subject and not think about the time I had almost lost Jolie.

"Have you tried with her near you?" he asked, looking at my chest.

"Perhaps you're holding back with her being away from you."

He could have a point, but—

"It wasn't an issue before I met her," I reminded him.

He shrugged. "Everything changes when you find your queen and mate," he said. "You should bring her here and try with her in the room."

It wasn't a bad idea.

"Okay," I agreed.

He glanced at the clock on the wall. "You should go shower and get ready. You're going to Katar's party, right?"

I nodded and then winced. Yet another surprise waiting for Jolie. Or, well, potential surprise.

"What's wrong?" Dad asked.

"Nothing," I said and sighed at his raised eyebrow. "Possibly nothing. I don't know. We'll see."

He chuckled and ruffled my hair like he used to when I was a boy. "You're always up to something, son. That hasn't changed." He stood and held out his hand. I accepted and let him pull me to my feet. "If you need anything, I'm always here."

I nodded. "I know. Thanks."

He started walking away, and I called out, "Dad?"

He turned to face me.

"What do you do when you screw up with Mom?"

Dad smiled. "I buy her gifts and remind her that she's my queen. The one goddess I worship, and that I'm an idiot for risking that."

I nodded.

"She loves you. She has sacrificed herself for you many times. Perhaps it is time for you to take over that role," he said and waved as he left the room.

My beautiful, infuriating mate was constantly throwing herself in danger. She wanted to protect us, I knew that, but just like she didn't want to lose us, we didn't want to lose her. We were in the beginnings of a war, and I had no idea what to expect. I wanted to protect her and to do that, I needed to be at my peak.

But, for quite a while now, I had been having issues with my scales. My scales used to automatically cover a part of my body that was in danger, but since that day I was shot, they hadn't been doing that. They hadn't been doing anything automatically, and I had no idea why.

With a sigh, I headed to the shower. Time to face our next ordeal.

CHAPTER 9

JOLIE

There were quite a few cars parked in front of Katar and Kara's house, and I could hear music playing.

Fox opened my door, and held out his hand. I let him help me from the car and smoothed down the dress I wore.

"You're gorgeous," he told me and kissed me deeply. "I love you."

"I love you, too," I said, smiling at him.

Fox lead me into the house, despite the party obviously going on in the backyard. I opened my mouth to ask what we were doing inside, when I saw my other mates waiting in the living room with Kara.

"What's going on?" I asked, planting my feet and coming to a halt in the hallway. This looked like an intervention. What the hell could I need an intervention for? I didn't smoke or do drugs. I enjoyed sweets, but so did all of my mates. I hadn't even been playing much videogames, so it couldn't be about that.

"Easy," Fox said, running a hand down my arm. "This isn't an intervention or anything."

He tried to pull me forward, but I yanked my hand away. "What's going on?" I asked again.

Kara walked to me, a smile on her face. She opened her arms, and I stepped forward to hug her. She smelled like flowers and gave motherly hugs that made you want to relax and tell her all the things going on in your life.

"The boys are worried about your health, so they asked me to check you out," she whispered into my ear. "They're being good mates, so please don't fight me on this."

I sighed and rested my head on her shoulder. "Okay, but I feel fine."

She pushed me back at arm's length and smiled. "Then this should be quick!"

Her eyes began to glow, and then she ran her hand from my head to my feet, and then back up again. She released the power, her eyes returning to normal as she smiled warmly at me. "Jolie, I need you to sit down."

Oh, no. That wasn't good.

Rhys brought me a chair, smiling at me with tears pooling in his eyes.

What was going on?

"Am I dying?" I asked softly.

My mates tensed and all eyes locked on me.

Kara chuckled softly. "No, darling daughter. You are not dying."

I sat in the chair and folded my arms across my chest. "Then, why am I being told to sit and why is Rhys trying not to cry?"

"I've got something in my eye," he lied, rubbing at his face.

Kara knelt in front of me and took my hands in hers. "You are pregnant, Jolie."

The world stopped, all sound disappeared, and I felt faint. This was why she had me sit down.

Pregnant? No. I'd been taking contraceptives. I had been careful to take them and never missed a day. My period was supposed to start in a day or two, so I wasn't technically late.

"You're sure?" I asked.

Kara nodded, smiling wider. "Yes. You are one hundred percent pregnant."

"Do you know whose it is?" I asked.

I saw my mates scowl out of the corner of my eye, but didn't turn to face them.

"No. We won't know for a few weeks," she said.

"Dammit," I whispered. Hot tears slid down my cheeks, and I sniffled. This wasn't supposed to happen yet. It wasn't the right time!

My four mates rushed to me, dropping to their knees and putting one hand each on me.

"What is it?" Fox asked. "Why are you upset? Why are you sad?"

"I thought you wanted children?" Rhys asked.

"I didn't want to have a child before we caught Brayden and Justina," I sobbed. "I didn't want to put yet another person in danger. It's hard enough keeping you four safe and now I have a baby to deal with! How am I going to protect the baby? What if she kills the baby?"

"We won't let her get to you. She can't harm our baby if she can't get to you," Deryn said, squeezing my leg. "We will protect you and our baby," he swore.

"Our baby is our top priority now," Rhys said with a nod. "We won't let anything happen to risk his or her life."

"No one's touching you," Fox growled, his eyes glowing.

"We will do everything we need to keep you both safe," Nico said. He rested his hand on my stomach and smiled, his eyes lighting with joy. "We're having a baby. This is a time to be happy."

"You keep saying 'our baby,' but you don't know whose it is," I said, wiping at my eyes.

"It doesn't matter who the technical father is," Rhys said. "We're all your mates and the baby will be all of ours."

"Just like the baby will be my grandchild, no matter who the father is," Kara said, wiping my cheeks with a soft cloth. "You and your baby are a treasure. You will be protected, and nothing will happen to you two. I will be your personal midwife, if you need it."

Rhys, Fox, and Deryn placed their hands on my stomach, and I felt a small magical spark zip between them and my stomach.

I was pregnant.

"We're having a baby," I whispered, tears returning to my eyes, but for a whole new reason. I had been worried I wouldn't be able to have a child, since sirens were almost infertile.

I stood, four sets of arms surrounded me, and each took turns kissing my cheek.

"What's going on?" Katar asked, worry evident in his tone.

The guys stepped away from me, except for Fox, who stood at my side with a proud smile.

"Happy birthday," he said to Katar.

"Thank you," Katar said, his eyes not leaving mine. "But, I'd like to know what's going on with my daughter."

I smiled at him and walked a step closer. "You're going to be a grandfather," I said.

His eyes widened and he looked at my stomach...then Kara, who nodded...and then back to me. "You're pregnant?"

I nodded, smiling wider.

He smiled, picked me up, and spun around in a circle while he cheered. "I'm going to be a grandpa!"

I chuckled and patted him on the shoulder.

He set me down and then reached towards my stomach, but stopped a few inches away, and looked at me. "May I?"

I nodded.

He set his hand on my stomach and tears sprang to his eyes. "A child. I can't wait to see it."

"Well, you'll have to wait nine months," I said and chuckled.

He looked up at me with furrowed brows. "What?"

"Nine months. That's a human gest—"

"You're not human," Nico reminded me.

"What?" I asked, turning to face him. I knew I wasn't human, but I didn't know that mattered.

"Our gestation periods aren't like humans," Rhys said. "They're faster."

"It's to make it easier to stay safe," Kara explained.

"How long?" I asked.

"Six months," Nico answered. "That's what the research I did on sirens said."

Six months! That was so soon.

"Easy," Deryn whispered, wrapping an arm around my waist, and pulling me against his side. "We've got plenty of time. It's six months still, that's half a year."

"I need to tell my dad," I whispered.

"How will you communicate with him?" Kara asked.

"I'll have to send a messenger to Atlantis," I said.

"Can we tell our dads?" Deryn asked.

"They're coming tonight, aren't they?" Katar asked.

Deryn and Rhys nodded.

I looked over at Nico, the only one who didn't have a father to tell, but he just smiled at me.

"Why don't we bring them in and tell them when they get here?" Katar suggested. "Then we can all celebrate together."

"I ruined your party," I realized and felt awful.

He shook his head and laughed. "Ruined it? This is the best present I have ever received!" He looked at my stomach again and said, "I'm going to spoil the shit out of this kid."

I laughed and tears sprang to my eyes.

"What's going on?" Dan asked from the entryway.

"Back here!" Katar called.

Deryn's grip on my waist tightened a moment, and then he relaxed.

"The host is missing from his own party," Dan said, smiling broadly as he clapped Katar on the back. "Happy birthday, old friend."

"Thank you, Dan," Katar replied.

"Where's Emrys?" Katar asked.

"Outside," Dan answered.

"I'll get him," Rhys said, and quickly left the room.

Dan looked at me and Deryn. "What's going on?"

Katar patted his shoulder. "All in good time, friend. Just wait until Emrys is here."

Emrys and Rhys came in, and Emrys paused by Dan, but frowned at me. "What's going on?"

"Jolie has some news," Katar said, beaming.

"You're all going to be grandfathers," I said, smiling.

Emrys's eyes widened, and he glanced at Rhys.

Dan whooped loudly and picked me up in a bone crunching hug. "Woohoo!" he yelled as he held me. He set me down, and I realized I had never seen him smile so wide before. "This is the best news, ever!"

"Congratulations," Emrys said, pulling me into a hug. "I can't wait to meet your child."

Was he worried it wouldn't be Rhys's? Why had he looked at Rhys when I told them?

"You're frowning," Emrys said. "Why?"

"I thought you'd be more excited," I said, which was partially true.

"I am very excited," he said, smiling. "I'm just not as rambunctious as some." He glanced at Dan and then focused on me again.

"We'll be able to tell who the father is in a few weeks," I said softly.

His smile wilted. "Okay."

Rhys came up behind me and wrapped his arms around me, resting both hands on my stomach. He dropped his head so his lips were right by my ear. "He doesn't care who the father is, baby."

"Why did he look at you like that, then?" I asked.

"Because I knew something was up, but hadn't thought it would be this," Emrys said. He smiled and rested a hand on my shoulder. "It doesn't matter who fathered the child. It's your child, and therefore it is my grandchild. That's all there is to it. Okay?"

I nodded quickly, trying to stop the tears threatening to spill over. It didn't make sense to me, but I was incredibly grateful.

"Come on! Let's go celebrate!" Katar said, tossing an arm around my shoulders and pulling me away from Rhys. "It's my birthday and I'm going to be a grandfather! I have two reasons to celebrate."

"No alcohol," Fox called after me.

I scowled and groaned. "Oh, dammit!"

Everyone laughed, but me.

"I'll get you a virgin daiquiri," Katar promised. "It will taste just as good."

"Alright," I pouted, but then smiled up at him and kissed his cheek. "Thank you."

"For?" he asked, and pushed open the back door.

There had to be over two hundred people. Some were dancing, most were drinking, and some were obviously drunk already.

"For being excited about this baby," I said. "I'm honestly still not sure I've wrapped my head around it yet."

"You realize that your mates are going to be even more protective, right?" he asked, leaning close so no one else would hear us.

I sighed. "Yeah. They're going to try to wrap me in bubble wrap."

"You'd just pop all the bubbles and make the wrap pointless," Katar teased.

I laughed. "Too true."

"Jolie, you can't put yourself in danger anymore. I know you want to keep your mates safe, but your job now is to keep your baby safe, which means you stay safe. So, no more heroics. Let your mates be the heroes. That's their job."

"I know," I whispered. "I just don't want to lose them."

"Losing you will devastate them. Losing you *and* your child will destroy them. I can't let that happen. If need be, I'll give you guards," Katar said.

We made our way through the people, and Katar smiled and talked to those he walked by.

"I'll be on my best behavior," I promised.

He chuckled. "That's not very reassuring."

We came to a stop at a temporary bar, where a woman was mixing drinks.

"Virgin daiquiri," Katar ordered for me.

"Right away, sir," she said, and poured what she'd mixed into a glass before handing it to a nearby person, and then starting on my drink.

"Stop stealing her from me," Dan growled, as he weaved through people and pulled me from Katar to drape an arm around my shoulders, and pulled me to his side.

"You see her more often than I do," Katar countered.

Deryn spun me away from Dan, snagging the drink the bartender held out as he did. "I'm stealing my mate back," he told them.

I laughed and took my drink from him. "Hello, handsome."

He kissed my cheek. "Hey, beautiful." He led me a little way away from the crowd, sliding his arm around my waist as we walked.

I took a drink and sighed happily. It was so good. "What are we doing over here?" I asked.

"We just wanted to get you a bit away from the crowd," Rhys said, coming to stand on my other side.

Nico slid his hands around my waist from behind and kissed the back of my neck. "Plus, you keep getting stolen from us."

I leaned back against him and turned my head to kiss his cheek. "You act like you like me, or something," I teased.

"Just a little bit," he whispered in my ear, resting his hands on my stomach.

"Everyone," Katar called.

The music stopped and everyone quieted.

"Thank you for coming to celebrate my birthday," Katar said, looking out over the crowd. "You've all made this one special day." His eyes settled on me and his smile widened. "So, let's enjoy the night with drinks and food!"

Everyone clapped and a dozen people came out of the main house, carrying trays of food.

"Food," I whispered, my stomach grumbling in agreement.

All four of my mates chuckled.

"I'll get her food," Fox said, kissing my cheek as he walked by.

"There are some seats over here," Deryn said, pointing to tables that had been set up.

I was incredibly unobservant tonight. I hadn't seen any of them.

"What's wrong?" Nico asked, coming to walk on my side as we headed to the tables.

"Just realizing I'm unobservant tonight," I admitted.

"You've got a lot on your mind," he said, linking our fingers together.

I leaned my shoulder against his as we walked. "Everything is going to be alright, isn't it?"

He squeezed my hand and smiled. "Yes, my queen. Everything is going to be just fine."

Fox brought me a huge plate of food and then sat with me while the others went to make their plates.

I sat with the four most important men in my life, eating at a birthday party for one of my fathers-in-law, and silently stressed. A baby was a huge change. We wouldn't be able to go out whenever we wanted. We wouldn't have free time. I would have a tiny being who depended on me to survive. Our lives would be focused on keeping this new being alive and healthy.

Fox set his hand on my leg while talking to the others. It did nothing to ease my worry.

I hadn't planned to have a child yet. Yes, I wanted a child, but not until we were safe. Though, if I were honest with myself, we were never safe. There were always random threats and there would always be evil in the world.

We had so much work to do to baby-proof the house. There were so many things we needed to buy. I didn't even know what dragon, wolf, mage, or elf babies were like. Did we run the risk of a dragon baby burning down the nursery?

Nursery. We needed to convert one of the rooms into a nursery.

"Jolie," Deryn whispered in my ear, his chin coming to rest on my shoulder. "What's wrong?"

"There's so much to do before the baby comes," I whispered.

He wrapped his arms around me. "We have plenty of time. We can figure out all the things we need to do tomorrow, and make a game plan. Okay?"

"I'm just not prepared," I whispered, closing my eyes. "I wasn't expecting this yet."

"None of us were," he reminded me. "But, we have each other, and we will get through it together."

He was right, but that didn't stop me from worrying.

"Have some cake," Rhys said, sliding a big slice of white cake with chocolate frosting on the table in front of me.

"Cake!" I gasped, leaning away from Deryn to grab a fork.

Deryn was right. We had each other. We could make a plan and get everything in order in the next six months.

I hoped.

CHAPTER 10
DERYN

Jolie was pregnant.

I stared at the wall of my bedroom, letting it sink in fully. Last night, when we had confirmed it, I'd wanted to steal her away and hide her from everyone.

My little siren was so danger prone, and I could not bear the thought of her or our child being injured.

I felt bad for wishing the child was mine, but I knew the others felt the same. We all wanted the child to be sired by us, but we would still love and raise the child as our own, even if it wasn't truly ours. What mattered was that it was Jolie's.

I had wanted to cry in joy, knowing that she was pregnant. We had all been worried she wouldn't be fertile enough to conceive, but that was obviously not the case.

"Hey," Rhys said from my doorway.

"What's up?" I asked, turning to face him.

"What are you thinking about?" he asked.

"The baby," I admitted.

He smiled, no, beamed. Rhys rarely beamed like that. "It's pretty awesome, right?"

I nodded. "I can't wait to see what the baby looks like."

"I know most dads want sons, but I would love to have a miniature Jolie running around," he said.

I felt the same.

"We're about to head out for the shopping trip," he said. "That's why I came to get you."

"Oh, right."

Jolie had decided she wanted to go to a baby store to look at furniture and begin decorating the nursery. We knew it would help ease her stress, or hoped it would, so we all agreed to go with her.

I followed Rhys down to the garage, where everyone was already inside one of our SUVs. Dad had ordered us to keep a guard and driver at all times, now that Jolie was pregnant. I knew he was just as excited as we were.

"Morning," I greeted Ezio.

Ezio nodded, but his eyes were focused on Jolie, who was fumbling with a pad of paper in her lap in the front passenger seat. Normally, I would have been jealous or angry at his attention on her, but for once, I was glad to have him. Ezio loved Jolie, and he would sacrifice himself in an instant for her. When I had told him Jolie was pregnant, he'd become even more protective. He hovered near her, ready to catch her if she tripped or fainted. Part of me knew that I should be the one hovering, but I also knew Jolie would hate to have us fawning over her so closely. She liked to be independent and strong, which she was, but for some reason, Ezio fawning over her didn't make her upset. Perhaps it was her knowledge that he wasn't her mate, so he was just being a doting friend? I wasn't certain. But, I could endure his presence, knowing it meant she would be safer.

"Buckle up," Ezio ordered Jolie.

She complied without even an eye roll.

She would have growled had I ordered her.

What was it about her exes that made her more compliant? Was she just more likely to rebel when it was a true authority figure, like her alpha or her mates? That had to be it.

"Do you have your list?" I asked her.

Fox rolled his eyes at me, and Nico snickered softly.

"Right here!" she announced happily, waving the pad of paper.

She'd become obsessed with lists lately.

"Alright, then let's go!" I said, smiling at her and sending all the love I felt for the beautiful woman in the front seat down our bond.

She still hadn't figured out how to communicate telepathically through the bond yet. Fox and Nico had tried to work with her on it, but she just became frustrated and angry. So, we decided to set that task aside until she wasn't so stressed out.

"*She quit,*" Nico said through our warrior bond, his head tilted so I could see his face.

My entire body tensed. "*What?*" I asked, turning to face him fully.

"*She sent in her resignation this morning,*" he explained. "*She told me that she was too stressed with the baby to even think about work and since we had all told her before she could quit and we would provide for her, she did it.*"

Wow. I never thought she would quit her job. She loved it. That's why we hadn't pushed her too much, because we could tell she truly loved her work.

"I should be happy," I whispered out loud to him, "but this just makes me worry even more."

He nodded. "Same."

CHAPTER II
JOLIE

The store I had chosen was three stories tall and had everything I would need for the baby. My mates hung back together, whispering to each other. Normally, I would have been irritated, but I had more important things on my mind.

"Ezio, can you get a shopping cart?" I asked. Ezio had been hovering over me ever since Dan had assigned him to me.

I had expected Deryn to growl at Ezio by now, but he hadn't so much as twitched his lip.

I glanced over at my mates.

They all smiled at me.

Suspicious.

I had known they would be happy once I was pregnant, but I'd underestimated how happy they would be. I had also underestimated the kings' reactions. Katar had warned me my mates would be overprotective, but the kings were much worse. Dan had tried to convince me to move into his house at the wolf den, stating it would be safer than our house. I had politely declined, and he had assigned Ezio to guard me.

Ezio returned with a cart. "Do you want to push it, so you can lean on it?" he asked, his brows narrowed.

I chuckled and patted his arm. "I'm barely pregnant, Ezio. I don't need help walking."

"I could carry you," he offered.

I put my hands on my hips. "You will do no such thing! I am perfectly capable of walking."

Fox slid his arm around my waist, and pulled me into his side. "I'll keep an arm around her," he said.

Ezio nodded in approval, and we started down the first aisle of the store.

The first stop was bottles. I stared at the wall of bottles. There were dozens of different shapes and sizes, and so many different nipple options that I didn't know where to begin. Some were marketed for werewolves and others for dragons. Maybe I should have waited until we found out who the sire was before choosing?

"Just get one of each," Fox suggested. "We can see what works and get more of that winning item."

I smiled and kissed his cheek. "Good idea."

Rhys leapt up to grab a bottle off the third shelf, and Deryn jumped up to grab one from the second shelf, tossing them into the cart Ezio was still standing behind.

"You could just ask for help," a store attendant said with a chuckle.

I turned and the older woman smiled at me. "First child?" she guessed.

I nodded.

"Who's the father?" she asked.

I glanced at my mates and bit my lip. "Um..."

"We are," All four said at the same time.

Her eyes widened. "Well, that doesn't really narrow down the specifics, but I suppose it is better to plan for every possibility. If you give me your list, I can help you find the items you need."

"Thanks, but I would prefer to look on my own," I told her, clutching my list a bit tighter.

"Nonsense, the Princess of the Four Clans of Jinla shouldn't have to do the shopping herself," she said, stepping closer to me with her hand out.

Ezio shot between us, his teeth bared. "She said, 'no thank you.' So, please leave her alone."

The woman had immediately taken several steps back, her eyes wide. "Yes, sir," she said and disappeared off into the store.

"Ezio," I said with a sigh.

"Sorry," he mumbled, dropping his head and going back to the cart.

"We'll get the rest of the bottles," Fox said, giving my side a squeeze.

I kissed his cheek and walked to Ezio, bumping my hip into his. "Hey. Talk to me."

He sighed. "I'm sorry. I just hate it when people can't take a hint. Or, straight answers. You clearly stated you didn't want her help. I don't want you getting stressed out or worked up. It could negatively impact the baby."

I hugged him, and he rested his chin on top of my head with a sigh. "Ezio, you are not responsible for me and the baby. Yes, we appreciate you being here to help keep me safe, but you don't need to stress yourself out trying to keep me from being stressed. You being stressed is going to stress me out. Understand?"

He growled and grumbled something that sounded like agreement, so I patted his back and continued on the shopping trip.

After three hours, I finally conceded defeat, leaning heavily against Fox as Deryn and Rhys paid for the shopping cart full of items we had gathered to purchase.

"What do you want to do now?" Fox asked, and rubbed his hand up and down my left arm.

"I think it's time to take you guys bulk food shopping," I said.

"More shopping?" Nico asked.

"We should eat first," I advised. "That way we aren't hungry while we're there."

"Plus, you need food," Ezio said, holding out a water bottle.

I drank it without argument and nodded. "I am hungry."

"Where would you like to eat?" Fox asked.

"Anywhere is fine," I said.

"Let's eat somewhere that's quick, so we can do our shopping, and then get her home," Nico suggested.

Fox nodded in agreement.

"Ready?" Deryn asked from the register. The cart was now full of shopping bags.

"Ready," I called back, heading towards them.

"We're going to get some quick food, and then Jolie wants to take us to another shopping place," Fox explained.

"This shopping trip wasn't enough for you?" Rhys teased.

I stuck my tongue out at him, ignoring his taunting.

They packed our purchases into the back, then went through a drive-through, purchasing ten bags of food. I scarfed down three burgers and a large fry before we reached the grocery store I had directed Ezio to.

"This looks like a regular grocery store," Deryn said.

"It's their bulk aisle that we're interested in today," I explained.

"I thought you were going to take us to that store where you can buy a hundred rolls of toilet paper at once," Nico said.

I chuckled. "No, that will have to be a different day. I don't have the energy for that store."

We all climbed out, and Deryn grabbed a shopping cart, standing on it and using one foot to propel it faster down the aisles.

"To the left, and then it will be the back right corner," I directed Deryn.

He nodded, sliding the cart around the corner without tipping it over.

"He's such a child," Fox said with a sigh.

I laughed. "You're one to talk."

He opened his mouth in mock shock. "Me?"

I kissed his cheek. "Your childlike joy is part of what I love about you."

He smirked, but said nothing.

Deryn did a small circle and then pushed his cart forward again, giving me a perfect view of his ass.

"Stop staring at his butt," Fox grumbled.

I snickered. "Well, it's there for my viewing. I can't help it."

"I need to do more squats," Fox mumbled.

Nico laughed and patted Fox's shoulder. "Just accept that Deryn's got the nicest butt out of all of us."

"No," Fox said. "I refuse to lose."

"What are you losing?" Ezio asked.

"Nicest ass," Fox replied.

Ezio threw back his head and laughed, the sound echoing off the tall shelves of the store.

We finally made it to the bulk food section and I smiled at my gathered guys. "Here. You take these bags." I tore a bag from the roll. "And, you fill it up with food from one of the bins."

"What do the bins hold?" Rhys asked, peering over at them.

"Spices, pasta shells, trail mix, chocolate, and more," I explained.

They looked at the bins with wide eyes.

"So, go ahead and get whatever you want," I said, heading towards the first bin where I could see malt chocolate balls.

"We just fill up the bags with as much of whatever item we want?" Fox asked.

I nodded. "And they charge you by weight."

Rhys started down the aisles, looking at each item. Deryn tore off five bags, and began spooning out various things into them.

"Make sure you label them with the item number from the bins," I called out before I forgot.

"Candy!" Fox called from the other side of the bins I was on.

I chuckled.

"Your mates are very easily entertained," Ezio said.

"They don't get out to experience human establishments often. The first time they went to a grocery store was a year ago when I had the flu."

"That must have been one strange trip," Ezio said. "I don't think Deryn has ever been around a sick human before."

"They thought I was dying," I said with a smirk.

He laughed. "I can imagine."

"Clearly you've been around humans more often than them," I commented. Truthfully, I knew very little about what had happened to Ezio between us breaking up and seeing him at the Summit.

He nodded. "I dated a couple humans, so I have a little experience with them."

"Someday, I'd like to hear your story," I told him, scooping some malt balls into my bag.

"Okay," he agreed.

"These bags aren't big enough," Rhys complained.

"Can we just take the entire barrel?" Deryn asked.

I laughed and shook my head. "No, just use the small bags. If you want to get a huge amount, we can order it. This was just supposed to be an adventure into the lives of humans for you. We don't buy huge bulks like you do, since we eat a lot less. One of these bags filled with taco seasoning lasted me over a year."

"A year?" Nico asked, scowling at the bag in his hand. "That's a long time."

"Well, I only made one pound of meat at a time, since I only ate a couple tacos each night," I admitted.

"Now you eat at least a pound of beef each night," Fox said. I still couldn't see him, since he was on the next aisle, but I could hear him just fine.

"And I suppose I'll be eating even more now?" I asked.

Ezio, Nico, Rhys, and Deryn all nodded their heads in response.

"You should pick out some treats," Nico said. "So we can keep them on hand when you get a craving."

That wasn't a bad idea. "Okay," I said, grabbing more bags and beginning my own adventure.

Our cart was half full of bags of items when we were finally done. I couldn't help chuckling at the strange looks we were getting from other shoppers.

"What else does this store have?" Fox asked, heading towards the nearest aisle.

"Yes, I'd like to see what else is here," Nico said, following Fox.

"Well, in that case, I'm going to get another cart," Ezio said. "Knowing you four, you're going to end up buying half of the store."

I didn't doubt it. "Just yell if you can't find us," I told him.

He scowled at me. "Jolie, I'm just going to follow your scent."

How had I forgotten that?

"Right," I said, smirking in embarrassment.

"Onward!" Deryn said, standing on one leg on the cart, then using the other to propel it forward again.

Rhys slipped his fingers into mine and tugged me close to his side. "Come on, beautiful. Let's go on an adventure."

I laughed. "The grocery store is hardly an adventure."

"We're exploring unfamiliar territories and leaving with treasures. Sounds like adventuring to me," he said.

I smirked. "Well, if this is an adventure, we already screwed up."

"How?" Rhys asked.

"We let our healer go first."

Rhys paused and then yelled, "Fox! Get back here!"

I laughed as we caught up to the other three, who had already filled the cart with several kinds of cereals and breakfast pastries.

"Sampling everything?" I asked.

They all nodded.

"After we figure out which of them are our favorites, we can order them in bulk," Fox explained.

"You realize there are like thirty more aisles and you've already filled the cart?" I said, smiling at the pure innocence they showed in situations like this.

"We can grab more carts if needed," Ezio said, pushing the new cart he brought into the middle of our group.

"Onward!" Rhys said. "We must continue our adventuring."

"Oh? Adventuring!" Fox said and smiled wide. "I'll stay in the middle in case we need healing."

"I've got the rear," Deryn said.

"I'm in front, Jolie behind me," Rhys said.

To anyone else, we must have sounded crazy, but this was our normal order when playing games together, and we easily fell into that mindset.

"Left," Rhys called over his shoulder.

We followed him to the left, down the next aisle.

"What's this?" Fox asked, picking up a can of frozen juice concentrate from the frozen bin.

"It's juice concentrate," I explained. "You put that in a container, and fill the container with water then mix it up, and you get juice."

His eyes widened, and he grabbed six different flavors, putting them in the second cart, which was already half full.

"This?" Deryn asked, holing up a box of frozen waffles.

"Frozen waffles," I said, smirking.

"You've never seen frozen waffles before?" Ezio asked Deryn.

Deryn shook his head. "So, you just heat them up?"

I nodded. "Microwave them or put them in a toaster."

"Get a bunch," Rhys said. "They'll make for a fast breakfast when we run behind."

Deryn nodded, and did as Rhys said.

"Is this really a pie?" Rhys asked, looking in the glass at the frozen chocolate pies.

"Yes. You just put them in the fridge to defrost, and eat when they're ready," I said.

"Get ten," Nico said.

I laughed and shook my head. "Where are you going to store all this frozen food?"

"We have a deep freeze in the kitchen," Rhys said.

I blinked in silence. "What? Since when?"

"We bought it last week," Nico answered.

"I totally missed that," I admitted.

"Ice cream!" Nico said, sounding like a giddy child.

"There are so many flavors!" Fox gasped.

"Get strawberry, please," I requested, staying by the cart so I was out of the way of their madness.

"I've never seen them like this before," Ezio whispered. He looked down at me. "You really do help them become more than they were."

"Stop," I said, blushing. "I'm just taking them shopping. Anyone could have done the same and had the same reactions from them."

He shook his head. "No. I don't think so, Jolie."

I didn't know what to say to that, but was saved because they headed to the next aisle, and I had to push the cart to catch up.

Our last aisle was the bread aisle.

Fox's eyes gleamed with joy. "So many different types!"

"Blueberry bagels and blueberry muffins for me," I requested.

Nico grabbed them for me, and then returned to staring at the bagels, a thoughtful expression on his face. "There's just so many different types and brands," he whispered.

"What about that aisle?" Rhys asked, pointing at the aisle across the way. "You had us skip it. Why?"

"That's the shampoo, hair dye, and feminine hygiene aisle. I didn't think you'd want to go down it," I explained.

"Do they have lots of shampoos?" Fox asked.

"With different scents?" Deryn asked.

Oh boy. Obviously, we were headed down the shampoo aisle.

"Yes, let's go."

They put their last bread choices in the cart, and then headed to the shampoo aisle. I watched with quiet fascination as they picked up various bottles, opened the lid, and took turns smelling the shampoos.

"That's disgusting!" Fox gagged. "Who would use that?"

"This one's not much better," Deryn said, holding a shampoo out to Fox.

Fox smelled it and gagged again.

"This one smells like Jolie," Nico said. The others reached for it, taking turns smelling it.

I smirked. "That's because that is the shampoo I use."

"Oh, smell this one," Rhys said, holding out a bottle that was covered in flower designs.

"Pretty," Fox said, tossing it into the cart. "I'm getting that."

"You're going to use flower scented shampoo?" I asked.

"Why not?" Fox asked, and all of them looked at me.

I raised my hands in surrender. "Nothing. It's fine. I was just asking."

They resumed smelling shampoos then moved to the conditioner and body washes next. I couldn't stand to see how much they spent, so I stood by the exit, with Ezio at my side.

"I'm hungry again," I complained. "I don't think I'm going to like being hungry so often."

He chuckled. "It just means you'll get to eat lots of delicious food."

"I want pizza," I said. "Pizza and chocolate."

"At the same time?" he asked.

I laughed, bending over to clutch at my stomach from the laughter tightening my stomach muscles. "No!"

He chuckled. "Well, I've heard of women eating lots of weird things while pregnant, so it wouldn't surprise me."

"Not this girl," I said with a smile. "At least, not yet."

The guys pushed the two overflowing shopping carts towards us.

"We're ready!" Fox said.

"I'm hungry," I announced, smiling.

"Well, then let's get the princess some food," Fox said.

CHAPTER 12

RHYS

"This is so good," Jolie moaned as she ate the last piece of the large pizza we'd gotten for her.

Deryn glanced at me, a smirk on his face. Yeah, she was already consuming more than she used to, now that she was pregnant.

"Do you want dessert?" Nico asked.

Jolie nodded, stuffing a pizza crust from Deryn's plate in her mouth.

I took a drink from my water to stop from laughing at her.

She was incredibly adorable, and I couldn't wait to see what she looked like with a cute, round belly.

"What?" Jolie asked, looking up at me.

Crap. She'd caught me staring.

"Nothing, beautiful. Just admiring you," I said.

She wiped her face with a napkin and frowned. "I'm eating a lot, aren't I?"

"No," I said immediately. "You need to eat twice what you normally do to get enough nourishment for the baby."

She scowled, her brows scrunching together into the most adorable face ever. "I still feel hungry, even though I already ate a lot."

"It's normal," Fox assured her, giving me a scowl.

My bad.

"Here, pick out dessert," Deryn said, setting a menu in front of her.

Her eyes lit up at the sight of the desserts, and she spent a solid minute in silence, deciding what she wanted.

"Chocolate cream pie," she said with a nod.

We all watched her eat it, our attentions focused on her, and that small spark of magic growing in her womb.

Whose would it be?

CHAPTER 13

JOLIE

Nico crawled out of bed, his movements slow, like he was trying not to wake me.

"Nico?" I asked, rubbing at my eyes. A glance at the clock confirmed it was still really early, only five in the morning.

He kissed my cheek. "I'm sorry. I didn't mean to wake you. I just need to go take care of something."

"You've been disappearing a lot lately. Where are you going?" I asked, standing to face him.

"It's nothing to worry about," he said, walking backwards, away from me. "I'll be back soon. The others are here to keep you company."

I reached out towards him just as he teleported away, my fingers brushing his shirt. His magic teleported him away, and when I looked down at my hand, a few of my fingers were missing.

I stared in disbelief as my mind tried to comprehend what had happened, screamed, and clutched at my hand. Had part of my fingers teleported with Nico? I dropped to my knees and closed my eyes, crying out in agony.

"Jolie!" Fox yelled, grabbing my shoulders.

I wrenched my eyes open and stared up into Fox's face. I bolted upright and glanced at my hand, which was whole. I turned to my right and glared at the spot Nico was supposed to be in.

"Where's Nico?" I asked, snarling.

"He left a couple of minutes ago," Fox said. "What happened? Why were you screaming?"

A dream. It must have been a dream.

"I dreamt he was leaving and I touched him as he teleported, and it teleported part of my fingers with him," I said, clutching my hand to my chest as the phantom pains still lingered.

"Your fingers are all there and accounted for," Fox said, kissing the tip of each one.

"Where does Nico keep sneaking off to?" I demanded, climbing out of bed and heading to my dresser.

"What are you doing?" Rhys asked, sitting up and rubbing his eyes.

"I'm going to find Nico," I explained, and pulled on a pair of pants.

"He's just with the mages, taking care of king things," Deryn said. "Come back to bed."

"He doesn't have to sneak out, if that's all he is doing," I argued.

"He leaves early so that he is gone mostly while you're asleep. He doesn't like to be away from you, even with all of us here, and Ezio downstairs," Fox explained.

Ezio had moved in yesterday, at Dan's urging. He had decided that it was better for Ezio to be my permanent guard, despite me already having four permanent guards who slept in my bed.

I gave up, stripped off my pants, and climbed back into bed. When Nico came back, I would talk with him. I understood he had more duties now that he was king, but I did not like him sneaking off without telling me. Plus, I had a niggling feeling that there was more going on than the other guys knew with Nico.

After breakfast, I went to the room across from mine, the nursery, and stood with my hands on my hips as I surveyed the empty room. We'd ordered some furniture, but I still needed to figure out how I wanted to paint it.

Green? Green was a neutral color, that would work for either gender, since we didn't know what it was yet.

It. I hated calling the baby I was growing 'it,' but until I knew at least the race, that was all I could call the little parasite.

"What are you doing?" Ezio asked from the doorway.

I wasn't surprised he had come looking for me. I had been here at least five minutes.

"Debating what color to paint the nursery. What do you think about green?" I asked.

"I'm not giving my input. This isn't my child," he said. "I don't want to sway you in anyway."

"I need to talk to you," I said, turning to face him.

Ezio scowled and crossed his arms over his chest. "About?"

"I need you to promise me something," I said softly. I didn't want my mates overhearing our discussion, so I peeked out the room, and then shut the door.

"I'm listening, but not agreeing yet," he told me.

"I know it's a very unlikely chance...a super rare occurrence...but if I die during childbirth—"

"You're not going to die," he growled. "We're going to have the top healers with you and—"

"Ezio!" I yelled, my eyes no doubt glowing with my anger. "Listen!"

His mouth snapped shut.

"If that happens, my mates are going to be beside themselves with grief. I need you to promise that you'll take care of the baby until they're sane again. Okay? The healers will be focused on me, and my mates won't be themselves, so I need someone I can trust who will focus on the baby." My voice cracked at the end, which I hated. I exhaled, trying to ease my worry. "Please, Ezio. I need you to do this. I need you to promise me that if something happens to me, the baby will be safe."

His arms had dropped during my explanation, and now he used them to hug me. "I promise," he whispered, stroking my hair. "I'll take care of the baby."

I hugged him back, wiping my tears off on his shirt. "Thank you."

"But, you're not going to die," he grumbled.

"Okay," I said with a nod. "I'll try my hardest."

"What's wrong?" Rhys asked, his voice more dragon than man.

"Nothing," I said. "Just worrying about the future."

Rhys looked at Ezio, but Ezio refused to meet his eyes, looking down at the floor instead.

"Jolie," Rhys growled.

I slipped my arms around his waist and rested my head on his chest. "I love you, Puff."

His anger melted away, and he wrapped me up in his arms. "I love you, too."

"Food?" I asked.

He chuckled. "Yeah, I've got some snacks for you."

"Yum!" I said, grabbed his hand, and dragged him after me so he couldn't grill Ezio.

Ezio followed on our heels, his brows furrowed, but he remained silent. Even if he told Rhys or Deryn, I didn't care. I needed to know someone would focus on the baby, and it honestly relieved some of my stress.

"What's on the agenda for today?" I asked.

"A trip to the elves," Rhys answered.

We entered the dining room, Fox stood, kissed my cheek, and pulled out my chair.

"What are we doing at the elves'?" I asked

"Uh, finding out the baby's race," Fox said, his body tense. "Did you forget?"

"I didn't realize it was happening today," I admitted. "Did you tell me?"

They all nodded.

I exhaled. "Sorry." I had been extremely forgetful lately.

"Have you been taking your pills?" Fox asked.

I chewed on the inside of my lip. "No."

He sighed. "Jolie, you know you're supposed to take them."

"They make me nauseous," I said, filling my plate with food from the table. Deryn must have cooked, since there were several types of meat on the table and that was his normal cooking procedure. Lots of meat, one type of vegetable, and several types of carbs.

"They are to ensure you and the baby are healthy," Rhys growled. "You have to take them."

"Whatever," I grumbled, but knew they were right. I tried to take them with and without food, but they always made me nauseous. "Maybe Kara will know some way for me to take them that won't make me want to throw up."

As soon as I finished eating, we all climbed into an SUV, and drove to the main house of the elves.

Katar and Kara met us outside, both hugging me and kissing my cheeks.

"Are you ready?" Kara asked.

"No," I mumbled. "Nico isn't here."

"Of course I am," Nico said from the doorway of the house, smiling.

I gave him my best glare. "You are in so much trouble."

His smile slipped. "What? Why?"

"Later," I growled, exhaled, and calmed myself. "Okay, let's get this over with."

"You act like it's a terrible thing," Katar said, laughing.

"It could be," I muttered as I walked by him into the house.

Kara had a room on the side of the house that she used for healing. She had a nice bed, that had decent padding. I started to climb up on it, but Rhys picked me up, and set me on it.

"I can do it," I growled.

"I know, but I don't want you straining," he said.

"I'm not *that* pregnant," I said and sighed.

"Lay back," Kara ordered me.

I obeyed, and two of my mates stood on each side of me.

She carried a weird looking wand and held it over my belly. "Ready?" she asked.

I nodded. All four of my mates nodded.

She whispered something, and the wand began to glow. The glow spread to my stomach, and then five colors rose into the air.

"What?" she said, frowning.

"What's wrong?" I asked.

"It's only supposed to show two colors," Katar said.

"Try again," Fox said.

"Let me help this time," Katar offered.

Kara grumbled something below her breath, but let Katar help, his hand on the wand, too, and his power mixing with hers.

The same five colors rose again.

"What the hell?" Deryn asked.

"Is that possible?" Rhys asked Kara, his brows furrowed.

"No, but we are talking about Jolie," she said and chuckled. "This girl always takes what is possible and tosses it out the window."

"Explain, please," I begged.

"It's supposed to show us two colors, the color of the being you're impregnated by and your color. But, it's showing colors for all of us," Nico said.

"Which would mean the baby is a mixture of me and the four of you?" I asked.

They nodded.

I was glad I was lying down. I relaxed on the bed, and stared up at the ceiling.

"Oh, dear," a female voice whispered.

We all spun, staring at my mother in her ghostly form.

"Mom?" I asked.

"Mom?" Kara asked. She looked at my mother and her eyes widened. "You're dead."

Mom smiled. "Hi, Kara. Long time no see."

"Don't you dare—" Kara began, but Katar grabbed her.

"What did you do?" I asked my mother.

"I fiddled with your hormones a bit, to help you get pregnant, and—"

"Mom!" I gasped. "Why would you do that? I wasn't planning to get pregnant yet. I wanted to kill our enemies first and—"

"There's never a right time to have a baby," she said. "Right, Kara?"

"Don't you talk to me," Kara growled.

"Aw, don't be like that. I really am dead. I only come back when I can convince the goddess to give me a few minutes with Jolie."

"So, you did this?" I asked.

She nodded. "You were so worried about who the father was going to be. This way, the baby is all of yours." She smiled, so proud of herself.

"Well, it does take away the stress you have been holding in," Nico said.

"Now we're just going to have to worry about how the baby will turn out," Fox mumbled.

"It'll be just like Jolie," Mom said. "It will be able to use all of your powers, and will be incredibly powerful."

"Have you been haunting Dad?" I asked.

She smirked. "Occasionally."

"He didn't have something to do with this, did he?" I asked.

She shrugged, but didn't respond.

"Of course," I said and sighed.

"I have to go," Mom said, then rested her hand on my stomach. "This baby is going to be glorious. And you're going to be a wonderful mother."

Tears brimmed in my eyes, and she kissed my forehead before disappearing.

"Well, that explains that," Katar said, smiling wide. "Now I really can't wait to play with my grandchild."

A hybrid.

I stared up at the ceiling and then started laughing. I laughed until I had to clutch my stomach.

"What?" Deryn asked.

"I've got one of the weirdest lives ever! I became the queen to the four princes when I drunkenly stumbled into a meeting, and ended the war by handing over a necklace from my grandma. Then I became your mates. Now, my dead mother is meddling in our affairs, and created a hybrid baby to make me happy." I laughed again, wiping at the tears coming from my eyes.

Everyone in the room laughed.

"Well, no one can say being mated to you is dull or uneventful," Fox said, smiling wide.

That was definitely true. Though, I wasn't certain that was a good thing.

CHAPTER 14
NICO

Rhys, Fox, Deryn, and I stood together in Fox's old bedroom in his parents' house. Jolie and Kara were talking, so it gave us a perfect chance to hide.

"We're going to have to isolate her," Rhys said.

Sadly, he was right.

"If the others find out she's having a hybrid, it could be chaos," Fox whispered. He looked at his wall, as though he could see through it, and see Jolie. "She's not going to like us hiding her away, even more than we have been."

"It's necessary to keep her safe," I said. "She'll hate us for a bit, but once our baby is born, she will thank us for it."

"Have you learned anything new?" Deryn asked me.

"About what?" I asked, scowling.

He gave me his, don't-act-stupid look. "Our enemies."

Did he know? Did they know?

"Nothing more than you know," I said and shrugged.

"So, you've been sneaking out and still haven't found anything useful?" Rhys asked, folding his arms over his chest.

Shit.

"How did you know?" I asked.

They all rolled their eyes.

"We've known you our whole lives, Nico," Fox said. "You can't hide shit from us. Jolie is pretty suspicious, too."

"Yeah. Be prepared for a lecture when we get home," Deryn said with a smirk.

Great.

"We're still no closer to finding them," I admitted.

"Maybe it is better if we stop looking," Rhys said.

All eyes turned to him. Rhys, the take charge guy, wanted to sit back?

"What brought this on?" I asked.

"Maybe, if we leave them alone for a bit, they will leave us alone. If we can keep Jolie out of harm's way long enough for her to have our baby, I would feel a lot better. I'm all for blowing them to smithereens, but her safety is our top priority. I just want the baby born without any issues."

"So, you want me to stop?" I asked. I knew I was scowling, but I wanted to find Justina. She'd severed our bonds and tortured Jolie, and I could not forgive her for that. I needed to find her and then tear her to pieces.

"For now," Rhys said with a nod.

"I agree," Deryn said.

"Same," Fox said.

I sighed and rubbed my temples. "Fine. Until she has the baby, we will lay low."

"Should we get more guards for the house?" Fox asked.

Now we were all looking at him.

"You think she needs more than the four of us, Ezio, Leona, and Thor since he is basically always over?" Deryn asked.

He shrugged. "It couldn't hurt to have one more from each of our clans, right? One more dragon, elf, and mage could make a huge difference."

"I don't want another mage," I said. "It will interfere with my ability to sense magic users."

"Okay, so another dragon and elf," Fox said.

"I bet Andras would be more than willing to come protect her," Deryn said.

I thought he was teasing Rhys at first, but then I realized he was serious.

"Really?" I asked.

Deryn nodded. "He flirts with her to rile Rhys up, but he really does care for her."

"Who would you bring?" I asked Fox.

He shrugged. "Not sure, but I can find someone."

"I'll ask Andras," Rhys agreed. "He has grown fond of her, so I know he'll do everything he can to keep her safe."

"If shit hits the fan, I'm calling in her exes," Fox said.

"No," Rhys growled.

Fox met his glare with one of his own. "Stop being a jealous ass and think about it. Who would be better to protect her than men who are in love with her? It's already programmed into them to protect her. When they see her with a child that's part of their race, their instincts will override any other thought."

He was right.

"Only if it is absolutely necessary," I agreed.

Fox nodded once.

"So, are we going to make a list of names we want her to consider for the baby?" Deryn asked, smiling wide.

"I've got one for a girl and one for a boy all ready," Fox said.

"How is she going to choose?" I asked.

"Draw from a hat?" Rhys asked, beaming.

This was what I had hoped for the first time I saw her with all of us. There was something special about Jolie, and I just knew that she would end up making us smile like fools. I had been right.

On more than one occasion, the four of us had felt joy above anything else we had ever experienced. We had also felt pain, but the joy was worth it. Our mate was pregnant. My mate was pregnant. I was going to be a dad.

Even though it was probably terrible of me, I was glad my father wasn't alive for this. He would have blown a gasket when he found out our child was a hybrid. It was bad enough Jolie was a siren, now we would have a siren, mage, dragon, wolf, elf as a child.

"We better get back to her, before she gets anxious," Fox said.

We nodded in agreement and filed out of the room.

CHAPTER 15

JOLIE

"More guards?" I asked, mouth hanging open as Andras hugged me.

"Just two more," Rhys said. "And, does Andras really count?"

Andras rested his hand on my stomach, which was already much larger than a month ago when I'd found out I was pregnant. The baby kicked at his hand, and Andras smiled.

"I'm just here to make sure nothing happens to my favorite sister-in-law, and my niece or nephew," Andras said, and kissed my cheek.

I grumbled, but he pulled me deeper into the house, to the dining room where everyone was gathered for dinner. Andras had shown up, and I'd come to see why he was here. We stepped into the room, and I stared at Silverowl, Fox's brother sitting next to Fox. His silver hair was braided along his skull, and secured in a ponytail on the back.

"Silver, what are you doing here?" I asked, walking to him.

He stood, and kissed me on the cheek. "My brother requested I come to keep you safe. I couldn't turn him down."

I glared at Fox. "Why do you guys keep doing things without asking me?"

He smiled. "Because we know you'll say no."

I growled, and the baby tumbled around inside my stomach, making me cringe and grip the back of Silver's chair.

"The baby's acting up again?" Fox asked.

"Yeah," I grumbled.

Fox rested his hand on my stomach, and the baby kicked his hand. Fox chuckled. "That feels wolf-ish to me."

Deryn immediately stood, walked to me, and put his hand in place of Fox's. The baby gently kicked his hand, and then stilled.

Somehow, the guys had figured out how to tell when one aspect of the baby's nature was acting up over the other. I couldn't tell the difference, which really bothered me.

"Spunky," Deryn whispered. He bent down, and placed his forehead against my stomach. I felt the baby move, and press against Deryn's forehead, but it wasn't a kick. It was like the baby was trying to mimic him, though I couldn't be too sure of that.

"When do you find out the gender?" Andras asked. He'd taken a seat while the baby had distracted me.

"Next month," Fox said.

"Do you have a name picked?" Silver asked.

I shook my head. "Not yet." The guys had given me their top choices for each gender the other night. I had purchased a white board, put it in the nursery, and wrote down all the names we were deciding between, separated by gender, on it. It made it easier for me to view them all at once. I'd gone in there a few times, and said the names while resting my hand on my stomach, but the baby hadn't reacted to any of them. Not that I genuinely thought it would, but it would have made my life easier.

Deryn pulled out my chair for me, and I sat down, immediately digging into the plate of food before me. The baby made me eat a lot now, even more than I had a month ago. I finished three plates of food, then two pieces of cake before I was finally full.

Andras walked beside me to the living room, staring at my stomach.

"What?" I asked.

"Just curious what the baby is going to look like," he admitted.

I sighed. "You and me both."

"Well, it's definitely going to be attractive," Deryn said, and draped an arm around my shoulders.

"Or, we could be that attractive couple that has an ugly kid," I said.

Deryn scoffed and rolled his eyes. "Not a chance."

"I still can't believe your dead mother interfered with your pregnancy," Andras whispered. "You guys have the craziest lives ever."

I sighed again, something I did a lot lately. "Yeah, I know."

Leona skipped down the stairs, and pulled me away from Deryn. "How's my favorite prego?"

"Pregnant and tired," I admitted.

"Come sit," she ordered me, pulling me to the living room, and to the love seat. She wrapped us both up in a fluffy, quilted blanket up to our chins, then smiled at the guys. "We should watch a movie."

"What do you want to watch?" I asked.

"Comedy?" she suggested.

"Definitely no romance movies," Fox said.

"Hey! It was sad!" I snapped at him, knowing he was saying that because the last time we'd watched a romance, I had bawled for an hour afterwards.

"No romances," Rhys agreed.

"What about action?" Andras asked.

"I'm up for an action flick," I agreed.

"Me, too," Leona agreed. She moved closer to me and smiled. "I have so many movies to make up for missing."

Growing up in Atlantis, she didn't get to see movies, or really anything, since they didn't have television, cable, or the internet down there. I was still trying to figure out how to get those things down to them. There had to be a way.

"I'll pick," Andras said, squatting down by our movie shelf, which was really a wall of shelves lined with movies. Fox and Nico had organized it by genre, and then alphabetically. There had to be at least one thousand movies, most likely more than that. It was an insanely massive collection built by the five of us merging our collections into one.

"Popcorn?" I asked.

"And candy!" Leona agreed.

"On it!" Fox said, heading to the kitchen.

"I'm so spoiled," I said with a happy sigh.

"Yes, you are, but you deserve it," Leona said, and rested her head on my shoulder.

Someone knocked on the door, and then Thor came into the living room. He kissed Leona on the cheek and sat on the floor in front of her.

"Hey, Thor," I said, smiling.

He glanced up at me and smiled. "Hey, Jo."

Fox returned, set up a tray with the snacks, and then sat on the floor in front of me. "Ready," he told Andras.

Andras nodded, and hit play. The rest of the guys took seats on the couches, or on the floor. Deryn shifted into his wolf form, and lay next to Fox, who occasionally tossed him a piece of popcorn, which Deryn caught in his wolf mouth.

I munched on popcorn, candy, and cuddled with my best friend, surrounded by my favorite guys. It was the perfect night.

When the movie finished, Deryn chose another one, and more popcorn was made. Nico stole me from Leona, cuddling with me on the couch with Rhys to our left. Thor took my vacated spot, and pulled Leona into his side with an arm around her shoulders.

I couldn't help smiling as I watched them feed each other popcorn. They were adorable together.

Halfway through the movie, someone pounded on our door, startling everyone in the room. Deryn, Rhys, and Andras left the room to investigate.

A moment later, Dan walked in, scowling. "You've been keeping her from me," Dan growled.

"No, we've just been staying home," Deryn argued.

"Which is keeping her from me," Dan growled. He looked around the room until he spotted me. Then he picked me up and hugged me, but much gentler than he usually did.

"Hi, Father," I said, smiling.

"I've come to commune with my grandchild," he said, and set me down.

"What?" I asked.

"He wants to talk to the baby," Deryn explained.

Dan got down on his knees and then sat back on his heels, trying to lower himself enough to reach my stomach, but he was still too tall, so he bent forward. He rested his hand on my stomach, and I felt the power zap him through my stomach. He snarled, but then immediately smiled. He leaned forward and whispered to my stomach, too softly for me to hear. The baby swirled around in my stomach, moving much faster than before.

"What are you telling the baby?" I asked. "I haven't felt it move so much."

"Just promising to spoil the little hybrid once released into the world," he said. He pressed his forehead to my stomach, just like Deryn had done, and I felt the baby lean into him the same way. Had Dan done this with Deryn when Deryn was still inside his mother? Was this how their bond started?

"It's already quite strong," Dan whispered.

Everyone was watching and stayed silent as Dan spoke.

"You're going to have your hands full, son. There is zero doubt that this little hybrid will be an alpha. Zero doubt," Dan said and stood. He rested his hand on my cheek and smiled. "You're glowing, daughter. Pregnancy looks great on you."

I blushed and rubbed my now calm stomach. "Thank you."

"This is why you came here?" Nico asked.

"It's a bonding thing," Dan said.

"Which is why we're all here," Katar said.

Dan stepped aside so I could see past his bulky frame. Katar, Kara, Emrys, and Adelaide stood in the doorway of the living room.

"What does this do?" Nico asked.

With his father being dead, and his mother being human, I wasn't surprised that he didn't know what the purpose was. I was glad I wasn't the only one in the dark.

"The more often a king or alpha interact with a fetus, the stronger the fetus is," Adelaide explained. "It ensures there are no miscarriages and that the baby is born healthy."

"Since this is a hybrid, we want to be sure we take every precautionary measure possible," Kara said.

"You guys could have told us," Fox grumbled.

"We hadn't thought we would need to," Katar said. "We didn't realize you were going to hide Jolie even from us."

"We didn't want to risk the car rides," Rhys explained.

"You have a mage," Adelaide said, pointing at Nico.

"It isn't worth the risk," Rhys said and shrugged.

Adelaide glared at him. "Visiting your family isn't worth the risk?" she asked.

"Addy, don't give your son a hard time," Emrys said. He walked to me, smiling, and then hugged me lightly. "How are you feeling?"

"Good, thanks," I replied as I hugged him back.

"May I?" he asked.

I nodded. I had quickly gotten over them touching my stomach. Most Others liked touching in general, and being able to touch my stomach was top of their priorities.

"You sure you don't want me to move Martin and his family in here?" Dan asked Deryn. "Sharla can help Jolie if she goes into labor too early, and it wouldn't hurt to have another male here."

"Thanks, Dad, but Andras and Silverowl are helping us now," Deryn said.

"Hello, blessed child," Emrys whispered to my stomach. He rested his hand on it, and immediately the baby zapped him. Emrys chuckled. "You weren't joking, Dan. This is one feisty baby."

"Just like the momma," Dan said, smiling proudly.

Emrys rested his forehead against my stomach, and once again, the baby pressed forward.

How strange was it that the unborn child would know what to do?

"My turn," Adelaide said, shoving Emrys aside. She kissed my cheek, knelt, and began whispering quickly to the baby. The baby did a few somersaults, then she pressed her forehead to my stomach and the baby met her.

By the time all of them were done, I was crying.

Fox wiped my face with his sleeve and hugged me.

"How often do you need to do this?" I asked, sniffling.

"We would prefer at least once a week," Dan said.

"Okay," I agreed, and wiped my face on Fox's shoulder.

"You need a milkshake," Kara said, smiling wide.

"Oh, yes!" Adelaide said. "She definitely needs a milkshake. Do you have ice cream?"

I nodded.

"Come, Kara. Let's make our daughter-in-law a milkshake," Adelaide said, looping her arm through Kara's. I was glad that Adelaide didn't feel the need to test me anymore. Now I wasn't on high alert all the time around her.

"We'll be right back," Kara called over her shoulder as they left.

"They enjoy having someone to fuss over," Emrys said, smirking. "Let's hope your pregnancy goes well, or she might decide to move in."

"Sit," Dan commanded me and guided me back to Nico who hadn't moved.

I sat beside Nico, and he kissed my temple.

"So, what are we watching?" Dan asked, sitting down on my left.

Deryn told him the name and then went to the kitchen to make more popcorn. Our group grew larger, as the parents of my guys joined us to finish the movie. Kara and Adelaide brought everyone milkshakes, and as soon as I took one sip, I moaned.

"We added some vitamins to it as well," Kara said. "To help you and the baby. So, it's actually a healthy milkshake."

"Can I have one of these every day?" I asked Nico.

He chuckled. "I'm sure they'll be willing to give us the recipe."

"Or, we could just make them every time we come over," Kara said in a singsong voice.

"Once-a-week milkshakes are fine with me," I said quickly, which made everyone laugh.

We returned to our companionable silence, only broken when something in the movie was funny and some would laugh.

What would it be like if my father was here? Would he get along with the other kings and the queens? I wanted to visit him, but I knew the guys would not let me travel that far when they wouldn't even let me travel to their parents' clans.

"What's wrong?" Dan asked, wiping a tear that had fallen down my cheek away.

"Just missing my dad," I admitted.

"I haven't talked to him in years," Emrys said.

"Me, neither," Dan agreed.

"We could invite him here," Fox offered. "I'm sure Sam can hold down Atlantis until he returns."

"I doubt he would come," I said, biting my lip.

"He'll want to come bond with the baby," Emrys said, and Dan and Katar nodded in agreement.

"Oh, are we bonding with the baby now?" Mom asked as she appeared in front of us.

"What?" Dan asked.

"You really are real," Emrys said.

Adelaide stood, hands fisted, and glared at mom. "You visit your daughter, but not your best friend?"

Best friend? My mother and Adelaide had been best friends?

Mom smiled. "Oh, Addy. I'm dead, silly. I'm meddling much more than I should be anyway."

"Yeah, about that," Dan said. "What are you doing meddling with your daughter and the baby?"

She glared at Dan. "Shush, Daniel. I do what I want."

"Obviously," he muttered.

"Mom," I said with an exasperated sigh.

She walked to me and then instead of resting her hand on my stomach, she slipped her incorporeal hand through my stomach. The baby shimmied, and then stilled a moment, before doing several somersaults.

"What did you do?" I asked.

"Just checked to make sure everything is going well. Our little bundle of joy is perfect. I can't wait for you to see him or her," she said and smirked.

"You know!" I gasped.

She shrugged. "Maybe."

"What is it?" I asked.

"Nope," she said and shook her head. "I've meddled too much." She blew me a kiss. "Love you."

Before I could open my mouth, she disappeared. I roared angrily. "You can't just come and go as you please! Ugh!"

"Technically, she can," Dan whispered.

I turned my glare on him, and he just smiled.

"Alright, I think that's enough excitement for Jolie for the night," Nico said. He put his arm around my shoulders, then teleported me to our room.

"What's wrong?" I asked.

He knelt in front of me, and whispered to the baby. Again, too low for me to hear. Then, he rested his forehead against my stomach. It took a minute, but the baby met him, and I felt Nico's joy through our bond.

"What's it feel like?" I asked him.

"It doesn't have a voice, yet I feel like it's communicating with me. I don't know how to explain it. But, I can feel the magic within it. It is going to be very strong." He stood, smiling, and kissed me lightly on the lips.

"Are you alright?" I asked.

"I'm just tired. I have a lot going on with the mages and the war. And, with our baby," he said.

"Anything I can do to help?" I asked, resting my right hand on his left cheek.

He set his hand over mine. "Cuddle with me?"

I smiled wide and climbed up onto the bed. He followed me, flopping down onto his back. On my side, I snuggled up to him, resting my head on his chest, and threw a leg over his legs.

He stroked his fingers up and down my side, and kissed the top of my head.

"This is my favorite place to be," he whispered and exhaled loudly.

"Hey! They're cuddling without us!" Fox said as he entered the room.

I raised my head to tell them to give us some time, but Nico patted the bed. "Come on, you pathetic little kit. Get in here."

Fox shifted into his fox form, leapt up onto the bed, and snuggled with his head resting on my neck. His fur was really soft, and his whiskers tickled the bottom of my chin.

"Cuddle puddle!" Deryn yelled, and charged into the room. He shifted into his wolf form, and spooned himself around my butt, resting his head on Nico's legs.

Rhys came in and scowled. "This is incredibly unfair."

Fox crawled over the top of me, being careful not to step on me, and lay across Nico's chest, resting his head on my neck again, but from the opposite side. Deryn moved down a bit, so Rhys had enough room to spoon me from behind.

Once Rhys was settled, everyone let out a collective sigh.

"My favorite place," I whispered, and leaned up to kiss Nico on the cheek.

"Are the parents gone?" Nico asked.

"Yes," Rhys said. "They all left."

"So, we can sleep now?" I asked, my eyelids already growing heavy.

"Yes, my queen. Go to sleep," Rhys whispered, and kissed my shoulder.

CHAPTER 16
JOLIE

"Dad!" Deryn roared, startling us all from our sleep.

At some point during the night, he'd shifted back into his human form.

"What is it?" I asked.

Deryn turned the light on, and put some clothes on. "Dad's hurt."

"How do you know?" I asked, climbing out of bed.

"I can feel it," Deryn growled.

I started to get dressed, but Rhys took my hands. "No."

"Dan—"

"No," Deryn growled. "Rhys, stay with her. If this is a trick, we need someone who can fly her away."

Nico and Fox had gotten dressed already, and Nico had his staff in hand. Fox and Deryn rested their hands on Nico's shoulder, and they teleported away.

"Andras, Ezio, and Silver," Rhys called.

All three appeared at the doorway the next moment.

"Secure the border," Rhys ordered them.

"Attack?" Ezio asked.

"Dan's injured. It could be a distraction, but we aren't sure yet," Rhys said.

Rhys waited until they were gone and then held out the clothes I had started to put on.

"Oh, now I can change?" I asked, but I knew why he had stopped me before. I changed and sat on the bed.

Rhys stood, his back rigid as he waited for the others to return and report. Several minutes later, they still hadn't returned. "Shit," he said. "Leona! Thor!"

Thor appeared in the doorway, holding Leona. "Yes?"

"I think we're under attack," Rhys said.

"Roof?" Thor asked.

Rhys picked me up, and then nodded. "Yes."

We raced to the roof, but paused at the door.

"Stay," Thor ordered Leona and set her down next to me. He shifted into his warrior's form, held his hammer in one hand, and pushed open the door. He darted out onto the roof, then a moment later came back. "Ten dhampirs to the south. They're fighting the three others. They're winning."

"Who is winning?" I asked, the blood pounding in my ears.

"Our side," Thor said.

"I'll fly the girls out. You go assist them," Rhys said.

"I don't need to be protected," Leona argued.

"I'm not protecting you," Rhys explained. "I want you to be with us to protect Jolie in case Trident Douche shows up."

That got her attention. She kissed Thor deeply and whispered, "Stay safe."

He kissed her forehead. "You, too."

Rhys set me down, shifted into his dragon form, and then waited as Leona and I climbed onto his back. As soon as we were settled, he took to the sky, circling higher and higher above the house.

I could see the others finally, and let out a breath. There were only five dhampirs left, and our side didn't appear wounded.

"This seems too small," Leona said. "Why only send ten dhampirs if they have an army?" she asked Rhys.

Rhys snarled, and then roared as something hit his neck. What-ever it was had bounced off his dragon scales, but it proved the ten weren't the only ones.

"Fly!" I ordered Rhys, fear making my order more of a scream.

He obeyed, flying away from the roof. As we flew over the trees, I saw the huge number of enemies swarming towards our house.

"They're not going to survive!" I told Rhys.

"Put a bubble around Rhys's head," Leona ordered me.

I did as she said, putting a silencing bubble around his head, so his ears were covered.

Leona inhaled, then began singing. The song was a haunting

melody, full of loss and sorrow. The enemies below turned away from the house, and started following us.

I extended the bubble to cover me, so I could talk to Rhys. "Rhys! Take us to the dragon's den!" I ordered him, and then made the bubble small again.

He banked left, following my orders. Leona continued to sing, her eyes closed as she used magic.

We arrived at the dragon's border, and Mawrth roared at us.

"What does that mean?" Leona asked, stopping in her singing.

"It means, we're in trouble," I said and released the bubble.

Mawrth and Emrys flew past us, their jaws snapped open, and fire poured out, covering the dhampirs who had been lured with us.

"Andras is fighting at the house!" I yelled to Mawrth. "He needs help!"

Mawrth roared at me.

I glared at him. "Do as I say! Go help your brother or I swear, I will tear every single one of your scales from your body, while Rhys holds you down!"

Mawrth's eyes widened and after a moment's hesitation, he turned to obey.

"Dang, girl," Leona said and chuckled.

"He was long overdue for me to put him in his place. I have a feeling I'm going to have to fight him for dominance before he relinquishes," I said.

Rhys snarled.

"No, you can't get involved. It's my fight. Besides, your brother is super slow," I said.

Rhys growled again.

"Just take us to the house," I said and rolled my eyes at Leona.

"You realize that I have no idea what he said, right?" she asked, smirking.

"How are you feeling?" I asked Leona.

"Tired, but I'm okay. Just need to rest my voice a bit."

"Then shut up," I said and laughed.

Emrys roared as he approached us.

"Dan's hurt. My other mates went to the werewolves. There was a large group of dhampirs attacking the house, but Leona lured most of them here," I explained.

Emrys snorted smoke.

"I don't know if the others were attacked or not," I admitted. "Did you have any attacks?"

He snorted again.

"That's a no," I told Leona with a smirk.

I pulled out my phone and dialed Kara. She answered immediately. "We weren't attacked. I'm on my way to Dan. It's not good, Jolie. Get to the pack as soon as you can."

"Dan! Take me to Dan!" I screamed at Rhys.

He turned, and Emrys flew closer, then shifted into his human form, dropping down onto Rhys's back beside me.

I started to protest. "What about your—"

"Adelaide is there. She's a force to be reckoned with. And, there are several of our strongest fighters posted nearby in case she happens to need help," he said. He looped his arm around me, and pulled me against his side. "You're too stressed. Try to calm down, please."

I relaxed against him, and sniffled. "I can't lose Dan."

He patted my shoulder. "Kara is on her way. She'll take care of him."

I hoped she arrived soon enough. Dan was like a second father to me. I didn't want to lose him. I couldn't think about losing him.

We flew into the werewolves' territory and to the house. Dan lay outside the house, with the pack standing in a loose circle around him.

Rhys landed just on the outside of the group, and I leapt down from him, charging through the group to get to Dan.

Deryn caught my shoulder, stopping me from going all the way to him.

There was a puddle of blood beneath Dan, and he had a hole in his stomach where I could see his intestines.

I turned and looked up at Deryn, not surprised that his eyes were wolf eyes. "What happened?"

"Dhampirs attacked. Hundreds of them," Deryn said, his voice more growl than human. "He killed a lot of them, but they came after the twins and he got hurt protecting them."

"Are they—"

"They're fine," Deryn said. He pulled me back into a hug, and rested his chin on top of my head.

"You're always such trouble," Kara grumbled to Dan as she healed him. "Can't you ever do anything halfway? I mean, you could have at least left your guts inside of your body for me."

"Sorry, Kara," Dan whispered. "I just know how much you love seeing intestines."

She huffed.

"Can I—" I started to ask.

Kara nodded. "Come, Jolie."

I moved forward, and sat next to Dan, avoiding his blood puddle. "Hello, Father. You're looking a bit pale," I said, trying to lighten the mood.

He smiled, and I slid my hand into his. "What are you doing here? You should be at home, where it's safe," he said.

"Our house was attacked, too," I explained. "And, I had to come see how you were. You've got a grandchild on the way, and he needs your expert spoiling."

Dan smiled, but closed his eyes. "I can't wait to meet your child. I'm going to spoil the hell out of that baby. It will have everything it wants, and will have the run of the pack."

I sniffled. "I'd have it no other way."

He had stopped bleeding, and new skin was beginning to grow over his stomach.

"Tell me, how you kings were all friends, yet at war with each other for so long?" I asked him.

He sighed. "I didn't want to be at war. I was against it from the beginning. But, the artifact is precious to us."

"It belongs to all three of you, though, right?" I asked.

"Yes. It actually belongs to Jinla. It helps protect us from things like demon portals. They still happen occasionally, but it is much harder for demons to enter Jinla now that the artifact is back in its rightful place," Dan explained.

"So, despite being at war, you guys managed to stay friends?"

"Yes. It was all due to everyone accusing each other of stealing the artifact. I tried several times to end the war, but they're a bunch of stubborn old men."

"Hey," Emrys barked.

Dan smiled. "Trespassing again?"

Emrys snorted. "I escorted our daughter here. I couldn't let her come unprotected."

"She was with me," Rhys said.

"More is better," Emrys said, dismissing his son.

"Have you picked names yet?" Dan asked and opened his eyes. Most of his stomach was closed with new skin now.

I shook my head. "Not yet. We have a board with the options listed, but I haven't been able to narrow it down yet."

"That was Milly's favorite part of being pregnant," Dan whispered. "She liked figuring out names, and then narrowing it down. She made a game of it."

Milly was Deryn's mother.

"How did she make a game of it?" I asked, rubbing the back of Dan's hand as Kara continued to heal him.

"She would pick five of the names, tell me them, and I would say pass or veto," he explained. "The ones I vetoed, she got a chance to argue for. The ones that passed, she wrote down on a new list. We had over one hundred names picked for Deryn in the beginning. It took us almost the entire pregnancy to settle on Deryn," Dan said. He turned his head to look at me and smiled. "She would have loved you, Jolie. You're exactly the type of woman she wanted for Deryn."

I blushed. "I wish I could have met her."

Dan nodded and then cringed.

"No moving," Kara snapped at him.

"Sorry, Kara," he whispered. "I know she would have loved to meet you. She did know your mother, though."

"Apparently everyone knows her," I mumbled.

"She was such a fiery woman. She didn't take crap from anyone, and that was what caught your dad's eye. Back before I was alpha, there was a nasty alpha in charge. He shifted into warrior form to try to intimidate your mom."

"It didn't work?" I asked.

He shook his head, laughter in his eyes. "She walked right up to him, his seven-foot-tall form towering above her, kicked him in the shin, and then sang him asleep."

I wish I could have seen that.

"Your father watched it happen, and within the next hour, he had asked her for a date," Dan said.

"She turned him down," Kara said, smiling. "She said just because he was royalty didn't mean she was going to bow to him and fawn over him."

"Oh, he told me about that," Dan said. "He said that was the moment he knew it was true love."

I chuckled.

"Sounds like someone else we know," Rhys said.

I stuck my tongue out at him and turned back to Dan. "So, Father, do you have any name suggestions?"

"Hey! He gets to offer names, but I don't?" Emrys demanded.

"I'm dying, of course I get extra benefits," Dan said.

"You're not dying," Kara said, rolling her eyes. "But, you would have if I hadn't shown up."

"Well?" I asked Dan.

He was silent a long time, and I thought he had fallen asleep, except his eyes were open.

"Sierra for a girl," he said. "And, Dameon for a boy."

"What is it with you and D names for boys?" Deryn asked.

Dan smirked, rolling his head to the side to look at his son. "Ladies love the d."

The sexual joke was so out of the blue that I burst into laughter, laughing so hard that I cried.

Kara sighed. "Laughing like that only encourages them, Jolie."

"I'm sorry, but that was hilarious," I said, wiping at the tears beneath my eyes.

Kara sighed. "I understand a bit better how you fit in with those four."

"Hey," Fox said. "What's that supposed to mean?"

She smiled. "I love you, Son."

Fox grumbled something, and Nico smiled while patting him on the back.

"So, what are we going to do now?" I asked.

"We're going to send more guards to your house, put up some major wards, and put you on lock down until our little bundle of joy is born," Dan said.

I wanted to argue. I would have argued, but I was okay with that.

"Okay," I said with a nod.

The baby started kicking, and kicked my rib really hard, making me gasp.

Dan reached up and set his hand on my stomach. "Easy, child. Your mom has had all the excitement she needs for one day."

The baby quieted, bumping Dan's hand once before going silent.

"You guys are like baby gurus," I whispered appreciatively.

Dan chuckled. "No, I could just smell the wolf on you."

"What?" I asked, looking at my mates.

"Sometimes it's strong enough we can smell it," Deryn agreed.

"Other times, once we touch you, we can sense what it is," Fox said.

"That's so weird," I whispered, looking down at my stomach.

"Alright, everyone back to their houses!" Deryn ordered the still-gathered werewolves.

They disbursed immediately, and Emrys walked over to help Katar assist Dan with standing up. He was healed, but they still wanted him to be careful.

I stood and then immediately dropped back to my knees.

"Jolie?" Dan asked, turning towards me.

"Dizzy," I whispered.

"Today was rather eventful," Kara said, setting her hand on my shoulder. She used her magic to check me. "She needs water and rest. Fox, carry your mate."

Fox jogged over and picked me up. "Yes, Mother."

"Nico, teleport back to the house," Kara said. "I'll be over shortly. Get her into bed, or at least on the couch, and give her a glass of water."

"Yes, ma'am," Nico said.

"I'm going to stay here for a bit," Deryn said, coming to kiss me on the cheek. "I'll come home soon."

"Stay safe," I whispered. My eyes widened and I gasped. "What about the others!"

"What?" Deryn asked.

"Andras, Silver, and—"

"They're safe," Rhys said. "They called me."

I exhaled and felt terrible for a moment.

"Don't worry, we won't mention that you forgot about them," Fox whispered.

"You better not!" I yelled.

"Easy," Rhys whispered, resting a hand on my arm. "Don't get so worked up."

I muttered under my breath, but didn't say anything else. Nico teleported us back to the house, into the living room.

Andras, Silverowl, and Mawrth sat in the living room drinking beers and eating pizza.

"Jolie!" Andras and Silver yelled as soon as they saw us.

"She's alright," Fox assured them. "Just needs to lie down."

"Yes, I'm sure she's had a rough day," Mawrth said with a roll of his eyes.

"Says the pampered prince who can't even win a fight against a pathetic, spoiled girl," I taunted.

"Not today," Rhys growled. "You're not shifting or fighting today."

I glared at him.

"I mean it," Rhys said and turned to face Mawrth. "Stop acting like a brat. You realize that if you fight her, I get to whip your ass afterwards, right? Doesn't matter if she wins or not. She's my mate, and I can fight you afterwards."

Mawrth's face paled a bit. "Whatever. I never said I was going to fight her."

"Pansy," I mumbled.

Fox set me on the couch with a sigh. "Stop."

"He is an ass," I said, pointing at Mawrth.

"And no one is denying that or contradicting you," Andras said. "But, for today you need to calm down and ignore him."

"Why do you always defend her? Did you fall in love with her? Or did she use her siren's ability to lure you in?" Mawrth asked.

Andras snapped, his body becoming covered in scales as he slammed Mawrth to the ground. "She isn't my mate, but she is my brother's, which means she is family. She is also carrying my future niece or nephew. Even Mother has let go of her issues and has welcomed Jolie. Why can't you?"

Mawrth glared at Andras, but no matter how hard he struggled, he couldn't free himself. Andras was stronger, and clearly more powerful, since I knew not many dragons could hold the form he was currently in.

"I'm going to check on Deryn," Nico said, kissed my cheek, and then teleported away.

"Nico?" a somewhat familiar voice called from the front room.

Andras, Rhys, and Silver disappeared from the room.

Fox picked me back up, and held me against his chest. Mawrth stood, brushing off his clothes.

The next second, Nico's brother Klaus appeared beside me. "My, your mates are awfully rude. I just came to see my brother, and—"

He stopped talking, and focused on my stomach, which was odd since I was in Fox's arms and I wasn't big enough to tell from just a look yet. How did he know?

"Klaus, Nico isn't here," I said.

"You know him?" Rhys asked as everyone reentered the room.

"He is one of Nico's half-brothers," I explained.

"You're pregnant," Klaus whispered.

"What?" I asked.

He reached out towards me, but Fox stepped away from him, curling his body around mine protectively.

"You've got a little bundle of magic in your belly," Klaus said. "I sense a bit of it being a mage, but there's other magic, too."

"It's a hybrid," I answered. "And, don't ask. The answer is strange and complicated."

"Nico's?" Klaus asked.

I nodded, since he was one of the fathers.

Klaus's eyes darkened, and he turned to face Rhys. "You're the dragon mate, yes?"

Rhys nodded.

"You and I need to speak in a room away from her," Klaus said. He turned and smiled at me. "No offense, sister, but your heartbeat is erratic and I don't want to get you anymore stressed."

Sister?

Rhys, Andras, and Klaus walked out of the room.

"Stay on the couch," Fox ordered me as he set me down.

"Okay," I agreed, laying down on the couch, and getting comfortable.

"I'm getting her water," Fox said. He looked at Silver. "Don't let her get up."

Silver smiled and sat on the end of the couch where my feet were. He picked them up, set them in his lap, and started massaging them.

I moaned and stayed very still as he massaged them.

"She's not going anywhere," Silver assured him.

Fox nodded and left the room.

"Is Dan alright?" Thor asked as he rejoined us.

Dear goddess! I'd completely forgotten about Leona, who had teleported with us, and Thor, who had been here!

"Yes," Leona answered. "Kara healed him in time."

I closed my eyes and looked away from them to hide my feelings. How had I ignored Leona? How had I forgotten she was there? She was my best friend.

"Jojo, what's wrong?" Leona asked as she knelt beside me.

"Nothing," I lied.

"Jojo," she said in reprimand.

"Later," I whispered. "When we're alone."

"Okay," she agreed, kissed my cheek, and left with Thor.

I exhaled and rubbed a hand down my face.

Silver found a particularly sore spot, and rubbed with his knuckle.

I gasped and wiggled my toes as he worked the knot loose.

"Does no one rub your feet?" Silver asked.

I opened my eyes and knew I was blushing. "Not often."

Fox had returned, and held out a water glass to me.

"She never asks for it," Fox said.

"She's pregnant. Pregnant women get a lot of swelling in their feet and ankles," Silver said. "You should rub her feet, the tops of them, and her ankles and shins."

"Noted," Fox said with a nod.

"How do you know about that?" I asked Silver.

"I've helped Mother with a lot of deliveries," he said nonchalantly.

"You're going to make some woman very happy," I said.

He blushed and turned his face away from me.

"Here," Rhys said, handing me a plate of several types of cut up fruits.

"Thanks," I whispered, set the plate on my lap, and began eating pieces.

"Can I go home now?" Mawrth asked.

"Yeah," Rhys said with a sigh. "Thanks for helping earlier."

Mawrth gave me a glare before he headed towards the stairs.

"I'm going to fight him," I told Rhys with a growl before shoving a piece of a pear into my mouth, glaring at the opening Mawrth had walked through.

Rhys sighed. "It won't fix anything. I don't know what you're going to do, but something will happen to change his mind, and it won't be you defeating him."

"A few hits to the head wouldn't hurt anything," I grumbled.

"She's not wrong," Andras muttered.

"Don't encourage her," Rhys said with a sigh. "Just, drop it for now."

"What did my brother-in-law have to say to you?" I asked, looking at Rhys.

"Nothing important," Rhys lied.

I snorted, shoved another piece of pear in my mouth, and then said, "You're a terrible liar."

"Can we turn a show on?" Fox asked, heading to get the remote.

"Yes!" I shouted, mouth still full of fruit.

Fox turned on a drama we'd recently started watching and sat on the floor in front of me.

Nico and Deryn returned shortly thereafter, but Rhys pulled them away before I could say anything to them.

I wanted to go confront them, but I'd promised to stay on the couch. So, I stayed. I finished off the fruit, set the plate on the floor beside Fox, and lay on my side, curling my legs up a bit.

CHAPTER 17

RHYS

"What are you doing here?" Nico demanded of Klaus.

I'd grabbed Nico and Deryn as soon as they had returned to come talk to Klaus. I could have just given them the message, but I thought it better for Klaus to deliver it himself.

"I came to warn you," Klaus said. "I spoke to our brother and—"

"Which one?" Nico asked. His face was drawn and he looked exhausted.

"What did you call him? Trident Douche?" Klaus asked with a smirk.

"Where is he?" Nico asked, his eyes glowing and sparks crackling around his hands.

Oh, boy. He was close to losing control.

"Nico," I warned.

He exhaled and relaxed.

"He is preparing for war," Klaus said, the smirk gone. "He means to kill you, your mate, and as many of your kind as possible." He looked at me. "Yours." He looked at Deryn. "And yours, too."

"What do you know?" I asked. "What else can you tell us?"

"He will wage war at each of your homes, but won't contain it to those spots. He means to wreak havoc, and start a panic as far as possible," Klaus said.

"What type of army does he have that he thinks he can defeat us with?" Nico asked.

"I'm not sure. He was just raving like a lunatic about killing you all and torturing your mate before killing her," he said and shook his head sadly.

"We won't let that happen," I growled, and Deryn growled as well.

"Thank you, for telling me," Nico said. "I appreciate the warning."

"I can't help you," Klaus said softly. Even I could see the war within his eyes. "I won't come between siblings."

Nico nodded. "It's alright, Klaus. I understand. If the tables were turned, I wouldn't want to come between siblings, either."

Klaus smiled and glanced at the door. "Keep her safe. There's something special about that girl."

"We know," Nico said, smiling. "We'll protect her at all costs."

Klaus nodded once more and then teleported out.

"How's everything at the werewolf den?" I asked, looking at Deryn.

"Good. Dad's already walking around, preparing everyone for a possible next attack," Deryn said. He sighed. "I still can't believe they hurt him so badly."

"We need to up our training," I said.

The other two nodded.

"We should get back out there or she's going to come looking for us," I warned.

"This war isn't going to end well for Jinla," Nico whispered. "If he uses his siren powers—"

"We've got Leona and Jolie," I reminded him. "Jolie can use her siren powers even from here."

"She's not trained well enough yet," Deryn argued.

"I have faith that our mate can cause wide-spread panic from her bed with just the twitch of her finger," I joked.

"Your words are too possible for my liking," Nico grumbled.

"I'll talk with Leona about focusing her training to be an asset against Trident Douche and his armies," I promised.

We returned to the living room, and all ignored Jolie's glare. I just hoped this war wouldn't start until after our child was born. Once our child was born, we would triple the guards, and kill anyone who entered our territory without permission. No one was going to hurt them. No one.

CHAPTER 18
JOLIE

"I thought I wasn't supposed to be using my powers or stressing myself while pregnant?" I asked Leona.

She stood across the grass from me, stretching her arms above her head.

"I've been asked to up your training and get you in fighting shape. Well, siren fighting shape anyway," she said, smiling wide.

"What type of torture must I endure today?" I asked, sighing in resignation. I knew they wanted me to be strong so I could protect myself. And, I wanted that, too.

"I'm going to teach you to cause anger," she said.

"What?"

"I'm going to teach you how to make others angry. It's something I'm sure you'll be great at," she said with a wide smile.

"I don't know if that's a compliment or not, but I've been trying it and haven't been able to. I hope you've got a trick up your sleeve," I said, returning her smile.

"Sit and close your eyes. This is going to be an emotional ride."

I obeyed.

"Focus on Deryn. You should be able to focus on him through your mate bond," she explained.

I opened my bond with Deryn more than it already was, narrowing my bonds with the others, to focus on him. "Okay," I whispered.

"Think of something that really pisses you off. Something that makes you want to tear people's heads off," she said.

That was easy. I thought about internet lag causing me to lose my connection to the *Ghost 2* servers, and causing the team to wipe during the last step of the hard raid boss's fight. That bastard had had only a tick of health left. All we had to do was hit him once, and we would have won. Unfortunately, I was the last one alive, and right when I was about to hit him, my internet gave out, wiping us, and making us start over.

The anger built in me.

"Channel that anger to Deryn. Think of it like pushing the feeling down your mate bond," she said.

I imagined the anger as a red aura, and slid that red glow down our bond, coating it, and sending a wave at Deryn.

We heard a roar inside, and something shattered.

My eyes flew open, and Deryn marched outside, eyes glowing. "What are you doing?" he demanded. His hands were bleeding.

I started to stand, but Leona put a hand on my shoulder. "She's working on her powers."

"Warn me next time," he growled.

"What happened to your hands?"

"I was holding a glass vase, and suddenly, got so mad that I just smashed it in my hands," he said. He started to pick out the pieces of glass, not even wincing.

"Sorry," Leona said, wincing for Deryn.

"She did it though, right?" he asked.

Nico teleported to us. "I've got an idea."

"Okay," Leona said.

"I'm going to bring the others out, and we are going to spar. I want you to randomly send emotions to us," Nico said. "I want to see how it effects our fighting."

Leona nodded. "Then, I want you to send one emotion to all of them at once. So, we can see how effective it is when you send to multiple people."

"Got it," I said, and shifted my butt on the ground to get a bit more comfortable. Our grass was incredibly soft and lush, though. So, I didn't have to shift much.

"Let us change, and then we'll be out," Nico said.

"Food?" I requested.

He smirked, bent to kiss my lips, and whispered, "As my queen orders."

I sat still, trying my best to meditate before my next attempt.

The guys returned, and Leona whispered, "Do not open your eyes."

"Why not?" I asked, but obeyed.

"Just, don't," she said.

"Is it bad?"

She sighed. "Are we friends?"

"Duh," I said with a closed eyes eye roll.

"Then keep your eyes shut, and don't open them until we finish this test," she ordered me.

"Fine," I grumbled, wondering what she saw that she thought might hinder my ability to focus.

"Ready," Deryn called from somewhere behind me.

"Begin sparring," Leona instructed them. "Then, I'll instruct her to start.

Leona sat next to me, leaning her shoulder against mine, but facing the opposite direction as me. I assumed she was facing the guys, but I didn't bother asking.

I could hear the guys sparring behind me, their feet shuffled along the grass, and there were smacks of flesh against flesh.

"Enrage Fox," she whispered.

I opened Fox's bond, remembered the game killing me for no reason, telling me I was killed by the "architects," and wiping the team. Anger built in me, and I sent the red aura down Fox's bond.

Instantly, Fox snarled, and the movements behind me increased.

"Enrage Deryn," she said, her voice just loud enough for me to hear.

I repeated the steps, but kept Fox's link open and some of the anger sliding down his bond as well.

Deryn growled, and the fighting intensified behind me.

"Now, all of them," she said. "At the same time. I want you to pull all of the anger back, form it into a tight ball of rage, and then send it down all four bonds at once."

I gritted my teeth, opened all four bonds, drew the anger back from Deryn and Fox, and built the anger up until the red ball almost filled me up. Then, I sent it down all four links.

All four roared, and I heard Deryn shift and Rhys shift as well. Then, I felt the ground moving, and fire behind me.

"Holy shit!" Deryn roared.

"This is amazing!" Fox screamed.

"Turn around," she said, "but keep those bonds filled with rage."

I opened my eyes, and turned, looking at my four mates in their most dangerous forms, fighting each other.

Damn, they were gorgeous. They wore only sweatpants, and their bodies were covered in sweat as they fought each other.

"Close your eyes, draw it all back, then send them all the love you can," she instructed me.

"Love?" I asked.

She nodded.

I closed my eyes, and obeyed. I drew the red back into me, and let it drown in a ball of silver. I thought of how much I loved them, and how happy they made me.

When I opened my eyes, the guys stood perfectly still, looking at me with tears in their eyes.

"Girl, that is amazing," Leona whispered.

The guys came to me, dropped to their knees, and took turns hugging me.

"We love you, too," Nico whispered in my ear.

"Well, it looks like that was a success," Andras said behind me.

"Ah, just who I wanted to find," Leona said.

I pulled away from Nico to look at Andras and Leona.

Andras arched a brow. "Me?"

She nodded, an evil smirk on her face. "I need you to spar with Rhys."

Andras walked to the spot they used for sparring, tossed his shirt to the ground, and took a fighting stance. "Ready."

"Damn, that is one fine male," Leona whispered.

"You're dating Thor," Fox whispered with a chuckle.

"I can appreciate the way another male looks. I just can't touch," She said. She looked at me. "Right?"

I raised my hands. "I'm not touching that conversation with a ten-foot pole."

"Traitor," she muttered. "Besides, we haven't become exclusive."

Rhys walked to Andras, stood a few feet away, and took a fighting stance. "Ready," he called out to me.

"Use your bond with Rhys, and then the dragon's bond to find Andras," she instructed me.

"Shouldn't she rest first?" Fox asked, folding his legs beneath him next to me.

"No. I need to see what she can do," Leona said.

"Okay," I agreed.

I closed my eyes, and focused. I opened Rhys's bond, and then used our bond to travel down the dragon's bond to Andras. I found him, easily enough. "Got him."

"On my mark, send the fury to Rhys, and then to Andras," she said.

I nodded to let her know I understood.

"Start sparring," Leona called out to Rhys and Andras.

They began.

"Focus on Andras," Leona whispered. "Don't let it go anywhere else."

Right.

"Now," she whispered.

I obeyed and heard Andras roar and shift.

"Holy crap," Rhys said. "You shifted into warrior form."

Andras responded by roaring, and continuing his attack.

"Draw it back," Leona whispered.

I obeyed, but couldn't get all of it. "I can't get it all," I choked.

"Calm down," she whispered, and a cool wind wrapped around me, easing my worry. "Try again."

I took a deep breath, and then imagined breathing in all of the red anger. Slowly, it pulled away from Andras, and back into me, where I smothered it with love again, but this time, I didn't send that out to Andras.

I heard Andras gasping, and opened my eyes to find him laying on the ground on his back with Rhys beside him.

"Is he alright?" I asked. "Are you alright?" I called to Andras.

Andras raised a hand with one thumb up.

I exhaled in relief and sagged against Leona's side. "No more," I begged. "I'm exhausted."

"That was amazing!" Andras roared, fists raised.

"He's never been able to take a warrior form before," Rhys said as they walked towards us.

"How many people could she do that to?" Andras asked.

"I'm not sure," Leona admitted. "Or how long she could hold it for."

"How does anger affect the elves?" I asked Fox.

"Similar to the others, but we don't have a form to shift into. Your rage did give me an extra boost of my earth affinity, though."

"I thought I'd felt the ground rumbling," I said. I lay on my back, and took several deep breaths.

"This is good," Nico said with a nod. "This is very good."

"Water," I requested.

Nico teleported away, and then returned the next moment with a bottle of water.

I drank it all in three gulps, gasping for breath when I was done, and wiped at the water that had dribbled down my chin.

"No more for today," Nico said, picked me up, and teleported me to our room.

"I'm fine," I assured him. "I'm just tired."

"Which is why I'm putting you in bed," he said. "The guys and I have some planning to do, and this will alter our original plan a bit. So, you rest here, while we discuss our strategy."

"I don't like that you plan things without me," I told him, but as I lay on the soft bed with the warm blanket now settled on me, I was having trouble keeping my eyes open.

"Rest, and when you wake up, I'll explain our plan to you. Okay?" He kissed my forehead, and teleported away before I could respond.

"Fine," I grumbled, but even though I wanted to argue, I was tired, and a nap sounded amazing.

CHAPTER 19

FOX

"How many are we going to leave to protect her? And which of us? I'm not leaving her without one of us here," I said as we stood over the map of Jinla in Deryn's office.

We had left Jolie to nap, so we could strategize and figure out our plan a, b, c, and d. Just in case. Since things involving our mate often went awry. Not usually because it was her fault, but still, it was better to be prepared.

"Who wants to stay behind?" Rhys asked.

No one spoke up. While we all wanted Jolie protected, we also wanted to be on the front lines, to kill the punk who had tried to erase our mate's memory.

"I'll stay," I said with a sigh. "You all are more powerful and needed on the front lines."

"You sure?" Rhys asked.

I nodded. "Yeah. Just give him a few extra hits from me."

Deryn bared his teeth. "You got it."

"Alright. So, we'll leave Fox, Andras, Martin, Sharla, and Silverowl here," Rhys said.

We all nodded.

"Thor and Leona will be coming with us," Rhys continued. "We need Leona on the front lines in case Douche shows up and starts using his siren powers. Nico, I'll put you in charge of them, so you can teleport them to wherever they're needed when he shows up."

Nico nodded. "Understood."

"Deryn, you and the wolves will need to split up. I want a few wolves on each corner of the city," Rhys said. He put a few metal pieces around the map of Jinla. "I also want five wolves at the den to protect the kids, and those unable to fight."

"We've got the group for that picked out already," Deryn said with a nod.

"Fox, have you decided your defenses yet?" Rhys asked.

"Most of our forces are going to the center of the city. We want to be there, ready to be dispatched where necessary. Our healers are going to be stationed here, here, and here," I said and put markers down on the map. "That way they are centralized and able to heal anyone who needs it."

"Three guards on each healer," Rhys said.

"One mage will be with each healer," Nico said, and put markers next to the ones I'd placed.

"I've changed my mind," Klaus said as he teleported into the room.

Rhys stopped his fist an inch away from Klaus's face, snarling. "Stop doing that!" Rhys growled.

"What did you change your mind to?" Nico asked.

"I can't let Jolie or the baby get hurt," Klaus said, scowling. "He wants to hurt them to get at you, but they're too precious to be killed."

"We don't know you. We can't trust you," Rhys said.

"That baby is the first hybrid in over two hundred years," Klaus said, folding his arms across his chest. "Jolie is unifying our clans, and so quickly that it's blowing the old males' minds. They have no way to combat it. She's unifying not just our clans, but the humans with us. Something not possible before. I will protect her. I will keep her and the baby alive. May I lose my magic, and life, if I fail."

He was being serious. He was telling the truth.

"I think we should let him stay with Jolie," I said, meeting Klaus's eyes. "If he betrays us, he knows we'll kill him."

Klaus smiled. "Exactly. And what idiot wants to anger the four princes?"

"Your brother," I reminded him.

He rolled his eyes. "That's because he's always been stupid and full of anger. He thinks this is revenge for not being able to take the siren throne."

"Fine," Rhys agreed with a slight snarl. "You stay and protect Jolie."

"How are we going to contact each other when this starts?" Klaus asked. "This could happen at any moment."

"Day Star," Nico said.

Day Star was a mage spell that sent a huge ball of light in the sky that flashed bright enough to blind you if you looked at it directly. The flash could be seen for hundreds of miles. It was the easiest way to send a signal to everyone. Most high-level mages could perform the spell, so no matter who saw the first attack, everyone would know it had started.

Klaus nodded.

"I have an idea," Leona said from the doorway.

We all spun, eyes wide since none of us had heard her approach.

"Sorry," she said and smirked. "Didn't mean to frighten you boys."

"What is it?" Rhys asked.

She set two silver cylinders on the table. They were small, and looked familiar.

"These are earplugs," she said.

"We can't be deaf while being attacked," I said.

She rolled her eyes at me. "I swear, you guys act like women are stupid sometimes and it's just so barbaric. I see why Jolie gets so worked up when discussing battles with you."

"We don't—" Deryn started, but she waved his words away.

"Look. These are magic ear plugs. They're designed to make you deaf to a siren's call. So, no matter what Trident Douche tries to sing, you won't be affected," she explained.

"What about Jolie's powers?" I asked.

She smiled, joy and pride shining in her eyes. "My girl can still use her powers on you because she's doing it through the bond, not through sound."

Well, that was good to know. Also, slightly terrifying.

"Martin and Sharla will be moving in tomorrow," Rhys told us.

"You didn't tell Jolie that," Leona said, eyes wide.

"No, we didn't," Nico said and sighed. "We had planned to, but forgot today."

"She's going to be mad," Leona said in a sing-song voice.

"We need Sharla here in case she goes into labor and Kara is unavailable," Nico explained.

"And, having Martin here to protect her doesn't hurt either. Since, we all know he still loves her even if it's no longer romantic," she said.

We all cringed slightly. He did still care for her. He loved his mate, but part of him still belonged to Jolie. Just like if she hadn't taken us as mates, we still would have belonged to her.

"He offered. Plus, we will have several powerful guards here, which makes his mate and daughters safer than just at the werewolf den," Deryn said.

She smiled. "Don't try to convince me, wolfie boy. It's your mate that you have to deal with."

"She'll understand," I said, confident.

"Of course, I will," Jolie said, leaning her shoulder against the doorjamb. "Although, I would rather be told things *before* they are decided on."

"You're supposed to be sleeping," Nico grumbled.

"I slept for thirty minutes and then couldn't stay asleep because *someone* decided to take up martial arts in my stomach," she explained, and glanced down.

We all looked at her stomach and saw the baby pressing against her skin from the inside, the perfect outline of a baby's foot visible through her skin. The foot disappeared, and her entire belly seemed to shift around as it moved. Damn, it was moving around a lot, and was considerably larger.

Deryn was closest, so he bent a sniffed. "Dragon."

Rhys walked over, knelt, and pressed his forehead to her belly.

The baby kicked him in the forehead.

I let out a bark of laughter and then clamped a hand over my mouth. "Sorry," I mumbled.

Deryn smirked, but had kept his laughter in somehow.

Rhys growled, and the baby instantly stilled.

"Don't scare the baby!" Jolie snapped, backing away from him and putting her hand to her stomach. The baby kicked her hand, and she scowled. "Fine, scare away."

"I'm not scaring the baby," Rhys said, pulling her by the hand so she came back closer to him. "It's a dominance thing. Our child is an alpha, and we only understand one thing, dominance."

"Because you're all so pigheaded and stubborn?" Jolie muttered beneath her breath.

"Yes," I agreed.

She looked up at me and smiled.

There it was. The most beautiful smile in the world. She glowed, radiating strength and beauty in her pregnancy. I was one lucky male.

"Child, we need you to calm down, so we can talk out how best to protect you and your mother," Rhys whispered. "Understand?"

The baby leaned into his forehead, and stilled.

Jolie's eyes filled with tears, but she quickly wiped them away, and turned on us with hands on her hips. "Fill me in." She looked around the room, and her eyes widened when she saw Klaus. "Klaus? What are you doing here?"

"He's decided to assist us after all," Nico explained.

Klaus smiled. "I've come to assist with guarding you," he explained and then looked at her stomach. "And your child."

"Thank you," she said. She came the rest of the way into the room, stopping on my right, and looked at the map. She scowled a moment, and pointed at the location of the new school she had created. "What about the school? What happens if they're attacked?" she asked.

We all looked at each other. We hadn't really thought about that.

"I'll have a few wolves go to guard it and the kids, but I don't think they'd stoop so low as to attack children," Rhys said.

"They're not really kids," she said. "They're teenagers. I would consider Gavin a threat, and they should as well. They may be young, but they can still do plenty of damage."

She wasn't wrong. Gavin may not have been as strong as Rhys or Andras, but he could kill plenty of humans and his fire would destroy vampires easily enough.

"Plus," she continued. "What better way to hurt people than to kill their children."

We all tensed at that, because she was right.

"Okay," Rhys said. "I'll get a few to protect them."

She nodded, and resumed looking at the map. "You think he'll attack Atlantis?"

"I doubt it," I told her. "He would have to get his armies to Atlantis first. Not even Nico can teleport there."

"It's warded," she said. "That's why." She was silent a moment and then snarled. "If they hurt Pookie, I'm going to tear their arms off."

"Pookie?" Klaus asked.

"Her pet kraken," I answered.

His eyes widened, and he looked at her with awe. Yeah, she was pretty awe-inspiring.

"I'm sure they won't hurt Pookie," I assured her. If they were smart, they would stay away from her pet. I didn't want to see the rage she'd unleash if they killed Pookie.

"They better," she growled, her eyes glowing a moment, but then reverting to normal as she resumed looking at the map.

"So, who is babysitting me?" she asked. "Aside from Martin, Sharla, and Klaus?"

"Andras, Silverowl, and me," I answered.

She looked at me with wide eyes. "You're staying behind?"

I shrugged. "The others will be more instrumental out there."

"And, you don't want to leave me without at least one of you here," she guessed, nodding. She took a step to the side, so our hips touched, and then leaned her head on my shoulder. I wrapped my arm around her, pulling her tightly against me. Touching her completed the bond, and everything felt perfect.

"You're still tired," Nico accused.

She glared at him, a glare that could frighten even alphas. "I told you, the baby woke me up. And, I'm *always* tired now."

"Jolie—" Rhys started, but she turned her glare on him.

"I'm not leaving," she said, finality in her words.

She could order us to do just about anything as our queen, and we would have to do it. Yet, she rarely chose to order us around. Normally, she gave us suggestions or asked us to do something to avoid the orders being backed with magic. It was extremely considerate, and we all appreciated it.

Nico disappeared, and then reappeared behind me with the love seat. "Sit," he ordered her.

She glared at him, but huffed and sat. I felt cold without her against my side, but shoved those feelings aside.

Leona sat next to Jolie, and started petting Jolie's hair. Jolie leaned into Leona, and her entire body relaxed.

Leona coming to live with us had worried me initially, but having a girlfriend here turned out to be just what Jolie needed. She needed another female she had a bond with that she could relax and vent to.

I would have preferred to fill that role, but I was happy with our current situation.

"What happens if they focus the attack?" Deryn asked Rhys.

Rhys sighed. "This is where it gets frustrating. Where would they focus an attack? Our house? Or the elves or dragons, since they already attacked the mages and the werewolves? Or simply the city to cause chaos?"

"I hope they start with us," I said, smiling. I was more than ready to crack that Trident Douche's head open. I had never hated anyone, but Justina had been the first, followed quickly by Trident Douche.

"It's hot when Fox is angry," Jolie whispered to Leona.

"I can hear you," I reminded her, turning to give her a smile.

She smiled back. "I know. Turn around. I was enjoying the view."

I obeyed and then flexed my buttock muscles a few times, which made her burst into a fit of giggles.

"Fox," Rhys growled.

I wiped the smile from my face. "Right, sorry. Serious, Fox."

CHAPTER 20
LEONA

I hadn't been too sure about these four males when I first met them. Jolie was special, much more special than any of them knew. She deserved to be worshipped, and surprisingly enough, these males seemed to worship her.

Well, not truly, but they genuinely loved her and would lay down their lives for hers, so it was enough.

And, they were pretty good guys.

I walked in my room and screeched. A huge frog sat on my bed. It made a ribbit sound, jumped off, and moved towards me. Only one person would pull a prank like this.

"Nico!" I screamed.

I heard him chuckle wherever he was in the house, and then he appeared in my room. "What?" he asked.

I pointed at the huge frog. "Don't 'what' me! Get that disgusting thing out of here!"

"Aw, you're going to hurt his feelings," he accused, as he headed towards the frog.

A week after I had moved in, Nico started pulling pranks on me.

The other guys told me it was his version of hazing. They said it would eventually taper off, but not soon enough for my liking.

"Sorry," he mumbled. "I couldn't resist. I saw it and just knew I'd get that screech out of you."

"Jerk," I mumbled and tore the blanket off my bed. "Now I have to wash this."

He disappeared with the frog, and I sighed.

All in all, it was worth it. There was so much here that we missed out on in Atlantis. I loved Atlantis, but I also really loved video games and movies.

"Another prank?" Deryn asked, leaning his shoulder against my doorjamb.

I nodded. "Big frog."

He smiled. "That means he likes you."

I rolled my eyes. "We're not toddlers."

He moved out of my way, and followed me down to the laundry room. "Where's Thor?"

I shrugged. "Not sure."

"You haven't talked to him today?" he asked, disbelief coloring his tone.

I stopped and sighed. "We had a fight."

"I'm sorry," Deryn said, and he genuinely sounded sorry.

I turned and looked at him. "Why are you werewolves so damn territorial? It's irritating."

He smirked. "What happened?"

"Some guy hit on me while we were at a bar, while he was in the bathroom. I turned him down, nicely, and that made Thor mad," I explained.

Deryn chuckled. "He'll apologize later today. I'd bet money on it."

"We'll see," I said, and resumed walking.

"Don't worry, he won't end your relationship over this," he said, still following me.

"How do you know?" I asked, stopping again to face him, hiking the blanket up higher in my arms.

He smiled. "I know wolves, and while I don't know Thor that well, I do know him a bit. He truly cares for you. He's just feeling hurt that you didn't tell the guy to take a hike. It's a stupid wolf thing. He'll realize he is overreacting and call and apologize."

"So, it's like the time you got all rage monster when you saw Martin hug Jolie?" I asked, smirking.

His eyes turned gold a moment, but it was gone before I could say anything. "Yes," he said. "Exactly like that."

"I hope so," I muttered, and returned to my trip to the laundry room.

"You know, if you love him, you should just tell him," Deryn whispered beside me.

I turned, wide-eyed. "What?"

He shrugged. "Just saying. If you do love him, it would help him calm down if you told him that. Knowing you love him would at least let him know you're not going to end the relationship anytime soon. It's not an agreement to be mates, but it soothes the beast in us so we aren't worried about staking a claim."

"Whatever," I mumbled, and pushed open the laundry door with my foot. I paused, and looked back at him. "Thanks, Deryn."

He smiled. "Anytime. Oh, and dinner will be ready in about an hour."

I let the door close behind me and exhaled. They sure didn't act like princes. But, I was glad for that. Especially, since Jolie definitely didn't act like a princess.

I smirked, remembering all the times we played in the mud, and how mad the guards would be when they took her home and had to explain why she was so filthy.

Eventually, her father stopped making her wear dresses, and just let her be.

Those were some of the best days of my life.

When she disappeared, exiled, it broke my heart. If I hadn't had Colton, I doubted I would have come out quite as sane. Not that I was fully sane, but I definitely would have lost a few more screws without him.

I needed to take a trip and go visit him. I'd have asked Jolie if he could move here, but I doubted the guys would be okay with that. As it was, if I ended up mating with Thor, I wasn't sure if I would be allowed to stay here and have him move in. Or, if I would have to move out with him. I didn't really want to leave Jojo. She needed me. Maybe not forever, but she needed someone who could contain her powers, at least until she mastered them.

Once her child was born, it would be easier to train her. As it was, the child added to her instability.

After we killed the Douche of Atlantis, our lives would improve dramatically.

I wanted to do it. I wanted to be the one who sung him into his grave. To watch his eyes and ears bleed as I punished him for what he had done to Atlantis, to me, and most of all, to Jolie.

CHAPTER 21
JOLIE

"Stop kicking me so hard," I grumbled at my belly as we drove to the elves' territory so Kara could tell us the gender.

"He or she is just excited," Rhys said and set a hand on my belly.

The baby kicked him three times, and then pushed against my rib cage so hard, that I gasped in pain.

"Shit," Fox whispered, and pressed against the lump near my ribs. "We've got to stop the baby from doing that. It'll end up breaking one of her ribs."

I gasped for breath and closed my eyes. I wasn't sure what was going on in there, but the baby had been extremely active lately.

"I've got this," Leona said, and leaned around from her seat in the front to sing softly to the baby.

I couldn't hear her words, but they were soothing, melodic, and it made us all relax.

"You've got to teach me that," I whispered, a smile on my face.

"Yes, Princess," she said with a teasing wink.

We climbed out of the vehicle, and Nico put a shield around us. I had been surprised when they agreed to go to Kara, instead of making her come to us.

They had kept me prisoner in the house for so long, I didn't even know what date it was anymore.

"There they are," Katar said, opening the door and smiling at us.

"Father," Fox said and hugged him.

"Shoo," Katar said, pushing Fox to the side. "I need to get to my favorite."

Fox's mouth dropped open. "I can hear you, you know?"

Katar hugged me and placed a hand on my stomach. "Hello, Daughter."

I smiled, leaned around him, and stuck my tongue out at Fox.

"Hello, Father," I replied.

"Ready?" he asked.

I exhaled. "As I'll ever be."

Honestly, I was more nervous than I wanted to admit. I didn't care what gender the baby was, but I also had a dozen names to pick from still.

We walked into the house, and Kara had me lay on the examining table. "It's going to be cold," she told me and squirted jelly on my stomach.

I shivered, which made Kara chuckle.

My four mates took up places around me. Fox stood at my head, rubbing my cheek with his thumb while his hand cupped my cheek.

The other three stood on my sides, staring at the screen that would show the ultrasound, and where Kara would be able to tell us if it was a boy or a girl.

Kara smiled at the guys. "Breathe, boys. It'll be okay."

They exhaled as one, apparently having been holding their breaths.

She placed the wand on my stomach, and a weird black and grey image shown on the screen. She moved it around, looking at the baby, but avoiding the baby's genital area.

"Everything looks good. Nothing is out of place," she said.

She started to move towards its butt, and then it shifted into a wolf pup. She sighed. "Deryn."

Deryn's mouth had dropped open. "Did it? How? What?"

"Son, order your child to switch back," Katar said, though his wide eyes made me believe this wasn't a normal occurrence.

Deryn leaned down and whispered, "Now is not the time to be a pup. Shift."

The baby squirmed a bit.

Deryn growled, his eyes turning into his wolf's eyes. "Shift," he ordered the baby.

The baby popped from wolf to human in a blink.

"Blue rupees!" I gasped.

"That is not normal," Leona whispered. "Right?"

"Definitely not," Deryn said.

Kara moved the wand again, unperturbed by my strange child. "It's a—"

"Boy!" my mother said as she popped into existence.

Kara's mouth snapped shut, her eyes narrowed, and then she yelled, "You're such a brat!"

Mother giggled, and then disappeared again.

"I swear, I'm going to figure out a way to make her corporeal just so I can smack her," Kara growled. She turned and smiled at us. "Congratulations. You are having a boy."

The guys were silent, which was worrying me.

Nico set his hand on Deryn, and then they all placed a hand on each other.

"What are you—" I started to ask, but they all blinked out of existence.

"Where did they go?" Leona asked with a scowl.

"To celebrate," Katar said with a smile. He walked to me and set his hand on mine. "Males always want a boy to take on their mantle. They wouldn't have been disappointed with a daughter, but they don't want you to see how much this excites them."

I rolled my eyes, and sighed. "Boys are so weird."

Leona came over and watched as Kara continued looking at the baby. "You're having a baby, Jolie. It's so crazy."

"I know," I whispered. "At least that narrows down the name decision by half."

Kara chuckled. "Still having trouble?"

I nodded. "I can't decide. I like several of them, but none of them feel like they're perfect. You know?"

She nodded. "I understand completely."

"Especially with it being a hybrid. If it had been Fox's then figuring out a name would have been at least a little easier. But I can't incorporate all the races in one name," I said.

"Well, technically the baby will have two names," Katar said.

"What?" I asked.

"The first name and the middle name," he reminded me.

"Oh, right," I said and nodded.

"Can we bond with our little boy before you leave?" Kara asked, already squatting down.

"You may," I said with a nod.

She whispered to the baby then put her head against my stomach and the baby pressed against her.

Katar took his turn and then led me to the living room. Kara brought me a milkshake, and I greedily gulped it down.

"So good," I gasped between gulps.

"Where'd they go?" Fox asked from the other room.

"Living room, dear," Kara called out to him.

They walked into the room and smiled at me.

"Done celebrating?" I asked, raising my eyebrows.

"Yes," Fox said unabashedly and sat beside me. "How's your milkshake?"

"Amazing," I answered and resumed drinking it.

"We should get home," Rhys said. "Martin and his family will be arriving soon."

I wanted to go home to see Martin and Sharla, but I wanted to finish my milkshake. I still had more than half of it left. I didn't want to chug it down without enjoying some of it.

"Take the glass," Kara said when she saw my internal dilemma.

I smiled, stood, and then kissed her cheek. "Thanks, Mother."

"Anytime, Daughter. Just bring it back when you come visit again. Or, remind me if we visit you first," she said and hugged me.

"Okay," I agreed, hugged Katar, and then waited by the door.

"I'm not sure how I feel about a little male Jolie running around," Leona whispered. "Add in those four, and it sounds like you're going to have your hands full for the next eighteen years."

"Don't remind me," I whispered. "I'm stressed enough with the pregnancy. And I'm trying really hard not to think about delivery."

She hugged me. "It'll be fine."

The drive was filled with quiet, excited murmuring from the guys, but I tuned them out as I looked at my hands, clasped in my lap.

How soon would the attack happen? Where was Justina? What was she planning? I wasn't defenseless and could cause some serious damage, but she had that damn knife. Would she attack me? Or would she attack my mates? I didn't like that we were going to be separated. I understood the reasoning, but I still didn't like it.

"Jolie," Nico whispered.

I jerked, shocked to find we had arrived home.

Nico's brows were furrowed. He picked me up before I could protest, and carried me into the house. For once, he walked instead of teleporting, which I found odd, but he was obviously worried, so I let him walk.

He set me on the bed when we arrived in the room, then stood before me with crossed arms. "What were you thinking about?"

"Justina," I answered immediately.

His arms dropped and he relaxed. "Oh."

"Come here," I requested and scooted back on the bed.

He sat on the bed between my legs, with his back to me.

I rubbed his tense shoulders. "You're too stressed, Nico. You've got a lot on your plate and I'm not helping. I'm sorry. Maybe you should just let the others worry about me."

He chuckled, captured one of my hands, and kissed my palm. "Love, it wouldn't matter if you had ten midwives, a thousand guards, and the kings guarding you. I would still worry. You're my world, and the thought you might be hurt, or worse, is always in the back of my mind."

"How can I help?" I asked. "There has to be some way for you to relax a bit."

He turned and kissed me lightly. "I'm fine. Although, you laying about more would ease some of my worry."

"All I do is sit around," I groaned.

He smirked. "It'll be over soon." He placed his hand on my stomach. "Then, we'll be able to hold our boy."

I climbed off the bed, headed to the nursery, and erased all the girl names. Nico stood behind me, wrapped his arms around my waist, and pulled me back against his chest. We stood like that for a long time. We probably would have continued, but we heard the door open downstairs.

"Let's go greet our guests," he said, slipping his fingers into mine then teleporting us to the foyer.

"Auntie!" Madison and Tamara yelled, and before I could hug them, shifted into their wolf forms and rubbed against my legs.

I squatted down and pet them. "Hello, girls."

Martin pulled me to my feet, scowling. "Don't squat like that. You're going to get stuck on the floor one of these days, unable to stand."

"Was he this crazy when you were pregnant?" I asked Sharla as I leaned around Martin to look at her.

She smiled, nodded, and then shoved him aside to hug me. She rested her hand on my stomach and the baby kicked her hand. She chuckled. "Do you know what gender?"

"Boy," I answered.

Her eyes lit up. "I can't wait to meet him." She opened her mouth again, but I cut her off.

"No, I haven't figured out a name yet," I said. "There's a board in the nursery with the contenders."

She kissed my cheek. "You'll figure it out."

"I hope so," I grumbled.

"Come on," Nico said. "I'll show you to your rooms."

The family followed Nico up the stairs, leaving me alone in the foyer.

"What are you doing by yourself?" Fox asked, walking down the hallway with a bowl of popcorn.

"Uh—"

He scowled. "Come on. You look like you need some comedy in your life."

I snorted. "I've got all the comedy a girl could want here."

"Want to play some games instead?" he asked.

I smiled and nodded vigorously.

He chuckled. "Why did I even ask? I knew the answer."

He held out the bowl of popcorn, and I gratefully grabbed a few pieces, popping them into my mouth immediately.

We walked side by side, and I already felt happier. A nice perk of being with Fox.

We entered the game room and found Deryn laying on the couch, asleep.

Fox pushed me towards him, nodded his head, and then left the room.

Slowly, and quietly, I lay on my side in front of Deryn. He wrapped his arm around my waist, scooted back to give me more room, and tugged me back.

I lay my head on his bicep, closed my eyes, and relaxed.

"I love you," he whispered.

"I love you, too, Moon Moon."

"You going to nap with me?" he asked.

"I wouldn't be laying here otherwise," I whispered.

He spooned himself around me, kissed the back of my head, and relaxed.

With him wrapped around me, I felt safe and so incredibly warm.

CHAPTER 22
RHYS

"What do you mean he got beaten up?" I asked Dad.

"Exactly that," he said. "Some guy at the school was starting trouble, and Gavin stepped in, but he bit off more than he could chew."

Gavin wasn't as strong as Andras, but he was strong, and smart. How had he been defeated?

"What was the kid?" I asked.

Dad shrugged. "Gavin won't tell me. He just told me to drop it when I showed up to get him from the principal's office."

"I'll talk to him," I said, and headed out of Dad's office.

"Go easy on him," Dad ordered me.

"I know," I called behind me.

Mawrth glared at me a moment then averted his eyes as we passed each other in the hallway. I hoped he would eventually get over his issues with me and Jolie, but I wasn't holding my breath.

I knocked on Gavin's door twice.

He opened it and smiled. "Rhys!"

I hugged him and ruffled his hair. "Hey, little bro. How's it going?"

He shrugged, stepped back to let me in his room, and then shut his door. "Did Dad send you in here?"

"No. I came to talk to you because I wanted to check on you," I said honestly.

He sat in his computer chair, and spun it around in a circle, tucking his legs up on the chair. "I'm fine. I got beat up, but it happens." He shrugged, and looked at me. "You've been beaten up before."

I nodded. "We all battle an enemy or two who turns out to be tougher than we thought."

"He was picking on a human," Gavin explained. "I couldn't let him do that. Jolie started the school so we would get along."

"What was he?" I asked.

"Werewolf," he said.

"Name?" I asked.

Gavin shook his head. "No way. You're going to tell Deryn, Deryn's going to lecture him, and then that guy is going to kick my butt again."

"How did he kick your butt anyway? You're not weak."

Gavin sighed. "The human was close to me. I didn't want to risk injuring her."

Ah, there it was. *Her.* I thought that might be the case.

"She pretty?" I asked with a smirk.

Gavin smirked and spun his chair again. "Beautiful."

"Did she fawn over you after you got beat up?"

His smirk turned into a smile. "Yeah."

I laughed. "Well, at least there was some good to the beating."

"He's going to be expelled from the school," Gavin said. "They told us that if anyone was caught fighting they would get expelled. They almost expelled me, but the surveillance showed he started it, and that I was protecting her."

"What's *her* name?" I asked.

"I don't know," he said and tilted his head to the side. "I forgot to ask."

"Well, you better rectify that tomorrow," I said.

He nodded. "I plan to."

"Well, it looks like you didn't need a pep talk from your older brother after all. Anything you want to talk about while I'm here? I've got about half an hour before I need to be anywhere."

"How's Jolie?" he asked.

He loved Jolie. He'd immediately taken to her, and it warmed my heart to know my little brother was so fond of her. Thankfully, he wasn't hitting on her like Andras did, but I knew better than to think he wasn't attracted to her. He was a teenage boy, after all.

"She's doing well. We found out we're having a boy," I told him, smiling.

"A nephew?" he asked, his eyes lighting up.

I nodded.

"Did you pick out a name yet?" he asked.

"No," I said and shook my head. "Jolie has a list she keeps staring at, hoping one of them sticks."

"I can't wait to play with him," Gavin said, looking up at the ceiling. His smile slipped and he asked, "How do you keep from hurting a human girl?"

I stopped his spinning chair, sat on his bed so we were face to face, and said, "You just have to keep your strength in mind at all times. Now that Jolie is stronger, I don't check myself like I used to. Just imagine you're touching a baby. That way you don't use too much strength."

"Have you ever hurt Jolie on accident?" he asked.

"I burned her once," I admitted.

He cringed.

"You'll figure it out. Just remember, your first girlfriend won't likely be your last. So, don't be afraid to end it and move on if things don't work out."

"Do you have any regrets?" he asked.

I shook my head. "I wouldn't change anything because if I did, it might mean I wouldn't be with Jolie and about to have a child with her."

"Does it bother you that the child is a hybrid?" he asked.

I shook my head again. "No. It's actually pretty awesome. I love knowing that my best friends and my mate are all part of our child."

"He's going to be magnificent," Gavin said smiling wide. "Just like Jolie."

"She is pretty magnificent," I agreed. Then growled. "And mine."

Gavin rolled his eyes, knowing I was just teasing him since my growl wasn't too deep. "Yeah. Yeah."

I stood, clapped him on the shoulder, and said, "Good luck with your human girl. Feel free to text or call me with questions."

He stood, hugged me, and walked me to the door. "Thanks, Rhys."

I entered Dad's office, shut the door, and smiled at him. "He was protecting a human girl."

Dad chuckled. "That's what it looked like on the surveillance video, but he didn't tell me the human was a girl."

"He likes her," I added.

"Not surprising."

"He asked about not hurting a human. You may want to talk to him some about how to control his strength. Maybe give him some training."

Dad nodded. "Thanks, Rhys."

I shrugged. "Just doing my job as the oldest."

"Mawrth still hate you and Jolie?" he asked.

I scoffed. "Yeah."

"You going to do something about it?" he asked with an arched brow.

"After Jolie gives birth, she's going to kick his ass to establish dominance. I'll take it from there."

Dad threw his head back as he laughed. "Oh, I want front row seats to that!"

"I don't understand how he thinks he will be able to beat her, since she beat Mom," I said.

"She didn't defeat me in a fight," Mom said as she entered.

"She can," I assured her.

"Well, I have no desire to fight my pregnant daughter-in-law," she assured me.

"Good, since she's carrying your grandson," I said with a wide smile.

Dad's eyes widened, and Mom squealed. I had never in my life heard my mother squeal.

She threw her arms around me and danced around. "A boy! A little grandson!"

"You're much more excited than I thought you would be," I admitted. "I thought you'd prefer a granddaughter to spoil."

"Boys are much easier. They like getting dirty and fighting. I'm much better at that," she said.

That was definitely true.

"How's Jolie dealing with being on house arrest?" Dad asked.

"I'm stopping by the game store on the way home to get her the two newest games. That should occupy her for a week or two."

"In other words, she's going crazy," Mom said with a smirk.

"She doesn't mind being home. She hates how much we hover," I said and shrugged. "I can't help it. She's pregnant with my child. I don't want to let her out of my sight, but I'm trying to work on that. That's part of why I'm here. I left her napping on the couch with Deryn."

"She needs as much sleep as she can get," Mom said. "Once the baby is born, she'll get very little sleep."

"Well, she has four mates to help with the baby instead of one, so it shouldn't be too bad," Dad said.

"True," Mom agreed.

"When are you coming over next?" I asked them. I'd rather be prepared than have them show up out of the blue.

"Tomorrow," Mom said. "I want to bond more now that I know the baby is a boy."

I nodded, kissed her cheek, hugged Dad, and then left the house.

At the gaming store, the female cashier couldn't keep her eyes off of me. I'd thought having the mating crystal would be more of a deterrent, but nothing had changed. I avoided eye contact, grabbing the games I knew Jolie would want to play.

"These two games are pretty fun," the cashier said with a smile as she rang them up.

"I hope so. My mate is going crazy at home without some new games," I said.

"Jolie, right?" she asked.

I nodded. So, she did know who I was.

"You should get this, too," she said, and pointed at another new game I hadn't even known was out, *Ghost 3*.

"Oh, she definitely needs that," I agreed.

"I saw her at the tournament," she told me. "She's pretty good."

I smiled, proud of my little gamer. "Yeah, she is."

"Well, I hope she has fun with these. Take care," she said, smiling as I walked away.

I exited the shop and scowled. Had I been wrong? Was she not checking me out?

I turned back and caught her looking at my butt.

My smile returned. Nope. I still had it!

CHAPTER 23

JOLIE

I yawned and stretched out flat on my back, smacking Deryn in the face as I did and almost fell off the couch. Only his strong arm kept me from falling.

"Sorry," I gasped, rolled on my side, facing Deryn, and kissed his face several times in apology.

"You can hit me more often if I get that type of apology," he grumbled, still half asleep.

Chuckling, I kissed his lips. "I'd rather not hurt you and just give you kisses."

"Mm, kisses."

He opened his eyes, smiled, and said, "You're so damn beautiful."

I smirked. "Thank you."

He tried to tug me into him, but my protruding belly kept me from getting any closer. He sighed. "Soon, that baby will be out of you, and I'm going to have my way with you."

"You know we can have sex while I'm pregnant, right?" I asked, arching an eyebrow.

He shook his head. "It's not the same for us. Sensing the baby makes having sex weird."

That explained a lot.

"I see," I said.

He kissed the tip of my nose. "Trust me, you're not the only one going through withdrawals."

I didn't respond, just laid my head back down on his bicep, and closed my eyes.

"Jolie," Rhys called in a sing song voice. "I have presents."

I bolted upright and then groaned as the baby flipped around in my stomach. "Too fast."

Deryn sat up, placed his hand on my stomach, and the baby settled.

"Sorry," Rhys said.

"What did you get me?" I asked with a wide smile.

He held out a bag from *GameStart*, the local video game store. "New games."

I screeched, grabbed the bag, pulled out the games, and then my mouth dropped open.

"No way! They released *Ghost 3*? I didn't even know it was in production," Deryn said.

I leapt up and hugged Rhys, then gave him a long, deep kiss with lots of tongue. "You're the best. I love you."

"Kiss ass," Deryn grumbled.

"Which do you want to play first?" Rhys asked, grabbing the games from me and beginning to take the annoying plastic wrap off of them. I always had problems getting the plastic off, so he did it for me.

"You choose," I said and grabbed a game controller.

"Really?" he asked, looking up at me.

I nodded. "I can't choose between them. I know you guys all wanted to play these, too. So, you choose which one we are going to play first."

"We're going to play together?" Deryn asked.

I smirked. "Well, we all live in the same house. It makes sense for us to sit together and play the game with one another. Unless you guys want to play on your own, so you can get all the trophies and stuff on your profiles. I can understand that."

"No, playing together sounds great," Rhys said.

"I'll get Nico and Fox," Deryn said.

"Food!" I yelled. "Please!"

"Yes, my queen!" Deryn called back.

"How was your trip to your parents' house?" I asked Rhys, getting comfortable on the couch.

"Good. Gavin's got a crush on a girl at school," he told me as he popped the disc into the console.

"Oh? A dragon?"

"No, a human," he said, and glanced up at me.

I blinked. "What? You think it's because of me? I'm not human."

"We all thought you were. And yes, I do think it's because of you. I think you showed him that it doesn't matter what race the girl is, as long as she's nice," he said.

"Can we please go by the school one of these days? I want to see how it's going," I begged. I gave him my best puppy dog eyes and pouted a bit.

"What is she asking for?" Nico said. "And what do we have to do to make it happen?"

I smiled, victorious.

"She wants to go to the school," Rhys said.

Nico scowled, then sighed. "Okay. We'll take you."

I blinked in a silent stupor. Nico had agreed? So quickly?

Nico smiled and sat beside me. "You know we'd do anything for you."

"Yeah, but you've been keeping me on lockdown. I didn't think you'd let me leave," I admitted.

"We're trying to keep you here as much as possible, but I know how much the school means to you," he said.

I kissed him. "You're the best."

"I thought I was the best?" Rhys asked and showed Nico the games he'd gotten.

"You know I don't have favorites," I said with a roll of my eyes.

"You guys can't be her favorite, because I am," Ezio said as he took the open seat on my side, and draped his arm around my shoulders.

I leaned into him a minute, and then straightened, not wanting the guys to get jealous or to be too touchy with a male who wasn't my mate. It was hard, because I was a very touchy person. I enjoyed hugging or leaning on someone. But, I knew the guys didn't like when I touched other males too long. So, I was working on it.

"What are we playing?" Fox asked as he walked in, a huge smile on his face.

"*Ghost 3*," Rhys answered.

Fox sat between my legs, leaning against the couch, and Nico sat in front of Fox, leaning his head back into Fox's lap.

"Play with my hair, Fox," Nico asked in his imitation of a woman's voice.

Fox ran his fingers through Nico's hair. "You should condition more," Fox told him.

Nico scoffed and sat up. "My hair is super soft."

"Not as soft as Fox's," I argued.

Fox stuck his tongue out at Nico.

"You do have favorites," Deryn accused.

"Pointing out that Fox's hair is softer than Nico's is not me picking a favorite," I argued. "That would be like me saying that Fox's ears are pointier and you thinking that makes him my favorite."

"Let's just all remember, I have the nicest ass," Deryn said, smiling broadly.

"I have the nicest chest," Rhys said, flexing his pecs while waggling his eyebrows at me.

"And, I've got the biggest—" Fox started to say, but stopped when Tamara and Madison ran into the room.

"Heart," I ended for him. "Hello, girls."

They were in wolf form still, which I found a bit odd, but didn't comment.

They pawed at Deryn, and he let them climb up into his lap. Deryn began petting them, scratching under their chins, and behind their ears. It was adorable to see him so relaxed with the girls.

"Food!" Fox yelled and leapt up. He looked at me with wide eyes. "We didn't bring you back food."

"Whoops," Deryn said. "Sorry. I knew I forgot something."

"It's okay. I'll just starve to death," I said overdramatically with a whimper.

That earned me three pairs of eye rolls from the mates left in the room. Fox had left to get some food.

I waited for Fox to return before starting the game, so he didn't miss the intro scenes.

While we all munched on food, we watched the intro. Aliens were angry at us for killing their leader. Now, they wanted revenge. It was our job to destroy them, before they destroyed our world.

The actual game started, so I picked up the controller. Then, immediately groaned. "Forced walk," I complained.

The guys groaned, hating when the game forced you to walk instead of allowing you to run or jump.

Finally, the game let me have control, and I headed into battle.

"Right!" Fox yelled.

I spun right, slammed my fist into the alien's face, and then shot him with my shotgun.

"Archers top left," Deryn called out.

Too late, the line rifle shot to the head killed me.

I handed the controller to Fox, and he took a turn trying to get through the battle.

For hours we played, taking turns fighting enemies, calling out warnings to each other. I hadn't played games with my clan in months, but these guys were my true clan.

That was how we needed to work together during the battle against Justina and Trident Douche. We needed to work together as a clan.

The girls fell asleep in Deryn's lap, but he could easily use the game controller by putting his arms around their little furred bodies, so we let them be.

Sharla and Martin came down at one point to collect the girls and take them to bed. Freed from the girls, Deryn got us more food, and we continued with our gaming marathon.

It wasn't until warm bodies pressed against mine that I realized I had fallen asleep at some point and one of them had carried me to bed. I cuddled up against Nico's back, while Deryn spooned himself behind me, and fell into a happy and peaceful sleep.

When Adelaide and Emrys came to bond with the baby, Leona asked Emrys to assist us with a test.

Emrys agreed, and the entire house came outside to watch.

Sitting on the grass, I tried to ignore all of the people around me.

"I would prefer if you didn't ask me to fight him," Rhys said. "If he does go all out, I won't survive long."

Emrys smiled smugly. "Oh, come on. When was the last time you and I sparred? It will be fun."

"What if it's all of you against him?" Leona asked.

She sat beside me, facing the guys. I was facing them, too, but would soon turn away to use my powers for her little experiment.

"Dad?" Rhys asked.

"Me, fight you four?" he asked.

Leona nodded.

Emrys beamed. "Challenge accepted."

Rhys sighed. "Oh, boy."

Rhys and Deryn removed their shirts, tossing them on the grass near me.

"That's a lot of muscle on display," Sharla whispered from my other side. "How is Jolie going to concentrate?"

"I make her turn away," Leona replied.

Sharla chuckled.

"You two are rude," I said. "I'm sitting right here between you."

Sharla patted my head. "We know, Darling."

Madison and Tamara played on the far end of the grass with Martin, all three in wolf form.

I turned around, ready to begin, but a SUV pulled up, making us all stop.

"Who is that?" Rhys asked.

"My dad," Deryn said, and walked towards the SUV. "What's up, old man?" he asked.

Dan stepped out of the SUV and hugged Deryn. Thor stepped out of the driver's seat, and Leona tensed next to me. She and Thor were still not speaking, which worried me.

"What are you all doing out here?" Dan asked.

"We're experimenting with Jolie's powers," Leona answered. "Care to participate?"

"Whoa, we are not fighting both of them," Fox said.

"I'll gladly participate," Dan said, bent, and kissed my cheek. "What do you need me to do?"

"Go spar with Emrys and the boys," Leona said.

Dan cracked his neck from side to side, smiling wide. "Oh, goodie. I haven't sparred in a few months."

"Dad, no shifting," Deryn ordered him.

"Same for you," Rhys said to Emrys.

"It's like they don't trust us," Dan said with a sigh.

"Children," Emrys said and shook his head.

"Alright, you six start sparring. I'll instruct Jolie from there," Leona ordered them.

"What is she going to do?" Emrys asked, and Dan looked over waiting for the answer, too.

Leona smirked. "You'll find out."

I turned around, set my hands in my lap, and closed my eyes.

I could hear them moving around, flesh hitting flesh, but softly, and they even said the occasional teasing remark.

"Enrage Emrys," Leona whispered.

I opened the bond I had with Rhys, traveled down the dragon's bond, and searched out Emrys. He was easy to find, since he was king. I sent the wave of red into him, and he roared behind me.

The sounds of fighting grew more intense.

"Draw it back and give it to Dan," Leona whispered.

I drew it all back in, and sent it to Dan, whose bond was easier to find, since I had a bond with the wolves aside from the mate bond.

Dan roared, and the fighting movements increased.

"Enrage Rhys," she whispered.

"Dan?" I asked.

"Leave him enraged," she instructed.

I exited Dan's bond, leaving the red energy with him, and went to Rhys, sending some at him.

Rhys growled, and Emrys cursed.

"Send it to all of them. All six," Leona ordered me.

I tried to send it all at once, but it was too difficult. So, I sent it individually until all of them were covered in my red energy.

The fighting behind me sounded brutal, and I could smell blood in the air.

"What did she do to them?" Adelaide asked softly.

"Enraged them," Leona explained.

"Leona?" I asked.

"I want to see how long you can sustain it," she said.

"They're bleeding," I whispered.

"Superficial cuts, Daughter. They're fine," Adelaide assured me.

I took deep, slow breaths and kept the red aura covering each of them. The ground started shaking as Fox used his powers.

"Pull it back," Leona said quickly.

I sucked it all back in, in one sharp intake of breath.

I turned and saw all of the guys stagger forward, then drop to sit on the ground, panting, covered in sweat, and bleeding a bit.

"That...that was exhilarating," Emrys gasped.

"That was fun!" Dan boomed, smiling wide.

"What were you going to do with the ground?" I asked Fox.

He glanced at me and smirked. "Use some roots to wrap around them to hold them."

Dan and Emrys exchanged a look, and then smiled.

"So, I..." My words failed to come out of my mouth, my head grew fuzzy, sound disappeared, and I fell onto my back.

Leona's face appeared over mine, her brows furrowed in worry, and her mouth moved, but I couldn't hear anything.

Fox's face appeared, and his hands started glowing as he reached towards me.

A few moments later, sound returned, my head cleared, and I could sit up.

"Whoa," several voices said as several pairs of hands pushed me back down on the ground.

"I'm fine," I whispered, but stayed lying on the ground.

"She just burned up too much magic," Leona explained. "She was just going to faint."

"Fainting isn't good for the baby," Rhys said.

"I'm fine," I assured him.

"What do you think your maximum number of people is?" Leona asked.

I thought about it. "I'm not sure. It depends on how long I have to hold it. It also takes me awhile to send the rage to each of them, because I have to travel down each bond. Dan and the wolves are easier to get to, but my mates are easiest."

"That was some intense power boost," Emrys said. "What happens if she uses it on someone who isn't a king?"

"Andras took on warrior form during it," Rhys answered.

They finally let me sit up, and I found Adelaide staring at me.

"What?" I asked her.

"Does distance matter?" she asked.

"Physical distance?" Leona asked back.

Adelaide nodded.

"No. Since she's using the bonds, the other person can be anywhere in the world," Leona explained.

Adelaide beamed. "You, my dear, may have just ensured our victory."

"How?" Sharla asked.

"When the battle starts, if she can send that rage out to the kings and princes, it won't matter how many of them there are against us. We will use that rage to destroy them all," Adelaide said.

"I wouldn't be able to send it to you for very long," I said.

She turned to Emrys. "How many dhampirs could you have killed during that rage?"

Emrys shrugged. "A hundred? Maybe more."

Dan nodded. "Yeah."

"That's all we would need," Adelaide said.

Leona looked at me and smiled. "That may work. Fox will be with her, so he can heal her if she uses too much magic. And, if we give her a crystal with some extra magic, she can last even longer."

"I'll start storing energy now," Emrys said.

The baby started kicking, but for once it wasn't painful.

I rested my hand on my stomach, smiling as he kicked my hand. "The baby agrees with this plan."

"Let's hope we don't have a battle until after he's born," Rhys grumbled.

We all knew that we rarely got what we wanted though.

CHAPTER 24

RHYS

Jolie's training intensified once Leona and Adelaide hatched their plan to have her enrage us on the battlefield.

I didn't like it. I was too worried she would overextend herself and cause harm to her and the baby.

But, I was outvoted, so I let the topic drop.

The rage boost would be a huge advantage to us when we fought against the enemy. There was no doubt about that.

"Come here," I requested of Jolie when she came back in from one of her trainings.

She plodded over to me, her movements slow due to her ever growing belly and her training. "Hm?" she asked.

I wanted to pick her up, but her belly was so large that picking her up caused her pain now.

"Let's go shower," I told her. "You're covered in sweat, dirt, and grass."

She nodded, and headed towards the stairs, gripping the rail.

I walked a step behind her, ready to catch her if she stumbled, but she made it to our floor without incident. I ushered her into the bathroom while I got a change of clothes for the both of us.

When I returned to the bathroom, clothes in hand, she had started the water, and managed to pull her shirt off, but then sat on the toilet's closed lid.

"Need some help?" I asked.

She glared at me, but nodded.

She didn't like asking for help. She didn't like needing help. My little fighter tried so hard to do things on her own, to keep from being a burden, but thankfully she had learned to accept our help recently. I helped her get the rest of her clothes off.

I stripped, noticing her watching with lust in her eyes. We hadn't slept with her since we found out she was pregnant. It bothered her, but she understood our reasoning. We wanted to sleep with her. We wanted to do a lot of things to her, but our baby was much too aware for us to be able to enjoy doing any of those things while he was inside of her.

I nudged her into the shower, she sighed, and stepped inside. After stepping under the warm water, she started to reach for the shampoo, but I pulled her hand back.

"Let me," I whispered.

"What?" she asked, slightly delirious from fatigue.

"Let me wash you," I said and smiled. "You can barely move and you need a good scrubbing."

"Okay," she said and stepped back.

I lathered up her hair, pushed her a step back into the spray of the water, and rubbed her hair as the soap rinsed out.

Then, I used the bar of soap to wash away the dirt and grass from her skin. She had closed her eyes as soon as I started lathering her hair, and they were still closed as I finished washing her.

"Want to sit in the shower for a bit?" I asked.

Her eyes flew open and she nodded vigorously. She had tried sitting in the shower a week ago, and had been unable to get up, yelling for us to help her stand with flushed cheeks.

I helped her sit down, and then sat on the opposite side of the shower, my feet next to her hips.

She leaned her head back against the tiled wall and closed her eyes. "I miss you," she whispered.

"I'm right here, baby."

She shook her head. "I feel like you're far away. Like we haven't spent much time together. I know we've been together most days, but that's just how I'm feeling. I know it doesn't make sense, but..."

I moved to sit behind her, slipped my arm around her sides, and pulled her head back to rest against my chest. "I'm sorry. I love you."

She sniffled. "Pregnancy hormones suck."

I held in my chuckle, not wanting to upset her because Mother had warned me about this possibility.

"You just tell me what you need, and I'll do it," I promised her.

"This," she whispered, snuggling my arms tighter where they lay just beneath her breasts.

"Would you prefer this in our bed?" I asked.

She shook her head. "I like the warm water."

I sat still, relaxing at the nearness of my mate. She had been through so much, and I feared what lay ahead of us would cause her grief as well. There was always the possibility of casualties in war, and you never knew who would be the one to die.

When she had thought Dan was dying, it had torn her apart. She had been breaking bit by bit until they assured her he would be fine. She hadn't believed them until his stomach had fully healed, though. I'd felt her pain, her sorrow, and knew if she lost Dan or the other kings, she would grieve heavily.

Not having grown up with a true father, she viewed them as fathers now. And, they loved her like a daughter.

Dan and Father had pulled me aside the day we had experimented with her power on them.

"She cannot die during our battle," Father said. "If she does, the battle will be lost."

"Because the four of us won't be able to contain our grief," I agreed with a nod.

Dan shook his head. "No, because you four, and the three of us will not be able to contain our grief. If she dies, the seven of us will fall as well."

I looked down at my mate, the small, adorable gamer girl that she was. She held so much power over kings and princes, and she had no idea. One girl's death would be the death of the city.

That was why she was to be protected at the house. That was why I had spent a few million dollars to hire contractors to add defensive weapons to the house.

I would *not* lose her.

"Rhys," she whispered.

"Yes?"

"We'll have our happily ever after, right? Our lives won't always be like this?"

Her voice was barely more than a whisper, emotions making it crack a bit.

"Yes. We will," I promised her.

She wiped her eyes, sat away from me, and said, "I'm sorry. I—"

I turned her back to face me. "Don't apologize. I want you to tell me how you feel."

"This is the pregnancy hormones talking," she said.

"It doesn't matter what is causing it. You can always tell us how you feel," I assured her.

She wasn't used to sharing her emotions and worries with us. It was something we were working on. We knew it wasn't easy for her. Her stepfather had been an abusive jerk, so it made sense that she wasn't used to sharing her feelings.

She leaned against me again, kissed my shoulder, and then rested her head on it. "I love you, Puff."

CHAPTER 25

JOLIE

The guys had finally broken down and agreed to let me go to the city for a group date. Nico didn't come and promised he would make it up to me later, but said he had important king stuff to take care of.

I wasn't the only one who didn't believe him. But, aside from ordering him to come, I couldn't do anything about it.

I walked through a baby store, grabbed a few adorable outfits and stuffed animals, and then stood with the guys at the register to pay.

The clerk's eyes widened when she spotted us. "You're the princess!" she gasped. "I didn't know you were pregnant!"

"We're trying to keep it a secret," I told her.

She eyed my huge stomach. "How?"

Rhys chuckled. "We've been keeping her out of public sight, but she begged us to go out today."

She muttered, "I wouldn't mind being stuck at home with them for a few months."

I suppressed my laugh, and just smiled at her, since I was certain she didn't realize that we could all hear what she had said.

Deryn slipped behind me, pressing his chest into my back, and whispered, "Where are we going next, my queen?"

"Game store!" I said a bit too loudly, getting weird looks from some of the older patrons. I covered my mouth with one of my hands and chuckled. "The game store, please," I said in a normal tone this time.

"Then what?" Fox asked while looking at some pacifiers.

"Food," I said with a wide smile.

"It is almost dinner time," Rhys said after looking at his phone.

The girl held out the bag with our items. "Have a great day, Your Highnesses."

I waved to her as we walked outside.

All of my happiness disappeared in an instant. The store must have had sound dampeners to keep us from hearing the pure chaos going on outside.

Ogres, trolls, goblins, demons, and dhampirs were attacking the city. Buildings were on fire and people were screaming as they ran for their lives.

"Shit," Deryn growled, moving closer to me.

The guys formed a protective triangle around me.

"The one day Nico takes off would be the day they attack," Rhys growled.

My stomach felt weird, and I felt something move inside my lady parts. I glanced down, like I could see inside. What was going on?

It felt like a balloon had slipped out of me, and then it popped and water filled my pants.

I gasped.

"My water broke!" I all but screeched.

"Shit," Fox said and pulled out his phone.

"We should fly out of here," Rhys said.

A young woman with a toddler screamed to our right as a goblin advanced on them, wielding a sword.

"You need to protect the city," I ordered him. "Fox can drive me home."

"Kara's going to be busy with healing everyone and won't be able to help you give birth," Deryn said.

Fox had been on the phone, but he hung up and said, "I've got it handled. You two help the people."

"You sure?" Deryn asked, looking at me with furrowed brows.

I kissed his lips and whispered, "Protect the people."

He kissed me again, rested his hand on my stomach a moment, and then ran to intercept the goblin.

Rhys snarled, kissed me, touched my stomach, and ran after a troll chasing a group of people down the street.

Fox took my hand. "You've teleported before. Do you think you can do it now?"

I nodded, closed my eyes, pictured home, and used Nico's powers to teleport. When I opened them, we stood in the center of our living room.

A contraction gripped me, and I grunted in pain, bending over slightly.

"Silver!" Fox yelled. "Sharla!"

Silver appeared first. "What?"

"Her water broke," Fox explained. "The city is under attack. The war has begun."

Silver's eyes widened. "Shit. Okay, let's find you a place to give birth. Do you want to try a tub birth or just on a table?"

"Table," I requested.

Sharla stepped into the room. "What's going..." Her eyes dropped to my pants and she rushed forward. "Oh, honey. Your water broke. How long ago?"

"Ten minutes," Fox answered for me.

"Okay," Sharla said softly. "Normally, we still have several hours before the baby comes. So, let's get you comfortable."

"There's going to be a lot of blood," I reminded her. "Where the hell am I supposed to have the baby? I don't want to get blood all over."

Fox was on the phone again, but I didn't pay attention, letting Silver and Sharla lead me to my bathroom.

Silver brought in a cot that had significant padding and was surprisingly comfortable. I lay on it, then grunted as another contraction hit.

"I'm going to grab the supplies," Silver told Sharla. "Stay with her."

Sharla nodded, and sat beside me, holding my hand. "How are you doing, hun?"

"Okay," I said. "It's not too painful, yet."

She smiled. "That's good."

Fox ran into the room. "They're attacking!"

"Go," Sharla snarled. "I've got this."

Martin ushered the girls into the bathroom. "Stay with your mother," he ordered them.

My eyes widened. "Sharla, I don't want them seeing—"

She interrupted me. "They'll stay behind so they won't see anything."

Ezio stood in the doorway, facing the hallway.

"You're on bodyguard duty?" I asked.

He nodded.

Martin kissed his wife and daughters then my cheek, and then left.

Silver returned with a huge bag of supplies, and set it on the bathroom counter. "How're you doing?" he asked.

"Good," I said and then grunted at another contraction.

We all stilled when we heard the sound of rapid gunfire.

"They've breached the wards," Silver said. "That's the turrets shooting."

"Fox?" I asked. "Where's Fox?"

"He's just in the surveillance room," Silver assured me, pressing on my shoulder to make me lie down again. "Martin is with him and the others are on their way."

I relaxed, but focused on my bonds to see how my other mates were. No one appeared to be injured, which made me relax more.

"Do you want me to bring a TV in?" Sharla asked.

"Is that a good idea?" Ezio asked. "I don't think it's a good idea to get her stressed out during labor."

"I need it so I know when I need to use my powers," I said.

"I'll get it," Silver said. "Sharla, get her changed and check how far along she is?"

Sharla nodded.

Silver left, and then Sharla shut the door so Ezio was outside of it. "Girls, I want you to sit on that bed I made for you," she instructed them. I hadn't seen a bed, but I wasn't really paying too much attention to anything right now.

Sharla helped me strip out of my clothes, and then she put a hospital gown on, and draped a big warm blanket over me. "Alright, spread 'em," she ordered me with a smile.

"This was not how I expected this delivery to go," I grumbled, but spread my legs. "And I did not expect you to be dealing with this."

"Good thing we're friends," she said with a wink. She felt around and her eyes widened. "Shit, you're ready to have him at any moment."

"I don't feel strong contractions yet," I reminded her.

She threw open the door. "Silver! I can already see his hair!"

I heard Silver cuss, and he ran into the room. "Ezio, set up the TV, please."

My stomach moved to one side as the baby made a sudden movement, and then he began thrashing around.

I yelled in pain, clutching at my stomach.

"We need alphas," Sharla snapped. "Ezio get in here!"

He looked back, wide eyed. "What?"

"She needs an alpha of each race to calm the baby!" Sharla snapped. "Get in here and put your hand on her stomach!"

I yelped as the baby pushed against my ribs, and then he kicked hard, and we all heard the snap just before I screamed.

"Who is nearby?" Silver asked. "Who can we ask?"

Yukio, Declan, and Kylan entered the bathroom.

"What are you three doing here?" I asked, tears rolling down my face.

"Fox called us. Said you would need alphas in case the baby started acting up," Kylan said.

The three came to me. Kylan sat at my head, stroking my hair softly. Yukio and Declan sat on my sides, setting their hands on my stomach where Ezio wasn't touching.

"We don't have a mage," I sobbed as the baby continued to kick me.

"Yes, you do," Nico said, and dropped to his knees next to me. It was a tight fit, but they all made room.

"Nico," I sobbed, my ribs feeling like they were going to break more.

"Son, you need to stop hurting your mother," Nico said to my stomach.

The baby kicked again.

"Do it," Nico said.

I wasn't sure what he meant, but all of the guys touching my stomach, gripped my stomach a bit, and magic flowed from them into me, and then into the baby.

But, the baby didn't stop.

"Siren," I gasped.

"No," Sharla whispered, her eyes wide.

The baby moved down, turned, and then kicked my other ribs, cracking one of them.

I closed my eyes, the pain almost unbearable as contractions began to come in rapid succession.

Another hand touched my stomach, and a new magic seeped in, instantly calming the baby.

I opened my eyes and Dad smiled at me. "Hello, Daughter."

"Dad," I sobbed.

"You didn't think I would miss my grandson being born, did you?" he asked and wiped the tears from my eyes.

"He keeps hurting her," Nico explained.

"I've got it," Dad said. He bent forward, and began singing Mom's lullaby.

The baby moved down again, his body going into the right position for birthing.

"Alright, hun. Push," Sharla ordered me, flipping the blanket up so she could see, but the others couldn't.

I pushed, and clutched Nico's hand with one of mine.

"You're doing great, love," he whispered.

"Again," Sharla said and smiled. "You're doing great."

I pushed, my body shuddering at the strain.

"I don't mean to hurry you," Nico whispered, "but the others need your magic."

I pushed again and again. And after another push, the baby slid out into Sharla's waiting arms.

Silver rushed over, cleaning out his nose and mouth, and the baby wailed.

I smiled and Nico kissed my lips softly. "You did great, Jolie."

Everyone moved back from me, no longer needing to touch my stomach.

Sharla pushed on my stomach and I gasped in pain.

"What are you doing?" I demanded.

"I've got to get the placenta out, hun. I'm sorry. I know it hurts, but I've got to do it," she said.

Fox ran to the door and his eyes widened when he saw his son. He looked up and our eyes met. "Are you okay?"

I nodded.

Sharla pushed again, and Fox's face drained of color as he saw what she was doing.

"Done," she announced.

Nico helped Silver clean up the baby, and then Dad cut the umbilical cord.

Everyone found a place away from me, averting their eyes, and Sharla pulled my top down.

Once he was ready, Nico set the baby on my naked chest.

"What's his name?" Nico asked me.

"Caleb," I whispered, cradling him close. "His name is Caleb."

"Hello, Caleb," Nico said.

Fox sat on my other side, smiling with tears in his eyes. "Hello, Caleb. Welcome to the family."

I cradled the adorable baby who had features from each of my mates, but most notably had Rhys's bright blue eyes.

Sharla cringed. "I need to stitch you up. Just a couple and then your mates' powers will heal you the rest of the way."

I nodded and then looked at the TV. There were thousands of beings fighting, the city was burning, and I couldn't tell who was winning.

"Fox, hold Caleb, please," I requested.

Fox took him, cradling him against his bare chest.

When had he taken his shirt off?

I pulled my shirt up, closed my eyes, and tapped each of my mate bonds. They tapped them back.

I looked at the screen, seeing Deryn overrun with goblins and dhampirs, Rhys battling demons, and the kings up to their necks in enemies. They didn't look like they were winning.

It was time.

I closed my eyes again, and gathered as much rage as I could. I opened my connections with them, and sent all of the rage I could to Rhys, Deryn, Emrys, Katar, and Dan.

I opened my eyes, watching as the five of them roared at the same time, and began flinging enemies like ragdolls.

"Damn," Nico whispered.

"Look, your daddies are killing lots of bad guys," Fox whispered to Caleb, who was curled up on his chest with his eyes closed.

They were killing a lot of people, but it wasn't enough.

"Crystals," I ordered Ezio.

Ezio ran out, then returned with dozens of crystals holding a ton of magic. They had been storing energy for me, and now was the time for me to use it. I grabbed a handful, sucked the energy into myself. Once I'd absorbed it, I focused on the bonds with the werewolves, and poured the rage down the pack bonds. Then, I focused on the dragons, and sent more.

"What's going on outside?" Nico asked Fox.

Fox gasped. "Shit, I forgot we were being attacked."

"I'll check," Ezio said and left.

"Jolie, don't overextend yourself," Nico ordered me.

I could hear the dragons and werewolves roaring on the TV.

"Crystals," I asked softly, my body so weak and tired.

He put more in my hands, and I drew it all in.

"Jolie, what are you doing?" Nico demanded.

I used my final two bonds, and sent all of the rage I could to the mages and elves.

"Holy shit," Dad whispered.

I opened my eyes, holding the rage, and drawing magic from the crystals to keep the rage going.

The tides had turned, and we were defeating the enemies.

I heard Andras roar outside, and hoped he was okay.

"We'll go assist," Declan said.

Everyone, but Nico, Dad, Sharla, the girls, and Silver left the bathroom.

"Jolie," Nico growled. "That's enough. You've helped enough."

"Just a bit longer," I gasped, taking the last crystals in my hands.

"You're going to kill yourself," Dad snapped. "Let it go!"

He was right. I was at my limit.

I released the power, but instead of drawing the rage back, I left it with the others. They would burn it out on their own.

I gasped and let my head drop as I released the crystals from my grip.

"Jolie?" Nico asked.

"I'm good," I panted.

"They're still enraged," Sharla said and looked at me.

I nodded. "I left the rage with them to burn off."

"You know how to do that?" she asked.

I shrugged and smirked. "Apparently."

"You are way more powerful than we thought," Dad said, pride coloring his tone.

"You need to try to feed him," Sharla said, taking Caleb from Nico and handing him to me.

"I'm going to go help outside," Dad said.

"I'm sorry I wasn't there earlier," Nico said, his eyes on his hands in his lap.

"Where were you?" I asked.

He sighed. "I've been tailing Trident Douche and Justina."

My eyes widened. "What?" I gasped. "For how long?"

He cringed. "Three or so months."

"You knew where they were for that long?" I asked, unsure whether to be angry or not.

"Yes, but I didn't want to tip them off or risk them attacking early," he explained. "Turned out it didn't matter."

"No, it didn't," Justina said from the doorway.

Nico stood up, putting a shield around the six of us still in the bathroom.

How had she gotten in?

Sharla backed up until she stood in front of her girls, crouched and ready to fight.

I couldn't sit up or stand yet, but I clutched Caleb to me. "Get out of here," I snarled.

"Oh, you've got a baby? Who is the lucky father?" she asked, snarling. "Doesn't matter. Once I'm done, none of you will be alive."

"You're not touching my mate or my child," Nico snarled, his staff in his hand.

She drew the knife she'd cut our bonds with and smiled at the fear she must have seen on my face. "I see you remember this blade. I'm going to enjoy severing your mate bonds with it."

If she severed our mate bonds, we'd be unable to form any new bonds. We would have no bonds left to make. No, I couldn't handle that. I couldn't let her sever the last bonds that we had.

Nico tapped his staff on the ground, and a blue circle spread around us. "You can't step foot in here," he told her.

She picked dirt out from under her nail with the dagger. "Oh, I don't need to get in there."

She threw the dagger, and Nico's smug smile of assurance that his shield would hold, disappeared as the dagger slipped right through, and embedded into his chest.

I screamed his name, and stood, holding Caleb in my arms as I went to Nico. He gasped in pain, blood pooling beneath him from the wound.

"No," I cried, and Caleb cried, too.

Nico was dying. I could feel our bond fading. The bond flickered and dimmed slightly. Dammit! What could I do? I couldn't let him die, but I couldn't take the knife out. I couldn't heal him.

"Nico," I sobbed.

"You see, you just weren't meant to ever be happy. You're worthless and you're going to die, after I cut all of your bonds again, and kill everyone you love," Justina said, pulling another dagger from a sheath on her side.

I backed up until I stood just before Sharla, and handed her Caleb.

"Jolie," she whispered as she took him.

"Protect the children," I ordered her, my skin shifting into dragon's scales. I kissed Caleb's forehead, and he blinked at me. "I love you," I whispered into his bright blue eyes.

"You think you can win? How cute," Justina taunted.

I felt Deryn and Rhys tugging on our bonds, and I jerked them hard. I needed them and I needed them now.

"Any last words?" I asked her, shifted my hands into werewolf paws, and then gathered magic to me. I didn't have much, since I'd drained it all earlier, but I would use what I had.

"Jolie," Nico gasped.

"Help is coming," I assured Nico. "I'm going to take care of this once and for all."

"I'm going to enjoy hearing you cry when he dies," she said smugly.

"You are mine," I snarled at Justina.

Justina snarled back, and launched herself at me.

I slammed into her, sending her back into the hallway, and then stabbed her in the chest with my claws.

CHAPTER 26
JOLIE

Justina screamed, and I roared in her face, tossing her down the hallway.

Fox and Silver ran into the foyer, looking up at us on the second floor.

"Heal Nico!" I ordered them.

Fox snarled, unable to disobey my direct order. They both ran past me and into the bathroom.

"Got 'em trained finally, huh?" Justina asked, standing to her feet and wiping blood from her mouth.

"Stop talking, wench," I ordered her. I lunged forward, grabbed her by the throat, and tossed her out the nearest window. I leapt out of the window after her, landing in a crouch.

To my left, Ezio and the others were battling a large group of ogres and dhampirs. They glanced at me, eyes wide.

"Jolie!" Declan yelled.

"Defeat your enemies. I'm fine," I called back.

Justina stood and brushed herself off.

"Your death has been a long time coming," I told her. "I'm really going to fucking enjoy this."

She pulled out another dagger and flipped it in the air, smiling. "Let's dance, bitch."

She tried to cut my arm, but I had dragon scales covering it, which made the dagger just glance off. She snarled, furious.

Could I project my emotions to her? I'd done it with Trident Douche.

She continued to try to stab me, but I blocked with my arms, punched her a few times, and then kicked her in the stomach hard enough to send her sliding back on the grass.

"Fear," I whispered, thinking of being locked in the cupboard.

Her body trembled and her mouth popped open.

"That is what I felt when my father tortured me as a child," I told her. "He wasn't a good person. He was a murderer. A torturer. He deserved to die."

"You didn't know him," she snapped.

"No!" I snapped back. "You didn't know him. He blinded you with promises, so you didn't see what a monster he truly was. We were friends! I would have never betrayed you. I would have saved you, but you let him use me. You were going to let him kill me! You're not a friend. You're pathetic."

"I'm pathetic? You're the one who latched onto the first guy who paid her any attention when she got here. Oh wait, make that *guys*. You're so terrified of being alone that you couldn't settle for one guy."

"*They* added me to their warrior's bond. I didn't add myself," I reminded her.

"Who wouldn't want a whore they could pass around?" she asked with a sneer.

I tried to punch her, but she dodged and sliced the blade across my cheek.

I screamed in pain, and stumbled back, my hand flying to the bleeding wound.

"You're nothing but trouble. All you do is bring chaos and destruction wherever you go. You should let me kill you, to save those boys from being brought down by you any further," she hissed.

"I am trouble," I agreed. "I was cursed. I brought that on them. But, I chose to remove the curse. I almost died removing that damn curse. So they would be safe. I've trained for hours and hours, bleeding and bruised, so I could learn to protect myself. So I wouldn't be a burden. They love me, and I love them."

I couldn't hold the dragon scales on all of my body, so I just kept them in the vital parts like my throat and abdomen.

"Do they love you? Or did you use your siren powers to make them think they love you?"

"I don't have that ability," I told her.

"Just because mommy dearest from the beyond told you that, doesn't make it true," she snarled.

I gaped at her. "How did you know about that?"

She threw one of her daggers, and I barely managed to move so it didn't strike my heart. It did slice open my shoulder as it sailed over my arm, though.

I gasped in pain and growled.

"I can't believe Brayden was going to mate with you. Look at you! What do you have that these males keep falling for?" she screeched.

"Maybe it's because I'm not a fucking psycho like you!" I yelled, swinging at her.

She and I danced around each other, landing a few punches, but nothing significant.

I had to hurry and finish this or I would run out of energy. I was already dangerously low. I couldn't let her win. I had to kill her and get back to Caleb. I'd been away from him for too long as it was.

I stopped chasing her, centered myself, and opened my bond with Rhys. He was close, but not close enough. I drew on his bond, letting my center grow warm.

She charged forward, and I opened my mouth, letting out a stream of flames.

She screamed and fell backwards, her hands covering her now burned face.

"Didn't know I could do that, did you?" I asked her smugly. I kicked the daggers out of her hands, and knelt by her. "No one fucking hurts my family. Had you killed me, this wouldn't have happened. If you hadn't cut my bonds, I would have left you alone. But, you destroyed me that day. You caused pain in my mates, a pain that haunts them to this day. That is something I cannot forgive."

"Fuck. You," she gasped.

"No, thanks. You're not my type," I replied.

Rhys and Deryn landed and helped attack the others, but when they looked over at me, they roared and headed towards us.

"Goodbye, Justina," I whispered. I picked up one of her daggers and stabbed her in the chest.

"That's rather inconvenient," Brayden said on a sigh behind me.

I spun, eyes wide, but it was too late. He grabbed my face, and darkness crowded my vision.

"No. Not this one, brother," Klaus said and knocked Brayden away from me.

I fell to my knees, gasping, as my vision returned to normal.

"What are you doing?" Brayden demanded. "You don't pick sides!"

"I pick her. You won't kill her or her child," Klaus said.

"Why are you protecting her?" Brayden snarled.

"Because she makes Nico happy," Klaus said. "And Nico deserves to be happy."

"What about me? Don't I deserve to be happy? She ruined my life!" Brayden snapped.

Deryn picked me up and moved away from the two brothers. "Baby, what are you doing out here?"

"How's Nico?" I asked instead of answering him.

"He's alive," Rhys said. "You would have felt it if he died."

He was right. I just wasn't thinking properly at the moment. Now that I wasn't fighting Justina, I was so tired.

"If you aren't with me, then you are against me," Brayden said.

"Don't do this," Klaus begged. "Please, don't make me fight you."

"Step out of the way, then," Brayden snapped, his bloodshot eyes deranged.

Klaus snapped his fingers and a staff, much like Nico's, appeared in his hand. "The line has been drawn. If you try to harm her or hers, I will defend them," Klaus said softly, calmly.

Brayden opened his mouth and started singing. I went to plug Deryn's ears, since he was holding me and couldn't do it himself, but he already had in the earplugs from Leona.

Klaus sighed, tapped his staff on the ground, and a bubble formed around the entire grounds of the house. He tapped again and a bubble formed around Brayden, locking his sound in with him. He flicked his finger, and Brayden, and the bubble he was in, moved out of the circle that encircled our grounds.

Klaus looked at me and smiled. "I'll take care of him, sister."

"Nico was stabbed," I told him.

His eyes widened and he glared down at Justina. "They planned this. Fine, I'm done playing pacifist."

"What are—" I didn't get to finish my question.

His eyes began to glow, the bubbles disappeared, and before Brayden could draw in a breath, Klaus clapped his hands together, and Brayden burst into a pile of ashes.

Deryn's and my mouths dropped open at the same time. I dropped my hands from Deryn's shoulders to stare at the ash pile.

Holy shit! That was some serious magic power.

I stared at the pile mutely.

"Is he really dead?" Deryn asked Klaus.

Klaus stopped glowing, and sighed, looking worn. "Yes."

Fox, Nico, and Silver came out of the house. Silver and Fox were holding Nico up between them.

"What are you doing?" I demanded.

"Why?" Nico asked Klaus instead of answering me.

Klaus smiled. "Your mate is doing good things for the world. Your baby will do even greater things." He looked at the pile that used to be Brayden. "And he was too far gone to be saved."

"He killed Dad," Nico said.

Klaus nodded, his lips pinched in a tight line. "I know."

Deryn walked to Nico, and let me hug him.

"How are you?" I asked him.

"Healing," he said. "How are you?"

"Tired," I admitted. I looked around. "Where's Rhys?"

Deryn turned so I could see where the last dhampirs were being killed by our troop.

"I need to see Caleb," I whispered.

"Caleb?" Deryn asked.

"Our son," I replied, smiling.

He smiled back. "I like that name. Caleb." He carried me upstairs, running when he heard Caleb crying, and Sharla immediately handed Caleb over when we entered the bathroom.

"Go feed him," she ordered me.

I bounced the crying infant in my arms, and Deryn carried us to the bedroom. I lay on my side, and began nursing him.

"He's beautiful," Deryn whispered as he stroked Caleb's dark hair, hair just like his.

"He is," I agreed.

"Dad's coming," he told me.

"My dad is here," I said.

"I saw him fighting outside."

"Can you get me some water?" I asked.

"I got it," Fox said, walked in the room, and handed me a cup with a straw.

I took a few small drinks and then handed the cup back to him.

"How's our boy doing?" Rhys asked, entering the room.

Caleb finished nursing, so I held him out to Rhys.

Rhys pulled his shirt off, and then took Caleb, cradling him against his chest, and making adorable noises to him.

I closed my eyes, resting now that it was over. It was finally over.

Tears slipped down my face, and Deryn climbed onto the bed behind me, wrapping his arms around me.

"It's over, baby. It's all over," he whispered.

Fox stroked my hair, sitting behind Deryn on the bed.

Rhys lay down beside me, putting Caleb between us.

Nico walked into the room, tugged Rhys off the bed, and took his place. He set his hand on my cheek. "Don't you ever do that again."

"You were dying," I whispered.

"I would never leave you, darling." He smiled and kissed my lips lightly. He looked down at our sleeping son and smiled. "He's got Rhys's eyes."

"Your nose," Rhys said to Nico.

"My hair," Deryn said.

"My jaw," Fox said.

"He's perfect," I sniffled.

Deryn kissed my shoulder, and I realized that I was naked.

"Why didn't you tell me I was naked?" I asked.

"We thought you knew," Rhys said with a chuckle.

"Are you telling me that I fought Justina while naked? And that Klaus and Brayden saw me naked?"

"Yeah," Nico said and chuckled. "As did everyone else who was fighting outside."

I threw my head back and laughed, then clutched at my stomach and grunted in pain.

"You need to lay here and rest," Nico ordered me.

"So, do you," Rhys said. "You're not completely healed either."

Caleb started to fuss, and then we all stared in disbelief as he turned into a wolf pup.

"That is not normal," Deryn informed us.

"I need clothes," I said. "The kings are going to want to see him, and I don't want to be naked in front of my fathers." Well, apparently, I'd already been naked outside, which my dad had seen. Whoops.

Rhys grabbed sweatpants from the dresser, and helped me put them on while still laying down. He then helped me put a nursing tank top on that had convenient snaps to let me pull out a boob to feed Caleb without pulling up my entire shirt.

"Now, rest. We'll feed everyone, and that should give you enough time to fully recover," Rhys said. He looked at the wolf pup now in our bed and smiled. "He's adorable."

I snuggled closer to Caleb, wrapping myself around him like a human cocoon.

"Yes, he is," I whispered happily, a huge smile on my face as I closed my eyes.

Nico lay behind me, put one arm beneath my pillow, and one around my stomach.

I was just about to fall asleep, when Sharla came in and pushed on my stomach several times, which hurt.

"Ouch," I growled at her without opening my eyes.

"Shush. We have to do this to ensure your uterus tightens up correctly. Go back to sleep," she ordered me, and then left.

Caleb shifted back into human form, so I tugged a blanket up to just below his belly button, wrapped my arm around his side, and cuddled him against the top of my chest, which was bare, so our skin was in contact. He sniffed loudly a few times then settled and went to sleep.

CHAPTER 27
FOXFIRE

"She gave me an order," I whispered to Rhys as we stood outside the bedroom, watching her, Nico, and Caleb sleep.

"What?" he asked. "When?"

"I came in when Justina was fighting her. I was going to kill that wench, but Jolie ordered me to heal Nico. She didn't ask. She ordered me to do it. Then she tossed Justina out the window."

"Wow," Rhys whispered.

"It was so hot watching her throw the bitch out the window," I admitted.

He chuckled. "I'm still surprised she gave you an order. She usually tries to avoid doing that."

I nodded. "I was really surprised. I was also pissed because I wanted to kill Justina, but it was clear she wanted to do it. I don't know how the heck she had the energy to do it. She'd just given birth, used all of the crystals to send out the rage power to everyone, and then she fought Justina."

"Wait, she used *all* of the crystals?" Rhys asked, eyes wide as he turned to face me fully.

I gently shut the door, and led him away from the room. Those three needed some rest. Soon, our parents would be here and demanding to see them.

"Yes. She used all of them. She grabbed fistfuls of them."

"I didn't even know she could send it to everyone," Rhys whispered. "I couldn't believe my eyes when even the weakest dragons of our clan were taking warrior forms."

"If we hadn't invited her exes here, I don't know if she would have survived delivery. Caleb was fighting her and Sharla said she had started to panic until they showed up," I told him.

"I'm glad Silver thought to let us know of the possibility," Rhys whispered.

"Yeah, I'm going to have to buy him an extra present this year," I said and chuckled.

"My scales seem to be working again," Rhys said. "Not sure what fixed it, but I'm back to normal."

"Maybe you just needed a child to motivate you to become stronger," I said with a smirk.

Rhys shrugged. "Whatever it was, I'm glad."

The front door flew open, and we both raced to the stairs, stepping into Dan's path.

"Wait," I ordered him.

He glared down at me. "Where is she?"

"She's sleeping. She battled Justina after giving birth and sending us that power. She needs to sleep for at least an hour. We'll get you and the others some food, and then you can meet your grandson," I explained.

He glared at me, but after a tense moment gave a slight nod, and stomped down to the dining room.

I exhaled. "He still scares me."

"Only a fool wouldn't be scared of Dan," Rhys whispered.

"He almost broke my jaw while we were sparring when Jolie enraged him," I muttered and rubbed at the phantom pain in my jaw.

Rhys clapped me on the shoulder and smiled. "Better you than me."

"You're such a good friend," I teased.

His parents entered, and he escorted them to the dining room.

I waited by the door for my parents, knowing they'd want to rush upstairs.

The entered, ignored me, and started to head up the stairs.

"Hey," I snapped at them.

They turned.

"She's sleeping," I said. "Leave her be for a bit."

"I'm going to heal her," Mother said. "Katar, go with your son."

"Mom," I sighed.

Dad draped his arm around my shoulders and tugged me away.

"Come on, let's go get food ready. Your mate is going to be ravenous when she wakes up."

"Isn't that how she is whenever she wakes up?" I asked with a smirk.

Dad laughed. "Too true."

"So, any casualties?" I asked when we entered the room where Emrys, Adelaide, Declan, Rhys, Dan, Kylan, Ezio, Deryn, Silver, Dalton, Klaus, Martin, Sharla, Madison, Tamara, and Yukio sat around our table.

Everyone shook their heads.

Wow. Jolie had no idea what she'd accomplished by enraging everyone. Normally, there were at least a dozen casualties in a battle that large.

"What are we eating?" Dad asked.

"Pizza," Rhys announced.

"It was the easiest and fastest thing we could get," Deryn explained.

"Are there any shops open?" I asked, thinking of the destruction I had seen going on in the city.

"Our shop is always open," Dan said with a wide smile.

I sat down, and leaned my head on my arms on the table. I was so tired.

"So, what is our grandson's name?" Dan asked.

"No," Deryn said immediately. "Jolie can introduce him when he comes down."

"Did you tell him?" Rhys asked Deryn.

"Tell me what?" Dan asked.

Deryn shook his head, smirking. "I want to see his reaction when it happens."

Dan scowled. "If there's something wrong—"

"It's not wrong," Deryn said and then scowled. "I don't think."

"That's super reassuring, Son," Dan grumbled.

Mom returned, kissed the back of my head, and sat beside me. "She's still sleeping," she advised everyone. "But, she's healthy and so is the baby and Nico."

"He almost died," I whispered, remembering that awful pain in my chest when the knife had gone into his.

"Where's that dagger?" Emrys asked.

"I put it in our vault," Rhys answered. "I'll give it to you three to decide what you want to do with it."

"We should just give it to the elders," I suggested.

Dan nodded. "That's my vote, too."

What? Dan agreed with me on something for once?

"I agree," Dad said.

Thor and Leona entered, and Leona searched the room, her eyes wide and frantic.

"Where is she?" she demanded.

"She's sleeping," Kara told her.

"Is she—"

"She's fine," Dalton assured her.

"But, all that power," Leona whispered.

Dalton nodded. "I know. It surprised me, too. She used dozens of crystals with stored magical energy to pull it off, but she is fine. Kara just went and checked on her."

Leona sagged into Thor, who wrapped his arm around her waist to hold her against his side.

"See, I told you she was fine," Thor whispered. "Jolie is resilient."

"Like a cockroach," Adelaide said.

Several around the room growled, myself included.

She scoffed and rolled her eyes. "I didn't mean it as an insult. Just that things which should normally kill one of her kind, she lives through. It's quite remarkable."

"Says the villain as she debates dissecting her," I whispered to Dad.

Dad snorted as he tried to keep his laughter in, and Mother pinched my side.

"Let's make the table bigger," I said to Rhys.

Everyone stood, and backed up a few steps. Rhys and I hit the buttons on each side of the table, then shoved it apart at the seam. The table was magical, and could seat anywhere from four to thirty. I was glad Rhys had designed the room to be so large. The first time I'd entered, I had thought it was ridiculously oversized, but now I understood his reasoning.

Mother set her hand on the back of my head, and I felt her warm energy filling me.

"Mom," I mumbled.

"Hush. You're tired and your mate needs you at one hundred percent, so she doesn't have to be the only one dealing with the baby," she told me.

I wouldn't argue with her on that. Plus, I felt like I had failed Jolie today. She'd been injured fighting Justina, when we had all agreed not to let her fight her. If she hadn't ordered me away, I would have killed Justina immediately.

"Why are you scowling?" Dad asked.

"Nothing," I lied.

He arched a brow at me.

I waved my hand. "It's really nothing. I'm just brooding."

The doorbell rang, and we all cringed when we heard Caleb cry.

"Whoops," Rhys said as he stood. "I hadn't thought about the doorbell waking him."

"You may want to unhook it until he's a bit older," Adelaide suggested.

I stood as well, knowing he would need help carrying the boxes.

The werewolf at the door looked stressed, but smiled as he spoke to us, and made three trips for all of the pizzas they had ordered.

We set them out on the table, then passed around paper plates.

"Here, you all are," Jolie said as she entered the room.

Deryn, Rhys, and I rushed to her side.

Caleb's eyes were closed again, and he was in human form. I looked at his ears and felt a smile tug up my lips. His ears were pointed at the top, something I had missed before.

"Stop hogging them," Adelaide complained.

Jolie stepped away from us, turned Caleb so he was leaning back against her chest, facing everyone in the room, with her arm around him and one under his butt. "Everyone, this is Caleb."

All of the grandparents started to stand, but then all froze.

"Dalton, you go," Dan said. "We've had chances to bond with him while he was in her womb."

Dalton smiled appreciatively, then walked to Jolie. He kissed her forehead and her eyes closed a moment as her smile spread. Dalton rested his forehead against Caleb's and whispered to him.

Caleb opened his eyes and made a cooing sound.

Dalton stepped back and turned his head away as he tried to discreetly wipe his eyes.

"My turn!" Dan said and rushed over. He kissed Jolie's cheek. "How are you feeling?"

"Tired, but good," she said.

Dan looked down at Caleb, bending so he was eye level with the child. "Hello, Son."

Caleb met Dan's eyes, then shifted into a wolf pup in Jolie's arms.

Dan's eyes widened and his mouth dropped open.

"That was the secret I was keeping," Deryn said, chuckling. "And it was so worth it to see your face."

"That's not normal?" Dalton asked.

Dan shook his head. "They're usually not able to shift until around five years old."

"He shifted in vitro," Kara told him.

"We thought we'd all hallucinated it," Deryn said. "Clearly, we hadn't."

"That's remarkable," Dan said. He brushed his fingers across Caleb's head, between his ears. "You're perfect, little one."

"Caleb," Jolie reminded him.

Dan smirked. "Yes, Caleb."

Caleb shifted back, and Jolie shifted her hold on him, so he lay on her arm, with his butt against the bend in her elbow, and his head in her palm. He seemed to enjoy that position.

"Who's next?" she asked, looking up with a wide smile.

Perfect. Yes. Those two were perfect.

I looked at my brothers, and saw the same feeling reflected in their eyes.

EPILOGUE

JOLIE

"Caleb, don't bite so hard," I growled at the rambunctious six-month-old.

Caleb opened his jaws, his needle-sharp puppy teeth loosening from my finger.

"Thank you," I whispered and ruffled his ears.

Deryn bounded up to us in his wolf form, wagging his tail with his tongue lolling out the side of his mouth.

Caleb yipped in delight, and ran to Deryn, rubbing along his legs, looking more like a cat than a wolf.

"Your turn," I told Deryn, and headed towards the house.

I cast one glance back, watching as the father and son ran into the forest to play.

"Ready?" Fox asked.

I yelped, since I hadn't heard him approach. "What?" I asked.

He smiled and then bowed. "Would you accompany me, my queen?"

I smiled back. "Okay."

He wrapped his arms around me, spun around, and dipped me as he kissed me. My head spun, and I wrapped my arms around his neck, even though I knew he would never drop me.

"Where are we going?" I asked when he righted us.

"Come on and you'll find out," he said, slipping his fingers between mine, and tugging me along.

I chuckled at my kind-hearted mate, and jogged along behind him. He led me to one of Dan's SUVs, where Ezio stood, waiting for us.

"Ready?" Ezio asked.

Fox nodded, and ushered me into the back seat.

Once we were buckled, Ezio drove out, whispering conspiratorially to Fox.

"What's going on?" I asked.

"You'll see," Fox said. "I'm not going to ruin it."

We pulled into a car dealership, and I looked at Fox, but he wasn't looking at me. When we stopped, Fox leapt out, and opened the door for me.

"Come on," he hurried me, took my hand, and led me to the middle of the lot, where Rhys stood with a car salesman.

Rhys kissed my cheek, and spread his arms. "Pick one."

I blinked. "What?"

"You don't have a car," Rhys said.

"And, we think it is time that you have one of your own," Fox added.

"You mean...I won't have a driver or bodyguard assigned to me?" I asked, my mouth open in disbelief.

Rhys picked up one of my hands and said, "We would prefer you to have a driver, ten bodyguards, and a dozen more on backup, but we know that you can take care of yourself. You proved that when you gave birth to a child, used your power to save the city, and then defeated Justina. We are overprotective jerks at times, and we are trying to work on that."

"So, we are taking this first step, by giving you a car of your own. One that you can drive wherever you want to go. We would still prefer if you took someone with you, but it's not something we are going to require. We want you to be safe, but we want you to be happy first and foremost," Fox said.

I hugged them both, and then looked at the cars around me. There was every type of car, and I didn't know where to start. So, I just walked to each car I liked, and inspected it. I narrowed it down to two cars, test drove them, and then picked the winner. A cute sports car that had enough room for four people, or three people and a baby car seat. I got it in white.

"Dan's going to have some improvements done to it, so you'll get it in about a week," Rhys told me.

I snickered. "Of course, Dan is."

"Let's go get the paperwork finalized," the salesman said.

I walked between Rhys and Fox, holding each of their hands.

"Thank you," I said, smiling up at them. "This really means a lot to me."

They each squeezed my hand, smiling in response.

I expected us to go to our house, but instead, they drove to Dan's pizza restaurant. When we walked in, my eyes widened at the huge crowd gathered. Emrys, Adelaide, Katar, Kara, Silverowl, Andras, Gavin, Gavin's human girlfriend, Mawrth, Rhian, Brenin, Dan, Deryn, Caleb, Ezio, Yukio, Declan, Martin, Sharla, Tamara, Madison, Zelphar, Kylan, Tobias, Lorenzo, Thor, Leona, Nico, and Tawny were all there.

"What's going on?" I asked.

"Happy birthday!" everyone yelled.

My mouth gaped open and shut, like a fish out of water. It was my birthday? I had totally forgotten!

The front door opened, and Dad, Colton, and Sam walked in, carrying a huge cake. They started singing, and the rest of them joined in.

Tears brimmed, as all of the people I cared about the most sang to me. I blew out the candles, but didn't have a single thing to wish for. I had everything I ever wanted or needed, right here.

If you love reverse harem romance full of laughs and action, grab a copy of Accidental Mobster: books2read.com/accidental-mobster

AFTERWORD

Thank you so much for taking this journey with me! I loved writing this series, and although I'm sad Jolie's series ends here, there will be more to come in this world.

Check out THE DEMON'S FAIR (http://books2read.com/demons-fair), which is a novella from Leona's point of view.

I hope you'll continue reading my books, and consider leaving a review if you enjoyed them. Thank you again, for taking a chance on me. I know you have a lot of options, and the fact that you chose my books is not something I take lightly.

To stay up to date on my writing and publishing schedule, join my newsletter (catbanks.co/newsletter) and follow me on facebook (facebook.com/catherinebanksauthor).

About the Author

Catherine Banks is a USA Today bestselling fantasy author who writes in several fantasy subgenres and has multiple pseudonyms. She began writing fiction at only four years old and finished her first full-length novel at the age of fifteen. She is married to her soulmate and best friend, Avery, who she has two amazing children with. After her full-time job, she reads books, plays video games, and watches anime shows and movies with her family to relax. Although she has lived in Northern California her entire life, she dreams of traveling around the world. Catherine is also C.E.O. of Turbo Kitten Industries™, a company with many hats including being a book publisher and Etsy store full of nerdy fun.

facebook.com/catherinebanksauthor

twitter.com/catherineebanks

amazon.com/author/catherinebanks

bookbub.com/authors/catherine-banks